"I am not cut out to be a warrior," said Thuro.

"You are my grandson and the son of Aurelius and Alaida," replied Culain. "I think you will find that blood runs true. We already know you can swing an axe. What other surprises do you hold in store?"

Thuro shrugged. "I do not want to disappoint you, as I disappointed my father."

"Lesson one, Thuro: from now on you have no one to disappoint but yourself. But first you must agree to abide by what I say and obey every word I utter. Will you do this?"

"I will."

"Then prepare to die," said Culain. And there was no humor in his eyes.

By David Gemmell
Published by Ballantine Books:

LION OF MACEDON
DARK PRINCE

KNIGHTS OF DARK RENOWN

MORNINGSTAR

The Drenai Saga
      LEGEND
      THE KING BEYOND THE GATE
      QUEST FOR LOST HEROES
      WAYLANDER

The Stones of Power Cycle
      GHOST KING
      LAST SWORD OF POWER
      WOLF IN SHADOW
      THE LAST GUARDIAN*
      BLOODSTONE*

*Forthcoming

Ghost King

The Stones of Power
Book One

David Gemmell

A Del Rey® Book

BALLANTINE BOOKS • NEW YORK

A Del Rey© Book
Published by Ballantine Books
Copyright © 1988 by David A. Gemmell

All rights reserved under International and Pan-American Copyright Conventions. Published in the United States by Ballantine Books, a division of Random House, Inc., New York. Originally published in Great Britain in 1988 by Century Hutchinson Ltd.

http://www.randomhouse.com

ISBN 0-345-37902-0

Manufactured in the United States of America

First American Edition: January 1996

10 9 8 7 6 5

Dedication

This book is dedicated with love to Stella Graham, to Tom Taylor, and to Jeremy Wells for the gift of friendship.

Also to the ladies of the Folkestone Herald—Sharon, Madders, Susie, and Carol—for Rocky. And to Pip Clarkson, who cast the pearls anyway.

Acknowledgments

So much in the literary world depends on the skill of those who take the manuscript and edit it for publication. A writer can all too easily take the wrong direction or lose the thread of the drama. A good editor will redirect skillfully and enhance greatly the work that will then accrue credit to the author. Similarly, a good copy editor can, with an inserted word or clever deletion, polish a dull sentence to diamond brightness.

My thanks to my editor Liza Reeves for making it all seem so easy, to copy editor Jean Maund for the fine-tuning and the elegant polishing, and to my agent, Pamela Buckmaster, for bringing us together.

Foreword

Ghost King is a fantasy novel and is not intended to be historically accurate. However, the cities of Roman Britain, as named, did exist in the areas suggested, as did certain of the characters who appear in these pages.

Cunobelin was certainly a powerful warrior king who earned the title Brittanorum Rex from the Roman writer Suetonius. Cunobelin reigned for forty years from his base at Camulodunum, possibly giving rise to the Arthurian legends.

Paullinus was also a true man of history and did defeat the Iceni of Boudicca during the ill-fated uprising. During the same period the Ninth Legion did indeed disappear. Some historians claim they were ambushed and destroyed; others suggest a mutiny that the Romans covered up.

The maneuvers of Roman military units are detailed as accurately as research and the needs of drama allow.

The language used is relatively modern, and undoubtedly there will be some students who find it jarring to read of arrows being "fired," when of course the expression evolved only after the introduction of matchlock muskets. Similarly "minutes" and "seconds" appear ahead of their time.

Such arguments as may be offered can be overcome by pointing out that since the language being spoken is not English but a bastardized form of Latin-Celtic, some license in translation should be allowed.

Of the life of Uther Pendragon, little is known. This is not a history of the man, but a fantasy.

In other words it is not the story as it was but as it *ought* to have been.

David A. Gemmell
Hastings, 1988

Principal Characters

(in alphabetical order)

ALHYFFA Daughter of Hengist, wife of Moret

BALDRIC Warrior of the Pinrae

CAEL Son of Eldared, King of the Brigante

CULAIN LACH FERAGH Warrior of the Mist, also known as the Lord of the Lance. Master of weaponry.

ELDARED Brigante King and Lord of Deicester Castle. Betrayed his brother Cascioc twenty years before to help Aurelius gain the throne.

GWALCHMAI King's retainer. Cantii tribesman

GOROIEN The Witch Queen, immortal and ruthless

HENGIST Saxon king, father to Horsa, the warlord

KORRIN ROGEUR Woodsman of Pinrae, brother to Pallin

LAITHA Ward of Culain

LUCIUS AQUILA General of the Romano-British forces

MAEDHLYN Lord Enchanter to Aurelius

MORET Son of Eldared

PALLIN Half man, half bear, tortured by the Witch Queen

PRASAMACCUS Brigante tribesman

SEVERINUS ALBINUS Roman legate of the Ninth Legion

THURO Son of High King Aurelius Maximus and the Mist Maiden, Alaida

VICTORINUS King's retainer and first centurion

Roman Names of British Settlements

ANDERITA—Pevensey
CALCARIA—Tadcaster
CAMULODUNUM—
  Colchester
CATARACTONIUM—
  Catterick
DUBRIS—Dover
DUROBRIVAE—
  Rochester
EBORACUM—York
LAGENTIUM—Castleford

LINDUM—Lincoln
LONDINIUM—London
LONGOVICIUM—Lancaster
PINNATA CASTRA—
  Inchtuthill
SKITIS ISLAND—Isle of Skye
VENTA—Winchester
VINDOLANDA—
  Chesterholm
VINDOMARA—Ebchester

◇ 1 ◇

THE BOY STARED idly at the cold gray walls and wondered if the castle dungeons could be any more inhospitable than this chilly turret room with its single window staring like an eye into the teeth of the north wind. True, there was a fire glowing in the hearth, but it might as well have been one of Maedhlyn's illusions for all the warmth it supplied. The great gray slabs sucked the heat from the blaze, giving nothing in return but a ghostly reflection that mocked the flames.

Thuro sat on the bed and wrapped his father's white bearskin cloak about his slender shoulders.

"What a foul place," he said, closing his eyes and pushing the turret room from his mind. He thought of his father's villa in Eboracum and of the horse meadows beyond the white walls where mighty Cephon wintered with his mares. But most of all he pictured his own room, cozy and snug away from the bitter winter winds and filled with the love of his young life: his books, his glorious books. His father had refused him permission to bring even one tome to this lonely castle in case the other war leaders should catch the prince reading and know the king's dark secret. For while it might be well known in Caerlyn Keep that the boy

1

Thuro was weak in body and spirit, the king's retainers guarded the sad truth like a family shame.

Thuro shivered and left the bed to sit on the goatskin rug before the fire. He was as miserable as he had ever been. Far below in the great hall of Deicester Castle his father was attempting to bond an alliance against the barbarians from across the sea, grim-eyed reavers who had established settlements in the far south from which to raid the richer northlands. The embassy to Deicester had been made despite Maedhlyn's warnings. Thuro had not wished to accompany his father, either, but not for fear of dangers he could scarcely comprehend. The prince disliked the cold, loathed long journeys on horseback, and, more important, hated to be deprived of his books even for a day—let alone the two months set aside for the embassy.

The door opened, and the prince glanced up to see the tall figure of Gwalchmai, his brawny arms bearing a heavy load of logs. He smiled at the lad, and Thuro noted with shame that the retainer wore only a single woolen tunic against the biting cold.

"Do you never feel the chill, Gwalchmai?"

"I feel it," he answered, kneeling to add wood to the blaze.

"Is my father still speaking?"

"No. When I passed by, Eldared was on his feet."

"You do not like Eldared?"

"You see too much, young Thuro; that is not what I said."

But you did, thought Thuro. It was in your eyes and the slight inflection when you used his name. He stared into the retainer's dark eyes, but Gwalchmai turned away.

"Do you trust him?" asked the boy.

"Your father obviously trusts him, so who am I to offer opinions? You think the king would have come here with only twenty retainers if he feared treachery?"

"You answer my question with questions. Is that not evasive?"

Gwalchmai grinned. "I must get back to my watch. But think on this, Thuro: It is not for the likes of me to criticize the great. I could lose the skin from my back—or, worse, my life."

"You think there is danger here?" persisted the prince.

"I like you, boy, though only Mithras knows why. You've a sharp mind; it is a pity you are weakly. But I'll answer your question after a fashion. For a king there is always danger; it is a riddle to me why a man wants such power. I've served your father for sixteen years, and in that time he has survived four wars, eleven battles, and five attempts on his life. He is a canny man. But I would be happier if the Lord Enchanter were here."

"Maedhlyn does not trust Eldared; he told my father so."

Gwalchmai pushed himself to his feet. "You trust too easily, Thuro. You should not be sharing this knowledge with me or with any retainer."

"But I can trust you, can I not?"

"How do you know that?" Gwalchmai hissed.

"I read it in your eyes," said Thuro softly.

Gwalchmai relaxed, and a broad grin followed as he shook his head and tugged on his braided beard. "You should get some rest. It's said there's to be a stag hunt tomorrow."

"I'll not be going," said Thuro. "I do not much like riding."

"You baffle me, boy. Sometimes I see so much of your father in you that I want to cheer. And then ... well, it does not matter. I will see you in the morning. Sleep well."

"Thank you for the wood."

"It is my duty to see you safe."

Gwalchmai left the room, and Thuro rose and wandered to the window, moving aside the heavy velvet curtain and staring out over the winter landscape: rolling hills covered in snow, skeletal trees black as charcoal. He shivered and wished for home.

He, too, would have been happier if Maedhlyn had journeyed with them, for he enjoyed the old man's company and the quickness of his mind—and the games and riddles the Enchanter set him. One had occupied his mind for almost a full day the previous summer, while his father had been in the south routing the Jutes. Thuro had been sitting with Maedhlyn in the terraced garden, in the shade cast by the statue of the great Julius.

"There was a prince," said Maedhlyn, his green eyes sparkling, "who was hated by his king but loved by the people. The king decided the prince must die, but fearing the wrath of the populace, he devised an elaborate plan to end both the prince's popularity and his life. He accused him of treason and offered him trial by Mithras. In this way the Roman god would judge the innocence or guilt of the accused.

"The prince was brought before the king, and a large crowd was there to see the judgment. Before the prince stood a priest holding a closed leather pouch, and within the pouch were two grapes. The law said that one grape should be white, the other black. If the accused drew a white grape, he was innocent. A black grape meant death. You follow this, Thuro?"

"It is simple so far, teacher."

"Now, the prince knew of the king's hatred and guessed rightly that there were two black grapes in the pouch. Answer me this, young quicksilver: How did the prince produce a white grape and prove his innocence?"

"It is not possible, save by magic."

"There was no magic, only thought," said Maedhlyn, tapping his white-haired temple for emphasis. "Come to me tomorrow with the answer."

Throughout the day Thuro thought hard, but his mind was devoid of inspiration. He borrowed a pouch and two grapes from Listra the cook, and sat in the garden staring at the items as if in themselves they harbored the answer. As dusk painted the sky Trojan red, he gave up. Sitting alone in the gathering gloom, he took one of the grapes and ate it. He reached for the other—and stopped.

The following morning he went to Maedhlyn's study. The old man greeted him sourly, having had a troubled night, he said, with dark dreams.

"I have answered your riddle, master," the boy told him. At that the Enchanter's eyes came alive.

"So soon, young prince? It took the noble Alexander ten days, but then, perhaps Aristotle was less gifted than myself as a tutor!" He chuckled. "So tell me, Thuro, how did the prince prove his innocence?"

"He put his hand into the pouch and covered one grape. This he removed and ate swiftly. He then said to the priest, 'I do not know what color it was, but look at the one that is left.' "

Maedhlyn clapped his hands and smiled. "You please me greatly, Thuro. But tell me, how did you come upon the answer?"

"I ate the grape."

"That is good. There is a lesson in that also. You broke the problem down and examined the component parts. Most men attempt to solve riddles by allowing their minds to leap like monkeys from branch to branch, without ever realizing that it is the root that needs examining. Always remember that, young prince. The method works with men as well as it works with riddles."

Now Thuro dragged his thoughts from the golden days of summer back to the bleak winter night. He removed his leggings and slid under the blankets, turning on his side to watch the flickering flames in the hearth.

He thought of his father: tall and broad-shouldered with eyes of ice and fire, revered as a warrior leader and held in awe even by his enemies.

"I don't want to be a king," Thuro whispered.

Gwalchmai watched as the nobles prepared for the hunt, his emotions mixed. He felt a fierce pride as he looked upon the powerful figure of his king, sitting atop a black stallion of seventeen hands. The beast was called Bloodfire, and one look in its evil eyes would warn any horseman to beware. But the king was at ease, for the horse knew its master; they were as alike in temperament as brothers of the blood. But Gwalchmai's pride was mixed with the inevitable sadness of seeing Prince Thuro beside his father. The boy sat miserably on a gentle mare of fifteen hands, clutching his cloak to his chest, his white-blond hair billowing about his slender ascetic face. Too much of his mother in him, thought Gwalchmai, remembering his first sight of the Mist Maiden. It was almost sixteen years ago now, yet his mind's eye could picture the queen as if but an hour had passed. She rode a white pony, and beside the warrior king she seemed as fragile and out of place as ice on a rose. Talk among the retainers was that their lord had gone for a walk with Maedhlyn into a mist-shrouded northern valley and had vanished for eight days. When he returned, his beard had grown a full six inches and beside him was this wondrous woman with golden hair and eyes of swirling gray like mist on a northern lake.

At first many of the people of Caerlyn Keep had thought her a witch, for even there the tales were told of the Land of Mist, a place of eldritch magic. But as the months passed, she charmed them all with her kindness and gentle spirit. News of her pregnancy was greeted with great joy and instant celebration. Gwalchmai would never forget the raucous banquet at the keep or the wild night of pleasure that had followed it.

But eight months later Alaida, the Mist Maiden, was dead and her baby son hovered on the brink of death, refusing all milk. The Enchanter Maedhlyn had been summoned, and he, with his magic, had saved young Thuro. But the boy was never strong; where the retainers had hoped for a young man to mirror the king, they were left with a solemn child who abhorred all manly practices. Yet enough of his mother's gentleness remained to turn what would have been scorn into a friendly sadness. Thuro was well liked, but men who saw him would shake their heads and think of what might have been.

All this was on Gwalchmai's mind as the hunting party set off, led by Lord Eldared and his two sons, Cael and Moret.

The king had never recovered from the death of Alaida. He rarely laughed and came alive only when hunting either beasts or men. He had plenty of opportunity in those bloody days, for the Saxons and Jutes were raiding in the south and the Norse sailed their Wolfships into the deep rivers of the East Country. Added to this, there were raiders aplenty from the smaller clans and tribes who had never accepted the right of the Romano-British warlords to rule the ancient lands of the Belgae, the Iceni, and the Cantii.

Gwalchmai could well understand this viewpoint, being pure-blood Cantii himself, born within a long stone's throw of the Ghost Cliffs.

Now he watched as the noblemen cantered toward the wooded hills, then returned to his quarters behind the long stables. His eyes scanned the Deicester men as they lounged by the alehouse, and he began to grow uneasy. There was no love lost between the disparate groups assembled there, though the truce had been well maintained—a broken nose here, a sprained wrist there, but mostly the retainers had kept to themselves. But today Gwalchmai sensed a tension in the air, a brightness in the eyes of the soldiers.

He wandered into the long room. Only two of the king's men were there: Victorinus and Caradoc. They were playing knucklebones, and the Roman was losing with good grace.

"Rescue me, Gwal," said Victorinus. "Save me from my stupidity."

"There's not a man alive who could do that!" Gwalchmai moved to his cot and his wrapped blankets. He drew his gladius and scabbard from the roll and strapped the sword to his waist.

"Are you expecting trouble?" asked Caradoc, a tall rangy tribesman of Belgae stock.

"Where are the others?" he answered, avoiding the question.

"Most of them have gone to the village. There's a fair organized."

"When was this announced?"

"This morning," said Victorinus, entering the conversation. "What has happened?"

"Nothing as yet," said Gwalchmai, "and I hope to Mithras nothing does. But the air smells wrong."

"I can't smell anything wrong with it," Victorinus responded.

"That's because you're a Roman," put in Caradoc, moving to his blanket roll and retrieving his sword.

"I'll not argue with a pair of superstitious tribesmen, but think on this: If we walk around armed to the teeth, we could incite trouble. We could be accused of breaking the spirit of the truce."

Gwalchmai swore and sat down. "You are right, my friend. What do you suggest?"

Victorinus, though younger than his companions, was well respected by the other men in the King's Guards. He was steady, courageous, and a sound thinker. His solid Roman upbringing also proved a perfect counterpoint to the unruly, explosive temperaments of the Britons who served the king.

"I am not altogether sure, Gwal. Do not misunderstand me, for I do not treat your talents lightly. You have a nose for traps and an eye that reads men. If you say something is amiss, then I'll wager that it is. I think we should keep our swords hidden inside our tunics and wander around the keep. It may be no more than a lingering ill feeling among the Deicester men for Caradoc here taking their money last night in the knife-throwing tourney."

"I do not think so," Caradoc said. "In fact, I thought they took it too well. It puzzled me at the time, but it did not feel right. I even slept with one hand on my dagger."

"Let us not fly too high, my friends," said Victorinus. "We will meet back here in an hour. If there is danger in the air, we should all get a sniff of it."

"And what if we find something?" asked Caradoc.

"Do nothing. If you can, walk away from trouble. Swallow pride."

"No man should be asked to do that," protested the Belgae.

"That may be true, my volatile friend. But if there is trouble, then let the Deicester men start it. The king will be less than pleased if you break the truce; he'll flay the skin from your back."

Gwalchmai moved to the window and pushed open the wooden shutters.

"I do not think we need to concern ourselves about hiding weapons," he said softly. "The Deicester men are all armed."

Victorinus swept up his blanket roll. "Gather your gear now and follow me. Swiftly."

"There are about a dozen of them coming this way with swords in their hands," said Gwalchmai, ducking down from the window. Gathering his belongings, he followed his two companions to the roughly carved wooden door leading to the stables. Drawing their swords, they stepped through and pulled the door shut behind them. Swiftly they saddled three horses and rode out into the yard.

"There they are!" someone shouted, and soldiers rushed out to block the riders. Victorinus kicked his mount into a gallop, crashing into the crowding warriors, who scattered and fell to the cobbles. Then the trio were thundering under the beamed gateway and out into the snow-swept hills.

They had not traveled more than a mile when they came upon the bodies of their comrades, lying in a hollow by a frozen stream. The retainers had been armed only with knives, but at least eleven of the seventeen had been killed by arrows. The rest had been hacked to death by swords or axes.

The three men sat their horses in silence. There was no point dismounting. They gazed at the dead faces of those who had been their friends or at the least their comrades in war. By a gnarled oak lay the body of Atticus, the rope walker. Around him the snow was stained with blood, and it was obvious that he alone of all the retainers had managed to inflict wounds on the attackers.

"At least three men," said Caradoc, as if reading the thoughts of his companions. "But then, Atticus was a tough whoreson. What do we do now, Victorinus?"

The young Roman stayed silent for a moment, scanning the horizon. "The king," he said softly.

"And the boy!" said Gwalchmai. "Sweet Juno! We must find them—warn them."

"They are dead," said Victorinus, removing his bronze helm and staring at his distorted reflection. "That is why the retainers were lured away and murdered and why the king was invited on the stag hunt. It was a royal stag they hunted. We must get back to Caerlyn and warn Aquila."

"No!" Caradoc shouted. "This treachery cannot go unpunished."

Victorinus saw the pain in the Belgae's eyes. "And what will you do, Caradoc? Ride back to Deicester and scale the walls to find Eldared?"

"Why not?"

"Because it would be futile—you would die before getting within a yard of Eldared. Think ahead, man. Aquila does not expect the king back until spring, and he will be unprepared. The first sight he will see coming from the north is the Deicester army and any allies Eldared has gained. They will seize Eboracum, and the traitor will have won."

"But we must find the king's body," said Gwalchmai. "We cannot leave it for the crows; it is not fitting."

"And suppose he is not yet dead?" offered Caradoc. "I would never forgive myself for leaving him."

"I know what you are feeling, and I grieve also. But I beg you to put aside emotion and trust Roman logic. Yes, we could bury the king—but what of Eboracum? You think the king's shade would thank us for putting his body before the fate of his people?"

"And if he is not dead?" persisted Caradoc.

"You *know* that he is," Victorinus said sadly.

◇ 2 ◇

THURO WAS LOST. It had happened soon after the riders had left the castle, when the dogs had picked up a scent and raced into the dark wood with the hunters thundering after them. Having no intention of galloping into the trees in hot pursuit, he had reined in the mare and followed at a sedate canter, but somewhere along the trail he had taken a wrong turn, and now he could no longer even hear the hounds. The wintry sun was high overhead, and Thuro was cold through to his bones . . . and he was hungry. The trees were thinner here, the ground slowly rising. The wind had dropped, and Thuro halted by a frozen stream. He dismounted and cracked the ice, dipping his head and sipping the cold fresh water. His father would be so angry with him. He would say nothing, but his eyes would show his displeasure and his face would turn away from the boy.

Thuro cleared the snow from a flat rock and sat down, considering all the options open to him. He could ride on blindly in the hope of stumbling upon the hunters, or he could follow his own tracks back to the castle. It was not hard to find the right course of action with options such as those. He mounted the mare and swung her back to the south.

A large stag stepped lightly onto the trail and stopped

to watch the rider. Thuro reined in and leaned forward on the pommel of his saddle. "Good morning, prince of the forest; are you also lost?" The stag turned contemptuously away and continued its leisurely pace across the trail and into the trees. "You remind me of my father," Thuro called after it.

"Do you often talk to animals?" Thuro turned in the saddle to see a young girl dressed like a forester in a green hooded woolen tunic, leather leggings, and knee-high moccasins fringed with sheepskin. Her hair was short and a mixture of autumnal colors: light brown with a hint of both gold and red. Her face was striking, without a hint of beauty, and yet . . .

Thuro bowed. "Do you live near here?" he asked.

"Perhaps. But obviously you do not. How long have you been lost?"

"How do you know that I am lost?" he countered.

The girl stepped away from the tree beside the trail, and Thuro saw that she was carrying a beautiful bow of dark horn. "You may not be lost," she said, smiling. "It may be that you found your tracks so fascinating that you decided you just had to see them again."

"I concede," he told her. "I am seeking Deicester Castle."

"You have friends there?"

"My father is there. We are guests."

"A fortune would not induce me to be a guest of that foul family," she told him. "Continue on this path until you come to a lightning-blasted oak, then bear right and follow the stream. It will save you time."

"Thank you. What is your name?"

"Names are for friends, young lordling, not to be bandied about among strangers."

"Strangers can become friends. In fact, all friends were at some time strangers."

"All too true," she admitted. "But to speak more bluntly, I have no wish to strike up a friendship with a guest of Eldared's."

"I am sorry that you feel this way. It seems a great shame that to sleep in a cold and drafty castle somehow stains the spirit of a man. For what it is worth, my name is Thuro."

"You do speak prettily, Thuro," she said, smiling, "and you have a wonderful eye for horses. Come, join me for the midday meal."

Thuro did not question her sudden change of heart but dismounted and led his horse away from the trail, following the girl into the trees and up a winding track to a shallow cave under a sandstone rock face. There a fire had burned low under a copper pot perched on two stones. Thuro tied the mare's reins to a nearby bush and moved to the fire, where the girl joined him. She added oats to the boiling water, along with a pinch of salt from a small pouch at her side. "Gather some wood," she told him, "and earn your food." He did as she had bidden, gathering thick branches from beside the track and carrying them back to the cave.

"Are you planning to light a beacon fire?" she asked when he returned.

"I do not understand," he said.

"This is a cooking fire. It is intended to heat the oats and water and to give us warmth for an hour or so. The wood you need should be dry and no thicker than a thumb joint. Have you never set a cooking fire?"

"No. I regret that that is a pleasure I have not yet encountered."

"How old are you?"

"I shall be judged a man next autumn," he said some-what stiffly. "And you?"

"The same as you, Thuro. Fifteen."

"I shall fetch some more suitable wood," he said.

"Get yourself a platter at the same time."

"A platter?"

"How else will you eat your oats?"

Thuro was angry as he left the cave, an emotion he rarely felt and one with which he was exceedingly un-comfortable. As he had followed the forest girl, he had become acutely aware of the rhythmic movement of her hips and the liquid grace of her walk. By contrast, he had begun to feel that he was incapable of putting one foot in front of the other without tripping himself. His feet felt twice their size. He longed to do something to impress her and for the first time in his young life wished he were a shade more like his father. Pushing the thoughts from his mind, he gathered wood for the fire, finding also a round flat stone to serve as a platter for his food.

"Are you hungry?" she asked.

"Not very." Using a short stick, she expertly lifted the pot from the flames and stirred the thick, milky con-tents. He passed her his rock, and she giggled.

"Here," she said, offering him her own wooden plate. "Use this."

"The rock will be fine."

"I am sorry, Thuro; it is unfair of me to mock. It is not your fault you are a lordling; you should have brought your servant with you."

"I am not a lordling, I am a prince: the son of Max-imus the High King. And doubtless were you to be sitting in the hall of Caerlyn, you would feel equally ill at ease discussing the merits of Plutarch's *Life of Lycurgus*."

Her eyes sparkled, and Thuro realized they echoed the russet tones of her hair: light brown with flecks of gold.

"You are probably correct, Prince Thuro," she said with a mock bow, "for I was never at ease with Lycurgus and I agree with Plutarch in his comparison with Numa. How did he put it? 'Virtue rendered the one so respectable as to deserve a throne, and the other so great as to be above it.' "

Thuro returned the bow, but without mockery. "Forgive my arrogance," he told her. "I am not used to feeling this foolish."

"You are probably more at ease chasing stags and practicing with sword and lance."

"No, I am rather poor in those quarters also. I am the despair of my father. I had hoped to impress you with my knowledge, for there is little else I have to brag of."

She looked away and poured the cooling oats to her platter, then passed the food to Thuro. "My name is Laitha. Welcome to my hearth, Prince Thuro." He searched her face for any hint of mockery, but there was none.

He accepted the food and ate in silence. Laitha put down the pot and leaned back against the cave wall, watching the young man. He was handsome in a gentle fashion, and his eyes were as gray as woodsmoke, softly sad and wondrously innocent. Yet for all the gentleness Laitha saw, she found no trace of weakness in his face. The eyes did not waver or turn aside; the mouth showed no hint of petulance. And his open admission of his physical shortcomings endeared him to

the girl, who had seen enough of loudmouthed brag-
garts vying to prove their strength and manhood.

"Why do you not excel?" she asked him. "Is your
swordmaster a poor teacher?"

"I have no interest in swordplay. It tires me, and then
I fall ill."

"In what way ill?"

He shrugged. "I am told I almost died at birth, and
since then my chest has been weak. I cannot exert myself without becoming dizzy—and then my head
pounds, and sometimes I lose my sight."

"How does your father react to all this?"

"With great patience and great sadness. I fear I am
not the son he would have preferred. But it does not
matter. He is as strong as an ox and as fearless as a
dragon. He will reign for decades yet, and perhaps he
will marry again and sire a proper heir."

"What happened to your mother?"

"She died two days after I was born. The birth was
early by a month, and Maedhlyn—our Enchanter—was
absent on the king's business."

"And your father never remarried? Strange for a
king."

"I have never spoken to him of it ... but Maedhlyn
says she was the still water in his soul, and after she
had gone, there was only fire. There is a wall around
Maximus and his grief. None may enter. He cannot look
me in the face, for I am much like my mother. And in
all the time I can remember he has never touched me—
not an arm on the shoulder or the ruffling of a single
hair. Maedhlyn tells that when I was four, I was struck
down with a terrible fever and my spirit was lost within
the darkness of the Void. He says my father came to me
then and took me in his arms, and his spirit searched for

mine across the darkness. He found me and brought me home. But I remember nothing of it, and that saddens me. I would like to be able to recall that moment."

"He must love you greatly," she whispered.

"I do not know." He looked up at her and smiled. "Thank you for the oats. I must be going."

"I will guide you to the ford above Deicester," she said.

He did not argue and waited while she cleaned her pot, platter, and spoon. She stowed them in a canvas pack that she slung to her shoulder, and then, taking up her bow and quiver, she set out alongside him. The snow was falling thickly, and he was glad she was traveling with him. Without tracks to follow, he knew he would have been lost within minutes.

They had gone but a little way toward the trail when they heard the sound of horses riding at speed. In the first second that he heard the horsemen Thuro was delighted—soon he would be back at the castle and warm again. But then he realized it would mean saying good-bye to Laitha, and on an impulse he turned from the path, leading the mare deeper into the trees and behind a screen of bushes below the trail.

Laitha joined him, saying nothing. There were four men, all armed with swords and lances. They drew up a little way ahead and were joined by three riders coming from the opposite direction.

"Any sign?" The words drifted to Thuro like whispers on the wind, and he felt ashamed to be hiding there. These men were out in the cold searching for him; it was unfair of him to put them to further trouble. He was just about to step into view when another man spoke.

"No, nothing. It's incredible. We kill the father in minutes, but the beardless boy causes more trouble."

"You are talking nonsense, Calin. The father killed six men—and that was with an arrow deep in his lungs. The boy is costing only time."

"Well, I intend to make him pay for wasting my time. I'll have his eyes roasting on the point of my dagger."

Thuro stood statue-still until long after the riders had moved on.

"I do not think you should go back to Deicester," Laitha whispered, laying a gentle hand on his shoulder.

Thuro stood unmoving, staring at the empty trail, his thoughts whirling and diving from fear to regret, from panic to sorrow. His father had been murdered, and Thuro's world would never be the same again. This morning he had been miserable and cold, seemingly alone in a cheerless castle. But now he knew that he had not been alone, that the giant strength of Aurelius Maximus, the High King, had covered him like a mantle and the companionship of men such as Gwalchmai and Victorinus had shielded him from grimmer realities. Laitha was right; he was a spoiled lordling who did not even know how to set a cooking fire. Now the world was once more in turmoil. Eldared, as Maedhlyn had feared, was a traitor and a regicide. The prince was now a hunted animal with no chance of escaping his hunters. Of what use would be his learning now? Plutarch, Aristotle, and Suetonius were no help to a weakly boy in a perilous wood.

"Thuro?"

He turned slowly and saw the concern in Laitha's eyes. "I think you would be wise to leave me," he said. "My company will bring danger to you."

"What will you do?"

He shrugged. "I will find my father's body and bury it. Then, I suppose, I will try to make my way back to Caerlyn."

"You are now the king, Thuro. What will you do when you get there?"

"I shall abdicate. I am not suited to govern others. My father's general, Lucius Aquila, is also his second cousin. He will rule wisely—if he survives."

"Why should he not?"

"Eldared has the equivalent of five legions and four hundred horsemen. At Caerlyn there are only two legions; the rest of my father's army is made up of militiamen who return to their homes in winter. The killing of my father will see the start of a war no one can afford. With the Saxons invading the south, Eldared's ambition is lunacy. But then, the Brigantes have always hated the Romans, even before Hadrian built the wall to torment them."

"I was taught that Hadrian built the wall because he feared them," said Laitha.

"If that were true, there would have been few north-facing gates. The gates were sally points for raids deep into Brigante territory." Thuro shivered and noticed that the snow was quickening beneath a thunder-dark sky. "Where is the nearest village?" he asked.

"Apart from Deicester Town, there is Daris, some eight miles to the southeast. But Eldared will have men there looking for you. Why not come to my home. You will be safe there."

"I will be safe nowhere. And I do not wish to place you in peril, Laitha."

"You do not understand. I live with my guardian, and he will allow no one to harm you."

Thuro smiled. "I have just told you that Eldared has five legions. He is also the man who murdered the High King. Your guardian cannot be as powerful as my enemies."

"If we stand and debate, we will freeze to death. Now, let your horse go and follow me. Trust me, Thuro, for I am your only chance for life."

"But why release my horse?"

"It cannot go where I will lead you. And perhaps more important, your hunters are seeking a boy riding and will not search the paths we will walk. Now, come on."

Thuro looped the mare's reins over her head and draped them over the saddle pommel. Then he followed the lithe form of the forest girl ever deeper into the trees, emerging at last at the foot of a high hill in the shadow of the northern mountains. Thuro's feet were cold, his boots wet through. A little way up the rise he stopped, his face white and his breathing ragged as he sank to the snow. Laitha had walked on maybe twenty paces when she turned and saw him beside the trail. She ran lightly back to him and knelt. "What is the matter?"

"I am sorry—I cannot go on. I must rest for a while."

"Not here, Thuro; we are in the open. Come on, just a little more." She helped him to his feet, and he staggered on for perhaps ten paces. Then his legs gave way beneath him. As Laitha bent to help him, she saw movement some two hundred paces back along the trail. Three riders emerged from the trees, saw the travelers, and kicked their horses into a gallop.

"Your enemies are upon us, Thuro!" she shouted, dropping the pack from her shoulder and swiftly stringing her bow of horn. Thuro rolled to his knees and tried to stand, but his strength had fled. He watched as the riders drew their swords and saw the gleam of triumph in their eyes, heard the malice in their screams. His eyes flickered to Laitha, who was standing coolly with her bow stretched, the string nestling against her cheek. Time seemed to slow, and Thuro viewed the scene with detached fascination as Laitha slowly released her breath and, in the moment between release and the need for more air, loosed the shaft. It took the lead rider between his collarbones and punched him from the saddle.

But the remaining riders were too close to allow such perfect timing again, and Laitha's next shaft was loosed too swiftly. It glanced from the second warrior's helm, snapping back his head; he almost lost his balance and his horse veered to the right, but the last man hurled himself from his saddle to crash into the forest girl as she vainly strove to draw another arrow from her quiver. Her hand flashed for the hunting knife in her belt, but he hammered his fist into her jaw and she fell to the snow, stunned. The other horseman, having gained control of his mount, stepped from the saddle and approached Thuro with his sword extended.

"Well, little prince, I hope you enjoyed the hunt."

Thuro said nothing, but he climbed slowly to his feet and met the assassin's eyes.

"Are you not going to beg for life? How disappointing! I thought at the least you would offer us a king's ransom."

"I do not fear you," Thuro said evenly. "You are a man of little worth. Come, then, childkiller; earn your salt!"

The man tensed and raised his sword, but then his eyes flickered to a point behind Thuro. "Who are you?" he asked, and Thuro turned his head. Behind him, seeming to appear from nowhere, was a man in a white bearskin cloak. His hair was black, and silver shone at the temples; his face was square-cut and clean-shaven, his eyes gray. He was dressed in a dark leather tunic over green woolen leggings, and he carried a silver staff with two ebony grips: one at the top, the second half-way down.

"I asked who you are," repeated the assassin.

"I heard you," the newcomer answered, his voice deep, and colder than the winds of winter.

"Then answer me."

"I am Culain lach Feragh, and you have attacked my ward."

The man glanced at the unconscious girl. "She is only stunned—and she killed Pagis."

"It was a fine effort, and I will compliment her when she wakes. You, boy," he said to Thuro softly, "move behind me," Thuro did as he was bidden, and Culain stepped forward.

"I do not like to kill," he said, "but unfortunately you and your companion cannot be allowed to leave here alive, so I am left with no choice. Come, defend yourselves."

For a moment the two assassins simply stood staring at the man with the staff. Then the first of them ran forward, screaming a battle cry.

Culain's hand dropped down the shaft to the central ebony grip and twisted. The staff parted, and a silver blade appeared in his right hand. He parried the wild cut and reversed a slashing sweep to the assassin's throat. The blade sliced cleanly free, and the man's head slowly toppled from his shoulders. For one terrible moment the body stood; then the right knee buckled, and it fell to rest beside the grisly head. Thuro swallowed hard and tore his eyes from the corpse.

The second assassin ran for his horse and, dropping his sword, vaulted to the saddle as Culain stepped over the corpse and retrieved Laitha's bow. He selected an arrow, drew the string, and loosed the shaft with such consummate skill and lack of speed that Thuro had no doubt as to the outcome even before the missile plunged into the rider's back. Culain dropped the bow and moved to Laitha, lifting her gently.

After a while her eyes opened.

"Will you never learn, Gian?" he whispered. "Another doe for your collection?"

"He is the son of the king. Eldared seeks to kill him." Culain turned, and as his eyes fastened on the prince, Thuro saw something new in his gaze, some emotion that the boy could not place. But then a mask covered Culain's feelings.

"Welcome to my hearth," he said simply.

◇ 3 ◇

ELDARED, KING OF the Brigantes, Lord of the North-ern Wall, sat silently listening to the reports of his huntsmen. His sons Cael and Moret sat beside him, aware that despite his apparent tranquillity, their father's mood was darkening moment by moment.

Eldared was fifty-one years of age and a veteran of dark intrigue. Twenty years earlier he had switched sides to support the young Roman Aurelius Maximus in his bid for the throne, betraying his own brother Cascioc in the process. Since that time his power had grown and his support for Maximus had earned him great wealth, but his ambition was not content with rul-ing the highlands. During the last five years he had steadily increased his support among the warring tribes of the high country and solidified his power base among the Britons of the south. All he needed for the throne to fall was the death of Aurelius and his weakling son. Af-ter that, a surprise raid on Eboracum would leave him in an unassailable position.

But now a plan of stunning simplicity had been re-duced to ashes by simple human error. Three retainers had escaped, and the boy, Thuro, was at large in the mountains. Eldared kept his face calm, his hooded eyes betraying no hint of his alarm. The boy was not a great problem in himself, for he was by all accounts spineless and weak. However, if he managed to get back to Caerlyn, then Lucius Aquila, the canniest of generals, would use him as a puppet to rally support against Eldared. Added to this, if any of the survivors lived long enough to warn Aquila, the raid on Eboracum would become doubly perilous.

Eldared dismissed his huntsmen and turned his gaze to his elder son, Cael, a hawkeyed warrior just past his twentieth birthday.

"Suggestions?" invited the king, and Cael smiled.

"You do not need me to state the obvious, Father."

"No. I need you to show me you *understand* the obvious."

Cael bowed. "At present the boy is of secondary importance. He is hidden somewhere deep in our lands, and we can deal with him at leisure. First we must find the three who escaped, most especially the Roman Victorinus. He is a man Aurelius had chosen for future command, and I believe it was he who stopped the others from returning to seek the king."

"Well and good, boy. But what do you suggest we *do*?"

"Concentrate our efforts in the southwest. Victorinus will cross the wall at Norcester and then cut east and south to Eboracum."

"Why would he take the long route?" asked Moret. "It only increases his danger."

Cael's eyes showed his contempt for the question, but his voice was neutral as he answered it. "Victorinus is no fool, Brother. He knows we will send men southeast, and he gains time by such a maneuver. We need to use Goroien."

Moret cleared his throat and shifted nervously in his seat. Eldared said nothing.

"What choice do we have, Father?" Cael continued.

"Choice?" snapped Moret. "Another dead Brigante babe for that foul woman!"

"And how many dead Brigante men will fall before the walls of Eboracum if we do *not* use the witch?" Cael replied. "If I thought it would guarantee victory, I would let Goroien sacrifice a hundred babes."

"Moret has a point," Eldared said softly. "In this deadly game I like to control events. This Mist Magic of hers can be a boon, but at what price? She plays her own game, I think." He leaned back in his chair, resting his chin on his steepled fingers. "We will give the huntsmen another two days to catch the retainers. If they fail, I will summon Goroien. As for the boy . . . I believe he could be dead somewhere in a snowdrift. But send Alantric into the high country."

"He will not like that," said Moret. "The King's Champion sent out after a runaway boy?"

"His likes and dislikes are mine to command—as are yours," said Eldared. "There will be many opportunities in the spring for Alantric to show his skills with a blade."

"And what of the sword?" Moret asked.

Eldared's eyes flashed, and his face darkened. "Do not speak of it! *Ever!*"

Victorinus sat near the narrow window of the alehouse tavern, staring out at the remains of the Antonine Wall, built far to the north of Hadrian's immense fortifications and stretching from coast to coast over forty miles. It was a turf wall on a stone foundation, and as he stared, the young Roman saw the ruins as a vivid physical reminder of the failing Roman Empire. Three hundred years earlier three legions would have patrolled this area, with a fortress every Roman mile. Now it was windswept and mostly deserted, except in remote villages such as Norcester, on the well-traveled trade roads. He sipped his ale and cast a covert glance across the room to where Gwalchmai and Caradoc were sitting together, just beyond the six Brigante tribesmen. The three had been journeying for nine days; they had managed to buy provisions and a change of clothing from a Greek merchant on the road south. Victorinus was now dressed in the garb of an Order Taker: a long woolen robe and a fur jerkin. Across his shoulders hung a leather satchel containing stylus, parchment and a letter from Publius Aristarchos naming him as Varius Seneca, an Order Taker from Eboracum.

The innkeeper, an elderly Romano-British veteran, moved onto the bench seat alongside Victorinus.

"How soon can delivery be made if I order goods from you?" he asked.

"They will be here in the second week of spring," answered Victorinus, acutely aware of the Brigantes who sat nearby. "Depending of course on what you need," he continued. "It's been a bad year for wine in Gaul, and supplies are not plentiful."

"I need salt a deal more than I need Gallic wine," said the man. "The hunting is good in these hills, but without salt I can save little meat. So tell me, what does your merchant charge for salt?"

Victorinus drew in a deep breath; he was no quartermaster and had no knowledge of such dealings.

"What are you charged currently?" he asked.

"Six sesterces a pound. Five if I take the bulk shipment and then resell to the tribesmen."

"The cost has risen," said Victorinus, "and I fear I cannot match that price."

"So what can you offer?"

"Six and a half. But if you can secure orders from surrounding villages, I will authorize a payment in kind. One bag in ten sold will come to you free."

"I do not know how you people have the nerve to sell at these prices. It is not as if we were at war. The trade routes are as safe now as they have ever been."

"Your thinking is a little parochial, my friend. Most of the trade routes in Brigante territory may be open, but there is a war in the south, and that has cut our profits."

A tall Brigante warrior with a deep scar across his cheek rose from his table and approached Victorinus.

"I have not seen you before," he said.

"Is there any reason why you should have?" Victorinus replied. "Do you travel much to Eboracum?"

"You look more like a soldier than an Order Taker."

"I earn more salt this way, friend, with a great deal less danger."

"Are you traveling alone?"

"Even as you see. But then, I carry little money, and there are few who would attack an Order Taker. They would much rather wait until I have fulfilled my duties and then raid the wagons on their way back."

The man nodded, but his keen blue eyes remained fixed on the young Roman. Finally he turned his back and rejoined his comrades. Victorinus returned to his conversation with the innkeeper while keeping a wary eye on the Brigantes. The scarred tribesman looked across at Caradoc and Gwalchmai.

"Where are you from?" he asked.

"South," said Caradoc.

"Belgae, are you?"

Caradoc nodded.

"I thought I could smell fish!" The other Brigantes chuckled, and Caradoc colored but tore his eyes from the warrior. "I had a Belgae woman once," continued Scarface. "She charged a copper penny. She looked like you; perhaps it was your mother."

Gwalchmai reached across the table and gripped Caradoc's arm just as the tribesman was reaching for his sword. "It could well have been his mother," Gwalchmai put in softly. "As I recall, she had a fondness for animals."

The Brigante rose from his bench. "Not wise to be insulting so far from your homeland."

"It's my upbringing," said Gwalchmai, rising smoothly. "I was taught always to silence a yapping dog."

Iron blades slid sibilantly from their scabbards. Gwalchmai upended the table and leapt to the right, drawing his gladius. Caradoc moved left, his sword extended.

"Six against two," said Gwalchmai, grinning. "Typical of the Brigantes!"

"The object of battle is to win," said Scarface, his eyes gleaming and his color deepening. Caradoc's left hand dropped to his belt, coming up with a heavy dagger. Just as the Brigantes tensed for the attack, Caradoc's arm flashed forward and the dagger entered Scarface's throat below the chin strap of his bronze helm. With a gurgling cry he sank to the floor as Caradoc and Gwalchmai charged into the mass, hacking and cleaving.

Victorinus cursed, drew his gladius from within his robe, and leapt to join them, plunging his blade deep into the back of a stocky warrior. The tavern was filled with the discordant sounds of battle: iron on iron, iron on flesh. Within seconds the fight was over. Victorinus dispatched two of the men, as did Gwalchmai. Caradoc finished his own opponent and then sank to the floor. Victorinus knelt beside him, staring in anguish at the sword that jutted from the Belgae's belly.

"I think he's finished me," said Caradoc, gritting his teeth against the pain.

"I am afraid that he has," Victorinus agreed gently.

"You'd better leave me here. I have much to consider."

Victorinus nodded. "You were a fine companion," he said.

"You, too—for a Roman!"

Gwalchmai joined them. "Is there anything I can do?"

"You could look after my woman, Gwal. She's pregnant again. You could . . ." His eyes lost their sparkle, and breath rattled from his throat.

Gwalchmai swore. "You think they guessed who we were?" he asked.

"Perhaps," replied Victorinus, "but it is more likely to have been the normal British penchant for tribal disharmony. Come, we had better be on our way."

"How far is it to the Wall of Hadrian?"

"Too far—unless the gods smile."

Cael chuckled at his brother's discomfort as they walked across the cobbled courtyard to the carles' quarters. "You should not have mentioned the sword," said the taller man.

"Go ahead, enjoy yourself, Cael. But I know what I

saw. When he threw that blade out over the ice, a hand came up out of the water and drew it down."

"Yes, Brother. Was it a man's hand?"

"Your mockery does not upset me. Two other men saw the hand even if you did not."

"I was too busy putting the finishing blow to the Roman's neck," Cael snapped.

"A blow, I notice, that came from behind. Even without his sword, you did not have the courage to cut him from the front."

"You speak of courage?" Cael sneered, pausing before the oak doors of the carles' quarters. "Where were you? You did not land a blow."

"I considered eighteen to one good enough odds even for you, Cael."

"You miserable sheep! Bleat all you want. I did not hear your voice raised in argument when Father's plan was made known."

"The deed was ignobly done. There is no credit in such a murder. And by all the gods beyond, he died well. Even you must admit that."

"He had a choice, then, you think? Even a cornered rat will fight for its life."

Cael finished the conversation by turning away from his brother and pushing ahead into the dimly lit quarters, seeking Alantric. Moret turned back across the courtyard and returned to his apartments, where his young wife, Alhyffa, waited. She was dark-haired and sloe-eyed, and Moret's passion for her grew daily. He had not wanted to wed the Saxon girl and had argued long into the night with his father. But in the end, as he had known he would, he had given in and the betrothal had been secretly agreed to. He had traveled by ship to meet his bride, all the way around the coast to the lands they were now calling the South Saxon.

Her father had met him in an inlet near Anderida forest, and he had been taken to the long hall to see his bride. His heart had been heavy until the moment she had entered the hall . . . then it had all but stopped. How could a barbarous animal like Hengist produce such offspring? As she approached, he bowed low, breaking all precedent. If she was surprised, she did not show it. He stopped her as she was about to kneel.

"You will never need to kneel before me," he whispered.

And he had been true to his word, a fact that had surprised Alhyffa, especially after her father's disparaging comments concerning the treacherous family.

"Have no fear," he had told her. "Within a few seasons I shall be at Deicester Keep with an army, and then we'll find a good husband for you."

Yet now Alhyffa was not sure that she wanted her father riding north to take her back. Her husband was not a powerful man or a weak one, but he was gentle and loving and aroused in her a feeling not unlike love. As he entered the room, she watched his expression move from his perennial look of sadness to an almost juvenile joy. He swept her into his arms and swung her high into the air.

She draped her arms over his broad shoulders and kissed him lightly.

"I have missed you," he said.

"You liar! You have not been gone an hour."

"It's true; I swear it."

"How went it with your father?"

He shrugged and released her, his face once more sad and wistful. "I have no use for his lust for power. And my brother is as bad—if not worse. You know, Aurelius Maximus was not a bad High King."

"My father spoke of him always with respect."

"And yet your father connived in his murder."

She pulled him to the window bench and sat beside him in the sunshine. "The High King would have connived in the murder of Hengist, yet I do not doubt that he also respected my father. There has never been a king with clean hands, Moret. You are altogether too sensitive." He grinned and looked so terribly young that she took his face in her hands and kissed his fair cheeks, running her fingers through his long blond hair. "You have given me happiness. I pray to Odin that you receive a proper reward for it."

"You are reward enough for any man."

"You say that now, young prince, but what when my beauty fades?"

"Ask me that in twenty years. Or thirty. Or forty. Or a hundred!"

Her face became serious. "Do not wish for the passing of time, Moret, my love. Who knows what the future holds for any of us?"

"Whisht! Do not look sad. The future is all gold, I promise you."

Alhyffa pulled his head into her breast and stroked his hair while her sky-blue eyes stared out toward the south. She saw three horsemen riding, and each was holding aloft a severed head. They came closer—riding across the sky toward the window where she sat—and the sky darkened, lightning flashing behind them. She could not see their faces, nor would she look at the heads they carried; she closed her mind's eye against them and heard the bitter laughter as they rode on:

Odin's messengers, the Stormcrows, taunting her with premonitions of disaster.

She had never loved her father and thus had never cared about his victories or setbacks. But now she was torn. Moret's family was linked with Hengist, and therefore she should wish him success. Yet once successful, her father would turn on Eldared and destroy him and all his get. Eldared with all his cunning could not fail to see this; therefore, he must be planning the same tactic. And then what would be the future for Hengist's daughter?

"Do not think of tomorrow, Moret. Enjoy the now, for it is all any of us ever have."

◇ 4 ◇

THURO AWOKE IN a narrow room with log walls and a single window looking out over the mountains. The room was ice-cold, and the young prince burrowed under the blankets, hugging them to his sleep-warm body. He could not remember coming to bed, only the seemingly endless journey to Culain's log cabin nestling in a wood of pine. At one point Thuro's legs had given way beneath him, and Culain had lifted him effortlessly and carried him like a babe across his chest. Thuro remembered being dumped in a wide leather chair as the warrior tindered a fire in the stone hearth, and he could recall staring into the growing flames. But somewhere about that time he must have passed out.

He looked out across the room and saw his clothes laid on a narrow chair. Glancing below the covers, he saw that he was naked. He hoped fervently that Laitha had not been present when he had been undressed.

The door opened, and Culain entered. His long dark hair was tied at the nape of his neck, and he was wearing a high-necked shirt of thick wool and dark leather leggings over mountain boots of cured sheepskin.

"Time to be up, Prince! And doing!"

He walked to the bed and dragged back the covers. "Dress yourself and join me in the other room."

37

"Good morning to you," Thuro told his departing back, but Culain did not respond. The prince climbed from the bed and into his green woolen leggings and shirt of cream-colored wool edged with braid. Then he pulled on his boots and returned to sit on the bed. The events of the previous day washed over him like icy water. His father was dead, and his own life was in peril. He was hundreds of miles from friends and home, at the mercy of a grim-faced stranger he did not know. "I could do with your help now, Maedhlyn," he whispered.

Taking a deep breath and offering a prayer to the Earth Goddess, he joined Culain in the main room. The warrior was stacking logs in the hearth when he entered and did not look up.

"Outside you will find an ax and a hatchet. Chop twenty logs no bigger than you see here. Do it now, boy."

"Why should I chop logs for you?" asked Thuro, disliking the man's tone.

"Because you slept in my bed, and I don't doubt you'll want to eat my food. Or is payment above you, Prince?"

"I will chop your logs, and then I will leave you," Thuro said. "I like nothing about your manners."

Culain laughed. "You are welcome to leave, but I will be interested to know in which snowdrift you are planning to die. You are weaker than any boy I have ever known. I doubt you have the strength to walk down the mountain, and you certainly do not have the wit to know which direction to take."

"Why should my fate concern you?"

"I'll answer that question when I'm ready," Culain said, rising to his feet and moving to tower over the youngster. Thuro stood his ground and answered the firm gaze with uplifted chin, giving not an inch.

Culain smiled. "Well, boy, you may have no strength in your arms, but your spirit is not lacking, thank the Source. Now, chop the logs and we'll discuss your departure over breakfast."

Thuro felt he had won a small victory, but he was not sure what the prize might be or whether the win was worth a lick of salt. He left the cabin and located the wood store some eighty feet away, near a stand of trees.

He found the ax embedded in a log and wrestled it clear. Then he lifted the log to stand on a thick ring of pine and hefted the ax over his head. His first swing saw the ax head miss the log, burying itself in the snow-covered ground. He wrenched it clear, steadied his feet, and tried once more. This time the head glanced from the log, tearing the ax from Thuro's slender fingers; he retrieved it. On the third swing the ax hit into the log, stopping half way through and trapping the head. After several minutes he worked it loose; then he stood and thought about the action necessary to complete the task. He planted his feet wider apart, with his right leg slightly ahead, swung the ax—and split the log. He continued work for some time, until his breathing became ragged and his face was white with exhaustion. He counted the logs. Eleven ... and Culain had asked for twenty! More slowly now he continued the chore. His hands hurt, and he put down the ax to check the skin; four large blisters decorated his palm. He glanced toward the cabin, but there was no sign of Culain. Once more he counted the logs: eighteen. He took the ax in his injured hand and set to work until twenty had been split, leaving forty solid chunks.

Returning to the cabin, he found Culain sitting in the

wide leather chair, his feet raised on a small table. The warrior looked up as he entered.

"I thought you'd fallen asleep out there, Prince."

"I did not fall asleep, and I dislike the tone in your voice when you use my title—you make it sound like a dog's name. My name is Thuro; if you are uncomfortable around royalty, you may use that."

"May I indeed. What a singular honor! Where is the wood?"

"It is all chopped."

"But it needs to be in here to be of any use, boy."

Swallowing his anger, Thuro returned to the wood store and hefted three chunks, which he carried with ease back to the cabin, up the three steps, and into the hearth. He repeated this maneuver eight times before his arms burned like fire and his feet dragged in the snow. Culain merely sat, offering no assistance. Twice more Thuro stumbled back bearing wood, then he staggered and fell to the cabin floor. Culain leaned from his chair and tapped the boy on the back.

"Seven more chunks, I think, young Thuro."

The prince rolled to his knees, anger giving him strength as he staggered out into the snow and this time hefted four pieces, which he carried slowly back. His right hand was hot and sticky, and as he dumped the wood in the hearth, he noticed that blood was leaking from the torn blisters. He returned to the wood store and with a supreme effort carried the last of the chunks back to the cabin.

"Never leave an ax naked to the air," said Culain. "Always embed it in wood; it protects the edge."

Thuro nodded but lacked the strength for a retort. Once more in the open, he took the ax and plunged the head into a log.

"Anything else?" he called. "Or is it part of the game that I return first?"

"Come and eat," Culain called.

The two broke fast with cold meat and cheese, and Thuro wolfed his small portion swiftly. This was followed by a dark ale so bitter that the prince choked. Culain said nothing, but Thuro finished the foul brew to preempt any sneer.

"How do you feel?" Culain asked.

"I am fine."

"Would you like me to tend to your hand?"

Thuro was about to refuse when he saw that that was what the other man expected. He recalled the advice of Ptolemy, as reported by Plutarch: "As long as you react, your enemy holds your destiny in the palm of his hand. When you force him to react, you hold his neck in yours." Thuro smiled. "That would be kind."

Culain's eyebrows rose. "Hold out your hand." Thuro did so, and the warrior tipped salt from the shaker directly onto the wound. It stung like needles of fire. "That should suffice," said Culain. "Now I would like you to do me a service."

"I owe you nothing. I have paid for my breakfast."

"Indeed you have, but I would like you to carry a message to Laitha. I don't suppose you would want to leave without wishing her good-bye."

"Very well. Where is she?"

"She and I built a cabin higher in the peaks. She likes the solitude. Go to her and tell her I would appreciate her company this evening."

"Is that all?"

"Yes."

"Then I shall bid you farewell, Culain lach Feragh—

whatever that title may mean—and thank you for your awesome hospitality."

"I think you should delay your departure—at least until you know where to find Laitha."

"Then be so kind as to tell me."

Culain gave him simple directions, and Thuro left without another word. The morning was bright and chilly without a trace of breeze, and he wandered through the bleak winter landscape for over an hour before coming to the path Culain had indicated, which was marked by a fallen tree. He turned to the right and continued the climb, stopping often to rest. It was almost dusk when the exhausted prince came to Laitha's small cabin. She helped him inside, and he sat slumped before a log fire for several minutes, gathering his breath.

"I thought I would die out there," he said at last.

She sat beside him. "Climb out of those wet clothes and get warm."

"It is not fitting," he replied, hoping she would offer an argument. She did not.

"I'll fetch you something to eat. Some bread and cheese, perhaps."

"That would be wonderful. I haven't been this hungry since . . . I can't remember."

"It's a long haul to my home. Why did you come?" She offered him some dark bread and a round of white cheese.

"Culain asked me to give you a message. He said he wanted your company this evening."

"How strange."

"The man is strange and quite the most discourteous individual I have ever met."

"Well, I think it best you gather your strength and

feed a little warmth into your body before we head back."

"I shall not be going back. I have said my farewells," Thuro told her.

"You must go back. It is the only way off the mountain, and it will be well after dark before we reach his cabin. You"ll have to spend at least one more night there."

"Can I not stay here? With you?"

"As you said, Prince Thuro, that would not be fitting."

"He knew that," said Thuro. "He knew I would be trapped here. What evil game is he playing?"

"I think you presume too much," she snapped. "You are speaking of a friend of mine—the greatest friend anyone could ever have. Perhaps Culain does not like spoiled young princelings. But he saved your life, as he saved mine ten years ago—at no small risk to himself. Did he ask you for payment for that, Thuro?"

Instinctively he reached out and touched her hand. She withdrew it as if stung. "I am sorry," he said. "I did not mean to offend you. North of the wall, you are now the only friend I have. But even you said it was strange that he asked me to come here. Why was that?"

"It does not matter. We should be going."

"But it *does* matter, Laitha. Let me hazard a guess. You were surprised because you were going to him anyway. Is that not true?"

"Perhaps. Or perhaps he forgot."

"He does not strike me as a forgetful man. He knew I would be forced back to his cabin."

"Ask him when you see him," she countered, donning a heavy sheepskin jerkin and opening the door of the cabin. Outside, a heavy snowfall was in progress and the wind was picking up alarmingly. With a curse Thuro had last heard from a soldier, she slammed the door. "We cannot leave now," she said. "You'll have to stay the night." Thuro's mood brightened considerably.

Just then the door opened, and Culain stepped inside, pausing to brush a dusting of snow from his shoulders.

"Not a good night for traveling, Prince," he said. "Still, one or two chores in the morning and you'll soon pay for your keep."

Victorinus and Gwalchmai had been riding for four days, and for the last two they had been without food. The Roman was concerned more about the state of their supplies than about the possibility of capture, for the horses needed grain, and without horses they had no chance of leaving the land of the Brigantes.

"What I would not give for a good bow," said Gwalchmai as they spotted several deer on the flanks of a low hill.

Victorinus did not respond. He was tired, and the growth of beard on his square chin made him irritable. He was a man who liked to be clean, and the smell of his own stale sweat also galled him as he scratched at his face, cursing the lack of a razor.

"You are beginning to look human," said Gwalchmai. "Another few months and I'll braid the beard for you; then you can walk in respectable company."

Victorinus grinned, and some of his ill humor evaporated. "We have no coin left, Gwal, but somehow we must find food for the horses."

"I suggest we aim for the high ground," said Gwalchmai, "and try to spot a village or settlement. We can trade some of Caradoc's gear; his sword should fetch a good price." Victorinus nodded, but he did not like the idea. The saddest fact about the British tribes was that they were incapable of mixing together without bloodshed. The thought of Gwalchmai riding into any Brigante or Trinovante settlement filled him with apprehension.

They camped that night in a glade nestling in the bowl of the hills and out of the wind. It snowed heavily, but the two men and their mounts were snug in the shelter of a heavily laden pine and the fire kept their blood from freezing.

The following morning they located a small settlement consisting of some twelve huts and rode warily in. Gwalchmai seemed unconcerned, and Victorinus marveled anew at the British optimism that pervaded the tribes. They had a total inability to learn from past mistakes and greeted each new day as an opportunity to replay the errors of the past twenty-four hours.

"Try not to insult anyone," urged Victorinus.

"Have no fear, Roman. Today is a good day."

They were met by the village headman, an elderly warrior with braided white hair and a blue tattoo on his forehead in the shape of a spider's web.

"Greetings, Father," said Gwalchmai as a small crowd gathered behind the headman.

"I am no father to you, South Rat," answered the man, grinning and showing only one tooth at the top of his jaw.

"Do not be too sure, Father. You look like a man who spread his seed wide as a youngster, and my mother was a woman who attracted such men."

The crowd chuckled, and the old man stepped forward, his blue eyes bright. "Now you mention it, there is a certain family resemblance. I take it you've brought a gift for your old father?"

"Indeed I have," said Gwalchmai, stepping down from the saddle and presenting the old man with Caradoc's best knife, an oval-bladed weapon with a hilt of carved bone.

"From across the water," said the old man, hefting the weapon. "Good iron—and a fine edge."

"It is pleasant to be home," said Gwalchmai. "Can we rest the night and feed our horses?"

"But of course, my son." The old man called forward two youngsters, and they led the horses back toward a paddock east of the settlement. "Join me in my hut."

The hut was sparsely furnished, but it was a welcome respite from the wind. There was a cot bed and several rugs, and an iron brazier was burning coal. An elderly woman bowed as they entered and fetched bowls of dark ale and some bread and cheese. The three men sat by the brazier, and the ancient identified himself as Golaric, once the champion of the old king, Cascioc.

"A fine king, good with sword or lance. He was murdered by his brother and that cursed Roman, Aurelius." Golaric's bright eyes switched to Victorinus. "It is not often that an Order Taker bothers to visit my small village."

"I am not an Order Taker," Victorinus owned.

"I know that. My teeth may be gone, but my mind is unaffected. You are Victorinus the centurion. And you, my wayward son, are Gwalchmai the Cantii, the Hound of the King. Word travels with exceptional speed."

"We are hunted men, Father," said Gwalchmai.

"Indeed you are. Is it true that bastard Roman is dead?"

"Yes," said Victorinus, "and I'll not hear that term used of him—alive or dead."

"Short-tempered, is he not?" asked Golaric, seeing Victorinus' hand straying toward his gladius.

"You know these Romans, Father. No control," said Gwalchmai. "Why are you so open with your knowledge?"

"It pleases me to be so."

Gwalchmai smiled. "I know something of Brigante history. Cascioc was Eldared's elder brother; he was slain in his bed. There was almost a civil war among the tribes of the old Caledonian Confederacy. What part did you play in that, Father?"

"As I said, I was the King's Champion. I had a good arm in those days, and I should have gone to Eldared and cut his throat, but I did not. The deed was done, and I was sworn on blood oath to defend the king with my life. But Eldared was now the king, so I left his service. And now he offers good gold to kill the men who are a danger to him. I am not interested in his gold; I am interested only in his downfall."

"I cannot promise that," said Victorinus. "All I can say is that he will succeed if we do not reach Eboracum. Eldared bragged of having around fifteen thousand men at his call. Lucius Aquila has only four thousand at Eboracum. Taken by surprise, he would be routed."

"I do not care whether a Roman survives at Eboracum, but I understand the point you are making. Your horses will be fed and watered tonight, but tomorrow you will leave. I will give you food to carry—not much, for we are a poor village. But be warned; there are hunting parties south and east of you. You must move west and then south."

"We will be careful, Father," said Gwalchmai.

"And you can stop calling me 'Father.' I never slept with a Cantii woman in my life—they were all bearded."

Gwalchmai chuckled. "He's right," he told Victorinus. "It's one reason I joined the king's army."

"There's something else for you to think of," said Golaric. "The huntsmen seem unconcerned about your capture; they say that Mist Magic is being used to track you. If that is true, I pity you."

The color drained from Gwalchmai's face. "What does he mean?" asked Victorinus.

"Death," Gwalchmai whispered.

Throughout the long day the two men rode together, and Victorinus grew steadily more uncomfortable with the silence. The land was open, the wind was bitterly cold, but it was Gwalchmai's frightened eyes that dominated the Roman's thinking. He had known Gwalchmai for four years, since arriving at Camulodunum as a raw eighteen-year-old fresh from Rome. In that time he had come to hold the man in high regard for his eternal optimism and reckless bravery, but now he rode like a man possessed, his eyes unseeing, his manner echoing his defeat. They camped in the lee of a rock face, and Victorinus prepared a fire.

"What is wrong with you, man?" he asked as Gwalchmai sat passively staring into the flames.

"It is well for you that you do not understand," said Gwalchmai.

"I understand fear when I see it."

"It is worse than fear; it is the foreknowledge of death. I must ready myself for the journey."

At a loss for a response, Victorinus laughed in his face. "Is this Gwalchmai I see before me? Is this the

King's Hound? More like a rabbit in the torchlight, waiting for the arrow to strike. What is the matter with you, man?"

"You do not understand," repeated Gwalchmai. "It is in the bones of this land ... in the gods of wood and lake. This land was once the home of the gods, and they still walk here within the Mist. Do not mock me, Roman, for I know whereof I speak. I have seen scaled dragons in the air. I have seen the Atrol walk. I have heard the hissing of dead men's breath. There is no escaping it; if the old gods walk our trail, there is nowhere to hide."

"You talk like an old woman. What I can see, I can cut. What I can cut, I can kill. There is no more to be said. Gods, indeed! Look around you. Where are the Atrols? Where are the dragons? Where are the dead that walk?"

"You will see, Victorinus. Before they take you, you will see."

A cloud obscured the moon, and an owl swooped over the campsite. "There is your dragon, Gwalchmai. Out hunting mice!"

"My father angered an Enchanter once," said Gwalchmai softly, "and he summoned a witch woman. They found my father on a hillside—or rather, they found the bottom half of him. The top had been ripped away, and I saw the fang marks on his back."

"Perhaps you are right," offered Victorinus, "and perhaps demons do walk. But if they do, a man must face them. Fear is the killer here, Gwal." A distant wolf howled, the sound echoing eerily through the glade. Victorinus shivered and cursed inwardly. He wrapped his blanket around his shoulders and stoked the fire, adding fresh branches to the blaze.

"I'll keep watch for a couple of hours," he said. "You get some sleep."

Obediently Gwalchmai wrapped himself in his blankets and lay down by the fire while Victorinus drew his gladius and sat with his back to a tree. The night wore on, and the cold grew. The Roman added more fuel to the fire until the last broken branch was all but finished, then he pushed himself to his feet and stretched his back, moving off into the darkness to gather more dead wood. He put down his gladius and had stooped to lift a long windfall branch when a low, whispering sound alerted him. Still on edge after the conversation with Gwalchmai, he dropped the wood, swept up his sword, and dived to the right. Something touched the skin of his back, and he rolled, gladius sweeping up into the darkness that threatened to overwhelm him. The blade struck something solid, and a bestial scream followed. Victorinus rolled once more as a dark shadow loomed over him, then with a battle cry he leapt to meet his assailant. His sword plunged home, then a blow to the side of the head sent him hurtling back into the campsite to skid across the glowing coals of the fire. The clouds parted, the moon shining its silver light on the scene. Victorinus came to his feet—and froze . . . Before him was a creature some nine feet tall, covered in long brown hair. Its eyes were red, shining like freshly spilled blood, and its fangs were the length of daggers and wickedly curved. The creature's arms were disproportionately long, hanging almost to the ground, and from the end of each of its four fingers grew gleaming serrated talons.

A gray mist swirled around Victorinus' legs, rising even as he noticed it. The creature advanced. The Roman swiftly wiped his sword hand free of sweat and gripped the leather hilt of his gladius. It was the wrong weapon for this beast; he needed a spear.

"Come forward and die!" he called. "Have a taste of Roman iron!"

The creature stopped—and spoke. Victorinus was so surprised that he almost dropped his sword.

"You cannot fight destiny, Victorinus," it said, its voice sibilant. "This is the day of your passing. Cease your struggle. Rest and know peace. Rest and know joy. Rest . . ." The voice was hypnotic, and as the beast advanced, Victorinus blinked and tried to rouse himself from the lethargy it induced in him. The mist rose about his shoulders, billowing like woodsmoke.

"No!" he said, backing away.

Suddenly an unearthly scream pierced the silence. The mist parted, and Victorinus saw Gwalchmai behind the beast, raising his bloody sword for a second strike. The Roman raced forward to plunge his blade into the hairy throat. The talons lashed at him, ripping the front of his robes and scoring the skin. Gwalchmai struck once more from behind, and the creature fell. The mist thickened and then vanished.

The beast was gone.

Victorinus staggered back to the campsite, gathering together the hot coals with his swordblade and blowing flames to life. Gwalchmai joined him, but they said nothing until the fire was once more lit.

"Forgive me," said the Roman. "I mocked in ignorance."

"There is nothing to forgive. You were right—a man must fight for life even when he believes all is lost. You taught me a lesson today, Roman. I will not forget it."

"This is obviously a day for lessons. What was that thing?"

"An Atrol—and a small one. We were lucky, Victorinus. By now they will know they have failed, and the next demon will not die as easily."

"Maybe not, but it *will* die."

Gwalchmai grinned and slapped him on the shoulder. "I believe you."

"One of us ought to," said the Roman.

"I think we should leave this place," offered Gwalchmai. "Now that they have the scent, they will be close behind us."

As if to emphasize his words, a dreadful howling came from the north. It was answered from the east and west.

"Wolves?" Victorinus asked, dreading the answer.

"Atrols. Let us ride."

◇ 5 ◇

THURO STARED AT the unsmiling Culain and for the first time in his young life felt hatred swell inside him. His father was dead, his own life was in ruins, and now he was at the mercy of this strange mountain man. He stood up from the floor before the fire.

"I'll work for my keep tonight," he said, "despite your trickery. But then I leave."

"I fear not, young prince," said Culain, stripping off his leather jerkin and moving to stand before the fire. "The lower valleys will be cut off by morning, and the snow will be drifting over ten feet deep. I am afraid we are forced to endure your company for at least two months."

"You are a liar!"

"Rarely is that true," Culain replied softly, kneeling to extend his hands to the flames. "And certainly not on this occasion. Still, look on the summer side, Thuro. You do not have to see much of me—a few simple chores and you can keep Laitha company. Added to this, you may not be able to leave, but neither can your enemies come upon you. By spring you will be able to make the journey home a far less dangerous one. You may even learn something."

"You have nothing to teach me. I need to acquire none of your ways."

Culain shrugged. "As you will. I am tired. I am not as young as once I was. May I rest my old bones upon your cot, Gian?"

"Of course," said Laitha. Thuro saw the look in her eyes and wished he could inspire such a reaction. Her love for Culain was a radiant thing, and Thuro was amazed that he had not realized it before. He felt like an interloper, an intruder, and his heart sank. Why should the forest girl not love this man of action, tall and oak-strong, mature and powerful? Thuro turned away from the love in her eyes and wandered to the far window. It was shut tight against the weather, and he made a point of examining the wood, noting the neatness with which it fit the frame. Not a breath of draft troubled him. When he turned back, Culain had gone into the back room, Laitha with him. Thuro returned to the fire. He could hear them speaking in low tones but could distinguish no words.

Laitha returned a few minutes later and lit two candles. "He is sleeping," she said.

"Forgive me, Laitha. I had not wished to intrude."

Her large brown eyes focused on him, her look quizzical. "In what way intrude?"

He swallowed hard, aware that he walked a dangerous path. "On you and Culain. You seem happy together and probably did not need . . . more company. I will be gone as soon as I am able."

She nodded. "You were wrong, Thuro. There is much you can learn here—if you use your time well. Culain is a good man, the best I have known. There is no malice in him—whatever you may think. But there is always a reason for his actions that has little to do with selfishness."

"I do not know him as well as you," said Thuro in his best neutral tone.

"Indeed you do not. But you might, if only you would start thinking instead of reacting."

"I do not understand your meaning. Thinking is perhaps the one strength I have. In all my life my mind has never let me down as have my legs and lungs."

She smiled and reached out to touch his shoulder, and he felt an almost electric thrill in his blood. "Then think, Thuro. Why is he here?"

"How can I answer that?"

"By examining the evidence before you and reaching a conclusion. Think on it as a riddle."

Here was a situation in which Thuro felt comfortable. Even the word "riddle" made him feel more at home, remembering his evenings with Maedhlyn in the oak-paneled study. His mind switched effortlessly to a new path. Culain had asked him to visit Laitha, bringing a message, but then had come himself, thus negating the need for Thuro's journey. Why? He thought of the long arduous climb to this lonely cabin and realized that the mountain man must have set out soon after he had. He looked up and found Laitha staring at him intently. He smiled, but her face remained fixed.

"Have you come upon the answer?" she asked.

"Perhaps. He was watching out for me in case I collapsed in the snow."

Now it was her turn to smile, and he watched the tension flow from her shoulders. "Do you still see him as an ogre?"

"The fact remains that there was no necessity for me to come here at all."

"Think about that, too," she said, rising smoothly and moving to a long chest by the far wall. She removed two blankets and passed them to him. "Sleep here before the fire. I will see you in the morning."

"Where will you sleep?" he asked.

"Alongside Culain."

"Oh. Yes, of course."

"Yes, of course," she repeated, the hint of fire in her eyes. He colored deeply and looked away.

"I did not mean to offend. Truly."

"Your words are not as offensive as the look in your eye."

He nodded and spread his hands. "I am jealous. Forgive me."

"Why should I forgive you? What is your crime? You see and you do not see. You make judgments on the flimsiest evidence. Do not be misled, Thuro, as to your strengths. True, your body is not as strong as your mind. But what does that tell us? Your body is so weak that you have mistakenly inflated the true power of your intellect. Your mind is undisciplined, and your arrogance unacceptable. Good night to you."

He sat for a long time watching the fire burn, adding logs and thinking on what she had said. He should have known that Culain had followed him from the moment the tall warrior had entered the cabin, just as he should have known why he had been told to come here. True, it was to trap him in the mountains for the remainder of the winter, but there was no gain in it for Culain, only for Thuro, safe now from his enemies. He lay on the floor with the blanket over his shoulders, feeling foolish and young and far out of his depth. Laitha first and then Culain had saved his life. He had repaid them with arrogance and lack of gratitude.

He awoke early, having slept dreamlessly. The fire was down to gray ash with an occasional glowing ember. He carefully shifted the ash, allowing air to circulate, and added the last of the logs. Then he rose and left the cabin. Outside, the snow had stopped and the air was fresh and bitterly cold. He located the wood store and took up a long-handled ax. His first stroke sliced a thick log, and he felt pride roar through him. He grinned and drew in a deep, searing breath. The blisters on his hand had dried, but the skin was still sore. He ignored the growing discomfort and continued to chop the wood until twenty logs had been rendered to forty-six chunks. Then he gathered them and sat down on the chopping ring, sweat dripping from his face. He no longer felt cold; he felt alive. His arms and shoulders burned with the raw physical effort, and he waited a little while until his breathing returned to normal. Then he took up three chunks and carried them back to the hearth. Just as he had the day before, he began to feel light-headed after several trips, so he slowed his action and rested often. In that way he completed his task without collapse and felt a ridiculous sense of achievement when the hearth was full. He returned to the wood store and hammered the ax blade into a log. His hand was bleeding again, and he sat staring at the congealing blood, as proud of it as of a battle scar.

A brightly colored bird fluttered down to sit on a branch above his head. Its breast was reddish brown, while its head was black, as if a little cap were perched there. On its back the feathers were gray, like a tiny cape, and the ends of its wings and tail were black with a white stripe, like the symbol of a Pilus Primus, a first centurion.

Thuro had seen birds like that before in Eboracum

wood but had never stopped to examine their beauty. It gave a soft, piping whistle and then vanished off into the woods.

"It was a Pyrrhula, a bullfinch," said Culain, and Thuro jumped. The man's approach had been as silent as the arrival of dawn. "There are many beautiful birds in the high country. Look there!" Thuro followed his pointing finger and saw the most comical sight. It was a small orange bird with a white beard and black mustache, looking for all the world like a tiny sorcerer. "That is a Panurus Biarmicus, a bearded tit," said Culain. "There are very few left now."

"It looks like a friend of mine. I wish he could see it."

"You speak of Maedhlyn, and he has already seen it."

"You know Maedhlyn?"

"I have known Maedhlyn since the world was young. We grew up in the city of Balacris before Atlantis sank. And you asked about my title—Culain lach Feragh: Culain the Immortal." He smiled. "But not any longer. Now I am Culain the man and the happier for it. I greet every new gray hair as a gift."

"You are from the Land of Mist?"

"Maedhlyn and I and several others created the land. It was not easy, and even now I am not sure it was worthwhile. What do you think?"

"How can I answer that? I have never been there. Is it wondrous?"

"Wondrously dull, boy! Can you imagine immortality? What is there that is new in the world to pique your interest? What ambitions can you foster that are not instantly achievable? What joy is there in an endless sequence of shifting seasons? Far better to be mortal and grow old with the world around you."

"There is love, surely," said Thuro.

"There is always love. But after a hundred years or a thousand, the flames of passion are little more than a glow in the ash of a long-dead fire."

"Is Laitha immortal?"

"No, she is not of the Mist. Are you taken with her, Thuro? Or are you bored, stuck in these woods?"

"I am not bored. And yes, she is beautiful."

"That is not what I asked."

"Then I cannot answer. But I would not presume to approach your lady even were she to receive me."

Culain's gray eyes sparkled, and a wide grin crossed his features. "Well said! However, she is not my lady. She is my ward."

"But she sleeps with you!"

"Sleeps, yes. Was life so sheltered for you in Eboracum? What can Maedhlyn have been thinking of?"

"And yet she loves you," said Thuro. "You cannot deny it."

"I would hope that she does, for I have been a father to her—as best I could."

For the first time in his short relationship with the Mist Warrior Thuro felt strangely superior. For he knew that Laitha loved Culain as a man; he could see it in her eyes and the tilt of her head. Yet Culain could not see it; this made him truly mortal, and Thuro warmed to him.

"How old are you?" he asked, switching the subject.

"The answer would dazzle you, and I shall not give it. But I will say that I have watched this island and its people for over seven hundred years. I was even the king once."

"Of which tribe?"

"Of all the tribes. Have you not heard of Cunobelin?"

"The Trinovante king? Yes. That was you?"

"For over forty years I ruled. I was a legend, they tell me. I helped build Camulodunum. Suetonius wrote of me that I was the Brittanorum Rex—the king of all Britain—the greatest of the Belgic kings. Ah, but I had an ego in those days, and I did like so to be flattered!"

"Some of the tribes believe that you will return when the land is threatened. It is taught around the campfires. I thought it a wonderful fable, but it could be true. You could come back; you could be king again."

Culain saw the brightness of hope in the boy's eyes. "I am not the king any longer, Thuro. And I have no wish to rule. But you can."

Thuro shook his head. "I am not like my father."

"No. There is a great deal of your mother in you."

"Did you know her?"

"Yes, I was there the day Maedhlyn brought your father home. Alaida gave up everything for him, including life. It is not a subject it pleases me to speak of, but you have a right. Alaida was my daughter, the only child I have fathered in my long life. She was nineteen when she left the Feragh, twenty when she died. Twenty! I could have killed Maedhlyn then. I nearly did. But he was so penitent, I realized it was a greater punishment to leave him be."

"Then you are my grandfather?" Thuro asked, savoring the feel of the word and seeing for the first time that Culain's eyes of woodsmoke gray were the image of his own.

"Yes," said Culain.

"Why did you never come to see me? Did you hate me for killing my mother?"

"I think that I did, Thuro. Great age does not always ensure great wisdom, as Maedhlyn knows! I could have

saved Alaida, but I refused to allow her to take a stone
from the Feragh."

"Are the stones magical there?"

"Not all of them, but there is a special stone we call
the Sipstrassi, and it is the source of all magic. What a
man can dream, he can create. The most imaginative of
men become Enhancers; they liven an otherwise tedious
existence with their living dreams."

"Maedhlyn is one of these," said Thuro, "I have seen
him conjure winged horses no longer than my fingers
and whole armies to battle on my father's desktop. He
showed me Marathon and Thermopylae, Platea and
Phillipi. I saw the great Julius fought to a standstill in
Britain by Caswallon. I listened to Antony's funeral
oration . . ."

"Yes, I, too, have seen these things," said Culain,
"but I was speaking of Alaida."

"I am sorry," said Thuro, instantly contrite.

"Do not be. Boys and magic make for excitement.
She had her own stone, but I would not allow her to
take it from the Feragh. I thought somehow that when
she needed me, she would call. I knew I would hear her
wherever I was. But she did not call. She chose to die.
Such was her pride."

"And you blame yourself for her death?"

"Who else would I blame? But that is in the past, and
you are the present. What am I to do with you?"

"Help me get back to Eboracum?"

"Not as you are, Thuro. You are only half a man. We
must make you strong; you will not survive a day as the
weakling prince."

"Will you use stone magic to make me strong?"

"No. Earth magic," said Culain. "We will look inside
you and see what we can find."

"I am not cut out to be a warrior."

"You are my grandson and the son of Aurelius and Alaida. I think you will find that blood runs true. We already know you can swing an ax. What other surprises do you hold in store?"

Thuro shrugged. "I do not want to disappoint you as I disappointed my father."

"Lesson one, Thuro: from now on you have no one to disappoint but yourself. But you must agree to abide by what I say and obey every word I utter. Will you do this?"

"I will."

"Then prepare to die," said Culain. And there was no humor in his eyes.

Thuro stiffened as Culain stood and pulled a gladius from a sheath behind his belt. The blade was eighteen inches long and double-edged, its hilt of leather. He reversed the weapon and handed it to Thuro. It felt blade-heavy and uncomfortable in his hand.

"Before I can teach you to live, you must learn to die—how it feels to be vanquished," Culain said. "Move onto open ground and wait." Thuro did as he was bidden and Culain produced a small golden stone from his pocket, closing his fist around it. The air thickened before Thuro, solidifying into a Roman warrior with a bronze breastplate and leather helm. He seemed young, but his eyes were old. The warrior dropped into a fighting crouch with his blade extended, and Thuro backed away, uncertain.

The warrior advanced, locking Thuro's gaze. The blade lunged. Instinctively Thuro parried, but his opponent's gladius rolled over his own and plunged into the boy's chest. The pain was sickening, and all strength fled from the prince. His knees buckled, and he fell with a scream as the Roman dragged free his blade.

Moments later Thuro rose out of darkness to feel the snow on his face. He pushed himself to his knees and felt for the wound. There was none. Culain's strong hand pulled him to his feet, and Thuro's head spun. Culain sat him on the chopping ring.

"The man you fought was a Roman legionary who served under Agricola. He was seventeen and went on to become a fine gladiator. You met him early in his career. Did you learn anything?"

"I learned I am no swordsman," Thuro admitted ruefully.

"I want you to use your brain and stop thinking with your feelings. You knew nothing of Plutarch before Maedhlyn taught you. There are no born swordsmen; it is an acquired skill, like any other. All it requires is good reflexes allied to courage. You have both. Believe it! Now follow me; there is something I want you to see."

Thuro offered the gladius to Culain, who waved it away. "Carry it with you always. Get used to the feel and the weight. Keep it sharp."

The Mist Warrior walked out past the cabin and down the slope toward the valley below. Thuro followed, his belly aching for food. The return trip to Culain's cabin was made in less than an hour, and the prince was frozen when they arrived. The cabin was cold, and there was no wood in the hearth.

"I shall prepare breakfast," Culain said. "You—"

"I know. Chop some logs."

Culain smiled and left the boy by the wood store. Thuro took up the ax in his sore hands and began his work. He managed only six logs and carried the chunks into the hearth. Culain did not berate him and gave him a wooden bowl filled with hot oats sweetened with honey. The meal was heavenly.

Culain cleared away the dishes and returned with a wide bowl brimming with clear water. He placed it before Thuro and waited for the ripples to settle.

"Look into the water, Thuro." As the prince leaned forward, Culain lifted a golden stone over it and closed his eyes.

At first Thuro could see only his reflection and the wooden beams above his head. But then the water misted, and he found himself staring down from a great height to the shores of a frozen lake. A group of riders was gathered there. The scene swelled, as if Thuro were swooping down toward them, and he recognized his father. A burning pain began in his chest, tightening his throat, and tears blurred his vision. He blinked them back. By the lake a man stepped from behind a rock, a longbow bent. The arrow flashed into his father's back, and his horse reared as his weight fell across its neck, but he held on. The other riders swarmed forward, and the king drew his sword and cut the first man from the saddle. A second arrow took his horse in the throat, and the beast fell. The king leapt clear and ran to the edge of the lake, turning with his back to the ice. The riders—seventeen of them—dismounted. Thuro saw Eldared at the rear with one of his sons. The group rushed forward, and the king, blood staining his beard, stepped in to meet them with his double-handed sword hacking and cleaving. The killers fell back in dismay. Five were now down, and two others had retired from the fray with deep wounds to arm and shoulder. The king stumbled and bent double, blood frothing from his mouth. Thuro wanted to look away, but his eyes were locked to the scene. An assassin ran in to plunge a dagger into the king's side; the dying monarch's blade sliced up and over, all but beheading the man. Then the king turned and staggered onto the ice and, with the last of his strength, hurled the sword far out over the lake. The assassins swarmed around the fallen king, and Thuro saw Cael deliver the death blow. And in that dreadful moment the prince watched as something akin to triumph flared in Aurelius' eyes. The sword hung in the air, hilt down, just above a spot at the center of the lake where the ice had broken. A slender hand reached up from below the water and drew the sword down.

The scene fragmented and blurred, and Thuro's astonished face appeared on the surface of the water in the bowl. He leaned back and saw Culain watching him intently.

"What you saw was the death of a man," said Culain softly, respectfully, as if conveying the greatest compliment. "It was meet that you should see it."

"I am glad that I did. Did you see his eyes at the end? Did I misread them, or was there joy there?"

"I wondered about that, and only time will supply an answer. Did you see the sword?"

"Yes. What did it mean?"

"Simply that Eldared does not have it. And without it he cannot become High King. It is the Sword of Cunobelin. My sword!"

"Of course. My father took it from the stone at Camulodunum; he was the first to be able to draw it."

Culain chuckled. "There was little skill in that. Aurelius had Maedhlyn to guide him, and it was Maedhlyn who devised the stone ploy in the first place. The reason no one could draw the sword was that it was always a heartbeat ahead in time. Draw it? No man could touch it. It was part of the legend of Cunobelin, a legend Maedhlyn and I established four hundred years ago."

"For what reason?" Thuro asked.

"Vanity. In those days, as I have told you, I had a great ego. And it was fun, Thuro, to be a king. Maedhlyn helped me age gracefully. I still had the strength of a twenty-five-year-old in a body that looked wonderfully wrinkled. But then I grew bored, and Maedhlyn staged my death—but not before I had dramatically planted my sword in the boulder and created the legend of my return. Who knew then but that I might want to? Unfortunately, events did not fare too well after my departure. A young man named Caractacus decided to anger the Romans, and they took the island by force. By then I was elsewhere. Maedhlyn and I crossed the Mist to another age. He had fallen in love with the Greek culture and became a traveling philosopher. But he couldn't resist meddling, and he trained a young boy and made him an emperor— conquered most of the world."

"What did you do?"

"I came home and did what I could for the Britons. I felt somewhat responsible for their plight. But I did not take up arms until the death of Prasutagas. After he died, the Romans flogged his wife, Boudicca, and raped his daughters. I raised the Iceni under Boudicca's banner, and we harried the invincible Roman army all the way to Londinium, which we burned to the ground. But the tribes never learned discipline, and we were smashed at Atherstone by that wily fox Paullinus. I took Boudicca and her daughters back to the Feragh, and they lived there in some contentment for many years."

"And did you fight again?" Thuro asked.

"Another day, Thuro. How do you feel?"

"Weary."

"Good." Culain removed his fur-lined jerkin and handed it to the boy. "This should keep you warm. I want you to return to Laitha's cabin, restore yourself in her good grace, and then return here."

"Could I not rest for a while?"

"Go now," said Culain. "And if you can, when you come in sight of her cabin, run. I want some strength built into those spindly legs!"

◇ 6 ◇

PRASAMACCUS WAS PROUD of his reputation as the finest hunter of the Three Valleys. He had worked hard on his bowmanship but knew that it was his patience that set him apart from the rest. No matter what the weather was, burning heat or searing cold, he could sit silently for hours waiting the right moment to let fly. No stringy meat for Prasamaccus, for his quarry dropped dead instantly, shot through the heart. No deer he killed had run for a mile with its lungs bubbling and its juices swelling the muscles to jaw-breaking toughness.

His bow was a gift from his clan leader, Moret, son of Eldared. It was a Roman weapon of dark horn, and he treasured it. His arrows were as straight as shafts of sunlight, and he trimmed each goose feather with careful cuts. In a tourney last Astarte Day, he had brought a gasp from the crowd when he had sliced to the bull through the shaft of his last hit. It was a fluke, yet it highlighted his awesome eye.

Now, as he sat hidden in the bushes of the hillside, he needed all his patience. The deer were slowly but steadily making their way toward him. He had been hidden there for two hours, and his blood felt like ice even through the sheepskin cloak gathered about his slender frame. He was not a tall man, and his face was thin and angular, blue eyes set close together. His chin was pointed, emphasized by a straggly blond beard. Crouched as he now was, it was impossible to spot the deformity that set him apart from his fellows, which had deprived this finest of hunters of a bride.

The deer were almost within killing range, and Prasamaccus chose a fat doe as his target. With infinite lack of speed he drew a long shaft from his doeskin quiver and notched it to the bowstring.

Just then the lead stag's head came up, and the small herd scattered. Prasamaccus sighed and stood. He limped forward, his twisted leg causing him to hobble in a sadly comical manner. When he had been a toddler, he had fallen in the path of a galloping horse that had smashed his left leg to shards. Now it was some eight inches shorter than the right, the foot mangled and pointing inward. He waited as the riders galloped toward him. There were two men, and their horses were lathered; they ignored him and thundered past. As a hunter himself, he knew they were being pursued and glanced back along the trail. Three giant beasts were loping across the snow, and Prasamaccus blinked. Bears? No bear could move that fast. His eyes widened. Lifting his hand to his mouth, he let out a piercing whistle, and a bay mare came galloping from the trees. He pulled himself into the saddle and slapped her rump. Unused to such treatment from a normally gentle master, the mare broke into a run. Prasamaccus steered her after the riders, swiftly overtaking their tired mounts.

"Veer left!" he shouted. "There is a ring of stones and a high hollow altar."

Without checking to see if they had followed him, he urged the mare up the snow-covered hill and over the crest, where black stones ringed the crown of the hill like broken teeth. He clambered from the saddle and limped to the center, where a huge altar stone was set atop a crumbling structure some eight feet high. Prasamaccus clawed his way to the top, swung his quiver to the front, and notched an arrow in his bow.

The two riders, their mounts almost dead from exhaustion, reached the circle scant seconds before the beasts. Prasamaccus drew back the bowstring and let fly. The shaft sped to the first beast as it towered over a running tribesman with a braided blond beard. The arrow took the beast in its right eye, and it fell back with a piercing scream that was almost human. The two men scrambled up alongside Prasamaccus, drawing their swords.

A mist sprang up around the circle, swirling between the stones and rising to stand like a gray wall beyond the monoliths. The two remaining Atrols faded back out of sight, and the three men were left at the center in ghostly silence.

"What are those creatures?" asked Prasamaccus.

"Atrols," Gwalchmai answered.

"I thought they must be, but I expected them to be bigger," said the bowman.

Victorinus smiled grimly. The mist around the stones was now impenetrable, but it had not pervaded the center. Victorinus glanced up. There was no sky, only a thick gray cloud hovering at the height of the stones.

"Why are they not attacking?" asked the Roman. Gwalchmai shrugged. From beyond the stones came a sibilant, whispering voice.

"Come forth, Gwalchmai. Come forth! Your father is here." A figure appeared at the edge of the mist, a bearded man with a blue tattoo on both cheeks. "Come to me, my son!" Gwalchmai half rose, but Victorinus grabbed his arm. Gwalchmai's eyes were glazed; Victorinus struck him savagely across the cheek, but the Briton did not react. Then the voice came again.

"Victorinus ... your mother waits." And a slender white-robed woman stood alongside the man.

An anguished groan broke from Victorinus' lips, and he released his hold on Gwalchmai, who scrambled down the altar. Prasamaccus, understanding none of this, pushed himself to his feet and sent an arrow into the head of Gwalchmai's father. In an instant all was changed. The image of the man disappeared, to be replaced by the monstrous figure of an Atrol tearing at the shaft in its cheek. Gwalchmai stopped, the spell broken. The image of Victorinus' mother faded back into the mist.

"Well done, bowman!" said Victorinus. "Get back here, Gwal!"

As the tribesman turned to obey, the mist cleared, and there at the edge of the stones were a dozen huge wolves standing almost as tall as ponies.

"Mother of Mithras!" Prasamaccus exclaimed.

Gwalchmai sprinted for the stones as the wolves raced into the circle. He leapt, reaching for Victorinus' outstretched hand. The Roman grabbed him and hauled him up just ahead of the lead wolf, whose jaws snapped shut bare inches from Gwalchmai's trailing leg.

Prasamaccus shot the beast in the throat, and it fell back. A second wolf leapt to the altar, scrabbling for purchase, but Victorinus kicked it savagely, and it pitched to the ground. The wolves were all around them now, snarling and snapping. The three men backed to the center of the altar. Prasamaccus sent two shafts into the milling beasts, but the rest ignored their wounded comrades. With only three shafts left, Prasamaccus refrained from loosing any more arrows.

"I don't like to sound pessimistic," said Gwalchmai, "but I'd appreciate any Roman suggestions at this point."

A wolf jumped and cleared the rock screen around the men. Gwalchmai's sword rammed home alongside Prasamaccus' arrow.

Suddenly the ground below began to tremble and the stones shifted. Gwalchmai almost fell but recovered his balance in time to see Victorinus slip from the shelter. The tribesman hurled himself across the altar, seizing the Roman's robe and dragging him to safety. The wolves also cowered back as the tremor continued. Lightning flashed within the circle, and a huge wolf reared up, his flesh transparent, his awesome bone structure revealed. As the lightning passed, the beast fell to earth and the stink of charred flesh filled the circle. Once more lightning seared into the wolves, and three died. The rest fled beyond the stones into the relative sanctuary of the mist.

A man appeared from within a glow of golden light beside the altar. He was tall and portly, a long black mustache flowing onto a short-cropped white beard. He wore a simple robe of purple velvet.

"I would suggest you join me," he said, "for I fear I have almost used up my magic."

Victorinus leapt from the altar, followed by Gwalchmai. "Hurry now, the gate is closing." But Prasamaccus, with his ruined leg, could not move at speed, and the golden globe began to shrink. Gwalchmai followed the wizard through, but Victorinus ran back to aid the bowman. Breathing heavily, Prasamaccus hurled himself through the light. Victorinus hesitated. The glow was no bigger than a window and was shrinking fast as the wolves poured into the circle. A hand reached through the golden light, hauling the Roman clear. There was a sensation like ice searing hot flesh, and Victorinus opened his eyes to see Gwalchmai still holding him by the robe ... only now they were standing in Caerlyn wood, overlooking Eboracum.

"Your timing is impeccable, Lord Maedhlyn," said Victorinus.

"Long practice," said the Enchanter. "You must take your report to Aquila, though he already knows that Aurelius is dead."

"How?" asked Gwalchmai. "Did someone else escape?"

"He knows because I told him," snapped Maedhlyn. "That's why I am an Enchanter and not a cheese maker, you ignorant moron."

Gwalchmai's anger flared. "If you are such an Enchanter, then why is the king dead? Why did your powers not save him?"

"I'll not bandy words with you, mortal," Maedhlyn hissed, looming over the tribesman. "The king is dead because he did not listen, but the boy is alive because I led him clear. Where were you, King's Hound?"

Gwalchmai's jaw dropped. "Thuro?"

"Is alive, no thanks to you. Now begone to the barracks." Gwalchmai stumbled away, and Victorinus approached the Enchanter.

"I am grateful, my lord, for your aid. But you were wrong to berate Gwalchmai. I led him from Deicester; we believed the boy dead."

Maedhlyn waved his hand as if swatting a fly. "Wrong, right! What does it matter? The clod made me angry; he was lucky I didn't turn him into a tree."

"If you had, my lord," said Victorinus with a hard smile. "I'd have slit your throat." He bowed and followed Gwalchmai toward the barracks.

"And what is your part in this?" Maedhlyn asked Prasamaccus.

"I was hunting deer. This has not been a good day for me."

Prasamaccus hobbled into the barrack square, having lost sight of the swifter men. Some children gathered to mock him, but he was used to that and ignored them. The buildings were grand, but even Prasamaccus could tell where the old Roman constructions had been repaired or renovated; the craftsmanship was less skilled than the older work.

The roads and alleyways were narrow, and Prasamaccus passed through the barracks square and on to the Street of Merchants, pausing to stare into open-fronted shops and examine cloth or pottery and even weapons in a larger corner building. A fat man wearing a leather apron approached him as he examined a curved hunting bow.

"A fine weapon," said the man, smiling broadly. "But not as fine as the one you are carrying. Are you looking to trade?"

"No."

"I have bows that could outdistance yours by fifty paces. Good strong yew, well seasoned."

"Vamera is not for sale," said Prasamaccus, "though I could use some shafts."

"Five denarii each."

Prasamaccus nodded. It had been two years since he had seen money coin, and even then it had not been his. He smiled at the man and left the shop. The day was bright, and the snow was absent from the town though still to be seen decorating the surrounding hills. Prasamaccus thought of his predicament. He was a hunter without a horse and with only two arrows in a land that was not his own. He had no coin and no hope of support. And he was hungry. He sighed and wondered which of the gods he had angered now. All his life people had told him that the gods did not like him. The injury to his leg was proof of that, they said. The only girl he had ever loved had died of the red plague. Not that Prasamaccus had ever told her of his love, but even so, as soon as his affection had materialized within him, she had been struck down. He turned his pale blue eyes to the heavens. He felt no anger at the gods. How could he? It was not for him to question their likes and dislikes. But he felt it would be pleasant at least to know which of them held him in such low esteem.

"What's wrong with your leg?" asked a small, fair-haired boy of around six years.

"A dragon breathed on it," Prasamaccus said.

"Did it hurt?"

"Oh, yes. It still does when the weather turns wet."

"Did you kill the dragon?"

"With a single shaft from my magic bow."

"Are they not covered with golden scales?"

"You know a great deal about dragons."

"My father has killed hundreds. He says you can only strike them behind their long ears; there is a soft spot there that leads to the brain."

"Exactly right," said Prasamaccus. "That's how I killed mine."

"With your magic bow."

"Yes. Would you like to touch it?" The boy's eyes

sparkled, and his small hand reached out to stroke the black, glossy frame.

"Will the magic rub off?"

"Of course. The next time you see a dragon, Vamera will appear in your hand with a golden arrow."

Without a good-bye the boy raced off shouting his father's name, desperate to tell him of his adventure. Prasamaccus felt better. He hobbled back into the barracks square and followed the smell of cooking meat to a wide building of golden sandstone. Inside was a mess hall with rows of bench tables and at the far end a huge hearth where a bull was spitted. Prasamaccus, ignoring the stares as he passed, moved slowly to the line of men waiting for food and picked up a large wooden platter. The line moved on, each man receiving two thick slabs of meat and a large spoonful of sprouts and carrots. Prasamaccus reached the server, a short man who was sweating profusely. The man watched him for a moment, offering no meat.

"What are you doing here, cripple?"

"I am waiting to eat."

"This is the auxiliaries' dining hall. You are no soldier."

"The Lord Maedhlyn said I could eat here," Prasamaccus lied smoothly. "But if you wish, I will go to him and say you refused. What is your name?"

The man dumped two slabs of meat on his plate. "Next!" he said. "Move along now."

Prasamaccus looked for a nearby empty table. It was important not to sit too close to other men, for all who saw him knew he was despised by the gods, and none would want that luck rubbing off. He found a table near the window and sat down; taking his thin-bladed hunting knife from its sheath, he sliced the meat and ate it slowly. It tasted fine, but the fat content was high. He belched and leaned back, content for the first time since the incident with the Atrols. Food was now no longer a problem. The magic name of Maedhlyn cast a powerful spell, it seemed.

A stocky, powerfully built man with a square-cut beard sat opposite him. Prasamaccus looked up into a pair of dark brown eyes. "I understand the Lord Enchanter told you to eat here," said the man.

"Yes."

"I wonder why," the man went on, his suspicion evident.

"I have just returned from the north with Gwalchmai and . . . the other fellow."

"You were with the king?"

"No. I met Gwalchmai and came with them."

"Where is he now?"

"Making a report." Prasamaccus could not remember the name of the clan leader used by Maedhlyn.

"What news from the north?" asked the man. "Is it true the king is dead?"

Prasamaccus remembered the savage joy in his own Brigante village on hearing the news. "Yes," he answered. "I am afraid that it is."

"You do not seem too concerned."

Prasamaccus leaned forward. "I did not know the man. Gwalchmai feels his loss keenly."

"He would," said the man, relaxing. "He was the King's Hound. How was the deed done?"

"I do not know all the facts. You must ask Gwalchmai and . . ."

"Who?"

"I am bad with names. A tall man, dark-haired, curved nose."

"Victorinus?"

"That was it," said Prasamaccus, remembering the sibilant calls of the Atrols.

"What happened to the others?"

"What others?"

"The king's retainers?"

"I do not know. Gwalchmai will answer all your questions."

"I am sure that he will, my Brigante friend, and until he arrives, you must consider yourself my guest." The man stood and called two soldiers over. "Take this man into custody."

Prasamaccus sighed. The gods were surely laughing today.

The two soldiers walked Prasamaccus across the square, keeping out of arm's reach of the cripple. One carried his bow and quiver; the other had taken possession of his hunting knife. They led him to a small room with a barred door and no window. Inside was a narrow pallet bed. He listened as the bar dropped into place and then lay down on the bed. There was a single blanket, and he covered himself. Food had been taken care of, and now they had given him a bed. He closed his eyes and fell asleep almost instantly.

His dreams were good ones. He had killed a Mist Demon—he, "Prasamaccus the Cripple." In his dreams, his leg was restored to health and beautiful maidens attended him.

He was not happy to be awakened.

"My friend, please accept my sincere apologies," said Victorinus as Prasamaccus sat up, rubbing his eyes. "I had to make my report, and I forgot all about you."

"They fed me and gave me a place to sleep."

"Yes, I see that. But I want you to be a guest in my home."

Prasamaccus swung his legs from the bed. "Can I have my bow back?"

Victorinus chuckled. "You can have your bow, as many arrows as you can carry, and a fine horse from my stable. Your own choice."

Prasamaccus nodded sagely. Perhaps he was still dreaming, after all.

◇ 7 ◇

FOR THREE WEEKS Thuro had followed the instructions of Culain. He had run over mountain trails, chopped and sawed, carried and worked, and been "killed" on countless occasions by a succession of swordsmen conjured by the Mist Warrior. His greatest moment had been when he had finally beaten the young Roman. He had noticed during their three previous bouts that his opponent was thick-waisted and unbending, so he had advanced, dropping to his knees, and thrust his gladius up into the man's groin. The soldier had vanished instantly. Culain had been well pleased but had added a cautionary note.

"You won and should enjoy your triumph. But the move was dangerous. Had he anticipated it, he would have had an easy kill with a neck thrust."

"But he did not."

"True. But tell me, what is the principle of swordfighting?"

"To kill your opponent."

"No. It is *not* to be killed *by* your opponent. It is rare that a good swordsman leaves an opening. Sometimes it is necessary, especially if you find your enemy is more skilled, but such risks are generally to be avoided."

After that Culain had conjured a Macedonian warrior

from the army of Alexander. This man, grim-eyed and dark-bearded, had caused Thuro great problems. The boy had tried the winning cut he had used against the Roman, only to feel the hideous sensation of a ghostly sword entering his neck. Shamefaced, he had avoided Culain's eye, but the Mist Warrior did not chide him.

"Some people always need to learn lessons the painful way," was all he said.

One morning Laitha came to watch him, but his limbs would not operate smoothly and he tripped over his apparently enlarged feet. Culain shook his head and sent the laughing Laitha away.

Thuro finally dispatched the Macedonian with a move Culain had taught him. He blocked the man's sweeping cut from the left, swung on his heel to ram his elbow into the man's face, and finished him with a murderous slice to the neck.

"Tell me, do they feel pain?"

"They?"

"The soldiers you conjure."

"They do not exist, Thuro. They are not ghosts; they are men I knew. I create them from my memories. Illusions if you like."

"They are very good swordsmen."

"They were bad swordsmen—that's why they are useful now. But soon you will be ready to tackle adequate warriors."

When he was not working, Culain would walk him through the woods, pointing out animal tracks and identifying them. Soon Thuro could spot the spoor of the red fox with its five-pointed pads and the cloven hooves of a trotting fallow deer, light and delicate on the trail. Some animals left the most bewildering evidence of their passing; one such they found by a frozen stream,

four closely set imprints in a tight square. Two feet farther on there were another four, and so on.

"It is a bounding otter," said Culain. "It kicks off
with its powerful hind legs and comes down on its front
paws. The rear paws then land just behind the front, and
the beast takes off for another bound, leaving four
tracks close together. Obviously it was frightened."

At other times Thuro would walk with Laitha, whose
interest was trees and flowers, herbs and fungi. In her
cabin she had sketches, richly colored, of all kinds of
plants. Thuro was fascinated.

"Do you like mushrooms?" Laitha asked, one day in
early spring.

"Yes, fried in butter."

"Does this look tasty?" She showed him a beautifully
sketched picture of four capped fungi growing from the
bole of a tree. They were the color of summer sunshine.

"Yes, they look delicious."

"Then you would be wise to remember what they
look like. They are sulphur tufts, and a meal of these
would leave you in great pain and probably kill you.
What of this one?" It was a foul-looking object in ca-
daver gray.

"Edible?"

"Yes, and very nutritious. It also tastes pleasant."

"What is the most dangerous?" he asked.

"You should be interested in the most nutritious, but
since you ask, it is probably this," she answered, producing a drawing of a delicate white and yellow-green
fungus. "It is usually found near oak," she said, "and is
called death cap; I leave it to you to guess why."

"Do you never get lonely up in the mountains?"

"Why should I?" she replied, putting down her drawings. "I have Culain as my friend and the animals and birds and trees to study and draw."

"But do you not miss people, crowds, fairs, banquets?"

"I have never been among crowds or to a banquet. The thought does not thrill me. Are you unhappy here, Thuro?"

He gazed into her gold-flecked eyes. "No, I am not lonely—not with you, anyway." He was aware that his tone was too intense, and he flushed deep red. She touched his hand.

"I am something you can never have," she told him. He nodded and tried to smile.

"You love Culain."

"Yes. All my life."

"And yet you cannot have him, as I can never have you."

She shook her head. "That has yet to be decided. He still sees me as the child he raised. It will take time for him to realize I am a woman."

Thuro closed his mouth, stopping the obvious comment from being voiced. If Culain could not see it now, he would never see it. Added to which, here was a man who had known life since the dawn of history. How many women had he known? How many had he wed? What beauties had lain beside him through the centuries?

"How did he find you?" Thuro asked, seeking to move from the painful subject.

"My parents were Trinovante, and they had a village some sixty miles south. One day there was a raid by Brigantes. I cannot remember much of it, for I was only five, but I can still see the burning thatch and hear the screams of the dying. I ran up into the hills, and two horsemen pursued me. Then Culain was there with his silver lance; he slew the riders and carried me high into the mountains. Later we returned, but everyone was dead. So he kept me with him; he raised me and taught me all I know."

"It is hardly a surprise that you love him. I wish you success . . . and happiness."

Every morning Culain would put Thuro through two hours of heavy exercise: running, lifting rocks, or making him hang by his arms from the branch of a tree and raise his weight until his chin touched the branch. At first Thuro could raise himself only three times before his arms would tremble and refuse the burden. But now, as spring painted its dazzling colors on the mountainside, he could manage thirty. He could run for an hour with no sign of fatigue, and he had dispatched twelve of the ghostly opponents Culain had created. The last had proved difficult; he was a Persian from the army of Xerxes, and he fought with dagger and saber. Four times he defeated Thuro before the youth won through. He did it by leaving a fractional opening twice and covering late; the third time he lured the Persian into a lunge, sidestepped, and cut his gladius into his opponent's neck. Culain had clapped him on the back and said nothing. Thuro was sweating hard, for the fight had lasted more than ten minutes.

"Now I think," said Culain, "that you are ready for the reasonable swordsmen."

A movement to Thuro's left, and a ghostly sword cut into his shoulder, numbing his left arm. He threw himself from the log on which he sat and rolled to his feet. The man before him was a blond giant over six feet tall, wearing a bronze helm adorned with a bull's horns. He held a longsword and was wearing a chain-mail vest.

Thuro blocked the man's sudden charge, but his opponent's shoulder crashed into him, sending him sprawling to the grass. Thuro rolled as the longsword flashed for his head. With his enemy off balance, he regained his feet and launched a blistering attack, but his arm was weary and he was beaten back. Three times he almost found a way through, but his opponent—with his longer sword and greater reach—fended him off. Sweat dripped into the youth's eyes, and his sword arm burned. The warrior lunged; Thuro parried, swung on his heel, and hammered his elbow into the man's face. The warrior staggered back, and Thuro, still moving around, plunged his sword into the man's chest. As his enemy disappeared, the young prince fell to his knees, his breath coming in great gasps. After several minutes his angry eyes locked on Culain.

"That was unfair!"

"Life is unfair. Do you think your enemies will sit back and wait until you are fresh? Learn to marshal your strength. Were I to produce another warrior now, you would not last five heartbeats."

"There is a limit to every man's strength," Thuro observed.

"Indeed there is—a good point to remember. One day, perhaps, you will lead an army into battle. You will be filled with the urge to draw your sword and fight alongside your men. You will think it heroic, but your enemy will rejoice, for it is folly. As the long day wears on, all enemy eyes will be upon you and your weakening body. All their attacks will be aimed at you. So always bear that in mind, young prince. There is a limit to every man's strength."

"And yet do the men you lead not need to know you

will fight alongside them? Will it not raise their morale?" Thuro asked.

"Of course."

"Then what is the answer to the riddle? Do I fight or not fight?"

"Only you can decide that. But use your head. At some time in every battle there is a moment when it can turn. Weaker men blame it on the gods, but it has more to do with the hearts of the warriors. You must learn to read those moments; that is when you enter the fray, to the bitter dismay of your enemies."

"How is such a moment recognized?"

"Most men recognize it only in hindsight. The truly great general sees it in an instant. But I cannot teach you that, Thuro. That is a skill you either have or do not have."

"Do you have it?"

"I thought that I did, but when Paullinus lured me to attack him at Atherstone, my talent deserted me. He sensed the moment and attacked, and my brave Britons collapsed around me. We outnumbered him twenty to one. An unpleasant man, Paullinus, but a wily general."

Often, when not with either Culain or Laitha, Thuro would wander the hillsides, enjoying the freshness of spring in the mountains. Everywhere was color: white-petaled wood anemone tinged with purple, golden celandine, mauve violets, snow-white wood sorrel, and the tall, glorious purple orchid with its black-spotted leaves and petals shaped like winged helms.

Early one morning, with his chores completed, Thuro wandered alone in the valley below Culain's cabin. His shoulders had widened, and he could no longer squeeze into the clothes he had worn a mere two months earlier.

Now he wore a simple buckskin tunic and woolen leggings over sheepskin boots.

He sat by a stream, watching the fish glide below the water, until he heard a horse moving along the path. Then he stood and saw a single rider. The man spotted him and dismounted. He was tall and slender with shoulder-length red hair and green eyes, and he wore a longsword at his waist. He walked to Thuro and stood with hands on hips.

"Well, it has been a long chase," he said, "and you are much changed." He smiled. His face was open and handsome, and Thuro could detect no malice there.

"My name is Alantric," said the newcomer, "I am the King's Champion." He sat down on a flat rock, tugged free a length of grass, and placed it between his teeth. "Sadly, boy, I have been instructed to find your body and bring your head to the king." The man sighed. "I do not like killing children."

"Then return and say you could not find me."

"I would like to . . . truly. But I am a man of my word. It is unfortunate that I serve a king whose character is less than saintly. Do you know how to use that sword, boy?"

"That you will find out," said Thuro, his heart rate increasing as fear wormed into his heart.

"I will fight you left-handed. It seems more fair."

"I wish for no advantage," Thuro snapped, regretting it as he spoke.

"Well said! You are your father's son, after all. When you meet him, tell him I had no part in his killing."

"Tell him yourself," said Thuro.

Alantric stood and drew his longsword, and Thuro's gladius flashed into the air. Alantric moved out onto open ground, then spun and lunged. Thuro sidestepped and blocked, rolling his gladius over the blade and slicing a thin cut on Alantric's forearm. "Well done!" said the champion, stepping back, his green eyes blazing. "You've been taught well." He advanced once more, this time with care. Thuro noted the liquid grace of his enemy's style, the perfect balance, and the patience he showed. Culain would have been impressed by this man. Thuro attacked not at all, merely blocking his opponent at every turn while studying his technique.

Alantric attacked, his sword flashing and cutting, and the discordant clash of iron on iron echoed in the woods. Suddenly the Brigante faked a cut, twisted his wrist, and lunged. Caught by surprise, Thuro parried hastily, feeling the razor-sharp blade slide across his right bicep. Blood began to seep through his shirt. A second attack saw Alantric score a similar wound at the top of Thuro's shoulder, close to the throat. The youth moved back, and Alantric sprang forward. This time Thuro read the attack, swayed, and lanced his gladius into Alantric's side. But the Brigante was fast, and he leapt back before the blade had penetrated more than an inch.

"You have been taught well," he said again. He raised his sword to his lips in salute, then attacked once more. Thuro, desperate now, resorted to the move Culain had taught him. He blocked a thrust and spun on his heel, his elbow flashing back—into empty air! Off balance, the young prince fell to the grass. He rolled swiftly but felt Alantric's sword resting on his neck.

"A clever move, Prince Thuro, but you tensed before you tried it and I read your intent in your eyes."

"At least I ..." In the moment of speaking Thuro kicked Alantric's legs from under him and rolled to his feet. The Briton sat up and smiled.

"You are full of surprises," he said as he stood and sheathed his sword. "I think that I could kill you, but the truth is I do not wish to. You are worth ten of Eldared. It seems I must break my word."

"Not at all," said Thuro, sheathing his gladius. "You were sent to look for my corpse. It is true to say that you did not find it."

Alantric nodded. "I could serve you, Prince Thuro . . . should you ever be a king."

"I will remember that," Thuro told him, "as I will remember your gallantry." Alantric bowed and walked to his horse.

"Remember, Prince Thuro, never to let your enemy read your eyes. Do not think of an attack—just do it!"

Thuro returned the bow and watched as the warrior mounted and rode from sight.

Prasamaccus followed Victorinus to the Alia stables, where the young Roman ordered a chestnut gelding with three white fetlocks to be saddled for the Brigante. Having not genuinely believed he would be allowed to pick his own mount, Prasamaccus was therefore not disappointed with the beast. Victorinus mounted a black stallion of some seventeen hands, and the two rode west along the wide Roman road outside Caerlyn. They skirted Eboracum and continued west for an hour until they came to the fortress town of Calcaria.

"My villa is beyond the next hill," said Victorinus. "We can rest there and bathe."

Prasamaccus smiled dutifully and wondered what, under the sun, was a villa. Still, the sun was shining, his leg felt almost at ease, and he was not yet hungry again. All in all, the gods must be sleeping. A villa, it turned out, was a Roman name for a palace: white walls covered with vines, a garden, terrace steps, and pretty maidens running to take the reins of their horses. Gorgeous young creatures—all with teeth.

He fought to look dignified, copying the solemn expression on Victorinus' swarthy face. Unfortunately, he could not slide from the saddle with the Roman's grace, but even so he climbed down sedately and made every effort to keep his limp to a minimum. It surprised him not at all when no one laughed. Who would laugh at the guest of so important a chieftain? They moved inside, and Prasamaccus looked around for evidence of a fire, but there was none. The mosaic floor depicted a hunting scene in glorious reds and blues, golds and greens. Beyond it was an arch, and there the two men were helped from their clothes and offered goblets of warmed wine. It seemed bland compared with the water of life distilled in the north, but even so Prasamaccus could feel its heat slipping through his veins.

Yet another room contained a deep pool, and Prasamaccus gingerly followed the Roman into the warm water. Below the surface there were seats of stone, and the Brigante leaned his head against the edge of the bath and closed his eyes. This, he thought, was the closest to paradise he had ever known. After some twenty minutes the Roman climbed from the water, and Prasamaccus dutifully followed. They sat together on a long marble bench, saying nothing. Two young girls, one as black as night, came from the archway bearing bowls of oil. If the bath had been paradise, there was little left to describe the sensation that followed as the oil was softly rubbed into their skin and then scraped away with rounded knives of bone.

"Would you feel better for a massage?" asked Victorinus as the girls moved away.

"Of course," said Prasamaccus, wondering if one ate it or swam in it.

Victorinus led them through to a side room where two tables had been placed next to each other. The Roman stretched his lean, naked frame out on the first, and Prasamaccus took the second. Two more girls entered and began to rub yet more oil into their bodies, but this they did not scrape off. Instead they kneaded the muscles of the upper back, stroking away knots of tension of which Prasamaccus had been unaware. Slowly their hands moved down, and the men's shoulders were covered with warm white cloths. The Brigante sensed the girl's uncertainty as she reached his ruined leg. Her fingers floated over the skin like moths' wings, and then she began, with skillful strokes, to ease the deep ache that was always with him. Her skill was beyond words, and Prasamaccus felt himself slipping toward the sleep of the blessed. Finally the girls stepped back, and two male servants approached with togas of white. Dressed in one of them, Prasamaccus felt faintly ridiculous and not a little overdressed. Yet another in an apparently interminable series of rooms followed. There two divans were set alongside a table laden with fruit, cold meats, and pastries. Prasamaccus waited while the Roman settled himself on a divan, leaning on his elbow; then the Brigante once more copied the pose.

"You are obviously a man of some breeding," said Victorinus. "I hope you will feel at home within my house."

"Of course."

"Your bravery in aiding us will not go unrewarded, though I can imagine that your distress at being taken from your home and family must be great."

Prasamaccus spread his hands and hoped his expression conveyed the right emotions—whatever they might be.

"As you no doubt know, there will be a war between the tribes that follow Eldared and our own forces. We will of course win, but the war will hamper our battles in the south against the Saxon and Jute. What I am saying is that it will be difficult to assist you in getting home. But you are welcome to stay."

"Here in your villa?" Prasamaccus asked.

"Yes, though I don't doubt you would rather risk the perils of the road north. If that is the case, as I said, you must pick your own horse from the stable, and I will assist you with supplies and coin."

"Does Gwalchmai live here?"

"No. He is a soldier and lives in the barracks at Caerlyn. He has a woman there, I believe."

"Ah, a woman. Yes."

"How foolish of me!" said Victorinus. "Any of the slaves who take your fancy, you may feel free to bed. I would recommend the Nubian, who will guarantee a good night's sleep. And now I must leave you. I have a meeting to attend at the castle, but I will be back at around midnight. My man, Grephon, will show you to your room."

Prasamaccus watched the Roman leave and then wolfed down the food. He was not hungry, but he had found that it never paid to waste the opportunity to eat.

The servant Grephon approached silently, then cleared his throat. He watched as the Briton gorged himself but kept his face carefully void of expression. If his master had chosen to bring this savage to the villa, there was obviously a good reason for it. At the very least the man must be a prince among the northern tribes and therefore, despite his obvious barbarism, would be treated as if he were a senator. Grephon was a life servant to the Quirina family, having served Victorinus' illustrious father for seven years in Rome; he ran the household with iron efficiency. He was a short man, stocky and bald—despite being only twenty-five—with round unblinking eyes that were dark as sable. Originally he had come from Thrace, a boy slave brought into the Quirina household as a stable boy.

His swift mind had brought him to the attention of Marcus Lintus, who had taken him into the household as a playmate for his son, Victorinus. As the years passed, Grephon's reputation grew. He was undeniably loyal and closemouthed, with an eye for organization. By the age of nineteen he was organizing the household. When Marcus Lintus had died four years earlier, young Victorinus had asked Grephon to accompany him to Britain. He had not wished to come and could have refused, for he had become a freedman on the death of Marcus. But the Quirina family was rich and Grephon's future was assured with them, so with a heavy heart he had made the long journey through Gaul and across the sea to Dubris and up through the cursed countryside to the villa at Calcaria. He had staffed it and run it to perfection while Victorinus followed the High King as Primus Pilus, the first centurion to Aurelius' ragbag auxiliaries. Grephon could not understand why a highborn Roman would concern himself with such a rabble.

He cleared his throat once more, and this time the savage noticed him. Grephon bowed.

"Is there anything you desire, sir?" The man belched loudly.

"A woman?"

"Yes, sir. Do you have a choice in mind?" The Briton's pale blue eyes fixed on Grephon. "No. You choose."

"Very well, sir. Let me show you to your room and I will send someone up to you."

Grephon moved slowly, aware of the guest's disability, and led him up a short stairway to a narrow corridor and an oak door. Beyond it was a wide bed surrounded by velvet curtains. It was warm, though there was no fire. Prasamaccus sat down on the bed as Grephon bowed and departed. Damned if he would send the Nubian to such as this, he decided. He walked briskly to the kitchen and summoned the German slave girl, Helga. She was short, with hair like flax and pale blue eyes devoid of passion. Her voice was guttural as she struggled with the language, and though she was good enough at heavy work, none had so far seen fit to bed her. She was certainly not good enough to catch Victorinus' eye.

He explained her duties and was rewarded by a look close to fear in her eyes. She bowed her head and walked slowly toward the inner house. Grephon poured himself a goblet of fine wine and sipped it slowly, eyes closed, picturing the vineyards beyond the Tiber.

Helga climbed the stairs with a heavy heart. She had known this day would come and had dreaded it. Ever since being captured and raped by men of the Fourth Legion in her native homeland, she had lived with the secret fear of being abused once more. She had almost come to feel safe in this household, for the men were happily indifferent to her. Now she was being used to humor a crippled savage, a man whose deformity would have ensured his death in her tribe.

She opened the door to the bedroom to see the British prince kneeling by a hot air vent and peering into the dark interior. He looked up and smiled, but she did not respond. She walked to the bed and unfastened her simple green dress, a color that did not match her eyes.

The Briton limped to the bed and sat down.

"What is your name?"

"Helga."

He nodded. "I am Prasamaccus." He gently touched the soft skin of her face, then stood and struggled to free himself from the toga. Once naked, he slipped under the covers and invited her to join him. She did so and lay back across his arm. They stayed motionless for several minutes, and then Prasamaccus, feeling her warmth against his body, drifted to sleep.

Helga gently raised herself on one elbow, looking down into his face. It was slender and fine-boned, lacking cruelty. She could still feel the soft touch of his hand on her cheek. She had no idea what to do now. She had been told to make him happy so that he could rest well. Now that he was resting, she should return to the kitchens. Yet if she did, they would question why she had returned so quickly; they would think he had sent her away and perhaps punish her. She settled down beside him and closed her eyes.

At dawn she awoke to feel a soft hand touching her body. She did not open her eyes, and her heart began to hammer within her. The hand slid slowly across her shoulder and down to cup her heavy breast. The thumb circled the nipple, then the touch moved on, up and over the curve of her hip. She opened her eyes and saw the Briton staring at her body, his face lost in a kind of wonderment. He saw that she was awake and flushed deep red, pulling the covers back over her. Then he lay down and moved his body more closely alongside her, softly kissing her brow, then her cheek, and finally her lips. Almost without thinking, she reached up and curled her arm over his shoulder. He groaned . . . and she knew. In that instant she knew it all, as if she held Prasamaccus' soul under her eyes.

For the first time in her life Helga knew the meaning of power. She could choose to give or not to give. The man beside her would accept her choice. Her mind flew back to the brutality of her captors, men she would have liked to have killed. But they had been men unlike this one.

The man left her free to choose, not even understanding that he did so. She looked into his eyes once more and saw that they were wet with tears. Leaning forward, she kissed each eye, then drew him to her.

And in giving freely, she received a greater gift.

Her memories of lust and cruelty dissolved and returned to the past, devoid of the power ever to haunt her again.

For several days Victorinus rose early and returned late, seeing little of his houseguest, who spent most of the time locked in his room with the kitchen maid. The Roman had weightier problems on his mind. The Fifth Legion was stationed at Calcaria, auxiliary militiamen who were allowed home in the spring to see to their farms and families. Now, with Eldared and his Selgovae and Novantae allies ready to invade and the Saxon king, Hengist, preparing to ravage the south, there was no way these auxiliaries could be allowed to disband for two months. Tension was running high among the men, many of whom had not seen their wives since the previous September, and Victorinus feared a mutiny.

Aquila had asked him to help build morale by offering coin and salt to the men, but that had not been enough and desertions were increasing daily. The choices were limited. If they allowed the men to go home, Eboracum and the surrounding countryside would be defended by only one regular legion—five thousand men. Ranged against them would be a possible thirty thousand. Alternatively, they could recall a legion from the south, but the gods knew how badly the general Ambrosius needed men around Dubris and Londinium.

The third choice was to recruit and train a new militia, but that would be the same as sending children out against wolves. The Brigante and their vassal tribes were renowned warriors.

Victorinus dismissed the Nubian slave, Oretia, and climbed from his bed. He dressed and made his way to the central room, where he found Prasamaccus sitting by the far window staring out over the moonlit southern hills.

"Good evening," Victorinus said. "How are you faring?"

"Well, thank you. You seem tired."

"There is much to do. Does Helga please you?"

"Yes, very much."

Victorinus poured himself a goblet of watered wine. It was almost midnight, and his eyes ached for the sleep he knew would evade him. It annoyed him that the Briton was still there after six days. He had invited him only to offset the rough treatment he had received in being gaoled; otherwise he would have placed him in the barracks with Gwalchmai. Now it looked as if he had a permanent houseguest. The small fortress town was alive with rumors concerning the Brigante; all had him marked as a prince at the very least. Grephon had purchased some new clothes for him, and they only added to the image: the softest cream wool edged with braid, leather trews decorated with silver disks, and fine riding boots of the softest doeskin.

"What is your problem?" Prasamaccus asked.

"Would that there were only one."

"There is always one larger than the others," said the Brigante.

Victorinus shrugged and explained—though he knew not why—the problems with the militiamen. Prasamaccus sat silently as the Roman outlined the choices.

"How much of this coin is available for the men?" he asked.

"It is not a great sum—perhaps a month's extra pay."

"If you allow some of the men home, the amount for each man left will grow, yes?"

"Of course."

"Then make known the total amount on offer and tell the men they can go home. But explain that the coin will be distributed among those who choose to remain."

"What will that serve? What if only one man remains? He would be as rich as Crassus."

"Exactly," agreed Prasamaccus, though he had no idea who Crassus was.

"I do not follow you."

"No; that is because you are rich. Most men dream of riches. Myself, I have always wanted two horses. But the men who want to go home will now have to wonder how much they lose by doing so. What if—as you say—only one is left? Or ten?"

"How many do you think will remain?"

"More than half if they are anything like the Brigantes I have known."

"It would entail great risk to do as you suggest, but

I feel it is wise counsel. We will attempt it. Where did you learn such guile?"

"It is the Earth Mother's gift to lonely men," Prasamaccus answered.

His advice was proved right when three thousand men chose to stay, earning an extra two months pay per man. It eased Victorinus' burden and earned him plaudits from Aquila.

Three days later an unexpected guest arrived at the villa. It was Maedhlyn, hot, dusty, and irritable from his ride. An hour later, refreshed by a hot bath and several goblets of warmed wine, he sat talking for some time to Victorinus. Then they summoned Prasamaccus. When the Brigante saw the portly Enchanter, his heart sank. He sat quietly, refusing the wine Victorinus offered.

Maedhlyn sat opposite him, fixing him with his hawklike eyes.

"We have a problem, Prasamaccus, one that we think you will be able to solve. There is a young man trapped in Brigante territory far to the north of the Antonine Wall in the Caledones mountains. He is important to us, and we want him brought home. Now, we cannot send our own men, for they do not know the land. But you do and could travel there without suspicion."

Prasamaccus said nothing, but he reached for the wine and took a deep draft. The gods give, the gods take away. But this time they had gone too far; they had allowed him to taste a joy he had previously believed to be fable.

"Now," said Maedhlyn persuasively, "I can magic you to a circle of stones near Pinnata Castra, some three days ride from Deicester Castle. All you will need to do is locate the boy, Thuro, and return him to the circle exactly six days later. I will be there, and I will return every night at midnight thereafter in case you are delayed. What do you say?"

"I have no wish to return north," said Prasamaccus softly. Maedhlyn swallowed hard and glanced at Victorinus as the Roman sat beside the Brigante.

"You would be doing us a great service and would be well rewarded," Victorinus told him.

"I will need a copper bracelet edged with gold, a small house, also enough coin to purchase a horse and supply a woman with food and clothing for a year. Added to this, I want the slave Helga freed to live in this house." As he had been speaking, the color had left his face, and he feared he had set the price at an awesome level.

"Is that all?" asked Victorinus, and Prasamaccus nodded. "Then it is agreed. As soon as you return, we will arrange it."

"No," said the Brigante sternly. "It will be arranged tomorrow. I am not a foolish man and know I may not survive this quest. The land of the Caledones is wild, and strangers are not welcome. Also the boy, Thuro, is the son of the Roman king. Eldared will wish him dead. It is not meet that you should ask me to undertake your duties, but since you have, then you must pay . . . and pay now."

"We agree," said Maedhlyn swiftly. "When do you wish the marriage to take place?"

"Tomorrow."

"As a Druid of long standing I shall officiate," Maedhlyn declared. "There is an oak tree back along the trail, and we shall travel there in time for the birth of the new sun. You had best tell your lady."

Prasamaccus stood and bowed and, with as much

dignity as was allowed a limping man, returned to his room.

"What was that about marriage?" asked Victorinus.

"The bracelet is for her. It marks the ring of eternity and the never-ending circle of life that springs from the union of love. Touching!"

◇ 8 ◇

ALANTRIC KNEW HIS life would be forfeit should anyone find out about his meeting with the prince, so the only person he told was his wife, Frycca, as she stitched the wound in his arm. Frycca loved him dearly and would do nothing to harm him, but she was proud of his gallantry and spoke of it to her sister, Marphia, swearing her to the strictest secrecy. Marphia told her husband, Briccys, who only told his dearest friend on the understanding that the secret was to remain locked within him.

Within two days of his return Alantric was dragged from his hut by three of Eldared's carles. Realizing at once that he was doomed, he turned and shouted back to Frycca: "Your loose tongue has killed me, woman!"

He did not struggle as they pulled him toward the horses but walked with head down, totally relaxed. The guards relaxed with him, and he tore his right arm free and smote the nearest man on the ear. As the guard staggered, Alantric pulled free the man's sword and plunged the blade into the heart of the second soldier. The third stepped back, dragging his blade into the air, and Alantric leapt for the nearest horse, but the beast shied. Now a dozen more guards came running, and the

King's Champion backed away to the picket fence, a wild smile on his features.

"Come, then, Brothers," he called. "Learn a lesson that will last all your lives!"

Two men rushed in. Alantric blocked a blow, sent a backhand cut to the first man's throat, and grunted as the second attacker's sword slid into his side. Twisting, he trapped the blade against his ribs and skewered the swordsman.

"Alive! Take him alive!" Cael screamed from the battlements above.

"Come down and do it yourself, whoreson!" Alantric shouted as the guards came in a rush. Alantric's blade wove a web of death, and in the melee that followed a sword entered his back, tearing open his lungs. He sank to the ground and was hauled into the castle; he died just as Cael ran into the portcullis entrance.

"You stupid fools!" Cael bellowed. "I'll see you flogged. Get his wife!" But Frycca, in her anguish, had cut her own throat with her husband's hunting knife and lay in a pool of blood by the hearth.

Eldared's torturer worked long into the night on the others who had shared the secret, emerging with only one indisputable fact: The boy prince was indeed alive and hiding in an unknown area of the Caledones mountains.

Eldared summoned Cael to him. "You will go to Goroien and tell her I need the Soul Stealers. We have six people below whose blood should please her and as many whelps as she needs. But I want the boy!"

Cael said nothing. Among all the dark legends of the Mist, the Soul Stealers alone made him shiver. He bowed and left the brooding king to sit alone, staring into the hills of the south.

* * *

Thuro awoke still feeling the pain of the wound that had killed him, a lightning-fast roll and thrust from the Greek's short sword. Culain helped him to his feet.

"You did well, better than I could have hoped. Give me another month and there will not be a swordsman to rival you in all of Britain."

"But I lost," said Thuro, recalling with a shiver the ice-cold eyes of his young opponent.

"Of course you lost. That was Achilles, the finest warrior of his generation, a demon with sword or lance. A magnificent fighter."

"What happened to him?"

"He died. All men die."

"I had already surmised that," said Thuro. "I meant how."

"I killed him," said Culain. "I had another name then; I was Aeneas, and Achilles killed a friend of mine during the war against Troy. Not only that but he dragged the body around and around the city behind his chariot. He humiliated a man of great courage and brought pain to the father."

"I have heard of Troy. It was taken by a wooden horse with men hidden inside."

"Do not be misled by Homer, for he was jesting. 'Wooden horse' is slang for a useless object or for something pretending to be what it is not. It was a man who went to the Trojans pretending to betray his masters, the Greeks. The king, Priam, believed the man. I did not. I left the city with those who would follow me and fought my way to the coast. Later we heard that the man, Odysseus, had opened a side gate to allow Greek soldiers to enter the city."

"Why did the king believe him?"

"Priam was a romantic who saw the best in everyone. That is how he allowed the war to begin, by seeing the best in Helen. The face that launched a thousand ships was merely a scheming woman with dyed yellow hair. The Trojan War was begun by her husband, Menelaus, and planned by Helen. She seduced Priam's son, Paris, into taking her to his city. Menelaus then sought the aid of the other Greek kings to get her back."

"But why go to so much trouble over one woman?"

"They did not do it for a woman or for honor. Troy controlled the trade routes and levied great taxes on ships bound for Greece. It was—as are all wars—fought for profit."

"I think I prefer Homer," said Thuro.

"Read Homer for enjoyment, young prince, but do not confuse it with life."

"What has made you go gloomy today?" asked Thuro. "Are you ailing?"

Culain's eyes blazed briefly, and he walked away toward his cabin. Thuro did not follow at first but noticed the Mist Warrior glance back over his shoulder. The prince grinned, sheathed his gladius, and followed to find Culain sitting at the table, nursing a goblet of strong spirit.

"It's Gian," said Culain. "I have caused her distress; it is not something I intended, but she rather surprised me."

"She told you she loved you?"

"Do not be too clever, Thuro," snapped Culain. He waved his hand as if to wipe away the angry words. "Yes, you are right. I was a fool not to see it. But she is wrong; she has known no other man and has lifted me to the skies. I should have taken her to a settlement long since."

"What did you tell her?"

"I told her I saw her as my daughter and could not love her more than that."

"Why?"

"What sort of a question is that? Why what?"

"Why could you not take her to wife?"

"There was my second mistake, for she asked the same question. I have already given my heart; there can be no one else for me while my lady lives." Culain smiled. "But she will not have me because I choose to be mortal, and I cannot love her while she remains a goddess."

"And this you told to Laitha?"

"Yes."

"It was not wise," said Thuro. "I think you should have lied. I am not versed in the ways of women, but I think Laitha would forgive you anything except being in love with someone else."

"I can do many things, Thuro, but I cannot turn back the hours of my life. I would not wish pain on Gian, but it is done. Go to her; help her to understand."

"Not an easy task, and the more difficult for me because I do love her and would take her to wife tomorrow."

"I know that; so does she. So you are the one who should go to her."

Thuro stood, but Culain waved him to his chair once more. "Before you go, there is something I want you to see and a gift I wish you to have." He fetched a bowl of water and placed it before the prince. "Look deeply into the water and understand." Culain took a golden stone from his pocket and held it over the bowl until the water misted. Then he left the cabin, pulling shut the door behind him.

Thuro gazed down to find himself staring into a candlelit room where several men stood silently around a wide bed in which lay a slender child with white-blond hair. A man Thuro recognized as Maedhyln leaned over and placed his hand on the child's head.

"His spirit is not here," came Maedhlyn's voice, whispering inside Thuro's mind. "He is in the Void; he will not return."

"Where is the Void?" came another voice that brought a pang of deep sadness to the boy. It was Aurelius, his father.

"It is a place between heaven and hell. No man can fetch him back."

"I can," said the king.

"No, sire. It is a place of Mist Demons and darkness. You will be lost, even as the boy is lost."

"He is my son. Use your magic to send me there. I command it!"

Maedhlyn sighed. "Take the boy into your arms and wait."

The water misted once more, and Thuro saw the child wandering in a daze on a dark mountainside, his eyes blank and unseeing. Around him stalked black wolves with red eyes and slavering jaws. As they crept toward the child, a shining figure appeared bearing a terrible sword. He smote the wolves, and they fled. Then he swept the child into his arms and knelt with him by a black stream where no flowers grew. The child awoke then and cuddled into the chest of the man, who ruffled his hair and told him all was well. Three terrible beasts approached from a sudden mist, but the king's sword shone like fire.

"Back!" he said. "Or die. The choice is yours."

The beasts looked at him, gauging his strength, then returned to the mist.

"I will take you home, Thuro," said the king. "You will be well again." His father kissed him then.

Thuro's tears splashed to the bowl, disturbing the scene, but just as it faded, a dark shadow flitted across his vision.

Culain entered silently. "Gian said you regretted having no memory of the scene. I hope it was a gift worth having."

Thuro cleared his throat and wiped his eyes. "I am more in your debt now than ever. He came into hell to find me."

"For all his faults, he was a man of courage. By all the laws of mystery he should have died there with you, but such men are made to challenge the immutability of such laws. Be proud, Thuro."

"One more question, Culain. What kind of man has a gray face and opal eyes?"

"Where did you see such a man?"

"Just as the vision faded, I saw a man in black running forward with a sword raised. His face was gray and his eyes were clouded, like a blind man—only he was not blind."

"And you felt he was looking at you?"

"Yes. There was no time to feel fear; it was gone in an instant."

"Fear is what you should feel, for the man was a Soul Stealer, a drinker of blood. They exist in the Void, and none know their origins. It was a source of great interest in the Feragh. Some contend that they are the souls of the evil slain; others, that they come from a race similar to our own. Whatever the truth, they are dangerous, for their speed is like nothing human and their strength is prodigious. They feed on blood and nothing else and cannot stand strong sunlight; it causes their skin to blister and peel and eventually can kill them."

"Why would I see one?"

"Why indeed? But remember that you were looking into the Void and that that is their home."

"Can they be slain?"

"Only with silver, but few men can stand against them even then. They move like shadows and strike before a warrior can parry. Their knives and swords do not cut; they merely numb. Then a man feels their long hollow teeth in his throat, drawing his lifeblood. Give me your gladius."

Thuro offered the weapon hilt first. Culain ran his golden stone along both edges of the blade, then returned it. The prince examined it but could see no change.

"Let us hope you never do," said Culain.

Thuro found Laitha in the upper mountains, sitting on a flat rock and sketching a purple butterbur. Her eyes were red-rimmed, and the sketch was not of her usual high quality.

"May I join you?"

She nodded and placed her parchment and charcoal stick to her left. She was wearing only a light green woolen tunic, and her fingers and arms were blue with cold. He removed his sheepskin jerkin and draped it over her shoulders.

"He told you, then," she said, not looking at him.

"Yes. It is cold here; let us go back to your cabin and light a fire."

"You must think me very foolish."

"Of course I do not. You are one of the brightest people I have ever met. The only foolishness is Culain's. Now, let's go back." She smiled wanly and climbed from the rock. The sun was sinking in fire, and a bitter wind was whispering through the rocks.

Back at the cabin, with the fire roaring in the hearth, she sat before the flames, hugging her knees. He sat opposite her, nursing a goblet of watered wine from a cask in the back room.

"He loves someone else," she said.

"He has loved her since before you were born—and he is not a fickle man. You would not love him yourself if he were."

"Did he ask you to speak for him?"

"No," Thuro lied. "He merely told me how distressed he was to cause you pain."

"It was my own fault. I should have waited a year; it was not so long. I am still lean like a boy; I will be more womanly next year. Perhaps by then he will realize his own true feelings."

"And perhaps not," Thuro warned softly.

"She is not here, whoever she is. I am here. He will come to me one day."

"You are already beautiful, Laitha, but I think you underestimate him. What is a year to a man who has tasted eternity? He will never love you in the way you desire. Your passion will hurt you both."

Her eyes came up, and the look hit him like a blow. "You think I don't know why you are saying this? You want me yourself. I can see it in your moon-dog eyes. Well, you won't have me. Ever! If I can't have Culain, I will have no man."

"Fifteen is a little young to make such a decision."

"Thank you for that advice, Uncle."

"Now you are being foolish, Laitha. I am not your enemy, and you gain nothing by hurting me. Yes, I love you. Does that make me a villain? Have I ever pressed my suit upon you?"

She stared into the flames for several minutes, then smiled and reached out to touch his hand. "I am sorry, Thuro. Truly. I am so hurt inside, I just want to strike out."

"I have something to thank you for," he said. "You told Culain about me wanting to recall the day my father held me, and he used his magic stone to bring it to pass." He went on to explain about the vision and how Culain had touched his sword.

"Let me see," she asked.

"There is nothing to see." He drew the gladius, and the blade shone like a mirror.

"He has turned it to silver," said Laitha.

A dark shadow flitted by the window, and Thuro hurled himself across the room just as the door began to open. His shoulder slammed into the wood, and the door closed with a crash. Thuro fumbled for the bar, dropping it into place.

"What is happening?" cried Laitha, and Thuro swung around. The window was shuttered and barred against the cold. The door to the back room opened, and a dark shadow swept across the hearth. Laitha, half rising, slumped to the floor as a gray blade touched her flesh. Thuro dived to his left, rolled, and rose. With preternatural speed the shadow closed on him, and his blade flashed up instinctively, slicing through the dark, billowing cloak. There was an unearthly cry, and Thuro saw a corpse-gray face and opal eyes just before the creature vanished in smoke. A stench filled the room that caused Thuro to retch. Dropping to his knees, he crawled to Laitha; her eyes were open, but she was un-moving. He ran into the back room just as a second shadow darkened the window; his sword snaked out, and the apparition fled back into the night. He slammed the shutters and barred them.

Returning to Laitha, he stared into her eyes. She blinked. "If you can hear me, blink twice." She did so. "Now blink once for yes, twice for no. Is there any movement at all in your limbs?" Twice she blinked.

A crash came at the window, and a sword blade shattered the wood. Thuro, his gladius burning with blue fire, ran to the window and waited. A second crash came from the back room; then another unearthly cry rose from outside the cabin, and Thuro risked a glance through the shattered window.

Culain was standing alone in the clearing, his silver lance in his hands. Three figures moved toward him with blistering speed. He dropped to his knees, the lance flashing and lunging. Two cloaked assassins fell. Thuro tore open the cabin door and rushed into the night as four others closed on Culain.

"No, Thuro!" Culain bellowed, but it was too late, for a Soul Stealer flew at the prince. Thuro blocked a thrust and sliced his silver blade across his enemy's throat, and the creature vanished. Two others were on their way. Culain attacked the two facing him, blocking and cutting, dispatching one with a thrust to the belly. The second advanced, but Culain pressed a stud in the lance, and a sharp silver blade flashed through the air and into the Soul Stealer's chest.

Thuro managed to kill the first of the assassins, but the second sank a cold knife between his ribs. All strength fled from him, and his legs gave way. He fell on his back and saw the gray face looming above him, huge hollow teeth descending toward his throat.

Culain ran forward three paces, then threw the heavy lance. It sliced into the creature's back, plunging through to jut from its chest. It vanished, and the lance fell to the ground beside Thuro.

Culain lifted the paralyzed prince and carried him into the cabin, where Laitha was beginning to stir. "Get the fire built up and lock the door," he said.

He moved to her bow and emptied her quiver. There were twenty arrows. He touched his Sipstrassi Stone to the head of each, but nothing happened. Culain lifted Thuro's gladius; once more it was iron.

"What were they?" Laitha asked, rubbing limbs that ached with cold.

"Void killers. We are no longer safe here. Come here!" As she approached, he lifted her hand. A copper bracelet graced her left wrist, and he touched the stone to it. "If ever it shines silver, you know what it will mean?"

She nodded. "I am sorry, Culain. Will you forgive me?"

"There is nothing to forgive, Gian Avur. I should have told you about my lady, but I have not seen her for more than forty years."

"What is her name?"

"Her name is an old one meaning 'Light into Life.' She is called Goroien."

Culain sat up through the night, but the Soul Stealers did not return. Thuro awoke in the morning, his head seemingly full of wool, his movements slow and clumsy. Culain took him outside, and the crisp air drove the drowsiness from him.

"They will come again," said Culain. "There is no

end to them. They did not expect you to be armed with silver."

"I cannot stand against them; they are too fast."

"I have spoken to you, Thuro, of Eleari-mas, the Emptying. It is something you will need to master. Skill is not enough; speed is insufficient. You must free your instinct, empty your mind."

"I have tried, Culain. I cannot master it."

"It took me thirty years, Thuro. Do not expect to excel in a matter of hours." The sun was shining with golden brilliance, and the events of the night seemed of another age. Laitha was still sleeping. The Mist Warrior looked gaunt and jaded, the silver at his temples shining like snow on the distant mountain peaks. Dark rings circled his eyes. "Eldared has recruited an ally from the Feragh," he said. "No one else could open the Void. I thank the Source that you saw the vision, but who knows what will come next? Atrols, serpents, dragons, demons. The perils of the Mist are infinite. I blame myself, for I first used the floating gateways."

"In what way?" Thuro asked.

"When I led Boudicca's Iceni against the Romans, there was an elite legion, the Ninth. They marched south from Eboracum to catch us and trap us between themselves and Paullinus. But I sent the Mist, and they marched onto it and out of history."

"The legendary Ninth," whispered Thuro. "No one has ever known of their fate."

"Nor will any man. Even I. They died out of sight of their friends, their families, and even their land."

"Five thousand men," said Thuro. "That is power indeed."

"I would not do such a thing again . . . but someone has."

"Who has the power?"

"Maedhlyn. Myself. Maybe a dozen others. But that presupposes the lack of intellect and imagination in any of a hundred thousand worlds within worlds that make up the Mist. Perhaps someone has traveled a new road."

"What can I do? I cannot just remain here until they find me, and it puts both you and Laitha in peril."

"You must find your father's sword and your own destiny."

"Find . . . ? It was taken by a ghostly hand below the surface of the lake. I cannot travel there."

"Would that it were truly so simple. But the sword is not in the lake—I have searched there. No, it is in the Mist, and we must travel there to find it."

"You said there were thousands of worlds within the Mist. How will we know where to search?"

"You are joined to the sword. We will take a random path and see where it leads us."

"You will forgive me for saying that it does not sound very hopeful."

Culain chuckled. "I will be with you, Thuro. Though, yes, it will be like searching for one pebble in a rock slide. But better than waiting here for the demons to strike, yes?"

"When do we leave?"

"Tomorrow. I must prepare the path."

"And we must spend one more night waiting for the Soul Stealers?"

"Yes, but we have an advantage now. We know they are coming."

"A slim advantage, indeed."

"Perhaps as slender as the difference between life and death."

◇ 9 ◇

PRASAMACCUS WAS GRATEFUL for the tears Helga shed so publicly as he mounted the huge black stallion chosen that morning from Victorinus' stable. No warrior should leave on a dangerous hunt without such a display from a loving wife. He had been lucky, for Maedhlyn had been forced to wait five weeks after his magic had disclosed to him that the passes into the Caledones mountains were all blocked by heavy snow. Prasamaccus had used the time well, getting to know Helga, and she him. Happily, they both liked what they found. The house on the outskirts of Calcaria had been bought by Grephon at a fraction of its value, the owner being terrified of the coming war. At the back of the small white building was a ramshackle paddock and two fields that could be given over to crops.

Now Prasamaccus leaned over his saddle. "Hush, woman!" he said. "This is not seemly." But Helga's tears would not cease, and it was with a happy heart that Prasamaccus rode alongside the Enchanter toward the remnants of the stone circle above Eboracum.

For his part Maedhlyn was less than happy with the choice of messenger-escort he was sending to Thuro. The slender blond cripple was obviously a man of wit but hardly a warrior. And could he be trusted?

The Brigante cared nothing for the doubts he saw in Maedhlyn's sullen expression. The Caledones were in fact sparsely peopled, and the Vacomagi who did dwell in the foothills were renowned as a friendly tribe. With luck his mission would require no more than a six-day journey and a swift return to his white palace. He glanced nervously at the sky; he had kept his face blank, but the gods had a way of reading men's eyes.

Only two broken teeth remained of the circle, and Prasamaccus stood now where he had appeared six weeks before, overlooking the fortress city.

"You understand? Six days," said Maedhlyn.

"Yes. I'll notch a stick," Prasamaccus replied.

"Do not be flippant. You will appear above Pinnata Castra. In the mountains you will meet a man named Culain; he is tall, with eyes the color of storm clouds. Do not anger him. He will take you to the prince."

"Storm eyes. Yes, I'm ready."

With a muttered curse Maedhlyn produced a yellow-gold stone and waved it over his head. A golden glow filled the circle. "Ride west," said the Enchanter, and Prasamaccus mounted and headed the stallion forward. It shied and came down running directly at the largest stone. Prasamaccus closed his eyes. A smell like oil burning on cloth smote his nostrils, and his ears ached. He opened his eyes as the horse charged out of the circle where he had killed the Atrol. He pulled Vamera from his saddle pouch and strung her swiftly. Then, with an angry oath, he hung the bow on his pommel.

"Stupid wizard," he said. "This is the wrong circle. I am days from the Caledones."

Throughout the day Culain worked to assemble a circle of slender golden wire in the clearing below his cabin.

He looped the wire around four birch trees, then marked
the earth within the circle in a series of pentangles highlighted with chalk. At the center of the circle he constructed a perfect square, measuring the distances with
great care from the angles of the square to the farthest
points of the pentangles.

At noon he stopped, and Thuro brought him a goblet
of wine, which he refused.

"This needs a clear head, Thuro."

"What are you doing?"

"I am recreating the base layout of a minor circle—
creating a gateway, if you like. But if I am more than a
hairbreadth off in my calculations, we will end up in a
world or a time we do not desire."

"Where is Laitha?"

"She is watching the valley for sign of Eldared's
hunters."

"Can I fetch you some food?"

"No. I must finish the circle and lay on the lines of
magic. It will work only once; we will not be able to return here."

"I will watch with Laitha."

"No," said Culain sharply, "you are necessary here.
This whole circle is geared to you and your harmony. It
is our only hope of finding the sword."

Toward dusk Laitha came running into the clearing.

"There is a single rider moving up the valley," she
said. "Shall I kill him?"

Culain looked bone-weary. "No. No needless slaying.
I am almost ready. Thuro, go with Laitha and see the
man. Gian, stay hidden, and if the rider has hostile intent, shoot him down."

"I thought you needed me," said Thuro.

"The work is nearly done, the destination set. We will leave at dawn."

"Would it not be safer to leave now?" asked Laitha.

"The sun is almost gone, and we need its energies. No, we must survive one more night in the mountains."

Thuro and Laitha set off to intercept the rider, moving swiftly down the forest trails. As Thuro ran behind the lithe girl, he found his mind straying from concern about the horseman to appreciation of the supple, liquid grace of Laitha's movements.

Thuro spotted the rider moving carefully up the mountain trail and squatted down with Laitha behind a thick bush. The man rode a tall black stallion of almost seventeen hands and was dressed in a cream woolen tunic edged with braid and black trews decorated with small silver disks; he carried a dark bow of horn. He was in his early twenties, with fair hair and a straggly blond beard.

Thuro stepped out onto the path as Laitha notched an arrow to her bow.

"Welcome, stranger," said Thuro.

The man reined in. "Prince Thuro?"

"Yes."

"I have been sent to find you."

"Then step down from your mount and draw your sword."

Laitha had no intention of allowing Thuro to fight and loosed her shaft. At that moment an owl fluttered from a nearby branch, and the stallion shied. Laitha's arrow took the horse in the throat, and it fell, throwing the rider into the bushes beside the trail. Thuro was furious. He ran forward and helped the man to his feet, noticing for the first time that the rider was a cripple. Laitha stood with a second arrow notched.

"Damn you!" Thuro yelled. "Get out of my sight!" He moved to the horse, which was writhing on the ground, and opened its jugular with his hunting knife. "I am sorry," he told the man. "It was none of my doing."

"It was a fine horse—best I ever owned. I hope you have others."

"No."

The man sighed. "The gods give, the gods take away."

"Where is your sword?" Thuro asked.

"For what should I need a sword?"

"To fight me, of course. Or were you intending to use your bow?"

"Maedhlyn sent me to fetch you home. My name is Prasamaccus; I have been staying with Victorinus."

"Thuro!" called Laitha. "Look!"

Farther down the trail some dozen riders were following the tracks left by Prasamaccus.

"Your friends have arrived," said the prince.

"No friends of mine. What I told you was true."

"Then you had better follow me," said Thuro. "Here, let me carry your bow."

Prasamaccus handed him the weapon, and the trio set off, keeping away from the path. The sun was sinking, and the three faded from sight in the gathering gloom. They moved on for more than a quarter of an hour, forced to walk slowly to allow the limping Prasamaccus to keep up.

They reached the cabin as the moon cleared the clouds, and Culain ran forward to meet them.

"Who is he?"

"He says Maedhlyn sent him," answered Thuro, "but

Eldared's hunters are only minutes behind us." Culain cursed.

A gasp came from Laitha, and the three men swung toward her. She was holding up her arm and staring at the bracelet on her wrist; it had begun to glow faintly.

"The Soul Stealers," whispered Thuro.

"Would it be possible to have my bow back?" asked Prasamaccus.

Culain drew a silver knife and held it gently to the Brigante's throat; then he took the Sipstrassi Stone from his pocket and touched it to the man's temple. "Tell me why Maedhlyn sent you."

"He said to bring the prince to the circle of stones near Pinnata Castra. Then he would spirit us both home."

The knife returned to Culain's sheath. "Give him his bow and let me have the arrows." The Mist Warrior touched his stone to each of the twenty arrowheads and handed the quiver to Prasamaccus.

He notched an arrow to the string. The head shone with a white-blue light. "Very pretty," he said. A dark shadow sped from the trees, and before Laitha could react, Prasamaccus had drawn and loosed. The shaft took the assassin in the chest; the dark cloak billowed and fell to the ground, the Brigante's arrow beside it.

"Into the circle!" Culain yelled. More dark shapes moved into sight. Prasamaccus and Laitha both loosed shafts, while Culain ran forward, sweeping up his lance from the ground beside the golden wire. "Move to the central square," said Culain. As Thuro, Laitha, and Prasamaccus clambered over the wire, the Mist Warrior swung in time to block the thrust of a gray blade, cutting the lance head through the assassin's neck. More of the shadows converged toward the circle. Culain leapt the wire, but a cold knife cut into his shoulder. As his limbs lost their power, he shouted one word. A golden light filled the circle, forcing the shadow killers back. Bright as noonday, the glare was blinding. When it faded, the circle was empty, the golden wire gone, the earth smoldering.

Culain awoke in a broken circle of stones on the side of a high hill overlooking a deserted Roman fortress. He sat up and breathed deeply until the unearthly drowsiness left his limbs. The fortress below had partially collapsed, and several huts nearby had been constructed partly of stone from the ruined building. Culain glanced at the sky; a single moon hung there. The sky was clear, and he examined the stars. He was still in Britain. He cursed loudly.

A glow began to his left, and he swept up his lance and waited. Maedhlyn appeared.

"Oh, it's you," said the Enchanter. "Where is the boy?"

"Gone seeking his father's sword."

"Alone?"

"No; he has a girl and a cripple with him."

"Wonderful," said Maedhlyn.

Culain pushed himself to his feet. "It is better than him being dead."

"Marginally," Maedhlyn agreed. "What happened?"

"Soul Stealers came upon us. I sent Thuro and the others through a gateway."

"Which one?"

"I made it."

"Made? Oh, Culain, that was foolhardy indeed."

"Worse than you know. I had to send them at night."

"Better and better." Maedhlyn sniffed loudly and

cleared his throat. "You look older," he said. "Do you need a stone?"

"I have one, and I look older because I choose to. It is time to die, Maedhlyn. I have lived too long."

"Die?" Maedhlyn whispered, his eyes widening. "What nonsense is this? We are immortal."

"Only because we choose to be. I choose not to be."

"What does Athena say about this?"

"Her name is Goroien. We left that Greek nonsense behind centuries ago, and I have not seen her in forty years."

"It is cold here. Let us return to my palace; we'll talk there."

Culain followed him within the glow, and the two walked down the long hill to Eboracum and the converted villa Maedhlyn owned near the southern wall. Inside a fire burned brightly in an ornate stone hearth. The Enchanter had always heartily disliked Roman central heating, claiming it made his head thick and disturbed his concentration.

"You used not to think it nonsense," said the Enchanter as they sat together drinking mulled wine by the fire. "You made a wonderful Ares, a fine god of war. And we did help the Greeks after a fashion; we gave them philosophy and algebra."

"You always were a capricious meddler, Maedhlyn. How do you maintain your appetite for it?"

"People are wonderful creatures," said the Enchanter. "So inventive. I never tire of them and their gloriously petty wars."

"Have I mentioned before that I dislike you intensely?"

"Once or twice, Culain, now I come to recall—

though I cannot understand why. You know I would have given my life to save Alaida."

"Do not speak of her!"

Maedhlyn settled back in his deep leather chair. "Getting old does not suit you," he said.

Culain chuckled, but there was little humor in the sound. "Getting old? I *am* old—as old as time. We should have died with the waves that destroyed Balacris."

"But we did not, thank the Source! Why did you leave Goroien?"

"She could not understand my decision to become mortal."

"That's understandable. If you remember, she fell in love with the hero Gilgamesh and watched him age; some problem with his blood that the stone could not overcome. But I can see how she would not want to watch such an event again."

"I liked him," said Culain.

"Even though he took Goroien from you? You are a strange man."

"It was a passing fancy, and it is truly ancient history. What are your plans now, my Lord Enhancer, now that someone else is playing your game?"

"Enchanter, if you please. And I am unconcerned. Whoever it is can never play as well as I. You should know that, Culain; you have witnessed my genius through the ages. Did I not inspire the building of Troy? Did I not take Alexander to the brink of domination? To name but two small achievements. You think Eldared's petty sorcerer can oppose me?"

"As always, your arrogance is a joy to behold. You seem to forget how it has humbled you in the past. Troy fell despite your attempts to save it. Alexander took a fever and died. And as for Caligula . . . what on earth did you see in that boy?"

"He was bright as a button—much maligned. But I take your point. So who do you think is behind Eldared?"

"I have no idea. Pendarric has the power, but he tired of mortals long ago. Brigamartis, perhaps."

"She took to playing the gods' game with the Norse, but she's gone now. I haven't heard of her in a century or more. What of Goroien?"

"She would never use the Soul Stealers."

"I think you forget how ruthless she could be."

"Not at all. But not for someone else—not a petty king like Eldared. He couldn't pay enough. However, that is your problem now, Enchanter. I want nothing more to do with it."

"You surprise me. If Eldared has the power to summon the Soul Stealers and open a gate on your mountain, then he has the power to send assassins after the boy wherever he is. I take it you left nothing belonging to the prince on the mountain."

Culain closed his eyes. "I left his old clothes in a chest."

"Then they can find him. Unless you stop them."

"What are you suggesting?"

"Find the power behind Eldared and slay it. Or slay the king."

"And what will you be doing while I am scouring the countryside?"

"I will use this," said the Enchanter, lifting a yellowed leather-covered wedge of parchment. "It is the most valuable possession Thuro had. The works of Plutarch. Much of his harmony remains in it. I shall follow him through the Mist."

* * *

Prasamaccus gazed around himself. The landscape had changed; it was more rugged and open, the mountains stretching out into the distance beyond an immediate wooded valley. And it was bright . . . he looked up, and his heart sank. Two moons hung in the sky, one huge and silver-purple, the other small and white. The Brigante feared he knew what such phenomena might mean, and it was not good news. There was no sign of the warrior with the storm-cloud eyes.

"Where is Culain?" screamed Laitha.

"He did not manage to reach the central square," Thuro said softly. His eyes met those of Prasamaccus, who understood the unspoken thought. Culain had fallen among the Soul Stealers; both had seen it. Laitha began to search beyond the circle of white stones, calling Culain's name. Thuro sat down alongside Prasamaccus.

"I did not think anything could kill him," said Thuro. "He was an amazing man."

"I regret not having known him," said Prasamaccus with as much sincerity as he could muster. "Tell me, how do we get home?"

"I have no idea."

"Strange, I thought you were going to say that. Do you know where we are?"

"I am afraid not."

"I should have been a fortune-teller. I am beginning to know the answers to these questions before you speak. One last question. Does that second moon mean what I think it means?"

"I am afraid so."

Prasamaccus sighed and opened his pouch, producing

a small seed cake. Thuro smiled; he was beginning to like the crippled archer.

"How did you meet Victorinus?"

Prasamaccus swallowed the last of the seed cake. "I was out hunting . . ." He told Thuro of seeing the Atrols and fleeing to a stone circle and of the journey with Maedhlyn back to Eboracum. He did not mention Helga; the thought of never seeing her again was too painful. Meanwhile Laitha wandered back into the circle and sat down, saying nothing. Prasamaccus offered her his last seed cake, but she refused.

"It's your fault, cripple," she snapped. "If we had not had to wait for you, we could have escaped with Culain."

Prasamaccus merely nodded. It did not pay to argue with women.

"Nonsense!" stormed Thuro. "If you had not killed the poor man's horse, we would have arrived the sooner."

"You are saying it is my fault he is dead?"

"You are the one who introduced the question of fault, not I. Now, if you cannot be civil, hold your tongue!"

"How dare you? You are not my kinsman or my prince. I owe you nothing."

"If I might—" began Prasamaccus.

"Be quiet!" Thuro snarled. "I may not be your prince, but you are my responsibility. It is what Culain would have wanted."

"How would you know what he wanted? You are a boy; he was a man." She stood and stalked off into the darkness.

"Arguing with women offers no reward," said Prasamaccus softly. "They are always right; I saw that in my village. You'll only have to apologize to her."

"For what?"

"For pointing out that she was wrong. What are your plans, Prince?"

Thuro sat back. "Are you not angry with her for accusing you?"

"Why should I be? She was right; I slowed you down."

"But—"

"I know, she killed my horse. But how far can we take this back? Had I not been riding into the mountains, you would not have been delayed at all. Had you not been missing, I would not have been riding. Is it your fault? Arguing about it will not light us a fire, or find food."

"You are very philosophical."

"Of course," agreed Prasamaccus, wondering what it meant. He stood and limped out beyond the circle, seeking twigs for a fire, but there were none. "I think we should camp in those woods until morning," he said.

"I'll fetch Laitha."

"I'll do it," said Prasamaccus swiftly, limping out to where she sat.

The trio found a sheltered hollow and lit a campfire against a fallen trunk. Without blankets or food they sat silently, each lost in thought. Laitha grappled with grief and ill-understood anger. Thuro wondered what plan Culain might have conceived following their arrival. Would he have known this land? And if he had not, what would he have done? Set off north? South? Prasamaccus lay down beside the fire and thought of Helga. Five weeks of bliss. He hoped she would not have to wait for him too long.

When Thuro awoke, Prasamaccus had already started a fire and four clay spheres were sitting in the flames. The prince stretched his cramped muscles. Laitha still slept.

"You are up early," said Thuro, glancing at the dawn sky.

"Best to catch pigeons while they sleep. Are you hungry?"

"Ravenous." Prasamaccus hooked a ball from the fire with a short stick, then cracked a rock to it. The clay split cleanly, taking all the feathers from the bird. The meat was dark and similar to beef, and Thuro devoured it swiftly, sucking clean the fragile bones.

"I found a high hill," said Prasamaccus, "and from there I studied the land. I could see no sign of building, but there is some evidence of tilled fields to the west."

He rolled another ball from the fire and split it; then he moved to where Laitha lay and gently pushed her shoulder. She awoke, and he smiled at her. "There is breakfast cooking. Come eat." She did so in silence, careful to avoid even looking at Thuro.

"Why did Storm-eyes send you here?" asked the Brigante.

"To find my father's sword, the Sword of Cunobelin. But I do not know where to look, and I am not even sure that this is the world we were meant to enter. Culain said we needed the power of the sun, and we certainly left without that."

Prasamaccus cracked another clay sphere and sat back quietly. He had Vamera and therefore a constant supply of food. When they found people, he could trade skins and meat and perhaps buy a horse eventually. He would not starve, but what of his wards? What skills could the young prince bring to bear on this new world where he was not even a prince? The girl was not a concern, for she was young and pretty and her hips looked good for childbirth. She would not go hungry. Suddenly an unpleasant thought struck him. This was another world. Suppose it was the world of the Atrols or other demons? He remembered the tilled fields and was partially relieved. Demons tilling fields were somehow less demonic.

"We will go west," said Thuro, "and find the owners of the field."

Prasamaccus was relieved that Thuro had decided to be the leader; he was much more content to follow and advise, and that way little blame could be attached to him if matters went awry. The trio set off through the woods, following obvious game trails and coming across the spoor of deer and goat. The tracks were somewhat larger than Prasamaccus had known but not so large that they gave cause for concern. By midmorning they spotted the first deer. It was almost six feet high at the shoulders, which were humped, and it had a flap of skin hanging on its throat. Its antlers were sharp, flat, and many-pointed.

"It would need a fine strike to kill that beast," said Prasamaccus. He said no more, for his ruined leg was beginning to ache from the long walk. Thuro noticed his limp growing more pronounced and suggested a halt.

"We have come only about three miles," protested Laitha.

"And I am tired," Thuro snapped, sitting down against a tree. The Brigante sank gratefully to the grass. The boy would make a fine leader if he lived long enough, he thought.

After a short rest it was Prasamaccus who suggested

that they move on, smiling his thanks to Thuro, and toward late afternoon they emerged from the wood into a rolling land of gentle hills and dales. The distant mountains reared white and blue against the horizon, and in their shadow—some two miles farther west—was a walled stockade around a small village. Cattle and goats could be seen grazing on a hillside.

Thuro gazed long at the village, wondering at the wisdom of walking in. Yet what choice did he have? They could not spend their lives hiding in the woods. The path widened, and they followed it until they heard the sound of horsemen. Thuro stood in the center of the road; Prasamaccus moved to the left, Laitha to the right.

There were four men in the party, all heavily armored and wearing high plumed helms of shining brass. The leader halted his mount and spoke in a language Thuro had never heard. The prince swallowed hard, for this was a consideration that had not occurred to him. Whatever it was that the man said, he repeated it, this time more forcefully. Instinctively, Thuro's hand curved around the hilt of his gladius.

"I asked what you were doing here," said the rider.

"We are travelers," Thuro answered, "seeking rest for the night."

"There is an inn yonder. Tell me, have you seen a young woman, heavily pregnant?"

"No, we have just come from the woods. Is she lost?"

"She is a runaway." The warrior turned to his men and lifted his arm, and the four horsemen thundered by. Thuro took a deep, calming breath. Prasamaccus limped toward him and spoke. The words were unintelligible, a seemingly rhythmless series of random sounds.

"What are you talking about?" asked the prince. Prasamaccus looked startled and swung toward Laitha, whose words were equally strange, though almost musical. Thuro clapped his hands, and they both turned toward him. He slowly pulled clear his gladius, offering the hilt to Prasamaccus; the Brigante reached out and touched it. "Now do you understand me?"

"Yes. How do you come by this magic?"

Laitha interrupted them with an incomprehensible question.

"Might be best to leave her like that," said Prasamaccus. Laitha was becoming angry and shook her fist at Thuro. As she did so, the copper bracelet on her arm slid down over her tunic sleeve and touched the skin of her wrist.

"Thuro, you miserable whoreson? Do not leave me like this."

"I will not," said Thuro. Her eyes closed in relief, then they flared open.

"What happened to us?"

"Culain touched my sword and your bracelet with his magic stone. I suspect we are now speaking whatever language is common to this world."

"What did the riders want?" asked Laitha, dismissing the previous problem from her thoughts.

"They were seeking a runaway woman, heavily pregnant."

"She is hiding in those rocks," Prasamaccus told them. "I saw her just as we heard the soldiers."

"Then let us leave her be," declared Thuro. "We want no trouble."

"She is hurt," said Prasamaccus. "I think she's been whipped."

"No! We have problems enough."

Prasamaccus nodded, but Laitha walked away from the path and up the short climb to the rocks. There she found a young girl, no older than herself. The girl's eyes widened in terror, and she bit her lip, her slender hand moving protectively across her swollen stomach.

"I shall not hurt you," said Laitha, kneeling beside her. The girl's shoulders were bleeding, and it was obvious that a whip had been laid there with considerable force. "Why are you hunted?"

The girl touched her belly. "I am one of the Seven," she said, as if that answered the question.

"How can we help you?"

"Take me to Mareen-sa."

"Where is that?" The girl seemed surprised, but she pointed up into the hills, where a shallow wood opened beyond a group of marble boulders. "Come, then," said Laitha, holding out her hand. The girl rose and with Laitha's support began the climb.

Below them, Prasamaccus sighed and Thuro fought to control his anger.

"Easier to tame a wild pony than a wild woman," muttered the Brigante. "Said to be worth the effort, though."

Thuro felt the anger seep from him in the face of the man's mildness.

"Does nothing disturb you, my friend?"

"Of course," said Prasamaccus, hobbling off in the wake of the woman.

Thuro followed, his eyes sweeping the hills for sign of the horsemen.

◇ **10** ◇

THE VANGUARD OF the Brigante army—some seven thousand fighting men—crossed the Wall of Hadrian at Cilurnum, moving on in a ragged line to the fortress town of Corstopitum. The force was led by Cael and spearheaded by seven hundred riders of the Novontae, skilled horsemen and ferocious swordsmen.

Corstopitum was a small town of fewer than four hundred people, and the council leaders sent messages of support to Eldared, promising supplies of food to the army on its arrival. They also ordered the withdrawal of the British garrison, and the hundred soldiers marched to Vindomara twelve miles southeast. The town leaders in this larger settlement had studied the omens and followed the example of their northern neighbors. Once more the garrison was expelled.

Eldared was winning the war even before the first battle lines had been drawn.

Now, kneeling behind a screen of bushes in the woods above Corstopitum, Victorinus studied the camp below. The Brigantes had pitched their tents in three fields outside the city; the Novontae riders were farther to the west beside a swiftly flowing stream.

Gwalchmai moved silently alongside the swarthy Roman. "At least two thousand more than we expected, and the main force still to come," said the Cantii.

"Eldared is hoping his show of force will cow Aquila."

"That is not unreasonable. The cities do not relish a war."

Behind the two men waited a full cohort of Alia, 480 handpicked fighting men trained for battle as either foot soldiers or *cohors equitana*, mounted warriors. Victorinus moved back from the bushes and summoned the troop commanders to him. As with the old Roman army, the cavalry was split into turma—or troops—of thirty-two men each, with sixteen turmae to a cohort.

The commanders gathered around Victorinus in a tight circle as he outlined the night's plan of action. Each commander was given a specific target and the various counteroptions open to him depending on the fortunes of the battle. In such a ferocious skirmish the best-laid plans could come to nothing, and Victorinus knew there would be no opportunity for tactical changes once the fight began. Each turma would accomplish its own task and then withdraw. Under no circumstances would one group go to the aid of another.

For more than an hour they discussed the options; then Victorinus walked among the soldiers, checking weapons and horses and talking to the men. He wore, as did they, a leather-ringed breastplate and a wooden helm covered with lacquered cowhide, with scimitar-shaped ear guards tied under the chin. His thighs were protected by a leather kilt split into five sections above copper-reinforced boots that had replaced the more traditional greaves. The men were nervous yet anxious to inflict punishment on the proud Brigantes.

At one hour after midnight, with the Brigante camp

silent, three hundred horsemen thundered down the hill. Four turmae rode to the Brigante supply wagons, overturning them and putting them to the torch. Another troop galloped to the Novontae picket line, killing the guards and driving the horses up and into the hills. Brigante warriors streamed from their tents, but a hundred veteran lancers led by Gwalchmai hammered into them, driving them back. Behind the lancers two turmae galloped around the tents, hurling flaming brands to the canvas. The camp was in an uproar.

High above Corstopitum, Victorinus watched with concern as the flames grew and the pandemonium increased.

"Now, Gwalchmai! Now!" whispered the Roman. But still the battle raged, and the Brigante leaders began to restore order. As Victorinus verged on the edge of rage, he saw Gwalchmai's lancers wheel into the flying arrow formation and charge. The wedge, with Gwalchmai at the point of the arrow, sundered the gathering Brigante, and the other turmae galloped in behind the wings of the lancers as they broke clear into the fields. Several horses went down, but the main force escaped into the hills. In their wake Victorinus viewed with pleasure the burning wagons and tents and the scores of Brigante bodies that littered the fields.

The days of blood had begun . . .

Bitterness was so much part of Korrin Rogeur's life that he was hard-pressed to remember a time when different emotions had fueled his spirit. He stood now on the outskirts of the forest of Mareen-sa, watching the small group make its way down the hill toward the trees. He recognized Erulda and was pleased at her escape—though not for her sake but for the chagrin it would cause the magistrate. In Korrin Rogeur's world the only moments of pleasure came when his enemies were discomfited.

He was a tall man, wand-slim and wearing hunting garb of browns and dark greens that allowed him to merge with the forest. By his side was a longsword, and across his back he wore a longbow of yew and a quiver of black-feathered arrows. His eyes were dark, and a permanent scowl had etched deep lines into his brow and cheeks, making him seem older than his twenty-four years.

As the group grew closer, he studied the woman helping Erulda. She was young, tall, and lithe, long-legged and proud as a colt. Behind her came a fair-haired young man, and behind him a cripple.

Korrin scanned the skyline for signs of soldiers lying in wait, aware that the arrival of Erulda could herald a trap. He signaled the men hiding in the bushes, then moved out onto open ground. Erulda saw him first and waved; he ignored her.

"And where do you think you are going, pretty?" he asked Laitha.

Laitha said nothing. Her upbringing with Culain had lacked some of the finer points of communication. She drew her hunting knife and stepped forward.

"My, my," said Korrin, "a ferocious colt! Do you plan to stick me with your pin?"

"State your business, ugly, and be done with it," she told him.

Korrin ignored her and turned to Thuro. "Your women fight for you, do they? How pleasant."

Thuro advanced to stand before the taller woodsman. "Firstly, she is not my woman. Secondly, I do not like your tone. That may seem a small matter, especially as you have five men in the bushes even now, with shafts aimed. However, believe me when I tell you I can kill you before they can aid you."

Korrin grinned and walked beyond Thuro to where Prasamaccus had seated himself on the grass. "Your turn to offer me violence, I believe."

"This is a foolish and foolhardy game," said the Brigante, rubbing his aching leg. "There are soldiers hunting this girl who could come riding over the rise at any moment. I take it from her reaction when she saw you that you are a friend, so why not act like one?"

"I like you, cripple. You are the first of your group to make sense. Follow me."

"No," Thuro said softly. "We are looking for no trouble with the soldiers. You have the girl; we will leave."

Korrin lifted his arm, and five men stepped from the trees, arrows notched to taut bowstrings. "I fear not," he said. "I must insist you join us for a midday meal. It is the least I can offer."

Thuro shrugged, pulled Prasamaccus to his feet, and followed the woodsman into the forest. Erulda ran forward to walk beside Korrin, linking her arm in his.

The pace was too swift for Prasamaccus despite the fist that kept prodding his back, and on a slippery patch where the path rose he fell. As Thuro leaned to assist him, a dark-bearded woodsman kicked Prasamaccus in the back, hurling him to the ground once more. Thuro hit the man backhanded across the face, spinning him to the grass. A second man leapt forward, but Thuro spun and hammered his elbow into his attacker's throat. Prasamaccus scrambled to his feet as the others swarmed in to tackle the prince.

"Stop!" bellowed Korrin, and the men froze. "What is going on?"

"He struck me," stormed the first woodsman, pointing at Thuro.

"You are a troublesome boy," Korrin said.

"Ceorl kicked the cripple," said another man. "He got what he asked for."

Ceorl swore and rounded on the speaker, but Korrin stepped between them.

"You fight when I tell you, never before. And you will not strike a brother, Ceorl. *Ever.* All we have is our bond, one to the other. Break it and I'll kill you." He swung on Thuro. "I will say this once: You are at present a guest, albeit a reluctant one. So curb your temper, lest you truly wish to be treated like enemy."

"There is a difference between the two?"

"Yes. We kill our enemies. Bear that in mind."

They walked on at a reduced pace, and Prasamaccus was pleased to note the absence of a fist in his back. Still, his leg was raging by the time they reached the campsite, a honeycomb of caves in a rocky outcrop. He, Thuro, and Laitha were left to sit in the open under the eyes of four guards while Korrin and Erulda vanished into a wide cave mouth.

"You must learn not to be so hotheaded," said Prasamaccus. "You could have been killed."

"You are right, my friend, but it was a reaction. How is your leg?"

"It hardly troubles me at all."

"She did not even thank me," said Laitha suddenly. Thuro took a deep breath, but Prasamaccus tapped his arm sharply.

"It was a fine gesture nonetheless," said the Brigante.

Laitha dipped her head. "I am sorry I said what I did, Prasamaccus. You did not cause Culain's death. Will you forgive me?"

"I rarely recall words said in anger or grief. There is nothing to forgive. What we must decide is how to deal with our current situation. We appear to be sitting at the heart of a war."

"Surely not," said Laitha. "This is just an outlaw band."

"No," put in Thuro, "the girl was some kind of hostage. And if these men were truly outlaws, they would have searched us for coin. They appear to be a brotherhood."

"And a small one," said the Brigante, "which probably makes them the losing side."

"Why does that affect us?" Laitha asked. "We mean them no harm."

"What we may intend is not the point," said Thuro. "This looks to be a more or less permanent camp, and now we know how to find it. If the soldiers question us, we could betray the brotherhood."

"So? What are you suggesting?"

"Simply that we will either be slain out of hand or offered a place among them. The latter is more likely since we were not killed back in the hills."

Prasamaccus merely nodded.

"So what should we do?" Laitha asked.

"We join them—and escape when we can."

Korrin emerged from the cave and summoned Thuro. "Leave your sword and knife with your friends and follow me." The prince did as he was bidden and walked behind the woodsman deep into the torchlit maze of caves, arriving at last at a wide doorway cut into the sandstone. Korrin halted. "Go inside," he said softly. From within the entrance came a deep, throaty growl, and Thuro froze.

"What is in there?"

"Life or death."

The prince stepped into the shadow-haunted interior. Only one flickering candle lit the room beyond, and Thuro waited as his eyes grew accustomed to the dark. In the corner sat a hunched figure, seemingly immense in the shadows. The prince approached, and the figure turned and rose, towering over him. The head was grotesque, bulging-eyed and savagely marked, while the face was a mixture of man and bear. Saliva dripped from the jaws, and though the figure was robed in white like a man, the huge paws that extended from the sleeves were clawed and bestial.

"Welcome to Mareen-sa," said the creature, its voice deep and rolling, its words slurred almost beyond recognition. "Tell me of yourself."

"I am Thuro. A traveler."

"A servant of whom?"

"I am no man's servant."

"Each man is a servant. From where have you traveled?"

"I have walked the Mist. My world is far away."

"The Mist!" whispered the creature, moving closer, its claws resting on Thuro's shoulder, close to his throat. "Then you serve the Witch Queen?"

"I have not heard of her. I am a stranger here."

"You know, do you not, that I am ready to slay you?"

"So I understand," Thuro replied.

"I do not wish to. I am not as you see me, boy. Once I was tall and fair like my brother Korrin. But it does not pay to fall into the clutches of Astarte. Worse it is to love her, as I loved her. For then she does not kill you. No matter ... go away, I am tired."

"Do we live or die?"

"You live ... today. Tomorrow? We will talk again tomorrow."

The prince backed from the chamber as the hunched figure settled down in the corner. Korrin was waiting.

"How did you enjoy your meeting?" asked the woodsman. Thuro looked deeply into his eyes, sensing the pain hidden there.

"Can we talk somewhere?" The man shrugged and walked back toward the light. In a side chamber containing a cot and two chairs Korrin sat down, beckoning Thuro to join him.

"What would you like to talk about?"

"This may seem hard to believe, but I and my companions know nothing of your lands or your troubles. Who is Astarte?"

"Hard to believe? No. Impossible. You cannot travel anywhere on the face of this world without knowing Astarte."

"Even so, bear with me. Who is she?"

"I have no time for games," said Korrin, rising.

"This is not a game. My name is Thuro, and I have traveled the Mist. Your land, your world, is new to me."

"You are a sorcerer? I find that hard to take. Or are you really hundreds of years old and only pretending to be a beardless boy?"

"I came here—was sent here—by a man of magic. He did it to enable us to escape being murdered. That is the simple truth—question my friends. Now, who is Astarte?"

Korrin returned to his seat. "I do not believe you, Thuro, but you gain nothing by hearing me speak of her, so I will tell you. She is the Dark Queen of Pinrae. She rules from ocean to ocean, and if sailors can be believed, she controls lands even beyond the waters. And she is evil beyond any dream of man. Her foulness is such that if you truly have not heard of her, you will not believe her depravity. The girl you helped was one of the Seven. Her fate was to be taken to Perdita, the Castle of Iron, and there to see her babe devoured by the Witch Queen. Think on that! Seven babes every season!"

"Eaten?" said Thuro.

"Devoured, I said, by the Bloodstone."

"But why?"

"How can you ask a sane man why? Why does she destroy rather than heal? Why did she take a man like Pallin and turn him into the beast that he is becoming? You know why she did that? Because he loved her. Now do you understand evil? Every day that good man becomes more of a beast. One day he will turn on us and rend and slay, and we will have to kill him. Such is the legacy of the Witch Queen, may the ghosts disembowel her!"

"I take it she has an army."

"Ten thousand strong, though she has disbanded twice that number following her conquests of the Six Nations. But she has other weapons, dread beasts she can summon to rip a man to bloody ribbons. Have you heard enough?"

"How is it that you survive against such a foe?"

"How indeed? If she killed us now, how would we suffer? Allowing us to live and watch Pallin go mad—that is wondrously venomous. When we have been forced to kill him and our hearts are broken, then they will come."

"She sounds vile indeed," said Thuro. "Now I understand what you meant about the bond of brotherhood.

But tell me, why do the people stand for such evil? Why do they not rise up in their thousands?"

Korrin leaned back, fixing his dark eyes on Thuro as if seeing him for the first time. "Why should they? I did not—until my wife's name was drawn from the list. Until they dragged her screaming from our home, carrying a babe I would never see. Life is not unpleasant in Pinrae. There is enough food and work, and there are no enemies any longer across the borders. Now the only danger is to pregnant women—and only twenty-eight of those a year from a nation of who knows how many thousand. No, why should a man seek to overthrow such a benign ruler? Unless his wife and child are slain . . . unless his brother is turned into a foul monster doomed to be killed by his own kin."

"How long has Astarte ruled Pinrae?"

Korrin shrugged. "That is a matter for historians. She has always been queen. And yet to look at her . . . My brother journeyed to the Castle of Iron to plead for Ishtura, my wife. The queen took him to her bosom, and he fell for her golden beauty. What a price he paid to bed her!"

"Why do you not flee the land?" asked the prince.

"To where? Across the oceans? Who knows what evil dwells there? No, I shall stay and attempt all in my power to destroy her and all who serve her. What a burning there will be on that glad day!"

Thuro rose. "Oil never killed a fire," he said softly. "I think I will return to my friends."

"The fire I shall light will never be put out," said Korrin, his eyes gleaming in the torchlight. "I have the names on a scroll of life. And when she is dead, others will be named, and they can follow her screaming into darkness."

"The names of people who did not fight her?"

"Exactly."

"Names like yours—before they took your wife?"

"You do not understand. How could you?"

"I hope I never do," said Thuro, walking out to the corridor and into the warmth of the afternoon sun.

Thuro and the others were not called to see the man-beast Pallin during the next four days, and Korrin Rogeur all but ignored them. Prasamaccus was infuriated at the lack of skill shown by the brotherhood's hunters, who returned empty-handed at dusk each day, complaining that the deer were too fast or too canny or that their bows were not strong enough, their shafts not straight enough. On the fourth day they brought back a doe whose meat was so tough as to be indigestible. Prasamaccus sought out Korrin as the woodsman was setting off to scout in the north.

"What is it, cripple? I have little time."

"And little food . . . and even less skill."

"Make your meaning plain."

"You do not have a huntsman in your tiny army who could hit a barn wall from the inside, and I am tired of chewing on roots or meat unfit for a hunter. Let me take my bow and bring some fresh meat to the caves."

"Alone?"

"No. Give me someone who has a little patience and will do as he is told."

"You are arrogant, Prasamaccus," said Korrin, using the Brigante's name for the first time.

"Not arrogant, merely tired of being surrounded by incompetents."

Korrin's eyebrows rose. "Very well. Do you have anyone in mind?"

"The quiet one who spoke out against Ceorl."

"Hogun is a good choice. I'll tell him to kill you if you so much as appear to be trying to escape."

"Tell him what you wish—but tell him now!"

Thuro watched as the two men left the clearing, Prasamaccus limping behind the taller Hogun. Korrin Rogeur approached him. "Can he use that bow?"

"Time will tell," said Thuro. Korrin shook his head and departed with four other men. Laitha sat beside the prince.

"They brought in three other pregnant women last night," she told him. "I heard them talking. It seems Korrin raided a convoy they were with: four soldiers killed and several others wounded."

Thuro nodded. "It is his only chance to hurt Astarte, rob her of her sacrifices. But he is doomed, poor man, just like his brother."

"While he lives, there is hope—so Culain used to say."

Thuro nodded. "There is truth in that, I suppose. But there are not more than fifty men here—against an army of ten thousand. They cannot win. And have you noticed the lack of organization? It is not just that they lack skill as huntsmen; they do nothing but sit and wait for Pallin to go mad. There are not enough scouts out to adequately protect the camp; they have no meetings to discuss strategy; they do not even practice with their weapons. A more disorganized band of rebels I have never heard of; they wear defeat like a cloak."

"Perhaps they were just waiting for a prince with your battle experience," snapped Laitha.

"Perhaps they were!" Thuro pushed himself to his feet and approached the nearest guard, a hulking youngster armed with a longbow. "What is your name?" asked Thuro.

"Rhiall."

"Tell me, Rhiall, if I were to walk from this camp, what would you do?"

"I would kill you. Would you expect me to wave?" This brought a chuckle from the other three guards who had gathered around.

"I do not think you could kill me with that bow—not were I ten feet tall, six feet wide, and riding a giant tortoise." The other men grinned at Rhiall's discomfort. "What is there for the rest of you to smile about? You!" Thuro hissed, pointing at a lean man with a dark beard and green eyes. "Your bow is not even strung. Were I to run yonder into the trees, you would be useless."

"It doesn't pay to be insulting, boy," said the huntsman.

"Wrong," Thuro told him. "It does not pay to insult *men*. What are you, runaway servants? Clerics? Bakers? There is not a warrior among you."

"That does it!" said the lean man. "It is time someone taught you a lesson in manners, boy." Thuro stepped back, allowing the man to draw his longsword; then the prince's gladius snaked into the sunlight.

"You are right about lessons, forester." The prince leapt lithely back as the huntsman raised his sword and charged, slashing the weapon in a vicious arc toward Thuro's left side. The prince blocked the sweep with ease, pivoted on his heel, and hammered the man from his feet. The huntsman's sword flew through the air to clatter against the trunk of a nearby tree. "Lesson one," said Thuro. "Rage is no brother to skill."

A second man came forward more carefully. Thuro engaged him, and their blades whispered together. He was more skillful than his comrade, but he had not been trained by Culain lach Feragh. Thuro stepped forward, rolled his sword over his opponent's blade, then flicked his wrist. The huntsman's sword followed that of his comrade, and the man backed away, but Thuro sheathed his gladius. "Laitha, come over here!"

Scowling, the forest girl obeyed. Thuro turned to the guards. "I will not lower myself to best you with the bow, but I'll wager my sword against your bows that even this woman can outshoot you."

"I'll take that wager," said the lean man.

"I'll not play your games," stormed Laitha. Thuro swung on her, lashing his open hand across her face; she staggered back, shocked and hurt.

"This time you will do exactly as I say," Thuro snapped, his eyes blazing. "I have had enough of your childish outbursts. We are here because of your stupidity. Act your age, woman! And think of Culain!"

At the mention of his name, Laitha's anger flowed from her and she walked to the nearest man. "Name a target," she whispered.

"The tree yonder," said Rhiall.

"I said a target, not a monument of nature!"

"Then you name one."

"Very well," Leaning forward, she deftly scooped Rhiall's dark cap from his head and walked to the tree he had indicated. There she drew her hunting knife and plunged it through the hat, pinning it to the trunk. Then she paced out thirty steps and waited for the men to join her.

Rhiall strung his bow and notched an arrow. "That was a good hat," he grumbled as he pulled back the string, aimed, and loosed. The shaft glanced from the trunk and vanished into the forest. The second man's shot missed the hat by a foot; the third man clipped the rim, bringing applause from the others. Lastly the lean huntsman took aim; his shaft hit the handle of Laitha's knife and failed to pierce the target.

"Shoot again," said Laitha. He did so and scored a full hit in the crown of the hat. Laitha took Rhiall's bow and paced off another ten steps. She turned, drew back the string, froze, released her breath, and loosed. The shaft slammed through the crown of the hat alongside the lean man's arrow.

He sniffed loudly and walked to her mark, then took aim and released the string. The arrow creased the rim. Laitha moved back another ten paces and pierced the hat again. Then she approached Thuro, dropped the bow at his feet, and leaned in close.

"Touch me again," she whispered, "and I'll kill you." Turning her back, she returned to her place near the circle of rocks. The lean huntsman stepped forward.

"My name is Baldric. Perhaps you would teach me the move that disarmed me."

"Gladly," said Thuro. "And if you wish to live beyond the spring, you should practice your skills. One day soon the soldiers will come."

"It's not the soldiers we fear," said Baldric, "It's the Vores."

"Vores? I have not heard the name."

"Great cats. They can crush an ox skull in their jaws. Astarte uses them for sport—hunting the likes of us. Once they are loosed in the forest, we are truly lost."

"If the beast is mortal, it can be slain. If one can be slain, ten can die—or a hundred. What you need is to plan for the moment the Vores are loosed."

"How can you plan to fight a creature that runs faster than a horse and kills with either paw or fang? There

used to be Vore hunts when I was a boy: twenty men
with bows, another ten on horseback with long lances.
And still men would die in the hunt. And here we are
talking of twenty Vores, or thirty. And we have no hunting horses and no lances."

"You are a pitiful bunch, to be sure. The Vores eat
meat?"

"Of course."

"Then set traps. Dig pits with sharpened stakes at the
foot. A man is never beaten until the last drop of his
blood drips from the wound. And if you haven't the
heart to fight, then leave the forest. But do not dither in
the shadows."

"What is your interest?" asked the hulking Rhiall.
"You are not one of us."

"Happily true. But I am here, and you need me."

"How so?" asked Baldric.

"To teach you to win. Savor the word. *Win.*"

A terrifying roar came from the cave mouth, and the
men swung toward it. There, stark against the rock face,
was a towering bear with no semblance of humanity. It
saw the men gathered around Thuro, dropped on all
fours . . . and charged.

The beast that had been Pallin moved at ferocious
speed, hammering into the group before they could run.
Rhiall, the slowest to move, was hurled ten feet in the
air to land unconscious by a tall rock. The others were
thrown to the ground, where they scrambled to their
feet to sprint for the relative safety of the trees. Thuro
dived to his left, rolling on his shoulder and rising as
the beast reared up on its hind legs, its great talons rak-
ing the air. The prince drew his gladius and backed
away. The bear advanced, dropped to all fours, and

charged again. This time Thuro leapt high, coming down on the beast's back with sword raised, but he could not plunge it into the creature's neck, knowing what it once had been. The bear began to thrash around, seeking to dislodge the young warrior. In his efforts to hold on, Thuro dropped his sword; it fell to the beast's back and a blinding white light blazed from the blade. The bear dropped without a sound, and Thuro jumped clear of the falling body. The bestial features softened, and the young Briton watched as the fur shrank back to reveal the half-human face he recalled from the first meeting deep in the caves. He retrieved his sword, noting the heat emanating from the blade, and the answer came to him.

"Laitha!" he shouted. "Come quickly!" She ran to him and gazed in horror at Pallin's deformed features.

"Kill it quickly before it recovers."

"Give me your bracelet. Now!" Swiftly she pulled the copper band clear, and Thuro took it and held it to the twisted face. Once more light blazed, and Pallin's features softened further.

"What about the arrows?" whispered Laitha. "Culain touched those also."

Thuro nodded, and she raced across the clearing to fetch her quiver. One by one Thuro touched the arrowheads to the stricken half beast, and each time more of the man emerged. At last the magic was exhausted and Pallin's face was clearly more human than before, but the taloned paws remained, along with the huge sloping, fur-covered shoulders. His eyes opened.

"Why am I not dead?" he asked, his anguish terrible to hear.

The guards ran forward and knelt before him.

"This young man restored you, lord," said Baldric.

"He touched you with his magic sword. Your face . . ."
Baldric swept off his brass helm and held it before
Pallin's eyes. The man-monster gazed at his distorted
reflection, then turned his sad blue eyes on Thuro.

"You have only delayed the inevitable, but I thank
you."

"My friend Prasamaccus has another twenty arrows
that were touched by magic. When he returns, I will
bring them to you."

"No! Against Astarte we have no magic. Keep them
safe. I am doomed, though your aid should grant me another month of life as a man." He looked down at his
terrible hands. "As a man? Sweet gods of earth and water! What kind of man am I?"

"A good man, I think," said Thuro. "Have faith.
What magic can do, magic can undo. Are there no En-
chanters in this world?"

"You mean the Dream Shapers?" answered the man
Baldric.

"If they work magic, yes."

"There used to be one in the Etrusces—mountains
west of here."

"Do you know where in the mountains he lived?"

"Yes; I could take you."

"No!" said Pallin. "I want no one to risk danger for
me."

"You think there is less danger in these woods?"
Thuro asked. "How long before the Vores or the soldiers rip your brotherhood to pieces or drag your people
before Astarte to suffer your fate?"

"You do not understand: this is all a game to the
Witch Queen," said Pallin. "She told me she could see
my every movement and would watch me being slain
by my brethren. Even now she has heard your plans and

therefore has negated it. The Dark Lady watches us at this moment."

The guards eased back from the stricken monster, glancing fearfully at the sky. Thuro himself felt a cold shiver on his back, but he forced a laugh and stood.

"Do you think she is the only power in the world?" he scoffed. "If she is so invincible, why are you not dead? Can you hear me, Witch Queen? Why is he not dead? Come, Baldric, lead me to the Dream Shaper."

Two hundred miles away the silvered mirror shimmered as Astarte passed an ivory hand before it.

"You interest me, sweet boy. Come to me. Come to Goroien!"

◇ **11** ◇

At sunset Prasamaccus limped into the camp as Thuro and Baldric were preparing for their journey. Behind him came the red-faced Hogun, staggering under the weight of the deer the crippled Brigante had killed two hours before. Prasamaccus sank to the ground beside Laitha.

"What is going on?"

"The noble prince has decided to take on the Witch Queen," she answered. "He is heading off to some mountain range to find a wizard."

"Why are you angry? He has obviously earned their confidence."

"He is a boy," she said dismissively.

Tired as he was, Prasamaccus rose and limped to the group, where Thuro outlined the events of the day. The Brigante said nothing, but he sensed the growing excitement among the men. The man-beast Pallin had returned to the caves.

"How will you find the Dream Shaper?" asked Thuro.

As Baldric was about to answer, Prasamaccus interrupted sharply: "A word with you, young prince?"

Thuro followed the Brigante to a sturdy oak. "You obviously disbelieve that the Witch Queen overlooks us,

154

but that is an assumption and therefore unwise. Let the man lead us, but do not discuss the exact location."

"She cannot be everywhere; she is not a goddess."

"We do not know that. But she must have known the length of her spell on Pallin, and she could have been watching for his death. Give me your sword."

Thuro did so, and Prasamaccus took three arrows from his quiver and ran them down the blade. "I do not know if the magic can be transferred in this way, but I see no reason why not." He returned the sword to the prince. "Now let us find this Enchanter."

"No, my friend. Pallin says that you and Laitha must remain. They will not allow all of us to leave the forest. Look after her and I will see you soon."

Prasamaccus sighed and shook his head, but he said nothing and watched silently as the two men walked away into the shadows of the trees. Helga seemed so far away. The camp women gathered around the deer, quartering it expertly, and the Brigante lay down beside Laitha, covering himself with a borrowed blanket.

"He did not even say good-bye," said Laitha.

Prasamaccus closed his eyes and slept.

Two hours later he was awakened by the point of a boot nudging his side. He sat up to see Korrin Rogeur squatting down beside him.

"If your friend does not return, I will cut your throat."

"You woke me to tell me what I already know?"

Korrin sat down and rubbed at tired eyes. "Thank you for the deer," he said, as if the words had been torn from him under duress, "and I am grateful that your friend helped my brother."

"Was your scouting mission successful?"

"Yes and no. There is an army camped now at the

northern border—a thousand men. At first we thought they would enter the forest, but then they were ordered to dismount and return to their camp. It would seem this was around the time that the boy used his magic on Pallin."

"Then he saved not only your brother but your people as well," said Prasamaccus.

"That is how it seems," admitted Korrin. "We are doomed here, and it galls me. When I was a child, my father told me wonderful stories of heroes who could overcome impossible odds. But that is not life, is it? There are thirty-four fighting men here. *Thirty-four.* Not exactly an army."

"Look at it from Astarte's point of view," said the Brigante. "You are important enough to merit the attention of one-tenth of her army. She must fear you for some reason."

"We have nothing she should fear."

"You have a flame here, Korrin. Admittedly it is a small flame, but I once saw an entire forest consumed from the glowing coals of a carelessly lit campfire. That is what she fears: that your flame will grow."

"I am tired, Prasamaccus. I will see you in the morning."

"Come hunting with me."

"Perhaps." Korrin stood and moved away toward the caves.

"You are a wise man," said Laitha, pushing back her blanket and joining Prasamaccus. He smiled.

"I wish that were true. But were it the case, I would be back in the Land between Walls or in Calcaria with my wife."

"You are married? You have not mentioned her."

"Memory is sometimes painful, and I try not to think

of her. Wherever she is now, she is not seeing the same stars as I. Good night, Laitha."

"Good night, Prasamaccus." For a few minutes there was silence, then Laitha whispered, "I am glad you are here."

He smiled, but did not answer. It was not a time for conversation ... not when Helga was waiting in his dreams.

Thuro and Baldric walked through most of the night in a forest lit by the bright light of two moons, a silvered, almost enchanted woodland that Thuro found bordering on the beautiful. They slept for two hours and at dawn were at the western edge of the forest, facing the open valleys before the white-blue mountains.

"Now the danger begins," said Baldric. "May the ghosts preserve us!"

The two men strode out into the open. Baldric strung his bow and walked with an arrow ready. Thuro scanned the skyline, but there was no sign of soldiers. Small huts and larger houses dotted the land, and there were cattle grazing on the hillsides.

"Who are these ghosts you pray to?" he asked Baldric.

"The Army of the Dead," answered the lean huntsman.

At noon they stopped at a farmhouse, and Baldric was offered a loaf of dark bread. The inhabitants, a young man and woman, seemed fearful and all too anxious for the travelers to move on. Baldric thanked them for the food, and they vanished into the house.

"You knew them?" asked the prince.

"My sister and her husband."

"They were not very friendly."

"To speak to me is death since the warrant went out."

"What was your crime?"

"I killed a soldier who came for my neighbor's wife. She was one of the Winter Seven."

"What happened to the woman?"

"Her husband handed her over two hours later, and named me as the killer. I ran and joined Korrin."

"I would have thought there would be more rebels."

"There were," said the huntsman. "An army of two thousand rose in the north, but they were taken and crucified on the trees of Caliptha-sa. Astarte wove a spell about them so that even when the crows had torn the flesh from their bones, they were still alive. Their screams came from the forest for more than two years before she relented and released their souls. Now there are not many rebels."

The two travelers came to the foothills of the Etrusces by midafternoon of the following day. The mountains reared above them, gaunt giants against the gathering storm clouds. "There is a cabin," said Baldric, "about a mile ahead in a narrow valley. We will stay the night there."

The building was deserted, the windows hanging open and their leather hinges rotted. But the night was not cold, and the two men sat before a fire, saying little. Baldric seemed an insular, introverted man.

Toward midnight the storm broke above the mountains; rain lashed the sides of the cabin and was driven through the open windows by a shrieking wind. Thuro wedged the broken windows into place and watched as lightning speared the sky. He was tired and hungry, and his mind drifted to thoughts of Culain. He had not realized how fond he had grown of the Mist Warrior. That he had died at the hands of the Soul Stealers was more than a travesty. At least Aurelius had had the small satisfaction of taking some of his killers with him on the dark road. At the thought of his father, Thuro's mood mellowed to the point of melancholy. He could remember only four long conversations with the king; all of them had concerned his studies. But they had never spoken as father and son ...

A shadow moved across the clearing before the cabin, and Thuro jerked upright, blinking rapidly to clear his vision; he could see nothing. He drew his sword; the blade was shining like dull silver.

The door exploded inward, but Thuro was already moving. The shadow swept toward him even as Baldric awoke, reaching for his bow. Thuro's mind emptied as his gladius blocked a gray blade and slashed through the dark cape and up into the corpse-gray face. The demon vanished in an instant, cape fluttering to the floor. Thuro ran to Baldric, touching his sword to the man's arrowhead. They waited, but nothing moved in the storm. Thuro glanced down at his sword. Was it still silver or iron gray? He could not tell, and a tense hour followed. Taking a risk, he moved to the door, lifting it back into place and wedging it shut.

Baldric's face was white, his eyes fearful. "What was that thing?"

"A creature from the Void. It is dead."

"From its face, it was dead before it came in. How did you match it? I have never seen anything as swift."

"I used a trick taught me by a master. It is called Eleari-mas—the Emptying." Thuro gave a silent prayer of thanks to the departed Culain and allowed his body to relax. He thrust the gladius into the wooden floor. "If the blade glows silver, it means they have returned," he told the huntsman.

"You are more than you seem, boy. A good deal more."

"I think I have passed from youth to manhood in but a few days. Do not call me boy. My name is . . ." He stopped and smiled. "I carry a boy's name still. My naming was due to have been conducted at Camulodunum in the summer, but I shall not be there. No matter. I need no druid or Enchanter to tell me that I am a man." He dragged the sword from the wood and held it aloft. "Thuro is now the memory the man carries, a memory of youth and lesser days. This sword is mine. It is the sword of Uther Pendragon, the man."

Baldric stood and offered his hand. Uther took it in the warrior's grip, wrist to wrist. "More than a man," said Baldric. "You are a brother."

Gwalchmai sat with head bowed, the bandage on his arm dripping blood to the grass. His turma had been cut to pieces in a raid three miles from the merchant town of Longovicium. Twenty-seven men were dead or captured; the remaining four sat with Gwalchmai in a small wood, thinking of their comrades: men who had awoken to a bright sun and this afternoon stared sightlessly at a darkening sky.

Summer had arrived in northern Britain, but it had brought no joy to the beleaguered army of Lucius Aquila. The Brigantes, under Eldared and Cael, had conquered Corstopitum, Vindomara, Longovicium, Voreda, and Brocavum. Now they besieged the fortress city of Cataractonium, pinning down six cohorts of fighting men from the Fifth Legion. News from the south was scarcely better; Ambrosius had been forced to retreat against Hengist, and the Saxon king had taken Durobrivae in the southeast.

A Jute named Cerdic had raided the southwest and sacked the town of Lindinis, destroying two cohorts of auxiliaries. No one talked of victory now, for the British army was running short of men and hope, and the early victory at Corstopitum no longer boosted morale. Rather, it was the reverse, for it had raised expectations that had not been realized.

Gwalchmai sat, watching the blood on his arm thicken and dry. He made a fist and felt the pain in his bicep. It would heal, given time. But how much time did he have?

"If the king were still alive . . ." muttered a short, balding warrior named Casmaris, not needing to finish the sentence.

"He is not," snapped Gwalchmai, torn between agreement with the unspoken sentiment and loyalty to Aquila. "What is the point of this endless hankering for things past? *If* the king were alive. *If* Eldared could have been trusted. *If* we had ten more legions."

"Well, I am tired of running and holding," said Casmaris. "Why can we not bring up the Fourth and take them on in one bloody battle?"

"All or nothing?" queried Gwalchmai.

"And why not? Nothing is what we will have anyway. This is the slow death we are suffering."

Gwalchmai turned away; he could not argue. He was a Cantii tribesman, a Briton by birth and temperament, and he did not understand the endless strategies. His desire was simple: meet the enemy head on and fight until someone lost. But Aquila was a Roman of infinite patience who would not risk an empire on one throw of the dice. Deep inside him Gwalchmai could feel that they were both wrong. Perhaps there was a time for patience, but there was also a time for raw courage and a defiance of the odds.

He pushed himself to his feet. "Time to ride," he said.

"Time to die," muttered Casmaris.

Uther awoke with his heart thumping erratically, fear making him roll and rise, groping for his sword. He had fallen asleep while on watch.

"Have no fear," said Baldric, who was honing the blade of his hunting knife as the dawn sunlight streamed through the open window. The storm had passed, and the morning was bright and clear under a blue sky.

Uther smiled ruefully. Baldric offered him the last of the black bread, which the prince was forced to dampen with water from his companion's canteen to make it edible. They set off minutes later, heading higher into the timberline of the mountains, following a narrow trail dotted with the spoor of mountain goats and bighorn sheep. At last, as the sun neared noon, they came to a high valley where a small granite-built house nestled in the hollow of a hill. The roof had been thatched but was now black and ruined by fire.

The two men waited in the tree line, scanning the countryside for signs of soldiers. Satisfied that they were alone, they descended to the house, stopping at a huge oak. Crucified on the trunk was the near skeleton of a man.

"This would be Andiacus," said Baldric, "and I do not think he can help us." The leg bones were missing, obviously ripped away by wolves or wild dogs, and the skull had fallen to the earth by the tree roots. Uther wandered to the house, which was well built around a central room with a stone hearth. Everywhere was chaos: books and scrolls littering the floor, drawers pulled from chests, tables overturned, rugs pulled up. The three back rooms were in similar condition. Uther righted a cane chair and sat, lost in thought.

"Time to be leaving," said Baldric from the doorway.

"Not yet. Whoever did this was searching for the source of the Enchanter's power. They did not find it."

"How can you say that? They have torn the place apart."

"Exactly, Baldric. There is no evidence of an end to the search. It follows that either they found the source at the very last, or they did not find it. The latter is more probable."

"If they did not find it, how can we?"

"We know where not to look. Help me clear the mess."

"Why? No one lives here."

"Trust me." Together the two men righted all the furniture, then Uther sat down once more staring at the walls of the main room. After a while he stood and moved to the bedroom. The quantity of books and scrolls showed Andiacus to be a studious man. Some of the manuscripts were still tied, and Uther studied them. They were carefully indexed.

"What are we looking for?" asked the huntsman.

"A stone. A golden stone, black-veined, possibly the size of a pebble."

"You think he hid it before they killed him?"

"No. I think he hid it as a matter of course, probably every night. And he did not have it with him when they captured him, which could mean they took him in his sleep."

"If he hid it, they would have found it."

"No. If *you* hid it, they would have found it. We are talking of an Enchanter and a magic stone. He hid it in plain sight, but he changed it. Now all we must do is think of what it might have been."

Baldric sat down. "I am hungry, I am tired, and I do not understand any of this. But last night a creature of darkness tried to kill us, and I would like to be gone from these mountains before nightfall."

Uther nodded. He had been thinking of the Soul Stealer and wondering whether it had been sent by Eldared or Astarte or was merely a random factor associated with neither. He pushed his fears from his mind and returned to the problem at hand. Maedhlyn had often told him not to waste his energies on matters beyond his knowledge.

The murdered Enchanter either had hidden the stone or had transformed it. If it had been hidden, the searchers would have found it. Therefore, it had been transformed. Uther rose from the bed. Any one of the scattered objects on the floor could be Sipstrassi. Think, Uther, he told himself. Use your mind. Why would the Enchanter disguise the stone? To safeguard it so that no one would steal it. Around the room were ornate goblets, gold-tipped quills, items of clothing, blankets, candle holders, even a lantern. There were scrolls, books, and charms of silver, bronze, and gold. All would be worth something to a thief and therefore useless as a disguise for a magic stone. Uther eliminated them from his thoughts, his eyes scanning the room, seeking an object that was functional yet worthless. There was a desk by the window, the drawers ripped out and smashed. Beside it lay piles of scattered papers ... and there in the corner, nestling against the wall, an oblong paperweight of ordinary granite.

Uther pushed himself from the bed and moved to the rock. It was heavy and ideal for the purpose it served. He held it over the desktop and concentrated hard. After several seconds, his hand grew warm and there appeared two platters of freshly roasted beef. The granite in his hand disappeared, to be replaced by a thumbnail-sized Sipstrassi Stone with thick black veins interweaving on the golden surface.

"You did it!" whispered Baldric. "The Dream Shaper's magic."

Uther smiled, holding his elation in check, savoring the feeling of triumph, the triumph of mind. "Yes," he said at last, "but the power of the stone is not great. As the magic is exhausted, these black veins swell. When the gold is used up, the power is gone. Enjoy the meat. We cannot afford to waste any more enchantment; we must heal Pallin."

The food was as close to divine as either man had tasted. Then, gathering their weapons, Uther and Baldric left the house, the younger man carrying the Sipstrassi Stone in his hand. As they passed the skeleton, the stone grew warmer and Uther paused. A whisper like a breeze through dry leaves echoed inside his head, and a single word formed.

"Peace." It was a plea born of immense suffering. Uther remembered Baldric's word about the army of rebels who had been crucified yet not allowed to die. Stooping, he lifted the skull, touching the stone to its temple. White light blazed, and the voice inside Uther's head grew in power.

"I thank you, my friend. Take the stone to Erin Plateau. Bring the ghosts home." The whisper faded and was gone, and the black threads on the stone had swelled still further.

"Why did you do that?" Baldric asked.

"He was not dead," answered Uther. "Let us go."

Maedhlyn hurled the black pebble to the tabletop, where Culain swept it up. Neither man said anything as Maedhlyn poured a full goblet of pale golden spirit and drained it at a swallow. The Enchanter looked to be in a dreadful condition, his face sallow, the skin sagging beneath his beard. His eyes were bloodshot, his movements sluggish. For seven days he had tried to follow Thuro, but the Standing Stones above Eboracum merely drained the power from his Sipstrassi. The two men had traveled to another circle to the west, outside Cambodunum. The same mysterious circumstances applied. Maedhlyn worked for days on his calculations, snatching only an hour's sleep in midafternoon. Finally he attempted to travel back to Eboracum, but even that could not be achieved.

The companions had returned on horseback to the capital, where Maedhlyn searched through his massive library, seeking inspiration and finding none.

"I am beaten," he whispered, pouring another goblet of spirit.

"How can it be that the Standing Stones no longer operate?" Culain asked.

"What do you think I have been working on this past fortnight? The rising price of apples?"

"Be calm, Enhancer. I am not seeking answers, I am searching for inspiration. There is no reason for the stones to fail. They are not machines; they merely resonate compatibly with Sipstrassi. Have you ever known a circle to fail?"

"No, not fail. And how can I be calm? The immutable laws of mystery have been overturned. Magic no longer works." Maedhlyn's eyes took on a fearful look. He sat bolt upright and fished in the pocket of his dark blue robe, producing a second Sipstrassi Stone. He held it over the table, and a fresh jug of spirit materialized; he relaxed. "I have used up the power of two stones that should have lasted decades, but at least I can still make wine."

"Have you ever been unable to travel?"

"Of course. No one can travel where they already are; you know that. Law number one. Each time scale sets up its own opposing forces. It pushes us on, makes us accept, in the main, linear time. At first I thought I could not follow Thuro because I was already there. No circle would accept my journey on that score. Wherever he is and in whatever time, then I am there also. But that is not the case. It would not affect a journey from Cambodunum to Eboracum in the same time scale. The circles have failed, and I do not understand why."

Culain stretched out his lean frame on the leather-covered divan. "I think it is time to contact Pendarric."

"I wish I could offer an argument," said Maedhlyn. "He is so dour."

"He is also considerably more wise than both of us, your arrogance notwithstanding."

"Can we not wait until tomorrow?"

"No, Thuro is in danger somewhere. Do it, Maedhlyn!"

"Dour is not the word for Pendarric," grumbled the Enchanter. Taking his stone, he held his fist over the table and whispered the words of family, the oath of Balacris. The air above the table crackled, and Maedhlyn hastily withdrew the two jugs of spirit. A fresh breeze filled the room with the scent of roses, and a window appeared onto a garden in which sat a powerful figure in a white toga. His beard was golden and freshly curled, his eyes a piercing blue. He turned, laying down a basket of perfect blooms.

"Well?" he said, and Maedhlyn swallowed his anger. There was a wealth of meaning in that single word, and the Enchanter remembered his father using the same tone when young Maedhlyn had been found with the maidservant in the hay wagon. He pushed the humiliating memory from his thoughts.

"We seek your advice, lord," muttered Maedhlyn, afraid that the words would choke him. Pendarric chuckled.

"How that must pain you, Taliesan. Or should I call you Zeus? Or Aristotle? Or Loki?"

"Maedhlyn, lord. The circles have failed." If Maedhlyn had expected Pendarric to be ruffled by the announcement, he was doomed to disappointment. The once king of Atlantis merely nodded.

"Not failed, Maedhlyn. They are closed. Should they remain closed, then yes, they will fail. The resonance will alter."

"How can this be? Who has closed them?"

"I have. Do you wish to dispute my right?"

"No, lord," said Maedhlyn hastily, "but might I ask the reason?"

"You may. I did not mind the more capricious of my people becoming gods to the savages—it amused them and did little real harm—but I will not tolerate the same lunacy we suffered before. And before you remind me, Maedhlyn, yes, it was my lunacy. But the world toppled. The tidal waves, the volcanoes, and the earthquakes almost ripped the world asunder."

"Why should it happen again?"

"One of our number has decided it is not enough to

play at being a goddess; she has decided to *become* one. She has built a castle spanning four gateways, and she is ready to unleash the Void upon all the worlds that are. So I have closed the pathways."

Maedhlyn spotted a hesitation in Pendarric's comment and leapt on it: "But not *all* of them?"

The king's face showed a momentary flash of annoyance. "No. You were always swift, Taliesan. I cannot close her world . . . not yet. But then, I did not believe any immortal would be foolish enough to repeat my error."

Culain leaned forward. "May I speak, lord?"

"Of course, Culain. Are you standing by your decision to become mortal?"

"I am. When you say your error, you do not mean the Bloodstone?"

"I do."

"And who is the traitor?" asked Culain, fearing the answer.

"Goroien."

"Why would she do it? It is inconceivable."

Pendarric smiled. "You remember Gilgamesh, the mortal who could not accept Sipstrassi immortality? It seems he had a disease of the blood, and he gave it to Goroien. She began to age, Culain. You, of all of us, know what that must have meant to her. She now drains the life force from pregnant women into her Bloodstone. It will not be enough; she will need more souls and more again. In the end a nation's blood will not satisfy her, or a world's. She is doomed and will doom us all."

"I cannot accept it," said Culain. "Yes, she is ruthless. Are we not all ruthless? But I have seen her nurse a sick faun, help in childbirth."

"But what you have not seen is the effect of the Bloodstones. They eat like cancers at the soul. I know, Culain. You were too young, but ask Maedhlyn what Pendarric was like when the Bloodstone ruled Atlantis. I ripped the hearts from my enemies. Once I had ten thousand rebels impaled. Only the end of the world saved me. Nothing will save Goroien."

"My grandson is lost in the Mist. I must find him."

"He is in Goroien's world, and she is seeking him."

"Then let me go there. Let me aid him. She will hate him, for he is Alaida's son, and you know Goroien's feelings for Alaida."

"Sadly, Culain, I know more than that. So does Maedhlyn. And, no, the gates stay closed—unless, of course, you promise to destroy her."

"I cannot!"

"She is not the woman you loved; there is nothing but evil left in her."

"I have said no. Do you know me not at all, Pendarric?"

The king sat silent for a moment. "Know you? Of course I know you. More, I like you, Culain. You have honor. If you should reconsider, journey to Skitis. One gateway remains. But you will have to slay her."

Storm clouds swirled in Culain's eyes, and his face was white. "You survived the Bloodstone, Pendarric, though many would have liked to slay you. Widows and orphans in their thousands would have sought your blood."

The king nodded in agreement. "Yet I was not diseased, Culain. Goroien must die. Not for punishment—though some would argue she deserves it—but because her disease is destroying her. At the moment she sacrifices two hundred and eighty women a year from ten nations under her control. Two years ago she needed only seven women. Next year, by my calculations, she will need a thousand. What does that tell you?"

Culain's fist rammed to the table. "Then why do you not hunt her? You were a warrior once. Or Brigamartis?"

"This would make you happy, Culain? Bring you contentment? No, Goroien is a part of you, and you alone can come close to her. Her power has grown. If it is left to me to destroy her, I will have to shatter the world in which she dwells. Then thousands will die with her, for I will raise the oceans. Your choice, Culain. And now I must go."

The window disappeared. Maedhlyn poured another goblet of spirit and passed it to Culain, but the Mist Warrior ignored it.

"How much of this did you know?" he asked Maedhlyn. The Enchanter sipped his drink, his green eyes hooded.

"Not as much as you think. And I would urge you to follow your own advice and be calm." Their eyes met, and Maedhlyn swallowed hard, aware that his life hung by a gossamer thread. "I did not know of Goroien's illness, only that she had taken to playing goddess once more. That I swear."

"But there is something else, Enhancer—something Pendarric is aware of. So out with it!"

"First you must promise not to kill me."

"I'll kill you if you do not!" stormed Culain, rising from his chair.

"Sit down!" snapped Maedhlyn, his fear giving way to anger. "What good does it do you to threaten me? Am I your enemy? Have I ever been your enemy? Think back, Culain. You and Goroien went your separate ways. You took Shaleat to wife, and she gave you Alaida. But Shaleat died, bitten by a venomous snake. You knew—and do not deny it—that Goroien killed her. Or if you did not know, you at least suspected. That is why you allowed Aurelius to take Alaida from the Feragh. You thought that Goroien's hatred would be nullified if Alaida chose mortality. You did not even allow her a stone."

"I do not want to hear this!" shouted Culain, fear shining in his eyes.

"Goroien killed Alaida. She came to her in Aurelius' castle and gave her poison. The babe took it in, and it changed Alaida's blood. When she gave birth, the bleeding would not stop."

"No!" whispered Culain, but Maedhlyn was in full flow now.

"As for Thuro, he had no will to live, and I used up a complete stone to save him. But Goroien was always close through those early years, and I could not allow Thuro to grow strong. I gave him the weakness in his chest. I robbed him of his strength. Goroien saw the king's suffering and let the boy live. She was always a vindictive witch, only you were too blind to see it. At last she decided the time had come to wreak her full vengeance. She it was who went to Eldared, lifting him with dreams of glory. Not to kill the king, but Alaida's child—your grandson.

"You blamed me for Alaida's death. I said nothing. But when I left her on that fateful morning, her pulse was strong, her body fit, her mind happy. She did not have the disease of kings at that time, Culain."

The Mist Warrior lifted his goblet and drained the spirit, feeling its warmth cut through him. "Have you ever loved anyone, Maedhlyn?"

"No," replied the Enchanter, realizing as he said it the regret he carried.

"You are right. I knew she killed Shaleat, yet I could not hate her for it. It was why I decided on mortality." Culain laughed without humor. "What a weak response for a warrior. I would die to punish Goroien."

"It is ironic, Culain. You are dying when you do not have to, and she is dying when she does not wish to. What will you do?"

"What choice do I have? My grandson is lost in her world, along with another I love dearly. To save them I must kill the woman I have loved for two thousand years."

"I will come with you to Skitis Island."

"No, Maedhlyn. Stay here and aid the Roman, Aquila. Hold the land for Thuro."

"We cannot hold. I was thinking of taking up my travels once more."

"What is left for you?" asked Culain. "You have enjoyed the glories of Assyria, Greece, and Rome. Where will you go?"

"There are other worlds, Culain."

"Give it a little time. We have both given a great deal to this insignificant island. I would rather Eldared did not inherit it—or the barbarian Hengist."

Maedhlyn smiled wistfully. "As you say, we have given a great deal. I will stay awhile. But I feel we are holding back the sea with a barrier of ice . . . and summer is coming."

◇ 12 ◇

Prasamaccus sat with Korrin Rogeur behind a screen of bushes on the eastern hills of Mareen-sa, watching a herd of flat-antlered deer grazing three hundred paces away.

"How do we approach them?" Korrin asked.

"We do not. We wait for them to approach us."

"And if they do not?"

"Then we go home hungry. Hunting is a question of patience. The tracks show that the deer follow this trail to drink. We sit here and let the hours flow over us. Your friend Hogun chose to sleep the time away, which is as good a way as any—so long as someone stays on watch."

"You are a calm man, Prasamaccus. I envy you."

"I am calm because I do not understand hate."

"Has no one ever wronged you?"

"Of course. When I was a babe, a drunken hunter rode his horse over me. All my life since I have known pain—the agony of a twisted limb, the hurt of being alone. Hatred would not have sustained me."

The dark huntsman smiled. "I cannot be like you, but being *with* you calms me. Why are you here in Pinrae?"

"I understand we are seeking a sword. Or rather that Thuro is seeking a sword. He is the son of a king—a

174

great king by all accounts—who was murdered a few months ago."

"From which land across the water do you come?"

Prasamaccus sat back and stretched his leg. "It is a land of magic and mist. It is called Britain by the Romans but in reality is many lands. My tribe is the Brigante, possibly the finest hunters of the world, certainly the most ferocious warriors."

Korrin grinned broadly. "Ferocious? They are not all like you, then?"

Before Prasamaccus could reply, the deer stampeded in a mad run toward the west. The Brigante pushed himself to his feet. "Quickly," he said. "Follow me!" He limped toward an ancient oak, and Korrin joined him.

"What are you doing?"

"Help me up." Korrin linked his hands and levered the Brigante high enough to grab an overhanging branch and haul his body across it.

"Swiftly now, climb!" urged Prasamaccus. The Brigante moved aside and strung Vamera, notching a long shaft to the string. A terrible roar reverberated through the forest, and Korrin leapt for the branch, pulling himself up just as the first Vore bounded into the clearing. Prasamaccus' arrow flashed into its throat, but its run continued unchecked.

A second shaft bounced from its skull as it sprang toward the hunters. Its claws scrabbled at the branch, but Korrin kicked out, his boot smashing into the gaping jaws. The beast fell back, and two others joined it, pacing around the tree. Prasamaccus sat very still, a third arrow ready, and stared at the great cats. They were each some eight feet long with huge flat faces, oval yellow eyes, and fangs as long as a man's fingers. The first beast sat down and worried at the arrow in its throat, snapping it with its paw. It then continued to prowl the tree. The beasts' backs were ridged with muscle, and the Brigante could see no easy way to kill them.

"Shoot at them!" Korrin urged. At the sound of his voice the beasts began to roar and leap for the branch, but none could get a hold. Prasamaccus lifted his finger to his lips and mouthed a single word.

"Patience!"

He swung his quiver to the front and began to examine his arrows. Some were single-barbed, others double. Some had smooth heads for easy withdrawal; some were light, others heavy. Finally he chose a double-barbed shaft with a strongly weighted head. He notched it. It seemed to the Brigante that the only weak spot the Vore had was behind the front leg at the back of the ribs. If he could angle a shot correctly ...

He waited for several minutes, occasionally drawing back the string but hesitating. The watching Korrin grew ever more tense, but he held his tongue. A Vore paced away from the tree, presenting his back, and Prasamaccus whistled softly. The beast stopped and turned. In that instant the arrow flashed through the air, slicing into the Vore's back and through to its heart. It slumped to the ground without a sound.

Selecting a fresh arrow, the Brigante waited. A second Vore approached the dead beast and began to push at the corpse with its snout, trying to raise it. Another arrow sang through the clearing, and the Vore reared and fell to its back, its hind legs kicking. Then it was still. The third beast was confused; it approached its comrades and then backed away, smelling blood. It roared its anger to the skies.

A single bugle call echoed through the forest, and the

Vore turned toward the sound, then padded away swiftly. For some minutes the two men remained where they were, and then Korrin made to climb down.

"Where are you going?"

"The beast is gone."

"There may be others farther west. Let us wait awhile."

"Good advice, my friend. How did you know the Vores were loose?"

"The deer did not just run, they fled in panic. A man's smell would not do that, nor would a wolf's. Since the wind was coming from behind and to the right of us, I reasoned the beasts must be close."

"You are a canny man to have around, Prasamaccus. Perhaps our luck has changed."

As if to evidence his words, a large Vore raced across the clearing before them, oblivious to their presence, and leapt over the corpses in a headlong rush toward the bugle call.

"You think it is safe now?" asked Korrin.

"A few more minutes." Prasamaccus could feel sadness riding him. Korrin had not yet stopped to consider the full meaning of the attack, and the Brigante hesitated to voice his fears. If four Vores had been loosed, why not all of them? And if that was the case, what had befallen the brotherhood at the caves? "I think it is safe now," he said at last.

Korrin sprang to the ground and waited to aid the slower Prasamaccus.

"I owe you my life. I shall not forget it."

He began to walk back toward the camp, but Prasamaccus' slender hand fell on his shoulder. "A moment, Korrin." The taller man swung toward him,

his face paling as he saw the look of concern in
Prasamaccus' eyes. Then realization struck.

"No!" he screamed, and tore himself from the Brigante's grip to race away through the trees. Prasamaccus
notched an arrow and followed at his own halting pace.
He did not hurry, having no wish to arrive too soon.
When at last he did come in sight of the caves, his
worst fears were realized. Bodies were scattered in the
clearing, and in his path was a leg dripping blood to the
grass. It was a scene of carnage. In the cave mouth
Korrin knelt alongside the giant body of his brother.
Prasamaccus approached. The man-beast lay beside the
bodies of three Vores, and his talons were red with their
blood. Beyond Korrin, cowering in the darkness, were
three children and Laitha. Part of his burden lifted as he
saw that she was safe. Korrin was weeping openly,
holding a bloodstained paw in his lap. The man-beast's
eyes opened.

Prasamaccus touched Korrin's shoulder. "He lives,"
he whispered.

"Korrin?"

"I am here."

"I stopped them, Korrin. The Witch Queen did me a
service, after all. She gave me the strength to stop her
own hunting cats." He took a deep shuddering breath,
and Prasamaccus watched as his lifeblood continued to
flow from the dreadful wounds.

"Four of the Seven are safe within the caves. Some
of the men ran into the forest; I do not know if they
survived. Get them away from here, Korrin."

"I will, brother. Rest. Be at peace." The body shimmered as if in a heat haze, then shrank to that of a normal man, slender and fine-boned, the face handsome
and gentle. "Oh, sweet gods," Korrin whispered.

"Very touching," came a woman's voice, and Prasamaccus and Korrin turned. Sitting on a nearby rock was a golden-haired woman in a dress of spun silver that looped over one ivory-skinned shoulder.

Korrin lunged to his feet, dragging his sword clear. He ran at the woman, who lifted a hand and waved her fingers as if casually swatting a fly. Korrin flew from his feet to land against the rocks ten feet away.

"I said I would watch him die . . . and I have. Bring my women to the camp in the north. Perhaps then I will allow the rest of you to live."

Prasamaccus laid down his bow, feeling her eyes on him.

"Why do you not attempt to kill me?" she asked.

"To what purpose, lady? You are not here."

"How perceptive of you."

"It takes no great perception to see that you cast no shadow."

"You are disrespectful," she chided. "Come to me." Her hand pointed, and Prasamaccus felt a pull at his chest hauling him to his feet. He stumbled on his bad leg and heard her soft lilting, mocking laughter. "A cripple? How delicious! I was going to play a game with you, little man, make you suffer as Pallin suffered. But I see there is no need. Fate has perhaps dealt with you more unkindly than I could. And yet you should suffer some pain for your insolent glances." Her eyes shone.

Prasamaccus was still holding the arrow he had notched earlier, and as her hand came up once more, he raised the arrowhead before him. A blaze of white light came from her fingers, touched the arrow, and returned to smite her in the chest. She screamed and stood . . . and in that moment Prasamaccus saw the golden hair show silver at the temples. Her hand shot to her aging face, and panic replaced the malevolent smile. She disappeared in an instant.

Korrin stumbled to the Brigante's side. "What did you do?"

Prasamaccus looked down at the arrow; the shaft was black and useless, the head a misshapen lump of metal. He hurled it aside. "We must get the women from here before the soldiers come, as surely they will. Is there another hiding place in the forest?"

"Where can we hide from her?"

"One step at a time, Korrin. Is there a place?"

"Perhaps."

"Then let us gather what is useful and go." As he spoke, five men emerged from the trees. Prasamaccus recognized the tall Hogun and the hulking Rhiall.

"So," said the Brigante, "the brotherhood still lives."

Laitha strode from the cave to the body of a dead warrior and unbuckled the man's sword belt. Swinging it around her lean hips, she drew the blade, hefting it for weight. The hilt was long and tightly covered with dark leather, and she could grip it double-handed for the cut or sweep. Yet the blade was not so long or heavy that she was unable to use it one-handed. She found a suitable whetstone and began to hone the edge. Prasamaccus joined her.

"I am sorry you had to suffer such an ordeal."

"I did not suffer; Pallin kept the Vores from me. But the screams of the dying . . ."

"I know."

"That woman radiated evil, and yet she was so lovely."

"There is no mystery in that, Laitha. Pallin was a

good man, yet sight of him would cause sleepless nights. All that is good is not always handsome."

"I do not like to admit this, but she frightened me. All the way down to my bones. Before we left Culain, I saw a Soul Stealer from the Void. Its face was the gray of death, yet it inspired less fear in me than the Witch Queen did. How was it that you were able to speak so to her?"

"I do not follow you."

"There was no fear in your voice."

"It was in my heart, but all I saw was an evil woman. All she could do was kill me. Is that so terrible? In fifty years no one will remember my name. I will be merely the dust of history. If I am lucky, I will grow old and rot. If not, I will die young. Whatever, I will still die."

"I never want to die—or grow old. I want to live forever," said Laitha. "Just as Culain had the chance to do. I want to see the world in a hundred years or a thousand. I never want the sun to shine without it shining on me."

"I can see how that would be . . . pleasant," said the Brigante, "but for myself I think I would rather not be immortal. If you are ready, we should be on our way."

Laitha looked deeply into his sad blue eyes, not understanding his melancholy mood. She smiled, rose smoothly, and pulled him to his feet. "Your wife is a lucky woman."

"In what way?"

"She has found a gentle man who is not weak. And yes, I am ready."

The small group, joined by four other survivors, numbered nineteen people as they headed high into the hills at the center of Mareen-sa. There were four pregnant women, three children, and, counting Laitha, twelve warriors.

Because of the advanced stage of one of the pregnancies, the pace was slow, and it was dusk when Korrin led them up a long hill to a circle of black stones each some thirty feet high. The circle was more than a hundred yards in diameter, and several deserted buildings had been constructed around the eight-foot altar. Korrin dragged open a rotted door and pushed his way into the largest building. Prasamaccus followed him. Inside was one vast room over eighty feet long. Ancient dust-covered tables were set at right angles to the walls, with bench seats alongside.

Korrin made his way to a large hearth, where a fire had been neatly laid. A huge cobweb stretched from the logs to the chimney breast. Korrin ignored it and sparked the tinder. Flames rose hungrily at the center of the dead wood, and a warm red light bathed the central hall.

"What is this place?" asked Prasamaccus.

"The Eagle sect once dwelled here—seventy men who sought to commune with the ghosts."

"What happened to them?"

"Astarte had them slain. Now no one comes here."

"I cannot bring myself to blame them," said the Brigante, listening to the wind howling across the hilltop. One of the women began to moan and sank to the floor. It was Erulda.

"The babe is due," said Hogun. "We'd best leave her to the women." Korrin led the men outside to a smaller building where a dozen rotted cot beds lined the walls. A rats' nest had been built against the far wall, and the room stank of vermin. Once more a fire had been laid, and Korrin ignited it.

Prasamaccus tested several beds, then gingerly laid himself down. There was no conversation, and the Brigante found himself thinking of Thuro and wondering if the Vores had killed him. He awoke an hour before dawn, half-convinced he had heard the sound of drums and marching feet. He stretched and sat up. Korrin and the other men were still sleeping around the dying fire. He swung his legs from the cot and stood, suppressing a groan as the weight came down on his twisted limb. Taking up his bow and quiver, he stepped out into the predawn light. The door of the main building opened, and Laitha moved into sight. She smiled a greeting, then ran across to him. "I have been waiting for you for a full hour."

"Did you hear the drums?"

"No. What drums?"

"I must have been dreaming. Come, we'll find some meat." The two of them, both armed with bows, set off down the hill.

On that day Prasamaccus could do no wrong. He killed two deer, and Laitha slew a bighorn sheep. Unable to carry the meat home, they quartered the beasts, hanging the carcasses from three high tree branches.

With Prasamaccus carrying the succulent loin section of the deer, Laitha stopped to gather several pounds of mushrooms, which she carried inside her tunic blouse; the two hunters were greeted with smiles on their return. After a fine breakfast Korrin sent Hogun, Rhiall, and a man called Logay to scout for the soldiers, while Prasamaccus told them where he had hidden the rest of the meat. Somehow the terrifying events of the previous day seemed less hideous in the wake of Erulda's delivering a fine baby son. His lusty cries were greeted with smiles among the women, and Prasamaccus marveled

anew at the ability of people to cope with terror. Even
Korrin seemed less tense.

There was a stream at the bottom of the hill, near a
basin of clay. The three remaining women spent the day
creating pitchers and firing them in a kiln built some
thirty feet from the stream. It made little smoke.
Prasamaccus watched them work and thought of Helga
back in Calcaria. Had the war reached her? How was
she faring? Did she miss his presence as much as he
missed hers, or had she even now found a fit husband
with two good legs? He would not blame her if she had.
She had given him a gift beyond price, and if he had
believed in benevolent gods, he would have prayed for
her happiness.

He glanced down at his leather leggings. They were
filthy and torn, and several of the silver disks had come
loose. His fine woolen tunic was grimy, and the gold
braid at the cuffs was frayed. He hobbled to the stream
and removed his tunic, dipping it in the cool water and
cleaning it against a rock. On impulse he stripped his
trews and sat in the water, splashing it to his pale chest.
The women nearby giggled and waved; he bowed
gravely and continued to wash. Laitha wandered down
the hill, and one of the women approached her, offering
her something Prasamaccus could not make out. The
forest girl smiled her thanks and removed her boots,
wading out to where Prasamaccus sat.

"What did she want?"

"She had a gift for the hunter," answered Laitha,
showing him a small vial stoppered with wax. "It is a
cleansing oil for the hair." So saying, she tugged him
backward, submerging him. He came up sputtering, and
she broke the wax seal, pouring half the contents over
his head. Tucking the vial into her belt, she began to

massage his hair, which was an experience to rival the ministrations of Victorinus' slaves. She spoiled it by ducking him again when she was done. He sat up to hear the chuckling of the working women and the rich, rolling laughter of the men who sat at the top of the hill.

The good humor lasted until Hogun and the others returned at dusk. Prasamaccus knew something was wrong, for they had not bothered to gather the meat. He limped across to Korrin, and the dark huntsman looked up from his seat.

"The soldiers are coming," he said simply.

The small amphitheater was bare of spectators except for the queen, who sat at the center on a fur-covered divan. Below her on the sand stood four warriors, their swords raised in salute. She leaned forward.

"You are each the finest gladiators of your lands. None of you has tasted defeat, and all have killed more than a score of opponents. Today you have the opportunity of carrying from Perdita your own weight in gems and gold. Does that excite you?" As she spoke, her right hand caressed the skin of her throat and neck, enjoying the smooth silky feel of young flesh. Her blue eyes raked the warriors: strong men, lean and wolflike, their eyes confident as they looked upon one another, each feeling he was destined to be the victor. Goroien smiled.

"Do not seek to gauge the men around you. Today you fight as a team, against the champion of my choosing. Kill him and all the rewards you have been promised will be yours."

"We are all to fight one man, lady?" asked a tall warrior with a jet-black beard.

"Just one," she whispered, her voice growing hoarse with excitement. "Behold!"

The men turned. At the far end of the arena stood a tall figure, a black helm covering his face. His shoulders were wide, his hips lean and supple. He wore a cutaway mail shirt and a loincloth and carried a short sword and a dagger.

"Behold," said the queen once more. "This is the queen's champion, the greatest warrior of this or any age. He, too, has never known defeat. Tackle him singly or all at once."

The four men looked at one another. The riches were there, so why take risks? They advanced on the tall helmed warrior, forming a half circle. As they approached, he moved with dazzling swiftness, seeming to dance through them. But in his wake two men fell, disemboweled. The others circled warily. He dived forward, rolling on his shoulder, the dagger slicing the air to plunge home in Blackbeard's throat. Continuing his roll, he came alongside the last man, blocked his lunge, and sent a dazzling riposte through his enemy's jugular. He walked forward and bowed to the queen.

"Always the best," she said, the color high on her cheeks. She held out her hand, and he rose through the air to stand before her. She stood and ran her hands over his shoulders and down his glistening flanks.

"Do you love me?" she whispered.

"I love you. I have always loved you." The voice was soft and distant.

"You do not hate me for bringing you back?"

"Not if you do as you promised, Goroien." His hand circled her back, pulling her to him. "Then I will love you until the stars die."

"Why must you think of him?"

"I must be the Lord of Battle. I have nothing else. I never had. I am faster now, more deadly. And still he haunts me. Until I kill him I will never be that which I desire."

"But he is no longer a match for you. He has chosen mortality and grows older. He is not what he was."

"He must die, Goroien. You promised him to me."

"What is the point? He could not have beaten you at his best. What will you prove by slaying a middle-aged man?"

"I will know that I am what I always was, that I am a warrior." His hands roved her body. "I will know that I am still a man."

"You are, my love. The greatest warrior who ever lived."

"You will bring him to me, then?"

"I will. Truly I will."

Slowly he removed the helm. She did not look at his eyes ... could not. Ever since the day she had brought him back from the grave, they had defeated her.

Glazed as they had been in death, the eyes of Gilgamesh remained to torment her.

Uther and Baldric entered the forest of Mareen-sa just after dawn, following a perilous journey from the Etrusces mountains. Three times they had hidden from soldiers, and once they had been pursued by four mounted warriors, escaping by wading through a narrow stream and climbing an almost sheer rock face. They were tired now, but Uther's spirits were high with the thought that they were almost home. He would lift the spell from the man-beast Pallin and then continue his search for his father's sword.

He was mildly ashamed of himself as he contemplated the jubilant scenes when Pallin was restored, the cheers and the congratulations and his modest reactions to their compliments on his heroism. He pictured Laitha, seeing the admiration in her eyes and her acceptance of his manhood. He grew almost dizzy with the fantasy and wrenched his thoughts back to the narrow trail they were following. As he did so, his eyes lit on a massive track beside the path. He stopped and stared; it was the pad of a giant cat.

Baldric, walking ahead, swung and saw the prince kneeling by the wayside. He strolled back, froze as he saw the print, and pulled an arrow from his quiver.

"The Vores are loose," he whispered, his eyes scanning the trail.

Uther stood, his gray eyes narrowed in concentration. There was a stream nearby, and the prince walked to it and began to dig a narrow channel in the bank.

"What are you doing?" asked Baldric, but Uther ignored him. He widened the channel into a circle and watched as the water slowly filled it. When it was still, he lay full-length and stared into it, raising the Sipstrassi Stone above the water, whispering the words of power Culain had used. The surface shimmered, and he saw the caves and the bodies. Two foxes were tugging at the flesh of a severed leg. He stood.

"They have attacked the camp. Many are dead, but there is no sign of Korrin, Prasamaccus, or Laitha."

"You think they have been taken?"

"I do not know, Baldric. Where else could they be?"

The man shrugged. "We are lost." He sat down and buried his face in his hands. Uther saw a shadow flash across the ground and glanced up to see a huge eagle circling high overhead. The prince gripped the stone and focused on the bird. His head swam, and his mind merged. The forest was far below him, and he could see as he never had before: a rabbit in the long grass, a fawn hidden in the undergrowth. And soldiers moving toward a high hill on which stood a circle of jutting black stones. There were some three hundred fighting men on foot, but walking ahead of them was a line of Vores held in check by forty dark-garbed woodsmen. Uther returned to his body, stumbled, and almost fell.

Taking a deep breath to steady himself, he began to run, ignoring the slumped Baldric. Up over the narrow trail and down into a muddy glen he slipped and slithered.

A huge stag bounded into his path. He lifted the stone, and the creature froze. Swiftly Uther clambered to its back; the deer turned and ran toward the hill. Several times Uther was almost dislodged, but his legs gripped firmly on the barrel of the creature's body. It leapt into the open and raced up the flanks of the hill, swerving to stand before the Vores. Behind him Uther had seen Prasamaccus, Laitha, and several others waiting with arrows ready. Ahead of him the soldiers came into view, dark-eyed men in helms of bronze, black cloaks billowing.

The stag stood statue-still.

"Withdraw or die!" called Uther. After the initial shock of seeing a blond youth riding a wild deer, there had been silence among the soldiers. Now laughter greeted his words. A command rang out, and the dark-garbed woodsmen released the chains on the forty Vores. They leapt forward, their roars washing over Uther like thunder. He lifted the stone, his gray eyes cold as Arctic ice.

The Vores stopped their charge and turned, raging down into the massed ranks of the soldiers. Claws raked flesh; fangs closed on skull and bone. Horses reared and whinnied in terror as the mighty beasts ripped into the startled fighting men. Within seconds the savage carnage gave way to a mass panic, and the soldiers fled in all directions as the Vores continued their destruction. Uther turned the stag and slowly rode up the hill. At the top he slid from the creature's back, patting its neck. The deer bounded away.

From the forest the awful screams of the dying filled the air. Korrin approached Uther.

"Are you a god?"

Uther glanced down at the stone. It was no longer gold with black threads but black with golden threads. There was little magic left.

"No, Korrin, I am not a god. I am just a man who arrived too late. Yesterday I could have saved Pallin and the others."

"It is good to see you, Thuro," said Prasamaccus.

"Not Thuro, my friend. The child is dead. The man walks. I am Uther Pendragon, son of Aurelius. And I am the king, by right and by destiny."

Prasamaccus said nothing, but he bowed low. The other men, still shocked after their escape, followed suit. Uther accepted the honor without comment and walked away to sit alone on a broken rock overlooking the stream, where Prasamaccus joined him.

"May I sit with you, lord?" he asked with no hint of sarcasm.

"Do not think me arrogant, Prasamaccus. I am not. But I have killed the undead and flown on the wings of an eagle. I have ridden the forest prince and destroyed an army. I know who I am. More, I know *what* I am."

"And what are you, Prince Uther?"

Uther turned and smiled softly. "I am a young man,

barely of age, who needs wise counsel from trusted friends. But I am also the king of all Britain, and I will reclaim my father's throne. No force of this world or any other will deter me."

"It is said," offered Prasamaccus, "that blood runs true. I have seen the reverse at times—the sons of brave fathers becoming cowards. But in your case, Prince Uther, I think it is true. You have the blood of a great king in your veins and also the spirit of the warrior Culain. I think I will follow you, though never blindly. And I will offer you counsel whenever you ask for it. Do I need to kneel?"

Uther chuckled. "My first command to you is that you never kneel in my presence. My second is that you must always tell me when you feel that arrogance is surfacing in my nature. I have studied well, Prasamaccus, and I know that power has many counterpoints. My father had a tendency to believe himself right at all times merely because he was the king. He dismissed from his service a warrior-friend who had grown up alongside him. The man disagreed with him on a matter of strategy, and my father had him branded disloyal. Yet Aurelius was not a bad man. I have studied the lives of the great, and all become afflicted with pride. You are my champion against such excesses."

"A heavy burden," said Prasamaccus, "but a burden for another day. Today you are not a king; you are a hunted man in the forest of another world. I take it from the manner of your arrival that you found the Dream Shaper."

"I did. He was dead, but I have the source of his magic."

"Is it strong enough to get us back home?"

"I do not think so. It is almost gone."

"Then what do you plan?"

"The spirit of the Dream Shaper came to me and told me to bring the ghosts home. Baldric says the ghosts are an army of the dead. I will try to raise them against the queen."

The Brigante shivered. "You will raise the dead?"

"I will if I can find Erin Plateau."

Prasamaccus sighed. "Well, that should not prove too arduous. You are sitting on Erin Plateau, and that is the sort of luck I have come to expect."

"I have little choice, Prasamaccus. I have no intention of dying here—not with my father's murderers tearing at the heart of my kingdom. If I could, I would summon the Demon King himself."

The Brigante nodded and rose. "I will leave you to your plans," he said sadly.

Two hours later Laitha sat shrouded in misery at the edge of the hill beneath the light of the two moons. Since Thuro's return he had not spoken to her or acknowledged her existence. At first she had been angry enough to ignore this, but as the day passed, her fury had melted, leaving her feeling lonely and rejected. He was the one link she had to the wonderful world of her childhood. He had known Culain and knew of her love for him. With him she should have been able to share her grief and perhaps exorcise it. Now he was lost to her, as much as she was lost to Culain and the Caledones mountains.

And he had struck her! Before all those men. In retrospect she had been shrewish, but it had been only to bolster her confidence. Her life with Culain had taught her self-sufficiency, but she had always had the Mist Warrior close when real fear pervaded their world. She had felt Thuro was a true friend and had grown to love him in those early weeks, when his gentle nature had shown itself. His lack of skill with weapons had made her feel protective. As he had grown in stature under Culain's tutelage, she had grown jealous of the time he had spent with her man. All nonsense now.

A chilly wind blew, and she hugged her shoulders, wishing she had brought out a blanket but not desiring to return inside to fetch one. She wondered if the pain of Culain's passing would ever leave her. Something warm draped her shoulders, and she looked up to see Prasamaccus standing by her. He had brought a blanket warmed by the fire. She gathered it around herself, then burst into tears. He sat beside her, pulling her to him, saying nothing.

"I feel so alone," she said at last.

"You are not alone," he whispered. "I am here. Uther is here.

"He despises me."

"I think that he does not."

"Uther!" she hissed. "Who does he think he is? A new name every day, perhaps?"

"Oh, Laitha! You cannot see, can you? The boy has flown. You have told me of the weakly child he was when you found him, but that is not him anymore. Look at his strength when he stood alone against the Vores. He could not be sure he had the strength or the power to turn those cats, yet he did it. That was the work of a man. He says the power is almost gone, and many men would flee. But not Uther. Other men would use the remaining magic to find the sword. Not Uther. He seeks to aid the people he has befriended. Do not judge him by yesterday's memories."

"He does not speak to me."

"All paths run in two directions."

"He once said he loved me."

"Then he loves you still, for he is not a fickle man."

"I cannot go to him. Why should I? Why should a man alone be allowed the virtue of pride?"

"I am not sure it is a virtue. However, I am here to be a friend. And friends are sometimes helpless between lovers."

"We are not lovers. I loved Culain . . ."

"Who is dead. But no matter—lovers or friends, there is really very little difference that I can see. You do not need me to tell you how perilous is our situation. None of us can expect to survive long against the Witch Queen. Tomorrow she may return with a thousand men—ten thousand. Then we will be dead, and your misery will seem even less important. Go to Uther and apologize."

"I will not. I have nothing to apologize for."

"Listen to me. Go to him and apologize. He will then tell you what you want to hear. Trust me . . . even if it means lying."

"And if he laughs in my face?"

"You have lived too long in the forest, Laitha; you do not understand the world. Men like to think they control it, but that is nonsense. Women rule, as they always have. They tell a man he is godlike. The man believes them and is in their thrall. For without them to tell him, he becomes merely a man. Go to him."

She shook her head but stood. "I will take your advice, friend. But in future call me Gian. It is special to me; it is the language of the Feragh: Gian Avur, fawn of the forest." Then she smiled and wandered to the main building. She opened the door and stepped inside. Uther was sitting with the other men, and they were listening intently to his words. He looked up and saw her. Conversation ceased as he rose smoothly and came to her, stepping out into the night. Prasamaccus was nowhere to be seen.

"You wanted me?" he asked, his chin held high, his tone haughty.

"I wanted to congratulate you, and . . .and to apologize."

He relaxed, and his face softened, breaking into the self-conscious grin she remembered from their first day.

"You have nothing to apologize for. It has been hard for me to become a man. Culain taught me to fight, and Maedhlyn to think. Bringing the two together was left to me. But you have suffered greatly, and I have been of little help. Forgive me?" He opened his arms, and she stepped into his embrace.

In the background, crouched behind the rocks, Prasamaccus sighed and hoped they would not stand too long in the cold. His leg was aching, and he yearned for sleep.

Uther returned to the building, gathered his blankets, and took Laitha to the west of the hilltop, where a great stone had fallen, making a windbreak. He gathered wood for a small fire and spread the blankets on the ground. All this was done in silence, amid a growing tension of their bodies that did not affect the communion of their eyes. With the fire glowing, they sat together and did not notice the limping Prasamaccus returning to his bed.

Uther dipped his head and kissed Laitha's hair, pulling her more closely to him. She lifted her face. He smelt the musky perfume of her skin and brushed his lips against her cheek. His head swam, and a dreamlike sensation swept over him. He, the night, and Laitha were one. He could almost hear the whispering memories of the giant stones, feel the pulsing distance of the stars. She lay back, her arms curling around his shoulders, drawing him to her. His hand moved slowly down the curve of her back, feeling the flesh beneath her tunic. He was torn between the urge to tear her clothes from her and the need to savor this moment of moments. He kissed her and groaned. She tugged gently away from him and removed her tunic and leggings. He watched as her skin emerged from the clothing; it gleamed and glistened in the firelight. Stripping himself naked, he hesitated to pull her to him, his eyes drinking in her beauty. His hands were trembling as he reached for her. Laitha's body melted against him, and everywhere she touched him seemed to burn. She pushed herself under him, but he resisted. Her eyes opened wide in surprise, but he smiled softly.

"Not swiftly," he whispered. "Never swiftly!"

She understood. His head lowered to kiss her once more, his hand moving over her skin as gentle and warm as morning sunlight, touching, stroking, exploring. Finally, his head pounding, he rose above her. Her legs snaked over his hips, and he entered her. Thoughts and emotions raged and swirled inside his mind, and he was surprised to find regret swimming amid the joy. This was a moment he had dreamed of, yet it could never come again. He opened his eyes, looking down on her face, desperate to remember every precious second.

Her eyes opened, and she smiled. Reaching up, she cupped his face, pulling him closer, kissing him with surprising tenderness. Passion swallowed his regret, and he passed into ecstasy.

For Laitha the sensation was different. She, too, had

dreamed of the day she would surrender her virginity to the man she loved. And in a way she had. For Uther was all that was left of Culain, and she could see the Mist Warrior in Uther's storm-cloud eyes. And Prasamaccus had been right. The weakly youth in the forest had gone forever, replaced by this powerful, confident young man. She knew she could grow to love him, but never with the wild, wonderful passion she had felt for Culain. As she thought of him, her mind blended her memories with the slow, rhythmic contact at the center of her being, and she felt it was the Lance Lord moving so powerfully above her. Her body convulsed in a searing sea of pleasure that bordered on pain. And in her ecstasy she whispered his name.

Uther heard it and knew he had lost her in the moment of gaining her . . .

◇ **13** ◇

BALDRIC RETURNED TO Erin Plateau early the following morning. When the Vores had turned on the soldiers, the lean huntsman had swiftly scaled a tree and watched as the carnage continued. The beasts had killed scores of men and horses, driving the army from the forest. Baldric had followed them for some distance and now reported that Mareen-sa was free of threat. Korrin sent out scouts to watch for the enemy's return, glancing at Uther for approval. Uther nodded.

"The enemy will return," said the prince, "but we must make the delay work for us." Uther summoned Prasamaccus, sending him and Hogun to hunt for fresh meat. Laitha went with them to gather mushrooms, herbs, and other edible roots. Rhiall and Ceorl were sent to the city of Callia to see what effect the news of the soldiers' defeat would have.

Finally Uther called Korrin to him, and the two men walked to the edge of the stone circle, looking out over the vast forest and the sweeping hills of Mareen-sa.

"Tell me about the ghosts," said Uther. The woodsman shrugged.

"I have seen them only once—and that from a distance."

"Then tell me the legend."

"Is it wise to raise an army of the dead?"

"Is it wise for nineteen people to rebel against a Witch Queen?" Uther responded.

"I take your point. Well, the legend says that the ghosts were soldiers of an ancient king, and when he died, they marched into the underworld to fetch him back. But they became lost and now march forever through the wilderness of the Void."

"How many are there?"

"I have no idea. When I saw them, I took only one swift glance, and that was over my shoulder while I was running."

"Where did you see them?"

"Here," said Korrin, "on Erin."

"Then why have we not seen them?"

"It is the moons—but then, you would not know that. On certain nights of the year the light of Apricus, the large moon, cannot be seen. Only Sennicus shines. On those nights the ghosts walk, and the circle is shrouded in mist."

"How soon before Sennicus shines alone?"

Korrin shrugged. "I am sorry, Uther, but I do not know. It happens about four times a year, sometimes six. Rhiall would know. His father studied the stars, and he must have learned something. When he gets back, I will ask him."

Uther spent the day exploring the woodland around the hill, seeking out hiding places and trails the rebels might be forced to take when the soldiers returned. His frustration was great as he walked, for all the warriors whose lives had been researched by Plutarch had had one thing in common. They each, at some time in their lives, had ruled armies. There was little Uther could achieve with ten woodsmen, a crippled hunter, and a forest girl skilled with the bow. And even if he could raise a force from among the population, how long would it take to train them? How much time would Astarte allow?

He shared the concern of both Prasamaccus and Korrin about using an army of corpses. Yet an army was an army. Without it they were lost.

Hungry and tired, he sat down by a shallow stream and allowed his thoughts to return to the subject he had forced from his mind. At the height of his passion Laitha had whispered the name of Culain, and this had caused a terrible split in his emotions. He had worshiped Culain and was now jealous of him, even as he loved Laitha and was now angry with her. His mind told him it was not her fault that she still loved Culain, but his heart and his pride could not accept second place.

"Greetings," said a voice, and Uther leapt to his feet, sword in hand. A young woman sat close by, dressed in a simple tunic of shining white cloth. Her hair was gold, her eyes blue.

"I am sorry," he said. "You startled me."

"Then it is I who am sorry. You seem lost in thought."

She was quite the most beautiful woman Uther had ever seen. She rose and walked to stand beside him, reaching out to touch his arm. As she looked into his eyes, he saw a strange look come into hers.

"Is something wrong, lady?"

"Not at all," she said swiftly. "Sit with me for a while." The songs of the forest birds faded into what was almost a melody of soft-stringed lyres. The sun bathed them both, and all the colors of the forest shone with ethereal beauty. He sat.

"You remind me of someone I once knew," she said, her face close to his, the perfume of her breath sweet and arousing.

"I hope it was someone you liked."

"Indeed I did. Your eyes, like his, are the colors of the Mist."

"Who are you?" he whispered, his voice husky.

"I am a dream, perhaps. Or a wood nymph. Or a lover?" Her lips brushed his face, and she lifted his hand, pressing it to her breast.

"Who are you?" he repeated. "Tell me."

"I am Athena."

"The Greek goddess?" She drew back from him then, surprised.

"How is it that you know of me? This world is far from Greece."

"I am far from home, lady."

"Are you of the Mist?"

"No. What other names have you?"

"You know of the Feragh, I see. I am also called Goroien."

Now it was Uther's turn to show surprise. "You are Culain's lady; he spoke of you often."

She moved subtly away from him. "And what did he say?"

"He said that he had loved you since the dawn of history. I hope you will forgive me for saying that I can see why."

She acknowledged his compliment with a slight smile. "His love was not so great as you think. He left me and chose to become mortal. How would you explain that?"

"I cannot, lady. But I knew Culain, and he thought of you always."

"You say 'knew' and 'thought.' Have you lost touch with him?"

Uther licked his lips, suddenly nervous. "He is dead, lady. I am sorry."

"Dead? How?"

"My enemies destroyed him: Soul Stealers from the Void."

"You saw him die?"

"No, but I saw him fall just before the circle brought us to Pinrae."

"And who are you?" she asked, smiling sweetly, her left hand on his back. As she spoke, the nails of the hidden hand grew long and silver and hovered over his heart.

"I am Uther." The talons vanished.

"I do not know the name," she said, rising and moving to the center of the clearing.

"Will you help us?" he asked.

"With what?"

"This world is ruled by a Witch Queen, and I seek to overthrow her."

Goroien laughed and shook her head. "Foolish boy! Sweet, foolish boy! I *am* the Witch Queen. This is my world."

Uther rose. "I cannot believe that!"

"Believe it, Prince Uther," said Prasamaccus, stepping from the shadow of the trees.

"Ah, the cripple," said Goroien, "with the magic arrows."

"Shall I kill her?" asked the Brigante, a shaft aimed at her heart. Goroien turned to Uther, her eyebrows raised.

"No!"

"A wise choice, sweet boy, for now I will let you

both live ... for a little while. Tell me, how long has your name been Uther?"

"Not long, lady."

"I thought not. You are the boy Thuro, the son of Alaida. Know this, Uther. I slew your mother, I planned your father's death, and I sent the Soul Stealers into the Caledones mountains."

"Why?"

"Because it pleased me." She turned on Prasamaccus. "Loose your arrow, fool!"

"No!" shouted Uther, but the Brigante had already released the string. The shaft flashed in the sunlight, only to be caught in a slender hand and snapped in two.

"You said sweet words to me, Uther. I will not kill you today. Leave this place; hide in the world of Pinrae. I shall not seek you. But in four days I will send an army into this forest with orders to kill all they find. Do not be here." She raised her hand in a cutting motion, and the air beside her parted like a curtain. Beyond her, in a room adorned with shields, swords, and weapons of war, Uther saw a tall man wearing a dark helm. And then they were both gone.

"She came to kill you," said Prasamaccus.

"But she did not."

"She is capricious. Let us fetch Laitha and leave this place."

"I must wait for the one moon."

"You asked me to be a wise counselor ..."

"This is not a time for wisdom," snapped Uther. "This is a time for courage."

Under a bright moon a lone figure scaled the outer wall of Deicester Castle, strong fingers finding the tiniest cracks and crevices. Culain moved slowly and with great care. His horse and lance had been hidden in the woods two miles away, and his only weapon was a long hunting knife in a scabbard at the back of his belt.

The climb would not have been difficult in daylight, for the castle was over two hundred years old and the outer walls were pitted and scarred. But at night he was forced to test every hand- and toehold. He reached the battlements just after midnight and was not surprised to find no sentries. For who did Eldared fear in the Caledones? What army could penetrate this far into his territory? He swung his body over the wall and crouched in the moon shadows below the parapet. He wore dark leggings of dyed wool and a close-fitting leather shirt as soft as cloth. He stayed motionless, listening to the sounds of the night. In the barracks below and to the right were only a dozen soldiers. He had counted them from his hiding place during the day; now he could hear some of them playing dice. To his left the gate sentry was asleep, his feet planted on a chair, a blanket around his shoulders. Culain moved silently to the stairwell. The steps were wooden, and he moved down them, keeping close to the wall, away from the center of the slats, where the movement and therefore the noise would be greatest. Earlier he had noted the flickering lights at the highest western window of the keep, the rest of the upper living quarters dark and silent.

He crossed the courtyard at a run, halting before the door beside the locked gates of the keep. It was open. Once inside, he waited until his eyes grew accustomed to the darkness within, then found the stairs and climbed to the upper levels. A dog growled close by, and Culain opened the pouch at his side and pulled clear a freshly cut slice of rabbit meat. He walked boldly into the corridor. The dog, a gray war hound, rose threateningly, its lips drawn back to reveal long fangs. Culain crouched down and offered his hand. The dog, smelling the meat, padded forward to snatch it from Culain's fingers. He patted the hound's wide head and moved on.

At the farthest door he stopped. A light still showed faintly in the cracks around the frame. He drew his hunting knife and stepped inside. A candle was guttering by the bedside, and in the broad bed lay a man and a woman. Both were young: the woman no more than sixteen, the man a few years older. They were asleep in each other's arms like children, and Culain felt a pang of regret. The woman's face was oval and yet strong even in sleep. The man was fair-haired and fine-boned. Culain touched the cold knife blade to the man's throat. His eyes flared open, and he jerked, cutting the skin alongside his jugular.

"Do not hurt her!" he pleaded. Culain was touched despite himself, for the man's first thought had been for the woman beside him. He gestured for Moret to rise and, gathering the candle, led him through the bedroom into a side chamber, pushing shut the door behind him.

"What do you want?"

"I want to know how you contacted the Witch Queen."

Moret moved to stand beside a high window overlooking the Caledones mountains. "Why do you wish to see her?"

"That is my concern, boy. Answer me and you may live."

"No," Moret said softly. "I need to know."

Culain hesitated, considering killing the man and questioning the woman. But then, if she knew nothing, his mission would be ruined, for Cael and Eldared were away at war.

"I plan to destroy her," he said at last.

Moret smiled. "Go from here to the Lake of Earn. You know it?" Culain nodded. "There is a circle of stones and a small hut. Before the hut is a tiny cairn of rounded rocks. Build a fire there when the wind is to the north. The smoke enters the hut, and Goroien comes forth."

"Have you seen her?"

"No; my brother travels there."

Culain returned his knife to his scabbard. "It is against my better judgment to allow you to live, but I shall. Do not make me regret the decision, for I am not an enemy you would desire."

"No man who seeks to destroy Goroien could be an enemy of mine," Moret answered. Culain backed to the door and was gone within seconds. Moret stood for a while by the window, then returned to his bed. Outside the door Culain heard the bed creak and returned his knife once more to its scabbard.

Rhiall and Ceorl returned from Callia in high spirits. Behind them was a convoy of three wagons, sixty-eight men, and twelve women, two of them pregnant. The huge youth bounded up the hill, grabbing Korrin's arm.

"The soldiers ransacked the town. They took twenty pregnant women and burned the shrine to Berec. Two council leaders were hanged. The place is in an uproar."

"What are they all doing here?" asked Korrin, staring down at the crowd forming a half circle below the hill.

"They've come to see Berec reborn. The story is spreading like a grass fire that Berec has returned to earth, riding a forest stag and ready to overthrow the Witch Queen."

"And you let them believe it?"

Rhiall's face took on a sullen look. "Who is to say it is not true? He did ride a stag, just like Berec, and his magic vanquished the soldiers."

"What is in the wagons?"

Rhiall's good humor returned. "Food, Korrin. Flour, salt, dried fruit, oats, wine, honey. And there are blankets, clothes, weapons."

Uther approached and stared down at the gathering, which grew hushed and silent. The sun was behind him, and he appeared to the crowd to be bathed in golden light. Many in the group fell to their knees.

Rhiall and Korrin joined him. "How many fighting men?" Uther asked.

"Sixty-eight."

Uther grinned and laid his hand on Rhiall's shoulder. "That is a good omen. In my land the men fight in centuries of eighty warriors each. With our own people and these we now have a century."

Korrin grinned. "Your arithmetic is not as strong as your magic. Surely a century is one hundred?"

"True, but with cooks, quartermasters, and camp followers the fighting strength is eighty. Our army is formed by such units. Six centuries equal 480 men, or one cohort, and ten cohorts make a legion. It is a small beginning but a promising one. Korrin, go down among them and find out who the leaders are. Get the men in groups of ten. Add one of your own men to each group, two to the last. Find the groups work to make them feel part of the brotherhood and weed out the weak in heart, for they will need to fight within four days."

"One small problem, Uther," said Korrin. "They think you are a god. When they find out you are a man, we could lose them all."

"Tell me about the god—everything you can remember."

"You will play the part, then?" Rhiall asked.

"I will not risk losing sixty-eight fighting men. And it is not necessary for me to lie or to use any deceit. If they believe it, let them continue. In four days we will either have an army or be dead on this forest floor."

"Does that not depend," put in Korrin, "on when Sennicus shines alone?"

"Yes." Both men turned to Rhiall. "When will such an event happen again?" Uther asked.

"In about a month," said the youngster. Uther said nothing, his face without expression. Korrin cursed softly.

"Get the men in groups," said the prince, walking away to the edge of the stone circle, holding the bitter edge of his anger in check. In four days a terrible enemy would descend on the forest. His one hope was the army of the dead, and they could not be seen for a month. He needed to think, to plan, yet how could he devise a strategy with such limited forces at his disposal? All his life he had studied war and the making of war, seen the plans of generals from Xerxes to Alexander, Ptolemy to Caesar, Paullinus to Aurelius. But never had they been in a position like his. The unfairness of his situation struck him like a coward's blow. But then, why should life be fair? he reasoned. A man could do only his best with the favors the gods bestowed.

Prasamaccus joined him, sensing his unease.

"Are the gods being kind?" asked the Brigante.

"Perhaps," Uther replied, remembering that he had not yet learned of the life of Berec.

"The burden of responsibility is not light."

Uther smiled. "It would be lighter if I had Victorinus and several legions behind me. Where is Laitha?"

"She is helping unload the wagons. Is all well between you?"

Uther closed his mouth, cutting off an angry retort, then looked into the Brigante's cool, understanding eyes.

"I love her, and she is now mine."

"But?"

"How do you know there is a but?"

Prasamaccus shrugged. "Is there not?"

"Where did you learn so much of life?"

"On a hillside between the walls. What is wrong?"

"She loved Culain, and it chains her still. I could not compete with him in life—nor in death, it seems."

Prasamaccus sat silently for a moment, marshaling his thoughts. "It must be exceptionally hard for her. All her life she has lived with this hero, worshiping him as a father, loving him as a brother, needing him as a friend. It is not difficult to see how she came to believe she wanted him as a lover. And you are right, Prince Uther; you cannot compete. But in time Culain will fade."

"I know it is arrogance," said Uther, "but I do not want a woman who sees me as the shadow of someone else. I made love to her, and it was beautiful ... and then she whispered Culain's name. She lay beneath me, and in her mind I was not there."

There was nothing for the Brigante to say, and he had the wisdom to know it. Laitha was a foolish, undisciplined child. It would not have mattered if she had screamed his name inside her mind, but to speak it at such a time showed a stupidity beyond comparison. It was with some surprise that Prasamaccus realized he was angry with her; it was not an emotion he usually carried. He sat in silence with the prince for some time, and then, when Uther was lost in thought, he rose and limped back to where Korrin waited with a group of strangers.

"These are the leaders of the Callia men," said the woodsman. "Is ... the god ready to receive them?"

"No, he is communing with the spirits," answered Prasamaccus. Some of the men backed away. The Brigante ignored them and wandered away to the long hall.

Uther the man stared out over the forest, while Thuro the boy sat inside his skull. Only a few short months earlier the boy had been weeping in his room, frightened of the dark and the noises of the night. Now he was acting the man, but the torments of adolescence were still with him. As summer was beginning outside Eboracum, the boy Thuro had wandered into the woods and played a game where he was a hero, slaying demons and dragons. Now, with the summer there once more, he sat on a lonely hill and all the demons were real. Only there was no Maedhlyn. No Aurelius with his invincible legions. No Culain lach Feragh. Only the pretend man, Uther. "I am the king, by right and by destiny." Oh how the words haunted him now in his despair!

A frightened child sat among the stones of another world, playing a game of death. His melancholy deepened, and he realized he would give his left arm if Maedhlyn or Culain could appear at this moment. More, he would offer ten years of his life. But the wind blew over the hilltop, and he was alone. He turned and gazed at the group waiting silently some thirty paces away. Young men, old men, standing patiently waiting for the "god" to acknowledge them and their fealty. Turning his face from them, he thought of Culain and smiled. Culain really had been a god: Ares, the god of war to the Greeks, who became Mars for the Romans. Immortal Culain!

Well, thought Uther, if my grandfather was a god, then why not me? If the fates have decided I shall die in this deadly game, then let me play it to the full.

Without looking back, he raised his hand, beckoning the group forward. There were twelve of them, and they shuffled hesitantly to stand before him. He spread his arms, gesturing at the ground, and they sat obediently.

"Speak!" he said, and Korrin introduced each of the men, though Uther made no effort to remember their names. At the end he leaned forward and looked deeply into each man's eyes. All looked away the moment his gaze locked on theirs. "You!" said Uther, gazing directly at the oldest man, gray-bearded and lean as a hunting wolf. "Who am I?"

"It is said you are the god Berec."

"And what do you say?"

The man reddened. "Lord, what I said last night was said in ignorance." He swallowed hard. "I merely voiced the doubts we all carried."

Uther smiled. "And rightly so," he said. "I have not come to guarantee victory, only to teach you how to fight. The gods give, the gods take away. All that is of worth is what a man earns with his sweat, with his courage, and with his life. Know this: you may not win. I shall not rise to the sky and destroy the witch with spears of fire. I am here because Korrin called me. I shall leave when I please. Do you have the heart to fight alone?"

The bearded man's head rose, his eyes proud. "I do. It has taken me time to know it, but I know it now."

"Then you have learned something greater than a god gift. Leave me—all but Korrin."

The men almost scrambled from his presence, some backing away, others bowing low. Uther ignored them all, and when they were out of earshot, Korrin moved forward.

"How did you know what that man said?" he asked.

"What do you think of them?"

The woodsman shrugged. "You picked the right man to speak to. He is Maggrig, the armorer. Once he was the most feared swordsman in Pinrae. If he stands, they all will. Do you wish me to tell you of Berec?"

"No."

"Are you well, Uther? Your eyes are distant."

"I am well, Korrin," answered the prince, forcing a smile, "but I need to think." The green-eyed huntsman nodded his understanding.

"I shall have food brought to you."

After he had gone, Uther ran his mind back over the meeting. It was no mystery how he had focused on Maggrig; the man's stance showed him to be a warrior, and he had been the first to come forward, the others crowding around him. It had been a pleasant surprise when Maggrig had misinterpreted Uther's question. But then, as Maedhlyn had always said, the prince had a swift mind.

Somehow the meeting left Uther feeling less melancholy. Was it so easy to be a god?

The answer would come within four days.

And it would be written in blood.

◇ **14** ◇

CULAIN LACH FERAGH sat before the cairn of stones, watching the smoke from his small fire wafting in through the shattered windows of the derelict house. The Mist Warrior laid his silver lance by his side and pulled on two leather gauntlets edged with silver. His long hair was bound at the nape of the neck, and over his shoulders he wore a silver-ringed protector expertly sewn to a short cape of soft leather. A thick silver-inlaid belt was buckled to his waist, and his legs were protected by thigh-length boots reinforced by silver strips on the front and sides. A flickering blue light began inside the dwelling, and Culain rose smoothly, placing a silver-winged helm on his head and tying the scimitar-shaped ear guards under his chin.

A slender figure came forward through the smoke, which billowed and died, the fire quenched in an instant. As he saw her, his mouth went dry and he longed to step forward and pull her into his arms. She in turn stopped in her tracks as she recognized him, her hand flying to her mouth.

"You are alive!" she whispered.

"Thus far, lady." She was wearing a simple dress of silver thread, her golden hair held in place by a black band at the brow.

"Tell me that you have come back to be with me."

"I cannot."

"Then why do you summon me?" she snapped, her blue eyes bright with anger.

"Pendarric says there is naught but evil in you, and he asked me to destroy you. But I cannot until I am convinced he is right."

"He was always an old woman. He had the world and lost it. Now it is the turn of others. He is finished, Culain. Come with me; I have a world to myself. Soon it will be four worlds. I have power undreamed of since the fall of Atlantis."

"And yet you are dying," he said, the words cutting him like knife wounds.

"Who says that I am?" she hissed. "Look at me! Am I any different? Is there a single sign of age or decay?"

"Not on the surface, Goroien. But how many have died . . . how many will die to keep you so?"

She moved toward him, and the music began in his mind. The air was still, and all the world was silent. Her arms came up around his neck, and he smelled the perfume of her skin, felt the warmth of her touch. Reaching up, he pulled her arms clear of him, pushing her away.

"What will you prove?" he asked. "That I love you still? I do. That I want you? That, too. But I will never have you. You killed Shaleat, you killed Alaida—and now you will destroy a world."

"What are these savages to you, with their ten-second lives? There will always be more to replace those who die. They are unimportant, Culain. They always were, only you were too obsessed to see it. What does it matter now that Troy fell or that your friend Hector was slain by Achilles? What does it matter that the Romans conquered Britain? Life moves on. These people are as shadows to you and me. They exist to serve their betters."

"I am one of them now, Goroien," he said. "My ten-second life is a joy. I never understood winter before or truly felt the joy of spring. Come with me. Live out a life unto death and we will see together what comes after."

"Never!" she screamed. "I will never die. You speak of pleasure. I see your decaying face, and it makes me want to vomit: lines by your eyes, and I don't doubt that under that helm the silver is spreading like a cancer through your hair. In human terms what are you now, thirty? Forty? Soon you will begin to wither. Your teeth will rot. Young men will push you aside and mock you. And then you will fall, and the worms will eat your eyes. How could you do this?"

"All things die, my love. Even worlds."

"Do not speak to me of love; you never loved me. Only one man ever loved me, and I have brought him back from the grave. That is what power is, Culain. Gilgamesh is with me once more."

He stepped back from the glare of triumph in her eyes. "That is not possible!"

"I kept his body throughout the centuries, surrounded by the glow of five stones. I worked and studied. And one day I succeeded. Go away and die somewhere, Culain, and I shall find your body and bring it back. Then you will be mine."

"I am coming to Skitis, Goroien," he said softly. "I shall destroy your power."

She laughed then, rich mocking laughter that caused the color to flood his cheeks. "*You* are coming? Once that would have put terror into my heart, but not now.

A middle-aged man, soft and decaying, is coming to challenge Gilgamesh? You have no idea how often he speaks of you, dreams of killing you. You think to stand against him? I will show you how your arrogance has betrayed you. You always liked the shade games—play this one." She gestured with her right hand, and the air shimmered. Before Culain stood a tall warrior with golden hair and bright blue-green eyes. He carried a curved sword and a dagger. "Here is Gilgamesh as he was." The warrior leapt forward, and Culain swept up the lance, twisted the handle, and pulled clear the hidden sword. He was just in time to block a savage cut. Then another . . . and another. Culain fought with all the skill of the centuries, but Goroien was right; his aging body was no longer equipped to tackle the whirlwind that was Gilgamesh, the Lord of Battle. Culain, growing desperate, took a chance, spinning on his heel in the move he had taught Thuro. His opponent leapt to the left, avoiding Culain's raised elbow, and a cold sword slid beneath the Mist Warrior's ribs.

He crumpled, hitting the hard clay ground on his face and dislodging the silver helm. He fought to stay conscious, but his mind fell into darkness. When he awoke, Goroien was still there, sitting by the cairn of stones.

"Go away, Culain," she said. "What you fought was Gilgamesh as he was. Now he is stronger and faster; he would kill you within seconds. Either that or use this." She dropped a yellow pebble on the ground before him; it was pure Sipstrassi with virtually no sign of black veins. "Become immortal again. Become what you were . . . what you should be. Then you will have a chance."

He pushed himself to his feet. "It is not usual to give your enemy a chance at life, lady."

"How could you be my enemy? I have loved you since before the fall. I will love you on the day the universe ends in fire."

"We will never be lovers again, lady," he said. "I will see you on Skitis Island."

She stood. "You fool! You will not see me. You will see your death coming toward you in every stride Gilgamesh takes."

She walked into the derelict house without a backward glance, and Culain slumped to the ground, tears in his eyes. It had taken all his strength to tell her their love was ended. He stared down at the Sipstrassi Stone and lifted it. She was right; he was in no condition to face Gilgamesh. Her voice drifted back to him as if from a great distance.

"Your grandson is a handsome boy. I think I will take him. Do you remember my time as Circe?" Her laughter echoed into silence.

Culain sat with head bowed. After the Trojan War Goroien had wreaked her vengeance on the Greeks, causing the bloody deaths of Agammemnon the warlord and Menelaus the Spartan king. But by far the most hideous of her vengeful acts had been the shipwreck of Odysseus. For Goroien, as Circe the witch, had turned some of the survivors into swine, tricking the others into cooking and eating them.

He picked up his sword and brushed the dirt from the blade.

Walking to his horse, he touched the Sipstrassi Stone to its temple and stepped back. The beast's body collapsed, then swelled and stretched, its smooth flanks growing silver-edged scales of deep rust-red. Its head shimmered, its eyes becoming slanted like a great cat's, its snout stretching, fangs erupting from a cavernous mouth. Huge wings unfolded from its ribs, and its hooves erupted into taloned claws. Its long neck arched back, and a terrible cry filled the air. Culain looked down at the black pebble in his hand and tossed it to the ground. Sliding his sword back into the haft of his lance, he climbed to the saddle on the dragon's back, whispering the word of command. The beast rose on its powerful legs, the wings spreading wide; then it soared into the night air heading northwest to Skitis.

On the third night a fearsome storm broke over Erin Plateau, with shafts of lightning spearing the sky. Uther remained where he had stayed for three days, sitting at the edge of the circle. Prasamaccus and Korrin gathered food and blankets for the prince and stepped out into the driving rain. At that moment lightning streaked the sky, and both men saw Uther stand and raise his arms over his head, his blond hair billowing in the shrieking wind. Then he vanished. Korrin ran to the stones, with Prasamaccus hobbling behind, but there was no sign of the prince.

The storm broke, the rain easing to a fine drizzle. Korrin sank to a rock.

"It is over," he said, bitterness returning to his voice for the first time since the Vores had turned on the soldiers. Korrin began to curse and swear, and the Brigante moved away from him; he, too, felt demoralized and beaten, and he sat on the fallen stone overlooking the forest.

"What will we tell them?" said Korrin. The Brigante gathered his cloak tightly around his slender frame. His leg ached, as it always did when the weather turned damp, and his heart told him he would never see Helga again. He could offer Korrin no advice. Just then the two moons appeared from behind the breaking clouds, and a third man joined them.

"Where is Berec?" asked Maggrig, but neither man answered. "So, we are alone, as he said we might be." He scratched his graying beard and sat beside Korrin. "We've set some snares and dug a few pits, which should slow them a little. And there are some five good ambush points."

Korrin glanced up, surprised. The news of Berec's departure seemed to affect Maggrig not at all. "We should hit them first at the Elm Hollow. The horsemen will not be able to charge up the rise, and we'll have a hundred feet of killing ground. Even our archers should be unable to miss at that distance. We could down perhaps a hundred men."

"You are talking of eighty men against an army," said Korrin. "Are you mad?"

"Eighty men is all we had yesterday. Gods, man, no one lives forever."

"Except the Witch Queen," said Korrin, adding a savage curse.

"Take some advice from an old warrior: tell no one Berec has gone for good. Just say he has . . . who knows? . . . journeyed back to his castle in the clouds. In the meantime, let us hit them hard."

"Good advice," said Prasamaccus. "We do not know how many soldiers are coming, and the forest is immense. We should be able to lead them a merry chase."

Below, in the tiny village of tents that had sprung up by the stream, a young woman wandered out into the forest to be alone for a while. As she entered the darkness, she caught sight of the moonlight reflecting from metal in the distance. She climbed a stout oak and peered to the west.

Moving silently through the trees came the army of Goroien.

For more than thirty hours Uther had been awake and worrying about the problem of the Void, searching every angle, exploring all the facts at his disposal. His reasoning and his training told him that he had overlooked a salient point, but try as he could, there seemed no way to home in on it.

And then, just as the storm broke, the answer sailed effortlessly into his mind. Just because the ghost army could not be *seen* did not necessarily mean they were not *there*.

It was so simple. The freezing rain was forgotten. Prasamaccus had told him that he had dreamed of drums and marching feet on his first night on Erin Plateau, and Uther should have leapt on that thought like a striking falcon.

All that was left now was to enter the Void—the home of Atrols and Soul Stealers. Yes, he thought, that is all. Do not stop to think, Uther, he told himself. Just do it! He stood, raised his arms above his head, gripped the stone tightly, and wished for the Void.

His head spun, and he fell. Around him the Mist swirled. Pushing himself to his knees, he drew his gladius. The Sipstrassi Stone was almost black. He risked touching his sword blade; it shone with a white light, and in the Mist he could see dark shadows and gray, cold faces. A long time ago, Thuro the child had wandered here in a fever dream and Aurelius had brought him back. The fear of that time returned to haunt him, and as his fear grew, the shadow shapes moved closer. Uther the man stood and steadied himself, lifting his sword high above his head. The light shone from the blade, pushing back both the Mist and the shadows within it.

As the Mist rolled away, Uther saw the desolate landscape of the Void, a place of ash-gray hills and long-dead trees beneath a slate-dark sky. He shivered. It was no place for a man to die. Far off to his right he caught the faint sound of drums. Holding his sword high like a lantern, he walked toward the sound. The shadows followed him, and he could hear whispering voices calling his name. The prince ignored them. He climbed a low hill and stopped in wonder. There, in a dusty valley, was a defensive enclosure made of mounds of gray earth thrown up from a huge square ditch. Sharpened stakes had been set into the banks. Within the enclosure were scores of tents, and at the center of the square stood a staff bearing a golden eagle, its wings spread. Uther stood for several minutes staring at the camp, unable to accept the vision before his eyes. Yet all the clues had been before him. Korrin had spoken of the Eagle sect that had tried to commune with the ghosts. The soldiers marched to the drum in perfect order.

And Culain had talked of his greatest regret, when he had consigned an army to the Mist.

Uther stood on the lonely hilltop and gazed in wonder at the eagle of the Ninth Legion.

The prince walked slowly down the hill to stand before the wide opening to the enclosure. Two legionaries stepped into his path, their eyes tired, their spears sharp. He was commanded to halt. The language was recognizable but lacked the later British additions. He thought back to his training under Maedhlyn and Decianus and answered them in their own archaic tongue.

"Who is your legate?"

The legionaries glanced at one another, and the taller man stepped forward.

"Are you Roman?"

"I am."

"Are we close to home?" The voice quavered.

"I am here to bring you home. Who is your legate?"

"Severinus Albinus. Wait here." The soldier raced away, and Uther stood, still holding the shining sword. Ten men returned some minutes later, and the prince was ushered into the enclosure, an honor guard of five legionaries on either side of him. Men rushed from their tents to see the stranger, their faces ashen, their eyes dull. The guard halted before a wide tent. Uther surrendered his weapons to the centurion at the entrance and ducked inside. A young man of maybe twenty-five, dressed in a polished bronze breastplate, was seated on a low stool.

"Your name?" he asked.

"You are Severinus Albinus?" responded Uther, aware that the success of his mission depended on maintaining the initiative.

"I am."

"The legate of Legio IX?"

"No. Our legate is Petillius Cerialis; he did not accompany us. Who are you?" Uther sensed that the young man, like all the men he had seen, was on the edge of desperation.

"I am Uther."

"Where is this place?" asked Severinus, rising. "We have marched here for months. No food. No water. Yet no thirst or hunger. There are creatures within the accursed Mist who drink blood. There are beasts the like of which I have never dreamed of. Are we all dead?"

"I can return you to Eboracum," said Uther, "but first

there is much you should know." He walked past the young soldier and seated himself on a divan at the back of the tent. Severinus Albinus joined him. "Firstly, you marched from Eboracum to aid Paullinus against the Iceni uprising. You entered the Mist, a world of the dead."

"I know all this," said Severinus. "How do we get home?"

Uther raised his hand. "Gently. Listen to every word. Paullinus defeated Boudicca more than four hundred years ago."

"Then we are dead. Sweet Jupiter, I cannot march any longer!"

"You are not dead, believe me. What I am attempting to tell you is that the world you knew is dead. The Roman Empire is fading. Britain no longer boasts a single Roman legion."

"I have a wife . . . a daughter."

"No," said Uther sadly. "They have been dead for four centuries. I can take you to Eboracum. The world is much changed, but the sun still shines, the grapes make wine, the streams flow clear, and the water is good to drink."

"Who rules in Britain now?" asked Severinus.

"The land is at war. The Brigantes have risen, and the Saxons and Jutes have invaded. The Romano-Britons led by Aquila, a pure-blooded Roman of noble family, are fighting for their lives. There was a king named Aurelius, but he was murdered. I am his son. And I have journeyed beyond the borders of death to bring you home."

"To fight for you?"

"To fight for me," said Uther, "and for yourselves."

"And you will take us to Eboracum?"

"Not immediately," said Uther, and told the Roman of the war in Pinrae and the rule of the Witch Queen. Severinus listened in silence.

"There was a time," he said when Uther fell silent, "that I would have mocked your tale. But not here, in this ashen wilderness. You want us to fight for you, Uther? I would sell my soul for one day in the sunshine. No, for a single hour. Just take us away from here."

Fear had brought Uther to the edge of panic. With the 4,600 men of the Ninth Legion marching behind him, he returned to the hill he had first encountered upon entering the Void. Now, after an hour, he still could not open the pathway between the worlds. He had willed himself back, the stone had glowed, and for a moment only he had seen the giant stones of Erin, misty shadows shimmering just out of reach. He heard Severinus Albinus behind him and waved the man back, fighting for calm. He glanced at the stone; only the thinnest thread of gold remained.

He knew now for certain that the power of the stone was insufficient to open a gateway large enough to allow the legion through. He was not even sure whether he himself could return, and his agile mind once more began the long slow examination of all the possibilities.

At last he decided on one supreme effort. He closed his eyes and pictured himself back in Pinrae, all the while holding the image of the Ninth Legion in his mind. Behind him Severinus saw Uther grow less tangible, almost wraithlike, but then he was back as before. The prince stared down at the black pebble in his hand and could not find the courage to turn and face the expectant soldiers.

Beyond the Void the army of Goroien had circled the

base of the hill, waiting for the order to attack. Maggrig and Korrin had placed archers all around the stones, but there was no way they could repel the armored soldiers. At best they would wound a score or so, and it seemed to Korrin that more than two thousand men were assembled below.

"Why do they not attack?" he asked the lean, wolf-like Maggrig.

"They are afraid of Berec's magic. But they will come soon."

Twenty paces to their left, kneeling behind a fallen stone, Laitha waited with an arrow notched, her eyes fixed on a tall warrior with a purple plume on his helm. She had already decided he would be her target for no other reason than that she disliked the arrogant way he strode among the men below, issuing orders. It made her feel somehow better to know that the strutting peacock would die before she did.

A hand touched her shoulder, and she turned to see a tall broad-shouldered man with a golden beard. She could not remember having seen him before.

"Follow me," he said, his manner showing that he was obviously used to being obeyed. He did not look back as Laitha followed him to the center of the plateau.

"Who are you?" she asked.

"Hold fast to your questions and climb the altar." She moved up on the broken central stones, clambering over the scarred and pitted runes worked into the surfaces.

The bearded man spoke just as she reached the highest point and stood precariously on the top stone, some six feet from the ground.

"Now lift your hand above your head."

"For what purpose?"

"You feel there is time for debate? Obey me."

Biting back her anger, she raised her right arm. "Higher!" he said. As she did so, her fingers touched something cold and clinging, and she withdrew her hand instinctively. "It is only water," he assured her. "Push high and open your fingers. Grasp what is there and draw it down."

Suddenly a great cry went up, a battle roar that chilled the blood, and the soldiers of Goroien swept up the hill. Arrows sang down to meet them, some glancing from armored breastplates or helms, others wedging in the flesh of bare legs and arms.

"Reach up!" ordered the tall stranger. "Swiftly, if you value your life."

Laitha pushed her hand through the invisible barrier of water and opened her fingers. She felt the cold touch of metal and the yielding warmth of leather. Grasping the object tightly, she drew it down. In her hand was a great sword with an upswept hilt of burnished gold and a silver blade, double-edged and engraved with runes she could not recognize.

"Follow me," said the man, running toward the rocks where Uther had last been seen. Halting, he pulled Laitha forward. "When I finish speaking, smite the air before you." The words that followed meant nothing to Laitha, but the air around him hissed and crackled as if a storm were due. "*Now!*" he shouted. The sword slashed forward, and a great wind blew up. Lightning flashed toward the sky, and the Mist billowed from where she struck. Laitha was hurled backward to the ground.

Uther leapt from the Mist, glancing around him. At the far end of the plateau the rebels began to stream back, and the prince could see the plumed helms of Goroien's soldiers. Just then Severinus Albinus stepped into the sunshine with the Ninth Legion following him. Some of the men fell to their knees as the sunshine touched them; others began to weep in joy and relief. Severinus, though young, was a seasoned campaigner, and he took in the situation in an instant.

"Alba formation!" he yelled, and Roman discipline was restored. Legionaries bearing embossed rectangular bronze shields drew their swords and formed a fighting line, pushing forward and spreading out to allow the spearmen through. As the rebels ran back, the line opened before them.

Goroien's soldiers had an opportunity then to rush the line, but they did not. They were mostly men of Pinrae, and they knew the legend of the ghost army. They stood transfixed as the legion formed a square and advanced with shields locked, long spears protruding. The soldiers of Pinrae were not cowards—they would face and had faced overwhelming odds—but they had already seen the coming of the god Berec. Now more and more spirits of the dead were issuing from the Mist, and this they could not bear. Slowly they backed away, returning to the base of the hill. The legion halted at the circle of stones, awaiting orders.

In the safety of the square Uther helped Laitha to her feet. "How did you do that? I thought I was fin—" He stumbled to a halt as he saw the great sword lying on the ground at Laitha's feet. He dropped to his knees, his hand curling around the hilt. "My father's sword!" he whispered. "The Sword of Cunobelin." He rose. "How?"

Laitha swung around, seeking the man with the golden beard, but he was nowhere in sight. She explained swiftly as Severinus Albinus approached.

"What are your orders, Prince Uther? Shall we attack?"

Uther shook his head and, carrying the longsword, strode to the edge of the square. The legionaries stepped aside, and he walked down the hill, halting some thirty feet from the enemy line. A bowman notched an arrow.

"Draw the string and I'll turn your eyes to maggot balls," said the prince. The man dropped both bow and arrow instantly.

"Let your leader step forward!"

A short, stocky middle-aged man in a silver breastplate walked from the line. He licked his lips as he came but held his shoulders back, pride preventing him from displaying fear.

"You know who I am," said Uther, "and you can see that the ghosts have come home. I gauge you are now outnumbered two to one, and I can see that your men are in no condition for battle."

"I cannot surrender," said the man.

"I see that, but neither would the queen desire you to throw away the lives of your men needlessly. Take your army from Mareen-sa and report to Astarte."

The man nodded. "What you say is logical. Might I ask why you are sparing us?"

"I am not here to see the men of Pinrae slaughter one another. I am here to destroy the Witch Queen. Do not misjudge my mercy. If we meet again on the field of battle, I will crush you and any who stand in my path."

The man bowed stiffly. "My name is Agarin Pinder, and if I am ordered to stand in your path, I will do so."

"I would expect no less from a man of duty. Go now!"

Uther swung on his heel and returned to the plateau,

calling Severinus to him. The young Roman followed him into the long building.

"Gods, I am hungry," said Severinus, "and what a wonderful feeling it is!" On the table was a flagon of wine, and Uther poured two goblets, passing one to the Roman.

"We must leave the forest and march on Callia, a town nearby," said Uther. "There are insufficient supplies here to feed a legion."

Severinus nodded. "You chose not to fight. Why?"

"The Roman army was once the finest the world had seen. The discipline was second to none, and many a battle turned on that. But your men were not ready, not after the creeping horror of the Void. They need time to feel the sunlight on their faces; then they will be truly Legio IX."

"You are a careful commander, Prince Uther. I like that."

"Speaking of care, I want you to take your men from the plateau and prepare your defensive enclosure below; there is a stream there. Do not allow your men to mix with the people of Pinrae. You have been part of their legends for hundreds of years, and on certain nights they even watch you march. It is a trick of the Mist. But the important point is this: They believe that you are of Pinrae and are part of their history. As such we will gain support from the country. Let no one suspect you are from another world."

"I understand. How is it that these people speak Latin?"

"They do not, but I'll explain that at another time. Send out a scouting troop to follow Goroien's soldiers from the forest. I will try to arrange some food for your men." Severinus drew himself upright and saluted, and Uther acknowledged the gesture with a smile.

As Severinus left the room, Korrin and Prasamaccus entered.

Korrin almost ran forward, his green eyes ablaze with excitement. "You did it!" he shouted, his fist punching the air.

"It is pleasant to be back," said Uther. "Where is the man with the golden beard?"

"I do not know who you mean," answered Korrin.

Uther waved his hand. "It does not matter. Tomorrow we march on Callia, and I want your best men, trusted men, to precede us. The ghost army of Pinrae is returning to free the land, and the word must be spread. With luck, the town will open its gates without a battle."

"I'll send Maggrig and Hogun. Gods, man, to think I almost killed you!"

Uther reached out and gripped Korrin's shoulder. "It is good to see you smile. Now leave me with Prasamaccus." The huntsman grinned, stepped back, and bowed deeply.

"Are you still set on leaving Pinrae?"

"I am, but not until Goroien is finished."

"Then that will suffice."

After he had gone, Prasamaccus accepted a goblet of wine and leaned in close, studying Uther's face. "You are tired, my prince. You should rest."

"Look," said Uther, lifting the sword. "The blade of Cunobelin, the Sword of Power, and I do not know how it came to Laitha. Or why. I was trapped in the Void, Prasamaccus, and was trying to find a way to tell almost five thousand men that I had raised their hopes for nothing. And just then, like a ghost, I saw Laitha raise a sword and cut the Mist as if it were the skin of a beast."

Prasamaccus opened his mouth to phrase a question but stopped, his jaw hanging. Uther turned to follow the direction of his gaze. Sitting by a new fire was the golden-bearded man, holding tanned hands toward the blaze.

"Leave us," Uther told the Brigante. Prasamaccus needed no second invitation and hobbled from the room as Uther approached the stranger.

"I owe you my life," he said.

"You owe me nothing," replied the man, smiling. "It is pleasant to meet a young man who holds duty so dear. It is not a common trait."

"Who are you?"

"I am the king lost to history, a prince of the past. My name is Pendarric."

Uther pulled up a chair and sat beside the man. "Why are you here?"

"We share a common enemy, Uther: Goroien. But aiding you was merely a whim—at least I think it was."

"I do not understand you."

"It is especially pleasant after so many centuries to find that I can still be surprised. Did Laitha tell you how she came by the sword?"

"She said she drew it through the air, and her hand was wet as if dipped in a river."

"You are a bright man, Uther. Tell me where she found the sword."

"How can I? I know of—" The prince stopped, his mouth suddenly dry. "Hers was the hand in the lake the day my father died. And yet she was with me in the mountains. How is this possible?"

"A fine question and one that I should like to answer.

One day, if you are still alive when I reach a conclusion, I shall come to you. All I know for certain is that it was right that it should happen. What will you do now?"

"I shall try to bring her down."

Pendarric nodded. "You are much like your grandfather: the same earnestness, the same proud sense of honor. It is pleasing to me. I wish you well, Uther, now and in the future."

"You are of the Feragh?"

"I am."

"Can you tell me what is happening in my homeland?"

"Aquila is losing the war. He smashed one Brigante army at Virosidum, and Ambrosius has destroyed Cerdic. But the Saxon Hengist is moving north with seven thousand men, hoping to link with Eldared for a conclusive battle at Eboracum."

"How soon will this happen?"

"It is not possible to say, Uther, any more than it is possible to predict your future. It may be that you will defeat Goroien and not be able to return home. It may be that you will return only to face defeat and death. I do not know. What I do know is that you are Rolynd, and that counts for more than crowns."

"Rolynd?"

"It is a state of being, a condition of harmony with the unknown universe. It is very rare—maybe only one man in ten thousand. In material terms it means you are lucky but also that you earn your luck. Culain is Rolynd; he would be proud of you."

"Culain is dead. The Soul Stealers killed him."

"No, he is alive—but not for long. He also is riding

to face Goroien, and there he will meet an enemy he cannot conquer. And now I must go."

"Can you not stay and lead the war against the Witch Queen?"

Pendarric smiled. "I could, Uther, but I am not Rolynd."

He reached out as if to shake Uther by the hand but instead dropped a Sipstrassi Stone into the prince's palm.

"Use it wisely," he said, and faded from sight.

◇ 15 ◇

L AITHA FOUND UTHER sitting alone, lost in thought, staring into the flickering flames. She approached him silently and drew up a chair near him. "Are you angry with me?" she asked, her voice soft and childlike. He shook his head, deciding it was better to lie than to face his pain. "You have not spoken to me for days," she whispered. "Was it . . . was I . . . so disappointing?" He turned to her then and realized that she did not know she had whispered Culain's name. He was filled with an urge to hurt her, to ram his bitterness home, but her eyes were innocent, and he forced back his wrath.

"No," he said, "you did not disappoint me. I love you, Laitha. It is that simple."

"And I love you," she told him, the words tripping so easily from her tongue that his anger threatened to engulf him. She smiled and tilted her head, waiting for him to reach out and draw her to him. But he did not. He turned once more to the fire. A great sadness touched her then, and she rose, hoping he would notice and bid her remain. He did not. She held back her tears until she was outside in the moonlight; then she ran to the edge of the stones and sat alone.

Inside the building Uther cursed softly. He had watched her leave, hoping this small punishment would hurt her, and now he found that it hurt him also. He had wanted to take her, to touch and stroke her skin, had needed to bury his head in her hair, allowing the perfume of her body to wash over him. And he had not told her that Culain was alive. Was that a punishment also—or a fear that she would turn from him? He wished he had never met her, for he sensed that his heart would never be rid of her.

He stood and looked down at his ragged, torn clothing. Not much like a god, Uther—more like a penniless crofter. On impulse he took up the stone and closed his eyes. Instantly he was clothed in the splendid armor of a first legate, a red cloak draped over a silver breastplate, a leather kilt decorated with silver strips, embossed silver greaves over soft leather riding boots. The stone still showed not a trace of a black vein.

He moved out into the night and wandered down to the square ditch enclosure where the legion had pitched its tents. The two legionary guards saluted him as he passed, and he made his way toward the tent of Severinus Albinus. Everywhere huge fires were burning under the carcasses of deer, elk, and sheep, and songs were being sung around several of the blazes. Severinus rose and saluted as Uther entered his tent. The young Roman was a little unsteady on his feet, and wine had stained the front of his toga. He grinned shamefacedly. "I am sorry, Prince Uther. You find me not at my best."

Uther shrugged. "It must have been good to see the sunshine."

"Good? I lost seventy men to the Void, and many of them returned to stand outside the camp and call to their comrades. Only their faces were gray, their eyes red—it was worse than death. I will have nightmares about it for all my life. But now I am drunk, and it does not seem so terrible."

"You have earned this night with your courage," said Uther, "but tomorrow the wax must stay firmly in place on the flagons. Tomorrow the war begins."

"We shall be ready."

Uther left the tent and returned to Erin, seeing Laitha sitting alone at the edge of the circle. He went to her, his anger gone.

"Do not sit here alone," he said. "Come join me."

"Why are you treating me this way?"

He knelt beside her. "You loved Culain. Let me ask you this: Had he taken you for his wife, would you have been happy?"

"Yes. Is that so terrible?"

"Not at all, lady. And if on your first night together he had whispered Goroien's name in your ear, would your happiness have continued?" She looked into his smoke-gray eyes—Culain's eyes—and saw the pain.

"Did I do that . . . to you?"

"You did."

"I am so sorry."

"As am I, Laitha."

"Will you forgive me?"

"What is there to forgive? You did not lie. Do I forgive you for loving someone else? That is not a choice you made; it is merely a truth. There is no need for forgiveness. Can I forget it? I doubt it. Do I still want you even though I know you will be thinking of another? Yes. And that shames me."

"I would do anything," she said, "to take away the hurt."

"You will become my wife?"

"Yes. Gladly."

He took her hand. "From this day forward we are joined, and I will take no other wives."

"From this day forward we are one," she said.

"Come with me." He led her to a small, still-deserted hut behind the main building. There he lifted his stone, and a bed appeared.

But the soaring passion of their first loving was not repeated, and both of them drifted to sleep nursing private sorrows.

The dragon circled Skitis Island twice before Culain directed it down to an outcrop of wooded hills some two miles from the black stone fortress Goroien had constructed. The edifice was huge, a great stone gateway below two towers and a moat of fire burning without smoke. Culain leapt from the dragon's back and spoke the words of power. The beast shrank back into the gray gelding it had been, and Culain stripped the saddle from its back and slapped its rump. The horse cantered away over the hillside.

The Mist Warrior took up his belongings and walked the half mile to the deserted cabin he had seen from the air. Once inside, he laid a fire, then stripped off his clothing and stepped naked into the dawn light. Taking a deep breath, he began to run. Within a short time his breathing became ragged, his face crimson. He pushed on, feeling the acids building in his limbs, aware of the pounding in his chest. At last he turned for home, every step a burning torture. Back at the cabin he stretched his aching legs, pushing his fingers deep into the muscles of his calves, probing the knots and strains. He bathed in an icy stream and dressed once more. Beyond the cabin was a rocky section of open ground. There he lifted two fist-sized stones and stood with his arms hanging loosely by his sides. Taking a deep breath, he raised his arms and lowered them, repeating the movement again and again. Sweat streamed from his brow, stinging his eyes, but he worked on until he had raised each rock-laden arm forty times. As dusk painted the sky, he set off for another run, shorter this time, loosening the muscles of his legs. Finally he slept on the floor before the fire.

He was up at dawn to repeat the torture of the previous day, driving himself even harder, ignoring the pain and discomfort, holding the one vision that could overcome his agony.

Gilgamesh, the Lord of Battle ...

The most deadly fighting man Culain had ever seen.

As Uther had hoped, the town of Callia opened its gates without a battle, the people streaming out to strew flowers at the feet of the marching legion. A young girl, no more than twelve, ran to Uther and placed a garland of flowers over his head.

Agarin Pinder and the army of Goroien had vanished like morning mist. The legion camped outside the town, and wagons bearing supplies rolled out to them. Uther met the town leaders, who assured him of their support. He found it distasteful that they flung themselves full-length on the ground before him but made no effort to stop them. By the following day six hundred erstwhile soldiers of the Witch Queen had come to him swearing loyalty. Korrin had urged him to slay them all, but Uther accepted their oaths, and they rode with him as the legion set off on the ten-day march to Perdita, the Castle of Iron.

Prasamaccus was sent with Korrin to scout ahead.

Each evening they returned, but no sign of opposition forces was found until the sixth day.

Tired and dust-covered, Prasamaccus gratefully accepted the goblet of watered wine and leaned back on the divan, rubbing his aching left leg. Uther and Severinus sat silently, waiting for the Brigante to catch his breath.

"There are eight thousand footmen and two thousand horse. They should be here late tomorrow morning."

"How was their discipline?" Severinus asked.

"They march in good order, and they are well armed." Severinus looked to Uther.

"Do they have scouts out?" the prince asked.

"Yes. I saw two men camped in the hills to the west watching the camp."

"Order the men to take up a defensive position on the highest hills," Uther told Severinus. "Throw up a rampart wall and set stakes."

"But Prince Uther—"

"Do it now, Severinus. It is almost dusk. I want the men working on the ramparts within the next hour." The Roman's face darkened, but he stood, saluted, and hurried from the tent.

"The Romans do not like fighting from behind walls," commented Prasamaccus.

"No more do I. I know you are tired, my friend, but locate the scouts and come to me when they have gone. Do not let them know you are there."

For two hours the men of the Ninth Legion constructed a six-foot wall of turf around the crown of a rounded hill. They worked in silence under the watchful eye of Severinus Albinus. An hour after dusk Prasamaccus returned to Uther's tent.

"They have gone," he said.

Uther nodded. "Fetch Severinus to me."

Dawn found Agarin Pinder and his foot soldiers twenty-two miles from the newly built fortress. He sent his mounted troops to engage the defenders and hold them in position until the infantry could follow. Then he allowed rations to be given to each man: a small loaf of black bread and a round of cheese. When they had broken their fast, they set off in columns of three on the long march to battle. He did not push them hard, for he wanted them fresh for the onslaught; he did not allow the pace to slacken, for he knew that fighting men did not relish a long wait. It was a fine line, but Agarin Pinder was a careful man and a conscientious soldier. His troops were the best trained of the Six Nations and also the best fed and best armed. The three, he knew, were inseparable.

At last he came in sight of the fortified hill. Already his mounted troops had circled the base, just out of arrow range. Agarin dismounted. It was nearing noon, and he ordered tents to be set up and cooking fires lit. He broke the columns and rode forward with his aide to check the enemy fortifications. As the tents were unrolled and the soldiers milled about the new camp, the Ninth Legion marched in two phalanxes from the woods on either side. They marched without drums and halted, allowing their five hundred archers to send a deadly rain of shafts into the camp. Hearing the screams of the dying, Agarin swung his horse and watched in disbelief as his highly trained troops milled in confusion. The legion, in close formation, advanced into the center of the camp, leaving two ranks of archers on the hills on either side.

Agarin cursed and hammered his heels into his horse's side, hoping to break through the red-cloaked enemy and rally his men. His horse reared and fell, an arrow in its throat. The general pitched over its neck, scrambled to his feet, and drew his sword. Turning to his aide, he ordered the man from the saddle. As he was dismounting, two arrows appeared in his chest. The stallion reared as the dying man's weight fell to its back, and it galloped away. The thunder of hooves from behind caused Agarin to spin on his heel as Uther and twenty men in the armor of Pinrae rode from the trees. The prince dismounted, drawing a longsword.

"I told you once. Now you must learn," said Uther. Agarin ran forward swinging his blade, but Uther blocked the blow, sending a vicious return cut through his enemy's throat. Agarin fell to his knees, his fingers seeking to stem the red rush of lifeblood. He pitched to his face on the grass.

In the camp all was chaos, slaughter, and panic. With no time to prepare, the men of Goroien's army either fought in small shield circles that were slowly and ruthlessly cut to pieces or ran back toward the east in frantic attempts to regroup. Some two thousand men managed to break from the camp under the command of three senior officers. They ran the deadly gauntlet of shafts from the bowmen on the hillsides and tried to form a fighting square, but then four hundred cavalry thundered from the woods with lances leveled. The square broke as panic blossomed and the soldiers fled, pursued and slain by the lancers.

They received no help from their own cavalrymen, who, seeing Agarin Pinder slain, rode south at speed. Within the hour the battle was over. Three thousand survivors threw away their weapons and pleaded for mercy.

The stench of death was everywhere, clinging and

cloying, and Uther rode to the fortress hill, where two hundred men of the legion waited. They cheered as he rode in, and he forced himself to acknowledge them with a smile. Korrin was ecstatic.

"What a day!" he said as Uther slid from the saddle.

"Yes. Five thousand slain. What a day!"

"When will you kill the others?"

Uther blinked. "What others?"

"Those who have surrendered," said Korrin. "They should all hang like the traitors they are."

"They are not traitors, Korrin; they are soldiers—men like yourself. Strong men, courageous men. I'll have no part in slaughter."

"They are the enemy! You cannot allow three thousand men—warriors—to go free. And we cannot feed and guard them."

"You are a fool!" Uther hissed. "If we kill them, no one will ever surrender again. They will fight like trapped rats, and that will cost me men. When these survivors go back, they will carry the word of our victory. They will say—and rightly so—that we are superb fighting men. That will weaken the resolve of those still to come against us. We are not here, Korrin, to start a bloodbath but to end the reign of the Witch Queen. And ask yourself this, my blood-hungry friend: When I leave this realm with my legion, from where will you recruit your own army? It will be from among the very men you want me to slay. Now, get away from me. I am tired of war and talk of war."

Toward midnight Severinus and two of his centurions entered Uther's tent. The prince looked up and rubbed his eyes. He had been asleep, Laitha beside him, and for the first time in weeks his dreams had been untroubled.

"Your orders have been obeyed, Prince Uther," said Severinus, his face set, his eyes accusing.

"What orders?"

"The prisoners are dead. The last of them tried to break free, and I lost ten men. But now it is done."

"Done! Three thousand men!" Uther rose to his feet, his eyes gleaming, and advanced on Severinus. "You killed them?"

"The man Korrin came to me with orders from you. We were to take the prisoners away in groups of a hundred and kill them out of earshot of the others. You did not give this order?"

Uther swung to the centurions. "Find Korrin and bring him here. *Now!*"

The two men backed away hurriedly. Uther pushed past Severinus into the night, sucking in great gasps of air. He felt he was suffocating. Laitha, dressed in a simple white tunic, came out and placed her hand on his arm. "Korrin has suffered greatly," she said. Uther shook her hand loose.

Minutes later the two centurions returned with Korrin behind them, his arms pinned by two legionaries.

Uther moved back into the tent, returning with the Sword of Cunobelin in his trembling hands.

"You wretch!" he told Korrin. "You had to have your blood, did you not?"

"You were too tired to know what you were doing," said Korrin. "You didn't understand or you would have given the order yourself. Now release me. We have work to do, strategies to think of."

"No, Korrin," Uther said sadly. "No more strategies for you. No more battles and no more murder. Today was the high point of your sad career. Today was the end. If you have a god, then make your prayer to him, for I am going to kill you."

"Oh, no! Not before the Witch Queen is overthrown. Don't kill me, Uther. Let me see Astarte slain. It is my dream!"

"Your dreams are drowned in blood."

"Uther, you cannot!" shouted Laitha.

The Sword of Cunobelin flashed up, entering Korrin's belly, sliding up under the rib cage, and cutting through his heart. The body slumped in the arms of the legionaries.

"Take this carrion and leave it for the crows," said Uther.

Back inside the tent Uther slammed the bloody sword into the hard-packed earth, leaving it quivering in the entrance. Laitha was sitting on the bed, her knees drawn up to her chest.

Severinus followed the prince inside.

"I am sorry," he said. "I should have queried an order of such magnitude."

Uther shook his head. "Roman discipline, Severinus. First, obey. Gods, I am tired. You had better send some men to the other Pinrae leaders: Maggrig, Hogun, Ceorl. Get them here."

"You think there will be trouble?"

"If there is, kill them all as they leave my tent." The soldier saluted and left. Uther moved to the sword jutting in the entrance, the blood staining the earth. He made as if to draw it clear, then stopped and returned to the divan beside the bed. Within minutes the rebel leaders were assembled outside, and Severinus led them in. Maggrig's eyes were cool and distant, his emotions masked. The others, as always, avoided Uther's eyes.

"Korrin Rogeur is dead," said Uther. "That is his blood."

"Why?" asked Maggrig.

"He disobeyed me and murdered three thousand men."

"Our enemies, Lord Berec."

"Yes, our enemies. That is not the point at issue. I had other plans for them, and Korrin knew that. His action was unforgivable. Now he has paid for it. You men have two choices. Either you serve me or you leave. But if you serve me, you obey me."

"Will you replace the Witch Queen?" asked Maggrig softly.

"No. When she is overthrown, I will leave Pinrae and return to my world. The ghost army will leave with me."

"And we are free to leave if we choose?"

"Yes," Uther lied.

"May I speak with the others?"

Uther nodded, and the men filed out. There was silence in the tent until their return. Maggrig, as always, was the spokesman.

"We will stay, Lord Berec, but Korrin's friends wish him to be buried as befits a war leader."

"Let them do as they please," said the prince. "In a few days we will reach Perdita. Strip the dead of weapons and arm your own men." He waved them away, aware that the sullen expressions were still evident.

"You have lost their love, I think," said Severinus.

"I want only their obedience. What were our losses today?"

"Two hundred and forty-one dead, eighty-six seriously wounded, and another hundred or so with light cuts. The surgeons are dealing with them."

"Your men fought well today."

Severinus accepted the compliment with a bow. "They are mostly Saxon, and as you know, they are fine warriors. They take to discipline well—almost as well as trueborn Romans. And if I may return the compliment, your strategy was exemplary. Eight thousand enemy casualties for the loss of so few of our own men."

"It was not new," said Uther. "It was used by Pompey and by the divine Julius. Antony executed a similar move at Philippi. Darius the Great was renowned for taking his Immortals on lightning marches, and Alexander conquered most of the world with the same strategy. The principle is a simple one: always act, never react."

Severinus grinned. "Do you always *react* so defensively to compliments, Prince Uther?"

"Yes," he admitted sheepishly. "It is a guard against arrogance."

After Severinus had left, Uther saw that Laitha still had not moved. She sat, hugging her knees and staring into the embers of the brazier fire. He sat beside her, but she pulled away from him.

"Speak to me," he whispered. "What is wrong?"

She swung on him then, her hazel eyes fierce in the candlelight. "I do not know you," she said. "You killed that man so coldly."

He said nothing for a moment. "You think I enjoyed it?"

"I do not know, Uther. Did you?"

He licked his lips, allowing the question to sink into his subconscious.

"Well?" she asked. He turned his face toward her.

"In that moment—yes, I did. All my anger was in that blow."

"Oh, Uther, what are you becoming?"

"How can I answer you?"

"But this war was being fought for Korrin. Now who is it for?"

"It is for me," he admitted. "I want to go home. I want to see Eboracum, and Camulodunum, and Durobrivae. I do not know what I am becoming. Maedhlyn used to say that a man is the sum total of all that happens to him. Some things strengthen; some things weaken. Korrin was like that. The death of his wife unhinged him, and his heart was like a burning coal, desiring only vengeance. He once told me that if he won, he would light fires under his enemies that would never go out. As for me, I am trying to be a man—a man like Aurelius or Culain. I have no one to turn to, Laitha. No one to say, 'You are wrong, Thuro. Try again.' Killing Korrin may have been a mistake, but if I had done it earlier, three thousand men would still be alive. And now—if we win—there will be no fires that never go out."

"There was such gentleness in you when we were back in the Caledones," she said, "and you were a hunted prince, ill suited to swordplay. Now you are acting the general and committing murder."

He shook his head. "That is the sad part. I am not *acting* the general, I *am* the general. Sometimes I wish this was all a dream and that I could wake in Camulodunum with my father still king. But he is dead, and my land is being torn apart by wolves. For good or ill I am the man who can stop it. I understand strategy, and I know men."

"Culain would never have killed Korrin."

"And such is the way of legends," he mocked. "No sooner does the man die than he becomes a wondrous figure. Culain was a warrior; that makes him a killer.

Why do you think the Ninth Legion was in the Void? Culain sent them there. He told me about it back in the Caledones. It was a regret he carried, but he did it while fighting a war against the Romans four hundred years ago."

"I do not believe you."

"You are a foolish child," he snapped, his patience gone.

"He was twice the man you are!"

Uther stood and took a deep breath. "And you are a tenth of the woman you ought to be. Maybe that's why he rejected you." She flew at him, her nails flashing toward his face, but he brushed aside her attack and hurled her facedown to the bed. Swiftly he straddled her back, pinning her. "Now, that is no way for a wife to behave." She struggled for some minutes, then relaxed, and he released her. She rolled to her back, her fist cracking against his chin, but he grabbed her arms and pinned her beneath him.

"I may not be right all the time," he whispered, "and I may have struck a bad bargain with you. But whatever I become, I will always need you. And always love you."

Outside, Prasamaccus heard the argument die away.

"I do not think they will want to see you now," whispered a sentry.

"No," Prasamaccus agreed, hobbling away into the darkness.

For two weeks Culain had toiled and struggled to regain lost strength and speed. He was now fitter and faster than he had been for years . . . and he knew it was not enough. Goroien had been right. In accepting mortality, Culain had lost the vital edge of youth. His doubts were many as he sat on the hard-packed ground before the cabin, watching the sun sink in fire.

Once, as Cunobelin the king, he had allowed his body to grow old and gray, but it had been a sham. Beneath the wrinkles his strength had remained.

For two days now he had exercised not at all, allowing his tired body to rest and replenish its lost energy. Tomorrow he would walk to the Castle of Iron and seek a truth he felt he already knew.

He was glad now that he had used up the stone in that wonderfully extravagant flight. The temptation to use its power on himself would today have proved irresistible. His thoughts turned to Gilgamesh, seeing the warrior as he had first known him, strong and proud, leading a hopeless fight against an invincible enemy. Goroien had taken pity on him, which was unlike her, and had helped him overthrow the tyrant king. Gilgamesh had known glory then and the adulation of a freed people. But it was not enough; there was a hunger in the Lord of Battle that no amount of victories could ease. Culain had never understood the demon that drove him. Three times Gilgamesh had challenged Culain, and three times the Mist Warrior had refused to be drawn. Many in the Feragh had wondered at Culain's reasons. Few had realized the truth. Culain lach Feragh was afraid of the strange, dark quality in Gilgamesh that made him unbeatable.

Then came the day when news of his death had reached Culain. His heart had soared, for deep inside he had begun to believe that the Lord of Battle would one day kill him. He recalled the day well: the sun clear in a cloudless sky, distant cornfields glowing gold, and the high white turrets of Babylon cloaked in dark shadows. Brigamartis had brought the news, her face flushed with excitement. She had never liked Gilgamesh. Before his arrival she had been considered one of the finest sword duelists in the Feragh, but he had defeated her with ease in the shade games.

"There was something wrong with his blood," Brigamartis said gleefully. "It would not accept Sipstrassi power. He aged wonderfully; in the last two years even Goroien would not visit him. He had begun to drool, you know, and he was half-blind."

Culain had waited five years before crossing the Mist. Goroien was as beautiful as ever and acted as if her affair with Gilgamesh had never taken place. His name did not cross her lips for another three centuries.

Now the Lord of Battle had returned, and Culain lach Feragh would truly taste the terrors of mortality. It was galling to live so long only to face such bitterness. Thuro and Laitha were trapped in a world he could not reach, victims of a goddess he could never kill and menaced by a warrior he could not conquer.

He lifted his lance and drew the hidden sword. The edge was lethally sharp, the balance magnificent. He looked down at his reflection in the silver steel, gazing into his own eyes as if expecting to see answers there.

Had he ever truly known courage? How simple it had been for an immortal warrior to battle in the world of men. Almost all wounds could be healed, and he had on his side the knowledge and acquired skill of centuries. Even the great Achilles had been a child by comparison, the outcome of their duel never in doubt. Only his opponents had known courage. Culain smiled. His fear of Gilgamesh had made him run like a child in terror of the dark, and like all runners, he had hurtled headlong into greater fear. If he had killed Gilgamesh all those centuries ago, Goroien would not now have taken into her body the dread disease that was killing her. From that he could reason that she might never have become the Witch Queen. So the terrors of this age came squarely to rest on Culain's shoulders.

He accepted the burden and sought the sanctuary of Eleari-mas, the Emptying. But his mind drifted into memory. He saw again the curiously beautiful end of the world. He was fifteen years old, standing in the courtyard of his father's house in Balacris. He saw the sun sink slowly into the west and then hurtle back into the sky. A great wind came up, and the palace of Pendarric began to glow. He heard someone scream and saw a woman pointing to the horizon. A colossal black wall was darkening the sky, growing ever larger. He stared at it for some moments, thinking it a great storm. But soon the terror struck. It was a thundering thousand-foot wall of water, drowning the land. The golden glow from the palace spread over the city, reaching the outer sections just as the sea roared over them all. Culain had been rooted to the spot, desperate to draw out the last second of life. As the sea struck him, he screamed and fell, only to open his eyes and gaze at the sun in a blue sky. He stood and found himself on a hillside with thousands of his fellow citizens. The horizon had altered; blue-tinged mountains and endless valleys stretched out before him.

It was the first day of the Feragh, the day Pendarric had rescued eight thousand men, women, and children, turning Balacris into a giant gateway to another world. Atlantis was now gone, its glory soon to be forgotten.

Thus began the long immortal life of Culain lach Feragh, the Warrior of the Mist.

Unable to reach the heights of Eleari-mas, Culain opened his eyes and returned to the present. A thought struck him, easing the tension in his soul. Achilles and all the other mortals who had died beneath Culain's blade must have felt as he did now. What hope was there for a mortal who stood against a god? Yet still they had taken swords in hand and opposed him, just as the mortal Culain would oppose the immortal, undead Gilgamesh. It was good that Culain's last earthly experience would be a new truth. At last he would know how they felt.

Later, as he sat in silent contemplation, Pendarric appeared, stepping into the cabin as if coming merely from another room.

Culain smiled and rose, and the two men gripped hands. A table appeared, then two divans, the table bearing flagons of wine and two crystal goblets.

"It is a fine night here," said Pendarric. "I have always loved the smell of lavender."

Culain poured a goblet of wine and stretched himself on the divan. The king looked much as he always did, his golden beard freshly curled, his body powerful, his eyes ever watchful and masked against intrusion into his thoughts.

"Why did you come?"

Pendarric shrugged and filled his own goblet. "I came to talk to an old friend on the night before he takes a long journey."

Culain nodded. "How is Thuro?"

"He is now Uther Pendragon, and he leads an army. I thought you would like to know how he found it."

Culain sat up. "And?"

"He journeyed into the Void and brought back the Ninth Legion."

"No."

"And he has your sword, though I still do not know how."

"Tell me . . . all of it."

And Pendarric did so, until he reached the point of calling Laitha to the central altar. "I still do not understand why I asked her to do it. It was like a voice in my mind. I was as surprised as she when she produced the sword—doubly so when the ramifications are considered. She reached back into the past, to a time and a place in which she already existed. As we both know, that is not possible. It is a wondrous riddle."

"You should speak to Maedhlyn," said Culain.

"I would, but I do not like the man. There is an emptiness in him; he does not know how to love. And I am not sure I want the riddle solved. One of the problems with being immortal is that there are few questions that escape answers over so many centuries. Let this be one of them."

"Can Thuro . . . Uther . . . defeat Goroien?"

Pendarric shrugged. "I cannot say. She has great power. But at this moment I am more concerned with Culain." He stretched his hand over the table and opened his fingers. A golden Sipstrassi Stone tumbled to the wood.

"I cannot take it," said Culain. "But believe me, I want to."

"Can you win without it?"

"Perhaps. I am not without skill."

"I never liked Gilgamesh, and it seemed to me that his inability to accept Sipstrassi power was a judgment far above mine. But it has to be said that he was a towering warrior, truly Rolynd."

"As am I."

"As are you," agreed Pendarric. "But he, I think, has no soul. There is nothing of greatness in Gilgamesh—there never was. I think for him the world was gray. When Goroien brought him back, she doomed herself, for the Bloodstone enhanced his disease, giving it the strength to infect her."

"I still love her," Culain admitted. "I could not hurt her."

"I know." The king poured more wine, his eyes moving from Culain. "There is something else, and I am not sure even now whether it will aid or condemn you." Pendarric's voice trembled, and Culain felt a strange tension seep into his body. The king licked his lips and sipped his wine. "Goroien does not know that I am in possession of this . . . secret." He lapsed into a silence Culain did not disturb. "I am sorry, my friend," said Pendarric. "This is harder for me than I can say."

"Then do not tell me," said Culain. "After tomorrow it will not matter."

Pendarric shook his head. "When I told you of Laitha and the sword, that was not all. Something . . . someone . . . bade me tell you the whole of the truth. So let it be done. You remember the days in Assyria when Goroien contracted a fever that brought her to the edge of madness?"

"Of course. She almost died."

"She believed she hated you, and she left you."

"Not for long!"

Pendarric smiled. "No, a mere two decades. When she returned, was all as it should have been?"

"After a while. The disease took almost a century to leave her."

"Did it ever truly leave? Did her ruthlessness not grow? Was the gentleness in her soul not vanished forever?"

"Yes, perhaps. What are you saying?"

Pendarric took a deep breath. "When she left you, she was pregnant."

"I do not want to hear this!" Culain screamed, leaping to his feet. "Leave me!"

"Gilgamesh is your son and her lover."

All the strength and anger flowed from Culain's body, and he staggered; at once Pendarric was beside him, helping him to the divan.

"Why? Why did she not tell me?"

"How can I answer that? Goroien is insane."

"And Gilgamesh?"

"He knows. It is why he hates you, why he has always desired your death. Whatever madness infected Goroien was carried on into him. When he could not accept immortality, he blamed you."

"Why did you tell me?"

"Had you accepted the Sipstrassi Stone, I would not have spoken."

"You think this knowledge will make me stronger?"

"No," Pendarric admitted, "but it might help explain why you were so loath to fight him."

"I was afraid of him."

"That, too. But the call of blood was touching your subconscious. I have seen you both fight, and I know that the Culain of old could defeat Gilgamesh. You were always the best; he knew that. It only added to his hatred."

"How did you find out?"

"During the last years of his life Goroien would not see him. I went to him two days before he died. He was senile then, and calling for his mother. It is not a pleasant memory."

"I could have raised him without hate."

"I do not think so."

"Leave me, Pendarric. I have much to consider. Tomorrow I must try to kill my son."

◇ 16 ◇

THE TEN COHORTS of Legio IX arrived at the plain before Perdita, the Castle of Iron, five days after the battle in which Agarin Pinder's army had been crushed. Uther ordered a halt, and the twenty wagons bearing supplies and equipment were drawn into a hastily dug defensive enclosure. The rebel army now numbered more than six thousand men, and Maggrig had been placed in command of the Pinrae warriors.

With Prasamaccus, Maggrig, and Severinus, Uther walked to the edge of the trees overlooking the fortress, a cold dread settling on him as he gazed on the black castle rearing from the mist-shrouded plain. It seemed to the prince to resemble a colossal demonic head, with a cavernous mouth of a gateway. No troops were assembled to defend it, and the plain sat silent and beckoning.

"When do we advance?" Maggrig asked.

"Why has no further attempt been made to stop us?" countered Uther.

"Why count the teeth of the gifted horse?" said Prasamaccus. Maggrig and Severinus nodded agreement.

"We are not engaging an enemy force," said Uther. "We are fighting a war against a Witch Queen. No attempt has been made on my life; no other fighting force has been raised to oppose us. What does that suggest to you?"

"That she is beaten," said Maggrig.

"No," Uther replied. "The opposite is the case. She used Agarin because his victory was the simple option, but she has other forces at her disposal." He turned to Severinus. "We have four hours before dusk. Leave a small force within the enclosure and march the legion to where we stand."

"And what of my men?" asked Maggrig.

"Wait for my order."

"What do you plan?" asked Severinus.

Uther smiled. "I plan to take the castle."

On the high tower Goroien's eyes opened, and she, too, smiled.

"Come to me, sweet boy," she whispered. Beside her Gilgamesh stood, his dark armor gleaming in the sunlight.

"Well?" he asked.

"They are coming ... as is Culain."

"I would have liked the opportunity to kill the boy."

"Be satisfied with the man."

"Oh, I will be satisfied, Mother." Under the helm Gilgamesh grinned as he saw her shoulders stiffen and watched a crimson blush stain her porcelain features. She swung on him, forcing a smile.

"I wonder," she said, her voice dripping venom, "if it has occurred to you that after today you will have nothing to live for."

"What do you mean?"

"All your life you have dreamed of killing Culain lach Feragh. What will you do tomorrow, Gilgamesh, my love? What will you do when there is no enemy to fight?"

"I will know peace," he said simply. The answer shook her momentarily, for his voice had carried a note she had never heard from the Lord of Battle, a softness like the echoes of sorrow.

"You will never know peace," she spit. "You live for death!"

"Perhaps that is because I am dead," he replied, the harsh edge returning.

"He is coming. You should prepare yourself."

"Yes. I long to see his face and read his eyes in the moment I tell him who I am."

"Why must you tell him?" she asked, suddenly fearful.

"What will it matter?" he responded. "He will die anyway." With that he turned and walked from the ramparts. Goroien watched him depart and felt again the curious arousal his movements inspired. So graceful, so strong—steel muscles beneath silk-soft skin. Once more she gazed at the line of trees in the distance, then she also returned to her rooms.

As she entered the inner sanctum, she stopped before a full-length mirror and closely examined her reflection. A hint of gray shone in the gold of her hair, and the finest of lines was visible beside her eyes. It was growing worse. She moved to the center of the room, where a boulder-sized Bloodstone rested on a tree of gold. Around it were the dried-out husks of three pregnant women. Goroien touched the stone, feeling its warmth spread into her. The corpses vanished, and a shadow moved behind her.

"Come forth, Secargus!" she commanded, and a hulking figure ambled into view. More than seven feet tall, he towered over the queen, his bestial face more wolf than man, his jaws slavering, his tongue lolling.

"Fetch five more."

He reached out a taloned hand to touch her, his eyes pleading.

"Tonight," she said. "I will make you a man again, and you can share my bed. Would you like that?" The huge head nodded, and a low growling moan escaped the twisted mouth. "Now fetch five more." He ambled away toward the dungeons where the women were kept, and Goroien moved to the stone; the black lines were thick in the red-gold. For some time she remained where she was, waiting for Secargus to bring the women to their timely deaths.

On the ramparts once more, Goroien waited patiently. The mist swirled on the plain, but her excitement grew as she waited for the inevitable moment of victory. With an hour to go before dusk she saw the legion march from the trees in battle order, ranks of five, spreading to form a long shield wall before the spearmen. On they came into the mist: five thousand men whose souls would feed her Bloodstone. Her hands were trembling as she watched them advance, their bronze shields gleaming like fire in the dying sunlight. She licked her lips and raised her arms, linking her mind with the dread stone.

Suddenly the plain was engulfed in fire, white-hot and searing, the heat reaching even there on the battlements. Within the mist the soldiers burned, human torches that crumpled to the earth, their bodies blistering and burning like living candles. Black smoke obscured her vision, and she returned to her rooms.

Culain would soon be arriving, and she transformed

her clothing into a tight-fitting tunic and leggings of forest green with a belt of spun gold. It had always been Culain's favorite.

Back at the edge of the woods Uther collapsed. Prasamaccus and Severinus knelt beside him.

"It is exhaustion," said Severinus. "Fetch some wine!"

Maggrig stood close by, staring into the Mist where the vision of death had appeared. He was appalled, for he would willingly have led his own men across that plain and now would be lying scorched and dead on the blackened earth. Berec-Uther had halted the legion in the woods, then had knelt facing the plain.

Under the startled eyes of the rebel army Berec had lifted his hand, which had glowed as if he held a ball of fire. Then a vision had appeared of the legion marching, a truly ghostly army. When the fire had erupted and the heat had washed over the watchers, Maggrig's stomach had heaved. The illusion had been so powerful, he had almost smelled burning flesh.

Uther groaned. Severinus lifted him to a sitting position and held a goblet of wine to his lips. The prince drank deeply. Dark rings circled his eyes, and his face was gaunt and gray.

"How did you know?" asked the Roman.

"I did not know. But she is too powerful not to have one more weapon."

"This fell from your hand," said Prasamaccus, offering Uther a black pebble with threads of gold. The prince took it.

"We will advance on the castle at midnight. Find me fifty men—the best swordsmen you have. The legion will follow at dawn."

"I will lead the raid," said Severinus.

"No, it is my duty," Uther responded.

"With respect, Prince Uther, that is folly."

"I know, Severinus, but I have no choice. I alone have a source of magic to use against her. It is weak now, but it is all we have. We do not know what terrors wait inside the castle: Void warriors, Atrols, were-beasts? I have the Sword of Cunobelin, and I have the stone Pendarric gave me. I must lead."

"Let me go with you," pleaded the Roman.

"Now, *that* would be folly, but I am grateful for the offer. If all goes well, the legion will follow at dawn and I shall greet you in the gateway. If not ..." His eyes locked to Severinus' gaze. "Make your own strategy—and a home for yourselves in Pinrae."

"I'll pick your men myself. They will not let you down."

Uther called Laitha to him, and the two of them wandered away from the gathered men to a sheltered hollow near a huge oak.

Swiftly he told her of the attack he would be leading, explaining, as he had with Severinus, the reasons for his actions.

"I will come with you," she said.

"I do not want you in danger."

"You seem to forget that I also was trained by Culain lach Feragh. I can handle a sword as well as any man here, probably better than most."

"It would destroy me if you were slain."

"Think back, Uther, to the day we met. Who was it who slew the first of the assassins? It was I. This is hard for me, for I accept that as your wife I must obey you. But please let me live as I have been taught."

He took her hand and drew her to him. "You are free, Laitha. I will never own you or treat you as a servant or slave. And I would be proud if you were to walk beside me through the gate."

The tension eased from her. "Now I can truly love you," she said, "for now I know that you are a man. Not Culain, not his shadow, but a man in your own right."

He grinned boyishly. "This morning I washed in a stream, and as I looked down, I saw this child's face staring up at me. I have not yet needed to shave. And I thought how amusing Maedhlyn would find all this—his weak student leading an army. But I am doing the best that I can."

"For myself," she admitted, "I saw a tree this afternoon that seemed to grow into the clouds. I wanted to climb it and hide in the topmost branches. I used to pretend I had a castle in the clouds where no one could find me. There is no shame in being young, Thuro."

He chuckled. "I thought I had put that name behind me, but I love to hear you say it. It reminds me of the Caledones, when I did not know how to light a fire."

Just short of midnight Severinus noisily approached the hollow, clearing his throat and treading on as many dry sticks as he could see. Uther came toward him, laughing, Laitha just behind.

"Is this Roman stealth I hear?" asked the prince.

"It is very dark," the Roman answered with a grin.

"Are the men ready?"

The grin vanished. "They are. I shall follow at dawn."

Uther offered his hand, which Severinus took in the warrior's grip, wrist to wrist.

"I am your servant for life," said the Roman.

"Be careful, Severinus, I shall hold you to that."

"Make sure that you do."

* * *

Culain lach Feragh stood before the gates of Perdita, the winds of Skitis Island shrieking over the rocks. He wore his black and silver winged helm and silver shoulder guard, but no other armor protected him. His chest was covered merely by a shirt of doeskin, and on his feet were moccasins of soft leather.

The black gate opened, and a tall warrior stepped into the sunshine, his face covered by a dark helm. Behind him came Goroien, and Culain's heart soared, for she wore the outfit he had first seen on the day they had met. Goroien climbed to a high rock as Gilgamesh advanced to stand before Culain.

"Greetings, Father," said Gilgamesh. "I trust you are well." The voice was muffled by the helm, but Culain could hear the suppressed excitement.

"Do not call me Father, Gilgamesh. It offends me."

"The truth is sometimes painful." Now there was disappointment in the voice. "How did you find out?"

"You told Pendarric, but probably you do not remember. I understand you were senile at the time."

"Happily you will not suffer the same fate," Gilgamesh hissed. "Today you die."

"All things die. Do you object to me saying farewell to your mother?"

"I do. My lover has nothing to say to you."

Suddenly Culain chuckled. "Poor fool," he said. "Sad, tormented Gilgamesh! I pity you, boy. Was there ever a day in your life when you were truly happy?"

"Yes—when I bedded your wife!"

"A joy shared by half the civilized world," Culain said, smiling.

"And there is today," said Gilgamesh, drawing two short swords. "Today my happiness is complete."

Culain removed the winged helm and placed it at the ground by his feet.

"I am sorry for you, boy. You could have been a force for good in the world, but luck never favored you, did it? Born to a mad goddess and diseased from the moment you first sucked milk. What chance did you have? Come, then, Gilgamesh. Enjoy your happiness." The lance split in two, revealing the slanted sword. Culain laid the haft next to the helm and drew a hunting knife from his belt. "Come, this is your moment!"

Gilgamesh advanced smoothly and then leapt forward, his sword hissing through the air. Culain blocked the blow, and a second, and a third. The two men circled.

"Remove your helm, boy. Let me see your face."

Gilgamesh did not answer but attacked once more, his swords whirling in a glittering web but always blocked by the blades of Culain. On the rocks above Goroien watched it all in a semidaze. It seemed to her as if she were viewing two dancers moving with impossible grace to the discordant music of clashing steel. Gilgamesh as always was beautiful, almost catlike in his movements, while Culain reminded her of a flame leaping and twisting in a fire. Goroien's heart was beating faster now as she tried to read the contest. Culain was stronger and faster than he had been when the shade of Gilgamesh had defeated him. And yet he was failing. Almost imperceptibly he was slowing. Gilgamesh, with the eye of the warrior born, saw the growing weakness in his opponent and launched a savage attack . . . but it was too early, and Culain blocked the blows and spun on his heel, his sword snaking out in a murderous riposte. Gilgamesh hurled himself backward as the silver blade scored his stomach, opening the top layers of skin.

"Never be hasty, boy," said Culain. "The best are never reckless." No blood seeped from the wound. Gilgamesh tore his helm from his head, his golden hair catching the last of the sunlight, and Culain saw him with new eyes. How could he ever have missed the resemblance to the mother? The Mist Warrior was growing tired—but not as weary as his body appeared. He was grateful now to Pendarric, for had he not known the truth, he would be dead by now. He could not have fought so well while struggling to come to terms with the awful knowledge.

"Are you beginning to know fear, little man?" he asked. Gilgamesh mouthed a curse and came forward.

"I could never fear you," he hissed, his dead gray eyes conveying no emotion.

Swords clashed, and Culain's hunting knife barely blocked a disemboweling thrust that had been superbly disguised. He leapt back, aware more than ever that he had to maintain his strategy, for there was more to a battle than mere skill with a blade.

"A nice move, but you must learn to disguise the thrust," he said. "Were you taught by a fishmonger?"

Gilgamesh screamed and attacked once more, his swords flashing with incredible speed. Culain blocked, twisted, moved, being forced back and back toward a jutting rock. He ducked under a whistling cut, hurled himself to the right, rolled on his shoulder, and came back to his feet. A trickle of blood was running from a slashing cut in his side.

"That was better," he said, "but you were still open to a blow on the left." It was a lie, but Culain said it with confidence.

"I never knew a man to talk as much as you," Gilgamesh answered. "When you are dead, I'll rip the tongue from your head."

"I should take the eyes," advised Culain. "Yours look as if the maggots still remain."

"Damn you!" Gilgamesh screamed. His blades flashed for Culain's face, and it was all the Mist Warrior could do to fend him off; there was no opportunity for a counterstrike. Three blows forced their way through his defenses only partially blocked, the first slashing a wide cut to his chest, the second piercing his side, and the third plunging into his shoulder. Once more he escaped by hurling himself sideways and rolling to his feet.

"Where are your taunts now, Father? I cannot hear you."

Culain steadied himself, his gray eyes focused on the lifeless orbs of his opponent. He knew now with a terrible certainty that he could not defeat Gilgamesh and live. He backed away, half stumbling. Gilgamesh raced forward, but Culain suddenly dived to the ground in a tumbler's roll, rising into Gilgamesh's path. The Lord of Battle's sword plunged home in Culain's chest, cleaving the lungs, but Culain's sword sliced up into the enemy's belly to cut through the heart. Gilgamesh groaned, his head sagging to Culain's shoulder.

"I beat you!" he whispered, "as I always knew I could."

Culain dragged himself clear of the body, which slumped facefirst to the ground. He stumbled, his lungs filling with blood and choking him. He fell to his knees and stared down at the hilt of the sword jutting from his chest. Blood rose in his throat, spraying from his mouth.

On the rock above Goroien screamed. She leapt to the ground and ran to Culain's side, grabbing the sword hilt and tearing it from his chest. As he sank to the ground, she pulled a small Sipstrassi Stone from her tunic pocket, but as she placed it over the wound, she froze, staring at her hands. They were wrinkled and stained with brown liver spots.

Yet it was impossible, for five thousand men had died to feed her Bloodstone. In that moment she knew that her only chance for life lay in the small Sipstrassi fragment held over Culain. She stared down at his face.

He tried to shake his head, willing her to live, then lapsed into the sleep of death.

Her hand descended, the power flowing into Culain, stopping the wound, healing the lungs, driving on and on, pushing back his mortality. His hair darkened, the skin of his face tightening. At last the stone was black.

Culain awoke to see a white-haired skeletal figure lying crumpled at his side. He screamed his anguish to the skies and tried to lift her, but a whisper stopped him. The rheumy eyes had opened. He crouched low over her and heard the last words of Goroien, the goddess Astarte, the goddess Athena, the goddess Freya.

"Remember me."

The last flickering ember of life departed, the bones crumbling to white dust that the wind picked up and scattered on the rocky ground.

Uther, Prasamaccus, and Laitha walked in silence, the fifty swordsmen of the legion moving in a line with shields raised on either side of them. The black castle grew ever more large and sinister. No lights shone in the narrow windows, and the gateway was darker than the night.

Prasamaccus walked with an arrow notched. Laitha kept close to Uther. Behind them came Maggrig and six Pinrae warriors; his eyes remained locked to Uther's back, for every time he looked at the castle, his limbs trembled and his heart hammered. But where Berec walked, so, too, would Maggrig, and when the Witch Queen was dead, the godling would follow. For Maggrig knew that the prince would never relinquish his hold on the people, and he was not prepared to allow another Enchanter to torment the land.

With each step the attackers grew more tense, waiting for the fire to reach out and engulf them, as it had the phantom legion Uther had conjured. Slowly they neared the castle, and at last Uther stepped onto the bridge before the gate towers. He drew the Sword of Cunobelin, glanced up at the seemingly deserted ramparts, and advanced.

At once a bestial figure ran from the darkness, a terrible howl ripping the silence. More than seven feet tall, the giant wolf-beast roared toward the prince, and in its taloned hands was an upswept ax. An arrow sang from Prasamaccus' bow, taking the creature in the throat, but its advance continued. Uther ran forward, leaping nimbly to his left as the ax descended. The Sword of Cunobelin swept up, shearing through the huge arm at the shoulder; the creature screamed, and the sword sliced down into its neck with all the power Uther could exert with his double-handed grip. Before the eyes of the attackers the giant body shrank, and Maggrig pushed forward to stare at the dead but now human face. "Secargus," he said. "I served with him ten years ago. Fine man."

At that moment a sound drifted to the tense warriors,

and men looked at one another in surprise. A baby's cry floated on the wind, echoing in the gateway.

"Take twenty men," Uther told a centurion named Degas. "Find out where it is coming from. The rest of you split into groups of five and search the castle."

"We will come with you, Lord Berec," said Maggrig, his hand on his sword. He did not meet Uther's gaze, for he was afraid that his intent would be read in his eyes. Uther merely nodded and moved through the gateway. Inside was a maze of tunnels and stairwells, and Uther climbed ever higher. The corridors were lit by lanterns, faintly aromatic and glowing with a blood-red light. Strangely embroidered rugs covered the walls, showing scenes of hunts and battles. Everywhere statues of athletes could be seen in various poses, throwing javelins, running, lifting, wrestling. All were of the finest white marble.

Near the topmost floor they came to the apartments of Goroien, where a massive bed almost filled a small room that had been created from silvered mirrors. Uther gazed around at a score of reflections. The sheets were of silk, the bed of carved ivory inlaid with gold.

"She certainly likes to look at herself," commented Laitha. Prasamaccus said nothing. He felt uncomfortable, and it had little to do with fear of Goroien. All she could do was kill him. Something else was in the air, and he did not like the way Maggrig kept so close to Uther and the other men of Pinrae also gathered around the prince. The group moved through to the far room, where a five-foot tree of gold supported a rounded black boulder veined with threads of dull red gold.

"The source of her power," said Uther.

"Can we use it?" Maggrig asked.

Without answering, Uther strode to the tree and

raised the Sword of Cunobelin high over his head. With one stroke he smashed the stone to shards. At once the room shimmered, the hangings, the carpets, and the furniture all disappearing. The group stood now in a bare, cold room lit only by the moonlight streaming in silver columns through the tall narrow windows.

"She is gone," said Uther.

"Where?" Maggrig demanded.

"I do not know. But the stone is now useless. Rejoice, man. You have won!"

"Not yet," Maggrig said softly.

"A moment of your time," Prasamaccus said as the wolflike Maggrig drew his knife. The warrior turned slowly to find himself facing a bent bow with the shaft aimed at his throat.

The other Pinrae men spread out, drawing their weapons. Laitha stepped forward to stand beside the stunned Uther.

"Did Korrin truly mean so much to you?" asked the Brigante.

"Korrin?" answered Maggrig with a sneer. "No, he was a headstrong fool. But you think I am foolish also? This is not the end of the terror, only the beginning of fresh evils. Your magic and your spells!" he hissed. "No good ever came of such power. But we'll not let you live to take her place."

"I have no wish to take her place," said Uther. "Believe me, Maggrig, the Pinrae is yours. I have my own land."

"I might have believed you, but you lied once. You told me we were free to serve you or leave, and yet the legion archers were waiting in the shadows. We would all have been slain. No more lies, Berec. Die!"

As he spoke, he hurled himself at Uther. The prince

leapt back, his sword slashing up almost of its own vo-
lition. The blade took Maggrig in the side, cleaving his
ribs and exiting in a bloody swath. The other warriors
charged, and the first fell to Prasamaccus—an arrow
through his temple—the second to Laitha.

"Halt!" Uther bellowed, his voice ringing with authority, and the warriors froze. "Maggrig was wrong!
There is no betrayal! I speak not from fear, for I think
you know we can slay you all. Now cease this madness." For a moment he had them, but one man suddenly hurled a dagger, and Uther swerved as the blade
flashed by his ear. Laitha plunged her gladius into the
chest of the nearest warrior, and Prasamaccus shot yet
another. The remaining pair rushed at Uther, and he
blocked one thrust, spinning on his heel to crash his elbow into the face of the second man. The Sword of
Cunobelin cut through the man's neck, toppling his
head to the floor. Laitha leapt forward, killing the last
man with a dazzling riposte that ripped open his throat.
In the silence that followed Uther backed away from the
bodies, an awful sadness gripping him.

"I liked him," he whispered, staring at the dead Maggrig. "He was a good man. Why did he do it, Prasamaccus?"

The Brigante turned away with a shrug. This was not
the time to talk of the circle of life and how a man's actions would always return to haunt him. Ever since, in
his rage, Uther had killed Korrin, Prasamaccus had been
waiting for the moment of Pinrae revenge. It was as inevitable as night following day.

"Why?" Uther asked again.

"This is a world of madness," said Laitha. "Put it
from your mind."

The trio left the room, slowly making their way to

the courtyard. There Degas was waiting with more than
forty pregnant women and one new mother. Some of
the women were crying, but they were tears of relief.
Two days earlier sixty women had been imprisoned in
Perdita.

"This is a strange castle," said Degas, a short powerfully built soldier. "There are three more gates, but they
lead nowhere: just blackness beyond them and a deadly
cold. And a little while ago all the lanterns vanished,
and the statues. Everything! All that is left is the building itself, and cracks have already started appearing
near the battlements." As he spoke, the gate tower
creaked and shifted.

"Let us leave," said Uther. "Are all the men here?"

"All the Romans, yes, but what of your guards?"

"They will not be coming. Let's get the women out."
A wall lurched behind them, giant stones shifting and
groaning as the legionaries helped the women to their
feet and out through the yawning gateway. Once on the
plain, Degas stopped to look back.

"Mother of Mithra!" he said. "Look!"

The great Castle of Iron was turning to dust, huge
clouds billowing in the predawn breeze. From the
woods the men of the Ninth Legion swarmed down,
their cheers ringing in the night. Uther was swept from
his feet and carried shoulder-high back to the camp. As
the dawn sun rose over the plain, the castle had completely disappeared. All that was left was a great circle
of black stones.

Uther left Severinus and the others and walked to the
entrance of the enclosure, looking out at the silent
camp of the Pinrae men. On impulse he strode from the
safety of the legion encampment and walked alone to
where the Pinrae leaders sat. Their eyes were sullen as

he approached, and several men reached for their weapons. They were seated in a circle with the warriors behind them, as if in an arena. Uther smiled grimly.

"Tomorrow," he said, "I leave the Pinrae. And there is no joy now in our victory. Several days ago I had to kill a man I had thought was my friend. Tonight I killed another whom I respected and hoped would lead you when I had gone." His eyes swept the faces around him. "I came here to aid you; I have no desire to rule you. My own land is far from here. Korrin Rogeur died because he could not control the hatred in his heart; Maggrig died because he could not believe there was none in mine. Tonight you must choose a new leader, a king, if you will. As for me, I shall return here no more."

Not a word was spoken, but their hands were no longer on their sword hilts. Uther looked at the men, recognizing Baldric, with whom he had traveled on the first quest for the stone. In his eyes there was only cold anger. Beside him sat Hogun, Ceorl, and Rhiall. They made no move, but their hatred remained.

Uther wandered sadly back to the enclosure. Only a short time earlier, as he had returned with Baldric, he had pictured their adulation. Now he felt he had learned a real lesson. During his short time in the Pinrae he had freed a people and risked his life, only to earn their undying enmity.

Here was a riddle for Maedhlyn to solve . . .

Prasamaccus met him at the entrance, and the prince clapped him on the shoulder. "Do you hate me also, my friend?"

"No. Neither do they. They fear you, Uther; they fear your power and your courage, but mostly they fear your anger."

"I am not angry."

"You were the night you killed Korrin. It was a bloody deed."

"You think I was wrong?"

"He deserved to die, but you should have summoned the people of Pinrae to judge him. You killed him too coldly and had his body thrown in a field for the crows to peck at. Anger overruled your judgment. That's what Maggrig could not forgive."

"But for you I would be dead now. I shall not forget it."

Prasamaccus chuckled. "You know what they say, Uther? That there are two absolutes with kings: the length of their anger and the shortness of their gratitude. Do not burden me with either."

"Not even with friendship?"

Prasamaccus placed his hand on Uther's shoulder. It was a touching gesture that Uther rightly sensed would never be repeated.

"I think, my lord, that kings never have friends, only followers and enemies. The secret is to know which are which."

The Brigante hobbled away into the night, leaving Uther more alone than he had ever been.

◇ 17 ◇

At dawn Uther walked alone to the circle of black stones on which Perdita had been constructed. The dawn shadows were shrinking, and a cool wind blew over the plain. At the center altar sat the man Pendarric, his large frame wrapped in a heavy purple cloak that was sheepskin-lined.

"You did well, Uther. Better than you know."

The prince sat beside him. "The people of Pinrae cannot wait to see my back. And if they see it for too long, they'll plunge knives in it."

"Such is the path of the king," said Pendarric. "And I *know*. You will find—if you live long enough—some splendid contradictions. A man can be a robber all his life and yet do one good deed and be remembered in song with great affection. But a king? He can spend his life in good works yet perpetrate one evil deed and be remembered as a tyrant."

"I do not understand."

"You will, Uther. The rogue is looked down upon, the king looked up to. That is why the rogue can always be forgiven. But the king is more than a man; he is a symbol. And symbols are not allowed human frailties."

"Are you seeking to dissuade me?"

"No, to enlighten you. Do you wish to go home?"

"Yes."

"Even if I tell you that the odds proclaim you will die there within the hour?"

"What do you mean?"

"Eldared and the Saxons have linked forces. As we speak, fewer than six thousand of your troops are surrounded by almost twenty-five thousand of the enemy. Even with the Ninth Legion, your chances of victory are remote."

"Can you get me to the battlefield?"

"I can. But think of this, Uther. Britain will be a Saxon land. They are many, but you are few. You cannot prevail forever. If you stay in the Pinrae, you can build an empire."

"Like Goroien? No, Pendarric. I promised the Ninth Legion I would take them home, and I keep my promises when I can."

"Very well. There is one other fact you should know. Goroien is dead; she died saving Culain. No, do not ask me why, but the Lance Lord is now restored to youth. One day he will return to your life. Be wary, Uther."

"Culain would never harm me," answered Uther, feeling a sudden premonitory chill as he pictured Laitha. His eyes met Pendarric's, and he knew the king understood. "What will be, will be," said Uther.

Victorinus slashed his sword across the face of a blond-bearded warrior, who fell, only to be trampled by the surging, screaming tide of men behind him. An ax crashed against Victorinus' shield, numbing his arm. His gladius ripped upward to plunge deep into the man's side. A sword cannoned from the Roman's helm and down to slice into the leather breastplate. A spear took the attacker in the chest, and two legionaries pushed forward to lock their shields before Victorinus. He leapt back, allowing them room. Sweat dripped from his brow, stinging his eyes. He glanced left and right, but the line held. On the hill to the right Aquila was surrounded, his seven cohorts forming a shield wall against the Brigantes. Victorinus and his six cohorts were similarly confronted by eight thousand Saxon warriors led by Horsa, son of the legendary Hengist.

This was the battle the Romans had sought to avoid. Ambrosius had harried the Saxon army throughout their long march north but then had been trapped at Lindum, his two legions smashed in four days of bloody fighting. With the three cohorts still left to him—1,440 men—Ambrosius had fled to Eboracum. Now Aquila had no choice but to risk the kingdom on one desperate battle. But he had waited too long.

Eldared and Cael had pushed the Brigante army of fifteen thousand men to the west of Eboracum, linking with Horsa at Lagentium.

Aquila had made one last attempt to split the enemy, attacking the Brigante and Saxon camps with two separate forces, but the plan had failed miserably. Horsa had hidden two thousand men in the high woodlands, and those men had hammered into Aquila's rear guard. The Romans had retreated in good order and linked forces on a range of hills a mile from the city, but now the Saxons had forced a wedge into the Roman line, which had buckled and regrouped as two fighting units. There was no hope of victory now, and the six-thousand-strong Romano-British army was being slowly cut to pieces by a force four times as powerful. Men fought merely to stay alive for a few more blessed hours, holding to impossible dreams of escape by night.

"Close up on the left!" yelled Victorinus, his voice

straining to rise above the cacophonous clash of iron on bronze as the Saxon axes and swords smashed at the shields and armor of the Roman soldiers.

The battle would have been over by then if it had not been for the Roman gladius. The weapon was a short sword, eighteen inches from hilt to blade tip; it had been designed for disciplined warfare where men would be required to stand close together in a tight fighting unit. But the Saxon and the Brigante used swords up to three feet long, and that meant they needed more space in which to swing the weapons. This caused problems for the attackers as they pressed against the shield wall, for the longswords became clumsy and unwieldy. Even so, sheer weight of numbers was forcing the wall to yield inch by bloody inch.

Suddenly a section gave way, and a dozen Saxon warriors led by a tall man with a double-headed ax raced into the center. Victorinus dashed forward, knowing that the rear guard would be following. He ducked under the swinging ax and buried his blade in the man's groin. A sword lanced for his face, his shield deflected it, and his attacker died with Gwalchmai's gladius in his heart.

The rear guard advanced in a half circle, closing the gap and forcing the Saxons back into a tight mass where the longsword was useless. The legionaries pushed forward, their blades plunging and cutting at the nearly helpless enemy. Within a few minutes the line was sealed once more, and Gwalchmai, his rear guard reduced to forty men, rejoined Victorinus.

"It does not look good!" he said.

At the center of the Roman square the two hundred archers had long since exhausted their shafts and waited stoically with hands on the hilts of their hunting knives.

They had little armor, and when the line broke, they would be slaughtered like cattle. Some of them pushed close to the fighting line, dragging back the injured or dead and stripping them of armor and weapons.

Victorinus stared out over the sea of Saxon fighting men. Tall men they were, mostly blond or red-haired, and they fought with a savage ferocity he was forced to admire. Earlier in the battle some twenty Saxons had ripped their armor from their chests and attacked the line, fighting on with terrible wounds. These were the feared Bare-sarks, or naked warriors—called Berserkers by the Britons. One man had fought on until he had trodden on his own entrails and slipped. Even then he had lashed out with his sword until he bled to death.

On the other hill Aquila calmly directed operations as if he were organizing a triumphal march. He carried no sword and moved about behind the wall, encouraging the men.

For two months now Victorinus had experienced mixed feelings about the old patrician. He had been exasperated by his reluctance to take risks but had always appreciated his courage and his caring for the welfare of the men under him. Under Aurelius he had been a careful and clever general, but without the charismatic monarch Aquila had been found wanting in the game of kings.

Three times the line buckled, and three times Gwalchmai led the rear guard into action to plug the gap. Victorinus gazed about him, sensing that the day was almost done. The Saxons could sense it, too; they fell back to regroup, then attacked with renewed frenzy. Victorinus wished the battle could fade away, if only for a few seconds, so he could tell the men around him how proud he was to die alongside them. They were not truly Roman soldiers, merely auxiliaries hastily trained, but no Roman legionary could have bettered them on this day.

Suddenly thunder rolled across the sky, so loud that some of the Saxons screamed in terror, believing that Donner the storm god walked among them. Lightning speared up from a hill to the east, and for a moment all fighting ceased. With the sun sinking behind him, Victorinus stared in disbelief as the sky over the distant eastern hill split apart like a great canvas to reveal a second sun blazing in the heavens. The field of battle was now lit like a scene from hell, double shadows and impossible brilliance blinding the warriors from both sides. Victorinus shielded his eyes and watched as a single figure appeared on the hill, holding aloft a great sword that shone like fire. Then warriors streamed out to stand alongside him, their shields ablaze.

And then the sky closed, the alien sun disappearing as if a curtain had been drawn across it. But the army remained. Victorinus blinked as he watched the new force close ranks with a precision that filled his heart with wonder. Only one army in the world could achieve such perfection ...

The newcomers were Roman.

This thought had obviously struck the Saxon leader, who split his force in two, sending a screaming mass of warriors to engage the new enemy.

The shield wall opened, and five hundred archers ran forward, the front line kneeling and the second rank standing. Volley after volley raked the Saxon line, which faltered halfway up the hill. A bugle sounded, and the archers ran back behind the shield wall, which advanced slowly. The Saxons regrouped and charged. Ten-foot spears appeared between the shields. The first of the Saxon warriors tried to halt, but the mass behind pushed them on and the spears plunged home. From within the square the archers—with the angle of the hill to aid them—continued their murderous assault on the Saxon line, and the Roman advance continued.

Back on the two hills the Romano-British army fought with renewed vigor. No one knew or cared where this ally force had originated from. All that mattered was that life and hope had been restored.

The Ninth Legion reached the bottom of the hill. The men to the left and right of the fighting square pulled back to create an arrow-shaped wedge at the center, which pushed on toward the raven banner, where Horsa directed the Saxon force.

Inside the fighting wedge Uther longed to hurl himself forward, but good sense prevailed. As with the Saxons' long blades, the great Sword of Cunobelin would be useless at present. Yard by yard the Saxons fell back, unable to penetrate the wall of shields; they began to throw axes and knives over the wall. Severinus bellowed an order, and the second rank of the square lifted their shields high, protecting the center.

The early advance began to falter. Even with the addition of almost five thousand troops, the Britons were still outnumbered two to one.

On the western hill Aquila read the situation and signaled to Victorinus, raising his arm, bent at the elbow, and making a stabbing motion into the joint with his other hand. Victorinus tapped his breastplate, showing that he understood; then he summoned Gwalchmai.

"We are going to attack," he said, and the Cantii grinned. It was the sort of madness a Briton could appreciate. Outnumbered and trapped yet holding the high ground, they would throw away their only advantage and hack and slash their way into the enemy ranks. He turned and ran back to the waiting archers.

"Arm yourselves!" he yelled. "We march!"

The archers moved forward, stripping breastplates from the dead, gathering swords and shields.

Gwalchmai ran along the line shouting instructions, then Victorinus pushed his way to the point at which the wedge would be formed. This was the moment of most extreme peril, for he would have to step in toward the enemy and the two men on either side of him would turn their shields outward to protect his flanks. If either failed, he would be isolated in the middle of the Saxons. A sword lunged for him, but he turned it on his shield and disemboweled the warrior. Gwalchmai's hand descended on his shoulder. "Ready!" the Cantii yelled.

"Now!" bellowed Victorinus, stepping forward and slashing open the throat of a Saxon warrior. The line yielded at the angles of the square. Victorinus, swinging his sword in a frenzy, forced his way deeper into the enemy line. The man to the left of him went down, an ax embedded in his neck. Gwalchmai hurdled the body and took the dead soldier's place. Slowly the wedge began to force its way downhill.

At the same time Aquila ordered his square to attack. The Brigantes fell back in dismay as the wedge cleaved the center of their line.

In the middle of the battle Uther watched the British cohorts struggling to join him. The battleground was condensing toward Horsa's raven banner and the red dragon of Eldared. Uther moved back alongside Severinus.

"Order your archers to drop their shafts around the dragon standard. That is where Eldared and his sons will be standing." Severinus nodded, and within moments a deadly hail of barbed arrows began to flash from the sky.

Eldared saw his closest carle fall beside him, along with a score of warriors. Others ran forward to raise their shields over the king.

The battle had reached a point of exquisite balance when the three Roman forces, heavily outnumbered, were still closing slowly on the enemy banners. If they could be held or pushed back, Eldared would win the day. If they could not, he would be dead. It was a time for courage of the highest order.

At the Saxon center Horsa, a blond giant in a raven-wing helm, bearing a longsword and rounded shield, gathered his carles and launched his own attack on the new enemy.

But Eldared had no wish to die; in his mind there would always be another day. With Cael beside him he fled the field, the Brigantes streaming after him. Horsa looked at his fleeing allies and shook his head; he had never liked Eldared. He glanced at the sky.

"Brothers in arms, brothers in Valhalla," he said to the man beside him.

"Let the swords drink one last time," replied the man.

The Saxons charged, almost cleaving the wedge, but fury and courage were no match for discipline. The Roman line swung out like the horns of a bull, encircling the surging Saxons. Victorinus and Aquila linked forces behind them, and the battle became a massacre.

Uther could contain himself no longer. Pushing his way to the front line, he snatched up a gladius and a shield and stepped into the fray, cutting a path toward the giant Saxon leader. Horsa saw the fighting figure in the silver breastplate and black-plumed helm and grinned. He, too, pushed his way forward, shouldering aside his own warriors. Behind him came the banner bearer and a score of carles. The men to the left and right of Uther fell. The prince stabbed an attacker with his gladius, which became embedded in the warrior's side. Dropping his shield, he drew the Sword of Cunobelin and began to cleave his way forward with slashing double-handed strokes, moving ever ahead of the square.

Horsa leapt to meet him, and their swords clashed. All around them the battle continued, until at last only Horsa and Uther still fought. The Saxon army had been destroyed utterly. Several Romans moved in, ready to kill the giant war leader, but Uther waved them back.

Horsa grinned again as he saw the massed Roman ranks about him. His banner bearer was dead, but in death he had plunged the banner staff into the ground, and the black raven still fluttered above him.

He stepped back, lowering his sword for a moment.

"By the gods," he said to Uther, "you are an enemy worth having."

"I make a better friend," Uther responded.

"You are offering me life?"

"Yes."

"I cannot accept. My friends are waiting for me in Valhalla." Horsa lifted his sword in salute. "Come," he said, "join me on the swan's path to glory. We will walk together into Odin's hall of heroes." He leapt forward, his sword flashing in the dying light, but Uther blocked the blow, sending a reverse cut that half severed the giant's neck. Horsa fell, losing his grip on his sword. His hand scrabbled for it, his eyes desperate. Uther knew that many Saxons believed they could not enter Valhalla if they died without a sword in their hands. He dropped to his knees, pressing his own sword into the dying man's hand as Horsa's eyes closed for the last time.

The prince rose, retrieving the Sword of Cunobelin, and ordered Horsa's body to be draped in the raven banner.

Lucius Aquila stepped forward, bowing low.

"Who are you, sir?" he asked.

The prince removed his helm. "I am Uther Pendragon, High King of Britain."

◇ *Epilogue* ◇

UTHER RETURNED IN triumph to Camulodunum, where he was crowned High King. The following spring he led the Ninth Legion into the Lands of the Wall, smashing the Brigante army in two battles at Vindolanda and Trimontium.

Eldared was captured and put to death, while Cael escaped by ship with two hundred retainers, sailing south to link with Hengist. After he received the news of the death of his son, Hengist had the Brigantes blood-eagled on the trees of Anderida, their ribs ripped open for the crows to devour.

Moret offered allegiance to Uther, who left him as the Brigante overlord.

Prasamaccus returned to the ruins of Calcaria and there found Helga, who was living once more with the servants of Victorinus. Their reunion was joyous. With the ten pounds of gold Uther had given him, Prasamaccus bought a large measure of land and set to breeding horses for the king's new *cohors equitana*.

Uther himself promoted Victorinus to head the legions, barring the Ninth, which the king kept as his own.

During the four bloody years that followed Uther harried the Saxons, Jutes, and newly arrived Danes, building a reputation as a warrior king who would never know defeat. Laitha remained a proud yet dutiful wife and rarely spoke of her days with Culain lach Feragh.

All that changed one summer's morning five years after the battle of Eboracum ...

A lone rider came to the castle at Camulodunum. He was tall and dark-haired with eyes the color of storm clouds. In his hands he carried a silver lance. He strode through the long hall, halting before the doors of oak and bronze.

A Thracian servant approached him. "What is your business here?"

"I have come to see the king."

"He is with his counselors."

"Go to him and tell him the Lance Lord is here. He will see me."

Culain waited as the man timidly opened the door and slipped inside.

Uther and Laitha were sitting at an oval table around which also sat Victorinus, Gwalchmai, Severinus, Prasamaccus, and Maedhlyn, the Lord Enchanter.

The servant bowed low. "There is a man who wishes to see you, sire. He says his name is Lancelot."

THE LAST GUARDIAN
The Stones of Power
Book Four
by David Gemmell

Read on for an excerpt from its opening chapter . . .

SOUTH OF THE PLAGUE LANDS—A.D. 2341

BUT HE DID not die. The flesh around the bullet wound over his hip froze as the temperature dropped to thirty below zero, and the distant spires of Jerusalem blurred and changed, becoming snow-shrouded pine. Ice had formed on his beard, and his heavy black double-shouldered topcoat glistened white in the moonlight. Shannow swayed in the saddle, trying to focus on the city he had sought for so long, but it was gone. As his horse stumbled, Shannow's right hand gripped the saddle pommel and the wound in his side flared with fresh pain.

He turned the black stallion's head, steering the beast downhill toward the valley.

Images rushed through his mind: Karitas, Ruth, Donna; the hazardous journey across the Plague Lands and the battles with the Hellborn; the monstrous ghost ship wrecked on a mountain. Guns and gunfire, war and death.

The blizzard found new life, and the wind whipped freezing snow into Shannow's face. He could not see where he was heading, and his mind wandered. He knew that life was ebbing from his body with each passing second, but he had neither the strength nor the will to fight on.

He remembered the farm and his first sight of Donna, standing in the doorway with an ancient crossbow in her

288

hands. She had mistaken Shannow for a brigand and had feared for her life and that of her son, Eric. Shannow had never blamed her for that mistake. He knew what people saw when the Jerusalem Man came riding—a tall, gaunt figure in a flat-crowned leather hat, a man with cold, cold eyes that had seen too much of death and despair. Always it was the same. People would stand and stare at his expressionless face; then their eyes would be drawn down to his guns, the terrible weapons of the Thundermaker.

Yet Donna Taybard had been different. She had taken Shannow into her hearth and her home, and for the first time in two weary decades the Jerusalem Man had known happiness.

But then had come the brigands and the warmakers and finally the Hellborn. Shannow had gone against them all for the woman he loved, only to see her wed another.

Now he was alone again, dying on a frozen mountain in an uncharted wilderness. And strangely, he did not care. The wind howled about horse and man, and Shannow fell forward across the stallion's neck, lost in the siren song of the blizzard. The horse was mountain-bred; he did not like the howling wind or the biting snow. Now he angled his way through the trees into the lee of a rock face and followed a deer trail down to the mouth of a high lava tunnel that stretched through the ancient volcanic range. It was warmer there, and the stallion plodded on, aware of the dead weight across his back. This disturbed him, for his rider was always in balance and could signal his commands with the slightest pressure or flick of the reins.

The stallion's wide nostrils flared as the smell of smoke came to him. He halted and backed up, his iron hooves clattering on the rocky ground. A dark shadow moved in front of him . . . in panic he reared, and Shannow tumbled from the saddle. A huge taloned hand caught the reins, and the smell of lion filled the tunnel. The stallion tried to rear again, to lash out with iron-shod hooves, but he was held tight and a soft, deep voice whispered to him, a gentle hand stroking his neck. Calmed by the voice, he allowed himself to be led into a deep cave, where a campfire had been set within a circle of round flat stones. He waited calmly as he was tethered to a jutting stone at the far wall; then the figure was gone.

Outside the cave Shannow groaned and tried to roll to his belly, but he was stricken by pain and deep cold. He opened his eyes to see a hideous face looming over him. Dark hair framed the head and face, and a pair of tawny eyes gazed down at him; the nose was wide and flat, the mouth a deep slash rimmed with sharp fangs. Shannow, unable to move, could only glare at the creature.

Taloned hands moved under his body, lifting him easily, and he was carried like a child into a cave and laid gently by the fire. The creature fumbled at the ties on Shannow's coat, but the thick pawlike hands could not cope with the frozen knots. Talons hissed out to sever the leather thongs, and Shannow felt his coat being eased from him. Slowly but with great care the creature removed his frozen clothing and covered him with a warm blanket. The Jerusalem Man faded into sleep—and his dreams were pain-filled.

Once more he fought the Guardian lord, Sarento, while the *Titanic* sailed on a ghostly sea and the Devil walked in Babylon. But this time Shannow could not win, and he struggled to survive as the sea poured into the stricken ship, engulfing him. He could hear the cries of drowning men, women, and children but could not save them. He awoke sweating and tried to sit. Pain ripped at his wounded side, and he groaned and sank back into his fever dreams.

He was riding toward the mountains when he heard a shot; he rode to the crest of a hill and gazed down on a farmyard where three men were dragging two women from their home. Drawing a pistol, Shannow kicked his stallion into a run and thundered toward the scene. When the men saw him, they flung the women aside and two of them drew flintlocks from their belts; the third ran at him with a knife. He dragged on the reins, and the stallion reared.

Shannow timed his first shot well, and a brigand was punched from his feet. The knife man leapt, but Shannow swung in the saddle and fired point-blank, the bullet entering the man's forehead and exiting from the neck in a bloody spray. The third man loosed a shot that ricocheted from the pommel of Shannow's saddle to tear into his hip. Ignoring the sudden pain, the Jerusalem Man fired twice. The first shell took the brigand high in the shoulder, spinning him; the second hammered into his skull.

In the sudden silence Shannow sat his stallion, gazing at the women. The elder of the two approached him, and he could see the fear in her eyes. Blood was seeping from his wound and dripping to the saddle, but he sat upright as she neared.

"What do you want of us?" she asked.

"Nothing, lady, save to help you."

"Well," she said, her eyes hard, "you have done that, and we thank you." She backed away, still staring at him. He knew she could see the blood, but he could not—would not—beg for aid.

"Good day to you," he said, swinging the stallion and heading away.

The younger girl ran after him. She was blond and pretty, and her face was leathered by the sunlight and the hardship of wilderness farming. She gazed up at him with large blue eyes.

"I am sorry," she told him. "My mother distrusts all men. I am so sorry."

"Get away from him, girl!" shouted the older woman, and she fell back.

Shannow nodded. "She probably has good reason," he said. "I am sorry I cannot stay and help you bury these vermin."

"You are wounded. Let me help you."

"No. There is a city near here, I am sure. It has white spires and gates of burnished gold. There they will tend me."

"There are no cities," she said.

"I will find it." He touched his heels to the stallion's flanks and rode from the farmyard.

A hand touched him, and he awoke. The bestial face was leaning over him.

"How are you feeling?" The voice was deep and slow and slurred, and the question had to be repeated twice before Shannow could understand it.

"I am alive thanks to you. Who are you?"

The creature's great head tilted. "Good. Usually the question is, *What* are you. My name is Shir-ran. You are a strong man to live so long with such a wound."

"The ball passed through me," said Shannow. "Can you help me sit up?"

"No. Lie there. I have stitched the wounds front and back, but my fingers are not what they were. Lie still and rest tonight. We will talk in the morning."

"My horse?"

"Safe. He was a little frightened of me, but we understand each other now. I fed him the grain you carried in your saddlebags. Sleep, man."

Shannow relaxed and moved his hand under the blankets to rest on the wound over his right hip. He could feel the tightness of the stitches and the clumsy knots. There was no bleeding, but he was worried about the fibers from his coat that had been driven into his flesh. It was these that killed more often than ball or shell, aiding gangrene and poisoning the blood.

"It is a good wound," said Shir-ran softly, as if reading his mind. "The issue of blood cleansed it, I think. But here in the mountains wounds heal well. The air is clean. Bacteria find it hard to survive at thirty below."

"Bacteria?" whispered Shannow, his eyes closing.

"Germs . . . the filth that causes wounds to fester."

"I see. Thank you, Shir-ran."

And Shannow slept without dreams.

were already familiar with the document and the arguments on each point. They were not only better prepared but better organized, and on the whole, made up of the more articulate elements in the community.

Much ink has been spilled by historians in debating the motivation of the advocates of the new Constitution. For more than a century the tendency prevailed to idolize the Founding Fathers who created what one nineteenth-century British statesman called "the most wonderful work ever struck off at a given time by the brain and purpose of man." In 1913, however, Charles A. Beard's book *An Economic Interpretation of the Constitution* advanced the amazing thesis that the Philadelphia "assembly of demi-gods" was made up of humans who had a selfish interest in the outcome. They held large amounts of depreciated government securities and otherwise stood to gain from the power and stability of the new order.

Beard argued that the delegates represented an economic elite of those who held mainly "personalty" against those who held mainly "realty." The first group was an upper crust of lawyers, merchants, speculators in western lands, holders of depreciated government securities, and creditors whose wealth was mostly in "paper": mortgages, stocks, bonds, and the like. The second group consisted of small farmers and planters whose wealth was mostly in land and slaves. The holders of western lands and government bonds stood to gain from a stronger government. Creditors generally stood to gain from the prohibitions against state currency issues and against the impairment of contract, provisions clearly aimed at the paper money issues and stay laws (granting stays, or postponements, on debt payments) then effective in many states.

Beard's thesis was a useful antidote to hero worship, and still contains a germ of truth, but he rested his argument too heavily on the claim that holders of personalty predominated in the convention. Most of the delegates, according to evidence unavailable to Beard, had no compelling stake in paper wealth, and most were far more involved in landholding. After doing exhaustive research into the actual holdings of the Founding Fathers, the historian Forrest McDonald announced in his book *We the People: The Economic Origins of the Constitution* that Beard's economic interpretation of the Constitution does not work." Prominent nationalists, including the "Father of the Constitution," James Madison himself, had no western lands. Much other personalty. Some opponents of the Constitution, on the other hand, held large blocks of personalty. None deny that economic interests figured in the process.

Signing the Constitution, September 17, 1787. *Thomas Pritchard Rossiter's painting shows George Washington presiding over what Thomas Jefferson called "an assembly of demi-gods."*

senators from the passing fancies of public passion by preventing the choice of a majority in any given year. Senators were expected to be, if not an American House of Lords, at least something like the colonial councils, a body of dignitaries advising the president as the councils had advised the governors.

And the president was to be an almost kingly figure. The chief executive was subject to election every four years, but the executive powers corresponded to those which British theory still extended to the king; in practice these powers actually exceeded the monarch's powers. This was the sharpest departure from the recent experience in state government, where the office of governor had commonly been downgraded because of the recent memory of struggles with the colonial executives. The president had a veto over acts of Congress, subject to being overridden by a two-thirds vote in each house, although the royal veto had long since fallen into complete disuse. The president was commander-in-chief of the armed forces, and responsible for the execution of the laws. The chief executive could make treaties with the advice and consent of two-thirds of the Senate, and had the power to appoint diplomats, judges, and other officers with the consent of a Senate majority.

The president was instructed to report annually on the state of the nation and was authorized to recommend legislation, a provision which presidents eventually would take as a mandate to form and promote extensive programs. Unlike the king, however, the president could be removed for cause, by action short of revolution. The House could impeach (indict) the chief executive—and other civil officers—on charges of treason, bribery, or "other high crimes and misdemeanors," and the Senate could remove an impeached president by a two-thirds vote upon conviction. The presiding officer at the trial of a president would be the chief justice, since the usual presiding officer of the Senate (the vice-president) would have a personal stake in the outcome.

The convention's nationalists—men like Madison, James Wilson, and Hamilton—wanted to strengthen the independence of the executive by entrusting the choice to popular election. At least in this instance the nationalists, often accused of being the aristocratic party, favored a bold new departure in democracy. But an elected executive was still too far beyond the American experience. Besides, a national election would have created enormous problems of organization and voter qualification. Wilson suggested instead that the people of each state choose presidential electors equal to the number of their senators and representatives. Others proposed that the legislators make the choice. Finally, late in the convention, it was voted to let the legislature decide the method in each state. Before long nearly all the states were choosing the electors by popular vote, and the electors were acting as agents of party will, casting their votes as they had pledged before the election. This method was contrary to the original expectation that the electors would deliberate and make their own choices.

On the third branch of government, the judiciary, there was surprisingly little debate. Both the Virginia and New Jersey plans had called for a Supreme Court, which the Constitution established, providing specifically for a chief justice of the United States and leaving up to Congress the number of other justices. The only dispute was on courts "inferior" to the Supreme Court, and that too was left up to Congress. Although the Constitution nowhere authorized the courts to declare laws void when they conflicted with the Constitution, the power of judicial review was almost surely intended by the framers, and was soon exercised in cases involving both state and federal laws. Article VI declared the federal constitution, federal laws, and treaties to be the "supreme law of the land," state laws or constitutions to the contrary notwithstanding. At the time the advocates of states' rights thought this a victory, since it eliminated the proviso in the Virginia plan for Congress to settle all conflicts with state authority. As it turned out the clause became the basis for an important expansion of judicial review.

While the Constitution extended vast new powers to the national government, the delegates' mistrust of unchecked power

is apparent in repeated examples of countervailing for separation of the three branches of government, the pre veto, the congressional power of impeachment and remo Senate's power over treaties and appointments, the co plied right of judicial review. In addition the new frame ernment specifically forbade Congress to pass bills of a (criminal condemnation by legislative act) or ex post fa (laws adopted after the event to make past deeds cri also reserved to the states large areas of sovereignty— tion soon made explicit by the Tenth Amendment.

The most glaring defect of the Articles of Confeder rule of unanimity which defeated every effort to ame led the delegates to provide a less forbidding though st method of amending the new Constitution. Amendm be proposed either by two-thirds vote of each house o vention especially called upon application of two-th legislatures. Amendments could be ratified by approv fourths of the states acting through their legislature conventions. The national convention has never however, and state conventions have been called o to ratify the repeal of the Eighteenth Amendment, w tablished Prohibition.

THE FIGHT FOR RATIFICATION   The old rule of unan plied to ratification of the Constitution itself, would ly have doomed its chances at the outset. The final Constitution therefore provided that it would beco upon ratification by nine states (not quite the thre jority required for amendment). Conventions were the proper agency for ratification, since legislatu expected to boggle at giving up any of their procedure, insofar as it bypassed the existing Confederation, constituted a legal revolution, but which the Confederation Congress joined. After forts to censure the convention for exceeding its Congress submitted its work to the states on S 1787.

In the ensuing political debate, advocates of t tution, who might properly have been called cause they preferred a strong central governme ore reassuring name of Federalists. Opponent ore decentralized federal system, became Ant tiative which the Federalists took in assuming racteristic of the whole campaign. They got t cs. Their leaders, who had been members o

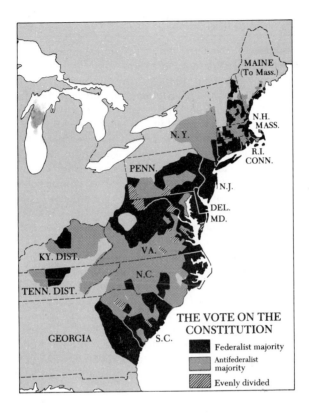

THE VOTE ON THE
CONSTITUTION

■ Federalist majority

▨ Antifederalist majority

▨ Evenly divided

functioned in a complex interplay of state, sectional, group, and individual interests which turned largely on how well people had fared under the Confederation.

There is evidence, however, in the voting and in the makeup of the ratifying conventions of divisions between "localist" and "cosmopolitan" elements, as the historian Jackson T. Main labeled them, who held to opposing worldviews because of their contrasting experiences. The localist tended to be a person "of narrow horizons—most often rural and sparsely educated—whose experience is limited to his own neighborhood," whereas the cosmopolitan was a person "of broad outlook, usually urban, urbane, and well-educated, who has traveled widely and has had extensive contacts with the world because of his occupation, the offices he has held, or his interests."

A large proportion of the localists were, to be sure, small farmers, but their leaders were often men of substance who were temperamentally or ideologically opposed to centralization. Two decades before Beard's interpretation appeared, another historian had mapped out the vote on ratification state by state and had observed that a line drawn fifty miles inland from Maine to Georgia would separate "pretty accurately" the Federalist tidewater from the Antifederalist interior. In general the idea works. Small farmers and frontiersmen saw little to gain from the promotion of interstate commerce and much to lose from prohibitions on paper money and stay laws, and many of them feared that an expansive land policy was likely to favor speculators.

There were, however, some notable exceptions. Some farmers in New Hampshire and western Massachusetts, for instance, felt they had an interest in promoting interstate commerce up and down the Connecticut River. In Virginia the Shenandoah Valley, running northeastward, encouraged strong ties with Maryland and Pennsylvania. Some parts of the frontier looked to a stronger government for defense against Indians: in the state of Georgia, for instance, fear of the Creek Indians motivated unanimous ratification by a state convention eager to promote a stronger central government—which, as it turned out, soon reached an understanding with the Creeks.

Charles A. Beard hardly made a new discovery in finding that people are selfish, but it would be simplistic to attribute all human action to hidden economic interest. One must give some credence to the possibility that people mean what they say and are often candid about their motives, especially in large matters of public affairs. The most notable circumstance of the times in fact was that, unlike so many revolutions, the American Revolution led not to general chaos and terror but, in the words of the social critic Hannah Arendt, to "a spontaneous outbreak of constitution-making." From the 1760s through the 1780s there occurred a prolonged debate over the fundamental issues of government which in its scope and depth—and in the durability of its outcome—is without parallel.

THE FEDERALIST   Among the supreme legacies of that debate was *The Federalist*, a collection of essays originally published in the New York press between October 1787 and July 1788. Instigated by Alexander Hamilton, the eighty-five articles published under the name "Publius" included about thirty by James Madison and five by John Jay. The authorship of some remains in doubt. Written in support of ratification, the essays defended the principle of a supreme national authority, but at the same time sought to reassure doubters that the people and the states had little reason to fear usurpations and tyranny by the new government. In perhaps the most famous single essay, No. 10, Madison argued that the very size and diversity of the country would make it impossible for any single faction to form a majority which could dominate the government. Republics, the conventional wisdom of the times insisted, could work only in small, homogeneous countries like Switzerland and the Netherlands. In larger countries they would descend into anarchy and tyranny through the influence of factions. Quite the contrary, Madison insisted. Given a balanced federal polity they could work in large and diverse countries probably better. "Extend the sphere," he wrote, "and you take in a greater variety of parties and interests; you make it less probable that a majority of the whole will have a common motive to invade the rights of other citizens. . . ."

The Federalists did try to cultivate a belief that the new union would contribute to prosperity, in part to link their movement with the economic recovery already under way. The Antifederalists, however, talked more of the dangers of power in terms that had become familiar during the long struggles with Parliament and the crown. They noted the absence of a Bill of Rights protecting the rights of individuals and states. They found the process of ratification highly irregular, as it was—indeed illegal under the Articles of Confederation. Patrick Henry "smelt a rat" from the beginning. Not only did he refuse to attend the Constitutional Convention, he demanded later that it be investigated as a conspiracy. The Antifederalist leaders—men like Henry and Richard Henry Lee of Virginia, George Clinton of New York, Sam Adams and Elbridge Gerry of Massachusetts, Luther Martin of Maryland—were often men whose careers and reputations had been established well before the Revolution. The Federalist leaders, on the other hand, were more likely to be younger men whose careers had begun in the Revolution and who had been "nationalized" in the fires of battle—men like Hamilton, Madison, and Jay.

The disagreement between the two groups, however, was more over means than ends. Both sides for the most part agreed that a stronger national authority was needed, and that it required an independent income to function properly. Both were convinced that the people must erect safeguards against tyranny, even the tyranny of the majority. Few of its supporters liked the Constitution in its entirety, but felt that it was the best obtainable; few of its opponents found it unacceptable in its entirety. Once the new government had become an accomplished fact, few diehards were left who wanted to undo the work of the Philadelphia convention.

THE DECISION OF THE STATES Ratification gained momentum before the year 1787 was ended, and several of the smaller states were among the first to act, apparently satisfied that they had gained all the safeguards they could hope for in equality of representation in the Senate. Delaware's convention was first, and ratified the Constitution unanimously on December 7; Pennsylvania approved by 46 to 23 on December 12; New Jersey on December 18 and Georgia on January 2 were unanimous; Connecticut voted in favor, 128 to 40, on January 9. Massachusetts, still sharply divided in the aftermath of Shays's Rebellion, was the first state in which the outcome was close. There the Federalists carried the day by winning over two hesitant leaders of the popular party. They dangled before John Hancock the possibility of becoming vice-president, and won the acquiescence of Samuel Adams when they agreed to recommend amendments designed to protect human rights, including one that would specifically reserve to the states all powers not granted to the new government. Massachusetts approved, by 187 to 168 on February 6. Maryland ratified on April 26, by 63 to 11; South Carolina on May 23, by 149 to 73. In New Hampshire one session had failed to agree, and the Federalists had won a delay during which they mobilized greater strength. On June 21, 1788, the reassembled delegates voted ratification by 57 to 47.

New Hampshire was the ninth to ratify, and the Constitution could now be put into effect, but the union could hardly succeed without the approval of Virginia, the largest state, or New York, the third largest, which occupied a key position geographically.

RATIFICATION OF THE CONSTITUTION

Order of Ratification	State	Date of Ratification
1	Delaware	December 7, 1787
2	Pennsylvania	December 12, 1787
3	New Jersey	December 18, 1787
4	Georgia	January 2, 1788
5	Connecticut	January 9, 1788
6	Massachusetts	February 7, 1788
7	Maryland	April 28, 1788
8	South Carolina	May 23, 1788
9	New Hampshire	June 21, 1788
10	Virginia	June 25, 1788
11	New York	July 26, 1788
12	North Carolina	November 21, 1789
13	Rhode Island	May 29, 1790

The August 2, 1788, Massachusetts Centinel *announces New York's vote to ratify the Constitution. It took almost two years for Rhode Island to complete "the beauteous DOME."*

Both states had a strong opposition. In Virginia Patrick Henry became the chief spokesman of backcountry farmers who feared the powers of the new government, but wavering delegates were won over by the same strategem as in Massachusetts. When it was proposed that the convention should recommend a Bill of Rights, Edmund Randolph, who had refused to sign the finished document, announced his conversion to the cause. Virginia's convention ratified on June 25, by a vote of 89 to 79. In New York, as in New Hampshire, Hamilton and the other Federalists worked for a delay, in the hope that action by New Hampshire and Virginia would persuade the delegates that the new framework would go into effect with or without New York. On July 26, 1788, they carried the day by the closest margin thus far, 30 to 27. North Carolina and Rhode Island remained the only hold-outs, and North Carolina stubbornly withheld action until amendments composing a Bill of Rights were actually submitted by Congress. On November 21, 1789, North Carolina joined the new government, which was already under way, 194 to 77. Rhode Island, true to form, continued to hold out, and did not relent until May 29, 1790. Even then the vote was the closest of all, 34 to 32.

Upon notification that New Hampshire had become the ninth state to ratify, the Confederation Congress began to draft plans for an orderly transfer of power. On September 13, 1788, Congress adopted an ordinance which placed the seat of the new government in New York and fixed the date for elections: January 7, 1789, for choice of electors; February 4 for their balloting. March 4, 1789, was the date set for the meeting of the new Congress. Each state would set the date for electing its first members. On October 10, 1788, the Confederation Congress transacted its last business and passed into history.

"Our constitution is in actual operation," the elderly Ben Franklin wrote to a friend; "everything appears to promise that it will last; but in this world nothing is certain but death and taxes."

FURTHER READING

Merrill Jensen's *The New Nation* (1950) presents the "consensus" view that downplays the extent of crisis under the Confederation. Another useful analysis of this period is Richard Buel, Jr.'s *Securing the Revolution: Ideology in American Politics, 1789–1815* (1974).° Relevant chapters of Gordon S. Wood's *The Creation of the American Republic, 1776–1787* (1969) trace the changing contours of political philosophy during these years. The behavior of Congress is the subject of Jack N. Rakove's *The Beginnings of National Politics* (1979).° Also useful is Jackson Turner Main's *Political Parties before the Constitution* (1973).

David P. Szatmary's *Shays' Rebellion* (1980) covers that fateful incident. For a fine account of cultural change during the period, see Joseph J. Ellis's *After the Revolution: Profiles of American Culture* (1979)° and Oscar Handlin and Lilian Handlin's *A Restless People: America in Rebellion, 1770–1787* (1982).

As noted in the text, Charles A. Beard's *An Economic Interpretation of the Constitution of the United States* (1913)° remained powerfully influential for more than a generation. For another view, see Forrest McDonald's *E Pluribus Unum: The Formation of the American Republic, 1776–1790* (2nd ed., 1979) and his *Novus Ordo Seclorum: The Intellectual Origins of the Constitution* (1985). Other interpretations are found in *Essays on the Making of the Constitution* (2nd ed., 1987), edited by Leonard W. Levy. Catherine Drinker Bowen's *Miracle at Philadelphia* (1966)° is a readable narrative of the convention proceedings.

Recent scholarship treats both sides of the ratification argument. The best introduction to the Federalist viewpoint remains their own writings, edited by Benjamin F. Wright, *The Federalist* (1972).° Garry Wills's *Explaining America: The Federalist* (1981) provides an interpretation of what they wrote. Biographies of Federalist writers are also helpful, among them Jacob E. Cooke's *Alexander Hamilton* (1982), Forrest McDonald's *Alexander Hamilton: A Biography* (1979), and Irving Brant's *James Madison: The Nationalist, 1780–1787* (1948).

Herbert J. Storing and Murray Dry have recently completed a multivolume compendium of the anti-Federalist documents. Their slim but incisive introduction is *What the Anti-Federalists Were For* (1981). For the Bill of Rights which emerged from the ratification struggles, see Robert A. Rutland's *The Birth of the Bill of Rights, 1776–1791* (1955).

For discussions of the problem of slavery in forming the Constitution, see the relevant sections of Donald L. Robinson's *Slavery in the Structure of American Politics, 1765–1820* (1970)° and James MacGregor Burns's *The Vineyard of Liberty: The American Experiment* (1982).°

°These books are available in paperback editions.

8

THE FEDERALISTS:
WASHINGTON AND ADAMS

A New Government

On the appointed date, March 4, 1789, the new Congress of the United States, meeting in New York, could muster only eight senators and thirteen representatives. A month passed before both chambers gathered a quorum. Only then could the temporary presiding officer of the Senate count the ballots and certify the foregone conclusion that George Washington, with sixty-nine votes, was the unanimous choice of the electoral college for president. John Adams, with thirty-four votes, the second-highest number, became vice-president.

Washington's journey from Mount Vernon to New York, where he was inaugurated on April 30, turned into a triumphal procession which confirmed the universal confidence he commanded, and the hopeful expectancy with which the new experiment was awaited. But Washington himself confessed to feeling like "a culprit who is going to his place of execution," burdened with dread that so much was expected of him. When the fifty-seven-year-old Washington delivered the inaugural address he trembled visibly and at times seemed barely able to make out the manuscript in front of him.

SYMBOLS OF AUTHORITY   The task before the president and the Congress was to create a government anew. From the Confederation Washington inherited but the shadow of a bureaucracy: a foreign office with John Jay and two clerks; a Treasury Board with little or no treasury; a secretary of war with an army of 672

Mary Varick's sampler celebrates George Washington's inauguration as president of the United States in 1789.

officers and men, and no navy at all; a dozen or so clerks who had served the old Congress; a heavy debt and almost no revenue, and no machinery for collecting one. There was the acute realization that anything done at the time would set important precedents for the future. Even the question of an etiquette suited to the dignity and authority of the new government occupied Congress to a degree that later Americans (and not a few at the time) would regard as absurd. A committee of Congress went so far as to suggest for a presidential title "His Highness, the President of the United States and Protector of Rights of the Same." A solemn discussion of the issue in Congress ended happily when the House of Representatives addressed the chief executive simply by his constitutional title: "President of the United States." One irreverent wag in the Congress suggested privately that a form of address appropriate to the vice-president's appearance would be "Your Rotundity."

The Congress nevertheless agreed with one representative who said on the floor of the House: "there are cases in which generosity is the best economy, and no loss is ever sustained by a decent support of the Magistrate. A certain appearance of parade and external dignity is necessary to be supported." To that end Congress set the president's salary at $25,000, an income far above that of any other official and probably all but a few Americans. The president obliged them with a show of pomp and circumstance. On public occasions he appeared in a coach drawn by four horses, sometimes six, escorted by liveried retainers. He held formal dinners for "official characters and strangers of distinction," but took no invitations himself. Every Tuesday from 3 to 4 p.m. he held a formal levee, clothed in black velvet, his hair in full dress, powdered and gathered, wearing yellow gloves and a finely polished sword, holding a cocked hat with cockade and feather. Visiting in Boston, Washington stubbornly declined to visit Gov. John Hancock until Hancock paid a call on him, thus making the point that a president takes precedence over a mere governor. Mixed emotions greeted the show of ceremony. Some members of Congress continued to fear that another president might make "that bold push for the throne" predicted by Patrick Henry. The antimonarchists did stop a move to stamp coins with the head of the incumbent president—preferring an emblem of Liberty instead.

A formal reception for the wife of the president. Many thought Washington's formality was well suited to the newly created office he held.

GOVERNMENTAL STRUCTURE   More than matters of punctilio occupied the First Congress, of course. In framing the structure of government it was second in importance only to the Constitutional Convention itself. During the summer of 1789 Congress authorized executive departments, corresponding in each case to those already formed under the Confederation. To head the Department of State Washington named Thomas Jefferson, recently back from his mission to France. As head of the Department of War, Gen. Henry Knox continued in substantially the same position he had occupied since 1785. To head the Department of the Treasury, Washington picked his old wartime aide Alexander Hamilton, now a prominent lawyer in New York. The new position of attorney-general was occupied by Edmund Randolph, former governor of Virginia. Unlike the other three Randolph headed no department but served as legal advisor to the government, and on such a meager salary that he was expected to continue a private practice on the side. Almost from the beginning Washington routinely called these men to sit as a group for discussion and advice on matters of policy. This was the origin of the president's cabinet, an advisory body for which the constitution made no formal provision—except insofar as it provided for the heads of departments.

The structure of the court system, like that of the executive departments, was left to Congress, except for a chief justice and Supreme Court. Congress determined to set the membership of the highest court at six: the chief justice and five associate justices. There was some sentiment for stopping there and permitting state courts to determine matters of federal law, but the Congress decided in favor of thirteen Federal District Courts. From these, appeals might go to one of three Circuit Courts, composed of two Supreme Court justices and the district judge, meeting twice a year in each district. Members of the Supreme Court, therefore, became itinerant judges riding the circuit during a good part of the year. All federal cases originated in the District Court, and if appealed on issues of procedure or legal interpretation, went to the Circuit Courts and from there to the Supreme Court. There were only two exceptions, both specified in the Constitution: the Supreme Court had original jurisdiction in cases involving states or foreign ambassadors, ministers, and consuls. As the first chief justice Washington named John Jay, who served until 1795.

THE BILL OF RIGHTS   In the House of Representatives James Madison made a Bill of Rights one of the first items of business. The lack of such provisions had been one of the Antifederalists' major objections to the Constitution as originally proposed. While at first Madison believed that the absence of a Bill of Rights made little difference, he recognized the need to allay the fears of Antifederalists and to meet the moral obligation imposed by those ratifying conventions which had approved the Constitution with the understanding that amendments would be offered.

In all 210 amendments had been suggested. From the Virginia proposals Madison drew the first eight amendments, modeled after the Virginia Bill of Rights which George Mason had written in 1776. These all provided safeguards for certain fundamental rights of individuals. The Ninth and Tenth Amendments addressed themselves to the demand for specific statements that the enumeration of rights in the Constitution "shall not be construed to deny or disparage others retained by the people" and that "powers not delegated to the United States by the Constitution, nor prohibited by it to the states, are reserved to the States respectively, or to the people." The Tenth Amendment was taken almost verbatim from the Articles of Confederation. The House adopted, in all, seventeen amendments; the Senate, after conference with the House, adopted twelve; the states in the end ratified ten, which constitute the Bill of Rights, effective December 15, 1791.

RAISING A REVENUE   Revenue was the government's most critical need and the Congress, at Madison's lead, undertook a revenue measure as another of the first items of business. Madison proposed a modest trade duty for revenue only, but the demands of manufacturers in the northern states for higher duties to protect them from foreign competition forced a compromise. Madison's proposed ad valorem duty of 5 percent (of the goods' value) applied to most items, but reached 7½ percent on certain listed items, and specific duties as high as 50 percent were placed on thirty items: steel, nails, hemp, molasses, ships, tobacco, salt, indigo, and cloth among them. Madison linked the tariff to a proposal for a mercantile system which would levy extra tonnage duties on foreign ships, an especially heavy duty on countries which had no commercial treaty with the United States.

Madison's specific purpose was to levy economic war against Great Britain, which had no such treaty but had more foreign trade with the new nation than any other country. Northern businessmen, however, were in no mood for a renewal of economic pressures, for fear of disrupting the economy. Secretary of the Treasury Hamilton agreed with them. In the end the only discrimination built into the Tonnage Act of 1789 was between American and all foreign ships: American ships paid a duty of 6¢

per ton; American-built but foreign-owned ships paid 30¢; and foreign-built and -owned ships paid 50¢ per ton. The disagreements created by the trade measures were portents of quarrels yet to come: whether foreign policy should favor Britain or France, and the more persistent question of whether tariff and tonnage duties should penalize farmers with higher prices and freight rates in the interest of northern manufacturers and shipowners. The latter in turn became a sectional question of South versus North.

Hamilton's Vision of America

But the tariff and tonnage duties, linked as they were to other issues, marked but the beginning of the effort to get the country on a sound fiscal basis. In finance, with all its broad implications for policy in general, it was Alexander Hamilton who, in the words of one historian, more than any other man "bent the twig and inclined the tree." The first secretary of the treasury was a protégé of the president, a younger man who had been Washington's aide during four years of the Revolution. Born out of wedlock on a Caribbean island and deserted by a ne'er-do-well father, Hamilton was left an orphan on St. Croix at thirteen by the death of his mother. With the help of friends and relatives, he found his way at seventeen to New York, attended King's College (later Columbia University), entered the revolutionary agi-

Alexander Hamilton in 1796.

tations as speaker and pamphleteer, and joined the service, where he came to the attention of the commander. "George Washington was an aegis essential to me," Hamilton wrote later, after the president's death. Married to the daughter of Gen. Philip Schuyler, he studied law, passed the bar examination, established a legal practice in New York, and became a self-made aristocrat, serving as collector of revenues and member of the Confederation Congress. An early convert to nationalism, he had a big part in promoting the Constitutional Convention. Hamilton had been a hero of the siege of Yorktown and he remained forever after a frustrated military genius, hungry for greater glory on the field of battle.

In a series of classic reports submitted to Congress in the two years from January 1790 to December 1791, Hamilton outlined his program for government finances and the economic development of the United States. The reports were soon adopted, with some alterations in detail but little in substance. The only exception was the last of the series, the Report on Manufactures, which outlined a neomercantilist program of protective tariffs and other governmental supports of business. This eventually would become government policy, despite much brave talk of laissez-faire.

ESTABLISHING THE PUBLIC CREDIT   Hamilton submitted the first and most important of his reports to the House of Representatives on January 14, 1790, at the invitation of that body. This First Report on the Public Credit, as it has since been called, was the cornerstone of the Hamiltonian program. It recommended two things mainly: first, funding of the federal debt at face value, which meant that the government's creditors could turn in securities for new interest-bearing bonds; and second, the federal government's assumption of state debts from the Revolution to the amount of $21 million. The report provided the material for lengthy debates before its substance was adopted on August 4, 1791. Then in short order came three more reports: on December 13, 1790, a Second Report on Public Credit, which included a proposal for an excise tax on distilled spirits to aid in raising revenue to cover the nation's debts (Hamilton meant this tax also to establish the precedent of an excise tax, and to rebuke elements that had been least friendly to his program). On the following day another report recommended a national bank, a revival of the Robert Morris idea that had led to the Bank of North America. On January 28, 1791, the secretary proposed a national mint—which was established the following year. And finally, on December 5, 1791, as the culmination of his basic reports, the Report on Manufactures proposed an extensive program of government aid and encouragement to the development of manufacturing enterprises.

Each of Hamilton's reports excited vigorous discussion and disagreement. His program was substantially the one Robert Morris had urged upon the Confederation a decade before, and one which Hamilton had strongly endorsed at the time. "A national debt," Hamilton had written Morris in 1781, "if it is not excessive, will be to us a national blessing; it will be a powerful cement of our union. It will also create a necessity for keeping up taxation to a degree which without being oppressive, will be a spur to industry. . . ." Payment of the national debt, in short, would be not only a point of national honor and sound finance, ensuring the country's credit for the future; it would also be an occasion to assert a national taxing power and thus instill respect for the authority of the national government. Not least, the plan would win the new government the support of wealthy, influential creditors.

Few in Congress would dispute this logic, although a number of members had come expecting at least some degree of debt repudiation to lessen the burden. What troubled them more were questions of simple equity, questions which Hamilton took pains to anticipate and answer in the First Report itself. Since many of the bonds had fallen into the hands of speculators, especially after the appearance of the First Report sent agents of speculators (including members of Congress) scurrying to buy them up, was it fair that the original buyers, who had been forced into selling their bonds at a reduced price, should lose the benefit of payment at face value? Hamilton answered the argument on both practical and moral grounds. Not only would it be impossible to judge who might have benefited from selling bonds and investing the proceeds in more productive ways, but speculators were entitled to consideration for the risk they had taken and the faith they had shown in the government.

SECTIONAL DIFFERENCES EMERGE It was on this point, however, that Madison, who had been Hamilton's close ally in the movement for a stronger government, broke with him for the second time (their first break had been over tonnage duties), and as in the first case the difference here had ominous overtones of sectionalism. Madison did not question that the debt should be paid; he was troubled, however, that speculators and "stock-jobbers" would become the chief beneficiaries, and troubled further by the fact that the far greater portion of the debt was held north of the Mason-Dixon line. Madison, whom Hamilton had expected to take the lead for his program in the House, therefore advanced an alternative plan to give a larger share to the first owners than to the later speculators. "Let it be a liberal one in favor of the present holders," Madison conceded. "Let them have the highest price which has prevailed in the market; and let the residue belong to the original sufferers." Madison's opposition touched off a vigorous debate, but Hamilton carried his point by a margin of three to one when the House brought it to a vote.

Madison's opposition to the assumption of state debts got more support, however, and set up a division more clearly along sectional lines. The southern states, with the exception of South Carolina, had whittled down their debts. New England, with the largest unpaid debts, stood to be the greatest beneficiary of the assumption plan. Rather than see Virginia victimized, Madison held out an alternative. Why not, he suggested, have the government assume state debts as they stood in 1783 at the conclusion of the peace? Debates on this point deadlocked the whole question of debt funding and assumption through much of 1790.

A resolution finally came when Hamilton accosted Thomas Jefferson on the steps of the president's home and suggested a compromise. The next evening, at a dinner arranged by Jefferson, Hamilton and Madison reached an understanding. In return for northern votes in favor of locating the permanent capital on the Potomac, Madison pledged to seek enough southern votes to pass the assumption, with the further arrangement that those states with smaller debts would get in effect outright grants from the federal government to equalize the difference. With these arrangements enough votes were secured to carry Hamilton's funding and assumption schemes. The capital would be moved to Philadelphia for ten years, after which time it would be settled at a Federal City on the Potomac, the site to be chosen by the president. In August 1790 Congress finally passed the legislation for Hamilton's plan.

A NATIONAL BANK   By this vast program of funding and assumption Hamilton had called up from nowhere, as if by magic, a great sum of capital. As he put it in his original report, a national debt "answers most of the purposes of money." Transfers of government bonds, once the debt was properly funded, would be "equivalent to payments in specie." This feature of the program was especially important in a country which had, from the first

The first Bank of the United States in Philadelphia. Proposed by Hamilton, the bank opened in 1791.

settlements, suffered a shortage of hard money. Having established the public credit, Hamilton moved on to a related measure essential to his vision of national greatness. He called for a national bank, which by issuance of banknotes (paper money) might provide a uniform currency. Government bonds held by the bank would back up the value of its new banknotes, needed as a medium of exchange because of the chronic shortage of specie. The national bank, chartered by Congress, would remain under governmental surveillance, but private investors would supply four-fifths of the $10 million capital and name twenty of the twenty-five directors; the government would provide the other fifth of the capital and name five directors. Government bonds would be received in payment for three-fourths of the stock in the bank, and the other fourth would be payable in gold and silver.

The bank, Hamilton explained, would serve many purposes. Its notes would become a stable currency, uniform in value because redeemable in gold and silver upon demand. Moreover, the bank would provide a source of capital for loans to fund the development of business and commerce. Bonds, which might otherwise be stowed away in safes, would instead become the basis for a productive capital by backing up banknotes available for loan at low rates of interest, the "natural effect" of which would be "to incease trade and industry." What is more, the existence of the bank would serve certain housekeeping needs of the government: a safe place to keep its funds, a source of "pecuniary aids" in sudden emergencies, and the ready transfer of funds to and from branch offices through bookkeeping entries rather than shipment of metals.

Once again Madison rose to lead the opposition. Madison could find no basis in the Constitution for such a bank. He himself had proposed in the Constitutional Convention a grant of power to charter corporations, but no specific provisions had been adopted. That was enough to raise in President Washington's mind serious doubts as to the constitutionality of the measure, which Congress passed fairly quickly over Madison's objections. Before signing the bill into law, therefore, the president sought the advice of his cabinet and found there an equal division of opinion. The result was the first great and fundamental debate on constitutional interpretation. Should there be a strict or a broad construction of the document? Were the powers of Congress only those explicitly stated or were others implied? The argument turned chiefly on Article 1, Section 8, which authorized Congress to "make all laws which shall be necessary and proper for carrying into execution the foregoing Powers."

Such language left room for disagreement and led to a confrontation between Jefferson, with whom Attorney-General Edmund Randolph agreed, and Hamilton, who had the support of Secretary of War Henry Knox. Jefferson pointed to the Tenth Amendment, which reserved to the states and the people powers not delegated to Congress. "To take a single step beyond the boundaries thus specially drawn around the powers of Congress, is to take possession of a boundless field of power, no longer susceptible of any definition." A bank might be a convenient aid to Congress in collecting taxes and regulating the currency, but it was not, as Article 1, Section 8, specified, *necessary*.

Hamilton had not expected the constitutionality of the bank to become a decisive issue, and in his original report had neglected the point, but he was prepared to meet his opponents on their own ground. In a lengthy report to the president, Hamilton insisted that the power to charter corporations was included in the sovereignty of any government, whether or not expressly stated. The word "necessary," he explained, often meant no more than "needful, requisite, incidental, useful, or conducive to." And in a classic summary, he expressed his criterion on constitutionality: "This criterion is the *end*, to which the measure relates as a *mean*. If the *end* be clearly comprehended within any of the specified powers, collecting taxes and regulating the currency, and if the measure have an obvious relation to that *end*, and is not forbidden by any particular provision of the Constitution, it may safely be deemed to come within the compass of the national authority. . . . ''

The president, influenced by the fact that the matter came within the jurisdiction of the secretary of the treasury, accepted Hamilton's argument and signed the bill. And he had indeed, in Jefferson's words, opened up "a boundless field of power" which in coming years would lead to a further broadening of implied powers with the approval of the Supreme Court. Under John Marshall the Court would eventually adopt Hamilton's words almost verbatim. On July 4, 1791, the bank's stock was put up for sale and in what seemed to Jefferson a "delirium of speculation" sold out within a few hours, with hundreds of buyers turned away. It cost the government itself nothing until later, for its subscription of $2 million was immediately returned by the bank in a loan of the same amount, with ten years for repayment.

THE AMERICAN DOLLAR   The Mint Act of April 2, 1792, based on Hamilton's report of the previous year, confirmed that the unit of currency in the United States thenceforth would be the "dollar." The word derived from the Joachimsthaler, first minted in 1517 in the Joachimsthal (James's Valley) of Bohemia, a region rich in silver. Later the German Reichsthaler (imperial thaler) entered the English language as the "rix-dollar." This coin has approximately the same size and silver content as the peso, which became the "Spanish dollar." These "pieces of eight" (eight reals or "bits") had circulated widely in the colonies, which were starved of British coins.

The long-familiar "dollar," therefore, became a natural unit for the Continental bills. In 1785 the Confederation Congress resolved that the "money unit of the United States of America be one dollar," to be divided on the decimal system into smaller units. The next year Congress specified that one-hundredth of a dollar should be a "cent" and one-tenth a "dime" (from the French dixième). The Bank of the United States (1791) issued its notes in dollars, and the Mint Act specified coinage of silver and gold in a ratio of fifteen parts silver to one part gold, which reflected the greater value of gold.

The dollar mark, thought by many to derive from superimposing the letters *U* and *S*, actually was already in use as a symbol for the Spanish dollar. Two parallel lines || symbolized the Pillars of

Hercules at Gibraltar, represented on a common design of the peso. The superimposed S signified the plural: pesos $.

The United States became, apparently, the first country to establish a currency on the decimal priniciple. In 1793 the French revolutionary government copied the American example and eventually it became a universal standard. Americans, however, failed to return the compliment. During the 1790s the French government established the metric system of weights and measures which (later refined) became a universal standard—though not in the United States. Widely adopted over the years for specialized scientific, medical, and mechanical purposes, it remains unfamiliar to most Americans. How much easier to remember how many pecks are in a bushel (4) than how many liters are in a kiloliter (1,000). For that matter, on down into the 1820s and perhaps later some American ledgers calculated in terms of twelve pence to the shilling and twenty shillings to the pound— so much easier, apparently, than learning the newfangled decimal system. Under the New Hampshire Constitution of 1784 the shilling remained technically the official unit of currency until 1948.

ENCOURAGING MANUFACTURES Hamilton's imagination and his ambitions for the new country were as yet unexhausted. In the last of his great reports, the Report on Manufactures, he set in place the capstone of his design: the active encouragement of manufacturing to provide productive uses for the new capital he had created by his funding, assumption, and banking schemes. A reading of this report will lay to rest any idea that the Founding Fathers abandoned mercantilism to embrace the newfangled laissez-faire principles of Adam Smith. "The extreme embarrassments of the United States during the late War, from an incapacity of supplying themselves, are still matter of keen recollection," Hamilton wrote. Multiple advantages would flow from the development of manufactures: the diversification of labor in a country given over too exclusively to farming; greater use of machinery; work for those not ordinarily employed, such as women and children; the promotion of immigration; a greater scope for the diversity of talents in business; a more ample and various field for enterprise; and a better domestic market for the products of agriculture.

To secure his ends Hamilton was ready to use the means to which other countries had resorted, and which he summarized: protective tariffs, or in Hamilton's words, "protecting duties," which in some cases might be put so high as to be prohibitive; re-

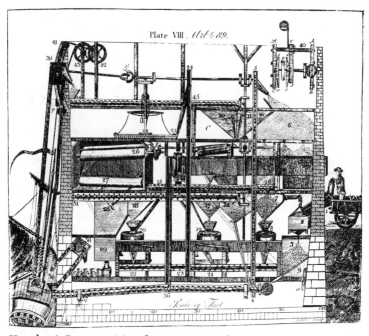

Plate VIII.

Hamilton's Report on Manufactures proposed protective duties to encourage innovation, as represented by this mechanized grain elevator patented by a Delaware resident in 1795.

straints on the export of raw materials; bounties and premiums to encourage certain industries; tariff exemptions for the raw materials of manufacturing, or "drawbacks" (rebates) to manufacturers where duties had been levied for revenue or other purposes; encouragements to inventions and discoveries; regulations for the inspection of commodities; and finally, the encouragement of internal improvements in transportation, the development of roads, canals, and navigable streams.

Some of his tariff proposals were enacted in 1792. Otherwise the program was filed away—but not forgotten. It became an arsenal of arguments for the advocates of manufactures in years to come, in Europe as well as in America. An outline can hardly do justice to a complex state paper that anticipated and sought to demolish all counterarguments, among them the ominous question which kept arising with Hamilton's schemes: "Ideas of a contrariety of interests between the northern and southern regions of the Union," which he found "in the Main as unfounded as they are mischievous." If, as seemed likely, the northern and middle states should become the chief scenes of manufacturing, they would create robust markets for agricultural products, some of which the southern states were peculiarly qualified to produce. North and South would both benefit, he argued, as more commerce moved between these regions than across the Atlantic, thus strengthening the Union: "every thing tending to establish *substantial* and *permanent order* in the affairs of a Country, to increase the total mass of industry and opulence, is ultimately beneficial to every part of it."

HAMILTON'S ACHIEVEMENT Largely owing to the skillful Hamilton, whom a student of the Federalist period called "the greatest administrative genius in America, and one of the greatest administrators of all time," the Treasury Department, which employed half or more of the civil servants at the time, was established on a basis of integrity and efficiency. The Revolutionary War debt was put on the way to retirement, a "Continental" became worth something after all (if only at a ratio of 100 to 1 in payments to the government), the credit of the government was secure, government securities sold at par, and foreign capital began to flow in once again. And prosperity, so elusive in the 1780s, began to flourish once again, although President Washington cautioned against attributing "to the Government what is due only to the goodness of Providence."

Still, the suspicion would not die that Hamilton's program was designed to promote a class and sectional interest, and some even thought a personal interest. There is, however, no evidence that Hamilton benefited personally in any way from his program, although Assistant Treasury Secretary William Duer, unbeknownst to Hamilton, did leak word of the funding and assumption message to favored friends in time for them to reap a speculative harvest from the rise in values. Duer himself later became involved in deals which landed him in prison.

There is no reason to believe that Hamilton's conscious aim was to benefit either a section or a class at the expense of the government. He was inclined toward a truly nationalist outlook. As a result of his early years in the islands he lacked the background of narrow localism that most of his contemporaries shared to some degree, although his failure to take that factor into full account was one of his weaknesses. Indeed he would have favored a much stronger central government, including a federal veto on state action, even a constitutional monarchy if that had been practicable. Hamilton believed that throughout history a minority of the strong dominated the weak. There was always a ruling group, perhaps military or aristocratic, and Hamilton had the wit to see now the rising power of commercial capitalism. He was in many ways a classic Whig who, like Britain's ruling oligarchy of the eighteenth century, favored government by the rich and well-born. The mass of the people, he once said, "are turbulent and changing; they seldom judge or determine right." And once, in his cups, he went further: "Your people, sir, is a great beast!" To tie the government closely to the rich and the well-born, then, was but to secure the interest of good government and to guard the public order against the potential turbulence which always haunted him.

Hamilton's achievement, however, was to tie more closely to the government those who were already on its side—and to overlook, or even antagonize, those who had their doubts. Hamilton never came to know the people of the small villages and farms, the people of the frontier. They were absent from his world, despite his own humble beginnings in the islands. And they, along with the planters of the South, would be at best only indirect beneficiaries of his programs. Below the Potomac the Hamiltonian vision excited little enthusiasm except in South Carolina, which had a large state debt to be assumed and a concentration of mercantile interests at Charleston. There was, in short, a vast number of people who were drawn into opposition to Hamilton's new engines of power. In part they were southern, in part backcountry, and in part a politically motivated faction opposing Hamilton in New York.

THE REPUBLICAN ALTERNATIVE

In this split over the Hamiltonian program lay the seeds of the first political parties of national scope. Hamilton became the embodiment of the party known as the Federalists; Madison and Jefferson became the leaders of those who took the name Republican and thereby implied that the Federalists really aimed at a monarchy. Parties were slow in developing, or at least in being acknowledged as legitimate. All the political philosophers of the age deplored the spirit of party or faction. The concept of a loyal opposition, of a two-party system as a positive good, was yet to be formulated. Parties, or factions, as eighteenth-century Englishmen and colonists knew them, were bodies of men bent upon self-aggrandizement through the favor of the government. They smelled of corruption. So it cannot be said that either side in the disagreement over national policy deliberately set out to create a party system, which indeed would not be firmly established nor widely accepted as a public good until the next century was more than a quarter spent.

But there were important differences of both philosophy and self-interest which simply would not dissolve. At the outset Madison, who had worked with Hamilton to build a national government, assumed leadership of Hamilton's opponents in the Congress. The states meant more to Madison than to Hamilton, who would as soon have seen a consolidated central government. And Madison, like Thomas Jefferson, was rooted in Virginia, where opposition to the funding schemes flourished. In December 1790 the Virginia Assembly bluntly protested Hamilton's funding schemes in a resolution drafted by Patrick Henry: "In an agricultural country like this . . . to erect, and concentrate, and perpetuate a large monied interest . . . must in the course of human events produce one or other of two evils, the prostration of agriculture at the feet of commerce, or a change in the present form of federal government, fatal to the existence of American liberty. . . . Your memorialists can find no clause in the Constitution authorizing Congress to assume the debts of the States!" To Hamilton this was "the first symptom of a spirit which must either be killed, or will kill the Constitution of the United States."

After the compromise which had assured the assumption of state debts Madison and Jefferson moved into ever more resolute opposition to Hamilton's policies: his move to place an excise tax on whiskey, which laid a burden especially on the trans-Appalachian farmers whose grain was best transported in liquid form; his proposal for the bank; and his report on manufactures. Against the last two both men raised constitutional objections. As the differences built, hostility between Jefferson and Hamilton grew and festered, to the distress of President Washington. Jefferson, the temperamentally shy and retiring secretary of state, then emerged as the leader of the opposition to Hamilton's policies; Madison continued to direct the opposition in Congress.

JEFFERSON'S AGRARIAN VIEW Thomas Jefferson, twelve years Hamilton's senior, was in most respects his opposite. In contrast to Hamilton, the careerist, the self-made aristocrat, Jefferson was to the manor born, his father a successful surveyor and land speculator, his mother a Randolph, from one of the First Families in Virginia. In contrast to Hamilton's ordered intensity, Jefferson conveyed a certain sense of aristocratic carelessness and a

Thomas Jefferson, in a portrait by Rembrandt Peale (1800).

breadth of cultivated interests that ranged perhaps more widely in science, the arts, and the humanities than those of any contemporary, even Franklin. Jefferson read or spoke seven languages. He was an architect of some distinction (Monticello, the Virginia Capitol, and the University of Virginia are monuments to his talent), a man who understood mathematics and engineering, an inventor, an agronomist. In his *Notes on Virginia* (1785) he displayed a knowledge of geography, paleontology, zoology, botany, and archeology. He collected paintings and sculpture. He knew music and practiced the violin, although some wit said only Patrick Henry played it worse.

Philosophically, Hamilton and Jefferson represented polar visions of the character of the Union in the first generation under the Constitution, and defined certain fundamental issues of American life which still echo two centuries later. Hamilton foresaw a diversified capitalistic economy, agriculture balanced by commerce and industry, and was thus the better prophet. Jefferson feared the growth of crowded cities divided into a capitalistic aristocracy on the one hand and a depraved proletariat on the other. Hamilton feared anarchy and loved order; Jefferson feared tyranny and loved liberty.

What Hamilton wanted for his country was a strong central government, run by the rich and well-born actively encouraging capitalistic enterprise. What Jefferson wanted was a republic of yeoman farmers: "Those who labor in the earth," he wrote, "are the chosen people of God, if ever he had a chosen people, whose breasts He has made His peculiar deposit for genuine and substantial virtue." Where Hamilton was the old-fashioned English Whig, Jefferson, who spent several years in France, was the enlightened *philosophe,* the natural radical and reformer who attacked the aristocratic relics of entail and primogeniture in Virginia; opposed an established church; proposed an elaborate plan for public schools; prepared a more humane criminal code; and was instrumental in eliminating slavery from the Old Northwest, although he kept the slaves he had inherited. On his tomb were finally recorded the achievements of which he was proudest: author of the Declaration of Independence and the Virginia Statute of Religious Freedom, and founder of the University of Virginia.

Jefferson set forth his vision of what America should be in his *Notes on Virginia*: "While we have land to labor then, let us never wish to see our citizens occupied at a work-bench, or twirling a distaff. . . . For the general operations of manufacture, let our work-shops remain in Europe. It is better to carry provisions and materials to work-men there, than bring them to the provisions and materials, and with them their manners and principles. . . . The mobs of great cities add just so much to the support of pure government, as sores do to the strength of the human body."

PARTY DISPUTES   The one thing that Jefferson and Hamilton had in common, it seemed, was their mutual enmity, which began with disagreement in the cabinet and soon became widely visible in a journalistic war of words between two editors with the curiously similar names of Fenno and Freneau. John Fenno's *Gazette of the United States,* founded in 1789, "to endear the General Government to the people," became virtually the official administration organ. It extolled Hamilton and his policies at every opportunity, and benefited from contracts for government printing. Philip Freneau, a poet and journalist, was enticed to Philadelphia from New York in 1791 to found the *National Gazette* and given a sinecure as translator for Jefferson's Department of State. Each man was compromised by his connection, but each loyally supported his benefactor out of real conviction.

In their quarrel Hamilton unwittingly identified Jefferson more and more in the public mind as the leader of the opposition to his policies; Madison was still a relatively obscure congressman whose central role in the Constitutional Convention was unknown. In the summer of 1791 Jefferson and Madison set out on a "botanizing" excursion up the Hudson, a vacation which many

Federalists feared was a cover for consultations with Gov. George Clinton, the Livingstons, and Aaron Burr, leaders of the faction in New York that opposed the aristocratic party of the De Lanceys, Van Rensselaers, and Philip Schuyler, Hamilton's father-in-law. While the significance of that single trip was blown out of proportion, there did ultimately arise an informal alliance of Jeffersonian Republicans in the south and New York which would become a constant if sometimes devisive feature of the party and its successor, the Democratic party.

Still, there was no opposition to Washington, who longed to end his exile from Mount Vernon and even began drafting a farewell address, but was urged by both Hamilton and Jefferson to continue in public life. He was the only man who could transcend party differences and hold things together with his unmatched prestige. In 1792 Washington was unanimously reelected, but in the scattering of second votes the Republican Clinton got fifty electoral votes to John Adams's seventy-seven.

Crises Foreign and Domestic

In Washington's second term the problems of foreign relations came to center stage, brought there by the consequences of the French Revolution, which had begun during the first months of Washington's presidency. Americans followed events in France with almost universal sympathy, up to a point. By the spring of 1792, though, the hopeful experiment in liberty, equality, and fraternity had transformed itself into a monster that plunged France into war with Austria and Prussia and began devouring its own children along with its enemies in the Terror of 1793–1794.

After the execution of King Louis XVI in January 1793, Great Britain entered into the coalition of monarchies at war with the French Republic. For the next twenty-two years Britain and France were at war, with only a brief respite, until the final defeat of French forces under Napoleon in 1815. The war presented Washington, just beginning his second term, with an awkward decision. By the treaty of 1778 the United States was a perpetual ally of France, obligated to defend her possessions in the West Indies. But Americans wanted no part of the war; on this much Hamilton and Jefferson could agree. Hamilton had a simple and direct answer to this problem: declare the alliance invalid because it was made with a government that no longer existed. Jefferson preferred to delay and use the alliance as a bargaining point with the British. But in the end Washington followed the advice of neither. Taking a middle course, on April 22, 1793, the president issued a neutrality proclamation that evaded even the word "neutrality." It simply declared the United States "friendly and impartial toward the belligerent powers" and warned American citizens that "aiding or abetting hostilities" or other unneutral acts might be prosecuted.

CITIZEN GENÊT At the same time, Washington accepted Jefferson's argument that the United States should recognize the new French government (becoming the first country to do so) and receive its new ambassador, Citizen Edmond Charles Genêt. Early in 1793 Citizen Genêt landed at Charleston, where he immediately organized a Jacobin Club, officially recognized in Paris by his fellow radicals. Along the route to Philadelphia the enthusiasm of his sympathizers gave Genêt an inflated notion of his potential, not that he needed much encouragement. In Charleston he began to authorize privateers to bring in British prizes, and in Philadelphia he continued the process. He intrigued with frontiersmen and land speculators, including George Rogers Clark, with an eye to an attack on Spanish Florida and Louisiana, and issued military commissions in an Armée du Mississippi and an Armée des Florides.

Genêt quickly became an embarrassment even to his Republican friends. Jefferson decided that the French minister had overreached himself when he violated a promise not to outfit a captured British ship as a privateer and sent out the *Little Sarah*, rechristened the *Petite Democrate*. When, finally, Genêt threatened in a moment of anger to appeal his cause directly to the American people over the head of their president, the cabinet unanimously agreed that he had to go and in August 1793 Washington demanded his recall. Meanwhile a new party of radicals had gained power in France and sent over its own minister, Citizen Fauchet, with a warrant for Genêt's arrest. Instead of returning to risk the guillotine, Genêt sought asylum, married the daughter of Governor Clinton, settled down as a country gentleman on the Hudson, and died years later an American citizen.

Genêt's foolishness and the growing excesses of the French radicals were fast cooling American support for their revolution. To Hamilton's followers it began to resemble their worst nightmares of democratic anarchy and infidelity. The French made it hard even for Republicans to retain sympathy, but they swallowed hard and made excuses. "The liberty of the whole earth was depending on the issue of the contest," the genteel Jefferson wrote, "and . . . rather than it should have failed, I would have seen half the earth devastated." Nor did the British make it easy for Federalists to rally to their side. Near the end of 1793 they informed the American government that they intended to occupy their northwest posts indefinitely and announced Orders in Council under which they seized the cargoes of American ships with provisions for or produce from the French islands.

Despite the offenses by both sides, the French and British causes polarized American opinion. In the contest, it seemed, one either had to be a Republican and support liberty, reason, and France, or become a Federalist and support order, faith, and Britain. And the division gave rise to some curious loyalties: slaveholding planters joined the yelps for Jacobin radicals who dispossessed aristocrats in France, and supported the protest against British seizures of New England ships; Massachusetts shippers still profited from the British trade and kept quiet. Boston, once a hotbed of revolution, became a bastion of Federalism.

JAY'S TREATY   Early in 1794 the Republican leaders in Congress were gaining support for commercial retaliation to bring the British to their senses, when the British gave Washington a timely opening for a settlement. They announced abandonment of the Orders under which American brigs and schooners were being seized, and on April 16, 1794, Washington named Chief Justice John Jay as a special envoy to Great Britain. Jay left with instructions to settle all major issues: to get the British out of the

John Jay, the first Chief Justice of the United States.

A 1794 watercolor of Fort Detroit, a major center of Indian trade which the British agreed to evacuate in Jay's Treaty.

western posts, and to secure reparations for the losses of American shippers, compensation for slaves carried away in 1783, and a commercial treaty which would legalize American commerce with the British West Indies.

Jay entered the negotiations with his bargaining power compromised by both Federalists and Republicans. In Philadelphia Hamilton indiscreetly told the British minister that the United States had no intention of joining the Armed Neutrality recently formed by Scandinavian countries to uphold neutral rights. In Paris the new American minister, James Monroe, spoke before the National Assembly and embraced both its president and its revolution. The British in turn demanded from Jay greater assurances that America would keep neutral.

To win his objectives, Jay was obliged to concede the British definition of neutral rights. He accepted the principles that naval stores were contraband, that provisions could not go in neutral ships to enemy ports, and the "Rule of 1756" by which trade with enemy colonies prohibited in peacetime could not be opened in wartime. Britain also gained most-favored-nation treatment in American commerce and a promise that French privateers would not be outfitted in American ports. Finally, Jay conceded that the old American debts to British merchants would be adjudicated and paid by the American government. In return for these concessions he won three important points: British evacuation of the northwest posts by 1796, reparations for the seizures of American ships and cargoes in 1793–1794, and legalization of trade with the British West Indies. But the last of these (Article XII) was so hedged with restrictions that the Senate eventually struck it from the treaty.

A public outcry of rage greeted the terms of the treaty when they were leaked and published in the Philadelphia *Aurora.* Even Federalist shippers, ready for settlement on almost any terms, were disappointed at the limitations on their privileges in the West Indies. But much of the outcry was simply expression of disappointment by Republican partisans who sought an escalation of conflict with "perfidious Albion." Some of it was the outrage of Virginia planters at the concession on debts to British merchants and the failure to get reparations for lost slaves. Given the limited enthusiasm of Federalists—Washington himself wrestled with doubts over the treaty—Jay remarked he could travel across the country by the light of his burning effigies. Yet the Senate debated the treaty in secret, and in the end quiet counsels of moderation prevailed. Without a single vote to spare, Jay's Treaty got the necessary two-thirds majority on June 24, 1795, with Article XII (the provision regarding the West Indies) expunged.

Washington still hesitated but finally signed the treaty as the best he was likely to get and out of fear that a refusal would throw the United States into the role of a French satellite. In the House opponents went so far as to demand that the president produce all papers relevant to the treaty, but the president refused on the grounds that treaty approval was solely the business of the Senate. He thereby set an important precedent of executive privilege (a term not used at the time), and the House finally relented, supplying the money to fund the treaty on a close vote.

THE FRONTIER STIRS   Other events also had an important bearing on Jay's Treaty, adding force to its settlement of the Canadian frontier and strengthening Spain's conviction that she too needed to reach a settlement of long-festering problems along America's southwestern frontier. While Jay was haggling in London, frontier conflict with Indians was moving toward a temporary resolution. Early in 1790 the northwestern tribes routed an American army under Gen. Josiah Harmar along the Maumee River. The next year Gen. Arthur St. Clair, governor of the Northwest Territory, gathered an army of militiamen and "men collected from the streets . . . from the stews and brothels of the cities," and went out to meet an even worse disaster. On November 4, 1791, the Indians surprised the American camp along the Wabash, singled out the officers, few of whom survived, and threw the militia into panic. Only about half of the men escaped unhurt. St. Clair himself, disabled by gout and propped up with pillows in a wagon to watch the battle, barely escaped. The de-

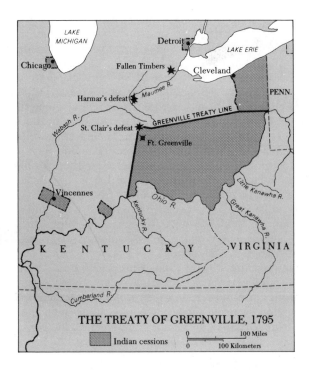

THE TREATY OF GREENVILLE, 1795

Indian cessions

0   100 Miles
0   100 Kilometers

feat resulted in the first congressional investigating committee, which finally put the blame on contractors who failed to supply the army properly.

Conditions along the northwestern frontier, on down into Kentucky, remained unsettled for three more years. Finally Washington named General Wayne, known as "Mad Anthony" since the storming of Stony Point in 1779, to head another expedition. In the fall of 1793 Wayne marched into Indian country with some 2,600 men, built Fort Greenville, and with reinforcements from Kentucky went on the offensive in 1794. On August, 4, 1794, the Indians, reinforced by some Canadian militia, attacked Wayne's force at the Battle of Fallen Timbers, but this time the Americans were ready and repulsed them with heavy losses, after which American detachments laid waste their fields and villages. Dispersed and decimated, they finally agreed to the Treaty of Greenville, signed in August 1795. In the treaty, at the cost of a $10,000 annuity, the United States bought from twelve tribes the rights to the southeastern quarter of the Northwest Territory (now Ohio and Indiana) and enclaves at the sites of Vincennes, Detroit, and Chicago.

THE WHISKEY REBELLION Wayne's forces were still mopping up after the Battle of Fallen Timbers when the administration resolved on another show of strength in the backcountry against the so-called Whiskey Rebellion. Hamilton's excise tax on strong drink, levied in 1791, had excited strong feeling along the frontier since it taxed a staple crop of the very people who had the least to gain from Hamilton's program. Their grain was more easily transported to market in concentrated liquid form than in bulk. The frontiersmen considered the tax another part of Hamilton's scheme to pick the pockets of the poor to enrich fat speculators. All through the backcountry, from Georgia to Pennsylvania and beyond, the tax gave rise to resistance and evasion. In the summer of 1794 the rumblings of discontent broke into open rebellion in the four western counties of Pennsylvania, where vigilantes organized to terrorize revenuers and taxpayers. They blew up the stills of those who paid the tax, robbed the mails, stopped court proceedings, and threatened an assault on Pittsburgh. On August 7, 1794, President Washington issued a proclamation ordering them home and calling out 12,900 militiamen from Virginia, Maryland, Pennsylvania, and New Jersey.

Washington as commander-in-chief reviews the troops mobilized to quell the Whiskey Rebellion in 1794.

Getting no response from the "Whiskey Boys," he issued a proclamation on September 24 for suppression of the rebellion.

Under the command of Gen. Henry Lee, a force larger than any Washington had ever commanded in the Revolution marched out from Harrisburg across the Alleghenies with Hamilton in their midst, itching to smite the insurgents. To his disappointment the rebels vaporized like corn mash when the heat was applied, and the troops met with little more opposition than a few Liberty Poles. By dint of great effort and much marching they finally rounded up twenty prisoners whom they paraded down Market Street in Philadelphia and clapped into prison. Eventually two of these were found guilty of treason, but were pardoned by Washington on the grounds that one was a "simpleton" and the other "insane." The government had made its point and gained "reputation and strength," according to Hamilton, by suppressing a rebellion which, according to Jefferson, "could never be found," but it was at the cost of creating or confirming new numbers of Republicans who scored heavily in the next Pennsylvania elections. Nor was it the end of whiskey rebellions, which continued in an unending war of wits between moonshiners and revenuers down to the day of twentieth-century rum-runners in hopped-up stock cars.

PINCKNEY'S TREATY   While these stirring events were transpiring in the Keystone State, Spain was suffering some setbacks to her schemes farther south. Spanish intrigues among the Creeks, Choctaws, Chickasaws, and Cherokees were keeping up the same turmoil the British fomented along the Ohio. Washington had sought to buy peace with $100,000 and a commission as brigadier-general to the Creek chief, Alexander McGillivray, the half-blooded son of a Scottish trader, but it was to no avail. In 1793, therefore, some settlers from East Tennessee took it upon themselves to teach the proud Cherokees a lesson by leveling a few of their villages, and in 1794 Tennesseans from around Nashville smote them again, burning and killing without pity.

The collapse of Spain's own designs in the west combined with Britain's concessions in the north to give some second thoughts to the Spanish, who were preparing to make peace with the French and switch sides in the European war. Among the more agreeable fruits of Jay's talks, therefore, were new parleys with the Spanish government, culminating in the Treaty of San Lorenzo (1795) in which Spain conceded every substantial point at issue. United States Minister Thomas Pinckney won acceptance of a boundary at the Thirty-first Parallel, free navigation of the

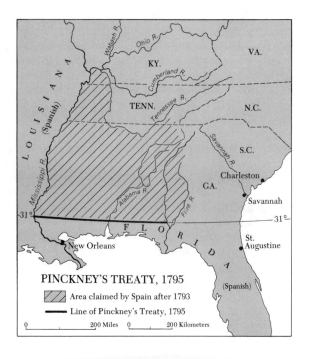

Mississippi, the right to deposit goods at New Orleans for three years with promise of renewal, a commission to settle American claims against Spain, and a promise on each side to refrain from inciting Indian attacks on the other. Ratification of the Pinckney Treaty ran into no opposition at all.

Now that Jay and Pinckney had settled things with Britain and Spain, and General Wayne in the Northwest and the Tennessee settlers to the south had smashed the Indians, the West was open for a renewed surge of settlers. New lands, ceded by the Indians in the Treaty of Greenville, revealed Congress once again divided on land policy. There were two basic viewpoints on the matter, one that the public domain should serve mainly as a source of revenue, the other that it was more important to accommodate settlers with low prices, maybe free land, and get the country settled. In the long run the evolution of policy would be from the first toward the second viewpoint, but for the time being the government's need for revenue took priority.

Opinions on land policy, like other issues, separated Federalists from Republicans. Federalists involved in speculation might prefer lower land prices, but the more influential Federalists like Hamilton and Jay preferred to build the population of the eastern states first, lest the East lose political influence and lose a labor force important to the future growth of manufactures. Men of their persuasion favored high land prices to enrich the treasury, sale of relatively large parcels of land to speculators rather than small amounts to actual settlers, and the development of compact settlements. In addition to his other reports, Hamilton had put out one on the public lands in which he emphasized the need for governmental revenues. Jefferson and Madison were prepared reluctantly to go along for the sake of reducing the national debt, but Jefferson expressed the hope for a plan by which the lands could be more readily settled. In any case, he suggested, frontiersmen would do as they had done before: "They will settle the lands in spite of everybody." The Daniel Boones of the West, always moving out beyond the settlers and surveyors, were already proving him right.

But for the time Federalist policy prevailed. In the Land Act of 1796 Congress resolved to extend the rectangular surveys ordained in 1785, but it doubled the price to $2 per acre, with only a year in which to complete payment. Half the townships would go in 640-acre sections, making the minimum cost $1,280, and alternate townships would be sold in blocks of eight sections, or 5,120 acres, making the minimum cost $10,240. Either was beyond the means of most ordinary settlers, and a bit much even for speculators, who could still pick up state lands at lower prices. By 1800 government land offices had sold fewer than

A newly cleared American farm.

50,000 acres under the act. Continuing pressures from the West led to the Land Act of 1800, which reduced the minimum sale to 320 acres and spread the payments over four years. Thus with a down payment of $160 one could get a farm. All lands went for the minimum price if they did not sell at auction within three weeks. Under the Land Act of 1804 the minimum unit was reduced to 160 acres, which became the traditional homestead, and the price per acre went down to $1.64.

WASHINGTON'S FAREWELL   By 1796 President Washington had decided that two terms in office were enough. Tired of the political quarrels and the venom of the partisan press, he was ready to retire once and for all to Mount Vernon. He would leave behind a formidable record of achievement: the organization of a national government with demonstrated power, a secure national credit, the recovery of territory from Britain and Spain, a stable northwestern frontier, and the admission of three new states: Vermont (1791), Kentucky (1792), and Tennessee (1796). With the help of Jay and especially Hamilton, Washington set about preparing a valedictory address, using a draft prepared by Madison four years before.

Washington's Farewell Address, dated September 17, 1796, was not delivered as a speech. It was first published in the Philadelphia *Daily American Advertiser* two days later. It stated first his resolve to decline being considered for a third term. After that, most of the message dwelled on domestic policy, and particularly on the need for unity among the American people in backing their new government. Washington decried the spirit of sectionalism. "In contemplating the causes which may disturb our union," he wrote in one prescient passage, "it occurs as a matter of serious concern that any ground should have been furnished for characterizing parties by geographical discriminations—*Northern* and *Southern*, *Atlantic* and *Western*—whence designing men may endeavor to excite a belief that there is a real difference of local interests and views." He decried as strongly the spirit of party, while acknowledging a body of opinion that parties were "useful checks upon the administration of the government, and serve to keep alive the spirit of liberty." From the natural tendency of men there would always be enough spirit of party, however, to serve that purpose. The danger was partisan excess: "A fire not to be quenched, it demands a uniform vigilance to prevent its bursting into a flame, lest, instead of warming, it should consume."

In foreign relations, he said, America should show "good faith

After two terms as president Washington was anxious to return with his family to his beloved Mount Vernon estate.

and justice toward all nations" and avoid either "an habitual hatred or an habitual fondness" for other countries. Europe, he noted, "has a set of primary interests which to us have none or a very remote relation. Hence she must be engaged in frequent controversies, the causes of which are essentially foreign to our concerns." The United States should keep clear of those quarrels. It was, moreover, "our true policy to steer clear of permanent alliances with any portion of the foreign world." A key word here is "permanent." Washington enjoined against any further permanent arrangements like that with France, still technically in effect. He did not speak of "entangling alliances"—that phrase would be used by Thomas Jefferson in his first inaugural address—and in fact specifically advised that "we may safely trust to temporary alliances for extraordinary emergencies."

Washington himself had not escaped the "baneful effects" of the party spirit, for during his second term the Republican press came to link him with the Federalist partisans. For the first time in his long career Washington was subjected to sustained, and often scurrilous, criticism. According to the editor of the Philadelphia *Aurora*, the president was "a man in his political dotage" and "a supercilious tyrant." Washington never responded to such abuse in public but in private he went into towering rages.

The effect of such abuse was to hasten his resolve to retire. On the eve of that event the *Aurora* proclaimed that "this day ought to be a Jubilee in the United States. . . . If ever a nation was debauched by a man, the American Nation has been debauched by Washington."

THE ADAMS YEARS

With Washington out of the race, the United States had its first partisan election for president. The logical choice of the Federalists would have been Washington's protégé Hamilton, the chief architect of their programs. But like many a later presidential candidate, Hamilton was not "available," however willing. His policies had left scars and made enemies. Nor did he suffer fools gladly, a common affliction of Federalist leaders, including the man on whom the choice fell. In Philadelphia, a caucus of Federalist congressmen chose John Adams as heir apparent with Thomas Pinckney of South Carolina, fresh from his

The Providential Detection. *An anti-Republican cartoon shows the American eagle arriving just in time to stop Thomas Jefferson from burning the Constitution on the "Altar to Gallic Despotism."*

triumph in Spain, as nominee for vice-president. As expected, the Republicans drafted Jefferson and added geographical balance to the ticket with Aaron Burr of New York, an ally of Clinton.

The rising strength of the Republicans, largely due to the smouldering resentment of Jay's Treaty, very nearly swept Jefferson into office, and perhaps would have but for the public appeals of the French ambassador for his election—an action which, like the indiscretions of Citizen Genêt, backfired. Then, despite a Federalist majority among the electors, Alexander Hamilton thought up an impulsive scheme which very nearly threw the election away after all. Between Hamilton and Adams there had been no love lost since the Revolution, when Adams had joined the movement to remove Hamilton's father-in-law, General Schuyler, from command of the Saratoga campaign. Thomas Pinckney, Hamilton thought, would be more subject to influence than the strong-minded Adams. He therefore sought to have South Carolina Federalists withhold a few votes from Adams and bring Pinckney in first. The Carolinians more than cooperated—they divided their vote between Pinckney and Jefferson—but New Englanders got wind of the scheme and dropped Pinckney. The upshot of Hamilton's intrigue was to cut Pinckney out of both offices and elect Jefferson vice-president with sixty-eight votes, second to Adams's seventy-one.

Adams had behind him a distinguished career as a Massachusetts lawyer, a leader in the revolutionary movement and the Continental Congress, a diplomat in France, Holland, and Britain, and as vice-president. In two treatises on politics, the three-volume *Defense of the Constitution of Government of the United States* (1787–1788) and the less formidable *Discourse on Davila°* (1790), he had formally committed to paper a political philosophy that put him somewhere between Jefferson and Hamilton. He shared neither the one's faith in the common people nor the other's fondness for an aristocracy of "paper wealth." He favored the classic mixture of aristocratic, democratic, and monarchical elements, though his use of "monarchical" interchangeably with "executive" exposed him to the attacks of Republicans who saw a monarchist in every Federalist. At times in his manner and appearance Adams was made out by his enemies to be a pompous ass, but his fondness for titles and protocol arose from a reasoned purpose to exploit men's "thirst for distinction." He was always haunted by a feeling that he was never

°An Italian historian.

John Adams.

properly appreciated— and he may have been right. He tried to play the role of disinterested executive which he outlined in his philosophy. And on the overriding issue of his administration, war and peace, he kept his head when others about him were losing theirs—probably at the cost of his reelection.

WAR WITH FRANCE   Adams inherited from Washington his cabinet —the precedent of changing personnel with each new administration had not yet been set—and with them a party division, for three of the department heads looked to Hamilton for counsel: Timothy Pickering at State, Oliver Wolcott at the Treasury, and Joseph McHenry at the War Department. Adams also inherited a menacing quarrel with France, a by-product of the Jay Treaty. When Jay accepted the British position that food supplies and naval stores—as well as war matériel—were contraband subject to seizure, the French reasoned that American cargoes in the British trade were subject to the same interpretation and loosed their corsairs in the West Indies with even more devastating effect than the British had in 1793–1794. By the time of Adams's inauguration in 1797 the French had plundered some 300 American ships, and had broken diplomatic relations. As ambassador to Paris, James Monroe had become so pro-French and so hostile to the Jay Treaty that Washington had felt impelled to remove him for his indiscretions. France then had refused to accept Monroe's replacement, Charles Cotesworth Pinckney, and ordered him out of the country.

Adams immediately acted to restore relations in the face of an outcry for war from the "High Federalists," including Secretary of State Pickering. Hamilton agreed with Adams on this point and approved his last-ditch effort for a settlement. In October 1797 C. C. Pinckney returned to Paris with John Marshall and Elbridge Gerry (a Massachusetts Republican) for further negotiations. After long, nagging delays, the three commissioners were accosted by three French counterparts (whom Adams labeled X, Y, and Z in his report to Congress), agents of Foreign Minister Talleyrand, a past master of the diplomatic shakedown. The three delicately let it be known that negotiations could begin only if there were a loan of $12 million, a bribe of $250,000 to the five directors then heading the government, and suitable apologies for remarks recently made in Adams's message to Congress.

Such bribes were common eighteenth-century diplomatic practice—Washington himself had bribed a Creek chieftain and ransomed American sailors from Algerian pirates, each at a cost of $100,000—but Talleyrand's price was high merely for a promise to negotiate. The answer, according to the commissioners' report, was "no, no, not a sixpence." When the XYZ Affair broke in Congress and the public press, this was translated into the more stirring slogan first offered as a banquet toast by Robert Goodloe Harper: "Millions for defense but not one cent for tribute." And the expressions of hostility toward France rose

A cartoon indicating the anti-French feeling generated by the XYZ Affair. The three American ministers at left reject the "Paris Monster's" demand for money.

to a crescendo—even the most partisan Republicans were hard put to make any more excuses, and many of them joined a cry for war. But Adams resisted a formal declaration of war; the French would have to bear the onus for that. Congress, however, authorized the capture of armed French ships, suspended commerce with France, and renounced the alliance of 1778, which was already a dead letter.

In 1798 George Logan, a Pennsylvania Quaker, visited Paris at his own expense, hoping to head off war. He did secure the release of some American seamen and won assurances that an American minister would be welcomed. The fruits of his mission, otherwise, were widespread denunciation and passage of the Logan Act (1799), which still forbids private citizens to negotiate with foreign governments without official authorization.

Adams proceeded to strengthen American defenses. An American navy had ceased to exist at the end of the Revolution. Except for revenue cutters of the Treasury Department, no armed ships were available when Algerian brigands began to war on American commerce in 1794. As a result Congress had authorized the arming of six ships. These were incomplete in 1796 when Washington bought peace with the Algerians, but Congress allowed work on three to continue: the *Constitution*, the *United States*, and the *Constellation*, all completed in 1797. In 1798 Congress authorized a new Department of the Navy. By the end of 1798 the number of naval ships had increased to twenty and by the end of 1799 to thirty-three. But before the end of 1798 an undeclared naval war had begun in the West Indies with the French capture of the American schooner *Retaliation* off Guadeloupe.

While the naval war went on, a new army was authorized in 1798 as a 10,000-man force to serve three years. Adams called Washington from retirement to be its commander, agreeing to Washington's condition that he name his three chief subordinates. Washington sent in the names of Hamilton, Charles C. Pinckney, and Henry Knox. In the old army the three ranked in precisely the opposite order, but Washington insisted that Hamilton be his second in command. Adams relented, but resented the slight to his authority as commander-in-chief. The rift among Federalists thus widened further. Because of Washington's age, the choice meant that Hamilton would command the army in the field, if it ever took the field. But recruitment went slowly until well into 1799, by which time all fear of French invasion was dispelled. Hamilton continued to dream of imperial glory, though, planning the seizure of Louisiana and the Floridas to keep them out of French hands, and even the invasion of South America, but these remained Hamilton's dreams.

Peace overtures began to come from Talleyrand by the autumn of 1798, before the naval war was fully under way. Adams decided to act on the information and took it upon himself, without consulting the cabinet, to name the American minister to the Netherlands, William Vans Murray, special envoy to Paris. The Hamiltonians, infected with a virulent attack of war fever, fought the nomination but finally compromised, in face of Adams's threat to resign, on a commission of three. After a long delay they left late in 1799 and arrived to find themselves confronting a new government under First Consul Napoleon Bonaparte. By the Convention of 1800 they got the best terms they could from the triumphant Napoleon. In return for giving up all claims of indemnity for American losses they got the suspension of the French alliance and the end of the quasi-war. The Senate ratified, contingent upon outright abrogation of the alliance, and the agreement became effective on December 21, 1801.

THE WAR AT HOME The real purpose of the French crisis all along, the more ardent Republicans suspected, was to create an excuse to put down the domestic opposition. The Alien and Sedition Acts of 1798 lent credence to their suspicions. These four measures, passed in the wave of patriotic war fever, limited freedom of speech and the press, and the liberty of aliens. Proposed by the High Federalists in Congress, they did not originate with Adams but had his blessing. Three of the four acts reflected hostility to foreigners, especially the French and Irish, a large number of whom had become active Republicans and were suspected of revolutionary intent. The Naturalization Act lengthened from five to fourteen years the residence requirement for citizenship. The Alien Act empowered the president to expel "dangerous" aliens on pain of imprisonment. The Alien Enemy Act authorized the president in time of declared war to expel or imprison enemy aliens at will. Finally, the Sedition Act defined as a high misdemeanor any combination or conspiracy against legal measures of the government, including interference with federal officers and insurrection or riot. What is more, the law forbade writing, publishing, or speaking anything of "a false, scandalous and malicious" nature against the government or any of its officers.

Considering what Federalists and Republicans said about each other, the act, applied rigorously, could have caused the impris-

Republican Rep. Matthew Lyon and the Connecticut Federalist Roger Griswald go at each other on the floor of the House (1798). Lyon soon became a target of the Sedition Act.

onment of nearly the whole government. But the purpose was transparently partisan, designed to punish Republicans whom Federalists could scarcely distinguish from Jacobins and traitors. To be sure, partisan Republican journalists were resorting to scandalous lies and misrepresentations, but so were Federalists; it was a time when both sides seemed afflicted with paranoia. But the fifteen indictments brought, with ten convictions, were all directed at Republicans and some for trivial matters. In the very first case one unfortunate was fined $100 for wishing out loud that the wad of a salute cannon might hit President Adams in his rear. The most conspicuous targets of prosecution were Republican editors and a congressman, Matthew Lyon of Vermont, a rough-and-tumble Irishman who published censures of Adams's "continual grasp for power" and "unbounded thirst for ridiculous pomp, foolish adulation, and selfish avarice." For such libels Lyon got four months and a fine of $1,000, but from his cell he continued to write articles and letters for the Republican papers. The few convictions under the act only created martyrs to the cause of freedom of speech and the press, and exposed the vindictiveness of Federalist judges.

Lyon and the others based a defense on the unconstitutionality of the Sedition Act, but Federalist judges were scarcely inclined to entertain such notions. It ran against the Republican grain, anyway, to have federal courts assume the authority to declare laws unconstitutional. To offset the Alien and Sedition Acts, therefore, Jefferson and Madison conferred and brought forth drafts of what came to be known as the Kentucky and Virginia Resolutions. These passed the legislatures of the two states in November and December 1798, while further Kentucky Resolutions, adopted in November 1799, responded to counterresolutions from northern states. These resolutions, much alike in their arguments, denounced the Alien and Sedition Acts as unconstitutional and advanced what came to be known as the state-compact theory. Since the Constitution arose as a compact among the states, the resolutions argued, it followed logically that the states should assume the right to say when Congress had exceeded its powers. The Virginia Resolutions, drafted by Madison, declared that states "have the right and are in duty bound to interpose for arresting the progress of the evil." The second set of Kentucky Resolutions, in restating the states' right to judge violations of the Constitution, added: "That a nullification of those sovereignties, of all unauthorized acts done under color of that instrument, is the rightful remedy."

The doctrines of interposition and nullification, revised and edited by later theorists, were destined to be used for causes unforeseen by the authors of the Kentucky and Virginia Resolutions. (Years later Madison would disclaim the doctrine of nullification as developed by John C. Calhoun, but his own doctrine of "interposition" would resurface as late as the 1950s as a device to oppose racial integration.) At the time, it seems, both men intended the resolutions to serve chiefly as propaganda, the opening guns in the political campaign of 1800. Neither Kentucky nor Virginia took steps to nullify or interpose its authority against enforcement of the Alien and Sedition Acts. Instead both called upon the other states to help them win a repeal. Jefferson counseled against any thought of violence, which was "not the kind of opposition the American people will permit." He assured a fellow Virginian that "the reign of witches" would soon end, that it would be discredited by the arrival of the tax collector more than anything else.

In 1798 Congress had imposed a direct tax on houses, land, and slaves. The Alien and Sedition Acts touched comparatively few individuals, but the tax reached every property holder in the country. In eastern Pennsylvania the general discontent with the tax reached the stage of armed resistance in Fries's Rebellion, an incident that scarcely deserves so impressive a name. John Fries, a Pennsylvania Dutch auctioneer, had led a group of armed men to force the release of two tax evaders imprisoned at Bethlehem.

To suppress this "insurrection" President Adams sent army regulars and militiamen into Northampton County. But like the Whiskey Rebellion five years before, the insurrection evaporated. The soldiers found not a rebellion but John Fries conducting an auction. He was arrested and brought to trial with two others on inflated charges of treason. The three men were found guilty twice, a second trial having been granted on appeal, and twice sentenced to hang. President Adams, however, decided that the men had not committed treason and granted them a pardon along with a general pardon to all participants in the affair.

REPUBLICAN VICTORY   Thus as the presidential election of 1800 approached, grievances were mounting against Federalist policies: taxation to support an army that had little to do but chase Pennsylvania farmers; the Alien and Sedition Acts, which cast the Republicans in the role of defending liberty; the lingering fears of "monarchism"; the hostilities aroused by Hamilton's programs; the suppression of the Whiskey Rebellion; and Jay's Treaty. When Adams decided for peace in 1800, he probably doomed his one chance for reelection: a wave of patriotic war fever with a united party behind him. His decision gained him much goodwill among the people at large, but left the Hamiltonians unreconciled and his party divided. In May 1800 the Federalists summoned enough unity to name as their candidates Adams and C. C. Pinckney, brother of Thomas Pinckney, who ran in 1796; they agreed to cast all their electoral votes for both. But the Hamiltonians continued to snipe at Adams and his policies, and soon after his renomination Adams removed two of them from his cabinet. Hamilton struck back with a pamphlet questioning Adams's fitness to be president, citing his "disgusting egotism." Intended for private distribution among Federalist leaders, the pamphlet reached the hands of Aaron Burr, who put it in circulation.

Jefferson and Burr, as the Republican candidates, once again represented the alliance of Virginia and New York. Jefferson, perhaps even more than Adams, became the target of villification as a Jacobin and an atheist. His election, Americans were warned, would bring "dwellings in flames, hoary hairs bathed in blood, female chastity violated . . . children writhing on the pike and halberd." Jefferson kept quiet, refused to answer the attacks, and directed the campaign by mail from his home at Monticello. He was advanced as the farmers' friend, the champion of states' rights, frugal government, liberty, and peace.

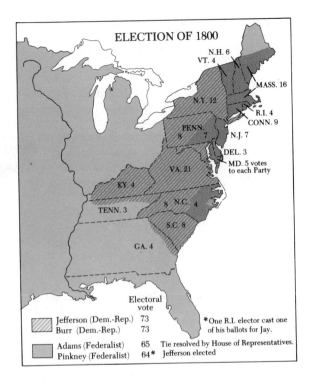

ELECTION OF 1800

N.H. 6
VT. 4
MASS. 16
N.Y. 12
R.I. 4
CONN. 9
PENN.
8   7
N.J. 7
DEL. 3
MD. 5 votes
to each Party
VA. 21
KY. 4
N.C. 4
TENN. 3   8
S.C. 8
GA. 4

Electoral
vote

Jefferson (Dem.-Rep.)   73   *One R.I. elector cast one
Burr (Dem.-Rep.)   73   of his ballots for Jay.

Adams (Federalist)   65   Tie resolved by House of Representatives.
Pinkney (Federalist)   64*   Jefferson elected

Adams proved more popular than his party, whose candidates generally fared worse than the president, but the Republicans edged him out by seventy-three electoral votes to sixty-five. The decisive states were New York and South Carolina, either of which might have given the victory to Adams. But in New York Burr's organization by vigorous activity won control of the legislature, which cast the electoral votes. In South Carolina, Charles Pinckney (cousin to the Federalist Pinckneys) won over the legislature by well-placed promises of Republican patronage. Still, the result was not final, for Jefferson and Burr had tied with seventy-three votes each, and the choice of the president was thrown into the House of Representatives, where Federalist diehards tried vainly to give the election to Burr. This was too much for Hamilton, who opposed Jefferson but held a much lower opinion of Burr. Burr refused to assent to the Federalist movement, but neither would he renounce it. Eventually the deadlock was broken when a confidant of Jefferson assured a Delaware congressman that Jefferson would refrain from wholesale removals of Federalists and uphold the new fiscal system. The representative resolved to vote for Jefferson, and several other

Federalists agreed simply to cast blank ballots, permitting Jefferson to win without any of them actually having to vote for him.

Before the Federalists relinquished power on March 4, 1801, their "lame duck" Congress passed the Judiciary Act of 1801. This act provided that the next vacancy on the Supreme Court should not be filled, created sixteen Circuit Courts with a new judge for each, and increased the number of attorneys, clerks, and marshals. Before he left office Adams named John Marshall to the vacant office of Chief Justice and appointed good Federalists to all the new positions, including forty-two justices of the peace for the new District of Columbia. The Federalists, defeated and destined never to regain national power, had in the words of Jefferson "retired into the judiciary as a stronghold."

FURTHER READING

The best introduction to the early Federalists remains John C. Miller's *The Federalist Era, 1789–1800* (1960).° Where Miller stresses narrative detail, more recent works analyze the ideological debates among the nation's first leaders. Richard Buel, Jr.'s *Securing the Revolution: Ideology in American Politics, 1789–1815* (1974),° Joyce Appleby's *Capitalism and a New Social Order* (1984), and Drew McCoy's *The Elusive Republic: Political Economy in Jeffersonian America* (1982)° trace the persistence and transformation of ideas first fostered during the Revolutionary crisis. John F. Hoadley's *Origins of American Political Parties, 1789–1803* (1986) provides a recent look at a subject limned by Joseph Charles's *The Origins of the American Party System* (1956) and Richard Hofstadter's *The Idea of a Party System* (1969).

The 1790s may also be understood through the views and behavior of national leaders. Among recent studies of Alexander Hamilton are Forrest McDonald's *Alexander Hamilton: A Biography* (1979)° and Gerald Stourzh's *Alexander Hamilton and the Idea of Republican Government* (1970). For the nation's first president, consult the two volumes by James T. Flexner, *George Washington and the New Nation, 1783–1793* (1970) and *George Washington: Anguish and Farewell, 1793–1799* (1972). Forrest McDonald's *The Presidency of George Washington* (1974) and John R. Alden's *George Washington: A Biography* (1984)° are also helpful. The second president is handled in Stephen G. Kurtz's *The Presidency of John Adams: The Collapse of Federalism, 1795–1800* (1957). The opposition viewpoint is the subject of Lance Banning's *The Jeffersonian Persuasion: Evolution of a Party Ideology* (1978).°

Federalist foreign policy is explored in Jerald A. Combs's *The Jay Treaty* (1970), William C. Stinchcombe's *The XYZ Affair* (1980), and

°These books are available in paperback editions.

Felix Gilbert's *To the Farewell Address: Ideas of Early American Foreign Policy* (1961).° Albert H. Bowman's *The Struggle for Neutrality* (1974), on Franco-American relations, is more interpretive.

For specific domestic issues, see Thomas Slaughter's *The Whiskey Rebellion* (1986) and Harry Ammon's *The Genet Mission* (1973).° Patricia Watlington's *The Partisan Spirit* (1972) examines the Kentucky Resolutions. The treatment of Indians in the old Northwest is explored in Richard H. Kohn's *Eagle and Sword: The Federalists and the Creation of the Military Establishment in America, 1783–1802* (1975). For the Alien and Sedition Acts, consult James Morton Smith's *Freedom's Fetters: The Alien and Sedition Laws and American Civil Liberties* (1956) and Leonard W. Levy's *Legacy of Suppression: Freedom of Speech and Press in Early American History* (1960). Daniel Sisson's *The American Revolution of 1800* (1974) is useful on that important election.

9

REPUBLICANISM: JEFFERSON AND MADISON

On March 4, 1801, Thomas Jefferson became the first president to be inaugurated in the new Federal City, Washington, District of Columbia. The location of the city on the Potomac had been the fruit of Jefferson's and Madison's compromise with Hamilton on the assumption of state debts. Choice of the site had been entrusted to President Washington, who picked a location upstream from his home at Mount Vernon. In 1791 Maj. Pierre L'Enfant, a French engineer who had served in the Revolution, drew up the original plan for the district. The design called for a gridwork of parallel streets overlaid with diagonal avenues which radiated from various centers, most conspicuously Jenkins's Hill (site of the Capitol) and the Executive Mansion, which faced each other along the length of Pennsylvania Avenue. L'Enfant also planned a third focus for the site of the Supreme Court, symbolizing the three branches of government, but that part of the plan was later abandoned, and the Court long occupied a room in the Capitol basement.

Work progressed on the public buildings and the city during the 1790s, and President Adams moved into his new home in September 1800. His wife Abigail arrived at the "great castle" in October. It was "in a beautiful situation" with a view of the Potomac and Virginia, but all the rooms were new and unfinished. By November the Adams family had to keep thirteen fires daily, she said, "or sleep in wet and damp places." Nearby Georgetown, D.C., where Abigail was obliged to market, was "the very

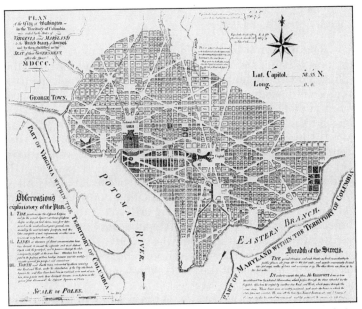

This Plan of the City of Washington *(1800) shows L'Enfant's detailed gridwork pattern of "Grand Avenues and Streets."*

dirtyest hole . . . for a place of any trade, or respectability of inhabitants."

When Jefferson took office, Washington was still an unprepossessing array of buildings around two centers, Capitol Hill and the Executive Mansion. Between them was a swampy wilderness traversed by the Tiber River and by Pennsylvania Avenue, still full of stumps and mud holes, but with a stone walkway which offered a vantage from which to shoot ducks, snipe, partridge, and, after rains, the perch in the Tiber River. The Congress, having met in eight different towns and cities since 1774, had at last found a permanent home, but as yet enjoyed few amenities. There were only a few sad houses, "most of them small miserable huts," according to one resident. To a French acquaintance one senator wrote: "We lack here only houses, wine cellars, learned men, amiable women, and other trifles to make our city perfect . . . it is the best city in the world to live in—in the future." There were two places of amusement, one a racetrack, the other a theater filled with "tobacco smoke, whiskey breaths, and other stenches, mixed up with the effluvia of stables, and miasmas of the canal." Practically deserted much of the year, the town came to life only when Congress assembled.

JEFFERSON IN OFFICE

The inauguration of Jefferson befitted the surroundings. The new president left his lodgings and walked two blocks to the unfinished Capitol, entered the Senate chamber, took the oath from Chief Justice John Marshall, read his inaugural address in a barely audible voice, and returned to his boarding house for dinner and the common table. John Adams was absent. He had quietly slipped away, which was just as well according to his descendant, the historian Henry Adams, since "he would have seemed, in his successor's opinion, as little in place as George III would have appeared at the inauguration of President Washington." A tone of simplicity and conciliation ran through Jefferson's inaugural address, its seeming artlessness the product of three laborious drafts: "We are all Republicans—we are all Federalists. If there be any among us who would wish to dissolve this Union or to change its republican form, let them stand undisturbed as monuments of the safety with which error of opinion may be tolerated where reason is left free to combat it."

After this eloquent affirmation of freedom, he proceeded to a ringing affirmation of republican govenment: "I know, indeed, that some honest men fear that a republican government cannot be strong; that this government is not strong enough. But would the honest patriot, in the full tide of successful experiment, abandon a government which has so far kept us free and firm, on

A pencil sketch of Thomas Jefferson, done around the time of his inauguration as president.

A watercolor of the president's house during Jefferson's term in office. Jefferson called it "big enough for two emperors, one pope, and the grand lama in the bargain."

the theoretic and visionary fear that this government, the world's best hope, may by possibility want energy to preserve itself? I trust not. I believe this, on the contrary, the strongest government on earth. I believe it is the only one where every man . . . would meet invasions of the public order as his own personal concern. Sometimes it is said that man cannot be trusted with the government of himself. Can he, then, be trusted with the government of others? Or have we found angels in the form of kings to govern him? Let history answer this question."

Jefferson's "happy faculty of condensing whole chapters into aphorisms," as one of his biographers put it, was displayed in his summary of the "essential principles" that would guide his administration: "Equal and exact justice to all men. . . ; peace, commerce, and honest friendship with all nations, entangling alliances with none. . . ; freedom of religion; freedom of the press; and freedom of person, under the protection of the habeas corpus; and trial by juries impartially selected. . . . The wisdom of our sages and the blood of our heroes have been devoted to their attainment."

The deliberate display of republican simplicity at Jefferson's inauguration would become the style of his administration. He took pains to avoid the occasions of pomp and circumstance which had characterized Federalist administrations and which to his mind suggested the trappings of kingship. Presidential messages went to Congress in writing lest they resemble the parliamentary speech from the throne. The practice also allowed Jefferson, a notoriously bad public speaker, to exploit his skill as a writer.

Jefferson discarded the coach and six in which Washington and Adams had gone to state occasions and rode about the city on horseback, often by himself. But this was, at least in part, therapy recommended by a doctor, and in part because Washington's rutted streets were hardly the place for a carriage. The formal levee was abandoned for an informal weekly reception to which all were invited. Dinners at the White House were held around a circular table, so that none should take precedence, and at social affairs the new president simply ignored the rules of protocol for what he called the rule of *pele mele,* in which the only custom observed was that the ladies went ahead of the men. "When brought together in society, all are perfectly equal," Jefferson said.

It was not that Jefferson had ceased to be the Virginia gentleman, nor that he had abandoned elegant manners or the good life. The cuisine of his French chef and the wines for his frequent dinners strained his budget to the point that he had to borrow money and he left office with a debt which was to pursue him the rest of his life. The dinners also strained the patience of the British minister, who had already taken umbrage at being received by a president "standing in slippers down at the heels, and both pantaloons, coat and underclothes indicative of an indifference to appearance." Perhaps it was a calculated slight to the minister of George III, who had behaved rudely when the author of the Declaration was presented to him in 1786.

Jefferson liked to think of his election as the "Revolution of 1800," but the margin had been close and the policies that he followed were more conciliatory than revolutionary. That they suited the vast majority of the people is attested to by his overwhelming reelection in 1804. Perhaps the most revolutionary thing about Jefferson's presidency was the orderly transfer of power in 1801, an uncommon event in the world of that day. "The changes of administration," a Washington lady wrote in her diary, "which in every age have most generally been epochs of confusion, villainy and bloodshed, in this our happy country take place without any species of distraction, or disorder." Jefferson placed in policy-making positions men of his own party, and was the first president to pursue the role of party leader, assiduously cultivating congressional support at his dinner parties and otherwise. It was a role he had not so much sought as fallen

*Philadelphia in 1800. The "Revolution of 1800" occurred peaceably,
"without any species of distraction, or disorder."*

into; he still shared the eighteenth-century distrust of the party
spirit. In the cabinet the leading fixtures were Secretary of State
James Madison, a longtime neighbor and political ally, and Secretary of the Treasury Albert Gallatin, a Pennsylvania Republican whose financial skills had won him the respect of Federalists.
In an effort to cultivate Federalist New England, Jefferson chose
men from that region for the positions of attorney-general, secretary of war, and postmaster-general.

In lesser offices, however, Jefferson refrained from wholesale
removal of Federalists, preferring to wait until vacancies appeared, a policy which led to his rueful remark that vacancies
obtained "by death are few; by resignation, none." But the pressure from Republicans was such that he often yielded and removed Federalists, trying as best he could to assign some other
than partisan causes for the removals. In one area, however, he
managed to remove the offices rather than the appointees. In
1802 Congress repealed the Judiciary Act of 1801, and so abolished the circuit judgeships and other offices to which Adams
had made his "midnight appointments." A new judiciary act restored to six the number of Supreme Court justices, and set up
six circuit courts, each headed by a justice.

MARBURY V. MADISON Adams's "midnight appointments" sparked
the case of *Marbury v. Madison*, the first in which the Supreme

Court declared a federal law unconstitutional. The case involved the appointment of one William Marbury as justice of the peace in the District of Columbia. Marbury's commission, signed by President Adams two days before he left office, was still undelivered when Madison took office as secretary of state, and Jefferson directed him to withhold it. Marbury then sued for a court order (a writ of mandamus) directing Madison to deliver his commission. The Court's unanimous opinion, written by John Marshall, held that Marbury was entitled to his commission, but then denied that the Court had jurisdiction in the case. Section 13 of the Judiciary Act of 1789, which gave the Court original jurisdiction in mandamus proceedings, was unconstitutional, the court ruled, because the Constitution specified that the Court should have original jurisdiction only in cases involving ambassadors or states. The Court, therefore, could issue no order in the case. With one bold stroke Marshall avoided an awkward confrontation with an administration that might have defied his order and at the same time established the precedent that the Court could declare a federal law invalid on the grounds that it violated provisions of the Constitution. The precedent of judicial review was not followed again for fifty-four years, but the principle was fixed for want of a challenge.

PARTISAN SQUABBLES The decision, about which Jefferson could do nothing, confirmed his fear of the judges' tendency to "throw an anchor ahead, and grapple further hold for future advances of power." In 1804 Republicans finally determined to use the impeachment power against two of the most partisan Federalist judges, and succeeded in ousting one of the two. The Republican House brought impeachments against District Judge John Pickering of New Hampshire and Justice Samuel Chase. Pickering was clearly insane, which was not a high crime or misdemeanor, but he was also given to profane and drunken harangues from the bench, which the Senate quickly decided was. In any event he was incompetent.

The case against Justice Chase, a much bigger matter, was less cut and dried. That he was highhanded and intemperate there was no question. Chase had presided at the sedition trials of two Republican editors, ordering a marshal to strike off the jury panel "any of those creatures or persons called democrats," and once attacked the Maryland consitution from the bench because it granted manhood suffrage, under which "our republican Constitution will sink into a mobocracy." But neither Jefferson nor the best efforts of John Randolph of Roanoke as prosecutor for the House could persuade two-thirds of the senators that Chase's vindictive partisanship constituted "high crimes and misdemeanors." His removal indeed might have set off the partisanship of Republicans in a political carnival of reprisals. His acquittal discouraged further efforts at impeachment, however, which Jefferson pronounced a "farce," after the failure to remove Chase.

DOMESTIC REFORMS   Aside from this setback, however, Jefferson for a while had things pretty much his own way. His first term was a succession of triumphs in both domestic and foreign affairs. He did not set out to dismantle Hamilton's program root and branch. Under Treasury Secretary Gallatin's tutoring he learned to accept the national bank as an essential convenience, and did not push a measure for the bank's repeal which more dogmatic Republicans sponsored. It was too late of course to undo Hamilton's funding and debt assumption operations, but none too soon in the opinion of both Jefferson and Gallatin to set the resultant debt on the way to extinction. At the same time Jefferson insisted on the repeal of the whiskey tax and other Federalist excises. Gallatin, former champion of the "whiskey boys" in Pennsylvania politics, had a change of heart after he took over the treasury, but Jefferson was adamant. The excises were repealed in 1802 and Jefferson won the undying gratitude of bibulous backwoodsmen.

Without the excises, frugality was all the more necessary to a government dependent for revenue chiefly on tariffs and the sale

Cincinnati in 1800, twelve years after its founding. Though its population was only about 750, its inhabitants were already promoting Cincinnati as "the metropolis of the north-western territory."

of western lands. Happily for Gallatin's treasury, both flourished. The tragedy of war that had engulfed Europe brought a continually increasing traffic to American shipping and thus revenues to the federal Treasury. And settlers flocked into the western lands, which were coming more and more within their reach. The admission of Ohio in 1803 increased to seventeen the number of states.

By the "wise and frugal government" promised in the inaugural, Jefferson and Gallatin reasoned, the United States could live within its income, like a prudent husbandman. The basic formula was simple: cut back expenses on the military. A standing army was a menace to a free society anyway, and therefore should be kept to a minimum and defense left, in Jefferson's words, to "a well-disciplined militia, our best reliance in peace, and for the first moments of war, till regulars may relieve them. . . ." The navy, which the Federalists had already reduced after the quasi-war with France, ought to be reduced further. Coastal defense, Jefferson argued, should rely on fortifications and a "mosquito fleet" of small gunboats.

In 1807 the record of Jeffersonian reforms was crowned by an act which outlawed the foreign slave trade as of January 1, 1808, the earliest date possible under the Constitution. At the time South Carolina was the only state that still permitted the trade, having reopened it in 1803. But for years to come an illegal traffic would continue. By one informal estimate perhaps 300,000 slaves were smuggled into the United States between 1808 and 1861.

THE BARBARY PIRATES Issues of foreign relations intruded on Jefferson early in his term. Events in the Mediterranean quickly gave him second thoughts about the need for a navy. On the Barbary Coast of North Africa the rulers of Morocco, Algeria, Tunis, and Tripoli had for years filled their coffers by means of piracy and extortion. After the Revolution American shipping in the Mediterranean became fair game, no longer protected by British payments of tribute. The new American government yielded up protection money too, first to Morocco in 1786, then to the others in the 1790s. In May 1801, however, the pasha of Tripoli upped his demands and declared war on the United States by the symbolic gesture of chopping down the flagpole at the United States Consulate. Rather than give in to this, Jefferson sent warships to blockade Tripoli.

A wearisome warfare dragged on until 1805, punctuated in 1804 by the notable exploit of Lt. Stephen Decatur who slipped into Tripoli harbor by night and set fire to the frigate *Philadel-*

phia, which had been captured (along with its crew) after it ran aground. Before the war ended William Eaton, consul at Tunis, staged an unlikely land invasion of Tripoli from Egypt. With fifteen United States Marines, about forty Greek soldiers, and some restless Arabs, he advanced across the desert and took Derna. But in 1805 the pasha settled for $60,000 ransom and released the crew of the *Philadelphia* (mostly British subjects) whom he had held hostage more than a year. It was still tribute, but less than the $300,000 the pasha had demanded at first, and much less than the cost of the war.

THE LOUISIANA PURCHASE It was an inglorious end to a shabby affair, but well before it was over events elsewhere had conspired to produce the greatest single achievement of the Jefferson administration, the Louisiana Purchase of 1803, which more than doubled the territory of the United States by bringing into its borders the entire Mississippi Valley west of the river itself. Louisiana, settled by the French, had been ceded to Spain in 1763. Since that time the dream of retaking Lousiana had stirred in the minds of Frenchmen. In 1800 Napoleon Bonaparte secured its return in exchange for a promise (never-fulfilled) to set up a Spanish princess and her husband in Italy as rulers of an enlarged Tuscany. When unofficial word of the deal reached Washington in May 1801, Jefferson hastened Robert R. Livingston, the new minister to France, on his way. Spain in control of the Mississippi outlet was bad enough, but Napoleon in control could only mean serious trouble. "There is on the globe one single spot the possessor of which is our natural and habitual enemy," Jefferson wrote Livingston. "The day that France takes possession of New Orleans . . . we must marry ourselves to the British fleet and nation," not at all the happiest prospect Jefferson ever faced.

Livingston had instructions to talk the French out of it, if it was not too late. If Louisiana had already become French he should try to get West Florida (once part of French Louisiana), either from France or with French help. Later Secretary of State Madison told him to seek a price for New Orleans and the Floridas, but Spain still held the Floridas, as it turned out. On into 1803 long and frustrating talks dragged out. Early that year James Monroe was made minister plenipotentiary to assist Livingston in Paris, but no sooner had he arrived in April than Napoleon's minister, Talleyrand, surprised Livingston by asking if the United States would like to buy the whole of Louisiana. Livingston, once he could regain his composure, snapped at the offer.

Napoleon's motives in the whole affair can only be surmised.

In 1802 Toussaint l'Ouverture led the slave revolt on Saint Domingue (later Haiti) depicted in this engraving.

At first he seems to have thought of a New World empire, but that plan took an ugly turn in French Sainte Domingue (later Haiti). There during the 1790s the revolutionary governments of France had lost control to a black revolt. In 1802, having just patched up the temporary Peace of Amiens with the British, Napoleon thought to improve the occasion by sending a force to subdue the island. By a ruse of war the French captured the black leader, Toussaint l'Ouverture, but then fell victim to guerrillas and yellow fever. Napoleon's plan may have been discouraged too by the fierce American reaction when the Spanish governor of Louisiana closed the Mississippi to American traffic in October 1802, on secret orders from Madrid. In the end Napoleon's purpose seems to have been simply to cut his losses, turn a quick profit, mollify the Americans, and go back to reshaping the map of Europe.

By the treaty of cession, dated April 30, 1803, the United States paid 60 million francs, approximately $11¼ million, for Louisiana. By a separate agreement the United States also assumed French debts owed to American citizens up to 20 million francs, or $3¾ million—making the total price about $15 million. In defining the boundaries of Louisiana the treaty was vague. Its language could be stretched to provide a tenuous claim on Texas and a much stronger claim on West Florida, from Baton Rouge on the Mississippi past Mobile to the Perdido River on the east. When Livingston asked about the boundaries, Talleyrand responded: "I can give you no direction. You have made a noble bargain for yourselves, and I suppose you will make the most of it." Napoleon himself observed: "If an obscurity did not exist, perhaps it would be good policy to put it there."

The turn of events had indeed presented Jefferson with a noble bargain, a great new "empire of liberty," but also with a constitutional dilemma. Nowhere did the Constitution provide for or even mention the purchase of territory. By a strict construction, which Jefferson had professed, no such power existed. Jefferson at first thought to resolve the matter by amendment, but his advisers argued against delay lest Napoleon change his mind. The power to purchase territory, they reasoned, resided in the power to make treaties. Jefferson relented, trusting, he said, "that the good sense of our country will correct the evil of loose construction when it shall produce ill effects." New England Federalists boggled at the prospect of new states that would probably strengthen the Jeffersonian party and centered their fire on a proviso that the inhabitants be "incorporated in the Union" as citizens. In a reversal that foretokened many future reversals on constitutional issues, Federalists found themselves arguing strict construction of the Constitution while Republicans brushed aside such scruples in favor of implied power.

In October 1803 the Senate ratified the treaty by an overwhelming vote of 26 to 6. Both houses of Congress voted the necessary money and made provision for the govenment of the new territory. On December 20, 1803, Gov. William C. C. Claiborne and Gen. James Wilkinson took formal possession of Louisiana from a French agent who had taken over from Spanish authorities only three weeks before. For the time the Spanish kept West Florida, but within a decade it would be ripe for the plucking. In 1808 Napoleon put his brother on the throne of Spain. With the Spanish colonial administration in disarray, American settlers in 1810 staged a rebellion in Baton Rouge and proclaimed the Republic of West Florida, quickly annexed and occupied by the United States as far eastward as the Pearl River. In 1812 the state of Louisiana absorbed the region—still known as the Florida parishes. In 1813, with Spain itself a battlefield for French and British forces, General Wilkinson took over the rest of West Florida, now the Gulf coast of Mississippi and Alabama. Legally, the American government has claimed ever since, all these areas were included in the original Louisiana Purchase.

EXPLORING THE CONTINENT   As an amateur scientist long before he was president, Jefferson had nourished an active curiosity about the Louisiana country, its geography, its flora and fauna, its pros-

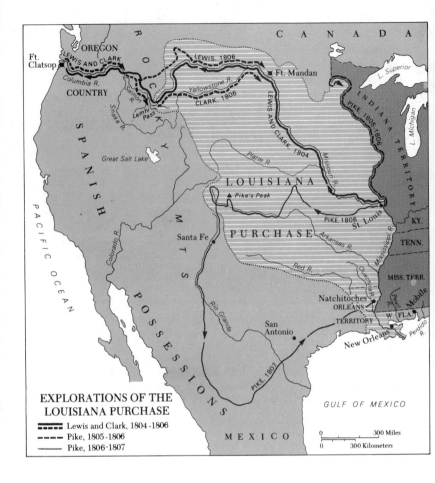

**EXPLORATIONS OF THE
LOUISIANA PURCHASE**

▬▬▬ Lewis and Clark, 1804-1806
- - - - Pike, 1805-1806
——— Pike, 1806-1807

pects for trade and agriculture. In January 1803 he asked Congress for money to send an exploring expedition to the far northwest, beyond the Mississippi, in what was still foreign territory. Congress approved and Jefferson assigned as commanders Meriwether Lewis, who as the president's private secretary had been groomed for the job, and another Virginian, William Clark, the much younger brother of George Rogers Clark.

During the winter of 1803–1804 a party of soldiers gathered at St. Louis and in May 1804 the "Corps of Discovery," numbering nearly fifty, set out to ascend the Missouri River. Six months later, near the Mandan Sioux villages in what was later North Dakota, they built Fort Mandan and wintered there in relative comfort, sending back downriver a barge loaded with specimens such as the prairie dog, previously unknown to science, and the magpie, previously unknown in America. Jefferson kept the great horns of a wapiti (elk) to display at Monticello. In the spring they added to the main party a French guide, who was little help, and his remarkable Shoshone wife, Sacajawea ("Canoe Launcher"), an enormous help as interpreter and go-between with the Indians of the region, and set out once again upstream. At the head of the Missouri they took the north fork, thenceforth the Jefferson River, crossed the continental divide at Lemhi Pass and in dugout canoes descended the Snake and Columbia Rivers to the Pacific. Near the later site of Astoria at the mouth of the Columbia they built Fort Clatsop in which they spent another winter. The following spring they headed back by almost the same route, and after a swing through the Yellowstone country, returned to St. Louis in September 1806, having been gone nearly two and a half years.

No longer was the Far West unknown country. Although it was nearly a century before a good edition of the *Journals of Lewis and Clark* appeared in print, many of their findings came out piecemeal, including an influential map in 1814. Convinced that they had found a practical route for the China trade, Lewis and Clark were among the last to hold out hope for a water route through the continent. Their reports of friendly Indians and abundant pelts quickly attracted traders and trappers to the region, and also gave the United States a claim to the Oregon country by right of discovery and exploration.

While Lewis and Clark were gone, Jefferson sent other explorers up the Ouachita and Red Rivers, but with little profit to

From the Journals of Lewis and Clark, *this is Clark's sketch of the head of a buzzard vulture, February 1806.*

geographical knowledge. More important were the travels of Lt. Zebulon Pike. Sent out in 1805–1806 to find the source of the Mississippi River, he mistakenly picked a tributary, later discoveries showed, but contributed to knowledge of the upper Mississippi Valley. Then, during 1806–1807, he went out to the headwaters of the Arkansas River as far as Colorado, discovered Pike's Peak but failed in an attempt to climb it, and made a roundabout return by way of Santa Fe, courtesy of Spanish soldiers who captured his party. Pike's account, while less reliable and less full than that of Lewis and Clark, appeared first and gave Americans their first overall picture of the Great Plains and Rocky Mountains. It also contributed to the widespread belief that the arid regions of the West constituted a Great American Desert, largely unfit for human habitation.

POLITICAL SCHEMES   Jefferson's policies, including the Louisiana Purchase, brought him almost solid support in the South and West. Even New Englanders were moving to his side. By 1809 John Quincy Adams, the son of the second president, would become a Republican! Die-hard Federalists read the handwriting on the wall. The acquisition of a vast new empire in the west would reduce New England to insignificance in political affairs, and along with it the Federalist cause. Under the leadership of Sen. Thomas Pickering, a group of Massachusetts bitter-enders called the Essex Junto began to think about secession from the Union, an idea that would simmer in New England circles for another decade. Rather than accede to a Union formed in the image of Jeffersonian Republicanism, they would withdraw.

Soon they hatched a scheme to link New York with New England and contacted Vice-President Aaron Burr, who had been on the outs with the Jeffersonians long since and who was, as ever, ready for subterranean schemes. Their plan depended on Burr's election as governor of New York. In April 1804, however, Burr was overwhelmed by the regular Republican candidate. The extreme Federalists, it turned out, could not even hold members of their own party to the plan, which Hamilton bitterly opposed on the grounds that Burr was "a dangerous man, and one who ought not to be trusted with the reins of government." When Hamilton's remarks appeared in the public press, Burr's demand for an explanation led to a duel at Weehawken, New Jersey, in which Hamilton was mortally wounded. Hamilton personally opposed dueling but his romantic streak and sense of honor compelled him to demonstrate his courage, long since established beyond any question at Yorktown. He went to his death, as his son had

Aaron Burr, the brilliant but erratic vice-president.

done in a similar affair the previous year, determined not to fire at his opponent. Burr was unhampered by such scruples. The death of Hamilton ended both Pickering's scheme and Burr's political career— but not his intrigues.

Meanwhile the presidential campaign of 1804 got under way when a congressional caucus of Republicans on February 25 renominated Jefferson and chose George Clinton for vice-president. Opposed by the Federalists Charles Coteworth Pinckney and Rufus King, Jefferson and Clinton won 162 of 176 electoral votes. Only Connecticut and Delaware recorded solid opposition. Jefferson's policy of conciliation had made him a national rather than a sectional candidate. With some pride, Jefferson said in his second inaugural address that he had carried out the general policies announced in the first: "The suppression of unnecessary offices, of useless establishments and expenses, enabled us to discontinue our internal taxes. . . . What farmer, what mechanic, what laborer ever sees a tax-gatherer of the United States?"

DIVISIONS IN THE REPUBLICAN PARTY

RANDOLPH AND THE *TERTIUM QUID* "Never was there an administration more brilliant than that of Mr. Jefferson up to this period," said John Randolph of Roanoke. "We were indeed in the full tide of successful experiment." But the Republican landslide had a sequel that would often follow such victories in later years.

The mercurial John Randolph of Roanoke, in a silhouette drawn from life.

Freed from a strong opposition—Federalists made up only a quarter of the new Congress—the majority began to lose its cohesion. Cracks appeared in the Republican facade, portents of major fissures that would finally split the party as the Federalists faded into oblivion. Ironically, John Randolph of Roanoke, a Jeffersonian mainstay in the first term, became the most conspicious of the dissidents. A brilliant but erratic Virginian, left frustrated by a hormonal deficiency, given to fits of insanity in his later years, gifted with a talent for invective delivered in a shrill soprano voice, the Virginia congressman flourished best in opposition. Few of his colleagues had the stomach for his tongue-lashings.

Randolph, too much a loner for leadership, was spokesman for a shifting group of "Old Republicans," whose adherence to party principles had rendered them more Jeffersonian than Jefferson himself. Their philosopher was John Taylor of Caroline, a Virginia planter-pamphleteer whose fine-spun theories of states' rights and strict construction had little effect at the time but delighted the logic-choppers of later years. Neither Randolph nor Taylor could accept his leader's pragmatic gift for adjusting principle to circumstance.

Randolph first began to smell a rat in the case of the Yazoo Fraud, a land scheme which originated in Georgia but entangled speculators from all over. In 1795 the Georgia legislature had sold to four land companies, in which some of the legislators were involved, 35 million acres in the Yazoo country (Mississippi and Alabama) for $500,000 (little more than a penny an acre). A new legislature rescinded the sale the following year, but not before some of the land claims had been sold to third parties. When Georgia finally ceded her western lands to federal authority in 1802, Jefferson sought a compromise settlement of the claims but Randolph managed to block passage of the necessary measures and in the ensuing quarrels was removed as Speaker of the House. The snarled Yazoo affair plagued the courts and Congress for another decade. Finally, in the case of *Fletcher v. Peck* (1810), Chief Justice Marshall ruled that the original sale, however fraudulent, was a legal contract. The repeal impaired the obligation of contract and was therefore unconstitutional. Final settlement came in 1814 when Congress awarded $4.2 million to the speculators.

Randolph's definitive break with Jefferson came in 1806, when the president sought an appropriation of $2 million for a thinly disguised bribe to the French to win their influence in persuading Spain to yield the Floridas to the United States. "I found I might co-operate or be an honest man—I have therefore opposed and will oppose them," Randolph said. Thereafter he resisted Jefferson's initiatives almost out of reflex. Randolph and his colleagues were sometimes called "Quids," or the *Tertium Quid* (the "third something"), and their dissents gave rise to talk of a third party, neither Republican nor Federalist. But they never got together. Some of the dissenters in 1808 backed James Monroe against Madison for the presidential succession, but the campaign quickly fizzled. The failure of the Quids would typify the experience of almost all third-party movements thereafter.

THE BURR CONSPIRACY John Randolph may have got enmeshed in dogma, but Aaron Burr was never one to let principle stand in the way. Born of a distinguished line of Puritans, including grandfather Jonathan Edwards, he cast off the family Calvinism early to pursue the main chance—and the women. Sheer brilliance and opportunism carried him to the vice-presidency. With a leaven of discretion he might easily have become heir-apparent to Jefferson, but a taste for intrigue was the tragic flaw in his character. Caught up in the dubious schemes of Federalist diehards in 1800 and again in 1804, he ended his political career once and for all when he killed Hamilton.

Searching then for new worlds to conquer, he turned to the West, and before he left office as vice-president he hatched the scheme that came to be known as the Burr Conspiracy. Just what he was up to probably will never be known, because Burr himself very likely was keeping some options open. He may have been getting up an expedition to conquer Mexico—some American freebooters had already pounced on Texas—or West Florida; he perhaps was out to organize a secession of Louisiana and set up an independent republic. On various pretexts he won the ear of the British and Spanish ministers in Washington (with whom he planted hints of a coup d'état in Washington), a variety of public figures in the East, and innumerable westerners, including two future presidents (William Henry Harrison and Andrew Jackson), and that noblest villain of them all, Gen. James Wilkinson, now governor of the Louisiana Territory but still in the pay of the Spanish government.°

In the summer of 1805 Burr sailed on a flatboat downriver all the way to New Orleans, propounding different schemes, lining up adventurers and dupes. By the summer of 1806 he was in Lexington, Kentucky, recruiting for an expedition to take up a land claim he had purchased in Arkansas, a likely staging area for a military enterprise or a fallback position if things went wrong. He arranged, but did not actually attend, the assembling of men, boats, and supplies on an island belonging to one of his confederates, a rich Irish refugee named Harmon Blennerhassett. Off they went, some sixty strong, to be joined downstream by Burr. But by now Burr's adventure had a cast of thousands, which was bound to cause talk. Rumors began to reach Jefferson, and in November 1806 so did a letter from Wilkinson warning of "a deep, dark, wicked and wide-spread conspiracy." Wilkinson was double-dealing with Spain and America, but Jefferson never guessed that he was anything but a patriot.

In January 1807, as Burr neared Natchez with his motley crew, he learned that Wilkinson had betrayed him and that Jefferson had ordered his arrest. He cut out cross-country for Pensacola, but was caught and taken off to Richmond for a trial, which, like the conspiracy, had a stellar cast. Charged with treason by the grand jury, Burr was brought for trial before Chief Justice Marshall, then riding circuit. The case revealed both Marshall and Jefferson at their partisan worst. Marshall was convinced that the "hand of malignity" was grasping at Burr, while Jefferson, determined to get a conviction at any cost, published

°The present state of Louisiana was then the Territory of Orleans. Wilkinson governed the rest of the Louisiana Purchase.

relevant affidavits in advance and promised pardons to conspirators who helped convict Burr. Marshall in turn was so indiscreet as to attend a dinner given by the chief defense counsel at which Burr himself was present.

The case established two major constitutional precedents. First, Jefferson ignored a subpoena requiring him to appear in court with certain papers in his possession. He refused, as Washington had refused, to submit papers to the Congress on grounds of executive privilege. Both believed that the independence of the executive branch would be compromised if the president were subject to a court writ. The second major precedent was the rigid definition of treason. On this Marshall adopted the strictest of constructions. Treason under the Constitution consists of "levying war against the United States or adhering to their enemies" and requires "two witnesses to the same overt act" for conviction. Since the prosecution failed to produce two witnesses to an overt act of treason by Burr, the jury brought in a verdict of not guilty.

Whether or not Burr escaped his just deserts, Marshall's strict construction of the Constitution protected the United States, as the authors of the Constitution clearly intended, against the capricious judgments of "treason" that governments through the centuries have used to terrorize dissenters. As to Burr, with further charges pending, he skipped bail and took refuge in France, but returned unmolested in 1812 to practice law in New York. He survived to a virile old age. At age eighty, shortly before his death, he was divorced on grounds of adultery.

WAR IN EUROPE

Oppositionists of whatever stripe were more an annoyance than a threat to Jefferson. The more intractable problems of his second term were created by the renewal of the European war in 1803, which helped resolve the problem of Louisiana but put more strains on Jefferson's desire to avoid "entangling alliances" and the quarrels of Europe. In 1805 Napoleon's smashing defeat of Russian and Austrian forces at Austerlitz made him the master of western Europe. The same year Lord Nelson's defeat of the French and Spanish fleets in the Battle of Trafalgar secured Britain's control of the seas. The war resolved itself into a battle of elephant and whale, Napoleon dominant on land, the British dominant on the water, neither able to strike a decisive blow at the other, and neither restrained by an overly delicate sense of neutral rights or international law.

HARASSMENT BY BRITAIN AND FRANCE   For two years after the renewal of hostilities things went well for American shipping, which took over trade with the French and Spanish West Indies. But in the case of the *Essex* (1805), a British prize court ruled that the practice of shipping French and Spanish goods through American ports while on their way elsewhere did not neutralize enemy goods. Such a practice violated the British rule of 1756 (laid down by the British courts during the Seven Years' War) under which trade closed in time of peace remained closed in time of war. Goods shipped in violation of the rule, the British held, were liable to seizure at any point under the doctrine of continuous voyage. In 1807 the commercial provisions of Jay's Treaty expired and James Monroe, ambassador to Great Britain, failed to get a renewal satisfactory to Jefferson. After that, the British interference with American shipping increased, not just to keep supplies from Napoleon's continent but also to hobble competition with British merchantmen.

In a series of Orders in Council adopted in 1806 and 1807 the British ministry set up a paper blockade of Europe from Copenhagen to Trieste. Vessels headed for continental ports had to get licenses and accept British inspection or be liable to seizure. Napoleon retaliated with his "Continental System," proclaimed in the Berlin Decree of 1806 and the Milan Decree of 1807. In the first he declared a blockade of the British Isles and in the second he ruled that neutral ships which complied with British regulations were subject to seizure when they reached continental ports. The situation presented American shippers with a dilemma. If they complied with the demands of one side, they were subject to seizure by the other.

It was humiliating, but the prospects for profits were so great that shippers ran the risk. For seamen the danger was heightened by a renewal of the practice of impressment. The use of press gangs to kidnap men in British (and colonial) ports was a longstanding method of recruitment for the British navy. The seizure of British subjects from American vessels became a new source of recruits, justified on the principle that British subjects remained British subjects for life: "Once an Englishman, always an Englishman." Mistakes might be made, of course, since it was sometimes hard to distinguish British subjects from Americans; indeed a flourishing trade in fake citizenship papers arose in American ports. The humiliation of impressment was mostly

Preparation for War to Defend Commerce. *In 1806 and 1807 American shipping was caught in the crossfire of war between Britain and France.*

confined to merchant vessels, but on at least two occasions before 1807 vessels of the American navy had been stopped on the high seas and seamen removed.

In the summer of 1807 the British *Leopard* accosted another American naval vessel, the frigate *Chesapeake*, just outside territorial waters off Norfolk. After the *Chesapeake*'s captain refused to be searched, the *Leopard* fired upon the American ship at the cost of three killed and eighteen wounded. The *Chesapeake*, unready for battle, was forced to strike its colors. A British search party seized four men, one of whom was later hanged for desertion from the British navy. Soon after the *Chesapeake* limped back into Norfolk, the Washington *Federalist* editorialized: 'We have never, on any occasion, witnessed the spirit of the people excited to so great a degree of indignation, or such a thirst for revenge. . . .'' Public wrath was so aroused that Jefferson could have had war on the spot. Had Congress been in session, he might have been forced into war. But Jefferson, like Adams before him, resisted the war fever and suffered politically as a result.

THE EMBARGO Jefferson resolved to use public indignation as the occasion for an effort at "peaceable coercion." In December 1807, in response to his request, Congress passed the Embargo Act, which stopped all export of American goods and prohibited American ships from clearing for foreign ports. The constitutional basis of the embargo was the power to regulate commerce, which in this case Republicans interpreted broadly as the power to prohibit commerce. "Let the example teach the world that our firmness equals our moderation," said the *National Intelligencer*, "that having resorted to a measure just in itself, and adequate to its object, we will flinch from no sacrifices which the honor and good of the nation demand from virtuous and faithful citizens."

But Jefferson's embargo was a failure from the beginning for want of a will to make the necessary sacrifices. The idealistic spirit which had made economic pressures effective in the prerevolutionary crises was lacking. Trade remained profitable despite the risks, and violation of the embargo was almost laughably easy. Enforcement was lax, and loopholes in the act permitted ships to clear port under the pretense of engaging in coastal trade or whaling, or under an amendment passed a few months after the act, for the purpose of bringing home American property stored in foreign warehouses. Some 800 ships left on such missions, but few of them returned before the embargo expired. Trade across the Canadian border flourished. As it turned out, France was little hurt by the act. Napoleon in fact exploited it to issue the Bayonne Decree (1808), which ordered the seizure of American ships in continental ports on the pretext that they must be British ships with false papers. Or if they truly were American, Napoleon slyly noted, he would be helping Jefferson enforce the embargo. Some British manufacturers and workers were hurt by the lack of American cotton, but they carried little weight with the government, and British shippers benefited. With American ports closed, they found a new trade in Latin American ports thrown open by the colonial authorities when Napoleon occupied the mother countries of Spain and Portugal.

The coercive effect was minimal, and the embargo revived the moribund Federalist party in New England, which renewed the charge that Jefferson was in league with the French. The embargo, one New Englander said, was "like cutting one's throat to cure the nosebleed." At the same time agriculture in the south

This 1807 Federalist cartoon compares Washington (left) to Jefferson (right). Washington is flanked by the British lion and the American eagle, while Jefferson is flanked by a snake and a lizard. Below Jefferson are volumes by French philosophers.

and west suffered for want of outlets for grain, cotton, and tobacco. After fifteen months of ineffectiveness, Jefferson finally accepted failure and on March 1, 1809, signed a repeal of the embargo shortly before he relinquished the "splendid misery" of the presidency.

In the election of 1808 the succession passed to another Virginian, Secretary of State James Madison. Presidential trial balloons for James Monroe and George Clinton, launched by the Quids, never got off the ground, and Jefferson used his influence in the caucus of Republican congressmen to win the nomination for Madison. Clinton was again the candidate for vice-president. The Federalists, backing Charles Cotesworth Pinckney and Rufus King of New York, revived enough as a result of the embargo to win 47 votes to Madison's 122.

THE DRIFT TO WAR   Madison was entangled in foreign affairs from the beginning. Still insisting on neutral rights and freedom of the seas, he pursued Jefferson's policy of "peaceful coercion" by different but no more effective means. In place of the embargo Congress had substituted the Non-Intercourse Act, which reopened trade with all countries except France and Great Britain and authorized the president to reopen trade with whichever of these gave up its restrictions. British Minister David M. Erskine assured Madison's secretary of state that Britain would revoke its restrictions on June 10, 1809. With that assurance, Madison reopened trade with Britain, but Erskine had acted on his own and the foreign secretary, repudiating his action, recalled him. Nonintercourse resumed, but it proved as ineffective as the embargo. In the vain search for an alternative, Congress on May 1, 1810, reversed its ground and adopted a measure introduced by Nathaniel Macon of North Carolina, Macon's Bill No. 2, which reopened trade with the warring powers but provided that if either dropped its restrictions non-intercourse would be restored with the other.

This time Napoleon took a turn at trying to bamboozle Madison. Napoleon's foreign minister, the duc de Cadore, informed the American minister in Paris that he had withdrawn the Berlin and Milan Decrees, but the carefully worded Cadore letter had strings attached: revocation of the decrees depended on withdrawal of the British Orders in Council. The strings were plain to see, but either Madison misunderstood or, more likely, went along in hope of putting pressure on the British. In response to the Cadore letter, he restored non-intercourse with the British. The British refused to give in, but Madison clung to his policy despite Napoleon's continued seizure of American ships. The seemingly hopeless effort did indeed finally work. With more time, with more patience, with a transatlantic cable, Madison's policy would have been vindicated without resort to war. On June 16, 1812, the British foreign minister, facing economic crisis, announced revocation of the Orders in Council. Britain preferred not to risk war with the United States on top of its war with Napoleon. But on June 1 Madison had asked for war, and by mid-June the Congress concurred.

THE WAR OF 1812

CAUSES The main cause of the war—the demand for neutral rights—seems clear enough. Neutral rights were the main burden of Madison's war message and the main reason for a mounting hostility toward the British. Yet the geographical distribution of the congressional vote for war raises a troubling question. The preponderance of the vote for war came from members of Congress representing the farm regions from Pennsylvania southward and westward. The maritime states of New York and New England, the region that bore the brunt of British attacks on

American trade, gave a majority against the declaration of war. One explanation for this seeming anomaly is simple enough. The farming regions were afflicted by the damage to their markets for grain, cotton, and tobacco, while New England shippers made profits in spite of British restrictions.

Other plausible explanations for the sectional vote, however, include frontier Indian depredations which were blamed on the British, western land hunger, and the desire for new lands in Canada and the Floridas. Indian troubles were endemic to a rapidly expanding West. Land-hungry settlers and speculators kept moving out ahead of government surveys and sales in search of fertile acres. The constant pressure to open new lands repeatedly forced or persuaded Indians to sign treaties they did not always understand, causing stronger resentment among tribes that were losing more and more of their lands. It was an old story, dating from the Jamestown settlement, but one that took a new turn with the rise of two Shawnee leaders, Tecumseh and his twin brother Tenskwatawa, "the Prophet."

Tecumseh, according to Gov. William Henry Harrison of the Indiana Territory, was "one of those uncommon geniuses, which spring up occasionally to produce revolutions and overturn the order of things." He saw with blazing clarity the consequences of Indian disunity, and set out to form a confederation of tribes to defend Indian hunting grounds, insisting that no land cession was valid without the consent of all tribes since they held the land in common. His brother supplied the inspiration of a religious revival, calling upon the Indians to worship the "Master of Life," to resist the white man's firewater, and lead a simple life within their means. By 1811 Tecumseh had matured his plans and

Tecumseh, the Shawnee leader who tried to unite the tribes in defense of their lands. He was killed in 1813 at the Battle of the Thames.

headed south to win the Creeks, Cherokees, Choctaws, and Chickasaws to his cause.

Governor Harrison saw the danger. He gathered a force and set out to attack Tecumseh's capital on the Tippecanoe River, Prophet's Town, while the leader was away. On November 7, 1811, the Indians attacked Harrison's encampment on the Tippecanoe River, although Tecumseh had warned against any fighting in his absence. The Shawnees were finally repulsed in a bloody engagement which left about a quarter of Harrison's men dead or wounded. Only later did Harrison realize that he had inflicted a defeat on the Indians, who had become demoralized and many of whom had fled to Canada. Harrison then burned their town and destroyed all its stores. Tecumseh's dreams went up in smoke, and Tecumseh himself fled to British protection in Canada.

The Battle of Tippecanoe reinforced suspicions that the British were inciting the Indians. Actually the incident was mainly Harrison's doing. With little hope of help from war-torn Europe, Canadian authorities had steered a careful course, discouraging warfare but seeking to keep the Indians' friendship and fur trade. To eliminate the Indian menace, frontiersmen reasoned, they needed to remove its foreign support, and they saw the province of Ontario as a pistol pointing at the United States. Conquest of Canada would accomplish a twofold purpose. It would eliminate British influence among the Indians and open a new empire for land-hungry Americans. It was also the only place, in case of war, where the British were vulnerable to American attack. East Florida, still under the Spanish flag, posed a similar menace. Spain was too weak or unwilling to prevent sporadic Indian attacks across the frontier. The British were also suspected of smuggling through Florida and intriguing with the Indians on the southwest border.

One historian of the quarrels with Britain has suggested that "scholars have overemphasized the tangible, rational reasons for action and . . . have given too little heed to such things as national pride, sensitivity, and frustration, although the evidence for this sort of thing leaps to the eye." Madison's drift toward war was hastened by the rising temperature of war fever. In the Congress which assembled in November 1811 a number of new members from southern and western districts began a chorus of orations, holding forth on "national honor" and British perfidy. Among them were Henry Clay of Kentucky, who became Speaker of the House, Richard M. Johnson of Kentucky, Felix Grundy of Tennessee, and John C. Calhoun of South Carolina.

John Randolph of Roanoke christened them the "War Hawks." After they entered the House, Randolph said "We have heard but one word—like the whip-poor-will, but one eternal monotonous tone—Canada! Canada! Canada!"

PREPARATIONS As it turned out, the War Hawks would get neither Canada nor Florida. For James Madison had carried into war a country that was ill-prepared both financially and militarily. In 1811, despite earnest pleas from Treasury Secretary Gallatin, Congress had let the twenty-year charter of the Bank of the United States expire. A combination of strict-constructionist Republicans and anglophobes, who feared the large British interest in the bank, did it in. Also, many state banks were mismanaged, resulting in deposits lost through bankruptcy. Trade had approached a standstill and tariff revenues had declined. Loans were needed for about two-thirds of the war costs while northeast opponents to the war were reluctant to lend money. Government bonds were difficult to float.

War had been likely for nearly a decade, but Republican economy had prevented preparations. When, finally, late in 1811 the administration decided to fill up the army to its authorized strength of 10,000 and add an additional force of 10,000, Madison still faced the old arguments against the danger of a standing army. Sen. William B. Giles of Virginia, one of the Old Republicans, suggested an additional force of 25,000 to serve five years. His purpose was to embarrass the administration, because such a volunteer force probably could not be raised and would strain the country's resources. The War Hawks nevertheless supported the measure, and in a law passed on January 9, 1812, raised the authorized force to 35,000. But when the war began the army numbered only 6,700 men, ill-trained, poorly equipped, and led by poorly prepared officers. The senior officers were still in large part veterans of the Revolution. The ranking general, Henry Dearborn, was a veteran of Bunker Hill, sixty-one at the outbreak of war.

The navy, on the other hand, was in comparatively good shape, with able officers and trained men whose seamanship had been tested in the fighting against France and Tripoli. Its ships were well outfitted and seaworthy—all sixteen of them. In the first year of the war it was the navy that produced the only American victories in isolated duels with British vessels, but their effect was mainly an occasional lift to morale. Within a year the British had blockaded the coast, except for New England where they hoped to cultivate antiwar feeling, and most of the little American fleet was bottled up in port.

THE WAR IN THE NORTH   The only place where the United States could effectively strike at the British was Canada. Only once, however, had a war in that arena proved decisive, late in the French and Indian War, when Wolfe took Québec and strangled the French Empire in America. A similar instinct for the jugular was Madison's best hope: a quick attack on Québec or Montréal would cut Canada's lifeline, the St. Lawrence River. Instead the old history of the indecisive colonial wars was repeated, for the last time.

Instead of striking directly at the lifeline, the administration opted for a three-pronged drive against Canada: along the Lake Champlain route toward Montréal, with Gen. Henry Dearborn in command; along the Niagara River, with forces under Gen. Stephen Van Rensselaer; and into Upper Canada (north of Lake Erie) from Detroit, where Gen. William Hull and some 2,000 men arrived in early July. In Detroit, Hull deliberated and vacillated while his position worsened and the news arrived that America's Fort Michilimakinac, isolated at the head of Lake Huron, had surrendered on July 17. British Gen. Isaac Brock cleverly played upon Hull's worst fears. Gathering what redcoats he could to parade in view of Detroit's defenders, Brock let it be known that thousands of Indian allies were at the rear and that once fighting began he would be unable to control them. Fearing massacre, Hull surrendered his entire force on August 16, 1812.

Along the Niagara front, General Van Rensselaer was more aggressive than Hull. On October 13 an advance party of 600 Americans crossed the Niagara River and worked their way up the bluffs on the Canadian side to occupy Queenstown Heights. The stage was set for a major victory, but the New York militia refused to reinforce Van Rensselaer's men on the claim that their military service did not obligate them to leave the country. They complacently remained on the New York side and watched their outnumbered countrymen fall to a superior force across the river.

On the third front, the old invasion route via Lake Champlain, the trumpet once more gave an uncertain sound. At first, when word came that the British had revoked the Orders in Council, General Dearborn accepted a temporary armistice. On November 19 he finally led his army north from Plattsburgh toward Montréal. He marched them up to the border, where the militia once again stood on its alleged constitutional rights and refused to cross, and then marched them down again.

Madison's navy secretary now pushed vigorously for American control of inland waters. At Presque Isle (Erie), Pennsylvania, twenty-eight-year-old Commodore Oliver H. Perry, already a

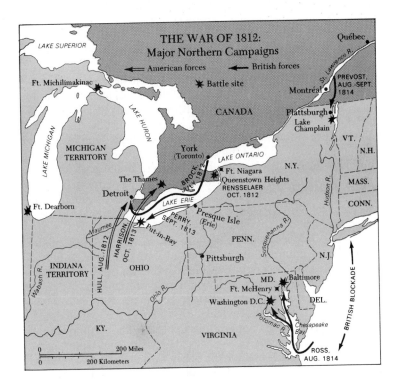

THE WAR OF 1812:
Major Northern Campaigns

⟵⟵ American forces   ⟵ British forces

✴ Battle site

LAKE SUPERIOR

Québec

Ft. Michilimakinac

PREVOST,
AUG.-SEPT.
1814

Montréal

CANADA

Plattsburgh
Lake
Champlain

VT.

N.H.

MICHIGAN
TERRITORY

LAKE MICHIGAN

LAKE HURON

York
(Toronto)

LAKE ONTARIO

N.Y.

Ft. Niagara
Queenstown Heights
RENSSELAER
OCT. 1812

MASS.

The Thames

BROCK JULY 1812

Detroit

Hudson R.

CONN.

LAKE ERIE

Ft. Dearborn

PERRY SEPT. 1813

Presque Isle

Put-in-Bay

Maumee

HARRISON OCT. 1813

HULL AUG. 1812

INDIANA
TERRITORY

OHIO

PENN.

Pittsburgh

Susquehanna R.

N.J.

Wabash R.

Ohio R.

MD.

Baltimore

Ft. McHenry

Washington D.C.

DEL.

BRITISH BLOCKADE

KY.

VIRGINIA

Potomac R.

Chesapeake
Bay

ROSS.
AUG. 1814

0   200 Miles
0   200 Kilometers

fourteen-year veteran who had seen action against Tripoli, was fetching hardware up from Pittsburgh and building ships from the wilderness lumber. By the end of the summer Perry had superior numbers and set out in search of the British, whom he found at Put-in Bay, near the mouth of the Sandusky, on September 10, 1813. Perry refused to quit when his flagship was shot out from under him. He transferred to another vessel, carried the battle to the enemy, and finally accepted surrender of the entire British squadron. To Gen. William Henry Harrison he sent the long-awaited message: "We have met the enemy and they are ours."

American naval control of waters in the region soon made Upper Canada untenable to the British. They gave up Detroit in September, and were dissuaded from falling back all the way to the Niagara only by the protests of Tecumseh and his Indian allies. When they took a defensive stand at the Battle of the Thames (October 5), General Harrison inflicted a defeat which eliminated British power in Upper Canada and released the Northwest from any further threat. In the course of the battle Tecumseh fell, and his dream of Indian unity died with him.

THE WAR IN THE SOUTH   In the Southwest too the war flared up in 1813. In April, Gen. James Wilkinson had occupied the remainder of Spanish West Florida, where British agents had been active, on the claim that it was part of the Louisiana Purchase. In July 1813 a group of American settlers clashed with the Creeks at Burnt Corn, north of Pensacola, and on August 30 the Creeks attacked Fort Mims, on the Alabama River above Mobile, killing almost half the people in the fort. The news found Andrew Jackson home in bed recovering from a street brawl with Thomas Hart Benton, later a senator from Missouri. As major-general of the Tennessee militia, Jackson summoned about 2,000 volunteers and set out on a campaign which utterly crushed the Creek resistance. The decisive battle came on March 27, 1814, at the Horseshoe Bend of the Tallapoosa River, in the heart of the upper Creek country. In the Treaty of Fort Jackson signed that August, the Creeks ceded two-thirds of their lands to the United States, including part of Georgia and most of Alabama.

Four days after the Battle of Horseshoe Bend, Napoleon's empire collapsed. Now free to deal with America, the British developed a threefold plan of operations for 1814. They would launch a two-pronged invasion of America via Niagara and Lake Champlain to increase the clamor for peace in the Northeast, extend the naval blockade to New England, subjecting coastal towns to raids, and seize New Orleans to cut the Mississippi River, lifeline of the West. Uncertainties about the peace settlement in Europe, however, prevented the release of British veterans for a wholesale descent upon the New World. War weariness, after a generation of conflict, countered the British thirst for revenge against the former colonials. British plans were stymied also by the more resolute young commanders Madison had placed in charge of strategic areas by the summer of 1814.

MACDONOUGH'S VICTORY   The main British effort was planned for the invasion via Lake Champlain. From the north Gen. George Prevost, governor-general of Canada, advanced with the finest army yet assembled on American soil: fifteen regiments of regulars, plus militia and artillerymen, a total of about 15,000. The front was saved only by Prevost's vacillation and the superb ability of Commodore Thomas Macdonough, commander of the American naval squadron on Lake Champlain. A land assault might have taken Plattsburgh and forced Macdonough out of his protected position nearby, but England's army bogged down while its flotilla engaged Macdonough in a deadly battle on September 11.

The British concentrated superior firepower from the flag-ship, the *Confiance*, on Macdonough's ship, the *Saratoga*. With his starboard battery disabled, Macdonough executed a daring maneuver known as "winding ship." He turned the *Saratoga* around while at anchor and brought its undamaged side into action with devastating effect. The *Saratoga* was so damaged that it had to be scuttled, but the battle ended with the entire British flotilla either destroyed or captured. After reading the news, the duke of Wellington informed the British ministry: "That which appears to me to be wanting in America is not a general, or a general officer and troops, but a naval superiority on the Lakes." Lacking this advantage the duke thought the British had no right "to demand any concession of territory from America."

FIGHTING IN THE CHESAPEAKE Meanwhile, however, American forces suffered the most humiliating experience of the war, the capture and burning of Washington, D.C. With attention focused on the Canadian front, the Chesapeake Bay offered the British a number of inviting targets, including Baltimore, now the fourth-largest city in America. Under the command of Gen. Robert Ross, a British force landed without opposition in June at

The Taking of the City of Washington in America. *An English cartoon depicts the taking of Washington, D.C., on August 24, 1814.*

Benedict, Maryland, and headed for Washington, forty miles away. To defend the capital the Americans had a force of about 7,000, including only a few hundred regulars and 400 sailors. At Bladensburg, Maryland, the American militia melted away in the face of the smaller British force. Only Commodore Joshua Barney's sailors held firm, pounding the British with five twenty-four-pound guns, but the sailors were forced to retire after half an hour.

On the evening of August 24, 1814, the British marched unopposed into Washington, where British officers ate a meal prepared for President and Mrs. Madison, who had joined the other refugees in Virginia. The British then burned the White House, the Capitol, and all other government buildings except the Patent Office. A tornado the next day compounded the damage, but a violent thunderstorm dampened both the fires and the enthusiasm of the British forces, who left to prepare a new assault on Baltimore.

The attack on Baltimore was a different story. With some 13,000 men, chiefly militia, some of them stragglers from Bladensburg, American forces fortified the heights behind the city. About 1,000 men held Fort McHenry, on an island in the harbor. The British landed at North Point, where an advance group of American militia inflicted severe casualties, including a mortal wound to General Ross. When the British finally came into sight of the city on September 13, they halted in the face of American defenses. All through the following night the fleet bombarded Fort McHenry to no avail, and the invaders abandoned the attack on the city as too costly to risk. Francis Scott Key, a Washington lawyer, watched the siege from a vessel in the harbor. The sight of the flag still in place at dawn inspired Key to draft the verses of "The Star Spangled Banner." Later revised and set to the tune of an English drinking song, it was immediately popular and eventually became the national anthem.

THE BATTLE OF NEW ORLEANS   The British failure at Baltimore followed by three days their failure on Lake Champlain, and their offensive against New Orleans had yet to run its course. Along the Gulf coast Andrew Jackson had been busy shoring up the defenses of Mobile and New Orleans. In November, without authorization, he invaded Spanish Florida and took Pensacola to end British intrigues there. Back in Louisiana by the end of November, he began to erect defenses on the approaches to New Orleans, anticipating a British approach by the interior to pick up Indian support and control the Mississippi. Instead the British

THE WAR OF 1812: Major Southern Campaigns

← American forces ✳ Battle site
← British forces

0   100 Miles
0   100 Kilometers

fleet, with some 7,500 European veterans under Gen. Sir Edwin Pakenham, entered Lake Borgne to the east of New Orleans, and eventually reached a level plain on the banks of the Mississippi just south of New Orleans.

Pakenham's painfully careful approach—he waited until all his artillery was available—gave Jackson time to throw up earthworks bolstered by cotton bales for protection. It was an almost invulnerable position, but Pakenham, contemptuous of Jackson's array of frontier militiamen, Creole aristocrats, free Negroes, and pirates, rashly ordered his veterans forward in a frontal assault at dawn on January 8, 1815. His redcoats ran into a murderous hail of artillery shells and deadly rifle fire. Before the British withdrew about 2,000 had died on the field, including Pakenham himself, whose body, pickled in a barrel of rum, was returned to the ship where his wife awaited news of the battle.

The Battle of New Orleans occurred after a peace treaty had already been signed, but this is not to say that it was an anticlimax or that it had no effect on the outcome of the war, for the treaty was yet to be ratified and the British might have exploited to advantage the possession of New Orleans had they won it. But the battle assured ratification of the treaty as it stood, and both governments acted quickly.

British General Pakenham's death at the Battle of New Orleans, January 8, 1815.

THE TREATY OF GHENT   Peace efforts had begun in 1812 even before hostilities got under way. The British, after all, had repealed their Orders in Council two days before the declaration of war and confidently expected at least an armistice. Secretary of State Monroe, however, told the British that they would have to give up the outrage of impressment as well. Meanwhile Czar Alexander of Russia offered to mediate the dispute, hoping to relieve the pressure on Great Britain, his ally against France. Madison then sent Albert Gallatin and James Bayard to join John Quincy Adams, American ambassador to Russia, in St. Petersburg. They arrived in July 1813, but the czar was at the warfront, and they waited impatiently until January 1814, but then the British refused mediation. Instead the British offered to negotiate directly, however. In February, Madison appointed Henry Clay and Jonathan Russell to join the other three commissioners in talks which finally got under way in the Flemish city of Ghent in August.

In contrast to the array of talent gathered in the American contingent, the British diplomats were nonentities, really messengers acting for the Foreign Office, which was more concerned with the effort to remake the map of Europe at the Congress of Vienna. The Americans had more leeway to use their own judgment, and sharp disagreements developed which had to be patched up by Albert Gallatin. The sober-sided Adams and the hard-drinking, poker-playing Clay, especially, rubbed each other the wrong way. The American delegates at first were instructed to demand that the British abandon impressment and paper blockades, and to get indemnities for seizures of American ships. The British opened the discussions with demands for territory in New York and Maine, removal of American warships from the Great Lakes, an autonomous Indian buffer state in the Northwest, access to the Mississippi River, and abandonment of American fishing rights off Labrador and Newfoundland. If the British insisted on such a position, the Americans informed them, the negotiations would be at an end.

But the British were stalling, awaiting news of victories to strengthen their hand. They withdrew the demand for an Indian buffer state and substituted *uti possidetis* (retention of occupied territory) as a basis for settlement. This too was rejected. The Americans countered with a proposal for the *status quo ante bellum* (the situation before the war). The news of American victory on Lake Champlain arrived in October and weakened the British resolve. Their will to fight was further weakened by a continuing power struggle at the Congress of Vienna, by the eagerness of British merchants to renew trade with America, and by the war-weariness of a tax-burdened public. The British finally decided that the game was not worth the candle. One by one demands were dropped on both sides until the envoys agreed to end the war, return the prisoners, restore the previous boundaries, and to settle nothing else. The questions of fisheries and disputed boundaries were referred to commissions for future settlement. The Treaty of Ghent was signed on Christmas Eve of 1814.

THE HARTFORD CONVENTION   While the diplomats converged on a peace settlement, an entirely different kind of meeting took place in Hartford, Connecticut. An ill-fated affair, the Hartford Convention represented the climax of New England's dissaffection with "Mr. Madison's war." New England had managed to keep aloof from the war and extract a profit from illegal trading and privateering. New England shippers monopolized the import trade and took advantage of the chance to engage in active trade with the enemy. After the fall of Napoleon, however, the British extended their blockade to New England, occupied Maine as far as the Penobscot River, and conducted several raids along the coast. Even Boston seemed threatened. Instead of rallying to the American flag, however, Federalists in the Massachusetts legislature on October 5, 1814, voted for a convention of New England states to plan independent action. The Constitution, they said, "has failed to secure to this commonwealth, and as they believe, to the Eastern sections of this Union, those equal rights and benefits which are the greatest objects of its formation."

On December 15 the Hartford Convention assembled with delegates chosen by the legislatures of Massachusetts, Rhode Island, and Connecticut, with two delegates from Vermont and one from New Hampshire: twenty-two in all. The convention included an extreme group, Timothy Pickering's "Essex Junto," who were prepared for secession from the Union, but it was controlled by a more moderate group led by Harrison Gray Otis, who wanted only a protest in language reminiscent of Madison's Virginia Resolutions of 1798. As the ultimate remedy for their grievances they proposed seven constitutional amendments designed to limit Republican influence: abolishing the three-fifths compromise, requiring a two-thirds vote to declare war or admit new states, prohibiting embargoes lasting more than sixty days, excluding the foreign-born from federal offices, limiting the president to one term, and forbidding successive presidents from the same state.

Their call for a later convention in Boston carried the unmistakable threat of secession if the demands were ignored. Yet the threat quickly evaporated. When messengers from Hartford reached Washington, they found the battered capital celebrating the good news from Ghent and New Orleans. The consequence was a fatal blow to the Federalist party, which never recovered from the stigma of disloyalty and narrow provincialism stamped on it by the Hartford Convention.

THE WAR'S AFTERMATH   Conveniently forgotten in the celebrations of peace were the calamities to which the Jeffersonian neglect of national defense had led. For all the fumbling ineptitude with which the War of 1812 was fought, it generated an intense feeling of patriotism. Despite the standoff with which it ended at Ghent, the American public came out of the war with a sense of victory, courtesy of Andrew Jackson and his men at New Orleans. Remembered were the heroic exploits of American frigates in their duels with British ships. Remembered too were the vivid words of the dying Capt. James Lawrence on the *Chesapeake* ("Don't give up the ship") and Oliver H. Perry on Lake Erie ("We have met the enemy and they are ours"), and the stirring stanzas of "The Star Spangled Banner." Under Republican leadership the nation had survived a "Second War of Independence" against the greatest power on earth, and emerged with

We Owe Allegiance to No Crown. *The War of 1812 generated a new feeling of nationalism.*

new symbols of nationhood and a new pantheon of heroes. The war also launched the United States toward economic independence, as the interruption of trade encouraged the growth of American manufactures. After forty years of independence, it dawned on the world that the new republic might be here to stay, and that it might be something more than a pawn in European power games.

As if to underline the point, Congress authorized a quick and decisive blow at the pirates of the Barbary Coast. During the War of 1812 the dey of Algiers had once again set about plundering American ships on the claim that he was getting too little tribute. On March 3, 1815, little more than two weeks after the Senate ratified the Peace of Ghent, Congress authorized hostilities against the pirates. On May 10 Capt. Stephen Decatur sailed from New York with ten vessels. In the Mediterranean he first seized two Algerian ships and then sailed boldly into the harbor of Algiers. On June 30, 1815, the dey of Algiers agreed to cease molesting American ships and to give up all American prisoners. In July and August Decatur's show of force induced similar treaties from Tunis and Tripoli. This time there was no tribute; this time, for a change, the Barbary pirates paid indemnities for the damage they had done. This time victory put an end to the piracy and extortion in that quarter, permanently.

One of the strangest results of a strange war and its aftermath was a reversal of roles by the Republicans and Federalists. Out of the wartime experience the Republicans had learned some lessons in nationalism. Certain needs and inadequacies revealed by the war had "Federalized" Madison, or "re-Federalized" this Father of the Constitution. Perhaps, Madison reasoned, a peacetime army and navy would not be such an unmitigated evil. Madison now preferred to keep something more than a token force. The lack of a national bank had added to the problems of financing the war. Now Madison wanted it back. The rise of new industries during the war led to a clamor for increased tariffs. Madison went along. The problems of overland transportation in the West had revealed the need for internal improvements. Madison agreed, but on that point kept his constitutional scruples. He wanted a constitutional amendment. So while Madison embraced nationalism and broad construction of the Constitution, the Federalists took up the Jeffersonians' position of states' rights and strict construction. It was the first great reversal of roles in constitutional interpretation. It would not be the last.

FURTHER READING

One of the classics of American history remains the survey of the Republican years found in Henry Adams's *History of the United States during the Administration of Thomas Jefferson* [and] *James Madison* (9 vols., 1889–1891). Marshall Smelser's *The Democratic Republic, 1801–1815* (1968) presents a more modern overview. James S. Young's *The Washington Community, 1800–1828* (1966)° provides an interesting look at both the mechanics of Jeffersonian politics and the design of the new national capital.

The standard modern biography is the multivolume work by Dumas Malone, *Jefferson and His Time* (6 vols, 1948–1981).° Forrest McDonald's *The Presidency of Thomas Jefferson* (1976) and Merrill Peterson's *Thomas Jefferson and the New Nation* (1970)° are shorter, yet incisive.

° These books are available in paperback editions.

Fawn Brodie's *Thomas Jefferson: An Intimate History* (1974)° offers a psychobiography. A good introduction to the life of Jefferson's friend and successor is Ralph L. Ketcham's *James Madison* (1971). Drew R. McCoy's *The Elusive Republic* (1982)° discusses the political economy of these years in the context of republicanism; Joyce Appleby's *Capitalism and a New Social Order* (1984)° deemphasizes the impact of republican ideology.

David Hackett Fischer's *The Revolution of American Conservatism: The Federalist Party in the Era of Jeffersonian Democracy* (1965), Shaw Livermore's *The Twilight of Federalism: The Disintegration of the Federalist Party* (1962), and Linda K. Kerber's *Federalists in Dissent* (1970) explore the Federalists while out of power.

The concept of judicial review and the courts can be studied in Richard E. Ellis's *The Jeffersonian Crisis* (1971). The most comprehensive work on John Marshall remains Albert J. Beveridge's *The Life of John Marshall* (4 vols., 1916–1919). Milton Lomask's two-volume *Aaron Burr: The Years from Princeton to Vice President, 1756–1805* (1979) and *The Conspiracy and the Years of Exile, 1805–1836* (1982) trace the career of that remarkable American.

For the Louisiana Purchase, consult Alexander De Conde's *This Affair of Louisiana* (1976). *The Journals of Lewis and Clark* (1953), edited by Bernard De Voto, and David F. Hawke's *Those Tremendous Mountains* (1980),° based on those journals, are both highly readable. Bernard W. Sheehan's *Seeds of Extinction* (1973) is more analytical about the Jeffersonians' Indian policy and the opening of the West. John C. Greene's *American Science in the Age of Jefferson* (1984) is a good summary of that topic.

Burton Spivak's *Jefferson's English Crisis: Commerce, the Embargo, and the Republican Revolution* (1979) discusses Anglo-American relations during Jefferson's administration; Clifford L. Egan's *Neither Peace nor War* (1983) covers Franco-American relations. A review of the events that brought on war in 1812 is presented in Robert A. Rutland's *Madison's Alternatives: The Jeffersonian Republicans and the Coming of War, 1805–1812* (1975). See also Roger H. Brown's *The Republic in Peril: 1812* (1964).° J. C. A. Stagg's *Mr. Madison's War* (1983) places the war in a larger historical context. Two recent works that concentrate on specific aspects of the war are Alan Lloyd's *The Scorching of Washington: The War of 1812* (1975) and William M. Fowler, Jr.'s *Jack Tars and Commodores* (1984), on the role of the navy.

10 ✒

NATIONALISM AND SECTIONALISM

ECONOMIC NATIONALISM

When did the United States become a nation? There is no easy answer to the question, for a sense of nationhood was a slow growth and one always subject to cross-currents of localism, sectionalism, and class interest, as indeed it still is. Americans of the colonies and the early republic by and large identified more closely with the local community and at most the province or state in which they resided than with any larger idea of empire or nation. Among the colonies there was no common tie equal to the connection between each and the mother country. The Revolution gave rise to a sense of nationhood, but that could hardly be regarded as the dominant idea of the Revolution. Men who, like Hamilton, were prepared to think continentally, strengthened the federal Union by the Constitution, but Jefferson's "Revolution of 1800" revealed the countervailing forces of local and state interest. Jefferson himself, for instance, always spoke of Virginia as "my country."

Immediately after the War of 1812, however, there could no longer be any doubt that an American nation existed. Nationalism found expression in economic policy and culture after 1815. An abnormal economic prosperity after the war fed a feeling of well-being and enhanced the prestige of the national government. Jefferson's embargo ironically had given impulse to the factories that he abhorred. His policy of "peaceful coercion," followed by the wartime constraints on trade, had caused capital in New England and the middle states to drift from commerce toward manufacturing. The idea spread that the strength of the country was dependent on a more balanced economy. After a

The Union Manufactories of Maryland in Patapsco Falls, Baltimore County, c. 1815. *A textile mill begun during the embargo of 1807; by 1825 the Union Manufactories would employ over 600 people.*

generation of war, shortages of farm products in Europe forced up the prices of American products and stimulated agricultural expansion, indeed a wild speculation in farmlands. Southern cotton, tobacco, and rice came to account for about two-thirds of American exports. At the same time planters and farmers could buy in a postwar market flooded with cheap English goods. The new American manufacturers would seek protection from this competition.

President Madison, in his first annual message to Congress after the war, recommended several steps toward strengthening the government: better fortifications, a standing army and a strong navy, a new national bank, effective protection of the new infant industries, a system of canals and roads for commercial and military use, and to top it off, a great national university. "The Republicans have out-Federalized Federalism," one New Englander remarked. Congress responded by authorizing a standing army of 10,000 and strengthening the navy as well.

THE BANK OF THE UNITED STATES   The trinity of economic nationalism—proposals for a second national bank, protective tariff, and internal improvements—inspired the greatest controversies of the time. After the national bank expired in 1811 the country had fallen into a financial muddle. State-chartered banks mushroomed with little or no control and their banknotes flooded the channels of commerce with money of uncertain value, which

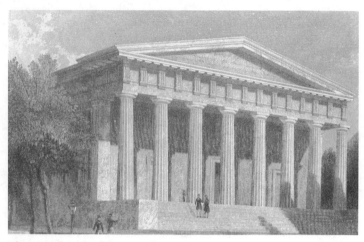

The second Bank of the United States.

often was not accepted at par. And this was the money on which Americans depended. Because hard money had been so short during the war, many state banks had suspended specie payments in redemption of their notes, thereby depressing the value of these notes further. The absence of the central bank had been a source of financial embarrassment to the government, which had neither a ready means of floating loans nor of transferring funds across the country.

Madison and most younger Republicans salved their constitutional scruples with a dash of pragmatism. The issue, Madison said, had been decided "by repeated recognitions . . . of the validity of such an institution in acts of the legislative, executive, and judicial branches of the Government, accompanied by . . . a concurrence of the general will of the nation." In 1816 Congress adopted over the protest of Old Republicans provision for a new Bank of the United States. Modeled after Hamilton's bank, it differed chiefly in that it was capitalized at $35 million instead of $10 million. Once again the charter ran for twenty years, once again the government owned a fifth of the stock and named five of the twenty-five directors, and again the bank served as the government depository. Its banknotes were accepted in payments to the government. In return for its privileges the bank had to take care of the government's funds without charge, lend the government $5 million on demand, and pay the government a cash bonus of $1.5 million.

The debate on the bank was noteworthy because of the leading roles played by the great triumvirate of John C. Calhoun of South Carolina, Henry Clay of Kentucky, and Daniel Webster of New Hampshire, later of Massachusetts. Calhoun, still in his youthful phase as a War Hawk nationalist, introduced the measure and pushed it through, justifying its constitutionality by the congressional power to regulate the currency, and pointing to the need for a uniform circulating medium. Clay, who had been in on the kill when Hamilton's bank expired in 1811, now confessed that he had failed to foresee the evils that resulted, and asserted that circumstances had made the bank indispensable. Webster, on the other hand, led the opposition of the New England Federalists, who did not want the banking center moved from Boston to Philadelphia. Later, after he moved from New Hampshire to Massachusetts, Webster would return to Congress as the champion of a much stronger national power, while events would carry Calhoun in the other direction.

A PROTECTIVE TARIFF The shift of capital from commerce to manufactures, begun during the embargo, had speeded up during the war. Peace in 1815 brought a sudden renewal of cheap British imports, and gave impetus to a movement for the protection of infant industries. The self-interest of the manufacturers, who as yet had little political impact, was reinforced by a patriotic desire for economic independence from Britain. Spokesmen for New England shippers and southern farmers opposed the movement, but both sections had sizable minorities who believed that the promotion of industry was vital to both sectional and national welfare.

The Tariff of 1816, the first intended more for the protection of industry against foreign competition than for revenue, passed by a comfortable majority. The South and New England registered a majority of their votes against the bill, but the middle states and Old Northwest cast only five negative votes altogether. Nathaniel Macon of North Carolina opposed the tariff and defended the Old Republican doctrine of strict construction. The power to protect industry, Macon said, like the power to establish a bank, rested on the doctrine of implied powers; Macon worried that implied powers might one day be used to abolish slavery. The minority of southerners who voted for the tariff, led by William Lowndes and John C. Calhoun of South Carolina, had good reason to expect that the South might itself become a manufacturing center. South Carolina was then developing a relatively diversified economy which included a few textile mills.

Clothing manufacturers, such as those represented in this advertisement for a New York sewing machine company, favored tariff protection from competing British goods.

According to the census of 1810 the southern states had approximately as many manufactures as New England. Within a few years New England moved ahead of the South, and Calhoun went over to Macon's views against protection. The tariff then became a sectional issue, with manufacturers, food growers, wool, sugar, and hemp growers favoring higher tariffs, while planters and shipping interests favored lower duties.

INTERNAL IMPROVEMENTS   The third major issue of the time was internal improvements: the building of roads and the development of water transportation. The war had highlighted the shortcomings of existing facilities. Troop movements through the western wilderness proved very difficult. Settlers found that unless they located near navigable waters, they were cut off from trade and limited to a frontier subsistence.

The federal government had entered the field of internal improvements under Jefferson, who went along with some hesitation. He and both of his successors recommended an amendment to give the federal government undisputed power in the field, but lacking that, the constitutional grounds for federal action rested mainly on provision for national defense and expansion of the postal system. In 1803, when Ohio became a state, Congress decreed that 5 percent of the proceeds from land sales in the state would go to building a National Road from the Atlantic coast into Ohio and beyond as the territory developed. In 1806 Jefferson signed a measure for a survey, and construction of the National Road got under way in 1811. By 1818 it was open from Cumberland, Maryland, to Wheeling on the Ohio River. Construction stopped temporarily during the business panic of 1819, but by 1838 the road extended all the way to Vandalia, Illinois.

In 1817 John C. Calhoun put through the House a bill to place in a fund for internal improvements the $1.5 million bonus the Bank of the United States had paid for its charter, as well as all future dividends on the government's bank stock. Once again opposition centered in New England and the South, which expected to gain least, and support came largely from the West, which badly needed good roads. On his last day in office Madison vetoed the bill. Sympathetic to its purpose, he could not overcome his "insuperable difficulty . . . in reconciling the bill with the Constitution" and suggested instead a constitutional amendment. Internal improvements remained for another hundred years, with few exceptions, the responsibility of states and private enterprise. Then and later Congress supported river and harbor improvements, and scattered post roads, but nothing of a systematic nature. The federal government did not enter the field on a large scale until passage of the Federal Highways Act of 1916.

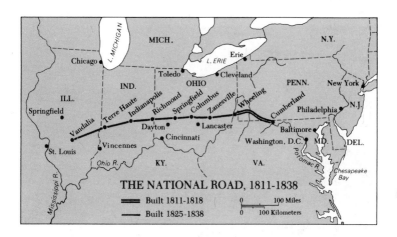

THE NATIONAL ROAD, 1811–1838
Built 1811–1818
Built 1825–1838

"Good Feelings"

JAMES MONROE   As Madison approached the end of a turbulent tenure he, like Jefferson, turned to a fellow Virginian, another secretary of state, as his successor: James Monroe. In the Republican caucus Monroe won the nomination, then overwhelmed his Federalist opponent, Rufus King of New York, 183 to 34 in the electoral college. The "Virginia Dynasty" continued. Like three of the four presidents before him, Monroe was a Virginia planter, but with a difference: Monroe came from the small-planter group. At the outbreak of the Revolution he was just beginning college at William and Mary. He joined the army at the age of sixteen, fought with Washington at Trenton, and was a lieutenant-colonel when the war ended. Later he studied law with Jefferson and absorbed Jeffersonian principles at the master's feet.

Monroe never showed the profundity of his Republican predecessors in scholarship or political theory, but what he lacked in intellect he made up in dedication to public service. His soul, Jefferson said, if turned inside out, would be found spotless. Monroe served in the Virginia assembly, as governor of the state, in the Confederation Congress and United States Senate, and as minister to Paris, London, and Madrid. Under Madison he had been secretary of state, and twice doubled as secretary of war. Monroe, with his powdered wig, cocked hat, and knee-breeches, was the last of the revolutionary generation to serve in the White House and the last president to dress in the old style.

To the postwar generation there was an air of nostalgic solidity

*James Monroe, portrayed as he
entered the presidency in 1816.*

about him, even though little more than twenty years before, as minister to Paris, he had defended the French radicals during their bloodiest exploits. Firmly grounded in Republican principles, he was never quite able to keep up with the onrush of the new nationalism. He accepted as accomplished fact the bank and the protective tariff, but during his tenure there was no further extension of economic nationalism. Indeed there was a minor setback. He permitted the National (or Cumberland) Road to be carried forward, but in his veto of the Cumberland Road Bill (1822) he denied the authority of Congress to collect tolls for its repair and maintenance. Like Jefferson and Madison, he also urged a constitutional amendment to remove all doubt about federal authority in the field of internal improvements, and in 1824 he signed the General Survey Bill, which authorized estimates of roads and canals needed for military, commercial, and postal purposes.

Whatever his limitations, Monroe surrounded himself with some of the strongest and ablest young Republican leaders. John Quincy Adams became secretary of state. William Crawford of Georgia continued in office as secretary of the treasury. John C. Calhoun headed the War Department after Henry Clay refused the job to stay on as Speaker of the House. The new administration found the country in a state of well-being: America was at peace and the economy was flourishing. Soon after his 1817 inauguration Monroe embarked on a goodwill tour of New England. In Boston, lately a hotbed of wartime dissent, a Federalist paper, the *Columbian Centinel,* ran a general comment on the president's visit under the heading "Era of Good Feelings." The label became a popular catch-phrase for Monroe's administration, and one that historians seized upon later. Like many a maxim, it conveys just enough truth to be sadly misleading. A resurgence of factionalism and sectionalism erupted just as the postwar prosperity collapsed in the Panic of 1819.

For two years, however, general harmony reigned, and even when the country's troubles revived, little of the blame sullied the name of Monroe. In 1820 he was reelected without opposition, even without needing nomination. The Federalists were too weak to put up a candidate, and the Republicans did not bother to call a caucus. Monroe got all the electoral votes except for three abstentions and one vote from New Hampshire for John Quincy Adams. The Republican party was dominant, or perhaps more accurately, was following the Federalists into oblivion. In the general political contentment the first party system was fading away, but rivalries for the succession soon commenced the process of forming new parties.

IMPROVING RELATIONS WITH BRITAIN Adding to the prevailing contentment after the war was a growing rapprochement with the recent enemy. Trade relations with Britain (and India) were restored by a Commercial Convention of 1815, which eliminated discriminatory duties on either side. The Peace of Ghent had left unsettled a number of minor disputes, but in the sequel two important compacts—the Rush-Bagot Agreement of 1817 and the Convention of 1818—removed several potential causes of irritation. In the first, effected by an exchange of notes between Acting Secretary of State Richard Rush and British Minister Charles Bagot, the threat of naval competition on the Great Lakes vanished with an arrangement to limit forces there to several revenue cutters. Although the exchange made no reference to the land boundary between the countries, its spirit gave rise to the tradition of an unfortified border, the longest in the world.

The Convention of 1818 covered three major points. The northern limit of the Louisiana Purchase was settled by extending the national boundary along the Forty-ninth Parallel west from Lake of the Woods to the crest of the Rocky Mountains. West of that point the Oregon country would be open to joint occupation, but the boundary remained unsettled. The right of Americans to fish off Newfoundland and Labrador, granted in 1783, was acknowledged once again.

The chief remaining problem was Britain's exclusion of American ships from the West Indies in order to reserve that lucrative trade for British ships. The Commercial Convention of 1815 did not apply there, and after the War of 1812 the British had once again closed the door. This remained a chronic irritant, and the United States retaliated with several measures. Under a Navigation Act of 1817, importation of West Indian produce was restricted to American vessels or vessels belonging to West Indian merchants. In 1818 American ports were closed to all British vessels arriving from a colony that was legally closed to vessels of the United States. In 1820 Monroe approved an act of Congress which specified total non-intercourse, in British vessels, with all British-American colonies, even in goods taken to England and reexported. The rapprochement with Britain therefore fell short of perfection.

JACKSON TAKES FLORIDA The year 1819 was one of the more fateful years in American history, a time when a whole sequence of developments came into focus. The bumptious new nationalism reached a climax with the acquisition of Florida and the extension of the southwestern boundary to the Pacific, and with three major decisions of the Supreme Court. But nationalism quickly began to run afoul of domestic cross-currents that would set up an ever-widening swirl in the next decades. In the calculus of global power, it was perhaps long since reckoned that Florida would some day pass to the United States. Spanish sovereignty was more a technicality than an actuality, and extended little beyond St. Augustine on the east coast and Pensacola and St. Marks on the Gulf. The thinly held province had been a thorn in the side of the United States during the recent war, a center of British intrigue, a haven for Creek refugees, who were beginning to take the name Seminole (runaway or separatist), and a harbor for runaway slaves and criminals. Florida also stood athwart the outlets of several important rivers flowing to the Gulf.

Spain was almost powerless at that point because of both internal and colonial revolt, and unable to enforce its obligations under the Pinckney Treaty of 1795 to pacify the frontiers. In 1816 American forces came into conflict with a group of escaped slaves who had taken over a British fort on the Appalachicola River. Seminoles who challenged the legality of Creek land cessions were soon fighting white settlers in the area. In November 1817 Americans burned the Seminole border settlement of Fowltown, killed four of its inhabitants, and dispersed the rest across the border into Florida.

At this point Secretary of War Calhoun authorized a campaign against the Seminoles, and summoned General Jackson from

Andrew Jackson, portrayed here at the time of his campaign against the Seminoles in Florida.

Nashville to take command. Jackson's orders allowed him to pursue the offenders into Spanish territory, but not to attack any Spanish post. A man of Jackson's direct purpose naturally felt hobbled by such a restriction, so he wrote to President Monroe that if the United States wanted Florida he could wind up the whole thing in sixty days. All he needed was private, unofficial word, which might be sent through Tennessee Rep. John Rhea. Soon afterward Jackson indeed got a letter from Rhea, and claimed that it transmitted cryptically the required authority, although Monroe always denied any such intention. The truth about the Rhea letter, which Jackson destroyed (at Monroe's request, he said), remains a mystery.

In any case, when it came to Spaniards or Indians, no white Tennessean—certainly not Andrew Jackson—was likely to bother with technicalities. Jackson pushed eastward through Florida, reinforced by Tennessee volunteers and a party of friendly Creeks, taking the Spanish post at St. Marks, and skirmishing with the Seminoles, destroying their settlements, and pursuing them to the Suwannee River. Two of their leaders, the prophet Francis and Chief Homollimico, Jackson hanged without any semblance of a trial. For two British intriguers in the area, a trader named Alexander Arbuthnot and a former British officer, Robert Ambrister, he convened a court-martial, but to the same end. Both had befriended the Seminoles, and Ambrister at least had offered them military training. In any case Jackson was convinced that the two were at the root of all the trouble, and the evidence did not much matter. Arbuthnot was hanged; Ambrister shot. Having mopped up the region from the Appalachicola to the Suwannee, Jackson then turned west and seized Pensacola, named one of his colonels civil and military governor of Florida, and returned home to Nashville. The whole thing had taken about four months; the Florida panhandle was in American hands by the end of May 1818.

The news created consternation in both Madrid and Washington. Spain demanded the return of its territory, reparations, and the punishment of Jackson, but Spain's impotence was plain for all to see. Monroe's cabinet was at first prepared to disavow Jackson's action, especially his direct attack on Spanish posts. Calhoun, as secretary of war, was inclined, at least officially, to discipline Jackson for disregard of orders—a stand which caused bad blood between the two men later—but privately confessed a certain pleasure at the outcome. In any case a man as popular as Jackson was almost invulnerable. And he had one important friend at court, Secretary of State John Quincy Adams, who real-

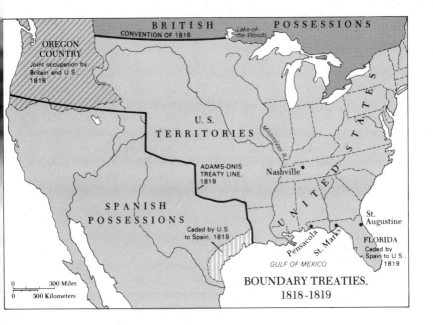

BOUNDARY TREATIES, 1818-1819

ized that Jackson had strengthened his hand in negotiations already under way with the Spanish minister, Luís de Onís y Gonzalez. American forces withdrew from Florida, but negotiations resumed with the knowledge that the United States could take Florida at any time.

The fate of Florida was a foregone conclusion. Adams now had his eye on a larger purpose, a definition of the western boundary of the Louisiana Purchase and—his boldest stroke—extension of a boundary to the Pacific coast. In lengthy negotiations Adams gradually gave ground on claims to Texas, but stuck to his demand for a transcontinental line. Agreement finally came early in 1819. Spain ceded all of Florida in return for American assumption of private American claims against Spain up to $5 million. The western boundary of the Louisiana Purchase would run along the Sabine River and then in stair-step fashion up to the Red River, along the Red, and up to the Arkansas River. From the source of the Arkansas it would go north to the Forty-second Parallel and thence west to the Pacific coast. A dispute over land claims held up ratification for another two years, but those claims were revoked and final ratifications were exchanged in 1821. Florida became a territory, and its first governor briefly was Andrew Jackson. In 1845 Florida eventually achieved statehood.

"A Firebell in the Night"

THE PANIC OF 1819   Adams's Transcontinental Treaty was a triumph of foreign policy and the climactic event of the postwar nationalism. Even before it was signed in February 1819, however, two thunderclaps signaled the end of the brief "Era of Good Feelings" and gave warning of stormy weather ahead. The two portents were the financial Panic of 1819 and the controversy over statehood for Missouri. The occasion for the panic was the sudden collapse of cotton prices in the Liverpool market. At one point in 1818 cotton had soared to 32½ cents a pound. The pressure of high prices forced British manufacturers to turn away from American sources to cheaper East Indian cotton. It proved unsatisfactory, but only after severe damage had been done in American markets. In 1819 cotton averaged only 14.3 cents per pound at New Orleans. The price collapse in cotton was the event that set off a decline in the demand for other American goods, and suddenly revealed the fragility of the prosperity that followed the War of 1812.

Since 1815 a speculative bubble had grown with expectations that expansion would go on forever. But American industry began to run into trouble finding markets for its goods. Even the Tariff of 1816 had not been enough to eliminate British competition. What was more, businessmen, farmers, and land jobbers had inflated the bubble with a volatile expansion of credit. The sources of this credit were both government and banks. Under the Land Law of 1800 the government extended four years' credit to those who bought western lands. After 1804 one could buy as little as 160 acres at a minimum price of $1.64 per acre (although in auctions the best lands went for more). In many cases speculators took up large tracts, paying one-fourth down, and then sold them to settlers with the understanding that the settlers would pay the remaining installments. With the collapse of prices, and then of land values, both speculators and settlers found themselves caught short.

The inflation of credit was compounded by the reckless practices of state banks. To enlarge their loans they issued banknotes far beyond their means of redemption, and at first were under little pressure to promise redemption in specie. Even the second Bank of the United States, which was supposed to introduce some order, was at first caught up in the mania. Its first president yielded to the contagion of get-rich-quick fever that was sweeping the country. The proliferation of branches combined with little supervision from Philadelphia to carry the bank into the same reckless extension of loans that state banks had pursued. In 1819, just as alert businessmen began to take alarm, a case of extensive fraud and embezzlement in the Baltimore branch came to light. The upshot of the disclosure was the appointment of Langdon Cheves, former congressman from South Carolina, as the bank's president and the establishment of a sounder policy.

Cheves reduced salaries and other costs, postponed dividends, restrained the extension of credit, and presented for redemption the state banknotes that came in, thereby forcing the state-chartered banks to keep specie reserves. Cheves rescued the bank from near-ruin, but only by putting heavy pressure on state banks. State banks in turn put pressure on their debtors, who found it harder to renew old loans or get new ones. In 1823, his job completed, Cheves relinquished his position to Nicholas Biddle of Philadelphia. The Cheves policies were the result rather than the cause of the Panic, but they were anathema to debtors who found it all the more difficult to meet their obligations. Hard times lasted about three years, and the bank took much of the blame in the popular mind. The Panic passed, but resentment of the bank lingered. It never fully regained the confidence of the South and the West.

THE MISSOURI COMPROMISE   Just as the Panic was breaking over the country, another cloud appeared on the horizon, the onset of a sectional controversy over slavery. By 1819 it happened that the country had an equal number of slave and free states, eleven of each. The line between them was defined by the southern and western boundaries of Pennsylvania and the Ohio River. Although slavery still lingered in some places north of the line, it was on the way to extinction there. Beyond the Mississippi, however, no move had been made to extend the dividing line across the Louisiana Purchase territory, where slavery had existed from the days when France and Spain had colonized the area. At the time the Missouri Territory embraced all of the Louisiana Purchase except the state of Louisiana (1812) and the Arkansas Territory (1819). In the westward rush of population, the old French town of St. Louis became the funnel through which settlers pushed on beyond the Mississippi. These were largely settlers from the south who brought their slaves with them.

In February 1819 the House of Representatives confronted legislation enabling Missouri to draft a state constitution, its population having passed the minimum of 60,000. At that point Rep. James Tallmadge, Jr., a congressman from New York, introduced

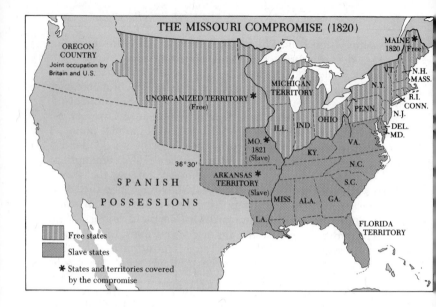

THE MISSOURI COMPROMISE (1820)

a resolution prohibiting the further introduction of slaves into Missouri, which had some 10,000 in 1820, and providing freedom at age twenty-five for those born after the territory's admission as a state. Tallmadge's motives remain obscure, but may have been very simply a moral aversion to slavery or perhaps a political aversion to having slavery and the three-fifths compromise extended any farther beyond the Mississippi River. After brief but fiery exchanges, the House passed the amendment on an almost strictly sectional vote and the Senate rejected it by a similar tally, but with several northerners joining in the opposition. With population at the time growing faster in the north, a balance between the two sections could be held only in the Senate. In the House, slave states had 81 votes while free states had 105; a balance was unlikely ever again to be restored in the House.

Congress adjourned in March, postponing further debate until the regular session in December. When the debate came, it was remarkable for the absence of moral argument, although repugnance to slavery and moral guilt about it were never far from the surface. The debate turned on the constitutional issue. Congress, Rufus King of New York asserted, was empowered to forbid slavery in Missouri as the Confederation Congress had done in the Northwest Territory. William Pinkney of Maryland asserted that the states were equal and that Congress could not bind a state. Southern leaders argued further that under the Fifth Amendment, slaveholders could not be denied the right to carry their property into the territory, which would be deprivation of property without due process of law. Henry Clay and others expressed a view, which Jefferson and Madison now shared, that the expansion and dispersal of slavery would ameliorate the condition of the slaves. Most of the constitutional arguments that would reverberate in later quarrels over slavery were already present in the argument over Missouri, but the moral issue of bondage had not yet reached the fevered condition it would later achieve, since few were yet prepared to defend slavery as a positive good. In fact the general abhorrence of slavery was still strong enough that during 1820 Congress defined the illegal foreign slave trade as piracy, subjecting those engaged in it to the death penalty. This penalty was not actually imposed, however, until the outbreak of the Civil War.

Maine's application for statehood made it easier to arrive at an agreement. Since colonial times Maine had been the northern province of Massachusetts. The Senate linked its request for separate statehood with Missouri's and voted to admit Maine as a free state and Missouri as a slave state, thus maintaining the balance in the Senate. An Illinois senator further extended the compromise by an amendment to exclude slavery from the rest of the Louisiana Purchase north of 36°30′N, Missouri's southern border. Slavery thus would continue in the Arkansas Territory and in the state of Missouri, and be excluded from the remainder of the area. But that was country which Zebulon Pike's and Stephen Long's reports had persuaded the public was the Great American Desert, unlikely ever to be settled. For this reason the

Henry Clay's compromise deflected a confrontation on the expansion of slavery. Clay is portrayed here in 1822.

arrangement seemed to be a victory for the slave states. The House at first refused to accept the arrangement, but the question went to a conference committee of the two houses for which Speaker Henry Clay had carefully chosen malleable members who accepted the Senate compromise. By a very close vote it passed the House on March 2, 1820.

Once that issue was settled, however, another problem arose. The proslavery elements which dominated Missouri's constitutional convention inserted in the new state constitution a proviso excluding free Negroes and mulattoes from the state. This clearly violated the requirement of Article IV, Section 2, of the Constitution: "The Citizens of each State shall be entitled to all Privileges and Immunities of Citizens in the Several States." Free Negroes were citizens of many states, including the slave states of North Carolina and Tennessee where, until the mid-1830s, they also voted.

The renewed controversy threatened final approval of Missouri's admission until Henry Clay, now beginning to earn his later title of the "Great Compromiser," formulated a "Second Missouri Compromise." Admission of Missouri as a state depended on assurance from the Missouri legislature that it would never construe the offending clause in such a way as to sanction denial of privileges that citizens held under the Constitution. It was one of the more artless dodges in American history, for it required the legislature to affirm that the state constitution did not mean what it clearly said, but the compromise worked. The Missouri legislature duly adopted the pledge, but qualified it by denying that the legislature had any power to bind the people of the state. On August 10, 1821, President Monroe proclaimed the admission of Missouri as the twenty-fourth state. For the time the controversy was settled. "But this momentous question," the aging Thomas Jefferson wrote to a friend after the first compromise, "like a firebell in the night awakened and filled me with terror. I considered it at once as the knell of the Union."

JUDICIAL NATIONALISM

JOHN MARSHALL, CHIEF JUSTICE   Meanwhile nationalism still flourished in the Supreme Court, where Chief Justice John Marshall preserved Hamiltonian Federalism for yet another generation. Marshall, a survivor of the Revolution, was among those who had been forever nationalized by the experience. In later years he said: "I was confirmed in the habit of considering America as my

Chief Justice John Marshall, pillar of judicial nationalism.

country and Congress as my government.'' The habit persisted through a successful legal career punctuated by service in Virginia's legislature and ratifying convention, as part of the "XYZ" mission to France, and as a member of Congress. Never a judge before he became chief justice in 1801, he established the power of the Supreme Court by force of mind and determination.

During Marshall's early years on the Court (altogether he served thirty-four years) he affirmed the principle of judicial review. In *Marbury v. Madison* (1803) and *Fletcher v. Peck* (1810) the Court first struck down a federal law and then a state law as unconstitutional. In the cases of *Martin v. Hunter's Lessee* (1816) and *Cohens v. Virginia* (1821) the Court assumed the right to take appeals from state courts on the grounds that the Constitution, laws, and treaties of the United States could be kept uniformly the supreme law of the land only if the Court could review decisions of state courts. In the first case the Court overruled Virginia's confiscation of Loyalist property because this violated treaties with Great Britain; in the second it upheld Virginia's right to forbid the sale of lottery tickets.

PROTECTING CONTRACT RIGHTS   In the fateful year 1819 came two more decisions of major importance in checking the states and building the power of the central government: *Dartmouth College v. Woodward*, and *McCulloch v. Maryland*. The Dartmouth College case involved an attempt by the New Hampshire legislature to alter a charter granted Dartmouth by George III in 1769 under which the trustees became a self-perpetuating board. In 1816 the state's Republican legislature, offended by this relic of monarchy and even more by the Federalist majority on the board, placed Dartmouth under a new board named by the governor. The original trustees sued, lost in the state courts, but with Daniel Webster as counsel, won on appeal to the Supreme Court. The charter, Marshall said for the Court, was a valid contract which the legislature had impaired, an act forbidden by the Constitution. This implied a new and enlarged definition of contract which seemed to put private corporations beyond the reach of the states that chartered them. But thereafter states commonly wrote into charters and general laws of incorporation provisions making them subject to modification. Such provisions were then part of the "contract."

STRENGTHENING THE FEDERAL GOVERNMENT   Marshall's single most important interpretation of the constitutional system came in the case of *McCulloch v. Maryland*. McCulloch, a clerk in the Baltimore branch of the Bank of the United States, failed to affix state revenue stamps to banknotes as required by a Maryland law taxing the notes. Indicted by the state, McCulloch, acting for the bank, appealed to the Supreme Court, which handed down a unanimous judgment upholding the power of Congress to charter the bank and denying any right of the state to tax the bank. In a lengthy opinion Marshall examined and rejected Maryland's argument that the federal government was the creature of sovereign states. Instead, he argued, it arose directly from the people acting through the conventions that ratified the Constitution. While sovereignty was divided between the states and the national government, the latter, "though limited in its powers, is supreme within its sphere of action."

Marshall then went on to endorse the doctrine of broad construction and implied powers set forth by Hamilton in his bank message of 1791. The "necessary and proper" clause, he argued, did not mean "absolutely indispensable." The test of constitutionality he summed up in almost the same words as Hamilton: "Let the end be legitimate, let it be within the scope of the constitution, and all means which are appropriate, which are plainly adapted to that end, which are not prohibited, but consistent with the letter and spirit of the constitution, are constitutional."

The state's effort to tax the bank conflicted with the supreme law of the land. One great principle which "entirely pervades the constitution," Marshall wrote, was "that the constitution and the laws made in pursuance thereof are supreme: that they control the constitution and laws of the respective states, and cannot be controlled by them." The tax therefore was unconstitutional for "the power to tax involves the power to destroy"—which was precisely what the legislatures of Maryland and several other states had in mind with respect to the bank.

REGULATING INTERSTATE COMMERCE Marshall's last great decision, *Gibbons v. Ogden* (1824), established national supremacy in regulating interstate commerce. In 1808 Robert Fulton and Robert Livingston, who pioneered commercial use of the steamboat, got from the New York legislature the exclusive right to operate steamboats on the state's waters. From them in turn Aaron

Deck Life on the *Paragon*, 1811–1812. *The* Paragon, *"a whole floating town," was the third steamboat operated on the Hudson by Robert Fulton and Robert R. Livingston. Fulton said the* Paragon *"beats everything on the globe, for made as you and I are we cannot tell what is in the moon."*

Ogden got the exclusive right to navigation across the Hudson between New York and New Jersey. Thomas Gibbons, however, operated a coastal trade under a federal license and came into competition with Ogden. On behalf of a unanimous Court, Marshall ruled that the monopoly granted by the state conflicted with the federal Coasting Act under which Gibbons operated. Congressional power to regulate commerce, the Court said, "like all others vested in Congress, is complete in itself, may be exercised to its utmost extent, and acknowledges no limitations other than are prescribed in the constitution."

The opinion stopped just short of stating an exclusive federal power over commerce, and later cases would clarify the point that states had a concurrent jurisdiction so long as it did not come into conflict with federal action. For many years there was in fact little federal regulation, so that in striking down the monopoly created by the state Marshall had opened the way to extensive development of steamboat navigation and, soon afterward, steam railroads. Economic expansion was often consonant with judicial nationalism.

Nationalist Diplomacy

THE NORTHWEST   In foreign affairs, too, nationalism continued to be an effective force. Within two years after final approval of Adams's Transcontinental Treaty, the secretary of state was able to draw another important transcontinental line. In 1819 Spain had abandoned her claim to the Oregon country above the Forty-second Parallel. Russia, however, had claims along the Pacific coast as well. In 1741 Vitus Bering, in the employ of Russia, had explored the strait which now bears his name, and in 1799 the Russian-American Company had been formed to exploit the resources of Alaska. Some Russian outposts reached as far south as the California coast. In September 1821 the Russian czar issued an *ukase* (proclamation) claiming the Pacific coast as far south as 51°, which in the American view lay within the "Oregon country."

In 1823 Secretary of State Adams contested "the right of Russia to any territorial establishment on this continent." The American government, he informed the Russian minister, assumed the principle "that the American continents are no longer subjects for any new European colonial establishments." The upshot of his protest was a treaty signed in 1824 whereby Russia, which had more pressing concerns in Europe, accepted the line of 54° 40′ as the southern boundary of its claim. In 1825 a similar agreement between Russia and Britain gave the Oregon country clearly defined boundaries, although it was still subject to joint occupation by the United States and Great Britain under their agreement of 1818.

LATIN AMERICA   Adams's disapproval of further colonization also had clear implications for Latin America. One consequence of the Napoleonic wars and French occupation of Spain and Portugal had been a series of wars of liberation in Latin America. Within little more than a decade after the flag of rebellion was first raised in 1811, Spain had lost its entire empire in the Americas. All that was left were the islands of Cuba, Puerto Rico, and Santo Domingo. The only possessions in the Americas left to European powers, 330 years after Columbus, were Russian Alaska, Canada, British Honduras, and Dutch, French, and British Guiana.

That Spain could not regain her empire seems clear enough in retrospect. The British navy would not permit it because Britain's trade with the area was too important. For a time, however, the temper of Europe after Napoleon was to restore "legitimacy" everywhere. The great European peace conference, the Congress of Vienna (1814–1815), returned that continent, as nearly as possible, to its status before the French Revolution and set out to make the world safe for monarchy. To that end the major powers (Great Britain, Prussia, Russia, and Austria) set up the Quadruple Alliance (it became the Quintuple Alliance after France entered in 1818) to police the European continent. In 1821 the Alliance, with Britain dissenting, authorized Austria to put down liberal movements in Italy. The British government was no champion of liberal revolution, but neither did it feel impelled to police the entire continent. In 1822, when the allies met in the Congress of Verona, they authorized France to suppress the constitutionalist movement in Spain and restore the authority of Ferdinand VII. At that point the British withdrew from the Concert of Europe, which in a few more years fell apart in a dispute over support of Greek rebellion against the Turks.

THE MONROE DOCTRINE   But in 1823 French troops crossed the Spanish border, put down the rebels, and restored King Ferdinand VII to absolute authority. Rumors began to circulate that France would also try to restore Ferdinand's "legitimate" power over Spain's American empire. Monroe and Secretary of War Calhoun were alarmed at the possibility, although John Quincy Adams took the more realistic view that such action was unlikely. After the break with the Quadruple Alliance, British Foreign

Minister George Canning sought to reach an understanding with the American minister to London that the two countries jointly undertake to forestall action by the Quadruple Alliance against Latin America. Monroe at first agreed, with the support of his sage advisors Jefferson and Madison.

Adams, however, urged upon Monroe and the cabinet the independent course of proclaiming a unilateral policy against the restoration of Spain's colonies. "It would be more candid," Adams said, "as well as more dignified, to avow our principles explicitly to Russia and France, than to come in as a cock-boat in the wake of the British man-of-war." Adams knew that the British navy would stop any action by the Quadruple Alliance in Latin America and he suspected that the alliance had no real intention to intervene anyway. The British wanted, moreover, the United States to agree not to acquire any more Spanish territory, including Cuba, Texas, or California, and Adams preferred to avoid such a commitment.

Indeed unbeknownst to Adams at the time Canning had already procured from French Foreign Minister Jules de Polignac a statement which renounced any purpose to reconquer or annex the former Spanish colonies. The Polignac Agreement was still unknown in the United States when Monroe incorporated the substance of Adams's views in his annual message to Congress on December 2, 1823. The Monroe Doctrine, as it was later called, comprised four major points: (1) that "the American continents . . . are henceforth not to be considered as subjects for future colonization by any European powers"; (2) the political system of European powers was different from that of the United States, which would "consider any attempt on their part to extend their system to any portion of this hemisphere as dangerous to our peace and safety"; (3) the United States would not interfere with existing European colonies; and (4) the United States would keep out of the internal affairs of European nations and their wars.

At the time the statement drew little attention either in the United States or abroad. Canning was more chagrined than anything else, since he had already achieved Monroe's objective two months before in the Polignac Agreement. In time the Monroe Doctrine, not even so called until 1852, became one of the cherished principles of American foreign policy, but for the time being it slipped into obscurity for want of any occasion to invoke it. In spite of Adams's affirmation, the United States came in as a cock boat in the wake of the British man-of-war after all, for the effectiveness of the doctrine depended on British naval supremacy. The doctrine had no standing in international law. It was merely a statement of intent by an American president to the Congress, and did not even draw enough interest at the time for European powers to renounce it.

ONE-PARTY POLITICS

Almost from the start of Monroe's second term the jockeying for the presidential succession had begun. Three members of Monroe's cabinet were active candidates: Calhoun, Crawford, and Adams. Henry Clay, longtime Speaker of the House, hungered and thirsted after the office. And on the fringes of the Washington scene a new force appeared in the person of Sen. Andrew Jackson, the scourge of the British, Spaniards, Creeks, and Seminoles, the epitome of what every frontiersman admired. All were Republicans, for again no Federalist stood a chance, but they were competing in a new political world, complicated by the cross-currents of nationalism and sectionalism. With only one party there was in effect no party, for there existed no generally accepted method for choosing a "regular" candidate.

PRESIDENTIAL NOMINATIONS   Selection by congressional caucus, already under attack in 1816, had disappeared in the wave of unanimity which reelected Monroe in 1820 without the formality of a nomination. The friends of Crawford sought in vain to breathe life back into "King Caucus," but only sixty-six congressmen appeared in answer to the call. They duly named Crawford for president and Albert Gallatin for vice-president, but the endorsement was so weak as to be more a handicap than an advantage. Crawford was in fact the logical successor to the Virginia dynasty, a native of the state though a resident of Georgia. He had flirted with nationalism, but swung back to states' rights and strict construction, and assumed leadership of a faction, called the Radicals, which included Old Republicans and those who distrusted the nationalism of Adams and Calhoun. Crawford's candidacy was a forlorn cause from the beginning, for the candidate had been stricken in 1823 by some unknown disease which left him half-paralyzed and half-blind. His friends protested that he would soon be well but he never did fully recover.

Long before the rump caucus met in early 1824, indeed for two years before, the country had broken out in a rash of presidential endorsements by legislatures and public meetings. In

July 1822 the Tennessee legislature named Andrew Jackson. In March 1824 a mass meeting of Pennsylvanians in Harrisburg added their endorsement, and Jackson, who had previously kept silent, responded that while the presidency should not be sought, it could not with propriety be declined. The same meeting named Calhoun for vice-president, and Calhoun accepted. The youngest of the candidates, he was content to take second place and bide his time. Meanwhile the Kentucky legislature had named its favorite son, Henry Clay, in November 1822. The Massachusetts legislature named Adams in 1824.

Of the four candidates only two had clearly defined programs, and the outcome was an early lesson in the danger of being committed on the issues too soon. Crawford's friends emphasized his devotion to the "principles of 1798," states' rights and strict construction. Clay, on the contrary, took his stand for the "American System": he favored the national bank, the protective tariff, and a national program of internal improvements to bind the country together and build its economy. Adams was close to Clay, openly dedicated to internal improvements but less strongly committed to the tariff. Jackson, where issues were concerned, remained an enigma and carefully avoided commitment. His managers hoped that, by being all things to all men, Jackson could capitalize on his popularity as the hero of New Orleans.

THE "CORRUPT BARGAIN" The outcome turned on personalities and sectional allegiance more than on issues. Adams, the only northern candidate, carried New England, the former bastion of Federalism, and most of New York's electoral votes. Clay took Kentucky, Ohio, and Missouri. Crawford carried Virginia, Georgia, and Delaware. Jackson swept the Southeast, plus Illinois and Indiana, and with Calhoun's support, the Carolinas, Pennsylvania, Maryland, and New Jersey. All candidates got scattered votes elsewhere. In New York, where Clay was strong, his supporters were outmaneuvered by the Adams forces in the legislature, which still chose the presidential electors.

The result was inconclusive in both the electoral vote and the popular vote, wherever the state legislature permitted the choice of electors by the people. In the electoral college Jackson had 99, Adams 84, Crawford 41, Clay 37. In the popular vote it ran about the same: Jackson 154,000, Adams 109,000, Crawford 47,000, and Clay 47,000. Whatever might have been said about the outcome, one thing seemed apparent. It was a defeat for Clay's American System: New England and New York opposed him on internal improvements; the South and Southwest on the protective tariff. Sectionalism had defeated the national program, yet the advocate of the American System now assumed the role of president-maker, since the election was thrown into the House of Representatives, where Speaker Clay's influence was decisive. Clay had little trouble in choosing, since he regarded Jackson as unfit for the office. He kept his own counsel until near the end, then threw his support to Adams. The final vote in the House, which was by state, carried Adams to victory with thirteen votes to Jackson's seven and Crawford's four.

It was a costly victory, for the result was to unite Adams's foes and to cripple his administration before it got under way. There is no evidence that Adams entered into any bargain with Clay to win his support, but the charge was made and widely believed after Adams made Clay his secretary of state, and thus put him in the office from which three successive presidents had risen. Adams's Puritan conscience could never quite overcome a sense of guilt at the maneuverings that were necessary to gain his election, but a "corrupt bargain" was too much out of character for credence. Yet credence it had with a large number of people, and on that cry a campaign to elect Jackson next time was launched almost immediately after the 1824 decision. The Crawford people, including Martin Van Buren, the "Little Magician" of New York politics, soon moved into the Jackson camp.

JOHN QUINCY ADAMS'S PRESIDENCY   John Quincy Adams was one of the ablest men and finest intellects ever to enter the White House, but he sadly lacked the common touch and the politician's gift for maneuver. He firmly refused to play the game of patronage, on the simple grounds that it would be dishonorable to dismiss "able and faithful political opponents to provide for my own partisans." In four years he removed only twelve officeholders. His first annual message to Congress was a grandiose blueprint for national development, set forth in such a blunt way that it became a disaster of political ineptitude. In the boldness and magnitude of its conception, the Adams plan outdid both Hamilton and Clay. The central government, the president said, should promote internal improvements, set up a national university, finance scientific explorations, build astronomical observatories ("lighthouses of the skies"), reform the patent laws, and create a new Department of the Interior. In general terms he proposed "laws promoting the improvement of the agriculture, commerce, and manufactures, the cultivation and encouragement of the mechanic and of the elegant arts, the advancement of

John Quincy Adams, a president of great intellect but without the common touch.

literature, and the progress of the sciences, ornamental and profound. . . . ''

To refrain from using broad federal powers "would be treachery to the most sacred of trusts." Officers of the government, he said, should not "fold up our arms and proclaim to the world that we are palsied by the will of our constituents. . . . '' Whatever grandeur of conception the message to Congress had, it was obscured by an unhappy choice of language. For a minority president to demean the sovereignty of the voter was tactless enough. For the son of John Adams to cite the example "of the nations of Europe and of their rulers" was downright suicidal. At one fell swoop he had revived all the Republican suspicions of the Adamses. To the aging Jefferson his message seemed like Federalism run riot, looking to "a single and splendid government of an aristocracy, founded on banking institutions, and moneyed incorporation under the guise and cloak of . . . manufactures, commerce, and navigation, riding and ruling over the plundered ploughman and beggared yeomanry." Jefferson did not see, though, that Adams's presidential message was the beginning of the definition of a new party system. The minority who cast their lot with Adams and Clay were turning into National-Republicans; the opposition, the growing party of Jacksonians, were the Democratic-Republicans, who would eventually drop the name Republican and become Democrats.

Adams's headstrong plunge into nationalism and his refusal to play the game of politics condemned his administration to utter frustration. Congress ignored his domestic proposals, and in foreign affairs the triumphs that he had scored as secretary of state had no sequels. In relations with Britain Adams had overreached himself by a "Perilous experiment" begun when he was secretary of state. By trying to force upon the British acceptance of American shipping on the same basis as British shipping in the West Indies, he passed up a chance for compromise on favorable terms, with the result that American shipping was banned altogether in 1826.

Before the year 1826 was out, Adams faced a showdown with the state of Georgia and meekly backed off. The affair began in 1825 when a federal Indian commissioner signed the fraudulent Treaty of Indian Springs with a group of Creek chieftains by which the Creeks lost 4.7 million acres in Georgia. Adams at first signed the treaty, but on further inquiry withdrew it and worked out the somewhat less stringent Treaty of Washington in 1826. The Georgia legislature denounced this annulment of the previous treaty as invalid and, by some obscure reasoning, called it a violation of states' rights. The governor mobilized the Georgia militia and notified Adams that the state would repel with force any attempt to void the earlier treaty. At this the administration simply abandoned the Creeks to their fate. The Cherokees were next on the agenda, but by the time Georgia got around to them, there was a president who supported the land grabbers.

The climactic effort to discredit Adams came on the tariff issue. The Panic of 1819 had given rise to action for a higher tariff in 1820, but the effort failed by one vote in the Senate. In 1824 the advocates of protection renewed the effort, with greater success. The Tariff of 1824 favored the Middle Atlantic and New England manufacturers with higher duties on woolens, cotton, iron, and other finished goods. Clay's Kentucky won a tariff on hemp, and a tariff on raw wool brought the wool-growing interests to the support of the measure. Additional revenues were provided by duties on sugar, molasses, coffee, and salt. The tariff on raw wool was in obvious conflict with that on manufactured woolens, but the two groups got together and reached an agreement. A bill to raise further the wool and woolens duties failed in 1827 only by the tie-breaking vote of Vice-President Calhoun, who was in retreat from his prior support of the tariff.

At this point the supporters of Jackson saw a chance to advance their candidate by an awkward piece of skulduggery. The plan, as later divulged by one of its authors, John Calhoun, was to present a bill with such outrageously high tariffs on raw materials that the manufacturers of the East would join the commercial interests there and with the votes of the agricultural South and

Southwest defeat the measure. In the process Jackson men in the Northeast could take credit for supporting the tariff, and Jackson men, wherever it fitted their interests, could take credit for opposing it—while Jackson himself remained in the background. John Randolph saw through the ruse. The bill, he asserted, "referred to manufactures of no sort or kind, but the manufacture of a President of the United States."

The measure served that purpose, but in the process Calhoun was hoist on his own petard. The idea was a shade too clever, and Calhoun calculated neither upon the defection of Van Buren, who supported a crucial amendment to satisfy the woolens manufacturers, nor upon the growing strength of manufacturing interests in New England. Daniel Webster, now a senator from Massachusetts, explained that he was ready to deny all he had said against the tariff because New England had built up her manufactures on the understanding that the protective tariff was a settled policy.

When the bill passed on May 11, 1828, it was Calhoun's turn to explain his newfound opposition to the gospel of protection, and nothing so well illustrates the flexibility of constitutional principles as the switch in positions by Webster and Calhoun. Back in his study at Fort Hill, Calhoun prepared the *South Carolina Exposition and Protest* (1828), which was issued anonymously along with a series of resolutions by the South Carolina legislature. In that document Calhoun set forth the right of a state to nullify an act of Congress which it found unconstitutional.

JACKSON SWEEPS IN   Thus far the stage was set for the election of 1828, which might more truly be called a revolution than that of 1800. But if the issues of the day had anything to do with the election, they were hardly visible in the campaign, in which politicians on both sides reached depths of scurrilousness that had not been plumbed since 1800. Jackson was denounced as a hot-tempered and ignorant barbarian, a co-conspirator with Aaron Burr, a participant in repeated duels and frontier brawls, a man whose fame rested on his reputation as a killer, a man whom Thomas Jefferson himself had pronounced unfit because of the rashness of his feelings—a remark inspired by Jackson's brief tenure in the Senate in 1797. In addition to that, his enemies dredged up the old story that Jackson had lived in adultery with his wife Rachel before they had been legally married; in fact they had lived together for two years in the mistaken belief that her

Jackson is to be President, and you will be HANGED. *This anti-Jackson cartoon, published during the 1828 campaign, shows him as a frontier ruffian.*

divorce from a former husband was final. The worry over this humiliation and her probable reception in Washington may have contributed to an illness from which Rachel died before her husband took office, and it was one thing for which Jackson could never forgive his enemies.

The Jacksonians, however, got in their licks against Adams, condemning him as a man who had lived his adult life on the public treasury, who had been corrupted by foreigners in the courts of Europe, and who had allegedly delivered up an American girl to serve the lust of Czar Alexander I. They called him a gambler and a spendthrift for having bought a billiard table and a set of chessmen for the White House, and a puritanical hypocrite for despising the common people and warning Congress to ignore the will of its constituents. He had finally reached the presidency, the Jacksonians claimed, by a corrupt bargain with Henry Clay.

In the campaign of 1828 when, the historian George Dangerfield said, "to betray an idea was almost to commit a felony," Jackson held most of the advantages. As a military hero he had some claim on patriotism. As a son of the West he was almost unbeatable there. As a planter and slaveholder he had the trust of southern planters. Debtors and local bankers who hated the national bank turned to Jackson. His vagueness on the issues protected him from attack by various interest groups. Not least of all, Jackson benefited from a spirit of democracy in which the commonality were no longer satisfied to look to their betters for

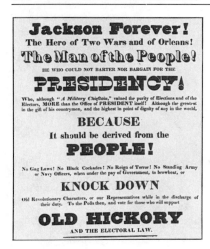

Jackson Forever!

The Hero of Two Wars and of Orleans!

The Man of the People!

HE WHO COULD NOT BARTER NOR BARGAIN FOR THE

PRESIDENCY!

Who, although "*A Military Chieftain*," valued the purity of Elections and of the Electors, MORE than the Office of PRESIDENT itself! Although the greatest in the gift of his countrymen, and the highest in point of dignity of any in the world,

BECAUSE

It should be derived from the

PEOPLE!

No Gag Laws! No Black Cockades! No Reign of Terror! No Standing Army or Navy Officers, when under the pay of Government, to browbeat, or

KNOCK DOWN

Old Revolutionary Characters, or our Representatives while in the discharge of their duty. To the Polls then, and vote for those who will support

OLD HICKORY

AND THE ELECTORAL LAW.

This 1828 handbill identifies Jackson, "The Man of the People," with the democratic impulse of the time.

leadership, as they had done in the lost world of Thomas Jefferson. It had become politically fatal to be labeled an aristocrat. Jackson's coalition now included even a seasoning of young Federalists eager to shed the stigma of aristocracy and get on in the world.

Since the Revolution and especially since 1800 manhood suffrage had been gaining ground. The traditional story has been that a surge of Jacksonian Democracy came out of the West like a great wave, supported mainly by small farmers, leading the way for the East. But there were other forces working in the older states toward a wider franchise: the revolutionary doctrine of equality, and the feeling on the parts of the workers, artisans, and small merchants of the towns, as well as small farmers and landed grandees, that a democratic ballot provided a means to combat the rising commercial and manufacturing interests. From the beginning Pennsylvania had opened the ballot box to all adult males who paid taxes; by 1790 Georgia and New Hampshire had similar arrangements. Vermont, in 1791, became the first state with manhood suffrage, having first adopted it in 1777. Kentucky, admitted in 1792, became the second. Tennessee (1796) had only a light taxpaying qualification. New Jersey in 1807, and Maryland and South Carolina in 1810, abolished property and taxpaying requirements, and the new states of the West after 1815 came in with either white manhood suffrage or a low taxpaying requirement. Connecticut (1818), Massachusetts (1821), and New York (1821) all abolished their property requirements.

Along with the broadening of the suffrage went a liberalization of other features of government. Representation was reapportioned more nearly in line with population. An increasing number of officials, even judges, were named by popular vote. Final disestablishment of the Congregational church in New England came in Vermont (1807), New Hampshire (1817), Connecticut (1818), Maine (1820), and Massachusetts (1834). In 1824 six state legislatures still chose the presidential electors. By 1828 the popular vote prevailed in all but South Carolina and Delaware, and by 1832 in all but South Carolina.

The spread of the suffrage brought a new type of politician to the fore: the man who had special appeal to the masses or knew how to organize the people for political purposes, and who became a vocal advocate of the people's right to rule. Jackson fitted the ideal of this new political world, a leader sprung from the people rather than an aristocratic leader of the people, a fron-

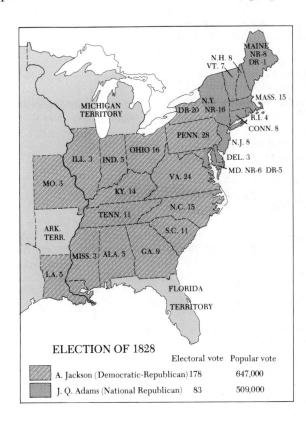

ELECTION OF 1828

		Electoral vote	Popular vote
	A. Jackson (Democratic-Republican)	178	647,000
	J. Q. Adams (National Republican)	83	509,000

tiersman of humble origin who had scrambled up by will and tenacity, a fighter, a defender of the liberties of the people, a man who made no pretence of profound learning. "Adams can write," went one of the campaign slogans, "Jackson can fight." He could write too, but he once said that he had no respect for a man who could think of only one way to spell a word.

When the 1828 returns came in, it was clear that Jackson had won by a comfortable margin. The electoral vote was 178 to 83, and the popular vote (the figures vary) was about 647,000 to 509,000. Adams won all of New England, except for one of Maine's nine electoral votes, sixteen of the thirty-six from New York and six of the eleven from Maryland. All the rest belonged to Jackson.

FURTHER READING

The standard overview of the Era of Good Feelings remains George Dangerfield's *The Awakening of American Nationalism, 1815–1828* (1965),° but his *The Era of Good Feelings* (1952) is an elegant synthesis. The gathering sense of a national spirit, hindered by an equally growing sectionalism, can be traced in Daniel J. Boorstin's *The Americans: The Nationalist Experience* (1965).° William H. Pease and Jane H. Pease's *The Web of Progress* (1985) shows the emerging sectionalism through a look at two cities, Boston, Massachusetts, and Charleston, South Carolina.

For discussions of the American System, see Bray Hammond's *Banks and Politics in America from the Revolution to the Civil War* (1957) and George R. Taylor's *The Transportation Revolution, 1815–1860* (1951). For an overview of all the economic trends of the period, see Douglass C. North's *The Economic Growth of the United States, 1790–1860* (1961).°

The political temper of the times is treated in biographical studies of principal figures: Harry Ammon's *James Monroe: The Quest for National Identity* (1971), Clement Eaton's *Henry Clay and the Art of American Politics* (1957), Samuel F. Bemis's *John Quincy Adams and the Union* (1956), Richard N. Current's *John C. Calhoun* (1963), and Chase C. Mooney's *William H. Crawford, 1772–1834* (1974).

On diplomatic relations after 1812, see Ernest R. May's *The Making of the Monroe Doctrine* (1975) and Dexter Perkins's *A History of the Monroe Doctrine* (1955).

Background on Andrew Jackson can be obtained from works cited in Chapter 11. The campaign which brought Jackson to the White House is analyzed in Robert V. Remini's *The Election of Andrew Jackson* (1963).°

°These books are available in paperback editions.

11 ∽

THE JACKSONIAN IMPULSE

Setting the Stage

INAUGURATION Inauguration Day, March 4, 1829, came in a welcome spell of balmy weather after a bitterly cold winter. For days before, visitors had been crowding the streets and rooming houses of Washington in hope of seeing the people's hero take office. When Jackson emerged from his lodgings, dressed in black out of respect to his late wife Rachel, a great crowd filled both the east and west slopes of Capitol Hill. After Chief Justice Marshall administered the oath, the new president delivered his inaugural address in a voice so low that few of the crowd could hear a word of it. It mattered little, for Jackson's advisers had eliminated anything that might give offense. On the major issues of the tariff, internal improvements, and the Bank of the United States, Jackson remained vague. Only a few points foreshadowed policies that the new chief executive would pursue: he favored retirement of the national debt, a proper regard for states' rights, a "just" policy toward Indians, and rotation in office, which he pronounced "a leading principle in the republican creed"—a principle his enemies would dub the "spoils system."

To that point all proceeded with dignity. Francis Scott Key, who witnessed the spectacle, declared: "It is beautiful, it is sublime!" After his speech Jackson mounted his horse and rode off to the White House, where a reception was scheduled for all who chose to come. The boisterous party that followed evoked the climate of turmoil that seemed always to surround Jackson. The crowd pushed into the White House, surged through the rooms, jostled the waiters, broke dishes, leaped on the furniture—all in

All Creation Going to the White House. *The scene following Jackson's inauguration as president, according to satirist Robert Cruikshank.*

an effort to shake the president's hand or at least get a glimpse of him. Surrounded by a group of his friends, the president soon made his escape by a side door and went back to his lodgings for the night. Somebody then had the presence of mind to haul tubs of punch out on the White House lawn, where the unruly crowd followed. To Justice Story, "the reign of 'King Mob' seemed triumphant."

APPOINTMENTS AND POLITICAL RIVALRIES   To the office seekers who made up much of the restless crowd at the inaugural, some of Jackson's words held out high expectations that he planned to turn the rascals out and let the people rule. So it seemed when Jackson set forth a reasoned defense of rotation in office. The duties of government were simple, he said. Democratic principles supported the idea that a man should serve a term in government, then return to the status of private citizen, for officeholders who stayed too long became corrupted by a sense of power. And democracy, he argued, "is promoted by party appointments by newly elected officials." Jackson hardly foresaw how these principles would work out in practice, and it would be misleading to link him too closely with the "spoils system," which took its name from an 1832 partisan assertion by Democratic Sen. William L. Marcy of New York: "To the victor belong the spoils." Jackson in fact behaved with great moderation compared to the politicians of New York and Pennsylvania, where the spoils of office nourished extensive political machines. And a number of his successors made many more partisan appointments. During his first year in office Jackson replaced only about 9 percent of the appointed officials in the federal government, and during his entire term fewer than 20 percent.

Jackson relied very little on his cabinet, which had little influence as an advisory group. More powerful was a coterie of men who had the president's ear and were soon dubbed his "Kitchen Cabinet." Among these, only Secretary of State Martin Van Buren headed a department, but most of the others were on the public payroll in some capacity. The most influential members seem to have been Amos Kendall of Kentucky, a former partisan of Clay; Duff Green, editor of the *United States Telegraph*, which had supported both Calhoun and Jackson; and Frank Blair, Sr., editor of the administration newspaper, the *Globe*.

Jackson's administration was from the outset a house divided between the partisans of Van Buren of New York and Vice-President Calhoun of South Carolina. Much of the political history of the next few years would turn upon the rivalry of the two, as each man jockeyed for position as the heir apparent to Jackson. It soon became clear that Van Buren held most of the advantages, foremost among them his skill at timing and tactics. As John Randolph put it, Van Buren always "rowed to his objective with muffled oars." Jackson, new to political administration, leaned heavily on him for advice and for help in soothing the ruffled feathers of rejected office seekers. Van Buren had perhaps more skill at maneuver than Calhoun, and certainly more freedom of maneuver since his home base of New York was more secure politically than Calhoun's base in South Carolina.

THE EATON AFFAIR   Van Buren also had luck on his side. Fate had quickly handed him a trump card: the succulent scandal of the Peggy Eaton affair. Peggy Eaton was the lively daughter of an Irish innkeeper whose place had been a Washington hangout for politicians, including at times Senators Jackson and Eaton of Tennessee. She was the widow of a navy purser whose death (capital gossip had it) was a suicide brought on by her affair with Senator Eaton. Her marriage to Eaton, three months before he entered the cabinet, had scarcely made an honest woman of her in the eyes of the proper ladies of Washington. Floride Calhoun, the vice-president's wife, pointedly snubbed her, and cabinet wives followed suit.

Peggy's plight reminded Jackson of the gossip that had pursued his own Rachel, and he pronounced Peggy "chaste as a virgin." To a friend he wrote: "I did not come here to make a

Cabinet for the Ladies of this place, but for the Nation." Despite their discomfort at Jackson's open displeasure, the cabinet members were unable to cure their wives of what Van Buren dubbed "the Eaton Marlaria." Van Buren, however, was a widower, and therefore free to lavish on poor Peggy all the attention that Jackson thought was her due. The bemused John Quincy Adams looked on from afar and noted in his diary that Van Buren had become the leader of the party of the frail sisterhood. Mrs. Eaton herself finally wilted under the chill, began to refuse invitations, and withdrew from society. The outraged Jackson came to link Calhoun with what he called a conspiracy, and drew even closer to Van Buren.

INTERNAL IMPROVEMENTS   While capital society weathered the chilly winter of 1829–1830, Van Buren prepared some additional blows to Calhoun. It was easy to bring Jackson into opposition to internal improvements and thus to federal programs with which Calhoun had long been identified: the Bonus Bill of 1817, the General Survey Bill of 1824, and Calhoun's own report on internal improvements made when he was secretary of war. Jackson did not oppose roadbuilding per se, but he had the same constitutional scruples as Madison and Monroe about federal aid to local projects. In 1830 the Maysville Road Bill, passed by Congress, offered Jackson a happy chance for a dual thrust at

King Andrew the First.
Opponents considered Jackson's Maysville veto an abuse of power. This cartoon shows King Andrew Jackson trampling on the Constitution, internal improvements, and the U.S. Bank.

both Calhoun and Clay. The bill authorized the government to buy stock in a road from Maysville to Clay's hometown of Lexington. The road lay entirely within the state of Kentucky, and though part of a larger scheme to link up with the National Road via Cincinnati, it could be viewed as a purely local undertaking. On that ground Jackson vetoed the bill as unconstitutional, to widespread popular acclaim.

But a foolish consistency about internal improvements was never Jackson's hobgoblin any more than it was his predecessors'. While Jackson continued to oppose federal aid to local projects, he supported interstate projects, such as the national road, as well as roadbuilding in the territories, and rivers and harbors bills, the "pork barrels" from which every congressman tried to pluck a morsel for his district. Even so, Jackson's attitude set an important precedent, on the eve of the railroad age, for limiting federal initiative in internal improvements. Railroads would be built altogether by state and private capital at least until 1850.

NULLIFICATION

CALHOUN'S THEORY   There is a fine irony to Calhoun's plight in the Jackson administration, for Calhoun was now in midpassage from his early phase as a War Hawk nationalist to his later phase as a states'-rights sectionalist—and open to thrusts on both flanks. Conditions in his home state had brought on this change. Suffering from agricultural depression, South Carolina lost almost 70,000 people to emigration during the 1820s, and was fated to lose nearly twice that number in the 1830s. Most South Carolinians blamed the protective tariff, which tended to raise the price of manufactured goods and, insofar as it discouraged the sale of foreign goods in the United States, reduced the ability of British and French traders to acquire the American money and bills of exchange with which to buy American cotton. This worsened problems of low cotton prices and exhausted lands. The South Carolinians' malaise was compounded by a growing reaction against the criticism of slavery. Hardly had the country emerged from the Missouri controversy when Charleston was thrown into panic by the Denmark Vesey slave insurrection of 1822, though the Vesey plot was nipped before it erupted.

The unexpected passage of the Tariff of Abominations (1828) left Calhoun no choice but to join those in opposition or give up his home base. Calhoun's *South Carolina Exposition and Protest* (1828), written in opposition to that tariff, actually had been an

John C. Calhoun. A War Hawk nationalist during the 1810s and 1820s, Calhoun was now becoming a states'-rights sectionalist.

effort to check the most extreme states'-rights advocates with a fine-spun theory in which nullification stopped short of secession from the Union. The statement, unsigned by its author, accompanied resolutions of the South Carolina legislature against the tariff. Calhoun, it was clear, had not entirely abandoned his earlier nationalism. His object was to preserve the Union by protecting the minority rights which the agricultural and slaveholding South claimed. The fine balance he struck between states' rights and central authority was not as far removed from Jackson's own philosophy as it might seem, but growing tension between the two men would complicate the issue. Jackson, in addition, was determined to draw the line at any defiance of federal law.

Nor would Calhoun's theory permit any state to take up such defiance lightly. The procedure of nullification, whereby a state could in effect repeal a federal law, would follow that by which the original thirteen states had ratified the Constitution. A special state convention, like the ratifying conventions embodying the sovereign power of the people, could declare a federal law null and void because it violated the Constitution, the original compact among the states. One of two outcomes would then be possible. Either the federal government would have to abandon the law or it would have to get a constitutional amendment removing all doubt as to its validity. The immediate issue was the constitutionality of a tariff designed mainly to protect American industries against foreign competition. The South Carolinians argued that the Constitution authorized tariffs for revenue only.

THE WEBSTER-HAYNE DEBATE   South Carolina had proclaimed its dislike for the impost, but had postponed any action against its enforcement, awaiting with hope the election of 1828 in which Calhoun was the Jacksonian candidate for vice-president. The state anticipated a new tariff policy from the Jackson administration. There the issue stood until 1830, when the great Hayne-Webster debate sharpened the lines between states' rights and the Union. The immediate occasion for the debate, however, was the question of public lands. Late in 1829 Sen. Samuel A. Foot of Connecticut, an otherwise obscure figure, proposed an inquiry looking toward restriction of land sales in the West. When the Foot Resolution came before the Senate in January 1830, Thomas Hart Benton of Missouri denounced it as a sectional attack designed to hamstring the settlement of the West so that the East might maintain its supply of cheap factory labor. Robert Y. Hayne of South Carolina took Benton's side. Hayne saw in the issue a chance to strengthen the alliance of South and West that the vote for Jackson reflected. Perhaps by supporting a policy of cheap lands in the West the southerners could get in return western support for lower tariffs. The government, said Hayne, endangered the Union by any policy that would impose a hardship upon one section to the benefit of another. The use of public lands as a source of revenue to the central government would create "a fund for corruption—fatal to the sovereignty and independence of the states."

Daniel Webster of Massachusetts rose to defend the East. Denying that the East had ever shown an illiberal policy toward the West, he rebuked those southerners who, he said, "habitually speak of the Union in terms of indifference, or even of disparagement." Hayne had raised the false spectre of "Consolidation!—That perpetual cry, both of terror and delusion—consolidation!" Federal moneys, Webster argued, were not a source of corruption but a source of improvement. At this point the Foot Resolution and the issue of western lands vanished from sight. Webster had adroitly shifted the grounds of debate, and lured Hayne into defending states' rights and upholding the doctrine of nullification instead of pursuing coalition with the West.

Hayne took the bait. After some personal thrusts, in which he harked back to Webster's early career as a Federalist, he launched into a defense of the *South Carolina Exposition,* appealed to the example of the Virginia and Kentucky Resolutions of 1798, and called attention to the Hartford Convention in which New Englanders had taken much the same position against majority measures as South Carolina did. The Union was created by a compact of the states, he argued, and the federal government could not be the judge of its own powers, else its

The eloquent Massachusetts Sen. Daniel Webster stands to rebut the argument for nullification in the Webster-Hayne debate.

powers would be unlimited. Rather, the states remained free to judge when their agent had overstepped the bounds of its constitutional authority. The right of state interposition was "as full and complete as it was before the Constitution was formed."

In rebuttal to the state-compact theory, Webster defined a nationalistic view of the Constitution. From the beginning, he asserted, the American Revolution had been a crusade of the united colonies rather than of each separately. True sovereignty resided in the people as a whole, for whom both federal and state governments acted as agents in their respective spheres. If a single state could nullify a law of the general government, then the Union would be a "rope of sand," a practical absurdity. Instead the Constitution had created a Supreme Court with the final jurisdiction on all questions of constitutionality. A state could neither nullify a federal law nor secede from the Union. The practical outcome of nullification would be a confrontation leading to civil war.

Hayne may have had the better of the argument historically in advancing the state-compact theory, but the Senate galleries and much of the country at large thrilled to the eloquence of "the Godlike Daniel." Webster's peroration became an American classic, reprinted in school texts and committed to memory by schoolboy orators: "When my eyes shall be turned to behold, for the last time, the sun in heaven, may I not see him shining on the broken and dishonored fragments of a once glorious Union. . . . Let their last feeble and lingering glance, rather, behold the gorgeous ensign of the republic . . . blazing on all its ample folds, as they float over the sea and over the land . . . Liberty and Union, now and forever, one and inseparable." In the practical world of coalition politics Webster had the better of the argument, for the Union and majority rule meant more to westerners, including Jackson, than the abstractions of state sovereignty and nullification. As for the public lands, the Foot Resolution was soon defeated anyway. And whatever one might argue about the origins of the Union, its evolution would more and more validate Webster's position.

THE RIFT WITH CALHOUN   As yet, however, the enigmatic Jackson had not spoken out on the issue. The nullificationists had given South Carolina's electoral vote to him as well as to Calhoun in 1828. Jackson, like Calhoun, was a slaveholder, albeit a westerner, and might be expected to sympathize with South Carolina, his native state. Soon all doubt was removed, at least on the point of nullification. On April 13, 1830, the Jefferson Day Dinner was held in Washington to honor the birthday of the former president. It was a party affair, but the Calhounites controlled the arrangements with an eye to advancing their own doctrine. Jackson and Van Buren were invited as a matter of course, and the two agreed that Jackson should present a toast which would indicate his opposition to nullification. When his turn came, after twenty-four toasts, many of them extolling states' rights, Jackson raised his glass and, pointedly looking at Calhoun, announced: "Our Union—It must be preserved!" (At the behest of Senator Hayne the first words were later published as "Our Federal Union.") Calhoun, who followed, trembled so that he spilled some of the amber fluid from his glass (according to Van Buren), but tried quickly to retrieve the situation with a toast to "The Union, next to our liberty most dear! May we all remember that it can only be preserved by respecting the rights of the States and distributing equally the benefit and the burthen of the Union!" But Jackson had set off a bombshell which exploded the plans of the states'-righters.

Nearly a month afterward a final nail was driven into the coffin of Calhoun's presidential ambitions. On May 12, 1830, Jackson first saw a letter containing final confirmation of reports that had been reaching him of Calhoun's stand in 1818, when as secretary of war the South Carolinian had proposed to discipline Jackson for his Florida invasion. A tense correspondence between Jack-

The Rats leaving a Falling House. *During his first term Jackson was beset by dissension within his administration. Here "public confidence in the stability and harmony of this administration" is toppling.*

son and Calhoun followed, and ended with a curt note from Jackson cutting it off. "Understanding you now," Jackson wrote two weeks later, "no further communication with you on this subject is necessary."

One result of the growing rift between the men was the appearance of a new administration paper. Duff Green's *United States Telegraph*, for two years the administration organ, was too closely allied with Calhoun. Jackson and his "Kitchen Cabinet" arranged to have Francis Preston Blair, Sr., of Kentucky, move to Washington and set up the Washington *Globe*, the first issue of which appeared before the end of 1830. Another result was a cabinet shakeup by Jackson, who was resolved to remove all Calhoun partisans. According to a plan contrived by Van Buren, he and Secretary of War Eaton resigned, offering as their reason a desire to relieve Jackson of the embarrassment of awkward controversy. Jackson in turn requested and got resignations of the others, and before the end of the summer of 1831 the president had a new cabinet entirely loyal to him.

Jackson then named Van Buren minister to London, pending Senate approval. The friends of Van Buren now importuned Jackson to repudiate his previous intention of serving only one term. It might have been hard, they felt, to get the nomination in 1832 for the New Yorker, who had been charged with intrigues against Calhoun, and the still-popular Carolinian might yet have carried off the prize. Jackson relented and in the fall of 1831 announced his readiness for one more term, with the idea of returning Van Buren from London in time to win the presidency in 1836. But in January 1832, when the Senate reconvened, Van Buren's enemies opposed his appointment as minister, and gave Calhoun, as vice-president, a chance to reject the nomination by a tie-breaking vote. "It will kill him, sir, kill him dead," Calhoun told Sen. Thomas Hart Benton. Benton disagreed: "You have broken a minister, and elected a Vice-President." So, it turned out, he had. Calhoun's vote against Van Buren provoked popular sympathy for the New Yorker, who would soon be nominated to succeed Calhoun.

Now that his presidential hopes were blasted, Calhoun came forth as the public leader of the nullificationists. These South Carolinians thought that, despite Jackson's gestures, tariff rates remained too high. Jackson, who accepted the principle of protection, nevertheless had called upon Congress in 1829 to modify duties by reducing tariffs on goods "which cannot come in competition with our own products." Late in the spring of 1830 Congress lowered duties on such consumer products as tea, coffee, salt, and molasses. In all it cut about $4.5 million from something over $20 million in tariff revenue. That and the Maysville veto, coming at about the same time, mollified a few South Carolinians, but nullifiers regarded the two actions as "nothing but sugar plums to pacify children." By the end of 1831 Jackson was calling for further reductions to take the wind out of the nullificationists' sails, and the tariff of 1832, pushed through by John Quincy Adams (back in Washington as a congressman), cut revenues another $5 million, again mainly on unprotected items. Average tariff rates were about 25 percent, but rates on cottons, woolens, and iron remained around 50 percent.

THE SOUTH CAROLINA ORDINANCE   In the South Carolina state elections of October 1832, all attention centered on the nullification issue. The nullificationists took the initiative in organization and agitation, and the Unionist party was left with a distinguished leadership but only small support, drawn chiefly from the merchants of Charleston and the yeoman farmers of the up-country. A special session of the legislature in October called for the election of a state convention. The convention assembled at Columbia on November 19 and on November 24 overwhelmingly adopted an ordinance of nullification which repudiated the tariff acts of 1828 and 1832 as unconstitutional and forbade collection of the duties in the state after February 1, 1833. The reassembled legislature then provided that any citizen whose property was seized by federal authorities for failure to pay the duty could get a state court order to recover twice its value. The legislature also chose Hayne as governor and elected Calhoun to succeed him as senator. Calhoun promptly resigned as vice-president in order to defend nullification on the Senate floor.

JACKSON'S FIRM RESPONSE   In the crisis South Carolina found itself standing alone, despite the sympathy expressed elsewhere. The Georgia legislature called for a southern convention, but dismissed nullification as "rash and revolutionary." Alabama pronounced it "unsound in theory and dangerous in practice"; Mississippi stood "firmly resolved" to put down nullification. Jackson's response was measured and firm, but not rash—at least not in public. In private he threatened to hang Calhoun and all other traitors—and later expressed regret that he had failed to hang at least Calhoun. In his annual message on December 4, 1832, Jackson announced his firm intention to enforce the tariff, but once again urged Congress to lower the rates. On December 10 he followed up with his Nullification Proclamation, which characterized the doctrine as an "impractical absurdity." Jackson said in part: "I consider, then, the power to annul a law in the United States, assumed by one state, incompatible with the existence of the Union, contradicted expressly by the letter of the Constitution, unauthorized by its spirit, inconsistent with every principle on which it was founded, and destructive of the great object for which it was formed." He appealed to the people of his native state not to follow false leaders: "The laws of the United States must be executed. I have no discretionary power on the subject; my duty is emphatically pronounced in the constitution. Those who told you that you might peaceably prevent their execution, deceived you; they could not have been deceived themselves. . . . Their object is disunion. But be not deceived by names. Disunion by armed force is treason."

CLAY'S COMPROMISE   Jackson sent Gen. Winfield Scott to Charleston Harbor with reinforcements of federal soldiers, who were kept carefully isolated in the island posts at Fort Moultrie and Castle Pinckney to avoid incidents. A ship of war and seven revenue cutters appeared in the harbor, ready to enforce the tariff before ships had a chance to land their cargoes. The nullifiers mobilized the state militia while unionists in the state organized a volunteer force. In January 1833 the president requested from Congress a "Force Bill," specifically authorizing him to use the army to compel compliance with federal law in South Carolina. Under existing legislation he already had such authority, but this affirmation would strengthen his hand. At the same time he gave his support to a bill in Congress which would have lowered duties to a maximum of 20 percent within two years. The nullifiers postponed enforcement of their ordinances in anticipation of a compromise. Passage of the bill depended on the support of Henry Clay, who finally yielded to those urging him to save the day. On February 12, 1833, he brought forth a plan to reduce the tariff gradually until 1842, by which time no rate would be more than 20 percent. It was less than South Carolina would have preferred, but it got the nullifiers out of the corner into which they had painted themselves.

On March 1, 1833, the compromise tariff and the Force Bill passed Congress and the next day Jackson signed both. The South Carolina Convention then met and rescinded its nullification, and in a face-saving gesture, nullified the Force Bill, for which Jackson no longer had any need. Both sides were able to claim victory. Jackson had upheld the supremacy of the Union and South Carolina had secured a reduction of the tariff.

JACKSON'S INDIAN POLICY

On Indian affairs Jackson's attitude was the typically western one, that Indians were better off out of the way. Jackson had already done his part in the Creek and Seminole Wars to chastise them and separate them from their lands. By the time of his election in 1828 he was fully in accord with the view that a "just, humane, liberal policy toward Indians" dictated moving them onto the plains west of the Mississippi. The policy was by no means new or original with Jackson; the idea had emerged gradually after the Louisiana Purchase in 1803. It had been formally set forth in 1823 by Calhoun, as secretary of war, and by now was generally accepted, that a permanent solution to the Indian "problem" would be their removal and resettlement in the "Great American Desert," which white men would never covet since it was thought fit mainly for horned toads and rattlesnakes.

INDIAN REMOVAL In response to Jackson's message, Congress in 1830 approved the Indian Removal Act and appropriated $500,000 for the purpose. Jackson's presidency saw some ninety-four removal treaties negotiated, and by 1835 Jackson

CHEROKEE PHŒNIX

NEW ECHOTÁ, THURSDAY FEBRUARY 21, 1828.

CONSTITUTION OF THE CHE-
ROKEE NATION,

*Formed by a Convention of Delegates
from the several Districts, at New E-
chota, July 1827.*

WE, THE REPRESENTATIVES of the
people of the CHEROKEE NATION in
Convention assembled, in order to establish justice, ensure tranquility,
promote our common welfare, and secure to ourselves and our posterity
the blessings of liberty; acknowledging with humility and gratitude the
goodness of the sovereign Ruler of the
Universe, in offering us an opportunity so favorable to the design, and im-
ploring his aid and direction in its ac-
complishment, do ordain and establish
this Constitution for the Government

readmission. *Moreover,* the Legislature shall have power to adopt such
laws and regulations, as its wisdom
may deem expedient and proper, to
prevent the citizens from monopoliz-
ing improvements with the view of
speculation.

ARTICLE II.

Sec. 1. THE POWER of this Government shall be divided into three
distinct departments;—the Legislative, the Executive, and the Judicial.

Sec. 2. No person or persons, belonging to one of these Departments,
shall exercise any of the powers properly belonging to either of the others, except in the cases hereinafter
expressly directed or permitted.

ARTICLE III.

The first issue of the Cherokee Phoenix *published the Constitution of the
Cherokee nation, which embraced "the lands solemnly guaranteed and
reserved forever to the Cherokee Nation by the Treaties concluded with
the United States."*

was able to announce that the policy had been carried out or was
in process of completion for all but a handful of Indians. The policy was effected with remarkable speed, but even that was too
slow for state authorities in the South and Southwest. Unlike the
Ohio Valley–Great Lakes region, where the flow of white settlement had constantly pushed the Indians westward before it, in
the Old Southwest settlement moved across Kentucky and Tennessee and down the Mississippi, surrounding the Creeks, Choctaws, Chickasaws, Seminoles, and Cherokees. These tribes of the
area had over the years taken on many of the features of white society. The Cherokees even had such appurtenances of "white
civilization" as a constitution, a written language, and black
slaves.

Most of the northern tribes were too weak to resist the importunings of Indian commissioners who, if necessary, used bribery
and alcohol to woo the chiefs, and if sometimes the tribesmen
rebelled, there was, on the whole, remarkably little resistance.
In Illinois and Wisconsin Territory an armed clash sprang up
from April to August 1832, which came to be known as the Black
Hawk War, when the Sauk and Fox under Chief Black Hawk
sought to reoccupy some lands they had abandoned in the pre-

vious year. Facing famine and hostile Sioux west of the Mississippi, they were simply seeking a place to get in a corn crop. The Illinois militia mobilized to expel them, chased them into Wisconsin Territory, and inflicted a gruesome massacre of women and children as they tried to escape across the Mississippi. The Black Hawk War came to be remembered later, however, less because of the atrocities inflicted on the Indians than because the participants included two native Kentuckians later pitted against each other: Lt. Jefferson Davis of the regular army and Capt. Abraham Lincoln of the Illinois volunteers.

In the South two nations, the Seminoles and Cherokees, put up a stubborn resistance. The Seminoles of Florida fought a protracted guerrilla war in the Everglades from 1835 to 1842. But most of the vigor went out of their resistance after 1837, when their leader Osceola was seized by treachery under a flag of truce to die a prisoner at Fort Moultrie in Charleston Harbor. After 1842 only a few hundred Seminoles remained, hiding out in the swamps. Most of the rest had been removed to the West.

THE CHEROKEES' TRAIL OF TEARS   The Cherokees had by the end of the eighteenth century fallen back into the mountains of northern Georgia and western North Carolina, onto land guaranteed to them in 1791 by treaty with the United States. But when Georgia ceded its western lands in 1802 it did so on the ambiguous condition that the United States extinguish all Indian titles within the state "as early as the same can be obtained on reasonable terms." In 1827 the Cherokees, relying on their treaty rights, adopted a constitution in which they said pointedly that they were not subject to any other state or nation. In 1828 Georgia responded with a law stipulating that after June 1, 1830, the authority of state law would extend over the Cherokees living within the boundaries of the state.

The discovery of gold in 1829 whetted the whites' appetite for Cherokee lands and brought bands of rough prospectors into the country. The Cherokees sought relief in the Supreme Court, but in *Cherokee Nation v. Georgia* (1831) John Marshall ruled that the Court lacked jurisdiction because the Cherokees were a "domestic dependent nation" rather than a foreign state in the meaning of the Constitution. Marshall added, however, that the Cherokees had "an unquestionable right" to their lands "until title should be extinguished by voluntary cession to the United States." In 1830 a Georgia law had required whites in the territory to get licenses authorizing their residence there, and to take an oath of allegiance to the state. Two New England missionaries among the Indians refused and were sentenced to four years at

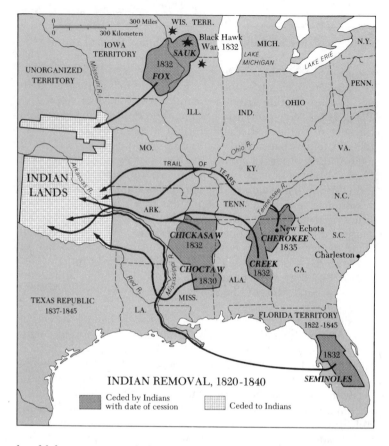

INDIAN REMOVAL, 1820-1840

Ceded by Indians with date of cession

Ceded to Indians

hard labor. On appeal their case reached the Supreme Court as *Worcester v. Georgia* (1832) and the court held that the Cherokee Nation was "a distinct political community" within which Georgia law had no force. The Georgia law was therefore unconstitutional.

Six years earlier Georgia had faced down President Adams when he tried to protect the rights of the Creeks. Now Georgia faced down the Supreme Court with the tacit consent of another president. Jackson is supposed to have said privately: "Marshall has made his decision, now let him enforce it!" Whether or not he put it so bluntly, Jackson did nothing to enforce the decision. In the circumstances there was nothing for the Cherokees to do but give in and sign a treaty, which they did in 1835. They gave up their lands in the Southeast in exchange for lands in the Indian Territory west of Arkansas, $5 million from the federal government, and expenses for transportation. By 1838 the Cherokees had departed on the "trail of tears" westward, following the

Choctaws, Chickasaws, Creeks, and Seminoles on a journey marked by the cruelty and neglect of soldiers and private contractors, and scorn and pilferage by whites along the way. A few held out in the mountains and acquired title to lands in North Carolina; thenceforth they were the "eastern band" of the Cherokees. Some Seminoles were able to hide out in the Everglades, and a scattered few of the others remained in the Southeast, especially mixed-blood Creeks who could pass for white.

THE BANK CONTROVERSY

THE BANK'S OPPONENTS   The overriding national issue in the campaign of 1832 was neither Jackson's Indian policy nor South Carolina's obsession with nullification. It was the question of rechartering the Bank of the United States. On the bank issue, as on others, Jackson had made no public commitment, but his personal opposition to the bank was already formed. Jackson had absorbed the western attitude of hostility toward the bank after the Panic of 1819, and held to a conviction that it was unconstitutional no matter what Marshall had said in *McCulloch v. Maryland*. Banks in general had fed a speculative mania, and Jackson, suspicious of all banks, preferred a hard-money policy. The general felt in his bones that the bank was wrong and did not need to form his opinions out of an intimate knowledge of banking. He was in fact blissfully ignorant of the subject.

Under the management of Nicholas Biddle the Bank of the United States had prospered and grown. Coming from a well-to-do Philadelphia family, Biddle had previously followed a career as editor, diplomat, and politician. He had little acquaintance with business when Monroe appointed him a government director of the bank, but he proved a quick study and by the time he became president of the bank in 1823 Biddle was well versed in banking.

The bank had worked to the benefit of business and performed the important function of supplying a stable currency by its policy of forcing state banks to keep a specie reserve (gold or silver) behind their notes. But arrayed against the bank were powerful enemies: some of the state and local banks which had been forced to reduce their note issues, debtor groups which suffered from the reduction, and businessmen and speculators "on the make" who wanted easier credit. States'-rights groups questioned the bank's constitutionality, though Calhoun, who had sponsored the original charter and valued the bank's function of regulating the currency, was not among them. Financiers of New

York's Wall Street resented the supremacy of the bank on Philadelphia's Chestnut Street.

Many westerners and workingmen, like Jackson, felt in their bones that the bank was, in Thomas Hart Benton's word, a "Monster," a monopoly controlled by a few of the wealthy with power that was irreconcilable with a democracy. "I think it right to be perfectly frank with you," Jackson told Biddle in 1829. "I do not dislike your Bank any more than all banks. But ever since I read the history of the South Sea Bubble I have been afraid of banks." This struck Biddle as odd, since he regarded his conservative policies as a safeguard against speculative manias like the eighteenth-century "South Sea Bubble," in which thousands of British investors had been fleeced. Jackson was perhaps right in his instinct that the bank lodged too much power in private hands, but mistaken in his understanding of the bank's policies.

Biddle at first tried to conciliate Jackson and appointed a number of Jackson men to branch offices of the bank. In his first annual message (1829), though, Jackson questioned the bank's constitutionality and asserted (whatever the evidence to the

This anti-Jackson cartoon depicts the president as an ass trampling on chicks that represent the branch banks of Biddle's Bank of the United States.

contrary) that it had failed to maintain a sound and uniform currency. Jackson talked of a compromise, perhaps a bank completely owned by the government with its operations confined chiefly to government deposits, its profits payable to the government, and its authority to set up branches in any state dependent on the state's wishes. But Jackson would never commit himself on the precise terms of compromise. Some of Jackson's cabinet members cautiously favored the bank, but the opposition of Amos Kendall and Francis P. Blair in the Kitchen Cabinet influenced him more. The defense of the bank was left up to Biddle.

BIDDLE'S RECHARTER EFFORT   Its twenty-year charter would run through 1836, but Biddle could not afford the uncertainty of waiting until then for a renewal. Biddle pondered whether to force the issue of recharter before the election of 1832 or after. On this point leaders of the National Republicans, especially Clay and Webster (who was counsel to the bank as well as a senator), argued that the time to move was before the election. Clay, already the candidate of the National Republicans, proposed to make the bank the central issue of the presidential canvass. Friends of the bank held a majority in Congress, and Jackson would risk loss of support in the election if he vetoed a renewal. But they failed to grasp the depth of prejudice against the bank, and succeeded mainly in handing to Jackson a popular issue on the eve of the election.

Both houses passed the recharter by comfortable margins, but without the two-thirds majority needed to override a veto. On July 10, 1832, Jackson vetoed the bill, sending it back to Congress with a ringing denunciation of monopoly and special privilege. In a message written largely by his confidant Amos Kendall, Jackson argued that the bank was unconstitutional, whatever the Court and Congress said. "Each public officer who takes an oath to support the Constitution swears that he will support it as he understands it, and not as it is understood by others. . . . The opinion of the judges has no more authority over Congress than the opinion of Congress had over the judges, and on that point the President is independent of both." Besides, there were substantive objections aside from the question of constitutionality. Foreign stockholders in the bank had an undue influence. The bank had shown favors to members of Congress and exercised an improper power over state banks. The bill, he argued, demonstrated that "Many of our rich men have not been content with equal protection and equal benefits, but have besought us to make them richer by act of Congress." An effort to overrule the veto failed in the Senate; a vote of 22 to 19 for the bank fell far short of the needed two-thirds majority. Thus the stage was set for a nationwide financial crisis.

CAMPAIGN INNOVATIONS   The presidential campaign, as usual, was under way early, the nominations having been made before the bank veto, two in fact before the end of 1831. For the first time a third party entered the field. The Anti-Masonic party was, like the bank, the object of strong emotions then sweeping the new democracy. The group had grown out of popular hostility toward the Masonic order, members of which were suspected of having kidnapped and murdered a bricklayer of Batavia, New York, for revealing the "secrets" of his lodge. Opposition to a fraternal order was hardly the foundation on which to build a lasting party, but the Anti-Masonic party had three important "firsts" to its credit: in addition to being the first third party, it was the first party to hold a national nominating convention and the first to announce a platform, all of which it accomplished in September

George Caleb Bingham's Verdict of the People *depicts the increasingly democratic politics of the early to mid–nineteenth century.*

1831 when it nominated William Wirt of Maryland for president.

The major parties followed its example by holding national conventions of their own. In December 1831 the delegates of the National Republican party assembled in Baltimore to nominate Henry Clay for president and John Sergeant of Pennsylvania, counsel to the bank and chief advocate of the recharter strategy, for vice-president. Jackson endorsed the idea of a nominating convention for the Democratic party (the name Republican was now formally dropped) to demonstrate popular support for its candidates. To that purpose the convention, also meeting at Baltimore, adopted the two-thirds rule for nomination (which prevailed until 1936), and then named Martin Van Buren as Jackson's running mate. The Democrats, unlike the other two parties, adopted no formal platform at their first convention, and relied to a substantial degree on hoopla and the personal popularity of the president to carry their cause.

The outcome was an overwhelming endorsement of Jackson in the electoral college by 219 votes to 49 for Clay, and a less overwhelming but solid victory in the popular vote, by 688,000 to 530,000. William Wirt carried only Vermont, with several electoral votes. South Carolina, preparing for nullification and unable to stomach either Jackson or Clay, delivered its eleven votes to Gov. John Floyd of Virginia.

REMOVAL OF GOVERNMENT DEPOSITS   Jackson took the election as a mandate to proceed further against the bank. He asked Congress to investigate the safety of government deposits in the bank, since one of the current rumors told of empty vaults, carefully concealed. After a committee had checked, the Calhoun and Clay forces in the House of Representatives united in the passage of a resolution affirming that government deposits were safe and could be continued. The resolution passed, by chance, on March 2, 1833, the same day that Jackson signed the compromise tariff and Force Bill. With the nullification issue out of the way, however, Jackson was free to wage his unrelenting war on the bank, that "hydra of corruption," which still had nearly four years to run on its charter. Despite the House study and resolution, Jackson now resolved to remove all government deposits from the bank.

When Secretary of the Treasury McLane opposed removal of the government deposits and suggested a new and modified version of the bank, Jackson shook up his cabinet. He kicked McLane upstairs to head the State Department, which Edward Livingston left to become minister to France. To take McLane's place at the Treasury he chose William J. Duane of Philadelphia, but by some oversight Jackson failed to explore Duane's views fully or advise him of the presidential expectations. Duane was antibank, but he was consistent in his convictions. Dubious about banks in general, he saw no merit in removing deposits from the Monster for redeposit in countless state banks. Jackson might well have listened to Duane's warnings that such action would lead to speculative inflation, but the old general's combative instincts were too much aroused. He summarily dismissed Duane and moved Attorney-General Taney to the Treasury, where the new secretary gladly complied with the presidential wishes, which corresponded to his own views.

The procedure was to continue drawing on governmental accounts with Biddle's Bank, and to deposit all new governmental receipts in state banks. By the end of 1833 there were twenty-three state banks which had the benefit of governmental deposits, "pet banks" as they came to be called. The sequel to Jackson's headlong plunge into finance, it soon turned out, was the precise opposite of what he had sought. As so often happens with complex public issues, dissatisfaction had become focused on a symbol. In this case the symbol was the "Monster of Chestnut Street," which had been all along the one institution able to maintain some degree of order in the financial world. The immediate result of Jackson's action was a contraction of credit by Biddle's bank in order to shore up its defenses against the loss of deposits. By 1834 the tightness of credit was creating complaints of business distress, which was probably exaggerated by both sides in the bank controversy for political effect: Biddle to show the evil consequences of the withdrawal of deposits, Jacksonians to show how Biddle abused his power.

The contraction brought about by the bank quickly gave way, however, to a speculative binge encouraged by the deposit of government funds in the pet banks. With the restraint of Biddle's bank removed, the state banks gave full rein to their wildcat tendencies. (The term "wildcat," used in this sense, originated in Michigan, where one of the fly-by-night banks featured a panther, or wildcat, on its worthless notes.) New banks mushroomed, printing banknotes with abandon for the purpose of lending to speculators. Sales of public lands rose from 4 million acres in 1834 to 15 million in 1835 and to 20 million in 1836. At the same time the states plunged heavily into debt to finance the building of roads and canals, inspired by the success of New York's Erie Canal. By 1837 total state indebtedness had soared to $170 million, a very large sum for this time. The supreme

The Downfall of Mother Bank. *In this pro-Jackson cartoon, the bank crumbles and Jackson's opponents flee in the face of the heroic president's removal of government deposits.*

irony of Jackson's war on the bank then was that it preceded a speculative mania that dwarfed even the South Sea Bubble.

FISCAL MEASURES The new bubble reached its greatest extent in 1836, when a combination of events conspired suddenly to deflate it. Most important among these were the Distribution Act, passed in June 1836, and the Specie Circular of July 1836. Distribution of the government's surplus funds had long been a pet project of Henry Clay. One of its purposes was to eliminate the surplus, thus removing one argument for cutting the tariff. Much of the surplus, however, was brought in by the "land office business" in western real estate, and was therefore in the form of banknotes that had been issued to speculators. Many westerners thought that the solution to the surplus was simply to lower the price of land; southerners preferred to lower the tariff—but such action would now upset the compromise achieved in the tariff of 1833. For a time the annual surpluses could be applied to paying off the government debt, but the debt, reduced to $7 million by 1832, was entirely paid off by January 1835.

Still the federal surplus continued to mount. Clay again proposed distribution, but Jackson had constitutional scruples about the process. Finally, a compromise was worked out whereby the government would distribute most of the surplus as loans to the states. To satisfy Jackson's scruples the funds were technically "deposits," but in reality they were never demanded back. Distribution was to be in proportion to each state's representation in the two houses of Congress, and was to be paid out in quarterly installments, beginning January 1, 1837.

About a month after passage of the Distribution Act came the Specie Circular of July 11, 1836, issued by the secretary of the treasury at Jackson's order. With that document the president belatedly applied his hard-money conviction to the sale of public lands. According to his order, after August 15 the government would accept only gold and silver in payment for lands—with the exception that for a brief time banknotes would be accepted for parcels up to 320 acres when bought by actual settlers or residents of the state in which the sale was made. The purposes declared in the circular were to "repress frauds," to withhold support "from the monopoly of the public lands in the hands of speculators and capitalists," and to discourage the "ruinous extension" of banknotes and credit.

Irony dogged Jackson to the end on this matter. Since few actual settlers could get their hands on specie, they were now left all the more at the mercy of speculators for land purchases. Both the distribution and the Specie Circular put many state banks in a precarious plight. The distribution reduced their deposits, or at least threw things into disarray by shifting them from bank to bank, and the increased demand for specie put an added strain on the supply of gold and silver.

BOOM AND BUST   But the boom and bust of the 1830s had causes larger even than Andrew Jackson, causes that were beyond his control. The inflation of mid-decade was rooted not so much in a prodigal expansion of banknotes, as it seemed at the time, but in an increase of specie payments from England and France, and especially from Mexico, for investment and for the purchase of America cotton and other products. At the same time British credits enabled Americans to buy British goods without having to export specie. Meanwhile the flow of hard cash to China, where silver had been much prized, decreased. The Chinese now took in payment for their goods British credits which they could in turn use to cover rapidly increasing imports of opium from British India.

Contrary to appearances, therefore, the reserves of specie in American banks kept pace with the increase of banknotes, despite reckless behavior on the part of some banks. But by 1836 a tighter British economy caused a decline in British investments

Broadway and Canal Street, New York City, 1836. New York's economy, and that of the nation, was strongly affected by world events in the mid-1830s.

and in British demand for American cotton just when the new western lands were creating a rapid increase in cotton supply. Fortunately for Jackson, the Panic of 1837 did not break until he was out of the White House and safely back at the Hermitage. His successor would serve as the scapegoat.

In May 1837 New York banks suspended specie payments on their banknotes and fears of bankruptcy set off runs on banks around the country, many of which were soon overextended. A brief recovery followed in 1838, stimulated in part by a bad wheat harvest at home which forced the British to buy American wheat. But by 1839 that stimulus had passed. The same year a bumper cotton crop overloaded the market and a collapse of cotton prices set off a depression from which the economy did not fully recover until the mid-1840s.

VAN BUREN AND THE NEW PARTY SYSTEM

THE WHIG COALITION   Before the crash, however, the Jacksonian Democrats reaped a political bonanza. Jackson had downed the dual monsters of nullification and the bank, and the people loved him for it. But out of the political wreckage that Jackson had inflicted on his opponents they began in 1834 to pull together a new coalition of diverse elements united chiefly by their hostility to Jackson. The imperial demeanor of that champion of democracy had given rise to the name of "King Andrew I"! His followers therefore were "Tories," supporters of the king, and his opponents became "Whigs," a name that linked them to the patriots of the American Revolution. This diverse coalition clustered around its center, the National Republican party of J. Q. Adams, Clay, and Webster. Into the combination came remnants of the Anti-Masons and Democrats who for one reason or another were alienated by Jackson's stands on the bank or state's rights. Of the forty-one Democrats in Congress who had voted to recharter the bank, twenty-eight joined the Whigs by 1836.

Whiggery always had about it an atmosphere of social conservatism and superiority. The core Whigs were the supporters of Henry Clay, men whose vision was quickened by the vistas of his "American System." In the South the Whigs enjoyed the support of the urban banking and commercial interests, as well as their planter associates, owners of most of the slaves in the region. In the West, farmers who valued internal improvements joined the Whig ranks. Most states'-rights supporters eventually dropped away, and by the early 1840s the Whigs were becoming more clearly the party of Henry Clay's nationalism, even in the South. Throughout their two decades of strength the Whigs were a national party, strong both North and South, and a cohesive force for Union.

THE ELECTION OF 1836 By the presidential election of 1836 a new two-party system was emerging out of the Jackson and anti-Jackson forces, a system that would remain in fairly even balance for twenty years. In May 1835, eighteen months before the election, the Democrats held their second national convention and nominated Jackson's handpicked successor, Vice-President Martin Van Buren, the Red Fox of Kinderhook. The Whig coalition, united chiefly in its opposition to Jackson, held no convention but adopted a strategy of multiple candidacies, hoping to throw the election into the House of Representatives.

The result was a free-for-all reminiscent of 1824, except that this time one candidate stood apart from the rest. It was Van Buren against the field. The Whigs put up three favorite sons: Daniel Webster, named by the Massachusetts legislature; Hugh Lawson White, chosen by anti-Jackson Democrats in the Tennessee legislature; and William Henry Harrison of Indiana, nominated by a predominantly Anti-Masonic convention in Harrisburg, Pennsylvania. In the South the Whigs made heavy

Martin Van Buren, the "Little Magician."

inroads on the Democratic vote by arguing that Van Buren would be soft on antislavery advocates and that the South could trust only a southerner—i.e., White—as president. In the popular vote Van Buren outdistanced the entire Whig field, with 765,000 votes to 740,000 votes for the Whigs, most of which were cast for Harrison. Van Buren had 170 electoral votes, Harrison 73, White 26, and Webster 14.

Martin Van Buren, the eighth president, was the first of Dutch ancestry and at the age of fifty-five the first born under the Stars and Stripes. Son of a tavernkeeper in Kinderhook, New York, he had been schooled in a local academy, read law, and entered politics. Although he kept up a limited practice of law, he had been for most of his adult life a professional politician, so skilled in the arts of organization and manipulation that he came to be known as the "Little Magician." In New York politics he became leader of an organization known as the "Albany Regency," which backed his election as senator and later as governor. In 1824 he supported Crawford, then switched to Jackson in 1828, but continued to look to the Old Republicans of Virginia as the southern anchor of his support. After a brief tenure as governor of New York he resigned to join the cabinet, and because of Jackson's favor became minister to London and then vice-president.

THE PANIC OF 1837 Van Buren owed much of his success to good luck, to having backed the right horse, having been in the right place at the right time. But once he had climbed to the top of the greasy pole, luck suddenly deserted him. Van Buren had inher-

ited Jackson's favor and a good part of his following, but he also
inherited a financial panic. An already precarious economy was
tipped over into crisis by depression in England, which resulted
in a drop in the price of cotton from 17½¢ to 13½¢ a pound, and
caused English banks and investors to cut back their commit-
ments in the New World and refuse extensions of loans. This was
a particularly hard blow since much of America's economic expansion depended on European—and mainly English—capital.
On top of everything else, in 1836 there had been a failure of the
wheat crop, the export of which in good years helped offset the
drain of payments abroad. As creditors hastened to foreclose, the
inflationary spiral went into reverse. States curtailed ambitious
plans for roads and canals, and in many cases felt impelled
to repudiate their debts. In the crunch a good many of the wildcat
banks succumbed, and the government itself lost some $9 mil-
lion it had deposited in pet banks.

Van Buren's advisors and supporters were inclined to blame
speculators and bankers but at the same time to expect that the
evildoers would get what they deserved in a healthy shakeout
that would bring the economy back to stability. Van Buren did
not believe that he or the government had any responsibility to
rescue hard-pressed farmers or businessmen, or to provide pub-

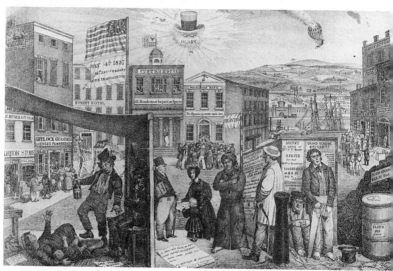

The Times. *This anti-Jacksonian cartoon depicts the effects of the
depression of 1837: a panic at the bank, beggars in the street.*

lic relief. He did feel obliged to keep the government itself in a healthy financial situation, however. To that end he called a special session of Congress in September 1837 which quickly voted to postpone indefinitely the distribution of the surplus because of a probable upcoming deficit, and also approved an issue of Treasury notes to cover immediate expenses.

AN INDEPENDENT TREASURY   But Van Buren devoted most of his message to his idea that the government cease risking its deposits in shaky banks and set up an Independent Treasury. Under this plan the government would keep its funds in its own vaults and do business entirely in hard money. Van Buren was opposed to the "blending of private interests with the operations of public business." The founders of the republic had "wisely judged that the less government interferes with private pursuits the better for the general prosperity." Webster's response typified the Whig reaction: "I feel . . . as if this could not be America when I see schemes of public policy proposed, having for their object the convenience of Government only, and leaving the people to shift for themselves." The Whiggish approach, presumably, would have been some kind of Hamiltonian program of government promotion of economic development, perhaps in the form of tariff or currency legislation. Good Jacksonians disapproved of such programs, at least when they were run from Washington.

Passage of the Independent Treasury was held up by opposition from a combination of Whigs and conservative Democrats who feared deflation. It took Van Buren several years of maneuvering to get what he wanted. Calhoun signaled a return to the Democratic fold, after several years of flirting with the Whigs, when he came out for the Independent Treasury. Van Buren gained western support by backing a more liberal land policy. He finally got his Independent Treasury on July 4, 1840. Although it lasted little more than a year before the Whigs repealed it in 1841, it would be restored in 1846.

The drawn-out hassle over the Treasury was only one of several that kept Washington preoccupied through the Van Buren years. A flood of petitions for Congress to abolish slavery and the slave trade in the District of Columbia brought on tumultuous debate, especially in the House of Representatives. Border incidents growing out of a Canadian insurrection in 1837 and a dispute over the Maine boundary kept British-American animosity at a simmer, but Gen. Winfield Scott, the president's ace trouble-shooter, managed to keep the hotheads in check along the border. These matters will be discussed elsewhere, but basic to the spreading malaise of the time was the depressed condition of the economy that lasted through Van Buren's entire term. Fairly or not, the administration became the target of growing discontent. The president won renomination easily enough, but could not get the Democratic convention to agree on his vice-presidential choice, which the convention left up to the Democratic electors.

THE "LOG CABIN AND HARD CIDER" CAMPAIGN The Whigs got an early start on their campaign when they met at Harrisburg, Pennsylvania, on December 4, 1839, to choose a candidate. Clay expected 1840 to be his year and had soft-pedaled talk of his American System in the interest of building broader support. Although he led on the first ballot, the convention was of a mind to look for a Whiggish Jackson, as it were, a military hero who could enter the race with few known political convictions or enemies. One possibility was Winfield Scott, but the delegates finally turned to William Henry Harrison, victor at the battle of Tippecanoe, former governor of the Indiana territory, briefly congressman and senator from Ohio, more briefly minister to Colombia. Another advantage of Harrison's was that the Anti-Masons liked him. To rally their states'-rights wing the Whigs chose for vice-president John Tyler of Virginia, a close friend of Clay.

The Whigs had no platform. That would have risked dividing a coalition united chiefly by opposition to the Democrats. But they had a slogan, "Tippecanoe and Tyler too," that went trippingly on the tongue. And they soon had a rousing campaign theme

In front of his log cabin, Old Tippecanoe pours cider for cheering supporters. Jackson and Van Buren, in back, try to stop the flow.

which a Democratic paper unwittingly supplied them when the Baltimore *Republican* declared sardonically "that upon condition of his receiving a pension of $2,000 and a barrel of cider, General Harrison would no doubt consent to withdraw his pretensions, and spend his days in a log cabin on the banks of the Ohio." The Whigs seized upon the cider and log cabin symbols to depict Harrison as a simple man sprung from the people. Actually he sprang from one of the first families of Virginia and lived in a commodious farmhouse.

Substituting spectacle for argument, the Whig "Log Cabin and Hard Cider" campaign featured such sublime irrelevancy as the country had never seen before. Portable log cabins rolled through the streets along with barrels of potable cider to the tune of catchy campaign songs in support of

> The iron-armed soldier, the true-hearted soldier,
> The gallant old soldier of Tippecanoe.

His sweating supporters rolled huge victory balls along the highways to symbolize the snowballing majorities. All the devices of hoopla were mobilized: placards, emblems, campaign buttons, floats, effigies, transparencies, great rallies, and a campaign newspaper, *The Log Cabin*. Building on the example of the Jacksonians' campaign to discredit John Quincy Adams, the Whigs pictured Van Buren, who unlike Harrison came of humble origins, as an aristocrat living in luxury at "the Palace":

> Let Van from his coolers of silver drink wine,
> And lounge on his cushioned settee;
> Our man on his buckeye bench can recline
> Content with hard cider is he!

The campaign left one lasting heritage in the American language, a usage now virtually worldwide. The expression "O.K." was picked up as an abbreviation for "Old Kinderhook," an affectionate name for Van Buren, whose supporters organized "O.K. Clubs" during the campaign. The Whigs gave the initials a jocular turn and a new meaning when they attributed them to Andrew Jackson's creative spelling. Jackson had marked certain papers with the initials, he was said to have told Amos Kendall, to signify that they were "oll korrect." Thereafter Whig cider barrels carried the same seal of approval.

"We have taught them to conquer us!" the *Democratic Review* lamented. The Whig party had not only learned its lessons well,

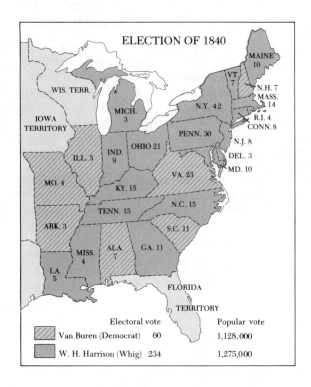

ELECTION OF 1840

	Electoral vote	Popular vote
Van Buren (Democrat)	60	1,128,000
W. H. Harrison (Whig)	234	1,275,000

it had learned to improve on its teachers in the art of campaigning. "Van! Van! Is a Used-up Man!" went one of the campaign refrains, and down he went by the thumping margin of 234 votes to 60 in the electoral college. In the popular vote it was closer: 1,275,000 for Old Tip, 1,128,000 for Van Buren.

Assessing the Jackson Years

The Jacksonian impulse had altered American politics permanently. Longstanding ambivalence about political parties had been purged in the fires of political conflict, and mass political parties had arrived to stay. They were now widely justified as a positive good. By 1840 both parties were organized down to the precinct level, and the proportion of adult white males who voted in the presidential election nearly tripled, from 26.5 percent in 1824 to 78.0 percent in 1840. That much is beyond dispute, but the phenomenon of Jackson, the great symbol for an age, has inspired among historians conflicts of interpretation as spirited as those among his supporters and opponents at the time. Jackson's personality itself seemed a compound of contradictions. His first major biographer discovered in different accounts that Jackson "was a patriot and a traitor. He was one of the greatest of generals, and wholly ignorant of the art of war. A writer brilliant, elegant, eloquent, without being able to compose a correct sentence or spell words of four syllables. The first of statesmen, he never devised, he never framed a measure. He was the most candid of men, and was capable of the profoundest dissimulation. A most law-defying, law-obeying citizen. A stickler for discipline, he never hesitated to disobey his superior. A democratic aristocrat. An urbane savage. An atrocious saint."

Interpretations of his policies, their sources, and their consequences have likewise differed. The earliest historians of the Jackson era belonged largely to an eastern elite nurtured in a "Whiggish" culture, men who could never quite forgive Jackson for the spoils system which in their view excluded the fittest from office. A later school of "progressive" historians depicted Jackson as the leader of a vast democratic movement which welled up in the West and mobilized a farmer-labor alliance to sweep the "Monster" bank into the dustbin of history. Some historians recently have focused attention on local power struggles in which the great national debates of the time often seem empty rhetoric or at most snares to catch the voters. One view of Jackson makes him out to be essentially a frontier nabob, an opportunist for whom democracy "was good talk with which to win the favor of the people. . . ."

Another school has emphasized the importance of cultural-

Andrew Jackson in 1845.
Jackson died shortly after
this daguerrotype was taken.

ethnic identity in deciding party loyalties. Jackson, according to this view, revitalized the Jeffersonian alliance of Virginia and New York, of individualistic southern planters and those elements of the North who stood outside the strait-laced Yankee culture created mainly by people of English origin. Though the political effects of ethnic identities were complex, in large measure such out-groups as the Scotch-Irish and the Catholic Irish felt more comfortable with the more tolerant Democratic party. If valid for the northern states, however, the cultural-ethnic interpretation needs qualification in the light of southern experience. Ethnic identities in the South had faded with the decline of immigration after the Revolution, but the South developed in the 1840s as vigorous a party division as the North.

There seems little question that, whatever else Jackson and his supporters had in mind, they followed an ideal of republican virtue, of returning to the Jeffersonian Arcadia of the Old Republic in which government would leave people largely to their own devices. In the Jacksonian view the alliance of government and business was always an invitation to special favors and an eternal source of corruption. The bank was the epitome of such evil. The right policy for government, at the national level in particular, was to refrain from granting special privileges and to let free competition in the marketplace reglate the economy.

In the bustling world of the nineteenth century, however, the idea of a return to agrarian simplicity was a futile exercise in nostalgia. Instead, laissez-faire policies opened the way for a host of aspiring entrepreneurs eager to replace the established economic elite with a new order of laissez-faire capitalism. And in fact there was no great conflict in the Jacksonian mentality between the farmer or planter who delved in the soil and the independent speculator and entrepreneur who won his way by other means. Jackson himself was all these things. What the Jacksonian mentality could not foresee was the degree to which, in a growing country, unrestrained enterprise could lead on to new economic combinations, centers of gigantic power largely independent of governmental regulation. But history is forever pursued by unintended consequences. Here the ultimate irony would be that the laissez-faire rationale for republican simplicity eventually became the justification for the growth of unregulated centers of economic power far greater than any ever wielded by Biddle's bank.

FURTHER READING

A survey of events covered in the chapter can be found in Glyndon Van Deusen's *The Jacksonian Era, 1828–1848* (1959).° Arthur M. Schlesinger, Jr.'s *The Age of Jackson* (1945)° emphasizes the role played by antibusiness interests in the agrarian South and the urban North. Richard Hofstadter's *The American Political Tradition and the Men Who Made It* (1948)° challenges this thesis. Lee Benson's *The Concept of Jacksonian Democracy* (1961) examines the ethnocultural basis for New York's politics of the common man. John W. Ward's *Andrew Jackson: Symbol for an Age* (1955)° assesses Jackson's impact on the psychology of mass politics. Edward Pessen's *Jacksonian America: Society, Personality, and Politics* (rev. ed., 1978) provides a recent overview of these arguments.

An introduction to the development of political parties of the 1830s can be found in Richard P. McCormick's *The Second Party System* (1966).° Richard Hofstadter's *The Idea of a Party System* (1969) traces the theories of political opposition which carried over from the first party system. In addition to the work by Benson, illuminating case studies include Ronald P. Formisano's *The Birth of Mass Political Parties* (1971), on Michigan; Formisano's *The Transformation of Political Culture* (1983), on Massachusetts; and Harry L. Watson's *Jacksonian Politics and Community Conflict: The Emergence of the Second American Party System in Cumberland County, North Carolina* (1981). Amy Bridges's *A City in the Republic* (1984) is on New York City politics. For an outstanding analysis of women in New York City during the Jacksonian period, see Christine Stansell's *City of Women* (1986). In *Chants Democratic* (1984) Sean Wilentz analyzes the social basis of working-class politics.

Biographies of Jackson include Robert V. Remini's *Andrew Jackson* (1966), which can serve as a good introduction. Also consult the three-volume biography by Remini: *Andrew Jackson and the Course of American Empire, 1767–1821* (1977), *Andrew Jackson and the Course of American Freedom, 1822–1832* (1981), and *Andrew Jackson and the Course of American Democracy, 1833–1845* (1984). On Jackson's successor, consult John Niven's *Martin Van Buren* (1983); Donald B. Cole's *Martin Van Buren and the Political System* (1984) is more critical.

The political philosophies of those who came to oppose Jackson are treated in Daniel W. Howe's *The Political Culture of Amercian Whigs* (1979). William P. Vaughn's *The Antimasonic Party in the United States, 1826–1843* (1983) discusses that group of Jackson's opponents.

Two studies of the impact of the bank controversy are William G. Shade's *Banks or No Banks: The Money Question in the Western States, 1832–1865* (1972) and James R. Sharp's *The Jacksonians versus the Banks: Politics in the States after the Panic of 1837* (1970). Daniel Feller's *The Public Lands in Jacksonian Politics* (1985) is a good introduction to that important topic.

°These books are available in paperback editions.

An outstanding book on the nullification issue is William W. Freeh-ling's *Prelude to Civil War: The Nullification Controversy in South Carolina, 1816–1836* (1966).° Grant Foreman's *Indian Removal* (1932) and Ronald N. Satz's *American Indian Policy in the Jacksonian Era* (1974) survey that tragedy; Michael P. Rogin's *Fathers and Children: Andrew Jackson and the Subjugation of the American Indian* (1975) is a psychological interpretaton of Jackson's Indian policy. The question of rising inequality in American cities is treated in Edward Pessen's *Riches, Class, and Power before the Civil War* (1973).

12

THE DYNAMICS OF GROWTH

Agriculture and the National Economy

COTTON "We are greatly, I was about to say fearfully, growing,"
John C. Calhoun told his congressional colleagues in 1816 when
he introduced his Bonus Bill for internal improvements. His pro-
phetic sentence expressed both the promise of national greatness and the threat of divisions that would blight Calhoun's own
ambition. But in the brief period of good feelings after the War of
1812, it was opportunity that seemed most conspicuously visible
to Americans everywhere, and nowhere more than in Calhoun's
native South Carolina. The reason was cotton, the new staple
crop of the South, which was spreading from South Carolina and
Georgia into the new lands of Mississippi and Alabama, where
Andrew Jackson had recently chastised the Creeks, and on into
Louisiana and Arkansas. Jackson himself had been set up as a
cotton planter at The Hermitage, near Nashville, Tennessee,
since the mid-1790s.

Cotton had been used from ancient times, but the Industrial
Revolution and its spread of textile mills created a rapidly growing market for the fluffy staple. Cotton had remained for many
years rare and expensive because of the need for hand labor to
separate the lint from the tenacious seeds of most varieties. But
by the mid-1780s in coastal Georgia and South Carolina a long-
staple Sea Island cotton was being grown commercially which
could easily be separated from its shiny black seeds by squeezing
it through rollers. Sea Island cotton, like the rice and indigo of
the colonial Tidewater, had little chance, though, in the soil and
climate of the up-country. And the green seed of the upland cotton clung to the lint so stubbornly that the rollers crushed the

seed and spoiled the fiber. One person working all day could manage to separate little if any more than a pound by hand. Cotton could not yet be king.

The rising cotton kingdom of the lower South came to birth at a plantation called Mulberry Hill in coastal Georgia, the home of Mrs. Nathanael Greene, widow of the Revolutionary War hero. At Mulberry Hill discussion often turned to the promising new crop and to speculation about better ways to remove the seeds. In 1792, on the way to a job as a tutor in South Carolina, young Eli Whitney, recently graduated from Yale, visited fellow graduate Phineas Miller, who was overseer at Mulberry Hill. Catherine Greene noticed her visitor's mechanical aptitude, which had been nurtured in boyhood by the needs of a Massachusetts farm. When she suggested that young Whitney devise a mechanism for removing the seed from upland cotton, he mulled it over and solved the problem in ten days. In the spring of 1793, his job as a tutor quickly forgotten, Whitney had a working model of a cotton gin.

By chance one of Mrs. Greene's daughters had bought some iron wire for a bird cage. Whitney used the wire to make iron pins which he inserted into a cylinder. When rotated, the cylinder passed cotton fiber through slots in an iron guard and the seeds dropped into a box below. Rotating brushes on the other side served as a doffer, removing the fiber as it passed through. With it one person could separate fifty times as much cotton as could be done by hand. The device was an "absurdly simple contrivance," too much so as it turned out. A simple description was all any skilled worker needed to make a copy, and by the time Whitney and Miller had secured a patent in 1794 a number of copies were already in use. Consequently the two men were never able to make good on the promise of riches that the gin offered, and spent most of their modest gains in expensive lawsuits. Improved models soon appeared. The use of a saw-toothed cylinder proved more effective than the original pins, and that device —which had occurred to Whitney at the start—appeared on the market as one of many designs contesting for patent rights.

Although Whitney realized little from his idea, he had unwittingly begun a revolution. Green-seed cotton first engulfed the up-country hills of South Carolina and Georgia, and after the War of 1812 migrated into the former Creek, Choctaw, and Chickasaw lands to the west. Cotton production soared. Slavery had found a new and profitable use. Indeed thereafter slavery became almost synonymous with the Cotton Kingdom in the popular view. Planters migrated westward with their gangs of

Whitney's cotton gin revolutionized the South's economy and breathed new life into slavery.

workers in tow, and a profitable trade began to develop in the sale of slaves from the coastal South to the West. The cotton culture became a way of life that tied the Old Southwest to the coastal Southeast in a common interest.

Not the least of the cotton gin's revolutionary consequences, although less apparent at first, was that cotton became almost immediately a major export commodity. Cotton exports averaged about $9 million in value from 1803 to 1807, about 22 percent of the value of all exports; from 1815 to 1819 they averaged over $23 million or 39 percent of the total, and from the mid-1830s to 1860 accounted for more than half the value of all exports. For the national economy as a whole, one historian asserted: "Cotton was the most important proximate cause of expansion." The South supplied the North both raw materials and markets for manufactures. Income from the North's role in handling the cotton trade then provided surpluses for capital investment. It was once assumed that the South supplied the Northwest with markets for foodstuffs, but recent research shows the Cotton Belt to have been self-sufficient in foodstuffs. The more likely explanation of growth in the Northwest now seems to be its own growing urban markets for foodstuffs, which supplemented the export market for grain.

FARMING THE WEST   The westward flow of planters and their slave gangs to Alabama and Mississippi during these flush times was paralleled by another migration through the Ohio Valley and the Great Lakes region, where the Indians had been steadily pushed westward until the risk was minimal. "Old America seems to be breaking up and moving westward," an English traveler observed in 1817 as he watched the migrants make their way along westward roads in Pennsylvania. Family groups, stages, light wagons, riders on horseback made up "a scene of bustle and business, extending over three hundred miles, which is truly wonderful." In 1800 some 387,000 settlers were counted west of the Atlantic states; by 1810, 1,338,000 lived over the mountains; by 1820, 2,419,000. By 1860 more than half the nation's expanded population resided in trans-Appalachia, and the restless movement had long since spilled across the Mississippi and touched the shores of the Pacific.

North of the expanding cotton belt in the Gulf states, the fertile woodland soils, riverside bottom lands, and black loam of the prairies drew farmers from the rocky lands of New England and the leached, exhausted soils of the Southeast. A new land law of 1820, passed after the Panic of 1819, eliminated the credit provisions of the 1800 act but reduced the minimum price from $1.64 to $1.25 per acre and the minimum plot from 160 to 80

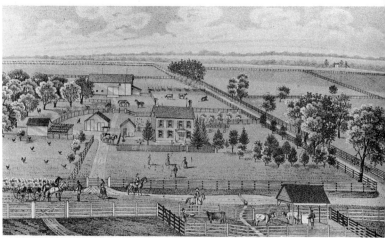

Farm Residence, Putnam County, Illinois. *Through the early decades of the nineteenth century migrants transformed midwestern plains to farmland.*

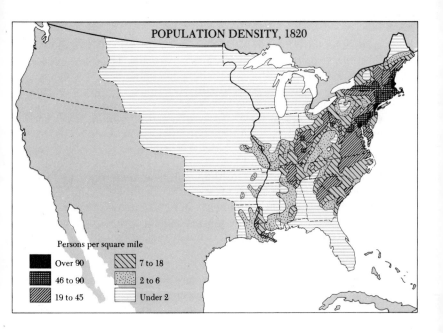

POPULATION DENSITY, 1820

Persons per square mile

- Over 90
- 46 to 90
- 19 to 45
- 7 to 18
- 2 to 6
- Under 2

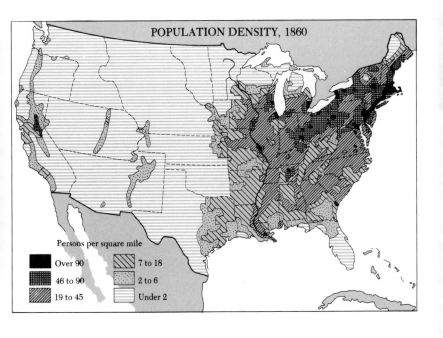

POPULATION DENSITY, 1860

Persons per square mile

- Over 90
- 46 to 90
- 19 to 45
- 7 to 18
- 2 to 6
- Under 2

acres. The settler could get a place for as little as $100, and over the years the proliferation of state banks made it possible to continue buying on credit. Even that was not enough for westerners, who began a long—and eventually victorious—agitation for further relaxation of the land laws. They favored preemption, the right of squatters to purchase land at the minimum price, and graduation, the progressive reduction of the price on lands that did not sell.

Success came ultimately with two acts of Congress. Under the Preemption Act of 1830, a renewable law made permanent in the Preemption Act of 1841, squatters could stake out claims ahead of the land surveys and later get 160 acres at the minimum price of $1.25. In effect the law recognized a practice enforced more often than not by frontier vigilantes. Under the Graduation Act of 1854, which Sen. Thomas Hart Benton had plugged since the 1820s, prices of unsold lands were to go down in stages until the lands could sell for 12½¢ per acre after thirty years.

The progress of settlement followed the old pattern of girdling trees, clearing land, and settling down at first to a crude subsistence. The development of effective iron plows greatly eased the backbreaking job of breaking the soil. As early as 1797 an American inventor had secured a patent on an iron plow, but a superstition that iron poisoned the soil prevented much use until after 1819, when Jethro Wood of New York developed an improved version with separate parts that could be replaced without buying a whole new plow complete. The prejudice against iron suddenly vanished, and the demand for plows grew so fast that Wood, like Whitney, could not supply the need and spent much of his remaining fifteen years fighting against patent infringements. The iron plow was a special godsend to those farmers who first ventured into the sticky black loams of the treeless prairies. Further improvements would follow, including John Deere's steel plow (1837) and the chilled-iron and steel plow of John Oliver (1855).

TRANSPORTATION AND THE NATIONAL ECONOMY

NEW ROADS The pioneer's life of crude subsistence eventually gave way to staple farming for cash income, as markets for foodstuffs grew both in the South and Northwest. Improvements in transportation were beginning to spur the development of a national market. As settlers moved west the demand went back east for better roads. In 1795 the Wilderness Road, along the trail blazed by Daniel Boone twenty years before, was opened to

The primitive condition of American roads is evident in this early-nineteenth-century watercolor.

wagon traffic, thereby easing the route through the Cumberland Gap into Kentucky and along the Knoxville and Old Walton Roads, completed the same year, into Tennessee. South of these roads there were no such major highways. South Carolinians and Georgians pushed westward on whatever trails or rutted roads had appeared.

To the northeast a movement for graded and paved roads (macadamized with crushed stones packed down) gathered momentum after completion of the Philadelphia-Lancaster Turnpike in 1794 (the term derives from a pole or pike at the tollgate, turned to admit the traffic). By 1821 some 4,000 miles of turnpikes had been completed, mainly connecting eastern cities, but western traffic could move along the Frederick Pike to Cumberland and thence along the National Road, completed to Wheeling on the Ohio in 1818, and to Vandalia, Illinois, by about mid-century; along the old Forbes Road from Philadelphia to Pittsburgh; and along the Mohawk and Genesee Turnpike from the Massachusetts line through Albany to Buffalo, whence one could take ship for points on the Great Lakes.

RIVER TRANSPORT   Once turnpike travelers had reached the Ohio they could float westward in comparative comfort. At Pittsburgh, Wheeling, and other points the emigrants could buy flatboats, commonly of two kinds: an ark with room for living

quarters, possessions, and perhaps some livestock; or a keelboat —similar but with a keel. For large flatboats—a capacity of forty tons was common—crews were available for hire. At the destination the boat could be used again or sold for lumber. In the early 1820s an estimated 3,000 flatboats went down the Ohio every year, and for many years after that the flatboat remained the chief conveyance for heavy traffic downstream.

By the early 1820s the turnpike boom was giving way to new developments in water transportation: the river steamboat and the canal barge, which carried bulk commodities far more cheaply than did Conestoga wagons on the National Road. As early as 1787 one inventor had launched a steamboat on the Delaware River, and in 1790 another carried passengers from Philadelphia to Trenton on a regular schedule, but technical problems continued to frustrate inventors. No commercially successful steamboat appeared until Robert Fulton and Robert R. Living-

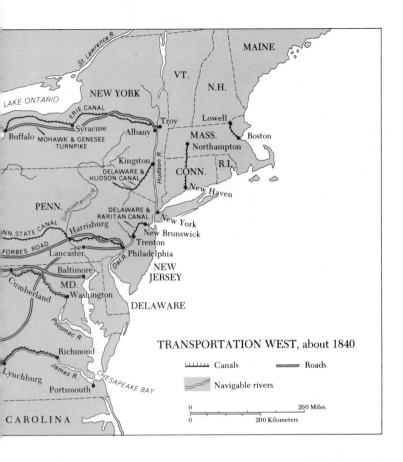

TRANSPORTATION WEST, about 1840

⊥⊥⊥⊥⊥ Canals   ══ Roads

Navigable rivers

0   200 Miles

0   200 Kilometers

ston sent the *Clermont* up the Hudson to Albany in 1807. After that the use of the steamboat spread rapidly to other eastern rivers, and in 1811 a business associate of Fulton launched a sidewheeler, the *New Orleans*, at Pittsburgh and sent it down the Ohio and Mississippi; thus began an era of steamboat transportation that opened nearly half a continent to water traffic. The *New Orleans* itself thereafter plied between New Orleans and Natchez, but in 1815 the *Enterprise* went all the way from New Orleans up the Ohio and another fifty miles up the Monongahela. In 1818 the *Walk-in-the-Water*, the first steamboat on Lake Erie, began a regular nine-day schedule between Buffalo and Detroit.

By 1836, 361 steamboats were registered to navigate the western waters. As the boats reached ever farther up the tributaries that connected to the Mississippi, their design evolved toward the familiar "steamboat Gothic," the glorified keelboat which one wit called "an engine on a raft with $11,000 worth of

The sumptuous interior of the steamboat Princess.

jig-saw work." By the 1840s shallow-draft ships that traveled *on* rather than *in* the water carried 50–100 tons of freight on twenty-four-inch drafts. These steam-powered rafts, the scorn of ocean-going salts, became the basis of the rivermen's boast that they could navigate a heavy dew, that they were "so built that when the river is low and the sandbars come out for air, the first mate can tap a keg of beer and run the boat four miles on the suds." These boats ventured into far reaches of the Mississippi Valley, up such rivers as the Wabash, the Monongahela, the Cumberland, the Tennessee, the Missouri, and the Arkansas.

The miracle of these floating palaces became one of the romantic epics of America. The tradition was fixed early. In 1827 a lyrical writer for Cincinnati's *Western Monthly Review* let himself go with a description of the "fairy structures of oriental gorgeousness and splendor . . . rushing down the Mississippi . . . or plowing up between the forests . . . bearing speculators, merchants, dandies, fine ladies, everything real and everything affected in the form of humanity, with pianos, and stocks of novels, and cards, and dice, and flirting, and love-making, and drinking, and champagne, and on the deck, perhaps, three hundred fellows, who have seen alligators and neither fear whiskey, nor gunpowder. A steamboat, coming from New Orleans, brings to the remotest villages of our streams, and the very doors of the cabins, a little Paris, a section of Broadway, or a slice of Philadelphia, to a ferment in the minds of our young people, the innate propensity for fashions and finery."

The prosaic flatboat, however, still carried to market most of the western wheat, corn, flour, meal, bacon, ham, pork, whiskey, soap and candles (the by-products of slaughterhouses), lead from Missouri, copper from Michigan, wood from the Rockies, and ironwork from Pittsburgh. But the steamboat, by bringing two-way traffic to the Mississippi Valley, created a continental market and an agricultural empire which became the new breadbasket of America. Farming evolved from a subsistence level to the ever-greater production of valuable staples. Along with the new farmers came promoters, speculators, and land-boomers. Villages at strategic trading points along the streams evolved into centers of commerce and urban life. The port of New Orleans grew in the 1830s and 1840s to lead all others in exports.

But by then the Erie Canal was drawing eastward much of the trade that once went down to the Gulf. In 1817 the New York legislature endorsed Gov. De Witt Clinton's dream of connecting the Hudson River with Lake Erie and authorized construction. Eight years later, in 1825, the canal was open for its entire 350 miles from Albany to Buffalo; branches soon put most of the state within reach of the canal. After 1828 the Delaware and

Lockport, New York, 1840. *This crucial point on the Erie Canal, "the most stupendous chain of artificial navigation" in the world, featured five ascending and five descending locks.*

Hudson Canal linked New York with the anthracite fields of northeastern Pennsylvania. The speedy success of the New York system inspired a mania for canals that lasted more than a decade and resulted in the completion of about 3,000 miles of waterways by 1837. But no canal ever matched the spectacular success of the Erie, which rendered the entire Great Lakes region an economic tributary to the port of New York. With the further development of canals spanning Ohio and Indiana from north to south, much of the upper Ohio Valley also came within the economic sphere of New York.

RAILROADS   The Panic of 1837 and the subsequent depression cooled the fever quickly. Some states that had borrowed heavily to finance canals had to repudiate their debts. The holders of repudiated bonds were left without recourse. Meanwhile a new and more versatile form of transportation was gaining on the canal: the railroad. Vehicles that ran on iron rails had long been in use, especially in mining, but now came a tremendous innovation—the use of steam power—as the steam locomotive followed soon after the steamboat. As early as 1814 the first practical steam locomotive was built in England. In 1825, the year the Erie Canal was completed, the world's first commercial steam railway began operations in England. By the 1820s the port cities of Baltimore, Charleston, and Boston were alive with schemes to tap the hinterlands by rail.

On July 4, 1828, Baltimore got the jump on other cities when Charles Carroll, the last surviving signer of the Declaration of Independence, laid the first stone in the roadbed of the Baltimore and Ohio (B&O) Railroad. Four years later the road reached seventy-three miles west of Baltimore. The Charleston and Hamburg Railroad, started in 1831 and finished in 1833, was at that time the longest railroad under single management in the world. It reached westward 136 miles to the hamlet of Hamburg, opposite Augusta, where Charleston merchants hoped to divert traffic from the Savannah River. Boston by 1836 had fanned out three major lines to Lowell, Worcester, and Providence.

By 1840 the railroads, with a total of 3,328 miles, had outdistanced the canals by just two miles. Over the next twenty years, though, railroads grew nearly tenfold to cover 30,626 miles; more than a third of this total was built in the 1850s. Several major east-west lines appeared, connecting Boston to Albany and Albany with Buffalo; combined in 1853, these lines became the New York Central. In 1851 the Erie Railroad spanned southern New York; by 1852 the Pennsylvania Railway connected

The New-York Central Rail Road connected Albany with New England and "All Points West, Northwest, and Southwest."

Philadelphia and Pittsburgh; in 1853 the B&O finally reached Wheeling on the Ohio. By then New York had connections all the way to Chicago, and in two years to St. Louis. Before 1860 the Hannibal and St. Joseph had crossed the state of Missouri. Farther south, despite Charleston's early start on both canals and railroads and despite the brave dream of a line to tap western commerce at Cincinnati, the network of railroads still had many gaps in 1860. By 1857 Charleston, Savannah, and Norfolk connected by way of lines into Chattanooga and thence along a single line to Memphis, the only southern route that connected the east coast and the Mississippi. In 1860 the North and South had only three major links: at Washington, Louisville, and Cairo, Illinois.

The proliferation of trunk lines had by then supplemented the earlier canals to create multiple ties between the Northwest and Northeast. But it was still not until the eve of the Civil War that railroads surpassed canals in total haulage: in 1859 they carried a little over 2 billion ton-miles compared to 1.6 billion on canals.

Travel on the early railroads was a chancy venture. Iron straps on top of wooden rails, for instance, tended to work loose and curl up into "snakesheads" which sometimes pierced railway coaches. The solution was the iron T-rail, introduced in 1831 and soon standard equipment on the best roads, but the strap-iron rail remained common because wood was so cheap. Wood was used for fuel too, and the sparks often caused fires along the way or damaged passengers' clothing. An English traveler reported seeing a lady's shawl ignited on one trip. She found in her own gown thirteen holes "and in my veil, with which I saved my eyes, more than could be counted." Creation of the "spark arrester"

THE GROWTH
OF RAILROADS,
1850

—— Railroads in 1850

and the use of coal relieved but never overcame the hazard. Until
after 1860 brakes had to be operated manually, crude pin-and-
link couplings were used, and adequate springs were unknown.
Different track widths often forced passengers to change trains
until a standard gauge became national in 1882. Land travel,
whether by stagecoach or train, was a jerky, bumpy, wearying
ordeal. An early stage rider on the Forbes Road said he alternately walked and rode and "though the pain of riding exceeded
the fatigue of walking, yet . . . it refreshed us by varying the
weariness of our bodies."

Water travel, where available, offered far more comfort, but
railroads gained supremacy over other forms of transport because of their economy, speed, and reliability. By 1859 railroads
had reduced the cost of transportation services by $150–$175
million, accounting for a social saving that amounted to some 4
percent of the gross national product. By 1890 the saving would
run up to almost 15 percent. Railroads provided indirect benefits
by encouraging settlement and the expansion of farming. During
the antebellum period the reduced costs brought on by the

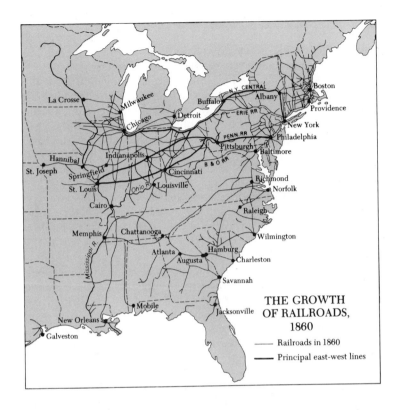

THE GROWTH
OF RAILROADS,
1860

—— Railroads in 1860
—— Principal east-west lines

railroads aided the expansion of farming more than manufacturing, since manufacturers in the Northeast, especially New England, had better access to water transportation. The railroads'
demand for rail iron and equipment of various kinds, however,
did provide an enormous market for the industries that made
these capital goods. And the ability of railroads to operate year
round in all kinds of weather gave them an advantage in carrying
finished goods too.

OCEAN TRANSPORT   For ocean-going traffic the start of service on
regular schedules was the most important change of the early
1800s. In the first week of 1818 ships of the Black Ball Line inaugurated a weekly transatlantic packet service between New
York and Liverpool. Beginning with four ships in all, the Black
Ball Line thereafter had one ship leaving each port monthly at an
announced time. With the business recovery in 1822 the packet
business grew in a rush. Runs to London and Le Havre were
added, and by 1845 some fifty-two transatlantic lines ran
square-riggers on schedule from New York, with three regular

sailings per week. Many others ran in the coastwide trade, to Charleston, Savannah, New Orleans, and elsewhere.

In the same year, 1845, came a great innovation with the building of the first clipper ship, the *Rainbow*. The clippers, built for speed, long and narrow with enormous sail areas, cut a dashing figure during their brief day of glory, which lasted less than two decades. In 1854 the *Flying Cloud* took eighty-nine days and eight hours to make the distance from New York to San Francisco, a speed that steamships took several decades to equal. But clippers, while fast, lacked ample cargo space, and after the Civil War would give way to the steamship.

The use of steam on ocean-going vessels lagged behind the development of steam riverboats because of the greater technological problems involved. In 1819 the first steamship to cross the Atlantic, the *Savannah*, used steam power for only eighty hours during a twenty-seven-day voyage from Savannah to Liverpool, relying on sails for most of the trip. It ended its days as a sailing vessel, stripped of its engines. On April 23, 1838, the British and American Steamship Navigation Company's ship *Sirius* arrived in New York, and another steamship, the *Great Western*, came in later the same day, but it would be another ten years before steamships began to threaten the sailing packets.

THE ROLE OF GOVERNMENT The massive internal improvements of the era were the product of both governmental and private initiatives, sometimes undertaken jointly and sometimes separately. Private investment accounted for nearly all the turnpikes in New England and the middle states. Elsewhere states invested heavily in turnpike companies and in some cases, notably South Carolina and Indiana, themselves built and owned the turnpikes. Canals were to a much greater extent the product of state investment, and more commonly state-owned and -operated. The Panic of 1837, however, caused states to pull back and leave railroad development mainly to private corporations. Most of the railroad capital came from private sources. Still, government had an enormous role in railroad development. Several states of the South and West built state-owned lines, such as Georgia's Western and Atlantic, completed from Atlanta to Chattanooga in 1851, although they generally looked to private companies to handle actual operations and in some cases sold the lines. States and localities along the routes invested in railroad corporations and granted loans; states were generous in granting charters and tax concessions.

The federal government helped too, despite the constitutional scruples of some against direct involvement. The government bought stock in turnpike and canal companies, and after the success of the Erie, extended land grants to several western states for the support of canal projects. Congress provided for railroad surveys by government engineers, and reduced the tariff duties on iron used in railroad construction. In 1850 Sen. Stephen A. Douglas of Illinois and others prevailed on Congress to extend a major land grant to support a north-south line connecting Chicago with Mobile. Grants of three square miles on alternate sides for each mile of railroad subsidized the building of the Illinois Central and the Mobile and Ohio Railroads. Regarded at the time a special case, the 1850 grant set a precedent for other bounties that totaled about 20 million acres by 1860—a small amount compared to the grants for transcontinental lines in the Civil War decade.

THE GROWTH OF INDUSTRY

While the South and West developed the agricultural basis for a national economy, the Northeast was laying foundations for an industrial revolution. Technology in the form of the cotton gin, the harvester, and improvements in transportation had quickened agricultural development and to some extent decided its direction. But technology altered the economic landscape even more profoundly by giving rise to the factory system.

EARLY TEXTILE MANUFACTURES   At the end of the colonial period manufacturing remained in the household or handicraft stage of development, or at most the "putting-out" stage, in which the merchant capitalist would distribute raw materials (say, leather patterns for shoes) to be worked up at home, then collected and sold. In 1815 *Niles' Weekly Register* described the town of Mount Pleasant, Ohio, with a population of barely over 500, as having some thirty-eight handicraft shops, including blacksmiths and bakers, and eight more shops engaged in tanning, textiles, and railmaking. Farmers themselves had to produce much of what they needed in the way of crude implements, shoes, and clothing, and in their simple workshops inventive genius was sometimes nurtured. As a boy Eli Whitney had set up a forge to make nails in his father's rural workshop. The transition from such production to the factory was slow, but one for which a base had been laid before 1815.

In the eighteenth century Great Britain had jumped out to a

long head start in industrial production. The foundations of Britain's advantage were: the development of iron smelting by coke when sufficient wood was lacking; the invention of the steam engine in 1705 and its improvement by James Watt in 1765; and a series of inventions that mechanized the production of textiles, including John Kay's flying shuttle (1733), James Hargreaves's spinning jenny (1764), Richard Arkwright's "water frame" (1769), and Samuel Crompton's spinning mule (1779). The last could do the work of 200 spinners. Britain also carefully guarded its hard-won secrets, forbidding the export of machines or descriptions of them, even restricting the departure of informed mechanics. But the secrets could not be kept. In 1789 Samuel Slater arrived from England with the plan of Arkwright's water frame in his head. He contracted with an enterprising merchant-manufacturer in Rhode Island to build a mill in Pawtucket, and in this little mill, completed in 1790, nine children turned out a satisfactory cotton yarn, which was then worked up by the putting-out system. In 1793 two Englishmen from Yorkshire built the first woolens mill, at Byfield, Massachusetts.

The beginnings in textiles were slow and faltering until Jefferson's embargo in 1807 and the War of 1812 restricted imports and encouraged the merchant capitalists of New England to switch their resources into manufacturing. New England, it happened, had one distinct advantage in that the fall line and the water power it provided stood near the coast where water trans-

New England Factory Village, 1830. *Mills and factories gradually transformed the New England landscape in the early nineteenth century.*

portation was also readily available. In 1813 Francis Cabot Lowell and a group of wealthy merchants known as the Boston Associates formed the Boston Manufacturing Company. At Waltham, Massachusetts, they built the first factory in which the processes of spinning and weaving by power machinery were brought under one roof, mechanizing every process from raw material to finished cloth. By 1815 textile mills numbered in the hundreds. A flood of British imports after the War of 1812 dealt a temporary setback to the infant industry, but the foundations of textile manufacture were laid, and they spurred the growth of garment trades and a machine-tool industry to build and service the mills.

TECHNOLOGY IN AMERICA Meanwhile American ingenuity was adding other bases for industrial growth. Oliver Evans of Philadelphia was a frustrated pioneer who had the misfortune to be ahead of his time. As a teenager he had been fascinated by steam engines but could not find the backing to pursue his ideas for steamboats and locomotives. As early as 1785 he built an automatic mill in which grain introduced at one end came out flour at the other, but could not get millers interested in trying it. Success eluded him until 1804, when he developed a high-pressure steam engine adapted to a variety of uses in ships and factories.

The practical bent of Americans was one of the outstanding traits noted by foreign visitors. In Europe, where class consciousness prevailed, Tocqueville wrote, men confined themselves to "the arrogant and sterile researches of abstract truths, whilst the social condition and institutions of democracy prepare them to seek immediate and useful practical results of the sciences." In 1814 Dr. Jacob Bigelow, a Harvard botanist, began to lecture on "The Elements of Technology," a word he did much to popularize. In his book of the same title he argued that technology constituted the chief superiority of moderns over the ancients, effecting profound changes in ways of living. Benjamin Silliman, Yale's first professor of chemistry, emphasized the application of science in his classes, publications (he founded the *American Journal of Science* in 1818), and public lectures.

One of the most striking examples of the connection between pure research and innovation, however, was in the work of Joseph Henry, a Princeton physicist. His research in electromagnetism provided the basis for Samuel F. B. Morse's invention of the telegraph and for electrical motors later on. In 1846 Henry became head of the new Smithsonian Institution, founded with a bequest from the Englishman James Smithson "for the increase and diffusion of knowledge among men." The year 1846 also saw the founding of the American Association for the Advancement of Science.

It would be difficult to exaggerate the importance of science and technology in changing the ways people live. All aspects of life—the social, cultural, economic, and political—were and are shaped by it. Invention often brought about completely new enterprises, the steamboat and the railroad being the most spectacular, without which the pace of development would have been slowed immeasurably.

Eli Whitney, whose cotton gin had deeply influenced the development of the South, also developed a basic principle which promoted the industrial growth of the North. In 1799 he won a government contract for the manufacture of muskets, and in his shop at New Haven developed machine tools to make parts with such precision as to be virtually identical. In a shop twenty miles away Simeon North began the same year with a contract for pistols. No one can say with assurance which man was the inventor. It was in fact more an evolution in machine tools than an invention, and the original idea seems to have been French. Its perfection, however, was an original American contribution.

Most basic inventions were imports from Europe. Preservation of food by canning, for instance, was unknown before the early nineteenth century when Americans learned of a new French discovery that food stayed fresh when cooked in airtight containers. By 1820 major canneries were in existence in Boston and New York. At the end of the 1830s glass containers were giving way to the "tin can" (tin-plated steel) brought in from England, and eventually used to market Gail Borden's new invention—a process for condensed milk. Among the outstanding American originals were Cyrus Hall McCormick of Virginia and Obed Hussey of Massachusetts, who separately invented practical reapers for grain at about the same time, a development as significant to the Northwest as the cotton gin was to the South. Hussey got a patent in 1833, McCormick in 1834. Competition between the two brought a rapid growth in the industry, but McCormick finally emerged on top because he had the foresight in 1847 to put his main plant at Chicago near the emerging wheat belt and the wit to accept improvements more quickly than Hussey.

A spate of inventions in the 1840s foretokened future changes in American life. In 1844 Charles Goodyear patented a process for vulcanizing rubber. In the same year the first intercity telegraph message was transmitted from Baltimore to Washington on the device Morse had invented back in 1832. The telegraph

"In this Field, July 25, 1831, will be Tried a new Patent Grain Cutter, worked by horsepower, invented by C. H. McCormick."

was slow to catch on at first, but seventeen years after that demonstration, with the completion of connections to San Francisco, an entire continent had been wired for instant communications. In 1846 Elias Howe invented the sewing machine, soon improved by Allen B. Wilson and Isaac Merritt Singer. The sewing machine, incidentally, was one invention that slowed the progress of the factory. Since it was adapted to use in the home, it gave the "putting-out" system a new lease on life in the clothing industry.

Examples can do no more than hint at the magnitude of change in technology and manufacturing. A suggestive if flawed measure was the growing number of patents issued. During the first twenty-one years of the Patent Office, 1790–1811, the number issued averaged only 77 per year; from 1820 to 1830 the average was up to 535; during the 1840s it was 646; and during the 1850s the number suddenly quadrupled to an average of 2,525 per year.

THE LOWELL SYSTEM Before the 1850s the factory still had not become typical of American industry. Handicraft and domestic production (putting-out) remained common. In many industries they stayed for decades the chief agencies of growth. Hatmaking in Danbury, Connecticut, and shoemaking in eastern Massachusetts, for instance, grew mainly by the multiplication of small shops and their gradual enlargement. Not until the 1850s did either begin to adopt power-driven machinery, usually a distinctive feature of the factory system.

The factory system sprang full-blown upon the American scene at Waltham, Massachusetts, in 1813, in the plant of the Boston Manufacturing Company. In 1822 its promoters, the Boston Associates, developed a new center at a village, renamed Lowell, where the Merrimack River fell thirty-five feet. At this "Manchester of America" the Merrimack Manufacturing Company developed a new plant similar to the Waltham mill. Another sprang up in 1823 at Chicopee and before 1850 textile mills appeared at many other places in Massachusetts, New Hampshire, and Maine. By 1850, as good waterpower locations were occupied, steam power was becoming common in textile manufacture.

Companies organized on the Waltham plan produced by 1850 a fifth of the nation's total output of cotton cloth. The chief features of this plan were large capital investment, the concentration of all processes in one plant under unified management, and specialization in a relatively coarse cloth requiring minimum skill by the workers. In the public mind, however, the system then and afterward was associated above all with the recruitment of young women from New England farms who lived in dormitories while they worked in the mills. The system offered reassurance to parents by providing strait-laced discipline supervised by respectable housemothers, regular curfews, and compulsory church attendance. Many women were drawn by the chance to escape the routine of farm life and to earn money which might be used to help the family or improve their own circumstances. Despite their twelve-hour day and seventy-hour week some of them found the time and energy to form study groups, publish a literary magazine, and attend lectures by Ralph Waldo Emerson and other luminaries of the era. Foreign travelers were almost universally charmed by the arrangement. It was hardly an idyllic existence, but few if any of the young women saw their work as a lifetime career. It was, rather, at worst a temporary burden, at best a preparation for life or an exciting interlude before settling into the routine of domesticity.

It was but an interlude in the history of American labor too. The "Lowell girls" drew attention less because they were typical than because they were special. An increasingly common pattern for industry was the family system, sometimes called the Rhode Island or Fall River system, which prevailed in textile manufactures outside of northern New England. Factories that relied on waterpower often rose in unpopulated areas, and part of their construction included tenements or mill villages. Whole families

Shortly after this Philadelphia dressmaker was depicted at work (1807), textile mills opened at Lowell (1822) and elsewhere transformed the nature of work for women and men.

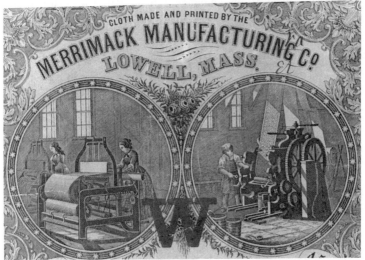

CLOTH MADE AND PRINTED BY THE
MERRIMACK MANUFACTURING Cọ
LOWELL, MASS.

might be hired, the men for heavy labor, the women and children for the lighter work. The system promoted paternalism. Employers dominated the life of the mill villages, often setting rules of good behavior. Wages under the system are hard to establish, for employers often paid in goods from the company store. The hours of labor often ran from sunup to sunset, and longer in winter—a sixty-eight- to seventy-two-hour week. Such hours were common on the farms of the time, but in factories the work was more intense and offered no seasonal let-up. The labor of children, common on the farm, excited little censure from communities still close to the soil. A common opinion at the time regarded the provision of gainful employment for the women and children of the lower orders as a community benefit.

CORPORATIONS AND INDUSTRY   In manufacturing the corporate form of organization caught on slowly. Manufacturing firms usually took the form of individual proprietorships, family enterprises, or partnerships. The success of the Boston Associates at Waltham and Lowell, and the growth of larger units, particularly in textiles, brought the corporate device into greater use. But until 1860 most manufacturing was carried on by unincorporated enterprises.

The corporate organization was more common for banking, turnpike, canal, and railroad companies, since many then believed that the form should be reserved for such quasi-public and quasi-monopolistic functions. The irregular practices of wildcat banks gave corporations a bad name throughout the period. Corporations were regarded with suspicion as the beneficiaries of special privileges, as threats to individual enterprises. "The very object of the act of incorporation is to produce inequality, either in rights, or in the division of property," one observer wrote in 1820. "*Prima facie*, therefore, all money corporations, are detrimental to national health. They are always for the benefit of the rich, and never for the poor." It would be many years before corporations came to be widely regarded as agencies of free enterprise.

Banks of the time supplied mainly short-term commercial loans and long-term secured loans, but even before 1815 some of them had become active as investment banks—that is, they would take government or private securities in wholesale lots and put them on the market. The New York Stock Exchange, started in 1817, soon became the chief exchange for these securities, and the Boston Stock Exchange was the one on which manufacturing securities were traded before the Civil War. Most of the capital that financed new factories through the purchase of securities came from profits made earlier in commerce. New England's head start in commerce fueled its head start in factories. Foreign investments were important in building the canals and railroads, but contributed little to manufacturing. The same was true of investments by the states.

As late as 1860 the United States was still preponderantly

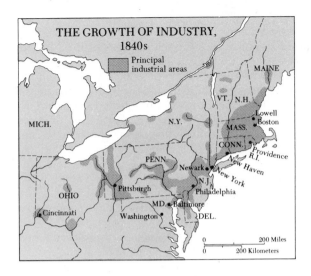

THE GROWTH OF INDUSTRY, 1840s

Principal industrial areas

MAINE

MICH.

N.Y.

VT. N.H.

MASS.

Lowell
Boston

CONN.

Providence
R.I.

PENN.

Newark

New Haven

New York

OHIO

Pittsburgh

N.J.

Philadelphia

Cincinnati

MD. Baltimore

Washington

DEL.

0   200 Miles
0   200 Kilometers

rural and agricultural. Industry was heavily concentrated in the Northeast. In southern New England, especially its coastal regions, and along the Hudson and Delaware Rivers, the concentration of industry rivaled that in any of the industrialized parts of Britain and exceeded that in most parts of the European continent.

In the 1860 Census of Manufactures cotton textiles stood ahead of all other categories in rank order of value added (value of product minus value of raw material). Recognizing the primacy of the fiber in exports as well, the census report began with these words: "The growth of the culture and manufacture of cotton in the United States constitutes the most striking feature of the industrial history of the last fifty years." In all, American industry in 1860 employed 1,311,000 workers in 140,000 establishments; with a capital investment of just over $1 billion, output amounted to $1.886 billion (up significantly from 1810's total output of $149 million), of which the value added by manufacturing was $854 million.

INDUSTRY AND CITIES   The rapid growth of commerce and industry impelled a rapid growth of cities. Using the census definition of "urban" as places with 8,000 inhabitants or more, the proportion of urban population grew from 3.3 percent in 1790 to 16.1 percent in 1860. Modern cities have served three major economic functions: they have been centers of trade and distribution, centers of manufacturing, and centers of administration. Until near the mid–nineteenth century American cities grew mainly in response to the circumstances of transportation and trade. Because of their strategic locations the four great Atlantic seaports of New York, Philadelphia, Baltimore, and Boston held throughout the antebellum period the relative positions of leadership they had gained by the end of the Revolution. New Orleans became the nation's fifth-largest city from the time of the Louisiana Purchase. Its focus on cotton exports, to the neglect of imports, however, caused it eventually to lag behind its eastern competitors. New York outpaced all its competitors and the nation as a whole in its population growth. By 1860 it was the first American city to reach a population of more than a million, largely because of its superior harbor and its unique access to commerce.

Pittsburgh, at the head of the Ohio, was already a center of iron production by 1800, and Cincinnati, at the mouth of the Little Miami, soon surpassed all other centers of meatpacking, with pork a specialty. Louisville, because it stood at the falls of the Ohio, became an important stop for trade and remained so after the short Louisville and Portland Canal bypassed the falls in 1830. On the Great Lakes the leading cities also stood at important breaking points in water transportation: Buffalo, Cleveland, Detroit, Chicago, and Milwaukee. Chicago was especially well located to become a hub of both water and rail transportation on into the trans-Mississippi West. During the 1830s St. Louis tripled in size mainly because most of the trans-Mississippi fur trade was funneled down the Missouri River. By 1860 St. Louis and Chicago were positioned to challenge Boston and Baltimore for third and fourth places.

St. Louis in the 1850s, looking east toward the Mississippi River. Steamboat traffic on the river was vital to the growth of St. Louis.

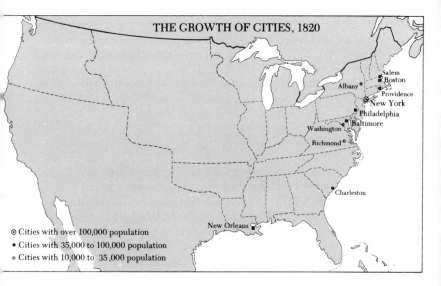

THE GROWTH OF CITIES, 1820

- ⊙ Cities with over 100,000 population
- ■ Cities with 35,000 to 100,000 population
- ○ Cities with 10,000 to 35,000 population

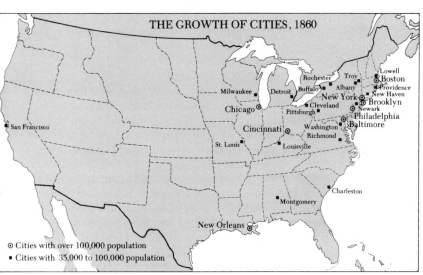

THE GROWTH OF CITIES, 1860

- ⊙ Cities with over 100,000 population
- ■ Cities with 35,000 to 100,000 population

Before 1840 commerce dominated the activities of major cities, but early industry often created new concentrations of population at places convenient to waterpower or raw materials. During the 1840s and 1850s, however, the stationary steam engine and declining transportation costs more and more offset the advantages of locations near waterpower and resources, and the attractions of older cities were enhanced: pools of experienced labor, capital, warehousing and trading services, access to information, the savings of bulk purchasing and handling, and the many amenities of city life. Urbanization thus was both a consequence of economic growth and a positive force in its promotion.

IMMIGRATION

Amid all the new economic growth, one condition of American life carried over beyond the mid–nineteenth century: land remained plentiful and relatively cheap, while labor was scarce and relatively dear. A decline in the birth rate coinciding with the onset of industry and urbanization reinforced this condition. The United States remained a strong magnet for immigrants, offering them chances to take up farms in the country or jobs in the cities. Glowing reports from early arrivals who made good reinforced romantic views of American opportunity and freedom. "Tell Miriam," one immigrant wrote back, "there is no sending children to bed without supper, or husbands to work without dinner in their bags." A German immigrant in Missouri wrote home applauding the "absence of overbearing soldiers, haughty clergymen, and inquisitive tax collectors."

During the forty years from the outbreak of the Revolution until the end of the War of 1812 immigration had slowed to a trickle. The wars of the French Revolution and Napoleon restricted travel until 1815. Within a few years, however, packet lines had begun to cross the north Atlantic, and competing shippers who needed westbound payloads kept the transatlantic fares as low as $30 per person. One informed estimate had it that from 1783 to 1819 total arrivals numbered about 250,000, or something under 7,000 per year. In 1820, when the government began to keep records, the number was 8,385. Thereafter the pace followed just behind the growth of business. For two decades the numbers rose steadily: 10,199 in 1825, 23,322 in 1830, 84,066 in 1840. After 1845 the tempo picked up rapidly. During the 1830s total arrivals had numbered fewer than 600,000. In the 1840s almost three times as many, or 1.7 million, immigrated, and during the 1850s 2.6 million more came. In 1850 the annual count went above 300,000 for the first time, then rose annually to a peak of 427,833 in 1854, a figure not equaled before 1880. The years from 1845 to 1854 saw the greatest proportionate influx of immigrants in American history, 2.4 million, or about 14.5 percent of the total population in 1845.

THE IRISH   In 1860 more than one of every eight persons in America was foreign born. The largest groups among them, by far, were 1.6 million Irish, 1.3 million Germans, and 588,000 British (mostly English). The Catholic Irish were the most conspicuous new element in the population. Ireland had long seethed with discontent at British rule, British landlords, and British taxes to support the Church of England. What sent the Irish fleeing their homeland was a chronic depression that set in with the nineteenth century. By the 1830s their numbers in America were quickly growing, and after an epidemic of potato rot in 1845 brought famine, the flow of Irish immigrants rose to a flood. The Irish disaster coincided with the end of depression and a rising tempo of business in the United States. In 1847 Irish arrivals numbered above 100,000 and stayed above that level for eight years, reaching a peak of 221,000 in 1851.

The Irish were mostly tenant farmers, but their experience had left them little taste for farm work and little money to travel or buy land. Great numbers of them hired on with construction gangs building the canal and railways—about 3,000 set to work on the Erie Canal as early as 1818. Few immigrants of any origin found their way into the South, but the Irish who did sometimes found work with planters who preferred not to risk valuable slaves at hazardous tasks. For the most part, however, the Irish congregated in the eastern cities, in or near their port of entry. Generally they worked as domestic servants or unskilled laborers, and clustered in shanty-towns and around Catholic churches, both of which became familiar features of the urban scene.

Experienced at organized resistance to rent and tax collectors, the Irish formed blocs of voters and found their way into American politics more quickly than any other immigrant group. Drawn mainly to the party of Jefferson and Jackson, "the party of the common man," they set a pattern of identification with the Democrats that other ethnic groups by and large followed. They also stimulated the growth of the Catholic church with their numbers and their more aggressive spirit. Years of persecution had instilled in them a fierce loyalty to the doctrines of the church.

THE GERMANS   When the new wave of German migration got under way in the 1830s there were still large enclaves of Germans in Pennsylvania and Ohio who had preserved their language and cultures, and in the Old World style, had clustered in agricultural villages. The new German migration peaked just a

A *Cincinnati* Turnverein, *or German gymnastic society.*

few years after the Irish, in 1854 when 215,000 arrived. Unlike the Irish, the Germans included fair numbers of independent farmers, skilled workers, and shopkeepers who arrived with some means to get themselves established in skilled labor or on the land. Three major centers of new settlement developed in Missouri and southwestern Illinois (around St. Louis), in Texas (near San Antonio), and in Wisconsin (especially around Milwaukee). The German migrants also included a large number of professional people, some of them refugees from the failure of liberal revolution in Germany, among whom was Carl Schurz, later senator from Missouri. The larger German communities developed traditions of good food, beer, and music along with German *Turnvereine* (gymnastic societies), sharpshooter clubs, fire engine companies, and kindergartens (introduced by Mrs. Carl Schurz).

THE BRITISH, SCANDINAVIANS, AND CHINESE Among the British immigrants too were large numbers of professionals, independent farmers, and skilled workers. Some British workers, such as Samuel Slater, helped transmit the technology of British factories into the United States. Two other groups that began to arrive in some number during the 1840s and 1850s were but the vanguard of greater numbers to come later. Annual arrivals from Scandinavia did not exceed 1,000 until 1843, but by 1860 a total of 72,600 Scandinavians lived in America. The Norwegians and Swedes gravitated to Wisconsin and Minnesota where the climate and woodlands reminded them of home. By the 1850s the sudden development of California was bringing in Chinese who, like the Irish in the East, did the heavy work of construction. Infinitesimal in numbers until 1854, the Chinese in America numbered 35,500 by 1860.

NATIVISM America had always been a land of immigrants, but the welcome accorded them had often been less than cordial. For many natives these waves of strangers in the land posed a threat of unknown tongues and mysterious ways. The greatest single group of newcomers were the Irish, who were mostly Catholic. The Germans too included many Catholics. This massive increase naturally aroused antagonisms which were rooted in the Protestant tradition of hostility to "popery" and aggravated by job competition in the cities where immigrants gathered. A militant Protestantism growing out of revivals in the early nineteenth century heated up the climate of opinion. There were fears of radicalism among the Germans and of voting blocs among the Irish, but above all hovered the menace of unfamiliar religious practices. Catholic authoritarianism was widely perceived as a threat to hard-won liberties, religious and political. The convenience of this, for political adventurers and fanatics, was that the Catholic church in most places remained small enough to be attacked with impunity.

In the 1830s nativism was conspicuously on the rise. Pointing to the Catholic missions sponsored by European groups, and to the pope's trappings of monarchy in Italy, overheated patriots envisaged conspiracy and subversion in America. Samuel F. B. Morse, already at work on his telegraph, took time out from his painting and inventing to write two books demonstrating his theory that Catholicism in America was a plot of foreign monarchs to undermine American liberty before its revolutionary message affected their own people. In 1836 he ran for mayor of New York on a Native American ticket, and his books went through numerous editions. But the literature of conspiracy could scarcely compete with a profitable trade in books which, in the guise of attacking evil, exploited salacious fantasies of sex in Catholic nunneries.

At times this hostility rekindled the spirit of the wars of religion. In 1834 a series of anti-Catholic sermons by Lyman Beecher and others aroused feelings to the extent that a mob attacked and burned the Ursuline Convent in Charlestown, Massa-

Americans Shall Rule America. *This 1856 sketch satirizes Baltimore nativists out to bully German and Irish immigrants.*

chusetts. In 1844 armed clashes between Protestants and Catholics in Philadelphia ended with about 20 killed and 100 injured. Sporadically, the nativist spirit took organized form in groups that proved their patriotism by hating foreigners and Catholics.

As early as 1837 a Native American Association was formed at Washington, but the most significant such group was the Order of the Star Spangled Banner, founded in New York in 1849. Within a few years this group had grown into a formidable third party. In July 1854 delegates from thirteen states gathered to form the American party, which had the trappings of a secret fraternal order. Members pledged never to vote for any foreign-born or Catholic candidate. When asked about the organization, they were to say "I know nothing." In popular parlance the American party became the Know-Nothing party. For a season it seemed that the American party might achieve major-party status. In state and local campaigns during 1854 the Know-Nothings carried one election after another. In November they swept the Massachusetts legislature, winning all but two seats in the lower house. That fall they elected more than forty congressmen. For a while they threatened to control New England, New York, and Maryland, and showed strength elsewhere, but the movement collapsed when slavery became the focal issue of the 1850s.

The Know-Nothings demanded the exclusion of immigrants and Catholics from public office and extension of the period for naturalization from five to twenty-one years, but the party never gathered the political strength to effect such legislation. Nor did Congress act during the period to restrict immigration in any way. The first federal law on immigration, passed in 1819, enacted only safety and health regulations regarding supplies and the number of passengers on immigrant ships. This and subsequent acts designed to protect immigrants from overcrowding and unsanitary conditions were, however, poorly enforced.

IMMIGRANT LABOR   After 1840 immigration became critical to the dynamics of growth. The increase in population it brought contributed to economic growth and demand, whether the newcomer took up land or went into the city. By meeting the demand for cheap, unskilled labor immigrants made a twofold contribution: they moved into jobs vacated or bypassed by those who went into the factories, and they themselves made up a pool of labor from which in time factory workers were drawn.

In New England the large numbers of Irish workers, accustomed to hard treatment, spelled the end of the "Lowell girls." By 1860 immigrants made up more than half the labor force in New England mills. Even so, their price was generally higher than that of the women and children who worked to supplement family incomes, and the flood of immigration never rose fast enough to stop the long-term rise in wages. So factory labor continued to draw people from the countryside. Work in the cities offered higher real wages than work on the farm, which kept manufacturers alert for ways to cut their labor costs by improving machines. The cost of labor also put a premium on mass production of low-priced goods for a mass market. Artisans who emphasized quality and craftsmanship for a custom trade found it hard to meet such competitive conditions. Many artisans in fact found that their skills were going out of style. Some took work as craftsmen in factories, while others went into small-scale manufacturing or shopkeeping, and some bought homesteads to practice their skills in the West.

ORGANIZED LABOR

EARLY UNIONS Few workers of the period belonged to unions, but in the 1820s and 1830s a growing fear that they were losing status led artisans of the major cities into intense activity in labor politics and unions. As early as the colonial period craftsmen had formed fraternal and mutual-benefit societies, much like the medieval guilds, through which they regulated a system for training apprentices. These organizations continued to flourish well into the national period. After the Revolution, however, organizations of journeymen carpenters, masons, shipfitters, tailors, printers, and cordwainers (as shoemakers were called) became concerned with wages, hours, and working conditions and began to back up their demands with such devices as the strike and the closed shop. These organizations were local, often largely social in purpose, and frequently lasted only for the duration of the dispute. The longest-lived was Philadelphia's Federated Society of Journeymen Cordwainers, which flourished from 1794 to 1806.

Early labor unions faced serious legal obstacles. Unions were prosecuted as unlawful conspiracies. In 1806, for instance, Philadelphia shoemakers were found "guilty of a combination to raise their wages." The decision broke the union. Such precedents were used for many years to hamstring labor organizations until the Massachusetts Supreme Court made a landmark ruling in the case of *Commonwealth v. Hunt* (1842). In this case the

The Shoemaker, *from* The Book of Trades, *1807. When boot- and shoemakers in Philadelphia went on strike in 1806, a court found them guilty of a "conspiracy to raise their wages."*

court ruled that forming a trade union was not in itself illegal nor was a demand that employers hire only members of the union.

Until the 1820s labor organizations took the form of local trade unions, confined to one city and one craft. During the ten years from 1827 to 1837 organization on a larger scale began to take hold. Philadelphia, in 1827, had the first city central, formed after the carpenters had lost a strike for the ten-hour day. The Mechanics' Union of Trade Associations included carpenters, shoemakers, bricklayers, glaziers, and other groups. In the mid-1830s still wider organizations were attempted. In 1834 the National Trades' Union was set up in the effort to federate the city societies. At the same time national craft unions were established by the shoemakers, printers, combmakers, carpenters, and hand-loom weavers, but all the national groups and most of the local ones vanished in the economic collapse of 1837.

LABOR POLITICS   With the removal of property qualifications for voting nearly everywhere, labor politics flourished briefly. In this, as in other respects, Philadelphia was in the forefront. A Working Men's party, formed there in 1828, gained the balance of power in the city council that fall. This success inspired other Working Men's parties in New York, Boston, and about fifteen states. In 1829 the New York party elected the head of the carpenters' union to the state legislature. The Working Men's parties were broad reformist groups devoted to the interests of labor. But they admitted to their ranks many who were not workers by any strict definition, and their leaders were mainly reformers and small businessmen. The labor parties faded quickly for a variety of reasons: the inexperience of labor politicians, which left the parties prey to manipulation by political professionals; the fact that some of their causes were espoused also by the major parties; and their vulnerability to attack on grounds of extreme radicalism or dilettantism. Additionally, they often splintered into warring factions, limiting their effectiveness.

Once the parties had faded, however, many of their supporters found their way into a radical wing of the Jacksonian Democrats. This wing became the Equal Rights party and in 1835 acquired the name "Locofocos" when their opponents from New York City's regular Democratic organization, Tammany Hall, turned off the gas lights at their meeting and the Equal Rights supporters produced candles, lighting them with the new friction matches known as Locofocos. The Locofocos soon faded as a separate group, but endured as a radical faction within the Democratic party.

While the labor parties elected few candidates, they did succeed in drawing notice to their demands, many of which attracted the support of middle-class reformers. Above all they carried on an agitation for free public education and the abolition of imprisonment for debt, causes that won widespread popular support. The labor parties and unions actively promoted the ten-hour day. In 1836 President Jackson established the ten-hour day at the Philadelphia Navy Yard in response to a strike, and in 1840 President Van Buren extended the limit to all government offices and projects. In private jobs the ten-hour day became increasingly common, although by no means universal, before 1860. Other reforms put forward by the workingman's parties included mechanics' lien laws, to protect workers against nonpayment of wages; reform of a militia system which allowed the rich to escape service with fines but forced the poor to face jail terms; the abolition of "licensed monopolies," especially banks; measures to ensure hard money and to protect workers against inflated banknote currency; measures to restrict competition from prison labor; and the abolition of child labor.

LABOR AND REFORM   After the Panic of 1837 the nascent labor movement went into decline, and during the 1840s the focus of its radical spirit turned toward the promotion of cooperative societies. During the 1830s there had been sporadic efforts to provide self-employment through producers' cooperatives, but the movement began to catch on after the iron molders of Cincinnati set up a successful shop in 1848. Soon the tailors of Boston had a cooperative workshop which employed thirty to forty men. New York was an especially strong center, with cooperatives among tailors, shirtmakers, bakers, shoemakers, and carpenters. Consumer cooperatives became much more vigorous and involved more people. The New England Protective Union, formed in 1845, organized a central purchasing agency for co-op stores and by 1852 was buying more than $1 million worth of goods while affiliated stores were doing in excess of $4 million in trade.

Both the producers' and consumers' movement benefited from the support of Associationists, who saw it as a possible first step on the road to utopia, but more people probably were drawn to the movement for practical reasons: to reduce their dependence on employers or to reduce the cost of purchases. After peaking in the early 1850s, however, cooperatives went into decline. The high mobility of Americans and the heterogenous character of the population as immigration increased created unfavorable conditions. Insufficient capital and weak, inexperienced management also plagued the cooperative movement.

THE REVIVAL OF UNIONS   The high visibility of reform efforts, however, should not obscure the continuing activity of unions, which began to revive with improved business conditions in the early 1840s. Still, the unions remained local, weak, and given to sporadic activity. Often they came and went with a single strike. The greatest single labor dispute before the Civil War came on February 22, 1860, when shoemakers at Lynn and Natick, Massachusetts, walked out for higher wages. Before the strike ended it had spread through New England, involving perhaps twenty-five towns and 20,000 workers. It stood out also as a strike the workers won. Most of the employers agreed to wage increases and some also agreed to recognize the union as a bargaining agent.

This reflected the growing tendency of workers to view their unions as permanent. Workers emphasized union recognition and regular collective bargaining agreements. They shared a growing sense of solidarity. In 1852 the National Typographical Union revived the effort to organize skilled crafts on a national scale. Others followed: the Hat Finishers National Association in 1854, the Journeymen Stone Cutters Association in 1855, the National Union of Iron Molders in 1859. By 1860 about twenty such organizations had appeared, although none was strong enough as yet to do much more than hold national conventions and pass resolutions.

JACKSONIAN INEQUALITY

During the years before the Civil War the United States had begun to develop a distinctive working class, most conspicuously in the factories and the ranks of common labor, often including many Irish or German immigrants. More and more craftsmen, aware that they were likely to remain wage earners, became receptive to permanent unions. But the American legend of "rags to riches," the image of the self-made man, was a durable myth. "In America," Tocqueville wrote, "most of the rich men were formerly poor." Speaking to the Senate on the tariff in 1832, Henry Clay said that almost all the successful factory owners he knew were "enterprising self-made men, who have whatever wealth they possess by patient and diligent labor." The legend had just enough basis in fact to lend credence. John Jacob Astor, the wealthiest man in America, worth more than $20 million at his death in 1848, came of humble if not exactly destitute origins. Son of a minor official in Germany, he arrived in 1784 with little or nothing, made a fortune first on the western fur trade, then parlayed that into a large fortune in New York real estate. But his and similar cases were more exceptional than common.

Researches by social historians on the rich in major eastern cities show that while men of moderate means could sometimes run their inheritances into fortunes by good management and prudent speculation, those who started with the handicap of poverty and ignorance seldom made it to the top. In 1828 the top 1 percent of New York's families (owning $34,000 or more) held 40 percent of the wealth, and the top 4 percent held 76 percent. Similar circumstances prevailed in Philadelphia, Boston, and other cities.

A supreme irony of the times was that the "age of the common man," "the age of Jacksonian Democracy," seems actually to have been an age of increasing social rigidity. Years before, the colonists had brought to America conceptions of a social hierarchy which during the eighteenth century corresponded imperfectly with the developing reality. In the late eighteenth century, slavery aside, American society probably approached equality more closely than any population its size anywhere else in the world. During the last half of the 1700s, one historian has argued, social mobility was higher than either before or since. By the time popular egalitarianism caught up with reality, reality was moving back toward greater inequality.

Why this happened is difficult to say, except that the boundless wealth of the untapped frontier narrowed as the land was occupied and claims on various opportunities were staked out. Such developments took place in New England towns even before the end of the seventeenth century. But despite growing social distinctions, it seems likely that the white population of America, at least, was better off than the general run of European peoples. New frontiers, geographical and technological, raised the level of material well-being for all.

FURTHER READING

On economic development in the nation's early decades, see W. Elliot Brownlee's *Dynamics of Ascent: A History of the American Economy* (2nd ed., 1979). Older, yet still valuable, are Douglass C. North's *The Economic Growth of the United States, 1790–1860* (1961)° and Thomas C. Cochran and William Miller's *The Age of Enterprise: A Social History of Industrial America* (rev. ed., 1961).°

°These books are available in paperback editions.

The resilient classic on transportation and economic growth is George R. Taylor's *The Transportation Revolution, 1815–1861* (1951).

Concurrent with transportation innovations was industrial growth. Thomas C. Cochran's *Frontiers of Change: Early Industrialism in America* (1981) is a recent survey. The business side of industrial growth can be studied in Elisha P. Douglass's *The Coming of Age of American Business* (1971). The impact of technology is traced in David J. Jeremy's *Transatlantic Industrial Revolution: The Diffusion of Textile Technologies between Britain and America* (1981) and Merritt R. Smith's *Harper's Ferry Armory and the New Technology: The Challenge of Change* (1977).

Richard D. Brown's *Modernization: The Transformation of American Life, 1600–1865* (1976) assesses the impact of technology on living patterns. How American values were affected by the new industrial system is assessed in John F. Kasson's *Civilizing the Machine: Technology and Republican Values in America, 1776–1900* (1976)° and Leo Marx's *The Machine in the Garden: Technology and the Pastoral Ideal in America* (1964).° Paul Johnson's *A Shopkeepers Millennium: Society and Revivals in Rochester, New York, 1815–1837* (1978) studies the role religion played in the emerging industrial order.

The attitude of the worker during this time of transition is surveyed in Joseph G. Rayback's *A History of American Labor* (rev. ed., 1966). Edward E. Pessen's *Most Uncommon Jacksonians: The Radical Leaders of the Early Labor Movement* (1967) concentrates on political reactions. Detailed case studies of working communities include Anthony F. C. Wallace's *Rockdale: The Growth of an American Village in the Early Industrial Revolution* (1978);° Thomas Dublin's *Women at Work: The Transformation of Work and Community in Lowell, Massachusetts, 1826–1860* (1979);° Stephan Thernstrom's *Poverty and Progress* (1964),° on Newburyport, Massachusetts; and Sean Wilentz's *Chants Democratic* (1984), on New York City. Walter Licht's *Working for the Railroad* (1983) is rich in detail.

For introductions to urbanization, see Sam Bass Warner, Jr.'s *The Urban Wilderness* (1972) and Richard C. Wade's *The Urban Frontier* (1959). A recent valuable case study is Edward K. Spann's *The New Metropolis: New York City, 1840–1857* (1981). Studies of the origins of immigration include Oscar Handlin's classic *The Uprooted* (2nd ed., 1973)° and Marcus Lee Hansen's *The Atlantic Migration, 1607–1860* (1940).

13

AN AMERICAN RENAISSANCE: ROMANTICISM AND REFORM

RATIONAL RELIGION

The American novelist Nathaniel Hawthorne once lamented "the difficulty of writing a romance about a country where there is no shadow, no antiquity, no mystery, no picturesque and gloomy wrong. . . . Romance and poetry, ivy, lichens, and wall-flowers, need ruin to make them grow." Unlike nations of the Old World, rooted in shadow and mystery, in historic cultures and traditions, the United States had been rooted in the ideas of the Enlightenment. Those ideas, most vividly set forth in Jefferson's Declaration, had in turn a universal application. In the eyes of many if not most citizens, the "first new nation" had a mission to stand as an example to the world, much as John Winthrop's "city upon a hill" had once stood as an example to erring humanity. The concept of mission in fact still carried spiritual overtones, for the religious fervor quickened in the Great Awakening had reinforced the idea of national purpose. In turn the sense of high calling infused the national character with an element of perfectionism—and an element of impatience when reality fell short of expectations. The combination brought major reforms and advances in human rights. It also brought disappointments that could fester into cynicism and alienation.

DEISM   The currents of the Enlightenment and the Great Awakening, now mingling, now parting, flowed on into the nineteenth century. By the turn of the century both had worked changes in the Calvinist orthodoxy of American religion. Many leaders of the Revolutionary War era, like Jefferson and Franklin, became deists, even while nominally attached to existent churches. Deism, which arose in eighteenth-century Europe, simply carried the logic of Sir Isaac Newton's world machine to its logical conclusion. The God of the deist, the Master Clockmaker in Voltaire's words, had planned the universe, built it, and then set it in motion. But men, on their own, by the use of reason might grasp the natural laws which govern the universe. Deism tended to be a benevolent force. Thomas Paine in *The Age of Reason* (1794) defined religious duties as "doing justice, loving mercy and endeavoring to make our fellow creatures happy," a message of Quaker-like simplicity. But ever the controversialist, Tom Paine felt obliged to assail the "superstition" of the Scriptures and the existing churches—"human inventions set up to terrify and enslave mankind and monopolize power and profit." Orthodox churchmen could hardly distinguish such doctrine from atheism.

The old Puritan churches around Boston proved most vulnerable to the logic of the Enlightenment. A strain of rationalism had run through Puritan belief all along in its stress on the need for right reason to interpret the Scriptures. Boston's progress from Puritanism to prosperity had persuaded many rising families that they were anything but sinners in the hands of an angry God. Drawn toward less strenuous doctrines, some went back to the traditional rites of the Episcopal church. More of them simply dropped or qualified their adherence to Calvinism while remaining in the Congregational churches.

UNITARIANISM By the end of the eighteenth century many New Englanders were drifting into Unitarianism, a belief which emphasized the oneness of God and put reason and conscience ahead of creeds and confessions. One stale jest had it that Unitarians believed in the fatherhood of God, the brotherhood of man, and the neighborhood of Boston. Boston was very much the center of the movement and it flourished chiefly within Congregational churches which kept their standing in the established order until controversy began to smoke them out.

It began in 1805 with the election of a liberal clergyman, Henry Ware, as Hollis Professor of Divinity at Harvard, followed by the choice of four more like-minded professors in as many years. In protest against Unitarian Harvard, the Rev. Jedediah Morse, the noted geographer, led a movement to establish Andover Theological Seminary as a center of orthodoxy. Thereafter more and more liberal churches accepted the name of Unitarian.

William Ellery Channing of Boston's Federal Street Church

emerged as the chief spokesman for the liberal position. "I am surer that my rational nature is from God," he said, "than that any book is an expression of his will." A "Conference of Liberal Ministers," formed in 1820, became in 1826 the American Unitarian Association with 125 churches (all but 5 of them in Massachusetts) including 20 of the 25 oldest Calvinist churches in the United States. That same year, when the Presbyterian minister Lyman Beecher moved to Boston, he lamented: "All the literary men of Massachusetts were Unitarian; all the trustees and professors of Harvard College were Unitarian, all the elite of wealth and fashion crowded Unitarian churches."

UNIVERSALISM   A parallel movement, Universalism, attracted a different social stratum: workers and the more humble. In 1779 John Murray, who had come from England as a missionary for the new doctrine, founded the first Universalist church at Gloucester, Massachusetts. In 1794 a Universalist convention in Philadelphia organized the sect. Universalism held to a belief in the salvation of all men and women, while holding intact most Calvinist doctrines. God, they taught, was too merciful to condemn anyone to eternal punishment. True believers could escape altogether through Christ's atonement; the unregenerate would suffer in proportion to their sins, but eventually all souls would come into harmony with God. "Thus, the Unitarians and Universalists were in fundamental agreement," wrote one historian of religion, "the Universalists holding that God was too good to damn man; the Unitarians insisting that man was too good to be damned."

THE SECOND AWAKENING

For all the impact of rationalism, however, Americans remained a profoundly religious people. There was, Alexis de Tocqueville asserted, "no country in the world where the Christian religion retains a greater influence over the souls of men than in America." Around 1800 a revival of faith began to manifest itself. Soon it grew into a Second Awakening. An early exemplar of the movement, Timothy Dwight, became president of Yale College in 1795 and set about to purify a place which, in Lyman Beecher's words, had turned into "a hotbed of infidelity," where students openly discussed French radicalism, deism, and perhaps things even worse. Like his grandfather, Jonathan Edwards, "Pope Timothy" had the gift of moving both mind and spirit, of reaching both the lettered and the unlettered. The result was a series of revivals that swept the student body and spread to all New England as well. "Wheresoever students were found," wrote a participant in the 1802 revival, "the reigning impression was, 'surely God is in this place.' "

After the founding in 1808, Jedediah Morse's Andover Seminary reinforced orthodoxy and the revival spirit so forcefully that its location came to be known as "Brimstone Hill." "Let us guard against the insidious encroachments of *innovation*—that evil and beguiling spirit which is now stalking to and fro in the earth, seeking whom it may devour." To avoid the fate of Harvard, Morse and his associates made professors give their assent to an Andover Creed of double-distilled Calvinism. The religious intensity and periodic revivals at Andover and Yale had their counterparts in many colleges for the next fifty years, since most were under the control of evangelical denominations. Hampden-Sydney College in Virginia had in fact got the jump on New England with a revival in 1787 which influenced many leaders of the awakening in the South.

REVIVALS ON THE FRONTIER   In its frontier phase the Second Awakening, like the first, generated great excitement and strange manifestations. It gave birth, moreover, to a new institution, the camp meeting, in which the fires of faith were repeatedly rekindled. Missionaries found ready audiences among lonely frontiersmen hungry for a sense of community. Among the established sects, the Presbyterians were entrenched among the Scotch-Irish from Pennsylvania to Georgia. They gained further

While Methodist preachers address the crowd at this revivalist camp meeting, a man in the foreground is overcome with religious ecstasy.

from the Plan of Union worked out in 1801 with the Congregationalists of Connecticut and later other states. Since the two groups agreed on doctrine and differed mainly on the form of church government, they were able to form unified congregations and call a minister from either church. The result through much of the Old Northwest was that New Englanders became Presbyterians by way of the "Presbygational" churches.

The Baptists had a simplicity of doctrine and organization which appealed to the common people of the frontier. Since each congregation was its own highest authority, a frontier congregation need appeal to no hierarchy before setting up shop and calling a minister or naming one of their own. Sometimes whole congregations moved across the mountains as a body. As Theodore Roosevelt later described it: "Baptist preachers lived and worked exactly as their flocks. . . . they cleared the ground, split rails, planted corn, and raised hogs on equal terms with their parishioners."

But the Methodists may have had the most effective method of all, the circuit rider who sought out people in the most remote areas with the message of salvation as a gift free for the taking. The system began with Francis Asbury, the founder. "When he came to America," a biographer wrote, "he rented no house, he hired no lodgings, he made no arrangements to board anywhere, but simply set out on the Long Road, and was traveling forty-five years later when death caught up with him." By the 1840s the Methodists had grown into the largest Protestant church in the country, with over a million members.

The frontier phase of the Second Awakening got its start in Logan County, Kentucky, an area notorious as a refuge of thieves and cutthroats. James McGready, a Presbyterian minister of Pennsylvania Scotch-Irish background, arrived there in 1796 after threats drove him out of the North Carolina Piedmont, where he was accused of running people distracted with his revivals. He had been influenced in his course by the Hampden-Sydney revival. Over the next few years he prepared a way for the Lord in the West. In 1800 a Methodist preacher conducted a meeting in the neighborhood, and so much excitement attended his preaching that other meetings were held near each of McGready's three churches. Through the summer people came from far and wide, prepared to stay on the grounds for several days. During August 1801 the preachings drew great crowds variously estimated at from 10,000 to 25,000.

The Great Revival spread quickly through the West and into more settled regions back east. Camp meetings came to be held typically in late summer or fall, when crops could be laid-by temporarily. People came from far and wide, camping in wagons, tents, brush arbors, or crude shacks. Mass excitement swept up even the most stable onlookers and the spirit moved participants to strange manifestations. Some went into cataleptic trances; others contracted the "jerks," laughed the "holy laugh," babbled in unknown tongues, danced like David before the Ark of God, or got down on all fours and barked like dogs to "tree the Devil." More sedate and prudent believers thought such rousements might be the work of the devil, out to discredit the true faith. But to dwell on the bizarre aspects of the camp meetings would be to distort an institution that offered a social outlet to an isolated people, that brought a more settled community life through the churches that grew out of it, that spread a more democratic faith among the common people. Indeed with time camp meetings became much more sedate and dignified affairs.

THE "BURNED-OVER DISTRICT" But little wonder that regions swept by such fevers might be compared to forests devastated by fire. Western New York state all the way from Lake Ontario to the Adirondacks achieved the name of the "Burned-Over District" long before 1821, when a "mighty baptism of the Holy Ghost" overwhelmed a young lawyer in the town of Adams. The spirit went through him "in waves and waves of liquid love," Charles Grandison Finney wrote years later. The next day he announced a new profession: "I have a retainer from the Lord Jesus Christ to plead his case," he told a caller. In 1823 the St. Lawrence Presbytery ordained Finney and for the next decade he subjected the Burned-Over District to yet another scorching.

Finney went on to become the greatest single exemplar of revivalism and, some would argue, the very inventor of professional revivalism. The saving of souls did not have to wait for a miracle, he argued; it could come from careful planning. Nor did Finney shrink from comparing his methods to those of politicians who used advertising and showmanship to get attention. The revivalist planned carefully to arouse excitement, not for its own sake but to rivet attention on the Word. "New measures are necessary from time to time to awaken attention and bring the gospel to bear on the public mind." To those who challenged such use of emotion Finney had a frank answer: "The results justify my methods." Finney carried the methods of the frontier revival into the cities of the East and as far as Great Britain.

Untrained in theology, Finney read the Bible, he said, as he would a law book, and worked out his own theology of free will.

Ohio's Oberlin College was the first in America to admit women or blacks. This graduating class is from the later nineteenth century.

His gospel combined faith and good works: one led to the other. "All sin consists in selfishness," he said, "and all holiness or virtue, in disinterested benevolence." Regeneration therefore was "a change from selfishness to benevolence, from having a supreme regard to one's own interest to an absorbing and controlling choice of the happiness and glory of God's Kingdom."

In 1835 Finney took the chair of theology in the new Oberlin College, founded by pious New Englanders in Ohio's Western Reserve. Later he served as its president. From the start Oberlin radiated a spirit of reform predicated on faith; it was the first college in America to admit either women or Negroes, and it was a hotbed of antislavery doctrine. Finney himself, however, held that men must be reformed from within, and cautioned against political action. In this, he held to a view which deeply influenced American social thought and action, a view which one historian has called romantic perfectionism: "Since social evils were simply individual acts of selfishness compounded, . . . it followed that . . . deep and lasting reform . . . meant an educational crusade based on the assumption that when a sufficient number of individual Americans had seen the light, they would automatically solve the country's social problems."

On the other hand the ardor aroused by revivals led to narrow sectarian bickerings, repeated schisms, and the phenomenon known as "come-outism" which further multiplied the sects—a phenomenon almost always noted by foreign travelers. James McGready's first revivals in Kentucky, for instance, created a tremendous demand for preachers which the Cumberland Presbytery met by ordaining men who lacked proper educational credentials. Independent congregations sprang up that recognized no other authority than the Bible. A similar movement arose independently in western Pennsylvania in 1809 led by Thomas and Alexander Campbell. The Campbellites adopted the name "Christian" and the practice of baptism by immersion. In 1832 a movement started in Lexington, Kentucky, to unite these churches as the Disciples of Christ—a name that came to be used interchangeably with Christian church.

THE MORMONS The Kentucky sects remained pretty much within the bounds of previous experience. The Burned-Over District, by contrast, gave rise to several new departures, of which the most important was the Church of Jesus Christ of Latter Day Saints, or the Mormons. The founder, Joseph Smith, Jr., born in Vermont, was the fourth child of wandering parents who finally settled in the village of Palmyra, New York. In 1820 young Smith (then fourteen) had a vision of "two Personages, whose brightness and glory defy all description." They identified themselves as the Savior and God the Father and cautioned him that all existing beliefs were false. About three years later the angel Moroni led Smith to the hill of Gumorah (its ancient name), where he found the Book of Mormon engraved on golden tablets in "reformed Egyptian." Later, with the aid of the magic stones Urim and Thummim, he rendered into English what he found to be a

The Mormon temple sits atop the highest hill in Nauvoo, Illinois, which the Mormons built into a city of 20,000 inhabitants in the early 1840s.

lost section of the Bible. This was the story of ancient Hebrews who had inhabited the New World and to whom Jesus had made an appearance.

After a slow start the church, founded April 6, 1830, gathered converts by the thousands. From the outset the Mormon saints upset the "gentiles" with their close pattern of community and their assurance of righteousness. In their search for a refuge from persecution the Mormons moved from New York to Kirtland, Ohio, then to several places in Missouri, and finally in 1839 to Nauvoo, Illinois, where they settled and grew in number for some five years. Through bloc voting they soon gathered political power in the Illinois state house, but finally offended both major parties with their demands. In 1844 a crisis arose when dissidents accused Smith of justifying polygamy and published in the *Nauvoo Expositor* an exposé of polygamy in theory and practice. When Smith tried to suppress the paper, the upshot was a schism in the church, a gathering movement in the neighboring counties to attack Nauvoo, and the arrest of Smith and his brother Hyrum. On June 27, 1844, an anti-Mormon lynch mob stormed the feebly defended jail and took out and shot both Joseph and Hyrum Smith.

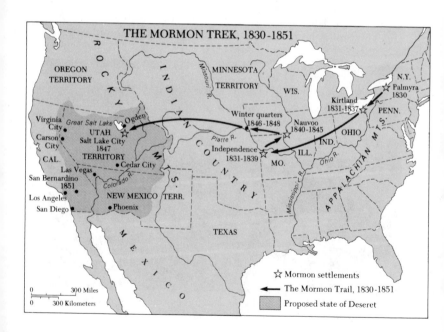

THE MORMON TREK, 1830–1851

☆ Mormon settlements
◄— The Mormon Trail, 1830–1851
▨ Proposed state of Deseret

In Brigham Young, successor to Joseph Smith and president of the Quorum of the Twelve, the Mormons found a leader of uncommon qualities: strong-minded, intelligent, and decisive. After the murder of the founder, Young patched up an unsure peace with the neighbors by promising to plan an early exodus from Nauvoo, Illinois. Before that year was out Young had chosen the place, sight unseen, from promotional literature on the West. It lay near the Great Salt Lake, guarded by mountains to the east and north, deserts to the west and south, yet itself fed by mountain streams of melted snow—"Truly a bucolic region," in John Charles Frémont's words. Despite its isolation, moreover, it was close enough to the Oregon Trail for the saints to prosper by trade with passing gentiles.

Brigham Young trusted God, but made careful preparations— no wandering in the wilderness for the Mormon Moses. As a result, the Mormon trek was better organized and less burdensome than most of the overland migrations of the time. Early in 1846 a small band crossed the frozen Mississippi into Iowa to set up the Camp of Israel, the first in a string of way stations along the route. By the fall of 1846 all 15,000 of the migrants had reached the prepared winter quarters on the Missouri River, where they paused until the first bands set out the next spring for the Promised Land. The first arrivals at Salt Lake in July 1847 found only "a broad and barren plain hemmed in by mountains . . . the paradise of the lizard, the cricket and the rattlesnake." But by the end of 1848 the Mormons had developed an efficient irrigation system and over the next decade, by cooperative labor, they brought about the greening of the desert. The Mormons had scarcely arrived when their land became part of the United States. They organized at first their own state of Deseret (meaning "land of the honey bee," according to Young) with ambitious boundaries that reached the Pacific in southern California. But the Utah Territory, which Congress created, afforded them almost the same control with Gov. Brigham Young the chief political and theocratic authority.

MILLENNIALISM   In the 1840s the Burned-Over District was once more swept by religious fervor, this time centered on millennialism and spiritualism. One William Miller, a Baptist farmer-preacher in upstate New York near the Vermont line, had become persuaded that the signs of the times pointed to an early Second Advent of Christ. The year 1843, which Miller called the last sure "year of time," brought widespread excitement and religious delusions. Miller had set no exact date, but when 1843

A satirical depiction of William Miller and his followers ascending to heaven at the millennium.

passed, some of his followers set October 22, 1844, as the date of the second coming. Even after that final disappointment Miller and others held to the belief that the millennium was near, however wrong their mathematics. In 1845 a loose organization was formed, which grew into the Advent Christian Association, from which in 1846 the Seventh Day Adventists broke away on the question of observing the Jewish Sabbath instead of the new Lord's Day.

Hard on the heels of the Millerite frenzy came the craze of "spirit-rapping" which began with Kate and Margaret Fox, daughters of a farmer near Rochester. In 1848 strange knocking sounds in the house began to keep their family awake. The girls soon identified the sounds as messages from the spirit world. As the word spread, the curious gathered for their revelations, and the Fox sisters were launched on a professional career of demonstrations as far away as England. Before long spirit mediums by the hundreds were staging seances, communicating with the dead, and spreading the vogue through spiritualist magazines.

This revival of faith was very much attuned to the rising democratic belief in the power and wisdom of the common man, with its preference for heart over head. No one expressed the hopefulness of this belief better than Andrew Johnson, political scourge of the Tennessee aristocrats:

> I believe that man can be elevated; man can become more and more endowed with divinity; and as he does he becomes more God-like in his character and capable of governing himself. Let us go on elevating our people, perfecting our institutions, until democracy shall reach such a point of perfection that we can acclaim with truth that the voice of the people is the voice of God.

ROMANTICISM IN AMERICA

Another great victory of heart over head was the romantic movement in thought, literature, and the arts. By the 1780s a revolt was brewing in Europe against the well-ordered world of the Enlightened thinkers. Were there not, after all, more things in this world than reason and logic can box up and explain: moods, impressions, feelings; mysterious, unknown, and half-seen things? A clear and lucid idea, organized and understandable, might well be superficial. Americans took readily to the romantics' emphasis on individualism, idealizing now the virtues of the common man, now the idea of original or creative genius in the artist, the author, or the great personality.

Where the Enlightened had scorned the Middle Ages, the romantic now looked back to the period with fascination. America, lacking a feudal history, nonetheless had an audience for the novels of Sir Walter Scott and copied the Gothic and even more exotic styles in architecture. More congenial to the American scene were the new themes in art. In contrast to well-ordered classical scenes, romantic artists such as Thomas Cole (1801–1848) and Thomas Doughty (1793–1856) preferred wild and misty landscapes which often evoked more than they showed.

The German philosopher Immanuel Kant gave the movement a summary definition in the title of his *Critique of Pure Reason* (1781), an influential book which emphasized the limits of human science and reason in explaining the universe. People have conceptions of conscience and beauty, the romantics believed, and religious impulses too strong to be dismissed as illusions. Where science can neither prove nor disprove, people are justified in having faith. The impact of such ideas was stated succinctly by a historian of American cultural life: "By degrees intu-

Kindred Spirits, *by Asher B. Durand, 1849. The artist depicts two friends and kindred spirits, the painter Thomas Cole and the poet William Cullen Bryant, standing amid a wild landscape in New York's Catskill Mountains.*

itive knowledge, during the period 1770–1830, took on validity equal to, or superior to, rational knowledge."

TRANSCENDENTALISM The most intense expression of such thought came in the Transcendentalist Movement of New England, which drew its name from its emphasis on those things which transcended (or rose above) the limits of reason. Transcendentalism, said one of its chroniclers, assumed "certain fundamental truths not derived from experience, not susceptible of proof, which transcend human life, and are perceived directly and intuitively by the human mind." If transcendentalism drew much from Kant, it was also rooted in New England Puritanism, to which it owed a pervasive moralism, and had a close affinity with the Quaker doctrine of the inner light. The inner light, a gift from God's grace, was transformed into intuition, a faculty of man's mind.

An element of mysticism had always lurked in Puritanism, even if viewed as a heresy—Anne Hutchinson, for instance, had been banished for claiming direct revelation. The reassertion of mysticism had something in common, too, with the meditative religions of the Orient—with which New England now had a flourishing trade. Transcendentalists steeped themselves in the teachings of Buddha, the Mohammedan Sufis, the Upanishads, and the Bhagavadgita.

In 1836 an informal discussion group soon named the Transcendental Club began to meet from time to time at the homes of members in Boston and Concord. A floating group, it drew at different times clergymen such as Theodore Parker, George Ripley, and James Freeman Clarke; writers such as Henry Thoreau, Bronson Alcott, Nathaniel Hawthorne, and Orestes Brownson; and learned women like Elizabeth and Sophia Peabody and Margaret Fuller. Fuller edited the group's quarterly review, *The Dial* (1840–1844), for two years before the duty fell to Ralph Waldo Emerson, soon to become the acknowledged high priest of transcendentalism.

EMERSON More than any other person, Emerson spread the Transcendentalist gospel. Sprung from a line of New England ministers, he set out to be a Unitarian parson, then quit before he was thirty. After travel to Europe, where he met England's great literary lights, Emerson settled in Concord to take up the life of an essayist, poet, and popular speaker on the lecture circuit. On the road he found a new ministry preaching the good news of optimism, self-reliance, and man's unlimited potential.

Emerson's lectures and writings hold the core of the Transcendentalist worldview. His notable lecture delivered at Harvard in 1837, "The American Scholar," essentially summarized his first book, *Nature*, published the previous year. In that lecture he urged his hearers to put aside their awe of European culture and explore their own new world. It was "our intellectual Declaration of Independence," said one observer. Emerson's lecture on "The Over-soul" set forth a kind of pantheism, in which the souls of all men commune with the great universal soul, of which they are part and parcel. His essay on "Self-Reli-

Ralph Waldo Emerson, author of Nature, *America's "intellectual Declaration of Independence."*

ance" (1841) has a timeless appeal to youth with its message of individualism and the cultivation of one's personality. Like most of Emerson's writings, it is crammed with quotable quotes:

> Whoso would be a man, must be a nonconformist. . . . Nothing is at last sacred but the integrity of your own mind. . . . It is easy in the world to live after the world's opinion; it is easy in solitude to live after our own; but the great man is he who in the midst of a crowd keeps with perfect sweetness the independence of solitude. . . . A foolish consistency is the hobgoblin of little minds, adored by little statesmen and philosophers and divines. . . . Speak what you think in hard words and tomorrow speak what tomorrow thinks in hard words again, though it contradict everything you said today. . . . To be great is to be misunderstood.

THOREAU Emerson's friend and Concord neighbor, Henry David Thoreau, practiced the self-reliance that Emerson preached. "If a man does not keep pace with his companion," Thoreau wrote, "perhaps it is because he hears a different drummer." And Thoreau marched to a different drummer all his life. After Harvard, where he exhausted the resources of the library in gargantuan bouts of reading, and after a brief stint as a teacher in which he got in trouble by his preference for persuasion over discipline, Thoreau settled down to eke out a living through his family's cottage industry of pencil making. But he made frequent escapes to drink in the beauties of nature. Not for him the contemporary scramble for wealth. "The mass of men," he wrote, "lead lives of quiet desperation."

His first book, *A Week on the Concord and Merrimack Rivers*

(1849), used the story of a boat trip with his brother as the thread on which to string his comments on life and literature. The second, *Walden, or Life in the Woods* (1854), used an account of his experiment in self-sufficiency to much the same purpose. On July 4, 1845, Thoreau took to the woods to live in a cabin he had built beside Walden Pond. He was out to demonstrate that a person could free himself from the products of commercialism and industrialism. His purpose was not to lead a hermit's life, but to test the possibilities. He would return to town to dine with his friends, and although he used manufactured lime to caulk his walls, he gathered clamshells and made enough himself to show it could be done. "I went to the woods because I wished to live deliberately," he wrote, ". . . and not, when I came to die, discover that I had not lived."

While Thoreau was at Walden the Mexican War broke out. Believing it an unjust war to advance the cause of slavery, he refused payment of his state poll tax as a gesture of opposition, for which he was put in jail (only for one night; an aunt paid the tax). The incident was so trivial as to be almost comic, but out of it grew the classic essay "Civil Disobedience" (1849) which was later to influence the passive-resistance movements of Mahatma Gandhi in India and Martin Luther King in the American South. "If the law is of such a nature that it requires you to be an agent of injustice to another," Thoreau wrote, "then, I say, break the law. . . ."

The broadening ripples of influence more than a century after Thoreau's death show the impact a contemplative man can have

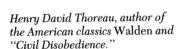

Henry David Thoreau, author of the American classics Walden *and* "Civil Disobedience."

on the world of action. Although both men lent their voices to worthy causes, Thoreau, like Emerson, shied away from involvement in public life. The Transcendentalists primarily supplied the force of an idea: men must follow their consciences. If these thinkers attracted only a small following among the public at large in their own time, they had much to do with pushing along reform movements and were the quickening force for a generation of writers that produced the first great classic age of American literature.

THE FLOWERING OF AMERICAN LITERATURE

HAWTHORNE   Nathaniel Hawthorne, the supreme artist of the New England group, never shared the sunny optimism of his neighbors nor their belief in reform. A sometime resident of Concord, but a native and longtime resident of Salem, he was haunted by the knowledge of evil bequeathed to him by his Puritan forebears—one of whom had been a judge at the Salem witchcraft trial. After college at Bowdoin, he worked for some time in obscurity in Salem, gradually began to place a few stories, and finally emerged to a degree of fame with his collection of *Twice-Told Tales* (1837). In these, as in most of his later work, his themes were the examination of sin and its consequences: pride and selfishness, secret guilt, selfish egotism, the impossibility of rooting sin out of the human soul. His greatest novels explored such burdens. In *The Scarlet Letter* (1850) Hester Prynne, an adulteress tagged with a badge of shame by the Puritan authorities, won redemption by her suffering, while the Rev. Arthur Dimmesdale was destroyed by his gnawing guilt and Roger Chillingworth by his obsession with vengeance.

The flowering of New England featured, too, a foursome of poets who shaped the American imagination in a day when poetry was still accessible to a wide public: Henry Wadsworth Longfellow, John Greenleaf Whitter, Oliver Wendell Holmes, Sr., and James Russell Lowell. But a fifth, Emily Dickinson, the most original of the lot, remained a recluse in the family home in Amherst. Only two of her poems had been published (anonymously) before her death in 1886 and the full corpus of her work remained unknown for years after that.

The half-decade of 1850–1855 saw the publication of *Representative Men* by Emerson, *Walden* by Thoreau, *The Scarlet Letter* and *The House of the Seven Gables* by Nathaniel Hawthorne, *Moby-Dick* by Herman Melville, and *Leaves of Grass* by Walt

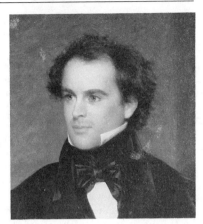

Nathaniel Hawthorne, author of
The Scarlet Letter.

Whitman. As the critic F. O. Mathiessen wrote in his book *American Renaissance:* "You might search all the rest of American literature without being able to collect a group of books equal to these in imaginative quality."

It had been little more than thirty years since a noted British critic asked in 1820: "In the four quarters of the Globe, who reads an American book?" Quoted out of context, the question rubbed Americans the wrong way, but the critic, an admirer of American institutions, foresaw a future flowering in the new country. He did not have long to wait, for within a year Washington Irving's *The Sketch Book* (1820), James Fenimore Cooper's *The Spy* (1821), and William Cullen Bryant's *Poems* (1821) were drawing wide notice in Britain as well as in America. Bryant's energies were drawn into journalism by his need to earn a living. As editor of the New York *Evening Post* he wielded an important influence in American life. Irving and Cooper went on to greater literary triumphs, and made New York for a time the national literary capital.

IRVING AND COOPER   Irving in fact stood as a central figure in the American literary world from the time of his satirical *Diedrich Knickerbocker's A History of New York* (1809) until his death fifty years later. He showed that an American could, after all, make a career of literature, and was a confidant and advocate of numerous other writers. During those years a flood of histories, biographies, essays, and stories poured from his pen. A talented writer, Irving was the first to show that authentic American themes could draw a wide audience. Yet, as Melville later noted, he was less a creative genius than an adept imitator. Even the most

"American" of his stories, "Rip Van Winkle" and "The Legend of Sleepy Hollow," drew heavily on German folk tales.

Cooper, a country gentleman, got his start as a writer on a bet with his wife that he could write a better novel than one they had just read. *Precaution* (1820) was an imitative story of manners in English high society, but the following year he brought out *The Spy* (1821), a historical romance based on a real incident of the American Revolution. In 1823 Cooper in *The Pioneers* introduced Natty Bumppo, an eighteenth-century frontiersman destined to be the hero of five novels known collectively as *The Leather-Stocking Tales*. Natty Bumppo, a deadshot also known as Hawkeye, and his Indian friend Chingachgook, the epitome of the noble savage, took a place among the most unforgettable heroes of world literature. The tales of man pitted against nature in the backwoods, of hairbreadth escapes and gallant rescues, were the first successful romances of frontier life and models for the later cowboy novels and movies set in the Far West. In addition to the backwoods tales, Cooper also was the virtual creator of the sea novel in *The Pilot* (1823), another romance of the Revolution.

POE AND THE SOUTH   By the 1830s and 1840s new major talents had come on the scene. Edgar Allan Poe, a native of Boston but reared in Virginia, was arguably America's most inventive genius in the first half of the century, and probably the most important American writer of the times in the critical esteem of Europeans. Poe's success had many dimensions. As a critic, he argued that the object of poetry was beauty (not truth) and that the writer should calculate his effect on the reader with precision. To that end he favored relatively short poems and stories, and wrote only one novel in his brief career. His poems, such as "The Raven," exemplified his theory, and although relatively few in number, won great fame. He was moreover a master of gothic horror in the short story and the inventor of the detective story and its major conventions. But the tormented, hard-drinking wanderer that Poe became hardly fit his countrymen's image of the proper man of letters.

Neither did a group of southern writers who came to be called the southwestern humorists. With stories of the backwoods from Georgia westward they exploited frontier tall tales and the raw, violent life of the region. Their number included Davy Crockett, a sort of real-life Natty Bumppo; George Washington Harris, whose hero, Sut Lovingood, lived up to his name; and Johnson Jones Hooper, author of *Some Adventures of Captain Simon*

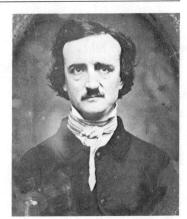

Edgar Allan Poe, perhaps the most inventive American writer of the period.

Suggs (1845), about a peerless con man whose motto became a national joke: "It is good to be shifty in a new country." Augustus Baldwin Longstreet, author of *Georgia Scenes* (1835), would hardly be remembered but for his stories about Ransy Sniffle and other examples of backwoods low life. Dismissed at the time as subliterary amusement, southwestern humor was later raised to the level of high art by Mark Twain.

Among southern authors, William Gilmore Simms best exemplified the genteel man of letters. Editor and writer in many genres, he had a prodigious output of poems, novels, histories, biographies, essays, short stories, and drama. He gained a wide audience with *Guy Rivers* (1834), first of a series of "Border Romances" set in frontier Georgia, but the peak of his achievement was in two novels published in 1835: *The Yemassee*, a story of Indian war in 1715, and *The Partisan*, first of seven novels about the Revolution in South Carolina. In his own time he was the preeminent southern author and something of a national figure, but he finally dissipated his energies in politics and the defense of slavery. He went down steadily in critical esteem, and most critics would agree with his own epitaph, that he had "left all his better works undone."

The duc de La Rochefoucauld-Liancourt, who visited the South in the 1790s, noted some cultural characteristics that continued to prevail in the nineteenth century: "In spite of the Virginian love for dissipation, the taste for reading is commoner there among men of the first class than in any other part of America; but the populace is perhaps more ignorant there than elsewhere." The readers of "the first class," however, tended to take their cues in literary and aesthetic matters from London or New York. They usually read English and northern authors to the neglect of their own, and took northern rather than southern magazines. And "men of the first class" who read widely tended to look upon literature as ornamental and a less praiseworthy activity than the high arts of oratory and statesmanship.

MELVILLE   Those southerners who followed the literary preferences of the North are likely to have passed over the work of Herman Melville, whose literary reputation went into a decline after his initial successes. In the twentieth century Melville's good reputation was dramatically revived, elevating him into the literary pantheon occupied by only the finest American authors. Born of distinguished ancestry on both sides, Melville suffered a sharp reversal of fortunes when his father died a bankrupt, and after various odd jobs, he shipped out as a seaman at age twenty. Some time later, after eighteen months aboard a whaler, he fetched up in the South Seas and jumped ship with a companion in the Marquesas Islands. After several weeks spent with a friendly tribe in the valley of the Typees, he signed onto an Australian whaler, jumped ship again in Tahiti, and finally returned home as a seaman aboard a frigate of the United States Navy. An embroidered account of his exotic adventures in *Typee* (1846) became an instant popular success, which he repeated in *Omoo* (1847), based on his stay in Tahiti.

So many readers took his accounts as fictional (as in part they were) that Melville was inspired to write novels of nautical ad-

Whaling off the Acushnet. *Melville's experiences on the ship informed his great novel,* Moby-Dick *(1851).*

ventures, and scored two successes after an initial failure. Then just five years after his first success, he produced one of the world's great novels in *Moby-Dick* (1851). In the story of Captain Ahab and his obsessive quest for the white whale that had caused the loss of his leg, Melville explored the darker recesses of the soul just as his good friend Hawthorne had done. The book was aimed at two audiences. On one level it was a ripping good yarn of adventure on the high seas. But Ahab's single-minded mission to slay the evildoer turned the captain himself into a monster of destruction who sacrificed his ship, his crew, and himself to his folly, leaving as the one survivor the narrator of the story. Unhappily, neither the public nor the critics at the time accepted the novel on either level. After that Melville's career wound down into futility. He supported himself for years with a job in the New York Custom House and turned to poetry, much of which, especially the Civil War *Battle-Pieces* (1866), gained acclaim in later years.

WHITMAN   Walt Whitman of Brooklyn had from the age of twelve worked mainly as a handyman and newspaperman, and remained relatively obscure until the first edition of *Leaves of Grass* (1855) caught the eye of contemporaries. Emerson found it "the most extraordinary piece of wit and wisdom that America has yet contributed," and greeted Whitman "at the beginning of a great career, which yet must have had a long foreground somewhere, for such a start"—an endorsement Whitman brazenly seized upon to promote the book. Yet it was appropriate that Emerson should endorse it for Whitman had taken to heart his argument that an American poet must exploit great American themes. The two greatest influences on him, Whitman said, were hearing Italian opera and reading Emerson: "I was simmering, simmering, simmering; Emerson brought me to a boil."

Whitman's life thereafter was in large measure given to "hackling" at his gargantuan *Leaves of Grass*, enlarging and reshaping it in successive editions. The growth of the book he identified with the growth of the country, which he proclaimed in all its variety. "I hear America singing," he wrote, "the varied carols I hear." He sounded his "barbaric yawp over the roofs of the world," and wrote unabashedly:

> Do I contradict myself?
> Very well then I contradict myself,
> (I am large, I contain multitudes.)

Walt Whitman, in an 1866 photograph.

While he celebrated America, he also set out to "celebrate myself and sing myself."

To his generation Whitman was a startling figure with his frank reminders of sexuality and "the body electric," which were not without homoerotic overtones. And he stood out from the pack of fellow writers in rejecting the idea that woman's proper sphere was a supportive and dependent role, just as he rejected the "empty dish, gallantry."

Later, during the Civil War, Whitman went to Washington to see about his injured brother. The injury was slight, but "the good gray poet" stayed on to visit the sick and wounded, to serve as attendant and nurse when needed. Out of his wartime service came *Drum Taps* (1865), containing his masterpiece of the 1860s, an elegy on the death of Lincoln: "When lilacs last in the dooryard bloom'd." In much of his prose Whitman vigorously defended democracy. In the postbellum *Democratic Vistas* (1871) he summoned Americans to higher goals than materialism.

THE POPULAR PRESS   The renaissance in literature came at a time of massive expansion in the popular press. The steam-driven Napier press, introduced from England in 1825, could print 4,000 sheets of newsprint in an hour. Richard Hoe of New York improved on it, inventing in 1847 the Hoe Rotary Press, which printed 20,000 sheets an hour. Like many advances in technology, this was a mixed blessing. The high cost of such a press made it harder for a man of small means to break into publishing. On the other hand it expedited production of cheap newspapers, magazines, and books—which were often cheap in more ways than one.

The New York *Sun*, in 1833 the first successful penny daily, and others like it, often ignored the merely important in favor of scandals and sensations, true or false. James Gordon Bennett, a native of Scotland, perfected this style on the New York *Herald*, which he founded in 1835. His innovations drew readers by the thousands: the first Wall Street column, the first society page (which satirized the well-to-do until it proved more gainful to show readers their names in print), pictorial news, telegraphic news, and great initiative in getting scoops. Eventually, however, the *Herald* suffered from dwelling so much on crime, sex, and depravity in general.

The chief beneficiary of a rising revulsion was the New York *Tribune*, founded as a Whig organ in 1841. Horace Greeley, who became the most important journalist of the era, announced that it would be a cheap but decent paper avoiding the "matters which have been allowed to disgrace the columns of our leading Penny Papers." And despite occasional lapses, Greeley's "Great Moral Organ" typically amused its readers with wholesome human-interest stories. Greeley also won a varied following by plugging the reforms of the day—those few he did not espouse he reported nonetheless. Socialism, land reform, feminism, abolitionism, temperance, the protective tariff, internal improvements, improved methods of agriculture, vegetarianism, spiritualism, trade unions—all got a share of attention. The *Trib-*

Reading Room, Astor House, 1840. *Offering "scraps of science, of thought, of poetry . . . in the coarsest sheet," inexpensive daily newspapers proliferated in the 1840s.*

une, moreover, set a new standard in reporting literary news. Margaret Fuller briefly served as critic; in 1856 the *Tribune* became the first daily to have a regular book-review column. For a generation it was probably the most influential paper in the country. By 1860 its weekly edition had a national circulation of 200,000. The number of newspapers around the country grew from about 1,200 in 1833 to about 3,000 in 1860.

Magazines found a growing market too. Periodicals of the eighteenth century typically had brief lives, but *The Port Folio* (1801–1827) of Philadelphia lasted an unusually long time. A monthly literary review edited at one time by Nicholas Biddle, it gave much attention to politics as well, from a Federalist viewpoint. *Niles' Weekly Register* (1811–1849) of Baltimore and Washington, founded by the printer Hezekiah Niles, was an early version of the twentieth-century news magazine. Niles got credit for accurate reports on the War of 1812 and made a reputation for good and unbiased coverage of public events—all of which make it a basic source for historians. The *North American Review* of Boston (1815–1940), started by a young graduate of Harvard, achieved high standing among scholarly readers. Its editor adorned the journal with materials on American history and biography. It also featured coverage of European literature.

More popular and more widely circulated than the others was *Graham's Magazine* of Philadelphia (1826–1858). Started as *The Casket: Flowers of Literature, Wit and Sentiment*, the magazine became a highly profitable enterprise after George R. Graham bought it in 1839, spicing it up with a "magazinish" style in contrast to the heavy review style of the day and decorating it with original artwork. As a result of the liberal payment he offered, Graham published the best authors of the day: Bryant, Longfellow, Cooper, Lowell, and Poe all appeared in its pages.

Harpers' Magazine (1850–present), originally the organ of the publishers Harper and Brothers, went Graham one better. Instead of showing that liberal rewards to authors paid off, the publisher built on a practice already profitable in book publishing—pirating the output of popular English writers in the absence of an international copyright agreement. Gradually, however, faced with an outcry against the practice, *Harpers'* instituted payment and published original material by American authors. *Frank Leslie's Illustrated Newspaper* (1855–1922) in New York used large and striking pictures to illustrate its material, and generally followed its founder's motto: "Never shoot over the heads of the people." *Leslie's* and a vigorous competitor of somewhat higher quality, *Harper's Illustrated Weekly* (1857–

1916), appeared in time to provide a thoroughgoing pictorial record of the Civil War.

The boom in periodicals gave rise to more journals directed to specialized audiences. Worthy of mention, among others, are such magazines as *Godey's Lady's Book* (1830–1898), *The Southern Literary Messenger* (1834–1864), *Hunt's Merchants' Magazine* (1839–1870), *DeBow's Commercial Review of the South and West* (1846–1880), and *The American Farmer* (1819–1897), the first important agricultural journal. The new methods of production and distribution gave a boost to the book market as well. The publisher Samuel Goodrich estimated gross sales of books in America at $2 million in 1820, $12 million in 1850, and nearly $20 million in 1860. From 1820 to 1850, he estimated, moreover, books by American authors increased their share of the market from about a third to about two-thirds.

EDUCATION

EARLY PUBLIC SCHOOLS Literacy was surprisingly widespread, given the condition of public education. By 1840, according to census data, some 78 percent of the total population and 91 percent of the white population could read and write. Ever since the colonial period, in fact, Americans had had the highest literacy rate in the Western world. Most children learned their letters from church or private "dame" schools, formal tutors, or from their families. When Abraham Lincoln came of age, he said, he did not know much. "Still, somehow, I could read, write and cipher to the rule of three, but that was all." At that time, about 1830, no state had a school system in the modern sense, although Massachusetts had for nearly two centuries required towns to maintain schools. Some major cities had the resources to develop real systems on their own. The Public School Society of New York, for instance, built a model system of free schools in the city, with state aid after 1815. In 1806 the society introduced the Lancasterian schools (after Joseph Lancaster, an English Quaker) in which teachers used monitors to instruct hundreds of pupils at once. By 1853 when the state took over its properties the society had provided schooling for more than 600,000 pupils.

A scattered rural popularion, however, did not lend itself so readily to the development of schools. In 1860, for instance, Louisiana had a population density of 11 per square mile, Virginia 14, while Massachusetts had 127. In many parts of the country, as in South Carolina after 1811, the state provided some aid to schools for children of indigent parents, but such institutions were normally stigmatized as "pauper schools," to be shunned by the better sort.

Beginning with Connecticut as early as 1750, and New York in 1782, most states built up "literary" or school funds—an idea which gained momentum when Ohio, upon achieving statehood in 1803, also got the sixteenth section of each township as endowment for education. The funds were applied to various purposes—usually at first to aid local schools either public or private.

By the 1830s the demand for public schools was rising fast. Reformers argued that popular government presupposed a literate and informed electorate. With the lowering of barriers to the ballot box the argument carried all the more force. Workers wanted free schools to give their children an equal chance. In 1830 the Working Men's party of Philadelphia resolved in favor of "a system of education that shall embrace equally all the children of the state, of every rank and condition." Education, it was argued, would be a means of reform. It would improve manners and at the same time lessen crime and poverty. Opposition was minor, but when it came it was from taxpayers who held education to be a family matter and from those church groups that maintained schools at their own expense.

Horace Mann of Massachusetts stood out in the early drive for statewide school systems. Trained as a lawyer, Mann sponsored through the legislature the creation of a state board of education, which he then served as secretary. Mann went on to sponsor many reforms in Massachusetts, including the first state-supported normal school for teachers, teacher-training institutes for refresher courses, a state association of teachers, and a minimum school year of six months. He made his twelve annual reports into instruments of propaganda for public education. In these papers he explored problems of methods, curriculum, school management, and much more. His final report in 1848 defended the school system as the way to social stability and equal opportunity. It had never happened, he argued, and never could happen, that an educated people could be permanently poor. "Education then, beyond all other devices of human origin, is a great equalizer of the conditions of men—the balance wheel of the social machinery."

In the South the state of North Carolina led the way. There Calvin H. Wiley played a role like that of Mann, building from a law of 1839 which provided support to localities willing to tax themselves for the support of schools. As the first state superintendent of public instruction he traveled to every county drumming up support for the schools. By 1860, as a result of his activities, North Carolina enrolled more than two-thirds of its white school population for an average term of four months. But the educational pattern in the South continued to reflect the aristocratic pretensions of the region: the South had a higher percentage of college students than any other region, but a lower percentage of public school students. And the South had some 500,000 white illiterates, more than half the total number in the country.

For all the effort, conditions for public education were seldom ideal. Funds were insufficient for buildings, books, and equipment; teachers were poorly paid, and often so poorly prepared as to be little ahead of their charges in the ability to read, write, and cipher. In many a rural schoolhouse the teacher's first task was to thrash the huskiest youth in the class in order to encourage the others. The teachers, consequently, were at first mostly men, often young men who did not regard teaching as a career but as a means of support while preparing for a career as a lawyer or preacher, or as part-time work during slack seasons on the farm. With the encouragement of educational reformers, however, teaching was beginning to be regarded as a profession. As the schools multiplied and the school term lengthened, women increasingly entered the field.

Still, given the condition of their preparation, teachers were heavily dependent on textbooks and publishers were happy to oblige them. The most common texts were Noah Webster's *Blue-Backed Spellers* and a series of six graded *Eclectic Readers* which William Holmes McGuffey, a professor and university president in Ohio, began to bring out in 1836 and completed in 1857. His books taught children to recite "Twinkle, Twinkle, Little Star," "The Boy Stood on the Burning Deck," "The Boy Who Cried Wolf," and the patriotic words of Washington, Patrick Henry, Webster, and Clay. The readers were replete with parables designed to instill thrift, morality, and patriotism. At the same time they carried selections from the masters of English prose and verse.

Most students going beyond the elementary grades went to private academies, often subsidized by church and public funds. Such schools, begun in colonial days, multiplied until there were in 1850 more than 6,000 of them. In 1821 the Boston English High School opened as the first free public secondary school, set up mainly for students not going on to college. By a law of 1827

Massachusetts required a high school in every town of 500; in towns of 4,000 or more the school had to offer Latin, Greek, rhetoric, and other college preparatory courses. Public high schools became well established in school systems only after the Civil War. In 1860 there were barely 300 in the whole country.

POPULAR EDUCATION   Beyond the schools there grew up many societies and institutes to inform the general public: mechanics' and workingmen's "institutes," "young men's associations," "debating societies," "literary societies," and such. Outstanding in the field was the Franklin Institute, founded at Philadelphia in 1824 to inform the public mainly in the fields of science and industry. Similar institutes were sponsored by major philanthropists like Lowell in Boston, Peabody in Baltimore, and Cooper in New York. Some cities offered evening classes to those who could not attend day schools. The most widespread and effective means of popular education, however, was the lyceum movement, which aimed to diffuse knowledge through public lectures. Professional agencies provided speakers and performers of all kinds, in literature, science, music, humor, travel, and other fields. Most of the major savants of the age at one time or another rode the lecture circuit: Emerson, Melville, Lyman Beecher, Daniel Webster, Harriet Beecher Stowe, Louis Agassiz, Benjamin Silliman.

Akin to the lyceum movement and ultimately reaching more people was the movement for public libraries. Benjamin Franklin's Philadelphia Library Company (1731) had given impulse to the growth of subscription or association libraries. In 1803 Salisbury, Connecticut, opened a free library for children and in 1833 Peterborough, New Hampshire, established a tax-supported library open to all. The opening of the Boston Public Library in 1851 was a turning point. By 1860 there were approximately 10,000 public libraries (not all completely free) housing some 8 million volumes.

HIGHER EDUCATION   The postrevolutionary proliferation of colleges continued after 1800 with the spread of small church schools and state universities. Nine colleges had been founded in the colonial period, all of which survived; but not many of the fifty that sprang up between 1776 and 1800 lasted. Among those that did were Hampden-Sydney, Charleston, Bowdoin, and Middlebury, all of which went on to long and fruitful careers. Of the seventy-eight colleges and universities in 1840, fully thirty-five had been founded after 1830, almost all as church schools. A

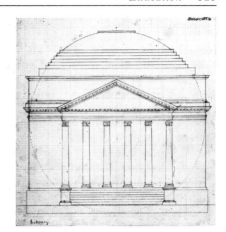

Jefferson's design for the rotunda at the University of Virginia, founded in 1819.

postrevolutionary movement for state universities flourished in those southern states that had had no colonial university. Federal policy abetted the spread of universities into the West. When Congress granted statehood to Ohio in 1803, it set aside two townships for the support of a state university and kept up that policy in other new states.

The coexistence of state and religious schools, however, set up conflicts over funding and curriculum. Beset by the need for funds, as colleges usually were, denominational schools often competed with tax-supported schools. Regarding curricula, the new Awakening led many of the church schools to emphasize theology at the expense of science and the humanities. On the other hand America's development required broader access to education and programs geared to vocations. The University of Virginia, "Mr. Jefferson's University," founded in 1819 within sight of Monticello, introduced in 1826 a curriculum which reflected Jefferson's own view that education ought to combine pure knowledge with "all the branches of science useful *to us, and at this day.*" The model influenced the other new state universities of the South and West.

Technical education grew slowly. The United States Military Academy at West Point, founded in 1802, and the Naval Academy at Annapolis, opened in 1845, trained a limited number of engineers. More were trained by practical experience with railroad and canal companies, and apprenticeship to experienced technologists. Similarly, most aspiring lawyers went to "read law" with an established attorney, and doctors served their apprenticeships with practicing physicians. The president of Brown University remarked that there were forty-two theological schools and forty-seven law schools, but none to provide "the agriculturalist, the manufacturer, the mechanic, and the merchant with any kind of professional preparation." There were few schools of this sort before 1860, but a promise for the future came in 1855 when Michigan and Pennsylvania each established an agricultural and mechanical college, now Michigan State and Pennsylvania State.

Elementary education for girls, where available for boys, met with general acceptance, but training beyond that level did not. Many men and women thought higher education unsuited to woman's destiny in life. Some did argue that education would make better wives and mothers, but few were ready yet to demand equality on principle. Progress began with the academies, some of which taught boys and girls alike. Good "female seminaries" like those founded by Emma Willard at Troy, New York (1824), and Mary Lyon at Mount Holyoke, Massachusetts (1836), prepared the way for women's colleges. Many of them, in fact, grew into such colleges, but Georgia Female College (later Wesleyan) at Macon, chartered in 1836, first offered women the A.B. in 1840. The work in female seminaries usually differed from the courses in men's schools, giving more attention to the social amenities and such "embellishments" as music and art. Vassar, opened at Poughkeepsie, New York, in 1865, is usually credited with being the first women's college to give priority to academic standards. Oberlin College in Ohio, founded in 1833, opened as both a biracial and a coeducational institution. Its first women students were admitted in 1837. In general the West gave the greatest impetus to coeducation, with state universities in the lead.

Some Movements for Reform

Alexis de Tocqueville, a French traveler who wrote a classic report on American society, *Democracy in America* (1835), commented on many things, including the role of education in the United States. Another matter caught his special attention: nothing, he wrote, "in my view, more deserves attention than the intellectual and moral associations in America." During his extended visit in 1831 he heard that 100,000 men had pledged to abstain from alcohol. At first he thought it was a joke. Why should these abstemious citizens not quietly drink water by their own firesides? Then he understood that "Americans of all ages, all stations to life and all types of dispositions are forever forming associations. There are not only commercial and industrial associations in which all take part, but others of a thousand different types—religious, moral, serious, futile, very general and very limited, very large and very minute."

Emerson spoke for his generation, as he so often did, when he asked: "What is man born for, but to be a Reformer, a Remaker of what man has made?" The urge to eradicate evil from nineteenth-century America had its roots in the widespread sense of mission, which in turn drew upon rising faith in the perfectibility of man. Belief in perfectibility had both evangelical and liberal bases. Transcendentalism, the spirit of which infected even those unfamiliar with the philosophy, offered a romantic faith in the individual and the belief that human intuition led to right thinking.

Few things escaped the ministrations of the reformers, however trivial or weighty: observance of the Sabbath, dueling, crime and punishment, the hours and conditions of work, poverty, vice, care of the handicapped, pacifism, foreign missions, temperance, women's rights, the abolition of slavery. Some crusaders challenged a host of evils; others focused on pet causes. One Massachusetts reformer, for example, insisted that "a vegetable diet lies at the basis of all reforms." The greatest dietary reformer of the age, however, was Sylvester Graham, who started as a temperance speaker in 1830 and moved on to champion a natural diet of grains, vegetables, and fruits, and abstinence from alcohol, coffee, tea, tobacco, and many foods. The Graham cracker is one of the movement's legacies to later times. Graham's ideas evolved into a way of life requiring proper habits of dress, hygiene, sex, and mind. The movement became a major industry, sponsoring health clubs, camps, sanitariums, magazines, and regular lecture tours by Graham, "the Peristaltic Persuader."

TEMPERANCE The temperance crusade, at which Tocqueville marvelled, was perhaps the most widespread of all, with the possible exception of the public school movement. The cause drew its share of spoilsports, but it also drew upon concern with a real problem. The census of 1810 reported some 14,000 distilleries producing 25 million gallons of spirits each year. With a hard-drinking population of just over 7 million, the "alcoholic republic" was producing well over three gallons per year for every man, woman, and child, not counting beer, wine, and cider. And the census takers no doubt missed a few stills. William Cobbett, an English reformer who traveled in the United States, noted in 1819 that one could "go into hardly any man's house without being asked to drink wine or spirits, even *in the morning*."

The movement for temperance rested on a number of arguments. First and foremost was the demand of religion that "soldiers of the cross" lead blameless lives. The bad effects of distilled beverages on body and mind were noted by the respected physician Benjamin Rush as early as 1784. The dynamic new economy, with factories and railroads moving on strict schedules, made tippling by the labor force a far greater problem than it had been in a simple economy. Humanitarians emphasized the relations between drinking and poverty. Much of the movement's propaganda focused on the sufferings of innocent mothers and children. "Drink," said a pamphlet from the Sons of Temperance, "is the prolific source (directly or indirectly) of nearly all the ills that afflict the human family."

The Way of Good & Evil. *Intemperance was one of the steps on the way of evil, leading to "everlasting punishment."*

In 1826 a group of ministers in Boston organized the American Society for the Promotion of Temperance. The society worked through lecturers, press campaigns, prize essay contests, and the formation of local and state societies. A favorite device was to ask each person who took the pledge to put by his signature a T for Total Abstinence. With that a new word entered the language: "teetotaler."

In 1833 the society called a national convention in Philadelphia where the American Temperance Union was formed. The convention revealed internal tensions, however: Was the goal moderation or total abstinence, and if the latter, abstinence merely from ardent spirits or also from wine, cider, and beer? Should the movement work by persuasion or by legislation? Like nearly every movement of the day, temperance had a wing of perfectionists who rejected counsels of prudence. They would brook no compromise with Demon Rum, and carried the day with a resolution that the liquor traffic was morally wrong and ought to be prohibited by law. The union, at its spring convention in 1836, called for abstinence from all alcoholic beverages —a costly victory that caused moderates to abstain from the movement instead.

The demand for the prohibition of alcoholic beverages led in the 1830s and thereafter to experiments with more stringent regulations and local option laws. In 1838 Massachusetts forbade the sale of spirits in lots of less than fifteen gallons, thereby cutting off sales in taverns and to the poor—who could not handle it as well as their betters, or so their betters thought. After repeal of the law in 1840, prohibitionists in Massachusetts turned to the towns, about a hundred of which were dry by 1845. In 1839 Mississippi restricted sales to no less than a gallon, but the movement went little further in the South. In 1846 Maine enacted a law against sales of less than twenty-eight gallons; five years later Maine forbade the manufacture or sale of *any* intoxicants. By 1855 thirteen states had such laws. Rum-soaked New England had gone legally dry, along with New York and parts of the Midwest. But most of the laws were poorly drafted and vulnerable to court challenge. Within a few years they survived only in northern New England. Still, between 1830 and 1860 the temperance agitation drastically reduced Americans' per-capita consumption of alcohol.

PRISONS AND ASYLUMS   The sublime optimism of the age, the liberal belief that people are innately good and capable of improvement, brought major changes in the treatment of prisoners, the handicapped, and dependent children. Public institutions arose dedicated to the treatment and cure of social ills. Earlier these had been "places of last resort," David Rothman wrote in *The Discovery of the Asylum*. Now they "became places of first resort, the preferred solution to the problems of poverty, crime, delinquency, and insanity." Removed from society, the needy and deviant could be made whole again. Unhappily, this ideal kept running up against the dictates of convenience and economy. The institutions had a way of turning into breeding grounds of brutality and neglect.

In the colonial period prisons were usually places for brief confinement before punishment, which was either death or some kind of pain or humiliation: whipping, mutilation, confinement in stocks, ducking, branding, and the like. A new attitude began to emerge after the Revolution. American reformers argued against the harshness of the penal code and asserted that the certainty of punishment was more important than its severity. Society, moreover, would benefit more from the prevention than the punishment of crime. The Philadelphia Society for Alleviating the Miseries of Public Prisons, founded in 1787, took the lead in spreading the new doctrines. Gradually the idea of the penitentiary developed. It would be a place where the guilty experienced penitence and underwent rehabilitation, not just punishment.

An early model of the new system, widely copied, was the Auburn Penitentiary, commissioned by New York in 1816. The prisoners at Auburn had separate cells and gathered for meals and group labor. Discipline was severe. The men were marched out in lock step and never put face to face or allowed to talk. But prisoners were at least reasonably secure from abuse by other prisoners. The system, its advocates argued, had a beneficial effect on the prisoners and saved money since the workshops supplied prison needs and produced goods for sale at a profit. By 1840 there were twelve prisons of the Auburn type.

It was still more common, and the persistent curse of prisons, for inmates to be thrown together willy-nilly. In an earlier day of corporal punishments jails housed mainly debtors. But as practices changed, debtors found themselves housed with convicts. In New York City, investigation showed about 2,000 debtors confined during 1816, as many as 600 at one time. Of the annual total, over 1,000 were held for debts less than $50, 700 for debts under $25. Without provision for food, furniture, or fuel, the debtors would have expired but for charity. The absurdity of the system was so obvious that the tardiness of reform seems strange. New York in 1817 made $25 the minimum for which one could

The Philadelphia Hospital was one of the few in eighteenth-century America to care for the mentally ill. It is depicted here in 1767.

be imprisoned, but no state eliminated the practice altogether until Kentucky acted in 1821. Ohio acted in 1828 and other states gradually fell in line, but it was still more than three decades before debtors' prisons became a thing of the past.

The reform impulse naturally found outlet in the care of the insane. The Philadelphia Hospital (1752), one of the first in the country, had a provision in its charter that it should care for "lunaticks," but before 1800 few hospitals provided care for the mentally ill. One notable exception was the hospital opened in Williamsburg in 1759 specifically for treatment of the mentally ill. The insane were usually confined at home with hired keepers or in jails and almshouses. In the years after 1815, however, asylums which housed the disturbed separately from criminals began to appear. Early efforts led to such optimism that a committee reported to the Massachusetts legislature in 1832 that with the right treatment "insanity yields with more readiness than ordinary diseases." These high expectations gradually faded with experience.

The most important figure in arousing the public conscience to the plight of these unfortunates was Dorothea Lynde Dix. A Boston schoolteacher called upon to instruct a Sunday school class at the East Cambridge House of Correction in 1841, she found there a roomful of insane persons completely neglected and left without heat on a cold March day. She then commenced a two-year investigation of jails and almshouses in Massachusetts. In a memorial to the state legislature in 1843 she began "I tell what I have seen," and went on to report "the *present* state of insane persons confined within the Commonwealth, in *cages, closets, cellars, stalls, pens! Chained, naked, beaten with rods, and lashed into obedience!*" Keepers of the institutions charged "slanderous lies," but she got the support of leading reformers

Dorothea Dix, one of the most influential of American reformers.

and won a large appropriation. From Massachusetts she carried her campaign throughout the country and abroad. By 1860 she had gotten twenty states to heed her advice. Of Dorothea Dix it was truly said that "Few persons have ever had such far-reaching effect on public policy toward reform."

WOMEN'S RIGHTS   While Dorothea Dix stood out as an example of the opportunity reform gave middle-class women to enter public life, Catherine Beecher, a leader in the education movement and founder of women's schools in Connecticut and Ohio, published a guide prescribing the domestic sphere for women. *A Treatise on Domestic Economy* (1841) became the leading handbook of what historians have labeled the "cult of domesticity." While Beecher upheld high standards in women's education, she also accepted the prevailing view that "woman's sphere" was the home and argued that young women should be trained in the domestic arts. Her guide, designed for use also as a textbook, led prospective wives and mothers through the endless rounds from Monday washing to Saturday baking, with instructions on health, food, clothing, cleanliness, care of domestics and children, gardening, and hundreds of other household details. Such duties, Beecher emphasized, should never be taken as "petty, trivial or unworthy" since "no statesman . . . had more frequent calls for wisdom, firmness, tact, discrimination, prudence, and versatility of talent."

The social custom of assigning the sexes different roles of course did not spring full-blown into life during the nineteenth century. In earlier agrarian societies sex-based functions were closely tied to the household and often overlapped. As the more complex economy of the nineteenth century matured, economic production came to be increasingly separated from the home, and the home in turn became a refuge from the cruel world outside, with separate and distinctive functions. Some have argued that the home became a trap for women, a prison that hindered fulfillment. But others have noted that it often gave women a sphere of independence in which they might exercise a degree of initiative and leadership. The so-called cult of true womanhood idealized woman's moral role in civilizing husband and family.

The status of women during this period remained much as it had been in the colonial era. Legally, a woman was unenfranchised, denied control of her property and even of her children. A wife could not make a will, sign a contract, or bring suit in court without her husband's permission. Her legal status was like that of a minor, a slave, or a free Negro. The organized movement for women's rights in fact had its origins in 1840, when the American antislavery movement split over the question of women's right to participate. American women decided then that they needed to organize on behalf of their own emancipation too.

In 1848 Lucretia Mott and Elizabeth Cady Stanton decided to call a convention to discuss "the social, civil, and religious condi-

An English print advises women of the early nineteenth century. "To Avoid Many Troubles Which Others Endure: Keep Within Compass and You Shall Be Sure."

tion and rights of women." The hastily called Seneca Falls Convention, the first of its kind, issued on July 19, 1848, a clever paraphrase of Jefferson's Declaration, the Declaration of Sentiments, mainly the work of Mrs. Stanton. The document proclaimed the self-evident truth that "all men and women are created equal," and the attendant resolutions said that all laws which placed woman "in a position inferior to that of men, are contrary to the great precept of nature, and therefore of no force or authority."

From 1850 until the Civil War the women's-rights leaders held annual conventions, and carried on a program of organizing, lecturing, and petitioning. The movement had to struggle in the face of meager funds and antifeminist women and men. What success the movement had was due to the work of a few undaunted women who refused to be overawed by the odds against them. Susan B. Anthony, already active in temperance and anti-slavery groups, joined the crusade in the 1850s. As one observer put it, Mrs. Stanton "forged the thunderbolts and Miss Anthony hurled them." Both were young when the movement started and both lived into the twentieth century, focusing after the Civil War on demands for woman suffrage. Many of the feminists like Stanton, Lucretia Mott, and Lucy Stone had supportive husbands, and the movement won prominent male champions like Emerson, William Ellery Channing, and William Lloyd Garrison. Editor Horace Greeley gave the feminists sympathetic attention in the New York *Tribune.*

The fruits of the movement were slow to ripen. The women did not gain the ballot, but there were some legal gains. The state

Elizabeth Cady Stanton (left) and Susan B. Anthony. Mrs. Stanton "forged the thunderbolts and Miss Anthony hurled them."

Margaret Fuller, one of the great American intellectuals of her time.

of Mississippi, seldom regarded as a hotbed of reform, was in 1839 the first to grant married women control over their property; by the 1860s eleven more states had such laws. In practice wives sometimes got separate estates, though probably more often to protect family property from the husband's creditors than to give the wives independent control.

Still, the only jobs open to educated women in any numbers were nursing and teaching, both of which extended the domestic roles of health care and nurture into the world outside. Both brought relatively lower status and pay than "man's work" despite the skills, training, and responsibility involved. Against the odds, a hardy band of women carved out professional careers. With the rapid expansion of schools, women moved into the teaching profession first. If women could be teachers, Susan Anthony asked, why not lawyers or doctors? Harriet Hunt of Boston was a teacher who, after nursing her sister through a serious illness, set up shop in 1835 as a self-taught physician and persisted in medical practice although twice rejected by Harvard Medical School. Voted into Geneva Medical College in western New York as a joke, Elizabeth Blackwell of Ohio had the last laugh when she finished at the head of her class in 1849. She founded the New York Infirmary for Women and Children and later had a long career as a professor of gynecology in the London School of Medicine for Women.

An intellectual prodigy among women of the time—the derisory term was "bluestocking"—was Margaret Fuller. A precocious child, she was force-fed education by a father who set her at Latin when she was six. As a young adult she moved in the literary circles of Boston and Concord, edited the *The Dial* for two years, and became literary editor and critic for Horace Greeley's New York *Tribune*. From 1839 to 1844 she conducted "conversations" with the cultivated ladies of Boston. From this classroom-salon emerged many of the ideas that went into her book *Woman in the Nineteenth Century* (1845), a plea for removal of all intellectual and economic disabilities. Minds and souls were neither masculine nor feminine, she argued. Genius had no sex. "What woman needs," she wrote, "is not as a woman to act or rule, but as a nature to grow, as an intellect to discern, as a soul to live freely and unimpeded, to unfold such powers as were given her when we left our common home."

UTOPIAN COMMUNITIES The quest for utopia flourished in the climate of reform. "We are all a little mad here with numberless projects of social reform," Emerson wrote in 1840. "Not a reading man but has a draft of a new community in his pocket." Drafts of new communities had long been an American passion, at least since the Puritans set out to build a Wilderness Zion. The visionary communes of the nineteenth century often had purely economic and social objectives, but those that were rooted in religion proved most durable. An early instance, an offshoot of the Mennonites in 1732, the Ephrata Community in Pennsylvania practiced an almost monastic life into the early nineteenth century. Founder Johann Conrad Beissel's emphasis on music left a lasting imprint on American hymnology. In 1803 George Rapp led about 600 Lutheran come-outers from Württemberg to Pennsylvania. They took the Bible literally, and like Beissel's group, renounced sex. Since the millennium was near they had to keep ready. No quarrel went unsettled overnight, and all who had sinned confessed to Rapp before sleeping. Industrious and disciplined, the Rappites prospered, and persevered to the end of the century.

More than a hundred utopian communities sprang up between 1800 and 1900. Among the most durable were the Shakers, officially the United Society of Believers, founded by Ann Lee Stanley (Mother Ann), who reached New York state with eight followers in 1774. Believing religious fervor a sign of inspiration from the Holy Ghost, they had strange fits in which they saw visions and prophesied. These manifestations later evolved into a ritual dance—hence the name Shakers. Shaker doctrine held God to be a dual personality: in Christ the masculine side was manifested, in Mother Ann the feminine element. Mother Ann preached celibacy to prepare Shakers for the perfection that was promised them. The church would first gather in the elect, and eventually in the spirit world convert and save all mankind.

Mother Ann died in 1784, but the group found new leaders. From the first community at Mount Lebanon, New York, the

A Shaker rocking chair, made around
1830–1840. Its simple elegance is typical of
Shaker crafts.

movement spread to new colonies in New England, and soon afterward into Ohio and Kentucky. By 1830 about twenty groups were flourishing. In Shaker communities all property was held in common. Governance of the colonies was concentrated in the hands of select groups chosen by the ministry, or "Head of Influence" at Mount Lebanon. To outsiders this might seem almost despotic, but the Shakers emphasized equality of labor and reward, and members were free to leave at will. The Shakers' farms yielded a surplus for the market. They were among the leading sources of garden seed and medicinal herbs, and many of their manufactures, including clothing, household items, and especially furniture, were prized for their simple beauty. By the mid–twentieth century, however, few members remained alive; they had reached the peak of activity in the years 1830–1860.

John Humphrey Noyes, founder of the Oneida Community, got religion at one of Charles G. Finney's revivals and entered the ministry. He was forced out, however, when he concluded that with true conversion came perfection and a complete release from sin. In 1836 he gathered a group of "Perfectionists" around his home in Putney, Vermont. Ten years later Noyes announced a new doctrine of complex marriage, which meant that every man in the community was married to every woman and vice versa. To outsiders it looked like simple promiscuity and Noyes was arrested. He fled to New York and in 1848 established the Oneida Community, which numbered more than 200 by 1851.

The group eked out a living with farming and logging until the mid-1850s, when the inventor of a new steel trap joined the community. Oneida traps were soon known as the best. The community then branched out into sewing silk, canning fruits, and making silver spoons. The spoons were so popular that, with the addition of knives and forks, tableware became the Oneida speciality. Community Plate is still made. In 1879, however, the community faced a crisis when Noyes fled to Canada to avoid prosecution for adultery. The members then abandoned complex marriage, and in 1881 decided to convert into a joint-stock company, the Oneida Community, Ltd. A similar fate overtook the Amana Society, or Community of True Faith, a German group that migrated to New York state in 1843 and on to Iowa in 1850. Eventually, in 1932, beset by the problems of the Great Depression, they incorporated as a joint-stock company making refrigerators and eventually a great variety of home appliances.

In contrast to these communities, Robert Owen's New Harmony was based on a secular principle. A British capitalist who worried about the social effects of the factory system, Owen built a model factory town, supported labor legislation, and set forth a scheme for a model community in his pamphlet *A New View of Society* (1813). Later he snapped at a chance to buy the Rappites' town of Harmony, Indiana, and promptly christened it New Harmony. In Washington an audience including President Monroe crowded the hall of the House of Representatives to hear Owen tell about his high hopes.

In 1825 a varied group of about 900 colonists gathered in New Harmony for a period of transition from Owen's ownership to the new system of cooperation. The group began to run the former Rappite industries, and after only nine months' trial Owen turned over management of the colony to a town meeting of all residents and a council of town officers. The high proportion of learned participants generated a certain intellectual electricity about the place. Schools sprang up quickly. Owen's two sons started a sprightly paper, the *New Harmony Gazette*. There were frequent lectures and social gatherings with music and dancing.

For a time it looked like a brilliant success, but New Harmony soon fell into discord. The *Gazette* complained of "grumbling, carping, and murmuring" members and others who had the "disease of laziness." The problem, it seems, was a problem common to reform groups. Every idealist wanted his own patented plan put into practice. In 1827 Owen returned from a visit to England to find New Harmony insolvent. The following year he dissolved the project and sold or leased the lands on good terms, in many cases to the settlers. All that remained he turned over to his sons, who remained and became American citizens.

The 1840s brought a flurry of interest in the ideas of Fourieristic socialism. Charles Fourier, a Frenchman, proposed to reorder society into small units, or "phalanxes," ideally of 1,620 members. All property would be held in common and each phalanx would produce that for which it felt itself best suited; the joy of work and communal living would supply the incentive. By example the phalanxes would eventually cover the earth and displace capitalism. Fourier remained a prophet without honor in his own country, but Arthur Brisbane's book *The Social Destiny of Man* (1840) brought Fourierism before the American public and Horace Greeley's New York *Tribune* kept it there.

Greeley was in such a hurry to try out the idea, however, that Brisbane thought him rash. Brisbane was right. The first community, the Sylvania Phalanx in northern Pennsylvania, founded with Greeley's help in 1842, lasted but a year. Sylvania picked up 2,300 acres of remote and infertile land at little cost. During their only season about 100 members produced just eleven bushels of grain on the four acres of arable land. Greeley lost $5,000. In all some forty or fifty phalansteries sprang up, but lasted on the average about two years.

Brook Farm was surely the most celebrated of all the utopian communities because it had the support of Emerson, Lowell, Whittier, and countless other well-known literary figures of New England. Nathaniel Hawthorne, a member, later memorialized its failure in his novel *The Blithedale Romance* (1852). George Ripley, a Unitarian minister and Transcendentalist, conceived of Brook Farm as a kind of early-day "think tank," combining high thinking and plain living. The place survived, however, mainly because of an excellent community school that drew tuition-paying students from outside. In 1844 Brook Farm converted itself into a phalanstery, but when a new central building burned down on the day of its dedication in 1846, the community spirit expired in the embers.

Utopian communities, with few exceptions, quickly ran into futility. Soon after Hawthorne left Brook Farm he wrote: "It already looks like a dream behind me." His life there was "an unnatural and unsuitable, and therefore an unreal one." Such experiments, performed in relative isolation, had little effect on the real world outside, where reformers wrestled with the sins of the multitudes. Among all the targets of reformers' wrath, one great evil would finally take precedence over the others— human bondage. The paradox of American slavery coupled with American freedom, of "the world's fairest hope linked with man's foulest crime," in Herman Melville's words, would inspire the climactic crusade of the age, abolitionism, one that would ultimately move to the center of the political stage and sweep the nation into an epic struggle.

FURTHER READING

Few single-volume works cover the diversity of early American reform and culture. A good start is Perry Miller's *The Life of the Mind in America: From the Revolution to the Civil War* (1965),° on the intellectual evolution which ran concurrent with reformist activity. Russel B. Nye's *Society and Culture in America, 1830–1860* (1974) provides a wide-ranging survey. On reform itself, consult Alice F. Tyler's *Freedom's Ferment: Phases of American Social History to 1860* (1944)° and Ronald G. Walter's *American Reformers, 1815–1860* (1978).°

Sydney E. Ahlstrom's *A Religious History of the American People* (1972) provides a solid survey of antebellum religious movements and developments. More interpretive is Martin E. Marty's *Righteous Empire: The Protestant Experience in America* (1970). Revivalist religion is discussed in Whitney R. Cross's *The Burned-Over District* (1950)° and John B. Boles's *The Great Revival* (1972). Donald G. Mathews, in *Religion in the Old South* (1977), dissects the concept of the evangelical mind.

For splinter sects, the scholarship is most voluminous on the Mormons. Among the most recent books are Klaus J. Hansen's *Mormonism and the American Experience* (1981), Leonard J. Arrington's *Brigham Young: American Moses* (1985), and Richard L. Bushman's *Joseph Smith and the Beginnings of Mormonism* (1984).

Francis O. Matthiessen's classic work *American Renaissance* (1941)° examines the literary history of the antebellum period. The best introduction to transcendentalist thought are the writings of the Transcendentalists themselves, collected in Perry Miller (ed.), *The Transcendentalists* (1950).° Also see Gay Wilson Allen's *Waldo Emerson: A Biography* (1981)° and Joel Porte's *Representative Man: Ralph Waldo Emerson in His Time* (1979). For Emerson's protégé, see Richard Le-Beaux's *Young Man Thoreau* (1977). A recent treatment of the poet Whitman is Justin Kaplan's *Walt Whitman: A Life* (1980).° A solid introduction to antebellum newspapers is Frank L. Mott's *American Journalism* (3rd ed., 1962). Barbara Novak's *Nature and Culture: American Landscape and Painting, 1825–1875* (1980)° provides an overview of the Hudson River School.

Several good works describe various aspects of the antebellum reform movement. For temperance, see W. J. Rorabaugh's *The Alcoholic Republic: An American Tradition* (1979).° Stephen Nissenbaum's *Sex, Diet, and Debility in Jacksonian America* (1980) looks at health reform. On prison reform and other humanitarian projects, see David J. Rothman's *The Discovery of the Asylum* (1971)° and Gerald N. Grob's *Mental Institutions in America* (1973). For the religious context of reform, consult Carroll Smith-Rosenberg's *Religion and the Rise of the American City: The New York Mission Movement* (1971).

Lawrence A. Cremin's *American Education: The National Experience, 1783–1876* (1980) traces early school reform. For other views, see Stan-

°These books are available in paperback editions.

ley K. Schultz's *The Culture Factory: Boston Public School, 1789–1860* (1973) and Carl F. Kaestle's *Pillars of the Republic* (1983).

The literature of feminism is both voluminous and diverse. Three surveys of feminist history that include the antebellum period are Carl N. Degler's *At Odds: Women and Family in America from the Revolution to the Present* (1980),° Gerda Lerner's *The Woman in American History* (1971), and Mary P. Ryan's *Womanhood in America* (3rd ed., 1983).° More particular to the antebellum period are Nancy F. Cott's *The Bonds of Womanhood: "Women's Sphere" in New England, 1780–1835* (1977)° and Ellen C. DuBois's *Feminism and Suffrage: The Emergence of an Independent Women's Movement in America, 1848–1869* (1978). Biographical studies include Alma Lutz's *Susan B. Anthony* (1959), Lois W. Banner's *Elizabeth Cady Stanton* (1980), and Paula Blanchard's *Margaret Fuller: From Transcendentalism to Revolution* (1978).

Perspectives on the family at this time can be gleaned from Milton A. Rugoff's *The Beechers* (1981) and Mary P. Ryan's *Cradle of the Middle Class* (1981).°

Michael Fellman's *The Unbounded Frame: Freedom and Community in Nineteenth Century Utopianism* (1973) surveys the utopian movements. Specific experiments are treated in Robert D. Thomas's *The Man Who Would Be Perfect* (1977), on John Humphrey Noyes; J. F. C. Harrison's *Quest for the New Moral World* (1969), on Robert Owens; Maren L. Carden's *Oneida* (1969); and Henri Desroche's *The American Shakers from Neo-Christianity to Pre-Socialism* (1971). Lawrence Foster's *Religion and Sexuality* (1981) discusses the Oneida, Shaker, and Mormon communities.

14 ✍

MANIFEST DESTINY

The Tyler Years

When William Henry Harrison took office in 1841, elected like Jackson mainly on the strength of his military record and without commitment on issues, the Whig leaders expected him to be a figurehead. At first it did seem that he would be a tool in the hands of Webster and Clay. Webster became secretary of state and, while Clay preferred to stay in the Senate, the cabinet was filled with his friends. Within a few days of the inauguration there were signs of strain between Harrison and Clay, whose disappointment at missing the nomination had made him peevish and arrogant. But the enmity never had a chance to develop, for Harrison served the shortest term of any president—after the longest inaugural address. At the inauguration on a chill and rainy day he caught cold. The importunings of office seekers in the following month filled his days and sapped his strength. On April 4, 1841, exactly one month after the inauguration, he died of pneumonia.

Thus John Tyler of Virginia, the first vice-president to succeed on the death of a president, was to serve practically all of Harrison's term. And if there was ambiguity about where Harrison stood, there was none about Tyler. At age fifty-one he already had a long career behind him as legislator, governor, congressman, and senator, and was on record on all the important issues. At an earlier time he might have been called an Old Republican, stubbornly opposed to everything that was signified by Clay's American System—protective tariffs, a national bank, or internal improvements at national expense—and in favor of strict construction and states' rights. Once a Democrat, he had broken with Jackson's stand on nullification and his imperious use of executive authority. Tyler had been chosen to "balance" the ticket, with no belief that he would wield power. And to compound the irony, because he was known as a friend of Clay, his choice had been designed in part to pacify Clay's disappointed followers.

DOMESTIC AFFAIRS   Given more finesse on Clay's part, personal friendship might have enabled him to bridge the policy divisions among the Whigs. But for once, driven by disappointment and ambition, the "Great Pacificator" lost his instinct for compromise. When Congress met in special session at the end of May 1841 Clay introduced, and the Whig majority passed, a series of resolutions designed to supply the platform that the party had evaded in the previous election. The chief points were repeal of the Independent Treasury, establishment of a third Bank of the United States, distribution to the states of proceeds from public land sales, and a higher tariff. Clay then set out to push his program through Congress. Despite the known views of Tyler, he remained hopeful. "Tyler dares not resist me. I will drive him before me," he said. Tyler, it turned out, was not easily driven.

By 1842 Clay's program was in ruins. He had failed to get a new bank, and distribution was abandoned with adoption of the high 1842 tariff. Even his successes were temporary—a Democratic Congress and president in 1846 restored the Independent Treasury and cut the tariff, leaving preemption (which legalized the frontier tradition of "squatter's rights") as the only major permanent achievement of the Whigs, something that had been no part of Clay's original scheme. If the program was in ruins, however, Clay's leadership of his party was fixed beyond question, and Tyler was left in the position of a president without a party.

FOREIGN AFFAIRS   In foreign relations, on the other hand, developments of immense significance were taking place. Several unsettled issues had arisen to trouble relations between Britain and the United States. In 1837 a forlorn insurrection in Upper Canada led to the seizure of the American steamboat *Caroline* by Canadians who set it afire and let it drift over Niagara Falls. In the course of the incident one American was killed. The British ignored all protests, but President Van Buren called out militia under Gen. Winfield Scott to prevent frontier violations in either direction. The issue faded until 1840 when Alexander McLeod, a Canadian, was arrested and brought to trial in New York state after he boasted of his participation in the incident and his responsibility for the killing. The British government now did admit that it had ordered destruction of the vessel and argued that McLeod could not be held personally responsible. The incident fortunately was closed when McLeod proved to have an airtight alibi—he was miles away and his story had been nothing but barroom braggadocio.

Another issue between the two nations involved the suppression of the African slave trade, which both the United States and Britain had outlawed in 1808. Congress failed to provide funds for American participation in the African slave patrol. In August 1841 Prime Minister Palmerston asserted the right of British patrols off the coast of Africa to board and search vessels flying the American flag to see if they carried slaves, but the American government remembered the impressments and seizures during the Napoleonic Wars and refused to accept it. Relations were further strained late in 1841 when American slaves on a brig, the *Creole*, bound from Hampton Roads to New Orleans, mutinied and sailed into Nassau, where the British set them free. Secretary of State Webster demanded that the slaves be returned as American property, but the British refused.

Fortunately at this point a new British ministry under Sir Robert Peel decided to accept Webster's overtures for negotiations and sent Lord Ashburton to Washington. Ashburton was widely known to be friendly to Americans, and the talks proceeded smoothly. The Maine boundary was settled in what Webster later called "the battle of the maps." Webster settled for about seven-twelfths of the contested lands along the Maine boundary,

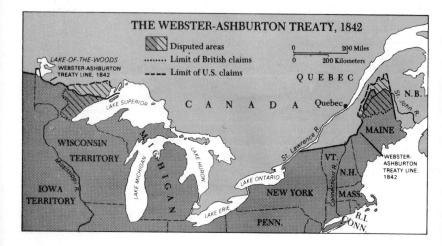

THE WEBSTER-ASHBURTON TREATY, 1842

and except for Oregon, which remained under joint occupation, he settled the other border disputes by accepting the existing line between the Connecticut and St. Lawrence rivers, and by compromising on the line between Lake Superior and the Lake-of-the-Woods. The Webster-Ashburton treaty (1842) also provided for joint patrols off Africa to repress the slave trade.

MOVING WEST

In the early 1840s the American people were no more stirred by the quarrels of Tyler and Clay over such issues as banking, tariffs, and distribution, important as they were, than students of history would be at a later date. Nor was the pulse much quickened by the adjustment of boundaries supposedly settled in 1783. What stirred the blood was the mounting evidence that the "empire of freedom" was hurdling the barriers of the "Great American Desert" and the Rocky Mountains, reaching out toward the Pacific coast. In 1845 John Louis O'Sullivan, editor of the *United States Magazine and Democratic Review*, gave a name to this bumptious spirit of expansion. "Our manifest destiny," he wrote, "is to overspread the continent allotted by Providence for the free development of our yearly multiplying millions." Traders and trappers, as always, were the harbingers of empire, and an unguarded boundary was no barrier to their entering Mexican borderlands sparsely peopled and scarcely governed from the remote capital.

REACHING THE ROCKIES   One of the first magnets to draw Americans was Santa Fe, a remote outpost of the Spanish empire founded in the seventeenth century, the capital and trading center for a population of perhaps 60,000 in New Mexico. In September 1821 an enterprising American merchant gathered a party to head up the Arkansas River on a horse-trading expedition. The men stumbled onto a group of Mexican soldiers who received them hospitably with the news that Mexico was newly independent and that American traders were welcome in Santa Fe, where the party then sold their goods for Spanish silver dollars. A second expedition in 1822 followed a new desert route along the Cimarron River. Word spread quickly and every spring thereafter merchants gathered at Independence, Missouri, for the long journey of wagon trains along the Santa Fe Trail. The trade never involved more than one or two hundred merchants, but it was a profitable enterprise in which American goods were traded for the gold, silver, and furs of the Mexicans. In 1843 trouble over the Texas question caused the Mexican government to close the trade.

The Santa Fe traders had pioneered more than a new trail. They showed that heavy wagons could cross the plains and penetrate the mountains, and they developed the technique of organized caravans for mutual protection. They also began to discover the weakness of Mexico's control over its northern borderlands, and to implant in American minds their contempt for the "mongrel" population of the region. From the 1820s on, however, that population had begun to include a few Americans who lingered in Santa Fe or Taos, using them as jumping-off points for hunting and trapping expeditions northward and westward.

The more important avenue for the fur trade, however, was the Missouri River with its many tributaries. The heyday of the mountain fur trade began in 1822 when a Missouri businessman

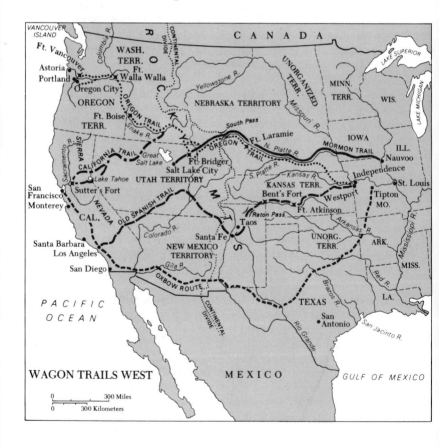

WAGON TRAILS WEST

George Caleb Bingham's Fur Traders Descending the Missouri *(1845).*

sent his first trading party to the upper Missouri. By the mid-1820s there developed the "rendezvous system," in which trappers, traders, and Indians from all over the Rocky Mountain country gathered annually at some designated place, usually in or near the Grand Tetons, in order to trade. But by 1840 the great days of the western fur trade were over. The streams no longer teemed with beavers. The country was trapped out, and the animals were saved from extinction only by the caprice of fashion, which now decreed that men's dress hats should be made of silk rather than beaver skins.

But during the 1820s and 1830s the trade had sired a uniquely reckless breed of "mountain men," who deserted civilization for the pursuit of the beaver, reverted to a primitive existence in the wilderness, sometimes in splendid isolation, sometimes in the shelter of primitive forts, and sometimes among the Indians. They were the first to find their way around in the Rocky Mountains and they pioneered the trails over which settlers by the 1840s were beginning to flood the Oregon country and trickle across the border into California.

THE OREGON COUNTRY   Beyond the mountains the Oregon country stretched from the Forty-second Parallel north to 54° 40′, between which Spain and Russia had given up their claims, leaving Great Britain and the United States as the only claimants. Under the Convention of 1818 the two countries had agreed to "joint occupation." Until the 1830s, however, joint occupation had been a legal technicality, because the only American pres-

ence was the occasional mountain man who wandered into the
Pacific slope or the infrequent trading vessel from Boston,
Salem, or New York.

The effective impulse for American settlement came finally
from an unlikely source. In 1833 the *Christian Advocate and
Herald,* a Methodist journal, published a fanciful letter from an
educated Wyandot Indian. It told of western tribesmen who
wanted the white man's "Book of Heaven" and missionaries to
instruct them in the Christian faith. Soon every pulpit and
church paper was echoing this fictitious request, and before the
year was ended the Methodist Missionary Society had established a mission in the fertile Willamette Valley, south of the Columbia.

Glowing reports returned east on the attractions of Oregon,
and the Methodist mission became the chief magnet for settlement there. By the late 1830s a trickle of emigrants was flowing
along the Oregon Trail. In 1841 and 1842 the first sizable wagon
trains made the trip, and in 1843 the movement began to assume
the proportions of mass migrations. That year about a thousand
overlanders followed the trail westward from Independence,
Missouri, along the Platte River into Wyoming, through South
Pass down to Fort Bridger (abode of a celebrated Mountain Man,
Jim Bridger), then down the Snake River to the Columbia and

Ferriage of the Platte, July 1849. *The Mormons did a thriving business
ferrying emigrants bound for Oregon across the Platte River. This sketch
shows overlanders improvising their own ferry.*

along the Columbia to their goal in the Willamette Valley. By 1845 there were about 5,000 settlers in the region.

EYEING CALIFORNIA   California, thinly peopled by mission friars and Mexican rancheros, had drawn New England ships into an illegal traffic in sea-otter skins before the end of the eighteenth century. By the late 1820s American trappers wandered in from time to time and American ships began to enter the "hide and tallow" trade. The ranchos of California produced cowhide and beef tallow in large quantity and both products enjoyed a brisk demand, cowhides mainly for shoes and the tallow chiefly for candles. Ships from Boston, Salem, or New York, well stocked with trade goods, struggled southward around Cape Horn and northward to the customs office at the California capital of Monterey. From there the ships worked their way down the coast, stopping to sell their goods and take on return cargoes. Richard Henry Dana's *Two Years before the Mast* (1840), a classic account of his adventures as a seaman in the trade, brought the scene vividly to life for his many readers and focused their attention on the romance and the potential of California.

By the mid-1830s shippers began setting up agents on the scene to buy the hides and store them until a company ship arrived. One of these agents, Thomas O. Larkin at Monterey, was destined to play a leading role in the American acquisition of California. Larkin stuck pretty much to his trade, operating a retail business on the side, while others branched out and struck it rich in ranching. The most noteworthy of the traders, however, was not American, but Swiss. John A. Sutter had tried the Santa Fe trade first, then found his way to California via Oregon, Hawaii, and Alaska. In Monterey he persuaded the Mexican governor to give him land on which to plant a colony of Swiss emigrés.

At the juncture of the Sacramento and American Rivers (later the site of Sacramento) he built an enormous enclosure that guarded an entire village of settlers and shops. At New Helvetia (Americans called it Sutter's Fort), completed in 1843, no Swiss colony materialized, but the enclosure became the mecca for Americans bent on settling the Sacramento country. It stood at the end of what became the most traveled route through the Sierras, the California Trail, which forked off from the Oregon Trail and led through the mountains near Lake Tahoe. By the start of 1846 there were perhaps 800 Americans in California, along with some 8,000–12,000 Californios of Spanish descent.

The way west remained fraught with the dangers of heat, cold, food and water shortages, disease, Indian conflict, and accident.

John Charles Frémont, the Pathfinder.

The most tragic case, no doubt, was the fate of the party led by George Donner, stranded by snow in the Sierras through the winter of 1846–1847. Several relief parties came to their rescue through the winter, but only forty of eighty-seven lived through the ordeal. The survivors resorted to cannibalism as their supplies ran out.

The premier press agent for California, and the Far West generally, was John Charles Frémont, the Pathfinder—who mainly found paths that the Mountain Men showed him. In the early 1840s his new father-in-law, Missouri Sen. Thomas Hart Benton, arranged the explorations toward Oregon that made him famous. In 1842 he mapped the Oregon Trail beyond South Pass—and met Christopher Carson, one of the most knowledgeable of the mountain men. Carson became Frémont's frequent associate, and as Kit Carson, the most famous frontiersman after Daniel Boone. In 1843–1844 Frémont went on to Oregon, then made a heroic sweep down the eastern slopes of the Sierras, headed southward through the central valley of California, bypassed the mountains in the south, and returned via Great Salt Lake. His reports on both expeditions, published together in 1845, enjoyed a career rare for a government document. In numerous popular reprints they gained a wide circulation.

American presidents, beginning with Jackson, tried to acquire at least northern California, down to San Francisco Bay, by purchase from Mexico. Jackson reasoned that as a free state California could balance the future admission of Texas as a slave state. But Jackson's agent had to be recalled after a clumsy effort to bribe Mexican officials. Tyler's minister to Mexico resumed talks, but they ended abruptly after a bloodless comic-opera conquest of Monterey by the commander of the American Pacific Fleet, who had heard a false rumor of war.

Rumors flourished that the British and French were scheming to grab California, though neither government had such intentions. Political conditions in Mexico left the remote territory in near anarchy much of the time, as governors came and went in rapid succession. Amid the chaos substantial Californios reasoned that they would be better off if they cut ties to Mexico altogether. Some favored an independent state, perhaps under French or British protection. A larger group, led by a Sonoma cattleman, admired the balance of central and local authority in the United States and felt their interests might best be served by American annexation. By the time the Americans were ready to fire the spark of rebellion in California, there was little will to resist.

ANNEXING TEXAS

AMERICAN SETTLEMENTS Manifest Destiny was most clearly at work in the most accessible of all the Mexican borderlands, Texas. There more Americans were resident than in all the other coveted regions combined. Many claimed in fact, if with little evidence, that Texas had been part of the Louisiana Purchase, abandoned only when John Quincy Adams had accepted a boundary at the Sabine River in 1819. Adams himself, as president, tried to make up for the loss by offering to buy Texas for $1 million, but Mexico refused both that and a later offer of $5 million, from Jackson. Meanwhile, however, it was rapidly turning into an American province, for Mexico welcomed American settlers there.

First and foremost among the promoters of Anglo-American settlement was Stephen F. Austin, a resident of Missouri, who gained from Mexico confirmation of a huge land grant originally given to his father by Spanish authorities. Indeed before Mexican independence from Spain was fully won he had begun a colony on the lower Brazos River late in 1821, and by 1824 had more than 2,000 settlers on his lands. In 1825, under a National Colonization Law, the state of Coahuila-Texas offered large tracts to *empresarios* who promised to sponsor immigrants. Most of the newcomers were southern farmers drawn to rich new cotton lands going for only a few cents an acre. By 1830 the coastal region of eastern Texas had approximately 20,000 white settlers and 1,000 Negro slaves brought in to work the cotton.

At that point the Mexican government took alarm at the flood of strangers who threatened to engulf the province. A new edict forbade further immigration, and troops moved to the frontier to enforce the law. But illegal American immigrants moved across the long border as easily as illegal Mexican immigrants would later cross over in the other direction. By 1835 the American population had grown to around 30,000, about ten times the number of Mexicans in Texas. Friction mounted in 1832 and 1833 as Americans organized conventions to demand a state of their own, separate from Coahuila. Instead of granting Texans their own state, General Santa Anna, who had seized power in Mexico, dissolved the national congress late in 1834, abolished the federal system, and became dictator of a centralized state. Texans rose in rebellion, summoned a convention which, like the earlier Continental Congress, adopted a "Declaration of Causes" for taking up arms, and pledged to fight for the old Mexican constitution. On March 2, 1836, however, the Texans declared their independence as Santa Anna approached with an army of conquest.

INDEPENDENCE FROM MEXICO   The Mexican army delivered its first blow at San Antonio, where it had already brought under siege a small Texas garrison holed up behind the adobe walls of an abandoned mission, the Alamo. On March 6, four days after the declaration of independence, the Mexican force of 4,000 launched a frontal assault and, taking fearful losses, finally swarmed over the walls and annihiliated the 187 Texans in the Alamo, including their commander William B. Travis and the frontier heroes Davy Crockett and Jim Bowie, slave smuggler and inventor of the Bowie knife. It was a complete victory, but a costly one. The defenders of the Alamo sold their lives at the cost of 1,544 Mexicans, and inspired the rest of Texas to fanatical resistance.

Commander-in-chief of the Texas forces was Sam Houston, a Tennessee frontiersman who had learned war under the tutelage of Old Hickory at Horseshoe Bend, had later represented the Nashville district in Congress, and had moved to Texas only three years before. Houston beat a strategic retreat eastward, gathering reinforcements as he went, including volunteer recruits from the United States. Just west of the San Jacinto River he finally paused near the site of the city that later bore his name, and on April 21, 1836, surprised a Mexican encampment there. The Texans charged, yelling "Remember the Alamo," over-

Sam Houston, president of the Republic of Texas before it was annexed by the United States.

whelmed the Mexican force within fifteen minutes, and took Santa Anna prisoner. The Mexican dictator bought his freedom at the price of a treaty recognizing Texan independence, with the Rio Grande as the boundary. The Mexican Congress repudiated the treaty, but the war was at an end.

THE MOVE FOR ANNEXATION   The Lone Star Republic then drafted a constitution, made Houston its first president, and voted almost unanimously for annexation to the United States as soon as the opportunity arose. Houston's old friend Jackson was still president, but even Old Hickory could be discreet when delicacy demanded it. The addition of a new slave state at a time when Congress was beset with abolitionist petitions threatened a serious sectional quarrel which might endanger the election of Van Buren. Worse than that, it raised the spectre of war with Mexico. Jackson kept his counsel and even delayed recognition of the Texas Republic until his last day in office. Van Buren shied away from the issue of annexation during his entire term as president.

Rebuffed in Washington, Texans turned their thoughts to a separate destiny. Under President Mirabeau Bonaparte Lamar, elected in 1838, they began to talk of expanding to the Pacific as a new nation that would rival the United States. France and Britain extended recognition and began to develop trade relations. Texas supplied them an independent source of cotton, new markets, and promised also to become an obstacle to American expansion. The British, who had emancipated slaves in their colonies in 1833, hoped Texans might embrace abolition as the price of guarantees against Mexico.

The Texans, however, had never abandoned their hopes of annexation. Reports of growing British influence created anxieties in the United States government and among southern slaveholders, who became the chief advocates of annexation. Secret negotiations with Texas began in 1843, and that April John C. Calhoun, Tyler's secretary of state, completed a treaty which went to the Senate for ratification.

Calhoun chose this moment also to send the British minister a letter instructing him on the blessings of slavery and stating that annexation of Texas was needed to foil the British abolitionists. Publication of the note fostered the claim that annexation was planned less in the national interest than to promote the expansion of slavery. It was so worded, one observer wrote Jackson, as to "drive off every northern man from the support of the measure." Sectional division, plus fear of a war with Mexico, contributed to the Senate's overwhelming rejection of the treaty. Solid Whig opposition contributed more than anything to its defeat.

POLK'S PRESIDENCY

THE ELECTION OF 1844 Prudent leaders in both political parties had hoped to keep this divisive issue out of the 1844 campaign. Clay and Van Buren, the leading candidates, had reached the same conclusion about Texas: when the treaty was submitted to the Senate, they both wrote letters opposing annexation because it would create the danger of war. Both letters, dated three days apart, appeared in separate Washington newspapers on April 27, 1844. Clay's "Raleigh letter" (written while he was on a southern tour) added that annexation was "dangerous to the integrity of the Union . . . and not called for by any general expression of public opinion." The outcome of the Whig convention in Baltimore seemed to bear out his view. Party leaders showed no qualms about Clay's stance. The convention nominated him unanimously, and the Whig platform omitted any reference to Texas.

The Democratic convention was a different story. Van Buren's southern supporters, including Jackson, abandoned him. With the convention deadlocked, on the eighth ballot expansionist forces brought forward James K. Polk of Tennessee, and on the ninth ballot he became the first "dark horse" candidate to win a major-party nomination. The party platform took an unequivocal stand favoring expansion, and to win support in the North and West as well as the South it linked the questions of Oregon and

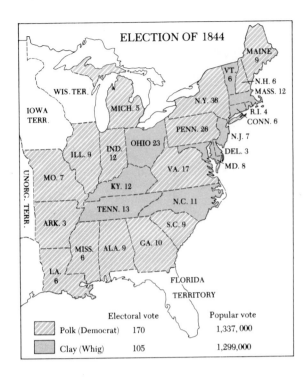

ELECTION OF 1844

	Electoral vote	Popular vote
Polk (Democrat)	170	1,337,000
Clay (Whig)	105	1,299,000

Texas: "our title to the whole of the territory of Oregon is clear and unquestionable," the party proclaimed, and called for "the reoccupation of Oregon and the reannexation of Texas."

The combination of southern and western expansionism was a winning strategy, so popular that Clay began to hedge his statement on Texas. While he still believed the integrity of the Union the chief consideration, he had "no personal objection to the annexation of Texas" if it could be achieved "without dishonor, without war, with the common consent of the Union, and upon just and fair terms." His explanation seemed clear enough, but prudence was no match for spread-eagle oratory and the emotional pull of Manifest Destiny. The net result of Clay's stand was to turn more antislavery votes to the Liberty party, which increased its count from about 7,000 in 1840 to more than 62,000 in 1844. In the western counties of New York the Liberty party drew enough votes away from the Whigs to give the state to Polk. With New York, Clay would have carried the election by seven electoral votes. Polk won a narrow plurality of 38,000 popular votes nationwide (the first president to win without a majority) but a clear majority of the electoral college, 170 to 105.

James Knox Polk, in a daguerrotype by Mathew Brady.

"Who is James K. Polk?" the Whigs scornfully asked in the campaign. But the man was not as obscure as they implied. He was a dark horse only in the sense that he was not a candidate before the convention. Born near Charlotte, North Carolina, trained in mathematics and the classics at the University of North Carolina, Polk had moved to Tennessee as a young man. A successful lawyer and planter, he had entered politics early, served fourteen years in Congress (four as Speaker of the House) and two as governor of Tennessee. Young Hickory, as his partisans liked to call him, had none of Jackson's charisma, but shared his prejudices and made up for his lack of color by stubborn determination and hard work, which destroyed his health during four years in the White House. March 4, 1845, was dark and rainy; Polk delivered his inaugural address to "a large assemblage of umbrellas," as John Quincy Adams described it. The speech was as colorless as the day, a recitation of Jeffersonian and Jacksonian principles in which Polk denounced protective tariffs, national banks, and implied powers, and again claimed title to Oregon.

POLK'S PROGRAM   In domestic affairs Young Hickory hewed to the principle of the old hero, but the new Jacksonians subtly reflected the growing influence of the slaveholding South within the party. Abolitionism, Polk warned, could bring the dissolution of the Union. Antislavery northerners had already begun to drift away from the Democratic party, which they complained was coming to represent the slaveholding interest.

Soon after Polk took office he explained his objectives to the historian George Bancroft, his navy secretary. His major objectives were reduction of the tariff, reestablishment of the Independent Treasury, settlement of the Oregon question, and the acquisition of California. He got them all. The Walker Tariff of 1846 replaced specific or flat duties with *ad valorem* (or percentage) duties, and in keeping with Democratic tradition, reduced the tariff to an average level of about 26.5 percent. In the same year Polk persuaded Congress to restore the Independent Treasury, which the Whigs had eliminated. Twice Polk vetoed internal improvement bills. In each case his blows to the American System of Henry Clay's Whigs satisfied the urges of the slaveholding South, but at the cost of annoying northern protectionists and westerners who favored internal improvements.

THE STATE OF TEXAS   But the chief focus of Polk's concern remained geographical expansion. He privately vowed to Bancroft his purpose of acquiring California, and New Mexico as well, preferably by purchase. The acquisition of Texas was already under way before Polk took office. In his final months in office President Tyler, taking Polk's election as a mandate to act, asked Congress to accomplish annexation by joint resolution, which required only a simple majority in each house and avoided the two-thirds Senate vote needed to ratify a treaty. Congress had read the election returns too, and after a bitter debate over slavery, the resolution passed by votes of 27 to 25 in the Senate and 120 to 98 in the House. Tyler signed the resolution on March 1, 1845, offering to admit Texas to statehood. The new state would keep its public lands but pay its own war debt, and with its own consent might be divided into as many as five states in the near future. A Texas convention accepted the offer in July, the voters of Texas ratified the action in October, and the new state formally entered the Union on December 29, 1845.

OREGON   Meanwhile the Oregon issue heated up as expansionists aggressively insisted that Polk abandon previous offers to settle on the Forty-ninth Parallel and stand by the platform pledge to take all of Oregon. The bumptious expansionists were prepared to risk war with Britain while relations with Mexico were simultaneously moving toward the breaking point. "Fifty-four forty or fight," they intoned. "All of Oregon or none." In his inaugural address Polk declared the American title to Oregon "clear and unquestionable," but privately he favored a prudent compromise. War with Mexico was brewing; the territory up to 54° 40′ seemed of less importance than Puget Sound or the ports of California, on which the British also were thought to have an eye.

Since Monroe each administration had offered to extend the boundary along the Forty-ninth Parallel. In July 1845 Polk renewed the offer, only to have it refused by the British minister, Richard Pakenham.

Polk withdrew the offer and went back to his claim to all of Oregon. In the annual message to Congress at year's end, he asked for permission to give a year's notice that joint occupation would be abrogated, and revived the Monroe Doctrine with a new twist: "The people of *this continent* alone have the right to decide their own destiny." To a hesitant congressman he avowed that "the only way to treat John Bull was to look him straight in the eye." After a long and bitter debate Congress adopted the resolution, but Polk was playing a bluff game. War with Mexico seemed increasingly certain and Secretary of State Buchanan privately assured the British government that any new offer would be submitted to the Senate.

Fortunately for Polk the British government had no enthusiasm for war over that remote wilderness at the cost of profitable trade relations with the United States. From the British viewpoint, the only land in dispute all along had been between the Forty-ninth Parallel and the Columbia River. Now the fur trade of the region was a dying industry. In early June 1846 the British government submitted a draft treaty to extend the border along the Forty-ninth Parallel and through the main channel south of Vancouver Island. On June 15 Buchanan and British Minister Pakenham signed it, and three days later it was ratified in the

American Settlement of Oregon City, 1846. *At the time the American settlement consisted of "two churches, and 100 houses, stores, & all of which have been built within five years."*

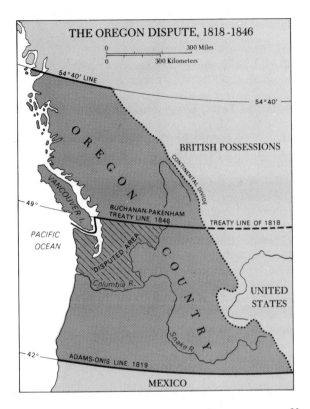

THE OREGON DISPUTE, 1818-1846

300 Miles

300 Kilometers

54°40' LINE

54°40'

BRITISH POSSESSIONS

CONTINENTAL DIVIDE

O R E G O N

VANCOUVER I.

49°

BUCHANAN-PAKENHAM
TREATY LINE 1846

TREATY LINE OF 1818

PACIFIC
OCEAN

DISPUTED AREA

Columbia R.

C O U N T R Y

UNITED
STATES

Snake R.

42°

ADAMS-ONIS LINE 1819

MEXICO

Senate, where the only opposition came from a group of bitter-end expansionists representing the Old Northwest who wanted more. Most of the country was satisfied. Southerners cared less about Oregon than about Texas, and northern business interests valued British trade more than they valued Oregon. Besides, the country was already at war with Mexico.

THE MEXICAN WAR

THE OUTBREAK OF WAR Relations with Mexico had gone from bad to worse. On March 6, 1845, two days after Polk took office, the Mexican ambassador broke off relations and left for home to protest the annexation of Texas. When an effort at negotiation failed, Polk focused his efforts on unilateral initiatives. Already he was egging on American intrigues in California. On October 17, 1845, he had written Consul Thomas O. Larkin in Monterey that the president would make no effort to induce California into the Union, but "if the people should desire to unite their destiny with ours, they would be received as brethren." Larkin, who could take a hint, began to line up Americans and sympathetic Californios. Meanwhile Polk ordered American troops under Gen. Zachary Taylor to take up positions on the Rio Grande in the new state of Texas. These positions lay in territory that was doubly disputed: Mexico recognized neither the American annexation of Texas nor the Rio Grande boundary.

The last hope for peace died when John Slidell, sent to Mexico City to negotiate a settlement, finally gave up on his mission in March 1846. Polk then resolved that he could achieve his purposes only by force. He sought and got the cabinet's approval of a war message to Congress. That very evening, May 9, the news arrived that Mexicans had attacked American soldiers north of the Rio Grande. Eleven Americans were killed, five wounded, and the remainder taken prisoner.

In his war message Polk could now take the high ground that the war was a response to aggression, a recognition that war had been forced upon the United States. "The cup of forbearance had been exhausted" before the incident; now, he said, Mexico "has passed the boundary of the United States, has invaded our territory, and shed American blood upon the American soil." The House quickly passed the war resolution, 174 to 14. The Senate followed suit on the next day by 40 to 2 with 3 abstentions, including Calhoun who feared that acquiring new territory would inflame the slavery issue. Polk signed the declaration of war on May 13, 1846. Both votes exaggerated the extent of support for the war. In the House twenty-seven members favored an amendment stating that the resolution should not be construed as approval of Polk's moving troops into the disputed area between the Nueces and the Rio Grande. The House authorized a call for 50,000 volunteers and a war appropriation of $10 million, but sixty-seven Whigs voted against that measure, another token of rising opposition to the war.

OPPOSITION TO THE WAR   In the Mississippi Valley, where expansion fever ran high, the war was immensely popular. But farther away from the scene of action there was less enthusiasm for "Mr. Polk's War." Whigs ranged from lukewarm to hostile. John Quincy Adams, who voted against participation, called it "a most unrighteous war." An obscure one-term congressman from Illinois named Abraham Lincoln, upon taking his seat in December 1847, began introducing "spot resolutions," calling on Polk to name the spot where American blood had been shed on American soil. If he were Mexican, Sen. Thomas Corwin of Ohio said, he would ask: "Have you not room in your own country to bury your dead men? If they come into mine, we will greet you, with bloody hands, and welcome you to hospitable graves."

Once again, as in 1812, New England was a hotbed of opposition, largely in the belief that this war was the work of "Land-Jobbers and Slave-Jobbers." As the Massachusetts poet James Russell Lowell put it in his *Biglow Papers*:

> They just want this Californy
> So's to lug new slave-states in
> To abuse ye, an' to scorn ye,
> An' to plunder ye like sin.

Some New England men, including Lowell, were ready to separate from the slave states, and the Massachusetts legislature formally pronounced the conflict a war of conquest. But before the war ended some antislavery men had a change of heart. Mexican territory seemed so unsuited to plantation staples that they endorsed expansion in hope of enlarging the area of free soil. Manifest Destiny exerted a potent influence even on those who opposed the war. *The Harbinger*, house organ of Brook Farm, managed to have it both ways. "This plundering aggression," the paper editorialized, "is monstrously iniquitous, but after all it seems to be completing a more universal design of Providence of extending the power and intelligence of advanced civilized nations."

PREPARING FOR BATTLE   Both the United States and Mexico approached the war ill-prepared. American policy had been incredibly reckless, risking war with both Britain and Mexico while doing nothing to strenghten the armed forces until war came. At the outset of war the regular army numbered barely over 7,000 in contrast to the Mexican force of 32,000. Before the war ended the American force grew to 104,000, of whom about 31,000 were regular army troops and marines. Most of these were six- and twelve-month volunteers from the West. Volunteer militia companies, often filled with frontier toughs, made up as raunchy a crew as ever graced the American military—innocent of uniforms, standard equipment, and discipline alike. One observer watched a band of such recruits with "torn and dirty shirts—uncombed heads—unwashed faces" trying to drill, "all hollowing, cursing, yelling like so many incarnate fiends." Repeatedly, despite the best efforts of the commanding generals, these undisciplined forces ran out of control in plunder, rape, and murder.

Nevertheless, being used to a rough-and-tumble life, they overmatched larger Mexican forces which had their own problems with training, discipline, and munitions. Mexican artillery pieces were generally obsolete, and the powder so faulty that American soldiers could often dodge cannon balls that fell short and bounced ineffectively along the ground.

The United States entered the war without even a tentative plan of action. One had to be worked out hastily, and politics complicated things. What Polk wanted, Thomas Hart Benton wrote later, was "a small war, just large enough to require a treaty of peace, and not large enough to make military reputations, dangerous for the presidency." Winfield Scott, general-in-chief of the army, was both a Whig and politically ambitious. Nevertheless Polk named him at first to take charge of the Rio Grande front. When Scott fell into disputes with Polk's secretary of war, the exasperated president withdrew the appointment. Scott, already known as "Old Fuss and Feathers" for his insistence on proper uniform, had also a genius for absurd turns of phrase. He began an indignant reply to the secretary of war with the remark that he got the secretary's letter as he "sat down to take a hasty plate of soup." One Washington wit promptly dubbed him Marshal Tureen.

There seemed now a better choice. Zachary Taylor's men had scored two victories over Mexican forces north of the Rio Grande, at Palo Alto (May 8) and Resaca de la Palma (May 9). On May 18 Taylor crossed over and occupied Matamoros, which a demoralized and bloodied Mexican army had abandoned. These quick victories brought Taylor instant popularity and the presi-

Zachary Taylor, "Old Rough and Ready." This daguerrotype was made around the time of the Mexican War.

dent responded willingly to the demand that he be made commander for the conquest of Mexico. "Old Rough and Ready" Taylor, a thickset and none-too-handsome man of sixty-one, seemed unlikely stuff from which to fashion a hero and impressed Polk as less of a political threat than Scott. Taylor acted at least as cautiously as Scott, awaiting substantial reinforcements and supplies before moving any deeper into Mexico. But without a major battle he had achieved Polk's main objective, the conquest of Mexico's northern provinces.

ANNEXATION OF CALIFORNIA Along the Pacific coast, conquest was under way before definite news of the Mexican war arrived. Near the end of 1845 John C. Frémont brought out a band of sixty frontiersmen ostensibly on another exploration of California and Oregon. "Frémont's conduct was extremely mysterious," John A. Sutter wrote. "Flitting about the country with an armed body of men, he was regarded with suspicion by everybody." When the commandant at Monterey ordered him out of the Salinas Valley, Frémont occupied the peak of Gavilan Mountain and defied the Mexicans to oust him, but soon changed his mind and headed for Oregon. In June 1846 Frémont and his men moved south into the Sacramento Valley. Americans in the area fell upon Sonoma on June 14, proclaimed a president of the "Republic of California," and hoisted the hastily designed Bear Flag, a California Grizzly and star painted on white cloth—a version of which became the state flag.

By the end of June Frémont had endorsed the Bear Flag Republic and set out for Monterey. Before he arrived, the commodore of the Pacific Fleet, having heard of the outbreak of hostilities, sent a party ashore to raise the American flag and proclaim California a part of the United States. The Republic of California had lasted less than a month and most Californians of whatever origin welcomed a change that promised order in preference to the confusion of the unruly Bear Flaggers.

Before the end of July a new commodore, Robert F. Stockton, began preparations to move against southern California. As senior officer on the scene, Stockton enlisted Frémont's band as the California Battalion and gave Frémont the rank of major. This group he sent down to San Diego too late to overtake the fleeing Mexican loyalists. In a more leisurely fashion, then, Stockton occupied Santa Barbara and Los Angeles. By mid-August resistance had dissipated. On August 17 Stockton declared himself governor, with Frémont as military commander in the north.

The Battle of the Plains of Mesa took place just before American forces entered Los Angeles. This sketch was made at the scene.

By August another expedition was closing on Santa Fe. On August 18 Stephen Kearny and his men entered the Mexican town, whence an irresolute governor had fled with its defenders. After setting up a civilian governor, Kearny divided his remaining force, leading 300 dragoons west toward California in late September. On October 6 they encountered a band of frontiersmen under Frémont's old helper, Kit Carson, who was riding eastward with news that California had already fallen. Kearny sent 200 of his men back and with the remaining 100 pushed west with Carson serving as a reluctant guide.

But after Carson's departure from the coast, the picture had changed. In southern California, where most of the poorer Mexicans and Mexicanized Indians resented American rule, a rebellion broke out. By the end of October the rebels had ousted the token American force in southern California. Kearny walked right into this rebel zone when he arrived. At San Diego he met up with Stockton and joined him in the reconquest of southern California, which they achieved after two brief clashes when they entered Los Angeles on January 10, 1847. Rebel forces capitulated on January 13.

TAYLOR'S BATTLES   Both California and New Mexico had been taken before Gen. Zachary Taylor fought his first major battle in northern Mexico. Having waited for more men and munitions, Taylor finally moved out of his Matamoros base in September 1846 and headed southward toward the heart of Mexico. His first goal was the fortified city of Monterrey, in Nuevo León, which he took after a five-day seige. Polk, however, was none too happy with the easy terms to which Taylor agreed, nor with Taylor's growing popularity. The whole episode merely confirmed the president's impression that Taylor was too passive to be trusted further with the major campaign. Besides, his victories, if flawed, were leading to talk of Taylor as the next Whig candidate for president.

But Polk's grand strategy was itself flawed. Having never seen the Mexican desert, Polk wrongly assumed that Taylor could live off the country and need not depend on resupply. Polk therefore misunderstood the general's reluctance to strike out across several hundred miles of barren land in front of Mexico City. The president was simply duped on another point. The old dictator Santa Anna, forced out in 1844, got word to Polk from his exile in

THE MEXICAN WAR:
MAJOR CAMPAIGNS
◄━ U.S. forces ◄━ Mexican forces
✳ Battle site
-·-·- Line set by Treaty of Guadalupe Hidalgo, 1848

0   400 Miles
0   400 Kilometers

Havana that in return for the right considerations he could bring about a settlement. Polk in turn assured the Mexican leader that Washington would pay well for any territory taken through a settlement. In August 1846, after another overturn in the Mexican government, Santa Anna was permitted to pass through the American blockade into Vera Cruz. Soon he was again in command of the Mexican army and then was named president once more. The consequence of Polk's intrigue was to put perhaps the ablest Mexican general back in command of the enemy army, where he busily organized his forces to strike at Taylor.

By then another front had been opened and Taylor was consigned to inactivity. In October 1846 Polk and his cabinet decided to move against Mexico City by way of Vera Cruz. Polk would have preferred a Democratic general, but for want of a better choice named Winfield Scott to the field command. In January 1847 Taylor was required to give up most of his regulars to Scott's force gathering at Tampico. Taylor, miffed at his reduction to a minor role, disobeyed orders and advanced beyond Saltillo.

There, near the hacienda of Buena Vista, Santa Anna met Taylor's untested volunteers with a large but ill-trained and tired army. In the hard-fought Battle of Buena Vista (February 22–23, 1847) neither side could claim victory on the strength of the outcome, but Taylor was convinced that only his lack of regulars prevented him from striking a decisive blow. In any case it was the last major action on the northern front, and Taylor was granted leave to return home.

SCOTT'S TRIUMPH   The long-planned assault on the enemy capital had begun on March 9, 1847, when Scott's army landed on the beaches south of Vera Cruz. It was the first major amphibious operation by American military forces, and was carried out without loss. Vera Cruz surrendered on March 27 after a weeklong siege. Scott then set out on the route taken by Cortés more than 300 years before. Santa Anna tried to set a trap for him at the mountain pass of Cerro Gordo, but Scott's men took more than 3,000 prisoners, large quantities of equipment and provisions, and the Mexican president's personal effects.

On May 15 Scott's men entered Puebla, the second city of Mexico. There Scott lost about a third of his army. Men whose twelve-month enlistments had expired felt free to go home, leaving Scott with about 7,000 troops in all. There was nothing to do but hang on until reinforcements and new supplies came up from the coast. After three months, with his numbers almost

Winfield Scott takes Mexico City after his defeat of Santa Anna.

doubled, Scott set out on August 7 through the mountain passes into the valley of Mexico, cutting his supply line to the coast. The aging duke of Wellington, following the campaign from afar, predicted: Scott "is lost—he cannot capture the city and he cannot fall back upon his base."

But Scott directed a brilliant flanking operation around the lakes and marshes which guarded the eastern approaches to Mexico City, then another around the Mexican defenses at San Antonio. In the battles of Contreras and Churubusco (both on August 20) Scott's army overwhelmed Mexican defenses on the way to the capital. In those defeats Santa Anna lost a third of his forces and had to fall back within three miles of the city. In fighting renewed after a lull, two strong points guarding the western approaches to Mexico City fell in the Battles of Molino del Rey (September 8) and Chapultepec (September 12–13). On September 13, 1847, American forces entered Mexico City and within three days mopped up the remnants of resistance. At the National Palace a batallion of marines ran up the flag and occupied the "halls of Montezuma."

THE TREATY OF GUADALUPE HIDALGO   After the fall of the capital, Santa Anna resigned and a month later left the country. Meanwhile Polk had appointed as chief peace negotiator Nicholas P. Trist, chief clerk of the State Department and a Virginia Democrat of impeccable partisan credentials. Trist was frustrated for want of anybody to negotiate with. In October Polk decided that the Mexican delays required a stronger stand and ordered Trist recalled, but before the message reached Mexico City things had changed. On November 11 the Mexican Congress elected an interim president, and on November 22 the new administration told Trist it had named commissioners to deal with him. Trist, having just received the recall notice, decided to go ahead with negotiations anyway. A sixty-five-page letter of justification did nothing to persuade Polk that he was anything but an "impudent and unqualified scoundrel," but Trist reasoned that it was better to continue than to risk a return of the war party or the disintegration of all government in Mexico.

Formal talks got under way on January 2, 1848, at the village of Guadalupe Hidalgo just outside the capital, and dragged out through the month. Finally Trist, fearing stronger orders from Washington at any time, threatened to end the negotiations and the Mexicans yielded. By the treaty of Guadalupe Hidalgo, signed on February 2, 1848, Mexico gave up all claims to Texas above the Rio Grande and ceded California and New Mexico to the United States. In return the United States agreed to pay Mexico $15 million and assume the claims of American citizens against Mexico up to a total of $3¼ million.

Miffed that Trist had ignored his orders, Polk nevertheless had little choice but to submit the treaty to the Senate. A growing movement to annex all of Mexico had impelled him to hold out for more. But as Polk confided to his diary, rejecting the treaty would be too risky. If he should reject a treaty made in accord with his own original terms in order to gain more territory, "the probability is that Congress would not grant either men or money to prosecute the war." In that case he might eventually have to withdraw the army and lose everything. The treaty went to the Senate, which ratified it on March 10, 1848. By the end of July the last remaining American soldiers had boarded ship in Vera Cruz.

THE WAR'S LEGACIES   The Mexican War had cost the United States 1,721 killed, 4,102 wounded, and far more, 11,155 dead of disease. The military and naval expenditures had been $97.7 million. For this price, and payments made under the treaty, the United States acquired more than 500,000 square miles of territory (more than a million counting Texas), including the great Pacific harbors of San Diego, Monterey, and San Francisco, with uncounted millions in mineral wealth. Except for a small addition by the Gadsden Purchase of 1853, these annexations rounded out the continental United States. Several important "firsts" are associated with the Mexican War: the first successful offensive war, the first major amphibious operation, the first occupation of an enemy capital, the first in which martial law was declared on foreign soil, the first in which West Point graduates played a major role, and the first reported by modern war correspondents like George W. Kendall of the New Orleans *Picayune*.

Manifest Destiny and images of the Golden West fired the imaginations of Americans, then and since. But the Mexican War somehow never became entrenched in the national legends. Within a few years it fell in the shadow of another and greater conflict, and was often recalled as a kind of preliminary bout in which Grant, Lee, and other great generals learned their trade as junior officers. The Mexican War never took on the dimensions of a moral crusade based on the defense of great principles. It was, transparently, a war of conquest provoked by a president bent on expansion. One might argue that Polk merely hastened, and possibly achieved at less cost in treasure and human misery, what the march of the restless frontier would soon have achieved anyway. During one term in office he annexed to Jefferson's "empire of liberty" more land than Jefferson himself, but the imperishable glamor that shone about the names of Caesar, Cortés, or Napoleon never brightened the name of Polk. For a brief season, however, the glory of conquest did shed luster on the names of Zachary Taylor and Winfield Scott. Despite Polk's best efforts, he had manufactured the next, and last, two Whig candidates for president. One of them, Taylor, would replace him in the White House, with the storm of sectional conflict already on the horizon.

FURTHER READING

For background on Whig programs and ideas, see Glyndon Van Dusen's *The Jacksonian Era, 1828–1848* (1959), Richard P. McCormick's *The Second American Party System* (1966), William R. Brock's *and Political Conscience* (1979), and Daniel W. Howe's *The Political Culture of the American Whigs* (1979).

Several works help interpret the concept of Manifest Destiny. Frederick Merk's *Manifest Destiny and Mission in American History* (1963) remains a classic. Merk takes a more diplomatic slant in *The Monroe Doctrine and American Expansionism, 1843–1849* (1966). Henry Nash

°These books are available in paperback editions.

Smith's *Virgin Land* (1950) is an interpretation of the role of the West in the American imagination.

Ray A. Billington's *Westward Expansion* (5th ed., 1982) and John D. Unruh's *The Plains Across: The Overland Emigrants and the TransMississippi West, 1840–1860* (1979)° narrate well the story of pioneer movement. Bernard De Voto's *the Wide Missouri* (1947)° concentrates on the fur trappers and the Mountain Men. Francis Parkman's *The California and Oregon Trail* (1848) is an enduring classic on the subject.

California was the promised land for many, and several scholars have concentrated on that area. Kevin Starr's *Americans and the California Dream, 1850–1915* (1973)° is a fine introduction. See also Earl Pomeroy's *The Pacific Slope: A History* (1965), which is helpful on the early history of Oregon. The Mormon migration to Utah is covered in Wallace E. Stegner's *The Gathering of Zion: The Story of the Mormon Trail* (1964), as well as works cited in Chapter 13.

The controversy over annexation of Texas is analyzed in David M. Pletcher's *The Diplomacy of Annexation: Texas, Oregon, and the Mexican War* (1973) and Frederick Merk's *Slavery and the Annexation of Texas* (1972).

Gene M. Brack's *Mexico Views Manifest Destiny, 1821–1846* (1975) takes Mexico's viewpoint on American designs on the West. On James K. Polk, see John H. Schroeder's *Mr. Polk's War* (1973). A survey of the military conflict is provided in K. Jack Bauer's *The Mexican War, 1846–1848* (1974). For a different perspective, see Robert W. Johannsen's *To the Halls of the Montezumas: The Mexican War in the American Imagination* (1984).

15

THE OLD SOUTH:
AN AMERICAN TRAGEDY

MYTH, REALITY, AND THE OLD SOUTH

SOUTHERN MYTHOLOGY Southerners, a North Carolina editor once wrote, are "a mythological people, created half out of dream and half out of slander, who live in a still legendary land." Most Americans, including southerners, carry in their minds an assorted baggage of myths about the South. Still the main burden of southern mythology is carried in those images of the Old South set during the nineteenth-century sectional conflict, or in modernized versions of them: the Sunny South of the plantation tradition or the Benighted South of the Savage Ideal.

The pattern of the first appeared full-blown at least as early as 1832 in John Pendleton Kennedy's romance, *Swallow Barn.* Every American is familiar with the euphoric pattern of kindly old massa with his mint julep on the white-columned piazza, happy "darkies" singing in fields perpetually white to the harvest, coquettish belles wooed by slender gallants underneath the moonlight and magnolias. The legend of the Southern Cavalier seemed to fulfill some psychic need for an American counterweight to the mental image of the grasping, money-grubbing Yankee.

But there are other elements in the traditional myth. Off in the piney woods and erosion-gutted clay hills, away from gentility, dwelt a depraved group known as the poor white trash: the crackers; hillbillies; sand-hillers; squatters; rag, tag, and bobtail; po' buckra to the blacks. Somewhere in the myth the respectable small farmer was lost from sight, perhaps neither romantic enough nor outrageous enough to fit in. He was absent too from the image of the Benighted South, in which the plantation myth simply appeared in reverse, as a pattern of corrupt opulence resting on human exploitation. Gentle old massa became the arrogant, haughty, imperious potentate, the very embodiment of sin, the central target of antislavery attack. He kept a seraglio in the slave quarters; he bred Negroes like cattle and sold them "down the river" to certain death in the sugar mills, separating families if that suited his purpose, while southern women suffered in silence the guilty knowledge of their men's infidelity. The "happy darkies" in this picture became white men in black skins, an oppressed people longing for freedom, the victims of countless atrocities, forever seeking a chance to follow the North Star to freedom. The masses of the white folks were, once again, poor whites, relegated to ignorance and degeneracy by the slavocracy.

THE SOUTHERN CONDITION   Everyone of course recognizes these pictures as overdrawn stereotypes, but as one historian has said, myths are made of tough stuff. Once implanted in the mind, they are hard to shake, partly because they have roots in reality. But to comprehend the distinctiveness of the Old South we must first identify the forces and factors that gave it a sense of unity. Efforts to do so usually turn on two lines of thought: the causal effects of environment (geography and climate), and the causal effects of human decisions and actions. The name of the historian Ulrich B. Phillips is associated with both. At the outset of his *Life and Labor in the Old South* (1929) Phillips wrote: "Let us begin by discussing the weather, for that has been the chief agency in making the South distinctive." It fostered the growing of staple crops, and thus the plantation system and black slavery. These things in turn brought sectional conflict and Civil War.

But while geography may render certain things possible and others impossible, explanations that involve human agency are more persuasive. In the 1830s Alexis de Tocqueville found the origins of southern distinctiveness in the institution of slavery. U. B. Phillips argued nearly a century later that with large numbers of blacks in the population, "the central theme" of southern history became "a common resolve indomitably maintained" by whites that they should retain their control. And this resolve in turn led to a sense of racial unity that muted class conflict among whites. But in the long run, the biracial character of the population influenced far more aspects of life than Phillips acknowledged. In making the culture of the South, W. J. Cash

A slave family in the cotton fields near Savannah, Georgia.

asserted in *The Mind of the South* (1941), "Negro entered into white man as profoundly as white man entered into Negro—subtly influencing every gesture, every word, every emotion and idea, every attitude." In shaping patterns of speech and folklore, of music and literature, black southerners immeasurably influenced and enriched the culture of the region.

The South differed from other sections too in its high proportion of native population, both white and black. Despite a great diversity of origins in the colonial population, the South drew few immigrants after the Revolution. One reason was that the main shipping lines went to northern ports; another, that the prospect of competing with slave labor was unattractive to immigrants. The South, one writer has said, "was created by the need to protect a peculiar institution from threats originating outside the region." After the Missouri Controversy of 1819–1821 the South became more and more a conscious minority, its population growth lagging behind that of other sections, its peculiar institution of slavery more and more an isolated and odious thing in Western civilization. Attitudes of defensiveness strongly affected its churches. The religious culture of the white South retreated from the liberalism of the Revolutionary War era into orthodoxy, which provided one line of defense against new doctrines of any kind, while black southerners found in a similar religious culture a refuge from the hardships of their lot, a promise of release on some future day of Jubilee.

Other ways in which the South was said to be different included its architecture, its peculiar work ethic, its penchant for the military, and its country-gentlemen ideal. One author, tongue in cheek, even suggested that the South was where the mule population was highest. The preponderance of farming remained a distinctive characteristic, whether pictured as the Jeffersonian yeoman living by the sweat of his brow or the lordly planter dispatching his slave gangs. In an agricultural society like the South there tended to be a greater "personalness" of human relations in contrast to the organized and contractual nature of relations in a more complex urban environment. But in the end what made the South distinctive was its people's belief, and other people's belief, that they *were* distinctive. Southernism, one historian asserted, was too elusive for a clear definition. "Poets," he wrote, "have done better in expressing the oneness of the South than historians in explaining it."

STAPLE CROPS The idea of the Cotton Kingdom is itself something of a mythic stereotype. Although cotton was the most important of the staple, or market, crops, it was a latecomer. Tobacco, the first staple crop, had earlier been the mainstay of Virginia and Maryland, and important in North Carolina. After the Revolution pioneers carried it over the mountains into Kentucky and as far as Missouri. Indigo, an important crop in colonial South Carolina, vanished with the loss of British bounties for this source of a valuable blue dye, but rice growing continued in a coastal strip that lapped over into North Carolina and Georgia. Rice growing was limited to the Tidewater because it required frequent flooding and draining of the fields, and along that sector of the coast the tides rose and fell six or seven feet. Since rice growing required substantial capital for floodgates, ditches, and machinery, its plantations were large and relatively few in number.

Sugar, like rice, called for a heavy capital investment in machinery to grind the cane, and was limited in extent because the cane was extremely susceptible to frost. An influx of refugees from the revolution in Haiti helped the development of a sugar belt centered along the Mississippi River above New Orleans. Some sugar grew in a smaller belt of eastern Texas. But it was always something of an exotic growth, better suited to a tropical climate. Since it needed the prop of a protective tariff, it produced the anomaly in southern politics of pro-tariff congressmen from Louisiana. Hemp had something of the same effect in the

Kentucky Blue Grass region and northwestern Missouri. Both flax and hemp were important to backcountry farmers at the end of the colonial era. Homespun clothing was most apt to be linsey-woolsey, a combination of linen and wool. But flax never developed more than a limited commercial market, and that mostly for linseed oil. Hemp, on the other hand, developed commercial

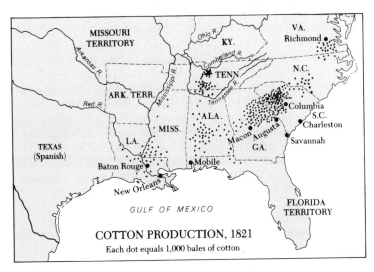

COTTON PRODUCTION, 1821
Each dot equals 1,000 bales of cotton

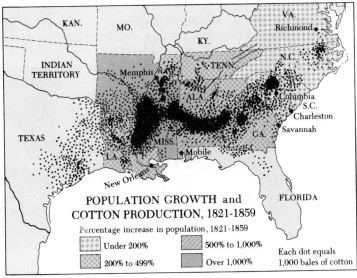

**POPULATION GROWTH and
COTTON PRODUCTION, 1821-1859**
Percentage increase in population, 1821-1859

Under 200%   500% to 1,000%

200% to 499%   Over 1,000%

Each dot equals
1,000 bales of cotton

possibilities in rope and cotton baling cloth, although it suffered heavy competition from a higher-quality Russian product.

Cotton, the last of the major staples, eventually outpaced all the others put together. At the end of the War of 1812 annual cotton production was estimated at less than 150,000 bales; in 1860 it was reported at 3.8 million. Two things accounted for the growth: the voracious market in British and French textiles, and the cultivation of new lands in the Southwest. Much of the story of the southern people—white and black—from 1820 to 1860 was their movement to fertile cotton lands farther west. The crop flourished best in the hot growing season of the Deep South. By 1860 the center of the cotton belt stretched from eastern North Carolina through the fertile Alabama-Mississippi black belts (so called for the color of both people and soil), on to Texas, and up the Mississippi Valley as far as southern Illinois. Cotton prices fell sharply after the Panic of 1837, and remained below 10¢ a pound through most of the 1840s, but they advanced above 10¢ late in 1855 and stayed there until 1860, reaching 15¢ in 1857—despite a business setback and a constantly increasing supply.

AGRICULTURAL DIVERSITY   The focus on cotton and the other cash crops has obscured the degree to which the South fed itself from its own fields. With 29.5 percent of the country's area in 1860, and 38.9 percent of its population, the slave states produced 52 percent of the nation's corn, 28.9 percent of the wheat, 19.2 percent of the oats, 19.4 percent of the rye, 10 percent of the white potatoes, and 94 percent of the sweet potatoes. The upper

Planting sweet potatoes on the Hopkinson plantation, Edisto Island, South Carolina, April 1862.

South in many areas practiced general farming in much the same way as the Northwest. Cyrus McCormick first tested his harvester in the wheatfields of Virginia. Corn grew everywhere, but went less into the market than into local consumption by man and beast, as feed and fodder, as hoecake and grits. On many farms and plantations the rhythms of the growing season permitted the labor force to alternate attention between the staples and the food crops.

Livestock added to the diversity of the farm economy. The South had in 1860 half of the nation's cattle, over 60 percent of the swine, nearly 45 percent of the horses, 52 percent of the oxen, nearly 90 percent of the mules, and nearly a third of the sheep, the last mostly in the upper South. Cattle herding prevailed on the southern frontier at one time, and persisted in areas less suited to farming, such as the piney woods of the coastal plains, the Appalachians, and the Ozarks and their foothills. Plantations and farms commonly raised livestock for home consumption.

Yet the picture was hardly one of unbroken prosperity. The South's staple crops quickly exhausted the soil, and open row crops like tobacco, cotton, and corn left the bare ground in between subject to leaching and erosion. Much of eastern Virginia by 1800 had abandoned tobacco, and in some places had turned to scrabbling wheat from the soil for the northern market. One ex-slave later recalled what he saw as a slave trader carried him across Virginia about 1805: "For several days we traversed a region, which had been deserted by the occupants—being no longer worth culture—and immense thickets of young red cedars now occupied the fields." In low-country South Carolina Sen. Robert Y. Hayne spoke of "Fields abandoned; and hospitable mansions of our fathers deserted . . . " The older farming lands had trouble competing with the newer soils farther west. But when the Panic of 1837 ended the flush times of Alabama and Mississippi, farm prices everywhere remained low until the mid-1850s. Soon western lands too began to show wear and tear. By 1855 Sen. C. C. Clay was writing of his home country in northern Alabama: "Our small planters, after taking the cream off their lands . . . are going further west and south in search of other virgin lands which they may and will despoil and impoverish in like manner." This of course happened all along the frontier. "If the Old South had greater ruins than did the other sections," one historian insisted, "it was largely because it had been more successful in quickly and cheaply garnering the riches which Nature offered and spending them in the far-away markets where the comforts and luxuries of a more advanced life might be secured."

So the Southeast and then the Southwest faced a growing sense of economic crisis as the century advanced. Proposals to deal with it followed two lines. Some argued for agricultural reform and others for diversification through industry and trade. Edmund Ruffin of Virginia stands out as perhaps the greatest of the reformers. After studying the chemistry of soils, he reasoned that most exhausted soils of the upper South had acid conditions which needed to be neutralized before they could become productive again. He turned his plantations into laboratories in which he discovered that marl from a shell deposit in eastern Virginia did the trick. Ruffin published the results in his *Essay on Calcareous Manures* (1832). Such publications and farm magazines in general, however, reached but a minority of farmers, mostly the larger and more successful planters. The same was true of the agricultural associations that sprang up in the Old South, though some of these sponsored experimental farms and agricultural fairs which became fairly common by the 1840s and 1850s, reaching farmers with examples put before their very eyes.

MANUFACTURING AND TRADE   By 1840 many thoughtful southerners reasoned that by staking everything on agriculture the region had wasted chances in manufacturing and trade. The census of 1810 had shown the South with more various and numerous manufactures than New England. The War of 1812 provided the South some stimulus for manufacturing, but the momentum was lost in the postwar flood of British imports. Then cotton growing swept everything before it. As the spread of landholding deflected concern with industry, the South became increasingly dependent on northern manufacturing and trade. Cotton and tobacco were exported mainly in northern vessels. In 1830 southern ship tonnage of 109,000 was less than a third of the North's 360,000; by 1860 the South's 855,000 was little more than a fifth of the North's 4 million. Southerners also relied on connections in the North for imported goods. The South became, economically if not formally, a kind of colonial dependency of the North.

The South's dependence on the North inspired a series of commercial conventions which commenced with a meeting at Augusta, Georgia, in 1837, and continued almost every year through the next two decades. The call for the first convention set forth a theme that would run through them all. The merchants of northern cities, it said, "export our . . . valuable productions, and import our articles of consumption and from this agency they derive a profit which has enriched them . . . at our expense."

Along with the call for direct trade in southern ships went a movement for a more diversified economy, for native industries to balance agriculture and trade. Southern publicists called attention to the section's great resources: its raw materials, labor supply, waterpower, wood and coal, and markets. The chief vehicle for the advocates of economic development, and the leading economic journal of the South, came to be *The Commercial Review of the South and the Southwest*, edited by James D. B. De Bow.

De Bow's contemporary, William Gregg, began promoting textiles in South Carolina during the 1840s, when he bought into an early cotton mill and successfully reorganized it. After travels in New England, he wrote a series of articles for a Charleston paper advocating southern industrial development. These pieces appeared in 1845 as a pamphlet: *Essays on Domestic Industry*. About a year later he began construction of the Graniteville Manufacturing Company. Built of native granite by local labor, the mill still survives. Adjoining the mill he built a model village with good homes, a school, library, churches, infirmary, and recreational facilities. The project was a success from the start, paying dividends in a few years of up to 8 percent.

In Richmond, Virginia, the Tredegar Iron Works grew into the most important single manufacturing enterprise in the Old South. Launched in 1837, the company in 1848 fell under the control of Joseph Reid Anderson, for several years its sales agent, before that a graduate of West Point and an army engineer. His military connections brought Tredegar contracts for cannon,

The Tredegar Iron Works in Richmond, Virginia.

shot, and shell, but the firm also made axes, saws, bridge materials, boilers, and steam engines, including locomotives. Unlike Gregg, Anderson used mainly slave workers, either hired from their owners or, more and more, owned by him outright.

Daniel Pratt of Alabama built Prattville, which grew into a model of diversified industry. Prattville ultimately had a gristmill, a shingle mill, a carriage factory, foundries, a tin mill, and a blacksmith shop. Pratt then launched into the iron business and coal mining, while on the side experimenting with vineyards and truck farming. Like Anderson he used both black and white labor; like Gregg he practiced paternalism. Profits from his company store went into churches, schools, a library, an art gallery, and a printing establishment—and into handsome dividends.

These men and others like them directed a program of industry that gathered momentum in the 1850s, and in its extent and diversity belied the common image of a strictly agricultural South. Manufactures were supplemented by important extractive industries such as coal, iron, lead, copper, salt, and gold, the last chiefly in North Carolina and Georgia. In manufacturing, altogether in 1860 the slave states had 22 percent of the country's plants, 17 percent of its labor, 20 percent of the capital invested, 17 percent of the wages generated, and 16 percent of the output, an impressive showing but still not up to the South's 29½ percent of the population. Also, southern industry was concentrated in the border states, which had many economic conditions in common with neighboring states of the North.

ECONOMIC DEVELOPMENT   There were two major explanations generally put forward for the lag in southern industrial development. First, blacks were presumed unsuited to factory work, perhaps because they could not adjust to the discipline of work by the clock. Second, the ruling orders of the Old South were said to have developed a lordly disdain for the practice of trade, because a certain aristocratic prestige derived from owning land and slaves, and from conspicuous consumption. But any argument that black labor was incompatible with industry simply flew in the face of the evidence, since factory owners bought or hired slave operatives for just about every kind of manufacture. Given the opportunity, a number of blacks displayed managerial skills as overseers. Nor should one take at face value the legendary indifference of aristocratic planters to the balance sheet. On the southwestern frontiers of the Cotton Kingdom, those who did fit that description became pathetic objects of humor, pushed aside by the hustlers.

More often than not the successful planter was a driving new-comer bent on maximizing profits. While the profitability of slav-ery has been a long-standing subject of controversy, in recent years economic historians have reached the conclusion that slaves on the average supplied about a 10 percent return on their cost. Slave ownership was, moreover, a reasonable speculation, for slave prices tended to move upward. By a strictly hardnosed and hardheaded calculation, investment in slaves and cotton lands was the most profitable investment available at the time in the South.

Despite the South's lag in trade and industry, incomes in the region fared well indeed, especially in the newer cotton lands of the Southwest. The census region comprising Arkansas, Loui-siana, Texas, and the Indian Territory (later Oklahoma) had a higher per-capita income than any other census region in 1860, $184 compared to a national average of $128. Since these calcu-lations included the total population, slave and free, some of the southwestern slaveholders clearly were rich beyond the dreams of avarice. The wealthiest regions at the time were the South-west and the Northeast, which had a per-capita income of $181 in 1860. The new cotton lands and the expanding factories en-joyed the most dynamic growth of the time.

The notion that the South was economically backward emerged from the sectional quarrels of the times, in which south-erners took a poorer-than-thou attitude, so to speak, in order to bolster their claims of northern exploitation. Antislavery ele-ments also contributed to this notion by way of arguing the fail-ure of a slave economy. It was true that in any comparison of the South with the North, the South usually came off second best. But in comparison with the rest of the world, the South as a whole was well off: its average per-capita income in 1860 ($103) was about the same as that of Switzerland, and was exceeded only by Australia, the North, and Great Britain, in that order.

WHITE SOCIETY IN THE SOUTH

If an understanding of the Old South must begin with a knowledge of social myths, it must end with a sense of tragedy. White southerners had won short-term gains at the costs of both long-term development and moral isolation in the eyes of the world. The concentration on land and slaves, and the paucity of cities and immigrants, deprived the South of the dynamic bases of innovation. The slaveholding South hitched its wagon not to a star, but to the world (largely British) demand for cotton, which had not slackened from the start of the Industrial Revolution. In the piping times of the late 1850s, it seemed that prosperity would never end. The South, "safely entrenched behind her cotton bags . . . can defy the world—for the civilized world depends on the cotton of the South," said a Vicksburg newspaper in 1860. "No power on earth dares to make war upon it," said James H. Hammond of South Carolina. "Cotton is king." The only perceived threat to King Cotton was the growing antislavery sentiment. The unperceived threat was an imminent slackening of the cotton market. The hey-day of expansion in British textiles was over by 1860, but by then the Deep South was locked into cotton production for generations to come.

THE PLANTERS   Although great plantations were relatively few in number, they set the tone of economic and social life in the South. What distinguished the plantation from the farm, in addition to its size, was the use of a large labor force, under separate control and supervision, to grow primarily staple crops for profit. A clear-cut distinction between management and labor set the planter apart from the small slaveholder, who often worked side by side with his bondsmen at the same tasks.

If, to be called a planter, one had to own 20 slaves, the South in 1860 numbered only 46,274 planters. Fewer than 8,000 owned 50 or more slaves, and the owners of over 100 numbered 2,292. The census enumerated only 11 with 500 and just 1 with as many as 1,000 slaves. Yet this small, privileged group tended to think of their class interest as the interest of the South, and to perceive themselves as community leaders in much the fashion of the English gentry. The planter group owned more than half the slaves, produced most of the cotton, tobacco, and hemp, and all of the sugar and rice. In a white population numbering just over 8 million in 1860, the total number of slaveholders came to only 383,637. But assuming that each family numbered five people, the whites with some proprietary interest in slavery came to 1.9 million, or roughly one-fourth of the white population. While the preponderance of southern whites belonged to the small-farmer class, the presumptions of the planters were seldom challenged. Too many small farmers aspired to rise in the world.

Often the planter did live in the splendor that legend attributed to him, with the wealth and leisure to cultivate the arts of hospitality, good manners, learning, and politics. More often the scene was less charming. Some of the mansions on closer inspection turned out to be modest houses with false fronts. A style of

The Fairntosh plantation house, North Carolina.

housing derived from the frontier log cabin grew to be surprisingly common. The one-room cabin would expand by the building of a second room with a sheltered open "dog trot" in the middle. As wealth increased, larger houses evolved from the plain log cabin and the dog trot grew into a central hall from the front to the rear of the house. In larger houses halls to one or both sides might be added.

The planter commonly had less leisure than legend would suggest, for he in fact managed a large enterprise. At the same time he often served as the patron to whom workers appealed the actions of their foremen. The quality of life for the slaves was governed far more by the attitude of the master than by the formal slave codes, which were seldom enforced strictly except in times of troubles. The mistress of the plantation, like the master, seldom led a life of idle leisure. She was called upon to supervise the domestic household in the same way the planter took care of the business, to see after food, linens, housecleaning, the care of the sick, and a hundred other details. Mary Boykin Chesnut of South Carolina complained that "there is no slave like a wife."

THE MIDDLE CLASS Overseers on the largest plantations generally came from the middle class of small farmers or skilled workers, or were younger sons of planters. Most aspired to become slaveholders themselves, and sometimes rose to that status, but others were constantly on the move in search of better positions. And their interests did not always coincide with the long-term interests of the planter. "Overseers are not interested in raising negro children, or meat, in improving land, or improving productive qualities of seed or animals," a Mississippi planter complained to

Frederick Law Olmsted, a northern visitor. "Many of them do not care whether property has depreciated or improved, so they make a crop to boast of." Occasionally there were black overseers, but the highest management position to which a slave could aspire was usually that of driver or leader, placed in charge of a small group of slaves with the duty of getting them to work without creating dissension.

The most numerous white southerners were the middle-class yeoman farmers. W. J. Cash, in his classic *The Mind of the South*, called the small farmer "the man at the center." The most prosperous of these generally lived in the mountain-sheltered valleys from the Shenandoah of Virginia down to northern Alabama, areas with rich soil but without ready access to markets, and so less suitable for staple crops or slave labor. But the more numerous yeomen lived in and around the plantation economy. Probably about 80 percent of them owned land. "Nearly all of them," Cash wrote, "enjoyed some measure of a kind of curious half-thrifty, half-shiftless prosperity—a thing of sagging rail fences, unpainted houses, and crazy barns which yet bulged with corn." The yeomen adapted from the planters certain traits of character. "The result was a kindly courtesy, a level eyed pride, an easy quietness, a barely perceptible flourish of bearing, which for all its obvious angularity and fundamental plainness, was one of the finest things the Old South produced."

THE "POOR WHITES" But outside observers often had trouble telling yeomen apart from the true "poor whites," a degraded class crowded off into the pine barrens. Stereotyped views of southern society had prepared many travelers to see only planters and "poor whites," and many a small farmer living in rude comfort, his wealth concealed in cattle and swine off foraging in the woods, was mistaken for "white trash." The type was a familiar one from the frontier days, living on the fringes of polite society. William Byrd of Virginia found them in "Lubberland" (his name for North Carolina) as early as 1730, and in the literature of the South, both fiction and nonfiction, their descendants appeared right on down to the twentieth-century Jeeter Lester of *Tobacco Road* and the Snopeses of William Faulkner's novels. One observer wrote in 1860: "There is no . . . method by which they can be weaned from leading the lives of vagrom-men, idlers, and squatters, useless to themselves and to the rest of mankind." They were characterized by a pronounced lankness and sallowness, given over to hunting and fishing, to hound dogs and moonshine whiskey.

Speculation had it that they were descended from indentured servants or convicts transported to the colonies, or that they were the weakest of the frontier population, forced to take refuge in the sand land, the pine barrens, and the swamps after having been pushed aside by the more enterprising and successful. But the problem was less heredity than environment, the consequence of infections and dietary deficiencies which gave rise to a trilogy of "lazy diseases": hookworm, malaria, and pellagra, all of which produced an overpowering lethargy. Many poor whites displayed a morbid craving to chew clay, from which they got the name "dirt eaters"; the cause was a dietary deficiency, although a folklore grew up about the nutritional and medicinal qualities of certain clays. Around 1900 modern medicine discovered the causes and cures for these diseases and by 1930 they had practically disappeared, taking with them many stereotypes of poor whites.

PROFESSIONALS AND OTHERS   "The social system of the South may be likened to a three-story white structure on a mudsill of black," as one historian put it. But that hardly exhausted the complexity of things. Manufacturers held their own with the planters, as did merchants, often called brokers or factors, who handled the planters' crops and acted as purchasing agents for their needs, supplying credit along the way. Professional people, including lawyers, doctors, and editors, stood in close relationship to the planter and merchant classes which they served and to which they sometimes belonged.

There was a degree of fluidity and social mobility in the class structure of the white South. Few indeed were the "cotton snobs" who lorded it over the lower orders. Planters were acknowledged as the social models and natural leaders of society by consensus. Planters risen from the ranks as often as not had close relatives still among the less well-to-do. Those who aspired to public office, especially, could not afford to take a lordly attitude, for every southern state by 1860 allowed universal white male suffrage. The voters, while perhaps showing deference to their "betters," could nevertheless pick and choose among them at election time.

Other groups stood farther from the mainstream. The mountain people of Appalachia engaged in subsistence farming, employed few or no slaves, and in attitude stood apart from the planter society, sometimes in open hostility toward it. Scattered in many of the flatland counties were small groups who sometimes fell even below the poor whites in the social scale. In some places the advance of the frontier had left behind pockets of Indians with whom passing whites and escaped slaves eventually mingled. The triple admixture of races produced islands of peoples known variously as brass ankles, Turks, redbones, yellow hammers, and Melungeons (derived apparently from "mélange," mixture).

BLACK SOCIETY IN THE SOUTH

"FREE PERSONS OF COLOR" Free Negroes, or "free persons of color," occupied an uncertain status, balanced somewhere between slavery and freedom, subject to legal restrictions not imposed on whites. In the seventeenth century a few blacks had been freed on the same basis as indentured servants. Over the years some slaves were able to purchase their freedom, while some gained freedom as a reward for service in American wars. Others were simply freed by conscientious masters, either in their wills, as in the case of George Washington, or during their lifetimes, as in the case of John Randolph. In one incredible case, a prince of the kingdom of Fita Jallon (in present-day Guinea), captured in warfare, turned up as a slave in Natchez, and after some years managed to get a letter in Arabic to the sultan of Morocco, who intervened in his favor. In 1827, after thirty-nine years of slavery, he gained his freedom and returned to Africa.

Yarrow Mamout was an African Muslim who was sold into slavery, purchased his freedom, acquired property, and settled in Georgetown (now part of Washington, D.C.). Charles Willson Peale executed this portrait of Mamout in 1819, when Mamout was over one hundred years old.

A badge, issued in Charleston, South Carolina, to be worn by free blacks.

The free persons of color included a large number of mulattoes. In urban centers like Charleston and especially New Orleans, "colored" society became virtually a third caste, a new people who occupied a status somewhere between black and white. Some of them built substantial fortunes and even became slaveholders. They often operated inns serving a white clientele. Jehu Jones, for instance, was the "colored" proprietor of one of Charleston's best hotels, which he bought in 1815 for $13,000. In Stateburg, South Carolina, a freed slave, William Ellison, prospered as a gin-wright and became himself a planter and slaveholder. In Louisiana a mulatto, Cyprien Ricard, bought an estate with ninety-one slaves for $250,000. In Natchez William Johnson, son of a white father and mulatto mother, operated three barbershops and owned 1,500 acres of land and several slaves.

But such cases were rare. Free blacks more often were skilled artisans (blacksmiths, carpenters, cobblers), farmers, or common laborers. The increase in their numbers slowed as legislatures put more and more restrictions on the right to free slaves, but by 1860 there were 262,000 free blacks in the slave states, a little over half the national total of 488,000. They were most numerous in the upper South. In Maryland the number of free Negroes very nearly equaled the number still held in slavery; in Delaware free Negroes made up 91.7 percent of the black population.

THE TRADE IN SLAVES The slaves stood at the bottom of the social hierarchy. From the first census in 1790 to the eighth in 1860 their numbers had grown from 698,000 to almost 4 million. The rise in the slave population came mainly through a natural increase, the rate of which was very close to that of whites at the

The end of the foreign slave trade in 1808 gave rise to a flourishing domestic trade in the United States. This watercolor depicts conditions on a slave ship.

time. When the African slave trade was outlawed in 1808, it seemed to many a step toward the extinction of slavery, but the expansion of the cotton belt, with its voracious appetite for workers, soon created such a vested interest in slaves as to dash such hopes. Shutting off the import of slaves only added to the value of those already present. Prices for prime fieldhands ranged between $300 and $400 in the 1790s, up to $1,000–$1,300 in the 1830s, peaked just before the onset of depression in 1837, and rose again in the great prosperity of the 1850s to $1,500–$2,000. Slaves with special skills cost even more.

The rise in slave value tempered some of the harsher features of the peculiar institution. Valuable slaves, like valuable livestock, justified some minimal standards of care. "Massa was purty good," one ex-slave recalled later. "He treated us jus' 'bout like you would a good mule." Another said his master "fed us reg'lar on good, 'stantial food, jus' like you'd tend to you hoss, if you had a real good one." Some owners hired wage laborers, often Irish immigrants, for ditching and other dangerous work rather than risk the lives of valuable slaves.

The end of the foreign slave trade gave rise to a flourishing domestic trade, with slaves moving mainly from the used-up lands of the Southeast into the booming new country of the Southwest. The trade peaked just before 1837, then slacked off, first be-

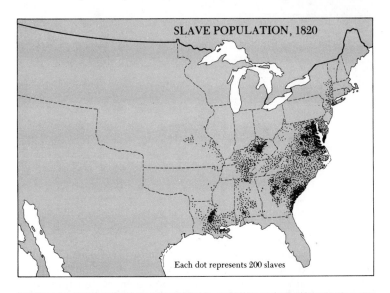

SLAVE POPULATION, 1820

Each dot represents 200 slaves

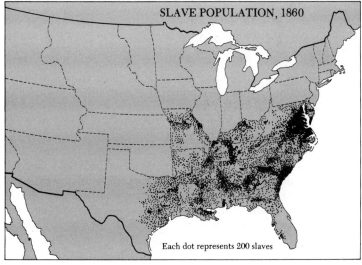

SLAVE POPULATION, 1860

Each dot represents 200 slaves

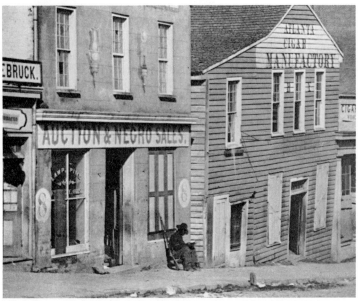

The offices of Pine, Birch & Co., dealers in slaves, Alexandria, Virginia.

cause of depression, then became agricultural reform and recovery renewed the demand for slaves in the upper South. Many slaves moved south and west with their owners, but there also developed an organized business with brokers, slave pens, and auctioneers. Franklin and Armfield, the leading traders, had their offices and collecting pens in Alexandria, Virginia, where they fattened and spruced up slaves for the auction block. From Alexandria slave coffles moved overland through the Ohio Valley or down the Piedmont, making sales along the way. Other groups went out by sea to Wilmington, Charleston, Savannah, or directly to Mobile, New Orleans, and on to Natchez, a leading market for the new districts.

While the mainstream of the trade moved southwestward, every town of any size had public auctioneers and dealers willing to buy and sell slaves—along with other merchandise—or handle sales on a commission. The worst aspect of the slave trade was its breakup of families. Only Louisiana and Alabama (from 1852) forbade selling a child under ten from its mother, and no state forbade separation of husband from wife. Many such sales are matters of record, and although the total number is controversial, it took only a few to damage the morale of all.

PLANTATION SLAVERY   The typical lot of the slave was plantation labor. More than half of all slaves in 1860 worked on plantations, and most of those were fieldhands. The best jobs were those of household servants and skilled workers, including blacksmiths, carpenters, and coopers. Others might get special assignments as, say, boatmen or cooks. Housing for the fieldhands was usually in simple one- or two-room wooden shacks with dirt floors, some without windows. Of food there was usually a rough sufficiency, but one slave recalled that "de flour dat we make the biscuits out of wus de third-grade shorts." A distribution of clothing commonly came twice a year, but shoes were generally provided only in winter. On larger plantations there was sometimes an infirmary and regular sick call, but most planters resorted to doctors mainly in cases of sickness. In a material way slaves probably fared about as well as the poor in the rest of the world, perhaps better than the peasants of eastern Europe.

To some extent, chiefly in the rice and tobacco belts, work was parceled out by the task. But more commonly fieldhands worked long hours from dawn to dusk, or "from kin [see] to kaint." The slave codes gave little protection from long hours. South Carolina's limit of fifteen hours in winter and sixteen in summer exceeded the hours of daylight most of the year. The slave codes adopted in each state concerned themselves mainly with the owner's interests, and subjected the slaves not only to his governance but to surveillance by patrols of county militiamen, who struck fear into the slave quarters by abusing slaves found at large without a good explanation. Evidence suggests that a majority of both planters and small farmers used the whip, which the slave codes authorized. The difference between a good owner and a bad one, according to one ex-slave, was the difference between one who did not "whip too much" and one who "whipped till he's bloodied you and blistered you."

The ultimate recourse of slaves was rebellion or flight, but most recognized the futility of such measures with whites wielding most of the power and weapons. In the nineteenth century only three slave insurrections drew much notice, and two of those were betrayed before they got under way. In 1800 a slave named Gabriel on a plantation near Richmond hatched a plot involving perhaps a thousand others in a scheme to seize key points in Richmond and start a general slaughter of whites. Twenty-five slaves involved in the plot were executed and ten others deported.

The Denmark Vesey plot in Charleston, discovered in 1822, was probably the plan of a free black to fall upon the white popu-

$200 Reward.

RANAWAY from the subscriber, on the night of Thursday, the 30th of Sepember,

FIVE NEGRO SLAVES,

To-wit : one Negro man, his wife, and three children.

The man is a black negro, full height, very erect, his face a little thin. He is about forty years of age, and calls himself *Washington Reed*, and is known by the name of Washington. He is probably well dressed, possibly takes with him an ivory headed cane, and is of good address. Several of his teeth are...

For slaves, escape was one means of resistance. This newspaper advertisement offers a $200 reward for the return of a slave family: husband, wife, and three children.

lation of the town, seize ships in the harbor, and make for Santo Domingo. In this case thirty-five were executed and thirty-four deported. The Vesey plot, however, remains an enigma. Some contemporaries in Charleston and historians since believed it had less to do with insurrection than with white hysteria, which fabricated a plot from rumors and the testimony of frightened slaves out to save their own skins by incriminating others.

Only the Nat Turner insurrection of 1831 in rural Southampton County, Virginia, got beyond the planning stage. Turner, a black overseer, was also a religious exhorter who professed a divine mission in leading the movement. The revolt began when a small group killed Turner's master's household and set off down the road repeating the process at other farmhouses, where other slaves joined the marauders. Before it ended at least fifty-five whites were killed. Eventually trials resulted in seventeen hangings and seven deportations, but the militia killed large numbers of slaves indiscriminately in the process of putting down the rebels.

Slaves more often retaliated against oppression by malingering, by pretending literal-mindedness in following orders, or by outright sabotage. There were constraints on such behavior, however, for laborers would likely eat better on a prosperous plantation than on one they had reduced to poverty. And the shrewdest slaveholders knew that they would more likely benefit from holding out rewards than from inflicting pain. Plantations based on the profit motive fostered between slaves and owners mutual dependency as well as natural antagonism. And in an agrarian society where personal relations counted for much, blacks could win concessions which moderated the harshness of slavery, permitting them a certain degree of individual and community development.

FORGING THE SLAVE COMMUNITY   To generalize about slavery is to miss elements of diversity from place to place and from time to time. The experience could be as varied as people are. Historians of slavery in recent years have transferred their perspectives from the institutional aspects of slavery to the human aspects: what it was like to be held in bondage. At its worst, the historian Stanley M. Elkins has argued, slavery, like the concentration camps of Nazi Germany, dehumanized its victims, and turned them into creatures who internalized their masters' image of them. The slave thus actually became what he seemed to whites to be, a "Sambo" who in Elkins's words "was docile but irresponsible, loyal but lazy, humble but chronically given to lying and stealing," an adult "full of infantile silliness" and "utter dependence and childlike attachment." Some slaves were no doubt so beaten down as to fit the description, but slave lore was too full of stories about "puttin' on ole massa" to permit the belief that Sambo was often anything more than a protective mask put on to meet the white folks' expectations—and not all slaves would demean themselves in that way.

Slaves were victims, there was no question about that. But to stop with so obvious a perception would be to miss an important story of endurance and achievement. If ever there was a melting pot in American history, the most effective may have been that in which Africans from a variety of ethnic, linguistic, and tribal origins fused into a new community and a new culture as Afro-Americans.

Recent scholarship on slavery has looked inside the slave community, once thought inaccessible, mainly by taking seriously firsthand accounts previously discounted as unreliable. Most useful among these have been the slave narratives, life stories of slaves and former slaves published in the 1800s. Among the more interesting are *The Narrative of the Life of Frederick Douglass* (1845) and *Twenty Years a Slave* (1853) by Solomon Northrup, a free man in the North who was kidnapped and sold south into slavery.

Members of the slave community were bound together in helping and protecting one another, which in turn created a sense of cohesion and pride. Slave culture incorporated many African survivals, especially in areas where whites were few. Among the Gullah Negroes of the South Carolina and Georgia coast, a researcher found as late as the 1940s more than 4,000 words still in use from the languages of twenty-one African tribes. But the important point, as another researcher put it, was not survivals which served "as quaint reminders of an exotic culture sufficiently alive to render the slaves picturesquely different but little more." The point was one of transformations in a living culture. Elements of African cultures thus "have continued to exist . . . as dynamic, living, creative parts of life in the United States," and have interacted with other cultures in which they came in contact.

SLAVE RELIGION AND FOLKLORE   Among the most important manifestations of slave culture was the slaves' religion, a mixture of African and Christian elements. Most Africans brought with them a concept of a Creator, or Supreme God, whom they could recognize in Jehovah, and lesser gods whom they might identify with Christ, the Holy Ghost, and the saints, thereby reconciling their earlier beliefs with the new Christian religion. Alongside the church they maintained beliefs in spirits (many of them benign), magic, and conjuring. Belief in magic is in fact a common human response to conditions of danger or helplessness. Conjurors plied a brisk trade in the slave community, and often exercised considerable influence by promising protection against floggings, separations, and other dangers.

But slaves found greater comfort in the church. Masters sought to instill lessons of humility and obedience, but blacks could identify their plight with that of the Israelites in Egypt or of the God who suffered as they did. And the ultimate hope of a better world gave solace in this one. Some owners openly encouraged religious meetings among their slaves, but those who were denied the open use of "praise houses" held "bush meetings" in secret. The preachers and exhorters who sprang up in the slave world commonly won the acceptance of the owners if only because efforts to get rid of them proved futile. The peculiar cadences of their exhortations, chants, and spirituals were to the whites at best exotic but fundamentally mystifying. The ecstatic "ring shout," in which the celebrants moved rhythmically in a circle, was not a dance—as whites tended to believe—because, the worshippers said, they never crossed their feet. Because slave religion was so widely misperceived by whites, one historian has called it the "invisible institution" of the antebellum South.

"African culture was much more resistant to the bludgeon of slavery than historians have hitherto suspected," one historian has written. African culture forms influenced a music of great rhythmic complexity, forms of dance and body language, spirituals and secular songs, and folk tales. Among oppressed peoples humor often becomes a means of psychological release, and there was a lively humor in the West African "trickster tales" of rabbits, tortoises, or Anansi the spider—relatively weak creatures who outwitted stronger animals. Afro-American folklore tended to be realistic in its images of wish-fulfillment. Until after emancipation there were few stories of superhuman heroes, except for tales about captive Africans who escaped slavery by flying back home across the ocean. For the most part whites remained strangely blind and deaf to the black culture around them.

THE SLAVE FAMILY   Whites showed much the same ambivalence toward the slaves' instinct for family life. Slave marriages had no legal status, but slaveowners generally seem to have accepted marriage as a stabilizing influence on the plantation. Sometimes they performed marriages themselves or had a minister celebrate a formal wedding with all the trimmings. A common practice was the "broomstick wedding," in which the couple was married by simply jumping over a broomstick, a custom of uncertain origin. But whatever the formalities, the norm for the

Several generations of a family raised in slavery. Plantation of J. J. Smith, Beaufort, South Carolina, 1862.

slave community as for the white was the nuclear family of parents and children, with the father regarded as head of the family. Slaves also displayed a lively awareness of the extended family of cousins. Most slave children were socialized into their culture through the nuclear family, which afforded some degree of independence from white influence.

Slaves were not always allowed to realize this norm. In some cases the matter of family arrangements was ignored or left entirely up to the slaves on the assumption that black females were simply promiscuous—a convenient rationalization for sexual exploitation, to which the presence of many mulattoes attested. The census of 1860 reported 412,000 persons of mixed ancestry in the United States, or about 10 percent of the Negro population, probably a drastic undercount. That planters and their sons took advantage of female slaves was widely admitted, and sometimes defended on the grounds that the practice protected the chastity of white women. "Like the partiarchs of old," wrote Mary Boykin Chesnut, a plantation mistress of South Carolina, "our men live all in one house with their wives and concubines." And, she observed, "any lady is ready to tell you who is the father of all the mulatto children in everybody's household but her own."

Antislavery Movements

EARLY OPPOSITION TO SLAVERY   From the Revolution to the early 1830s few southern whites showed much disposition to defend the peculiar institution. But in the oft-used figure of speech, they had the wolf by the ears and could not let go. Such scattered antislavery groups and publications as existed in those years in fact were found mainly in the upper South. In 1815, for instance, a Quaker preacher founded the Tennessee Manumission Society, and four years later the *Manumission Intelligencer*, soon renamed *The Emancipator*, began publication in Jonesboro, Tennessee. In 1821 Benjamin Lundy established in Ohio the *Genius of Universal Emancipation*, later published at Greenville, Tennessee, and Baltimore. In 1827 Lundy counted 106 emancipation societies, with 5,150 members, in the slave states and only 24, with 1,475 members, in the free states. The North Carolina Manumission Society held meetings as late as 1834. These groups and publications urged masters to free their slaves voluntarily.

The emancipation movement got a new thrust with the formation of the American Colonization Society in 1817. The society

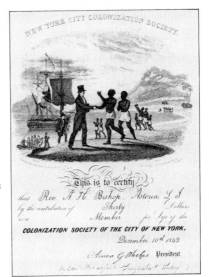

A certificate of membership in the New York City Colonization Society. It shows natives of Liberia welcoming society members and a ship carrying freed slaves from America.

proposed to colonize freed slaves in Africa, or as one historian put it, "more truly, away from America." Its supporters included such prominent figures as James Madison, James Monroe, Henry Clay, John Marshall, and Daniel Webster, and it appealed to diverse opinions. Some backed it as an antislavery group, while others saw it as a way to bolster slavery by getting rid of potentially troublesome free Negroes. Articulate elements of the free black community denounced it from the start. About a month after the group's founding, when James Forten, a successful sailmaker and Revolutionary War veteran, called upon the assembled free blacks of Philadelphia to vote on the proposition, he got a long, tremendous "No" which, he wrote, "seemed as if it would bring down the walls of the building." America, the blacks insisted, was their native land.

In 1821, nevertheless, agents of the Society acquired from local chieftains in West Africa a parcel of land which became the nucleus of a new country. In 1822 the first freed slaves arrived there, and twenty-five years later the society relinquished control to the independent republic of Liberia. But given its uncertain purpose, the colonization movement fell between two stools. It got meager support from either antislavery or proslavery elements. In all, up to 1860 only about 15,000 blacks migrated to Africa, approximately 12,000 with the help of the

Colonization Society. The number was infinitesimal compared to the number of slave births.

FROM GRADUALISM TO ABOLITIONISM   Meanwhile in the early 1830s the antislavery movement took a new departure. Three dramatic events marked its transition from favoring gradualism to demanding the immediate end of slavery. In 1829 a pamphlet appeared in Boston: *Walker's Appeal . . . to the Colored Citizens of the World.* Its author, David Walker, born a free Negro in North Carolina, preached insurrection and violence as a proper response to the wrongs that blacks suffered. Over the next few years Walker circulated the pamphlet widely among blacks and white sympathizers. While free Negroes in parts of the South were known to have read it, the message appears to have reached few slaves.

Two other major events followed in close sequence during 1831. On January 1, William Lloyd Garrison began publication in Boston of a new antislavery newspaper, *The Liberator.* Garrison, who rose from poverty in Newburyport, Massachusetts, had been apprenticed to a newspaperman and had edited a number of papers. For two years he worked on Benjamin Lundy's *Genius of Universal Emancipation* in Baltimore, but became restless with Lundy's moderation. In the first issue of his new paper he renounced "the popular but pernicious doctrine of gradual emancipation" and vowed: "I will be as harsh as truth, and as uncompromising as justice. On this subject, I do not wish to think, or speak, or write, with moderation. . . . I am in earnest—I will not equivocate—I will not excuse—I will not retreat a single inch AND I WILL BE HEARD."

William Lloyd Garrison.

And he was heard, mainly at first because his language provoked outraged retorts from slaveholders who publicized the
paper more than his own supporters did. Circulation in fact was
never very large, but copies went to papers with much wider cir-
culations. In the South, literate blacks would more likely encounter Garrison's ideas in the local papers than in what few
copies of *The Liberator* found their way to them. Slaveholders'
outrage mounted higher after the Nat Turner insurrection in
August 1831. Garrison, they assumed, bore a large part of the responsibility for the affair, but there is no evidence that Nat
Turner had ever heard of him, and Garrison said that he had not
a single subscriber in the South at the time. What is more, however violent his language, Garrison was a pacifist, opposed to the
use of physical violence.

THE AMERICAN ANTI-SLAVERY SOCIETY   A period of organization followed these events. In 1832 Garrison and his followers set up the
New England Anti-Slavery Society. In 1833 two wealthy New
York merchants, Arthur and Lewis Tappan, founded a similar
group in their state and the same year took the lead in starting a
national society with the help of Garrison and a variety of other
antislavery people. They hoped to exploit the publicity gained
by the British antislavery movement, which that same year had
induced Parliament to end slavery, with compensation to slaveholders, throughout the British Empire.

The American Anti-Slavery Society conceded in its constitution the right of each state to legislate on its domestic institutions, but set a goal of convincing fellow citizens "that
Slaveholding is a heinous crime in the sight of God, and that the
duty, safety, and best interests of all concerned, require its *immediate abandonment*, without expatriation." The society went
beyond the issue of emancipation to argue that blacks should
"share an equality with the whites, of civil and religious privileges."

The group set about organizing a barrage of propaganda for its
cause, including periodicals, tracts, agents, lecturers, organizers,
and fund-raisers. Probably its most effective single agent was
Theodore Dwight Weld of Ohio, a convert and disciple of the
great evangelist Charles Grandison Finney. In 1834 Weld led a
group of students at Lane Theological Seminary in Cincinnati in
a protracted discussion of abolition. Efforts of its president,
Lyman Beecher, and the trustees to repress this interruption of
normal routine led to a mass secession from Lane and the start of
a new theological school at the recently opened Oberlin College.

The move won the financial and moral support of the Tappans.

Weld and a number of the "Lane rebels" set out to evangelize the country for abolition. Weld earned the reputation of trouble-maker and "the most mobbed man in the United States," but at the same time he displayed a genius for turning enemies into disciples. In 1836 Weld conducted a New York training school for lecturers from which seventy apostles went out two by two to weave a network of abolitionist organizations across the North. Publications by Weld included *The Bible Against Slavery* (1837) and *American Slavery as It Is: Testimony of a Thousand Witnesses* (1839), the latter including examples of atrocities against slaves gathered from news accounts. The book sold 100,000 copies in its first year.

THE MOVEMENT SPLITS   As the movement spread, debates over tactics inevitably grew. The Garrisonians, mainly New Englanders, were radicals who felt that American society had been corrupted from top to bottom and needed universal reform. Garrison embraced just about every important reform movement that came down the pike in those years: antislavery, temperance, pacifism, and women's rights. Deeply affected by the perfectionism of the times, he refused to compromise principle for expediency, to sacrifice one reform for another. Abolition was not enough. He opposed colonization of freed slaves and stood for equal rights. He broke with the organized church, which to his mind was in league with slavery. The federal government, with its Fugitive Slave Law, was all the more so. The Constitution, he said, was "a covenant with death and an agreement with hell." Garrison therefore refused to vote. He was, however, prepared to collaborate with those who did or with those who disagreed with him on other matters.

Other reformers saw American society as fundamentally sound and concentrated their attention on purging it of slavery. Garrison struck them as an impractical fanatic. A showdown came in 1840 on the issue of women's rights. Women had joined the movement from the start, but quietly and largely in groups without men. The activities of the Grimké sisters brought the issue of women's rights forward. Sarah and Angelina Grimké, daughters of a prominent South Carolina family, had moved north to embrace antislavery and other reforms. Their publications included Angelina's *Appeal to the Christian Women of the South* (1836), calling on southern women to speak and act against slavery, and Sarah's *Letter on the Equality of the Sexes and the Condition of Women* (1838). Having attended Weld's school for antislavery apostles in New York (Angelina later married Weld), they set out speaking to women in New England and slowly widened their audiences to "promiscuous assemblies" of both men and women. Such unseemly behavior inspired the Congregational clergy of Massachusetts to pontificate in a pastoral letter: "If the vine . . . thinks to assume the independence and overshadowing nature of the elm, it will not only cease to bear fruit, but fall in shame and dishonor in the dust." But the Grimké sisters declined the role of clinging vines.

At the Anti-Slavery Society's meeting in 1840 the Garrisonians insisted on the right of women to participate equally in the organization, and carried their point. They did not commit the group to women's rights in any other way, however. Contrary opinion, mainly from the Tappans' New York group, ranged from outright antifeminism to simple fear of scattering shots on too many reforms. The New Yorkers broke away to form the American and Foreign Anti-Slavery Society. Weld, who had probably done more than anybody else to build the movement, declined to go with either group. Like the New Yorkers, he preferred to focus on slavery as the central evil of the times, but he could not accept their "anti-woman" attitude, as he saw it. Discouraged by the bickering, he drifted away from the movement he had done so much to build and into a long-term teaching career.

BLACK ANTISLAVERY Antislavery men also balked at granting full recognition to black abolitionists of either sex. Often blindly patronizing, white leaders expected blacks to take a back seat in the movement. Not all blacks were easily put down, and most became exasperated at whites' tendency to value purity over results, to strike a moral posture at the expense of action. But despite the invitation to form separate black groups, black leaders were active in the white societies from the beginning. Three attended the organizational meeting of the American Anti-Slavery Society in 1833, and some became outstanding agents for the movement, notably the former slaves who could speak from firsthand experience. Garrison pronounced such men as Henry Bibb and William Wells Brown, both escapees from Kentucky, and Frederick Douglass, who fled Maryland, "the best qualified to address the public on the subject of slavery."

Douglass, blessed with an imposing frame and a gift of eloquence, became the best-known black man in America. "I appear before the immense assembly this evening as a thief and a robber," he told a Massachusetts group in 1842. "I stole this head, these limbs, this body from my master, and ran off with them." Fearful of capture after publishing his *Narrative of the*

Frederick Douglass (left) *and Sojourner Truth* (right) *were both leading abolitionists.*

Life of Frederick Douglass (1845), he left for an extended lecture tour of the British Isles and returned two years later with enough money to purchase his freedom. He then started an abolitionist newspaper for blacks, the *North Star*, in Rochester, New York.

Douglass's *Narrative* was but the best known among a hundred or more such accounts. Escapees often made it out on their own —Douglass borrowed a pass from a free black seaman—but many were aided by the Underground Railroad, which grew in legend into a vast system to conceal runaways and spirit them to freedom, often over the Canadian border. Levi Coffin, a North Carolina Quaker who moved to Cincinnati and did help many fugitives, was the reputed president. Actually, there seems to have been more spontaneity than system about the matter, and blacks contributed more than was credited in the legend. Experience had conditioned escapees to distrust whites. One escapee recalled later: "We did not dare ask [for food], except when we found a slave's or a free colored person's house remote from any other, and then we were never refused, if they had food to give." A few intrepid refugees actually ventured back into slave states to organize escapes. Harriet Tubman, the most celebrated, went back nineteen times. Most refugees came from the upper South. Among the few who made it out of the Deep South, William and Ellen Craft of Macon, Georgia, devised one of the cleverest ruses. Being light-skinned she disguised herself as a decrepit planter accompanied north for medical aid by a faithful servant.

REACTIONS TO ANTISLAVERY Even the road north, many blacks found to their dismay, did not lead to the Promised Land. North of slavery, they encountered much of the discrimination and segregation that freed slaves would later encounter in the southern states. When Prudence Crandall of Connecticut admitted a black girl to her private school in 1833, she lost most of her white pupils. She held out in the face of insults, vandalism, and a law which made her action illegal, but closed the school after eighteen months and left the state. Garrison, Douglass, Weld, and other abolitionists had to face down hostile crowds who disliked blacks or found antislavery agitation bad for business. In 1837 a hostile mob in Alton, Illinois, killed the antislavery editor Elijah P. Lovejoy, giving the movement a martyr to both abolition and freedom of the press.

By then proslavery southerners, by seeking to suppress discussion of emancipation, had already given abolitionists ways to link antislavery with the cause of civil liberties for whites. In the summer of 1835 a mob destroyed several sacks of abolitionist literature in the Charleston post office. The postmaster had announced that he would not try to deliver such matter. Bitter debates in Congress ensued. President Jackson wanted a law against handling "incendiary literature," but Congress failed to oblige him. The postmaster-general, nevertheless, did nothing about forcing delivery.

One shrewd political strategy, promoted by Weld, was to deluge Congress with petitions for abolition in the District of Columbia. Most such petitions were presented by former President John Quincy Adams, elected to the House from Massachusetts in 1830. In 1836, however, the House adopted a rule to lay abolition petitions automatically on the table, in effect ignoring them. Adams, "Old Man Eloquent," stubbornly fought this "Gag Rule" as a violation of the First Amendment, and hounded its supporters until the Gag Rule was finally repealed in 1844.

Three years before, in 1841, Adams argued before the Supreme Court the *Amistad* case, established that blacks caught in the illegal African slave trade were free. In 1839 a Cuban schooner, the *Amistad*, was taking African captives to a Caribbean plantation when they rebelled, seized the ship, and ordered the owners to sail for Africa. Actually the ship arrived off Long Island, and the Africans were charged in an American court with murdering two crew members. Thirty-two survivors of the original fifty-seven were returned to their homeland.

Meanwhile, in 1840, the year of the schism in the antislavery movement, a small group of abolitionists called a convention in Albany, New York, and launched the Liberty party, with James

G. Birney, one-time slaveholder of Alabama and Kentucky, as its candidate for president. Birney, converted to the cause by Weld, had tried without success to publish an antislavery paper in Danville, Kentucky. He then moved it to Ohio and in 1837 became executive secretary of the American Anti-Slavery Society. In the 1840 election he polled only 7,000 votes, but in 1844 his vote rose to 60,000, and from that time forth an antislavery party contested every national election until Abraham Lincoln won the presidency.

THE DEFENSE OF SLAVERY   Birney was but one among a number of southerners propelled north during the 1830s by the South's growing hostility to emancipationist ideas. Antislavery in the upper South had its last stand in 1831–1832 when the Virginia legislature debated a plan of gradual emancipation and colonization, then rejected it by a vote of 73 to 58. Thereafter, leaders of southern thought worked out an elaborate intellectual defense of slavery, presenting it as a positive good rather than, in the words of Tennessee's constitutional convention of 1834, "a great evil" that "the wisest heads and most benevolent hearts" had not been able to dispose of.

In 1832 Prof. Thomas R. Dew of the College of William and Mary published the most comprehensive defense of slavery produced to that time, his *Review of the Debate of the Virginia Legislature of 1831 and 1832*. In it he made the practical argument that the natural increase of the slave population would outrun any colonization effort. But he went on to justify slavery as required by the circumstances of southern life and the condition of human inequality, citing as authorities the Bible, Aristotle, and Edmund Burke.

The biblical argument became one of the most powerful. The evangelical churches, which had widely condemned slavery at one time, gradually turned proslavery. Ministers of all denominations joined in the argument. Had not the patriarchs of the Old Testament held bondsmen? Had not Noah, upon awakening from a drunken stupor, cursed Canaan, son of Ham, from whom the Negroes were descended? Had not Saint Paul advised servants to obey their masters and told a fugitive servant to return to his master? And had not Jesus remained silent on the subject, at least so far as the Gospels reported his words? In 1843–1844 disputes over slavery split two great denominations along sectional lines and led to the formation of the Southern Baptist Convention and the Methodist Episcopal Church, South.

Presbyterians, the only other major denomination to split, did not divide until the Civil War.

Another, and fundamental, feature of the proslavery argument developed a theory of the intrinsic inferiority of Negroes. Most whites, blind and deaf to the complexity of black culture, assumed that the evidence of their eyes and ears confirmed their own superiority. The weight of scientific opinion, which was not above prejudice on such matters, was on their side, but it is doubtful that many felt the need of science to prove what seemed so obvious to them. Stereotyping the poor and powerless as inferior is an old and seemingly ineradicable human habit. There was in fact a theory championed by Dr. Josiah C. Nott, a physician of Mobile, Alabama, that blacks were the product of a separate creation, but this challenged orthodox faith in the biblical account of creation and was generally rejected.

Other arguments took a more "practical" view of slavery. Not only was slavery profitable, it was a matter of social necessity. Jefferson, for instance, in his *Notes on Virginia* (1785), had argued that emancipated slaves and whites could not live together without risk of race war growing out of the recollection of past injustices. What is more, it seemed clear that blacks could not be expected to work under conditions of freedom. They were too shiftless and improvident, the argument went, and in freedom would be a danger to themselves as well as to others. White workmen, on the other hand, feared their competition. Whites were also struck with fear by the terrible example of the bloody rebellion in Santo Domingo.

In 1856 William J. Grayson of Charleston published a lengthy poem, *The Hireling and the Slave*, which defended slavery as better for the worker than the "wage slavery" of northern industry. George Fitzhugh of Virginia developed the same argument, among others, in two books: *Sociology for the South; or, The Failure of a Free Society* (1854) and *Cannibals All! or, Slaves Without Masters* (1857). Few if any socialists ever waxed more eloquent over the evils of industrial capitalism than these proslavery theorists. The factory system had brought abuses and neglect far worse than those of slavery. Slavery, Fitzhugh argued, was the truest form of socialism, for it provided security for the workers in sickness and old age, whereas workers in the North were exploited for profit and then cast aside without compunction. Men were not born equal, he insisted: "It would be far nearer the truth to say that some were born with saddles on their backs, and others booted and spurred to ride them—and the riding does them good." Fitzhugh argued for an organic, hierarchical society, much like the family, in which each had a place with both rights and obligations. Calhoun endorsed slavery with the more popular argument that it freed masters from drudgery to pursue higher things, and thus made possible a Greek democracy—or what one historian has more aptly tagged a "Herrenvolk [master race] democracy."

Within one generation such ideas had triumphed in the white South over the postrevolutionary apology for slavery as an evil bequeathed by the forefathers. Opponents of the orthodox faith in slavery as a positive good were either silenced or exiled. Freedom of thought in the Old South had become a victim of the nation's growing obsession with slavery.

FURTHER READING

Those interested in the problem of discerning myth and reality in the southern experience should consult *Myth and Southern History* (1974), edited by Patrick Gerster and Nicholas Cords, for various essays on the topic. William R. Taylor's *Cavalier and Yankee: The Old South and American National Character* (1961) remains helpful. W. J. Cash's *The Mind of the South* (1941)° is a classic on the subject.

The dominance of the plantation system is analyzed in Ulrich B. Phillip's *Life and Labor in the Old South* (1929). Frank L. Owsley's *Plain Folk of the Old South* (1949) argues that yeoman farmers were dominant in many aspects of antebellum agriculture. Bruce Collins's *White Society in the Antebellum South* (1985) sees broad consensus among all classes of whites. Contrasting analyses of the plantation system are Eugene D. Genovese's *The World the Slaveholders Made* (1969) and Gavin Wright's *The Political Economy of the Cotton South* (1978).° Why southern industry lagged behind agriculture is treated in relevant chapters of Geneovese's *The Political Economy of Slavery* (1965).

Other works on southern culture and society include Bertram Wyatt-Brown's *Southern Honor* (1982),° Jane T. Censer's *North Carolina Planters and Their Children, 1800–1860* (1984), and Catherine Clinton's *Plantation Mistress* (1982).° William J. Cooper, Jr.'s *Liberty and Slavery* (1983)° and Robert F. Durden's *The Self-Inflicted Wound* (1985) cover southern politics of the era.

The historiography of slavery and racism contains some of the most exciting and controversial scholarship in American letters. The first major work, Ulrich B. Phillips's *American Negro Slavery* (1918), stressed a benign paternalism among planters. That view went generally unchallenged until Kenneth M. Stampp's *The Peculiar Institution* (1956)° discussed the conditions in which slaves were forced to live. A provocative

° These books are available in paperbook editions.

discussion of the psychology of black slavery can be found in Stanley M. Elkins's *Slavery: A Problem in American Intellectual Life* (3rd ed., 1976).° More recent scholarship emphasizes the self-generative, dynamic character of black society under slavery. George P. Rawick's *From Sundown to Sunup* (1972), John W. Blassingame's *The Slave Community: Plantation Life in the Antebellum South* (rev. ed., 1979),° Eugene D. Genovese's *Roll, Jordon, Roll: The World the Slaves Made* (1974),° and Herbert G. Gutman's *The Black Family in Slavery and Freedom, 1750–1925* (1976)° all stress the theme of a persisting and identifiable slave culture.

On the question of slavery's profitability, see Robert W. Fogel and Stanley L. Engerman's *Time on the Cross: The Economics of Negro Slavery* (2 vols., 1974),° which argues that not only did planters benefit from bondage, but the slaves themselves incorporated a Victorian work ethic based on incentives. Herbet G. Gutman reviewed this controversy in *Slavery and the Numbers Game* (1975).

Other recent works on slavery include Lawrence W. Levine's *Black Culture and Black Consciousness: Afro-American Folk Thought from Slavery to Freedom* (1977), Albert J. Raboteau's *Slave Religion: The "Invisible Institution" in the Antebellum South* (1978),° Joel Williamson's *New People: Miscegenation and Mulattoes in the United States* (1980), and his recent *The Crucible of Race* (1985). For an oral history of slavery, see *Slave Testimony* (1977), edited by John W. Blassingame. Charles Joyner's *Down by the Riverside* (1984) offers a vivid reconstruction of one slave community.

Useful surveys of abolitionism include Merton L. Dillon's *The Abolitionists: The Growth of a Dissenting Minority* (1974),° Ronald G. Walters's *The Antislavery Appeal* (1976),° and James B. Stewart's *Holy Warriors: The Abolitionists and American Slavery* (1976).°

Numerous biographies of the leading abolitionists contribute to an understanding of the movement: John L. Thomas's *The Liberator: William Lloyd Garrison* (1963), Gerda Lerner's *The Grimké Sisters from South Carolina: Rebels against Slavery* (1967), Bertram Wyatt-Brown's *Lewis Tappan and the Evangelical War against Slavery* (1969), and Robert H. Abzug's *Passionate Liberator: Theodore Dwight Weld and the Dilemma of Reform* (1980).°

On the role of free blacks in the antislavery movement, see Benjamin Quarles's *Black Abolitionists* (1969)° and Jane H. Pease and William H. Pease's *They Who Would Be Free* (1974). For a captivating first-person account, see *The Autobiography of Frederick Douglass* (1967).° Surveys of black history for the period include John B. Boles's *Black Southerners, 1619–1869* (1983), Leon F. Litwack's *North of Slavery: The Negro in the Free States, 1790–1860* (1961), and Ira Berlin's *Slaves without Masters* (1974), on southern free blacks.

For the proslavery argument as it developed in the South, see William J. Cooper's *The South and the Politics of Slavery, 1828–1856* (1978), James Oakes's *The Ruling Race: A History of American Slaveholders* (1982),° and *Slavery Defended* (1963), edited by Eric L. McKitrick, the last a collection of proslavery writings. The problems southerners had in justifying slavery is explored in Drew G. Faust's *A Sacred Circle: The Dilemma of the Intellectual in the Old South, 1840–1860* (1977) and Carl N. Degler's *The Other South: Southern Dissenters in the Nineteenth Century* (1974). George M. Fredrickson's *The Black Image in the White Mind* (1971) examines a variety of racial stereotypes held by white southerners.

16

THE CRISIS OF UNION

SLAVERY IN THE TERRITORIES

John C. Calhoun and Ralph Waldo Emerson had little else in common, but both men sensed in the Mexican War the omens of a greater disaster. Mexico was "the forbidden fruit; the penalty of eating it would be to subject our institutions to political death," Calhoun warned. "The United States will conquer Mexico," Emerson conceded, "but it will be as the man swallows the arsenic. . . . Mexico will poison us." Wars, as both men knew, have a way of breeding new wars, often in unforseen ways. Like Britain's conquest of New France, America's winning of the Southwest gave rise in turn to quarrels over newly acquired lands. In each case the quarrels set in train a series of disputes: Britain's crisis of empire had its counterpart in America's crisis of union.

THE WILMOT PROVISO   The Mexican War was less than three months old when the seeds of a new conflict began to sprout. On Saturday evening, August 8, 1846, a sweltering House of Representatives reassembled to clear its calendar for adjournment. Polk had sent Congress that noon a hurried request for $2 million to expedite negotiations with Mexico. He expected little hindrance, since party discipline had already whipped through most of his program. But the House, resentful of Polk's triumphs, was ripe for revolt when a freshman Democrat from Pennsylvania, David Wilmot, stood up. He favored expansion, Wilmot explained, even the annexation of Texas as a slave state. But slavery had come to an end in Mexico, and if free soil should be acquired, "God forbid that we should be the means of planting this institution upon it." Drawing upon the words of the Northwest Ordinance, he offered a fateful amendment to Polk's appropriations bill: in lands acquired from Mexico, "neither slavery nor involuntary servitude shall ever exist in any part of said territory, except for crime, whereof the party shall first be duly convicted."

Within ten minutes an otherwise obscure congressman had immortalized his name. The Wilmot Proviso, although never a law, politicized slavery once and for all. For a generation, since the Missouri Controversy of 1819–1821, the issue had been lurking in the wings, kept there most of the time by politicians who feared its disruptive force. From that day forth, for two decades the question would never be far from center stage.

The first flurry of excitement passed quickly, however. The House adopted the Wilmot Proviso that Saturday night. The following Monday the Senate refused to concur and Congress adjourned without giving Polk his $2 million. When Congress reconvened in December 1846, Polk prevailed on Wilmot to withhold his amendment when he asked for the money again, but by then others were ready to take up the cause. When a New York congressman revived the proviso he signaled a revolt by the Van Burenites in concert with the antislavery forces of the North. Once again the House approved the amendment. Once again the Senate refused. In March the House finally gave in, but in one form or another Wilmot's idea kept cropping up. Abraham Lincoln later recalled that during one term as congressman, 1847–1849, he voted for it "as good as forty times."

John C. Calhoun meanwhile devised a thesis to counter the proviso and set it before the Senate in four resolutions on February 19, 1847. The Calhoun Resolutions, which never came to a vote, argued that since the territories were the common possession of the states, Congress had no right to prevent any citizen from taking slaves into them. To do so would violate the Fifth Amendment, which forbade Congress to deprive any person of life, liberty, or property without due process of law, and slaves were property. Thus by a clever stroke of logic Calhoun took that basic guarantee of liberty, the Bill of Rights, and turned it into a basic guarantee of slavery. The irony was not lost on his critics, but the point became established southern dogma—echoed by his colleagues and formally endorsed by the Virginia legislature.

Sen. Thomas Hart Benton of Missouri, himself a slaveholder but also a Jacksonian nationalist, found in Calhoun's resolutions a set of abstractions "leading to no result." Wilmot and Calhoun between them, he said, had fashioned a pair of shears. Neither blade alone would cut very well, but joined together they could sever the ties of union. Within another year Benton was complaining that the slavery issue had become like the plague of frogs in Pharaoh's Egypt, with "this black question, forever on the table, on the nuptial couch, everywhere."

POPULAR SOVEREIGNTY   Many others, like Benton, refused to be polarized, seeking to bypass the conflict that was brewing. President Polk was among the first to suggest extending the Missouri Compromise dividing free and slave territory at latitude 36° 30′ all the way to the Pacific. Sen. Lewis Cass of Michigan suggested that the citizens of a territory "regulate their own internal concerns in their own way," like the citizens of a state. Such an approach would combine the merits of expediency and democracy. It would take the issue out of the national arena and put it in the hands of those directly affected.

Popular sovereignty, or squatter sovereignty, as the idea was alternatively called, had much to commend it, including an ambiguity which improved the presidential prospects of Cass. Without directly challenging the slaveholders' access to the new lands, it promised to open them quickly to free farmers who would almost surely dominate the territories. With this tacit understanding the idea prospered in Cass's Old Northwest, where Stephen A. Douglas of Illinois and other prominent Democrats soon endorsed it. Popular sovereignty, they hoped, might check the magnetic pull toward the opposite poles of Wilmot and Calhoun.

When the Mexican War ended in 1848, the question of bondage in the new territories was no longer hypothetical—unless one reasoned, as many did, that their arid climate excluded plantation crops and therefore excluded slavery. For Calhoun, who leaned to that opinion, that was beside the point since the right to carry slaves into the territories was the outer defense line of the peculiar institution, not to be yielded without opening the way to further assaults. In fact there is little reason in retrospect to credit the argument that slavery had reached its natural limits of expansion. Slavery had been adapted to occupations other than plantation agriculture. Besides, on irrigated lands, cotton later became a staple crop of the Southwest.

Nobody doubted that Oregon would become free soil, but it too was drawn into the maelstrom of controversy. Territorial status, pending since 1846, was delayed because its provisional government had excluded slavery. To concede that provision would imply an authority drawn from the powers of Congress, since a territory was created by Congress. Finally, a Senate committee proposed to let Oregon exclude slavery but to deny the territories of California and New Mexico any power to legislate at all on the subject, thus passing the issue to the courts. The question of slavery, previously outlawed under Mexican rule, could rise on appeal to the Supreme Court and thus be kept out of the political arena. The Senate accepted this but the House rejected it, and finally an exhausted Congress let Oregon organize without slavery, but postponed decision on the Southwest. Polk signed the bill on the principle that Oregon was north of 36°30′.

Polk had promised to serve only one term; exhausted by his labors and having reached his major goals, he refused to run again. In the Democratic convention Lewis Cass took an early lead and won nomination on the fourth ballot. The Democratic party had endorsed the author of squatter sovereignty, but its platform simply denied the power of Congress to interfere with slavery in the states and criticized all efforts to bring the question before Congress. The Whigs devised an even more artful shift. Once again, as in 1840, they passed over their party leader, Clay, for a general, Zachary Taylor, whose fame and popularity had grown since the Battle of Buena Vista. He was a legal resident of Louisiana who owned more than a hundred slaves, an apolitical figure who had never voted in a national election. Once again, as in 1840, the party adopted no platform at all. While most of Taylor's support came from the South, Thurlow Weed and William H. Seward of New York had favored him and helped engineer a vice-presidential nomination for New Yorker Millard Fillmore.

THE FREE-SOIL COALITION   But the antislavery impulse was not easily squelched. Wilmot had raised a standard to which a broad coalition could rally. Men who shied away from abolitionism could readily endorse the exclusion of slavery from the territories. The Northwest Ordinance and the Missouri Compromise supplied honored precedents. By doing so, moreover, one could strike a blow for liberty without caring about slavery itself, or about the slaves. One might simply want free soil for white farmers, while keeping the unwelcome blacks far away in the South, where they belonged. Free soil, therefore, rather than abolition, became the rallying point—and also the name of a new party.

Three major groups entered the free-soil coalition: rebellious Democrats, antislavery Whigs, and members of the Liberty party, which dated from 1840. Disaffection among the Democrats centered in New York, where the Van Burenite "Barnburners" squared off against the pro-administration "Hunkers" in a factional dispute which had as much to do with personal ambitions as with local politics. Each group gave the other its name, the one for its alleged purpose to rule or ruin like the farmer who burned his barn to get rid of the rats, the other for hankering or "hunkering" after office.

As their conflict grew, however, the Barnburners seized on the free-soil issue as a means of winning support. When the Democratic convention voted to divide the state's votes between contesting delegations, they bolted the party and named Van Buren as their candidate for president on a free-soil platform. Other Wilmot Democrats, including Wilmot himself, joined the revolt. Revolt among the Whigs centered in Massachusetts where a group of "conscience" Whigs battled the "cotton" Whigs. The latter, according to Charles Sumner, belonged to a coalition of northern businessmen and southern planters, "the lords of the lash and the lords of the loom." Conscience Whigs rejected the slaveholder, Taylor. The third group in the coalition, the abolitionist Liberty party, had already nominated Sen. John P. Hale of New Hampshire for president.

In August these groups—Barnburners, Conscience Whigs, and Liberty party men—organized the Free Soil party in a convention at Buffalo. Its presidential nomination went to Martin Van Buren by a close margin over Hale, while the vice-presidential nomination went to Charles Francis Adams, a Conscience

An 1848 Free Soil party banner promotes Martin Van Buren for president, Charles F. Adams for vice-president. The party's slogan was "Free Soil, Free Labor, Free Speech."

Whig. The old Jacksonian and the son of John Quincy Adams made strange bedfellows indeed! The Liberty party was rewarded with a platform plank that pledged the government to abolish slavery whenever such action became constitutional, but the party's main principle was the Wilmot Proviso and it entered the campaign with the catchy slogan of "free soil, free speech, free labor, and free men."

Its impact on the election was mixed. The Free Soilers split the Democractic vote enough to throw New York to Taylor, and the Whig vote enough to give Ohio to Cass, but Van Buren's total of 291,000 votes was far below the popular totals of 1,361,000 for Taylor and 1,222,000 for Cass. Taylor won with 163 to 127 electoral votes, and both major parties retained a national following. Taylor took eight slave states and seven free; Cass just the opposite, seven slave and eight free.

TOWARD STATEHOOD FOR CALIFORNIA Meanwhile a new dimension had been introduced into the question of the territories. On January 24, 1848, nine days before Trist signed the Mexican peace treaty, gold was discovered in California. The word spread quickly, and Polk's confirmation of the discovery in his last annual message, on December 5, 1848, turned the gold-fever into a worldwide contagion.

During 1849, by the best estimates, more than 80,000 persons reached California. Probably 55,000 went overland; the rest went by way of Panama or Cape Horn. Along the western slopes of the Sierra Nevada they thronged the valleys and canyons in a wide belt from LaPorte southward to Mariposa. The village of San Francisco, located near the harbor entrance Frémont had aptly named Golden Gate, grew rapidly into a city. The influx quickly reduced the Mexicans to a minority, and sporadic conflicts with the Indians of the Sierra Nevada foothills decimated the native peoples. In 1850 Americans already accounted for 68 percent of the population and there was a cosmopolitan array of "Sydney Ducks" from Australia, "Kanakas" from Hawaii, "Limies" from London, "Paddies" from Ireland, "Coolies" from China, and "Keskydees" from Paris (who were always asking "Qu'est-ce qu'il dit?").

The new president did not remain an enigma for long. Born in Virginia, raised in Kentucky, Zachary Taylor had been a soldier most of his adult life, with service in the War of 1812, the Black Hawk and Seminole Wars, as well as in Mexico. Constantly on the move, he had acquired a home in Louisiana and a plantation in Mississippi. Southern Whigs had rallied to his support, ex-

The discovery of gold in California transformed San Francisco from a village into a city. The busy harbor of San Francisco is depicted here in 1851.

pecting him to uphold the cause of slavery. Instead they had turned up a southern man with Union principles, who had no more use for Calhoun's proslavery abstractions than Jackson had for his nullification doctrine. Innocent of politics Taylor might be, and to southern Whigs it was ominous that the antislavery Seward had his ear, but "Old Rough and Ready" had the direct mind of the soldier he was. Slavery should be upheld where it existed, he felt, but he had little patience with abstract theories about slavery in territories where it probably could not exist. Why not make California and New Mexico into states immediately, he reasoned, and bypass the whole issue?

But the Californians, in need of organized government, were already ahead of him. By December 1849, without leave of Congress, California had a free-state government in operation. New Mexico responded more slowly, but by June 1850 Americans there had adopted another free-state constitution. The Mormons around Salt Lake, meanwhile, drafted a basic law for the imperial state of Deseret, which embraced most of the Mexican Cession, including a slice of the coast from Los Angeles to San Diego.

In Taylor's annual message on December 4, 1849, he endorsed immediate statehood for California and enjoined Congress to "abstain from . . . those exciting topics of sectional character which have hitherto produced painful apprehensions in the public mind." The new Congress, however, was in no mood for simple solutions.

THE COMPROMISE OF 1850

THE GREAT DEBATE   The spotlight fell on the Senate, where a stellar cast enacted one of the great dramas of American politics, the Compromise of 1850: the great triumvirate of Clay, Calhoun, and Webster, with a supporting cast that included William H. Seward, Stephen A. Douglas, Jefferson Davis, and Thomas Hart Benton. Henry Clay once again took the role of "Great Pacificator," which he had played in the Missouri and nullification controversies. In January he presented a package of eight resolutions which wrapped up solutions to all the disputed issues. He proposed to (1) admit California as a free state, (2) organize the remainder of the Southwest without restriction as to slavery, (3) deny Texas its extreme claim to a Rio Grande boundary up to its source, (4) compensate Texas for this by assuming the Texas debt, (5) uphold slavery in the District of Columbia, but (6) abolish the slave trade across its boundaries, (7) adopt a more effective fugitive slave act, and (8) deny congressional authority to interfere with the interstate slave trade. His proposals, in substance, became the Compromise of 1850, but only after a prolonged debate, the most celebrated, if not the greatest, in the annals of Congress—and the final great debate for Calhoun, Clay, and Webster. Calhoun, already dying, would be gone on March 31, and Clay and Webster two years later, in 1852.

On February 5–6 the aging Clay summoned all his eloquence in a defense of the settlement. In the interest of "peace, concord and harmony" he called for an end to "passion, passion—party, party—and intemperance." California should be admitted on the terms that its own people had approved. As to the remainder of the new lands, he told northerners: "You have got what is worth more than a thousand Wilmot provisos. You have nature on your side. . . ." Secession, he warned southerners, would inevitably bring on war. Even a peaceful secession, however unlikely, would gain none of the South's demands. Slavery in the territories and the District, the return of fugitives—all would be endangered.

The debate continued sporadically through February, with Sam Houston rising to the support of Clay's compromise, Jefferson Davis defending the slavery cause on every point, and none rising to any effective defense of President Taylor's straightforward plan. Then on March 4 Calhoun left his sickbed to sit, a gaunt figure with his cloak draped about his shoulders, as Senator Mason of Virginia read the "sentiments" he had "reduced to writing."

"I have, Senators, believed from the first that the agitation of the subject of slavery would, if not prevented by some timely and effective measure, end in disunion," said Calhoun. Neither Clay's compromise nor Taylor's efforts would serve the Union. The South needed but an acceptance of its rights: equality in the territories, the return of fugitive slaves, and some guarantee of "an equilibrium between the sections." The last, while not spelled out in the speech, referred to Calhoun's notion of a "concurrent majority" by which each section could gain security through a veto power, perhaps through a dual executive, an idea which would be elaborated in his posthumous *Discourse on the Constitution.*

Three days later Calhoun returned to hear Daniel Webster. The assumption was widely held that the "godlike Daniel," long since acknowledged the supreme orator of an age of oratory, would stick to his mildly free-soil views. In a sense he did, but his central theme, as in the classic debate with Hayne, was the preservation of the Union: "I wish to speak today, not as a Massachusetts man, not as a Northern man, but as an American. . . . I speak today for the preservation of the Union. 'Hear me for my cause.'" The extent of slavery was already determined, he insisted, by the Northwest Ordinance, by the Missouri Compromise, and in the new lands by the law of nature. The Wilmot Proviso was superfluous: "I would not take pains to reaffirm an

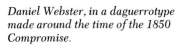
Daniel Webster, in a daguerrotype made around the time of the 1850 Compromise.

ordinance of nature nor to re-enact the will of God." Both sections, to be sure, had legitimate grievances: on the one hand the excesses of "infernal fanatics and abolitionists" in the North; and on the other hand southern efforts to expand slavery and southern slurs on northern workingmen. But "Secession! Peaceable secession! Sir, your eyes and mine are never destined to see that miracle." Instead of looking into such "caverns of darkness," let men "enjoy the fresh air of liberty and union." Let them look to a more hopeful future.

The March 7 speech was a supreme gesture of conciliation, and Webster had knowingly brought down a storm upon his head. New England antislavery leaders virtually exhausted the vocabulary of abuse against this new "Benedict Arnold" who had betrayed his section. John Greenleaf Whittier lamented in "Ichabod":

> So fallen! so lost! the light withdrawn
> Which once he wore!
> The glory from his gray hairs gone
> Forevermore!

But Webster had also revived hopes of compromise in both North and South. Agreement, wrote one observer, "will be mainly owing to the conciliatory tone taken by Mr. Webster." Georgia's Senator Toombs found "a tolerable prospect for a proper settlement of the slavery question, probably along the lines backed by Webster."

On March 11 William H. Seward, freshman Whig senator from New York, gave the antislavery reply to Webster. As the confidant of Taylor he might have been expected to defend the president's program. Instead he stated his own view that compromise with slavery was "radically wrong and essentially vicious." There was, he said, "a higher law than the Constitution," thus leaving some doubt, according to the historian David Potter, whether he was floor leader for Zachary Taylor or for God.

In mid-April a select Committee of Thirteen bundled Clay's suggestions (insofar as they concerned the Mexican cession) into one comprehensive bill, which the committee reported to the Senate early in May. The measure was quickly dubbed the "Omnibus" bill because it resembled the contemporary vehicle that carried many riders. Taylor continued to oppose Clay's compromise and the two men came to an open break which threatened to split the Whig party wide open. Another crisis loomed when word came near the end of June that a convention in New Mexico was applying for statehood, with Taylor's support, and with boundaries that conflicted with the Texas claim to the east bank of the Rio Grande.

TOWARD A COMPROMISE On July 4 friends of the Union staged a grand rally at the base of the unfinished Washington Monument. Taylor went to hear the speeches, lingering in the hot sun. Back at the White House he quenched his thirst with iced water and milk, ate some cherries, cucumbers, or cabbage, and was stricken with cholera morbus (gastroenteritis). Five days later he was dead. The outcome of the sectional quarrel, had he lived, probably would have been different, whether for better or worse one cannot know. In a showdown Taylor had put everyone on notice that he would be as resolute as Jackson. "I can save the Union without shedding a drop of blood," he said. On the other hand a showdown might have provoked civil war ten years before it came, years during which the northern states gained in population and economic strength.

Taylor's sudden death, however, strengthened the chances of compromise. The soldier in the White House was followed by a politician, Millard Fillmore. The son of a poor farmer in upper New York, Fillmore had come up through the school of hard knocks. Largely self-educated, he had made his own way in the profession of law and the rough-and-tumble world of New York politics. Experience had taught him caution, which some thought was indecision, but had made up his mind to support Clay's compromise and had so informed Taylor. It was a strange switch. Taylor, the Louisiana slaveholder, had been ready to

Millard Fillmore, whose support of the Compromise of 1850 helped the Union muddle through the crisis.

make war on his native region; Fillmore, whom southerners thought was antislavery, was ready to make peace.

At this point young Sen. Stephen A. Douglas of Illinois, a rising star of the Democratic party, came to the rescue of Clay's faltering compromise. Never sanguine about the Omnibus, he had refused service on the Committee of Thirteen, and with Clay's consent, kept himself ready to lead an alternative strategy. His strategy was in fact the same one that Clay had used to pass the Missouri Compromise thirty years before. Reasoning that nearly everybody objected to one or another provision of the Omnibus, Douglas worked on the principle of breaking it up into six (later five) separate measures. Few members were prepared to vote for all of them, but from different elements Douglas hoped to mobilize a majority for each.

It worked. Thomas Hart Benton described the sequel. The separate items were like "cats and dogs that had been tied together by their tails four months, scratching and biting, but being loose again, every one of them ran off to his own hole and was quiet." By September 17 it was over, and three days later Fillmore had signed the last of the five measures into law. The Union had muddled through, and the settlement went down in history as the Compromise of 1850. For the time it defused an explosive situation and settled each of the major points at issue.

First, California entered the Union as a free state, ending forever the old balance of free and slave states. Second, the Texas and New Mexico Act made New Mexico a territory and set the Texas boundary at its present location. In return for giving up its claims east of the Rio Grande Texas was paid $10 million, which secured payment of the Texas debt and brought a powerful lobby of bondholders to the support of compromise. Third, the Utah Act set up another territory. The territorial act in each case omitted reference to slavery except to give the territorial legislature authority over "all rightful subjects of legislation" with provision for appeal to federal courts. For the sake of agreement the deliberate ambiguity of the statement was its merit. Northern congressmen could assume that territorial legislatures might act to exclude slavery on the unstated principle of popular sovereignty. Southern congressmen assumed that they could not.

Fourth, a new Fugitive Slave Act put the matter wholly under federal jurisdiction and stacked the cards in favor of slave-catchers. Fifth, as a gesture to antislavery forces the slave trade, but not slavery itself, was abolished in the District of Columbia: more specifically, no slave could be brought into the District for

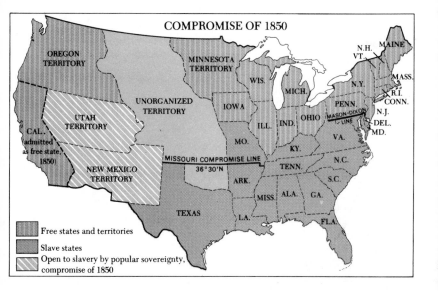

COMPROMISE OF 1850

OREGON TERRITORY

MINNESOTA TERRITORY

WIS.

UNORGANIZED TERRITORY

UTAH TERRITORY

IOWA

MICH.

N.Y.

N.H.
VT.

MAINE

MASS.

R.I.
CONN.

N.J.

PENN.

MASON-DIXON LINE

DEL.
MD.

CAL. (admitted as free state, 1850)

ILL. IND. OHIO

VA.

MO.

KY.

MISSOURI COMPROMISE LINE 36°30'N

NEW MEXICO TERRITORY

TENN.

N.C.

ARK.

S.C.

MISS. ALA. GA.

TEXAS

LA.

FLA.

Free states and territories

Slave states

Open to slavery by popular sovereignty, compromise of 1850

the purpose of sale or be held in a depot for transfer and sale elsewhere. The spectacle of slave coffles passing through the streets of the capital was brought to an end. Calling these five measures the Compromise of 1850 was an afterthought. Actually they were the result less of a sectional bargain than of a parliamentary maneuver. They were nevertheless an accomplished fact, and a large body of citizens welcomed the outcome, if not with joy, at least with relief. Millard Fillmore's message to Congress in December 1850 pronounced the measures "a final settlement."

Still, doubts lingered that either North or South could be reconciled to the measures permanently. In the South the disputes of 1846–1850 had transformed the abstract doctrine of secession into a movement animated by such fire-eaters as Robert Barnwell Rhett of South Carolina, William Lowndes Yancey of Alabama, and Edmund Ruffin of Virginia.

But once the furies aroused by the Wilmot Provisio were spent, the compromise left little on which to focus a proslavery agitation. The state of California was an accomplished fact, and, ironically, tended to elect proslavery men to Congress. New Mexico and Utah were far away, and in any case at least hypothetically open to slavery. Both in fact adopted slave codes, but the census of 1860 reported no slaves in New Mexico and only twenty-nine in Utah. The Fugitive Slave Law was something else again. It was the one clear-cut victory for the cause of slavery, but a pyrrhic victory if ever there was one.

Practical Illustration of the Fugitive Slave Law. *This cartoon depicts the divisive effects of the law.*

THE FUGITIVE SLAVE LAW   Southern intransigence had presented abolition its greatest gift since the Gag Rule, a new focus for agitation and one that was far more charged with emotion. The fugitive slave law did more than stack the deck in favor of slave-catchers; it offered a strong temptation to kidnap free Negroes. The law denied alleged fugitives a jury trial and provided that special commissioners got a fee of $10 when they certified delivery of an alleged slave but only $5 when they refused certification. In addition federal marshals could require citizens to help in enforcement; violators could be imprisoned up to six months and fined $1,000. A Massachusetts man said it fixed the value of a Carolina slave at $1,000, of a Yankee soul at $5.

"This filthy enactment was made in the nineteenth century, by people who could read and write," Emerson marveled in his journal. He advised neighbors to break it "on the earliest occasion." The occasion soon arose in many places, if not in Emerson's Concord. Within a month of the law's enactment claims were filed in New York, Philadelphia, Harrisburg, Detroit, and other cities. Trouble soon followed. In Detroit only military force stopped the rescue of an alleged fugitive by an outraged mob in October 1850.

There were relatively few such incidents, however. In the first six years of the fugitive act only three fugitives were forcibly rescued from the slave-catchers. On the other hand probably fewer than 200 were remanded to bondage during the same years. More than that were rescued by stealth, often through the Underground Railroad. Still, the Fugitive Slave Act had tremendous effect in widening and deepening the antislavery impulse in the North.

UNCLE TOM'S CABIN   Antislavery forces found their most persuasive appeal not in the fugitive slave law but in the fictional drama of Harriet Beecher Stowe's *Uncle Tom's Cabin,* a combination of unlikely saints and sinners, stereotypes and melodramatic escapades—and a smashing commercial success. The long-suffering Uncle Tom, the villainous Simon Legree, the angelic Eva, the desperate Eliza taking her child to freedom across the icy Ohio —all became stock characters of the American imagination. Slavery, seen through Mrs. Stowe's eyes, subjected its victims either to callous brutality or, at the hands of indulgent masters, to the indignity of extravagant ineptitude and bankruptcy. It took time for the novel to work its effect on public opinion, however. Neither abolitionists nor fire-eaters represented their sections at the time. The country was enjoying a surge of prosperity, and the course of the presidential campaign in 1852 reflected a common desire to lay sectional quarrels to rest.

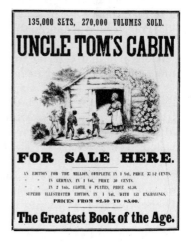

"The Greatest Book of the Age." Uncle Tom's Cabin, *as this advertisement indicates, was a tremendous commercial success.*

FOREIGN ADVENTURES

The Democrats, despite a fight over the nomination, had some success in papering over the divisions within their party. As their nominee for president they turned finally to Franklin Pierce of New Hampshire. The platform pledged the Democrats to "abide by and adhere to a faithful execution of the acts known as the Compromise measures. . . . " The candidates and the platform generated a surprising reconciliation of the party's factions. Pierce rallied both the Southern Rights men and the Barnburners, who at least had not burned their bridges with the Democrats. The Free Soilers, as a consequence, mustered only 156,000 votes for John P. Hale in contrast to the 291,000 they got for Van Buren in 1848.

The Whigs were less fortunate. They repudiated the lackluster Fillmore, who had faithfully supported the Compromise, and once again tried to exploit martial glory. It took fifty-three ballots, but the convention finally chose Winfield Scott, the hero of Lundy's Lane and Mexico City, a native of Virginia backed mainly by northern Whigs, including Seward. The convention dutifully endorsed the Compromise, but with some opposition from the North. Scott, an able commander but politically inept, had gained a reputation for antislavery and nativism, alienating German and Irish ethnic voters. In the end Scott carried only Tennessee, Kentucky, Massachusetts and Vermont. Pierce overwhelmed him in the electoral college 254 to 42, although the popular vote was closer: 1.6 million to 1.4 million.

Pierce, an undistinguished but handsome and engaging figure, a former congressman, senator, and brigadier in Mexico, was, like Polk, touted as another "Young Hickory." But he turned out to be made of more pliable stuff, unable to dominate the warring factions of his party, trying to be all things to all men, but looking more and more like a "Northern man with Southern principles."

"YOUNG AMERICA" Foreign diversions now distracted attention from domestic quarrels. After the Mexican War the spirit of Manifest Destiny took on new life in an amorphous movement called "Young America." The Spirit of Young America was full of spread-eagle bombast, buoyant optimism, and enthusiasm for economic growth and territorial expansion. The dynamic force of American institutions would somehow transform the world. On February 21, 1848, just two days after word of the Mexican treaty reached Washington, an uprising in Paris signaled the Revolutions of 1848, which set Europe ablaze. The Young Americans greeted that new dawn with all the ardor Jeffersonians had lavished on the first French Revolution. And when it all collapsed, the result seemed all the more to confirm the belief that Europe was, in the words of Stephen A. Douglas, "antiquated, decrepit, tottering on the verge of dissolution . . . a vast graveyard."

CUBA   Closer to home, Cuba, one of Spain's earliest and one of its last possessions in the New World, continued to be an object of American concern. In the early 1850's a crisis arose over expeditions launched against Cuba from American soil. Spanish authorities retaliated against these provocations by harassment of American ships. In 1854 the Cuban crisis expired in one final outburst of braggadocio, the Ostend Manifesto. That year the Pierce administration instructed Pierre Soulé, the minister in Madrid, to offer $130 million for Cuba, which Spain peremptorily spurned. Soulé then joined the American ministers to France and Britain in drafting the Ostend Manifesto. It declared that if Spain, "actuated by stubborn pride and a false sense of honor refused to sell," then the United States must ask itself, "does Cuba, in the possession of Spain, seriously endanger our internal peace and existence of our cherished Union?" If so, "then, by every law, human and divine, we shall be justified in wresting it from Spain. . . . " Publication of the supposedly confidential dispatch left the administration no choice but to disavow what northern opinion widely regarded as a "slaveholders' plot." The last word on this and other such episodes perhaps should go to the staid London *Times*, which commented near the end of 1854: "The diplomacy of the United States is certainly a very singular profession."

So was the practice of filibustering which, again, was more bluster than action. Little wonder the word has come to suggest gas-bag as well as freebooter, and the double-meaning is appropriate for the 1850s. William Walker, a Tennessean by birth who went to California and began to fancy himself a new Cortés, reached his supreme moment in 1855 when this "grey-eyed man of destiny" sailed with sixty followers, "the immortals," to mix in a Nicaraguan civil war. Before the year was out he had made himself president of a republic which Franklin Pierce promptly recognized. Walker was deposed in 1857, and in 1860 was executed by a firing squad in Honduras.

DIPLOMATIC GAINS IN THE PACIFIC   In the Pacific, however, American diplomacy scored some important achievements. American trade with China dated from 1785, but was allowed only through the port of Canton. In 1844 the United States and China signed the Treaty of Wanghsia, which opened four ports, including Shanghai, to American trade and for the first time granted America "extraterritoriality," or special privileges, including the right of Americans in China to remain subject to their own law. The Treaty of Tientsin (1858) opened eleven more ports and granted Americans the right to travel and trade throughout China. China quickly became a special concern of American Protestant missionaries as well. About fifty were already there by 1855, and for nearly a century China remained far and away the most active mission field for Americans.

Japan meanwhile had remained for two centuries closed to American trade. Moreover, American whalers wrecked on the shores of Japan had been forbidden to leave the country. Mainly in their interest President Fillmore entrusted a special Japanese expedition to Commodore Matthew C. Perry, who arrived in Tokyo on July 8, 1853. Japan's actual ruler, the Tokugawa shogun, was already under pressure from merchants and the educated classes to seek wider contacts in the world. He agreed to deliver Perry's letter to the emperor. Negotiations followed, and in the Treaty of Kanagawa (March 31, 1854) Japan agreed to an American consulate, promised good treatment to castaways, and permitted visits in certain ports for supplies and repairs. Broad commercial relations came after the first envoy, Townsend Harris, negotiated the Harris Convention of 1858, which opened five ports to American trade and made certain tariff concessions. In 1860 a Japanese diplomatic mission, the first to enter a Western country, visited the United States for three months.

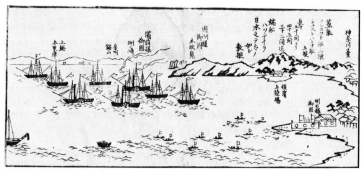

A Japanese view of Commodore Perry's Landing in Yokohama Harbor.

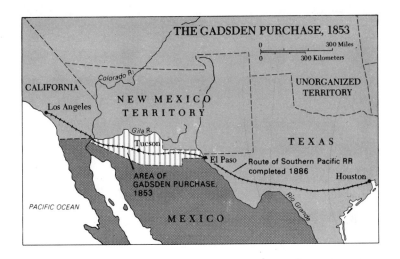

THE GADSDEN PURCHASE, 1853

0   300 Miles
0   300 Kilometers

CALIFORNIA

Los Angeles

Colorado R.

N E W   M E X I C O
T E R R I T O R Y

Gila R.

Tucson

El Paso

AREA OF
GADSDEN PURCHASE,
1853

PACIFIC OCEAN

UNORGANIZED
TERRITORY

T E X A S

Route of Southern Pacific RR
completed 1886

Houston

Rio Grande

M E X I C O

The Kansas-Nebraska Crisis

During the 1850s the only land added to the United States
was a barren stretch of some 30,000 square miles south of the
Gila River in present New Mexico and Arizona. This Gadsden
Purchase of 1853, which cost the United States $10 million, was
made to acquire land offering a likely route for a Pacific railroad.
The idea of building a railroad linking together the new continental domain of the United States, though a great national goal,
spawned sectional rivalries in still another quarter and reopened
the slavery issue. Among the many transcontinental routes projected, the four most important were the northern route from
Milwaukee to the Columbia River, a central route from St. Louis
to San Francsico, another from Memphis to Los Angeles, and a
more southerly route from New Orleans to San Diego via the
Gadsden Purchase.

DOUGLAS'S PROPOSAL   In 1852 and 1853 Congress debated and
dropped several likely proposals. For various reasons, including
terrain, climate, and sectional interest, Secretary of War Jefferson Davis favored the southern route and encouraged the Gadsden Purchase. Any other route, moreover, would go through the
Indian country which stretched from Texas to the Canadian
border.
    Stephen A. Douglas of Illinois had an even better idea: Chi-
cago ought to be the eastern terminus. Since 1845, therefore,
Douglas and others had offered bills for a new territory in the
lands west of Missouri and Iowa, bearing the Indian name Ne-

Sen. Stephen A. Douglas (D-Ill.)

braska. In January 1854, as chairman of the committee on territories, Senator Douglas reported yet another Nebraska bill. Unlike the others this one included the entire unorganized portion of the Louisiana Purchase to the Canadian border. At this point fateful connections began to transform his proposal from a railroad bill to a proslavery bill. To carry his point Douglas needed the support of southerners, and to win that support he needed to make some concession on slavery. This he did by writing popular sovereignty into the bill in language which specified that "all questions pertaining to slavery in the Territories, and in the new states to be formed therefrom are to be left to the people residing therein, through their appropriate representatives."

It was a clever dodge since the Missouri Compromise would still exclude slaves until the territorial government had made a decision, preventing slaveholders from getting established before a decision was reached. Southerners quickly spotted the barrier and Douglas as quickly made two more concessions. He supported an amendment for repeal of the Missouri Compromise insofar as it excluded slavery north of 36° 30', and then agreed to organize two territories, Kansas, west of Missouri; and Nebraska, west of Iowa and Minnesota.

Douglas's motives are unclear. Railroads were surely foremost in his mind, but he was influenced also by his proslavery friend, Sen. David Atchison of Missouri, by the desire to win support for his bill in the South, by the hope that popular sovereignty would quiet the slavery issue and open the Northwest, or by a chance to split the Whigs. But he had blundered, had damaged his presidential chances, and had set his country on the road to civil war. The tragic flaw in his plan was his failure to gauge the depth of antislavery feelings. Douglas himself preferred that the territories become free. Their climate and geography excluded plantation agriculture, he reasoned, and he could not comprehend how people could get so wrought up over abstract rights. Yet he had in fact opened the possibility that slavery might gain a foothold in Kansas.

The agreement to repeal the Missouri Compromise was less than a week old before six antislavery congressmen published a protest, the "Appeal of the Independent Democrats." The tone of moral indignation which informed their protest quickly spread among those who opposed Douglas. The document arraigned his bill "as a gross violation of a sacred pledge," and as "part and parcel of an atrocious plot" to create "a dreary region of despotism, inhabited by masters and slaves." They called upon their fellow citizens to protest against this "atrocious crime."

Across the North editorials, sermons, speeches, and petitions echoed this indignation. What had been radical opinion was fast becoming the common view of people in the North. But Douglas had the votes and, once committed, forced the issue with tireless energy. President Pierce impulsively added his support. Southerners lined up behind Douglas, with notable exceptions like Texas Sen. Sam Houston, who denounced the violation of two solemn compacts: the Missouri Compromise and the confirmation of the territory to the Indians "as long as grass shall grow and water run." He was not the only one to think of the Indians, however. Federal agents were already busy extinguishing Indian titles. But Douglas and Pierce whipped reluctant Democrats into line (though about half the northern Democrats refused to yield), pushing the bill to final passage in May by 37 to 14 in the Senate and 113 to 100 in the House.

Very well, many in the North reasoned, if the Missouri Compromise was not a sacred pledge, then neither was the Fugitive Slave Act. On June 2 Boston witnessed the most dramatic demonstration against the act. After several attempts had failed to rescue a fugitive named Anthony Burns, a force of soldiers and marines marched him to a waiting ship through streets lined with people shouting "Kidnappers!" past buildings draped in black, while church bells tolled across the city. The event cost the federal government $14,000. Burns was the last to be returned from Boston, and was himself soon freed through purchase by the black community of Boston.

THE EMERGENCE OF THE REPUBLICAN PARTY   What John C. Calhoun had called the cords holding the Union together had already begun to part. The national church organizations of Baptists and Methodists, for instance, had split over slavery by 1845. The national parties, which had created mutual interests transcending sectional issues, were beginning to unravel under the strain. The Democrats managed to postpone disruption for yet a while, but their congressional delegation lost heavily in the North, enhancing the influence of the southern wing.

The strain of the Kansas-Nebraska Act, however, soon destroyed the Whig party. Southern Whigs now tended to abstain from voting while Northern Whigs moved toward two new parties. One was the new American (Know Nothing) party, which had raised the banner of native Americanism and the hope of serving the patriotic cause of Union. More Northern Whigs joined with independent Democrats and Free Soilers in spontaneous antislavery coalitions with a confusing array of names, including "anti-Nebraska," "Fusion," and "People's party." These coalitions finally converged in 1854 on the name "Republican," evoking the memory of Jefferson. The Know-Nothings and the Republicans, paradoxically, appealed to overlapping constituencies. As the historian David Potter aptly pointed out, "much of the rural, Protestant, puritan-oriented population of the North was sympathetic to antislavery and temperance and nativism and unsympathetic to the hard-drinking Irish Catholics."

"BLEEDING" KANSAS   After passage of the Kansas-Nebraska Act, attention swung to the plains of Kansas where opposing elements gathered to stage a rehearsal for civil war. All agreed that Nebraska would be free, but Kansas soon exposed the potential for mischief in popular sovereignty. The ambiguity of the law, useful to Douglas in getting it passed, only added to the chaos. The people of Kansas were "perfectly free to form and regulate their domestic institutions in their own way, subject only to the Constitution." That in itself was subject to conflicting interpretations, but the law was completely silent as to the time of decision, adding to each side's sense of urgency about getting control of the territory.

The settlement of Kansas therefore differed from the usual pioneering efforts. Groups sprang up North and South to hurry right-minded settlers westward. The first and best known was the New England Emigrant Aid Society. During 1855 and 1856 it sent fewer than 1,250 colonists, but its example encouraged other groups and individuals to follow suit. Southern efforts of the same kind centered in Missouri, which was separated from Kansas only by a surveyor's line. When Kansas's first governor

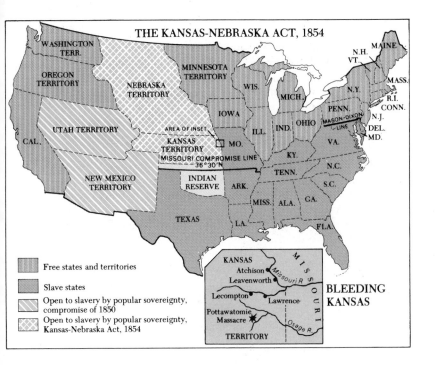

THE KANSAS-NEBRASKA ACT, 1854

WASHINGTON TERR.
OREGON TERRITORY
NEBRASKA TERRITORY
MINNESOTA TERRITORY
MAINE
N.H.
VT.
WIS.
MICH.
N.Y.
MASS.
R.I.
CONN.
IOWA
PENN.
N.J.
MASON-DIXON LINE
DEL.
MD.
UTAH TERRITORY
AREA OF INSET
ILL.
IND.
OHIO
CAL.
KANSAS TERRITORY
MO.
KY.
VA.
MISSOURI COMPROMISE LINE 36°30'N
NEW MEXICO TERRITORY
INDIAN RESERVE
ARK.
TENN.
N.C.
S.C.
MISS.
ALA.
GA.
TEXAS
LA.
FLA.

Free states and territories

Slave states

Open to slavery by popular sovereignty, compromise of 1850

Open to slavery by popular sovereignty, Kansas-Nebraska Act, 1854

KANSAS
Atchison
Leavenworth
Missouri R.
Lecompton
Lawrence
Pottawatomie Massacre
Osage R.
TERRITORY

BLEEDING KANSAS

arrived in October 1854, he found several thousand settlers already on the ground. He ordered a census and scheduled an election for a territorial legislature in March 1855. When the election took place, several thousand "Border Ruffians" crossed over from Missouri and swept the polls for proslavery forces. The governor denounced the vote as a fraud, but did nothing to alter the results. The legislature so elected expelled the few antislavery members, adopted a drastic slave code, and made it a capital offense to aid a fugitive slave and a felony even to question the legality of slavery in the territory.

Free-state men rejected this "bogus" government and moved directly toward application for statehood. In October 1855 a constitutional convention, the product of an extralegal election, met in Topeka, drafted a state constitution excluding both slavery and free Negroes from Kansas, and applied for admission to the Union. By March 1856 a free-state "governor" and "legislature" were functioning in Topeka. But the prospect of getting any government to command general authority in Kansas seemed dim, and both sides began to arm. The Emigrant Aid Society was soon in the business of gun-running as well as helping settlers. The Rev. Henry Ward Beecher's name became especially identified with gun-running because of "Beecher's Bibles," which were rifles supplied by his congregation.

Finally, confrontation began to slip into conflict. In May 1856 a proslavery mob entered the free-state town of Lawrence and began a wanton destruction of property. They smashed newspaper presses and tossed them into the river, set fire to the free-state governor's home, stole property that was not nailed down, and trained five cannon on the Free State Hotel, destroying it.

The "sack of Lawrence" resulted in just one casualty, but the excitement aroused a fanatical free-soiler named John Brown, who had a history of instability. A minister with whom he stayed in Kansas described him later as one "impressed with the idea that God had raised him up on purpose to break the jaws of the wicked." Two days after the sack of Lawrence, Brown set out with four sons and three other men toward Pottawatomie Creek, site of a proslavery settlement, where they killed five men in cold blood, ostensibly as revenge for the deaths of free-state men. The Pottawatomie Massacre (May 24–25, 1856) set off a running guerrilla war in the territory which lasted through the fall when a new governor restored a semblance of order with the help of federal soldiers. Altogether, by the end of 1856 Kansas lost about 200 killed and $2 million in property destroyed.

VIOLENCE IN THE SENATE   Violence in Kansas spilled over into the rhetoric of Congress, where angry legislators began to trade recriminations, coming to the verge of blows. On May 22, the day after the sack of Lawrence, two days before the Pottawatomie Massacre, a sudden flash of violence on the Senate floor electrified the whole country. Just two days earlier Sen. Charles Sumner of Massachusetts had finished a speech on "The Crime against Kansas." Sumner, elected five years earlier by a coalition of Free Soilers and Democrats, was a complex mixture of traits: capable at once of eloquence and excess, a man of principle with limited tolerance for opinions different from his own. He had intended his speech to be "the most thorough philippic" ever heard.

What he produced was an exercise in pedantry and studied insult. The treatment of Kansas was "the rape of a virgin territory," he said, " . . . and it may be clearly traced to a depraved longing for a new slave State, the hideous offspring of such a crime. . . . " Sen. A. P. Butler of South Carolina became a special target of his censure. Like Don Quixote in choosing Dulcinea, Butler had "chosen a mistress . . . who . . . though polluted in the sight of the world, is chaste in his sight—I mean the harlot, Slavery."

"Bully" Brooks's attack on Charles Sumner. The incident worsened the strains on the Union.

Sumner said that Butler betrayed "an incapacity of accuracy," a constant "deviation of truth."

Sumner's rudeness might well have discredited the man, if not his cause, had it not been for Preston S. Brooks, a congressman from Edgefield, South Carolina. For two days Brooks brooded over the insult to his uncle, Senator Butler. Knowing that Sumner would refuse a challenge to a duel, he considered but rejected the idea of taking a horsewhip to him. Finally, on May 22 he found Sumner writing at his Senate desk after an adjournment, accused him of libel against South Carolina and Butler, and commenced beating him about the head with a cane. Sumner, struggling to rise, wrenched the desk from the floor and collapsed.

Brooks had created a martyr for the antislavery cause. Like so many other men in those years, he betrayed the hotspur's gift for snatching defeat from the jaws of victory. For two and a half years Sumner's empty seat was a solemn reminder of the violence done to him. Some thought the senator was feigning injury, others that he really was physically disabled. In fact, although his injuries were bad enough, including two gashes to the skull, he seems to have suffered a psychosomatic shock which left him incapable of functioning adequately. When the House censured Brooks, he resigned, went home to Edgefield, and returned after being triumphantly reelected. His admirers showered him with new canes. Southerners who never would have done what Brooks did now hastened to make excuses for him. Northerners who never would have said what Sumner said now hastened to his defense. Men on each side, appalled at the behavior of the other, reasoned that North and South had developed into different civilizations, with incompatible standards of honor. "I do not see," Emerson confessed, "how a barbarous community and a civilized community can constitute one state. We must either get rid of slavery, or get rid of freedom."

SECTIONAL POLITICS Within the span of five days in May "Bleeding Kansas," "Bleeding Sumner," and "Bully Brooks" had set the tone for another presidential year. The major parties could no longer evade the slavery issue. Already in February it had split the hopeful American party wide open. Southern delegates, with help from New York, killed a resolution to restore the Missouri Compromise, and nominated Millard Fillmore for president. Later, what was left of the Whig party endorsed the same candidate.

At its first national convention the new Republican party passed over its leading figure, William H. Seward, who was awaiting a better chance in 1860. Following the Whig tradition they sought out a military hero, John C. Frémont, the "Pathfinder" and leader in the conquest of California. The Republican platform owed much to the Whigs too. It favored a transcontinental railroad and, in general, more internal improvements. It condemned the repeal of the Missouri Compromise, the Democratic policy of expansion, and "those twin relics of barbarism—Polygamy and Slavery." The campaign slogan echoed that of the Free Soilers: "Free soil, free speech, and Frémont." It was the first time a major party platform had taken a stand against slavery.

The Republican position on slavery, the historian Eric Foner has argued, developed from an ideology of free labor. "Political anti-slavery was not merely a negative doctrine, an attack on southern slavery and the society built on it," Foner wrote; "it was an affirmation of the superiority of the social system of the North—a dynamic expanding capitalist society, whose achievements and destiny were almost wholly the result of the dignity and opportunities which it offered the average laboring man." Such a creed, he argued, could accommodate a variety of opinions on race, economics, or other issues, but it was "an ideology which blended personal and sectional interest with morality so perfectly that it became the most potent political force in the nation."

The Democrats, meeting two weeks earlier in June, had rejected Pierce, the hapless victim of so much turmoil. Douglas too was left out because of the damage done by his Kansas-Nebraska Act. The party therefore turned to its old wheelhorse, James Bu-

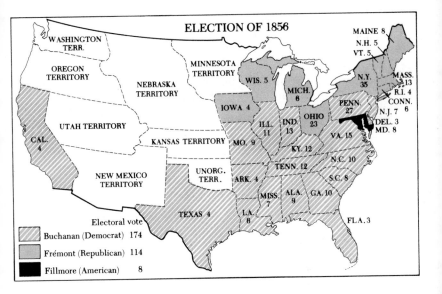

ELECTION OF 1856

Electoral vote
Buchanan (Democrat) 174
Frémont (Republican) 114
Fillmore (American) 8

chanan of Pennsylvania, who had long sought the nomination. The party and its candidate nevertheless hewed to the policies of Pierce. The platform endorsed the Kansas-Nebraska Act and nonintervention. Congress, it said, should not interfere with slavery in either states or territories. The party reached out to its newly acquired ethnic voters by condemning nativism and endorsing religious liberty.

The campaign of 1856 resolved itself into two sectional campaigns. The "Black Republicans" had few southern supporters, and only a handful in the border states, where fears of disunion held many Whigs in line. Buchanan thus went to the country as the candidate of the only remaining national party. Although Fillmore won a larger vote in the South than Scott had, the slave states were safe for Buchanan. Frémont swept the northernmost states, with 114 electoral votes, but Buchanan added five free states to his southern majority for a total of 174: Pennsylvania, New Jersey, Illinois, Indiana, and California, all but the last of which bordered on slave states.

Few presidents before Buchanan had a broader experience in politics and diplomacy. His career went back to 1815 when he started as a Federalist legislator in Pennsylvania before switching to Jackson in the 1820s. He had been over twenty years in Congress, minister to Russia and Britain, and Polk's secretary of state in between. His long quest for the presidency had been built on a southern alliance, and his political debts reinforced his belief that saving the Union depended on concessions to the South. Republicans belittled him as another "doughface" like Pierce, lacking the backbone to stand up to the southerners who dominated the Democratic majorities in Congress. His choice of four slave-state and only three free-state men for his cabinet seemed another bad omen.

The Deepening Sectional Crisis

THE DRED SCOTT CASE   An old saying has it that troubles come in threes. In 1856 Lawrence, the Brooks-Sumner affair, and Potta-wotamie came in quick succession. During Buchanan's first six months in 1857 he encountered the Dred Scott decision, new troubles in Kansas, and a business panic. On March 6, 1857, two days after the inauguration, the Supreme Court rendered a decision in the long-pending case of *Dred Scott v. Sandford.* Dred Scott, born a slave in Virginia about 1800, had been taken to St. Louis and sold to an army surgeon, Dr. John Emerson. In 1834 Emerson took him as body servant to Fort Armstrong, Illinois, then to Fort Snelling in Wisconsin Territory (later Minnesota), and finally returned him to St. Louis in 1838. After Emerson's death in 1843 Scott apparently had tried to buy his freedom. In 1846, with help from white friends, he brought suit in Missouri

Dred Scott (left) and Chief Justice Robert B. Taney (right). The Supreme Court's decision on Dred Scott's suit for freedom fanned the flames of discord.

courts claiming that residence in Illinois and Wisconsin Territory had made him free. A jury decided in his favor, but the state supreme court ruled against him. When the case rose on appeal to the Supreme Court, the country anxiously awaited its opinion on the issue of slavery in the territories.

Each of the nine justices filed a separate opinion, except one who concurred with Chief Justice Taney. By different lines of reasoning seven justices ruled that Scott remained a slave. The aging Taney, whose opinion stood as the opinion of the Court, ruled that Scott lacked standing in court because he lacked citizenship. Taney argued that one became a federal citizen either by birth or by naturalization, which ruled out any former slave. He further argued that no state had ever accorded citizenship to Negroes—a statement demonstrably in error. At the time the Constitution was adopted, Taney further said, Negroes "had for more than a century been regarded as . . . so far inferior, that they had no rights which the white man was bound to respect."

To nail down further the definition of Scott's status, Taney moved to a second major question. Residency in a free state had not freed him since, in line with precedent, the decision of the state court governed. This left the question of residency in a free territory. On this point Taney argued that the Missouri Compromise had deprived citizens of property in slaves, an action "not warranted by the constitution." He strongly implied, but never said explicitly, that the compromise had violated the due process clause of the Fifth Amendment, as Calhoun had earlier argued. The upshot was that the Supreme Court had declared an act of Congress unconstitutional for the first time since *Marbury v. Madison* (1803), and a major act for the first time ever. Congress had repealed the Missouri Compromise in the Kansas-Nebraska Act three years earlier, but the decision now pointed a thrust at popular sovereignty. If Congress itself could not exclude slavery from a territory, then presumably neither could a territorial government created by act of Congress.

By this decision six justices of the Supreme Court had thought to settle a question which Congress had dodged ever since the Wilmot Proviso surfaced. But far from settling it, they had only fanned the flames of dissension. Little wonder that Republicans protested: the Court had declared their program unconstitutional. It had also reinforced the suspicion that the slavocracy was hatching a conspiracy. Were not all but one of the justices who joined Taney southerners? And had not Buchanan chatted with the chief justice at the inauguration and then urged the people to accept the early decision as a final settlement, "Whatever this may be"? (Actually, Buchanan already knew the outcome because two other justices had spilled the beans in private letters.) Besides, if Dred Scott were not a citizen and had no standing in court, there was no case before it. The majority ruling was an *obiter dictum*—a statement not essential to deciding the case and therefore not binding, "entitled to just so much moral weight as would be the judgment of a majority of those congregated in any Washington bar-room."

Proslavery elements, of course, greeted the court's opinion as binding. Now the fire-eaters among them were emboldened to yet another demand. It was not enough to deny Congress the right to interfere with slavery in the territories; Congress had an obligation to protect the property of slaveholders, making a federal slave code the next step. The idea, first broached by Alabama Democrats in the "Alabama Platform" of 1848, soon became orthodox southern doctrine.

THE LECOMPTON CONSTITUTION   Out in Kansas, meanwhile, the struggle continued. Just before Buchanan's inauguration the proslavery legislature called an election of delegates to a constitutional convention. Since no provision was made for a referendum on the constitution, the governor vetoed the measure and the legislature overrode his veto. The Kansas governor resigned on the day Buchanan took office and the new president replaced him with Robert J. Walker. A native Pennsylvanian who had made a political career in Mississippi and a former member of Polk's cabinet, Walker had greater prestige than his predecessors, and like contemporaries such as Houston of Texas, Foote of Mississippi, and Benton of Missouri, put the Union above slavery in his scale of values. In Kansas he scented a chance to advance the cause of both the Union and his party. Under popular sovereignty, fair elections would produce a state that was both free and Democratic.

Walker arrived in May 1857, and, with Buchanan's approval, pledged to the free-state elements that the new constitution would be submitted to a fair vote. But in spite of his pleas, he arrived too late to persuade free-state men to vote for convention delegates in elections they were sure had been rigged against them. Later, however, Walker did persuade the free-state leaders to vote in the October election of a new territorial legislature.

As a result a polarity arose between an antislavery legislature and a proslavery constitutional convention. The convention, meeting at Lecompton, drew up a constitution under which

President James Buchanan, whose support of the Lecompton Constitution drove another wedge into the Democratic party.

Kansas would become a slave state. A referendum on the document was cunningly contrived so that voters could not vote against the proposed constitution. They could only accept it "with slavery" or "with no slavery," and even the latter meant that property in slaves already in Kansas would "in no measure be interfered with." The vote was set for December 21, 1857, with rules and officials chosen by the convention.

Although Kansas had only about 200 slaves at the time, free-state men boycotted the election on the claim that it too was rigged. At this point President Buchanan took a fateful step. Influenced by southern advisers and politically dependent upon southern congressmen, he decided to renege on his pledge to Walker and support the action of the Lecompton Convention. Walker resigned and the election went according to form: 6,226 for the constitution with slavery, 569 for the constitution without slavery. Meanwhile, the acting governor had convened the antislavery legislature, which called for another election to vote the Lecompton Constitution up or down. The result on January 4, 1858, was overwhelming: 10,226 against the constitution, 138 for the constitution with slavery, 24 for the constitution without slavery.

The combined results suggested a clear majority against slavery, but Buchanan stuck to his support of the Lecompton Constitution, driving another wedge into the Democratic party. Senator Douglas, up for reelection, could not afford to run as a champion of Lecompton. He broke dramatically with the president in a tense confrontation, but Buchanan persisted in trying to drive Lecompton "naked" through the Congress. In the Senate, administration forces held firm, and in March 1858 Lecompton was passed. In the House, enough anti-Lecompton Democrats combined to put through an amendment for a new and carefully supervised popular vote in Kansas. Enough senators went along to permit passage of the House bill. Southerners were confident the vote would favor slavery, because to reject slavery the voters would have to reject the constitution, which would postpone statehood until the population reached 90,000. On August 2, 1858, Kansas voters nevertheless rejected Lecompton by 11,300 to 1,788. With that vote Kansas, now firmly in the hands of its antislavery legislature, largely ended its role in the sectional controversy.

THE PANIC OF 1857   The third crisis of Buchanan's first half year in office, a financial crisis, broke in August 1857. It was brought on by a reduction in demand for American grain caused by the end of the Crimean War (1854–1856), a surge in manufacturing which outran the growth of markets, and the continued weakness and confusion of the state banknote system. Failure of the Ohio Life Insurance and Trust Company on August 24, 1857, precipitated the panic, which was followed by a depression from which the country did not emerge until 1859.

Everything in those years seemed to get drawn into the vortex of sectional conflict, and business troubles were no exception. Northern businessmen tended to blame the depression on the Democratic Tariff of 1857, which had put rates at their lowest level since 1816. The agricultural South weathered the crisis better than the North. Cotton prices fell, but slowly, and world markets for cotton quickly recovered. The result was an exalted notion of King Cotton's importance to the world, and apparent confirmation of the growing argument that the southern system was superior to the free-labor system of the North.

DOUGLAS VS. LINCOLN   Amid the recriminations over Dred Scott, Kansas, and the depression, the center could not hold. The Lecompton battle put severe strains on the most substantial cord of Union left, the Democratic party. To many, Douglas seemed the best hope, one of the few remaining Democratic leaders with support in both sections. But now Douglas was being whipsawed between the extremes. Kansas-Nebraska had cast him in the role of "doughface." His opposition to Lecompton, the fraudulent fruit of popular sovereignty, however, had alienated him from Buchanan's southern junta. But for all his flexibility and opportunism, Douglas had convinced himself that popular sovereignty was a point of principle, a bulwark of democracy and local self-government. In 1858 he faced reelection to the Senate against the opposition of Buchanan Democrats and Republicans. The year 1860 would give him a chance for the presidency, but first he had to secure his home base in Illinois.

To oppose him Illinois Republicans named Abraham Lincoln of Springfield, former Whig state legislator and one-term congressman, a moderately prosperous small-town lawyer. Lincoln's early life had been the hardscrabble existence of the frontier farm. Born in a Kentucky log cabin in 1809, raised on frontier farms in Indiana and Illinois, the young Lincoln had the wit and will to rise above his beginnings. With less than twelve months of sporadic schooling he learned to read, studied such books as came to hand, and eventually developed a prose style as muscular as the man himself. He worked at various farm tasks, operated a ferry, and made two trips down to New Orleans as a flatboatman. Striking out on his own, he managed a general store in New Salem, Illinois, learned surveying, served in the Black Hawk War (1832), won election to the legislature in 1834 at the age of twenty-five, read law, and was admitted to the bar in 1836. As a Whig regular, he adhered to the philosophy of Henry Clay. He stayed in the legislature until 1842, and in 1846 won a term in Congress. After a single term he retired from active politics to cultivate his law practice.

In 1854 the Kansas-Nebraska debate drew him back into the political arena. When Douglas appeared in Springfield to defend popular sovereignty, Lincoln spoke in refutation from the same platform. In Peoria he repeated the performance of what was known thereafter as the "Peoria Speech." This speech began the journey toward his appointment with destiny, preaching an old but oft-neglected doctrine: hate the sin but not the sinner.

> When Southern people tell us they are no more responsible for the origin of slavery, than we; I acknowledge the fact. When it is said that the institution exists; and that it is very difficult to get rid of it, in any satisfactory way, I can understand and appreciate the saying. . . .
>
> But all this, to my judgment, furnishes no more excuse for permitting slavery to go into our own free territory, than it would for reviving the African slave trade by law.

At first Lincoln held back from the rapidly growing new party, but in 1856 he threw in his lot with the Republicans, getting over 100 votes for their vice-presidential nomination, and gave some

A Republican party parade sweeps past the house of Abraham and Mary Lincoln during the Illinois senatorial campaign of 1858. During the campaign Lincoln and Stephen Douglas held their legendary debates.

fifty speeches for the Frémont ticket in Illinois and nearby states. By 1858 he was the obvious choice to oppose Douglas for the Senate seat, and Douglas knew he was up against a formidable foe. Lincoln resorted to the classic ploy of the underdog: he challenged the favorite to debate with him. Douglas had little relish for drawing attention to his opponent, but agreed to meet him in seven places around the state. Thus the legendary Lincoln-Douglas debates took place, August 21 to October 15.

At the time and since, much attention focused on the second debate, at Freeport, where Lincoln asked Douglas how he could reconcile popular sovereignty with the Dred Scott ruling that citizens had the right to carry slaves into any territory. Douglas's answer, thenceforth known as the Freeport Doctrine, was to state the obvious. Whatever the Supreme Court might say about slavery, it could not exist anywhere unless supported by local police regulations.

Douglas tried to set some traps of his own. It is standard practice, of course, to put extreme constructions upon an adversary's stand. Douglas intimated that Lincoln belonged to the fanatical sect of abolitionists who planned to carry the battle to the slave states, just as Lincoln intimated the opposite about Douglas. Douglas accepted, without any apparent qualms, the conviction of black inferiority which most whites, North and South, shared at the time, and sought to pin on Lincoln the stigma of advocating racial equality. The question was a hot potato, which Lincoln handled with caution. There was "A physical difference between the white and black races" and it would "forever forbid the two races living together on terms of social and political equality," he said. He simply favored the containment of slavery where it existed so that "the public mind shall rest in the belief that it is in the course of ultimate extinction." But the basic difference between the two men, Lincoln insisted, lay in Douglas's professed indifference to the moral question of slavery: "He says he 'don't care whether it is voted up or voted down' in the territories. . . . Any man can say that who does not see anything wrong in slavery, but no man can logically say it who does see a wrong in it; because no man can logically say he don't care whether a wrong is voted up or down. . . . "

If Lincoln had the better of the argument, at least in the long view, Douglas had the better of the election. The voters actually had to choose a legislature, which would then elect the senator. Lincoln men won the larger total vote, but its distribution gave Douglas the legislature, 54 to 41. As the returns trickled in from the fall elections in 1858—there was still no common election date—they recorded one loss after another for Buchanan men. When they were over, the administration had lost control of the House. But the new Congress would not meet in regular session until December 1859.

STORM WARNINGS   After the Lecompton fiasco the slavery issue was no longer before Congress in any direct way. The gradual return of prosperity in 1859 offered hope that the storms of the 1850s might yet pass. But the sectional issue still haunted the public mind, and like sheet lightning on the horizon, warned that a storm was still pending. In the spring there were two warning flashes. The Supreme Court finally ruled in the case of *Ableman v. Booth*, which had arisen in 1854 when an abolitionist editor in Milwaukee, Sherman M. Booth, roused a mob to rescue a fugitive slave. Convicted in federal court of violating the Fugitive Slave Act, he got the Wisconsin Supreme Court to order him freed on the ground that the act was unconstitutional. A unanimous Supreme Court made short work of Wisconsin's interposition. Chief Justice Taney's opinion denied the right of state courts to interfere and reaffirmed the constitutionality of the Fugitive Slave Act. The Wisconsin legislature in turn responded with states'-rights resolutions that faintly echoed the Virginia and Kentucky Resolutions of 1798–1799.

The episode, like others at the time, illustrated the significant fact that both North and South seized on nationalism or states' rights for their own purposes—neither was a point on which many men could claim consistency. Since the early 1840s the Garrisonian abolitionists had openly championed disunion, but they were a small, if vocal, minority in the North. In the South few denied a state's right to dissolve the bond of Union in the same way that the original states had ratified it. And as the South became increasingly a conscious minority, beset by antislavery forces and aware of its growing isolation in the Western world, more and more were willing to consider secession a possibility. By 1855, when Peru acted to abolish slavery, the peculiar institution was left only in Brazil, in the Spanish colonies of Cuba and Puerto Rico, in the Dutch colonies of Guiana and the West Indies, and in the American South.

JOHN BROWN'S RAID   For a season sectional agitations were held in check. But in October 1859 John Brown once again surfaced. Since the Pottawatomie Massacre in 1856 Brown had led a furtive existence, engaging in fundraising and occasional bushwhacking. Finally, on October 16, 1859, he was ready for his supreme gesture. From a Maryland farm he crossed the Potomac with nineteen men, including five Negroes, and under cover of darkness occupied the federal arsenal in Harper's Ferry, Virginia (now West Virginia). His scheme was foredoomed from the start, and any attempt at a rational explanation probably misses the point. His notion seems to have been that he would arm the many slaves who would flock to his cause, set up a black stronghold in the mountains of western Virginia, and provide a nucleus of support for slave insurrections across the South.

What he actually did was to take the arsenal by surprise, seize a few hostages, and sit there until he was surrounded and captured. He had even forgotten to bring food. Militiamen from the surrounding country rallied by the next afternoon, and the next evening Lt.-Col. Robert E. Lee, U.S. Cavalry, arrived with his aide, Lt. J. E. B. Stuart, and a force of marines. On the morning of October 18 Brown refused a call to surrender. The marines stormed the arsenal and took Brown prisoner, with a painful wound. Altogether Brown's men killed four people (including one marine) and wounded nine. Of their own force, ten died (including two of Brown's sons), five escaped, and seven were captured.

Brown was turned over to Virginia authorities, quickly tried for treason against the state and conspiracy to incite insurrection, convicted on October 31, and hanged on December 2 at Charlestown. Six others died on the gallows later. If Brown had

John Brown.

failed in his purpose—whatever it was—he had achieved two things. He had become a martyr for the antislavery cause, and he had set off panic throughout the slaveholding South. At his sentencing he delivered one of the classic American speeches: "Now, if it is deemed necessary that I should forfeit my life for the furtherance of the ends of justice, and mingle my blood further with the blood of my children and with the blood of millions in this slave country whose rights are disregarded by wicked, cruel, and unjust enactments, I say, let it be done."

When Brown, still unflinching, met his end, it was a day of solemn observances in the North. Prominent Republicans, including Lincoln and Seward, repudiated Brown's coup, but the discovery of Brown's correspondence revealed that he had enjoyed support among prominent antislavery leaders who, whether or not they knew at the time what they were getting into, later defended his deeds. "That new saint," Emerson said, " . . . will make the gallows as glorious as the cross." Garrison, the lifelong pacifist, now wished "success to every slave insurrection at the South and in every slave country."

By far the gravest after-effect of Brown's raid was to leave southerners in no mood to distinguish between John Brown and the Republican party. The southern mind now merged those who would contain slavery with those who would drown it in blood. All through the fall and winter of 1859–1860 rumors of conspiracy and insurrection swept the region. Every northern visitor, commercial traveler, or schoolteacher came under suspicion, and many were driven out. "We regard every man in our midst an enemy to the institutions of the South," said the Atlanta *Confederacy,* "who does not boldly declare that he believes African slavery to be a social, moral, and political blessing." Francis Lieber, a German exile, political scientist, and dedicated nationalist, survived in discomfort for yet a while at the College of South Carolina. But relations between the sections reminded him of what Thucydides had said about the Peloponnesian War of antiquity: "The Greeks did not understand each other any longer, though they spoke the same language."

The Center Comes Apart

The first session of the new Congress, which convened three days after the death of John Brown, confirmed Lieber's melancholy thought. The Democrats still controlled the Senate, but the House once again was thrown into deadlock over the choice of a Speaker. John Sherman of Ohio, the Republican candidate for Speaker, had committed the unforgivable sin in southern eyes of supporting the distribution of Hinton R. Helper's *The Impending Crisis of the South* (1857). Helper was a former North Carolinian who sought to demonstrate that slavery had impoverished nonslaveholding white southerners. The issue of "Helperism" kept enough votes from Sherman to prevent his selection. The House finally turned to William Pennington of New Jersey, an old Whig who supported the Fugitive Slave Act but also favored exclusion of slavery from the territories. He soon lined up with the Republicans. On the day after Pennington's election as Speaker, Jefferson Davis stood up in the Senate to introduce a set of resolutions for the defense of slavery, the main burden of which was a demand that the federal government extend "all needful protection" to slavery in the territories. Davis in effect asked for a federal slave code.

THE DEMOCRATS DIVIDE   Thus amid emotional hysteria and impossible demands the nation ushered in the year of another presidential election, destined to be the most fateful in its history. Four years earlier, in a moment of euphoria, the Democrats had settled on Charleston, South Carolina, as the site for their 1860 convention. Charleston in April, with the azaleas ablaze, was perhaps the most enticing city in the United States, but the worst conceivable place for such a meeting, except perhaps Boston. It was a hotbed of extremist sentiment, and lacked adequate accommodations for the crowds thronging in. South Carolina itself had chosen a remarkably moderate delegation, but the extreme southern-rights men held the upper hand in the delegations from the Gulf states.

PROGRESSIVE DEMOCRACY—PROSPECT OF A SMASH UP.

Prospect of a Smash Up. *This 1860 cartoon shows the Democratic party—the last remaining national party—about to be split by sectional differences and the onrushing Republicans led by Lincoln.*

Douglas men preferred to stand by the platform of 1856, which simply promised congressional noninterference with slavery. Southern firebrands, however, were now demanding federal protection for slavery in the territories. Buchanan supporters, hoping to stop Douglas, encouraged the strategy. The platform debate reached a heady climax when the Alabama fire-eater Yancey informed the northern Democracy that its error had been the failure to defend slavery as a positive good. An Ohio senator offered a blunt reply: "Gentlemen of the South," he said, "you mistake us—you mistake us. We will not do it."

When the southern planks lost, Alabama walked out of the convention, followed by the other Gulf states, Georgia, South Carolina (except for two stubborn up-country Unionists), and parts of the delegations from Arkansas and Delaware. This pattern foreshadowed with some fidelity the pattern of secession, in which the Deep South left the Union first. The convention then decided to leave the overwrought atmosphere of Charleston and reassemble in Baltimore on June 18. The Baltimore convention finally nominated Douglas on the 1856 platform. The Charleston seceders met first in Richmond, then in Baltimore, where they adopted the slave-code platform defeated in Charleston, and named Vice-President John C. Breckinridge of Kentucky for president. Thus another cord of union had snapped: the last remaining national party.

*Abraham Lincoln at the time of his
nomination for the presidency.*

LINCOLN'S ELECTION   The Republicans meanwhile gathered in
Chicago, in a gigantic hall jocosely called the "Wigwam." There
everything suddenly came together for "Honest Abe" Lincoln,
"the Railsplitter," the uncommon common man. Lincoln had
suddenly emerged in the national view during his senatorial
campaign two years before, and had since taken a stance designed to make him available for the nomination. He was strong
enough on the containment of slavery to satisfy the abolitionists,
yet moderate enough to seem less threatening than they were. In
February 1860 he had gone east to address an audience of influential Republicans at the Cooper Union in New York City, where
he emphasized his view of slavery "as an evil, not to be extended,
but to be tolerated and protected only because of and so far as its
actual presence among us makes that toleration and protection a
necessity."

Chicago provided surroundings that gave Lincoln's people
many advantages. His managers, for instance, could pack the galleries with noisy supporters. They started out with little more
support than the Illinois delegation, but worked to make Lincoln
everybody else's second choice. William H. Seward was the
early leader, but he had been tagged, perhaps wrongly, as an extremist for his earlier statements about an "irrepressible conflict" and a "higher law." On the first ballot Lincoln finished in
second place. On the next ballot he drew almost even with Seward, and when he came within one and a half votes of a majority
on the third count, Ohio quickly switched four votes to put him

over the top. Later the same day Sen. Hannibal Hamlin of Maine, a former Democrat, became the vice-presidential nominee.

The platform foreshadowed future policy better than most. It denounced John Brown's raid as "among the gravest of crimes," and promised the "maintenance inviolate of the right of each state to order and control its own domestic institutions." The party reaffirmed its resistance to the extension of slavery, and in an effort to gain broader support, endorsed a protective tariff for manufacturers, free homesteads for farmers, a more liberal naturalization law, and internal improvements, including a Pacific railroad. With this platform Republicans made a strong appeal to eastern businessmen, western farmers, and the large immigrant population.

Both major conventions revealed that opinion tended to become more radical in the upper North and Deep South. Attitude followed latitude. In the border states a sense of moderation, perhaps due to the fear that they would bear the brunt of any calamity, aroused the diehard Whigs there to make one more try at reconciliation. Meeting in Baltimore a week before the Republicans met in Chicago, they reorganized into the Constitutional Union party and named John Bell of Tennessee for president. Their only platform was "the Constitution of the Country, the Union of the States, and the Enforcement of the Laws."

Of the four candidates not one was able to command a national following, and the campaign resolved into a choice between Lincoln and Douglas in the North, Breckinridge and Bell in the South. One consequence of these separate campaigns was that each section gained a false impression of the other. The South never learned to distinguish Lincoln from the radicals; the North failed to gauge the force of southern intransigence—and in this Lincoln was among the worst. He stubbornly refused to offer the South assurances or to amplify his position, which he said was a matter of public record. The one man who tried to break through the veil that was falling between the sections was Douglas, who tried to mount a national campaign. Only forty-seven, but already weakened by drink, ill-health, and disappointments, he wore himself out in one final glorious campaign. Early in October 1860, at Cedar Rapids, Iowa, he got the news of Republican state victories from Pennsylvania and Indiana. "Mr. Lincoln is the next President," he said. "We must try to save the Union. I will go South." Down through the hostile areas of Tennessee, Georgia, and Alabama he carried appeals on behalf of the Union. "I do not believe that every Breckinridge man is a disunionist," he said, "but I do believe that every disunionist is a Breckinridge man." He was in Mobile when the election came.

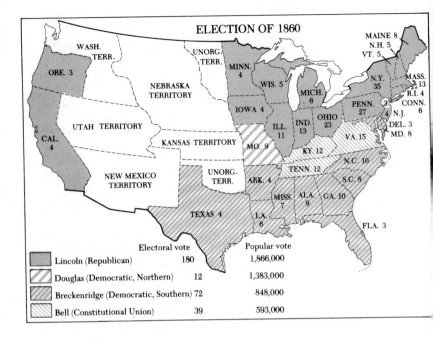

ELECTION OF 1860

	Electoral vote	Popular vote
Lincoln (Republican)	180	1,866,000
Douglas (Democratic, Northern)	12	1,383,000
Breckenridge (Democratic, Southern)	72	848,000
Bell (Constitutional Union)	39	593,000

By midnight of November 6 Lincoln's victory was clear. In the final count he had about 39 percent of the total popular vote, but a clear majority with 180 votes in the electoral college. He carried every one of the eighteen free states, and by a margin enough to elect him even if the votes for the other candidates had been combined. Among all the candidates, only Douglas had electoral votes from both slave and free states, but his total of 12 was but a pitiful remnant of Democratic Unionism. He ran last. Bell took Virginia, Kentucky, and Tennessee for 39 votes, and Breckinridge swept the other slave states to come in second with 72.

SECESSION OF THE DEEP SOUTH   Soon after the election the South Carolina legislature, which had assembled to choose the state's electors, set a special election for December 6 to choose delegates to a convention. In Charleston on December 20, 1860, the convention unanimously voted an Ordinance of Secession, declaring the state's ratification of the Constitution repealed and the union with other states dissolved. A Declaration of the Causes of Secession reviewed the threats to slavery, and asserted that a sectional party had elected to the presidency a man "whose opinions and purposes are hostile to slavery," who had declared "Government cannot endure permanently half slave,

CHARLESTON

MERCURY

EXTRA:

Passed unanimously at 1.15 o'clock, P. M., December 20th, 1860.

AN ORDINANCE

To dissolve the Union between the State of South Carolina and other States united with her under the compact entitled "The Constitution of the United States of America."

We, the People of the State of South Carolina, in Convention assembled, do declare and ordain, and it is hereby declared and ordained,

That the Ordinance adopted by us in Convention, on the twenty-third day of May, in the year of our Lord one thousand seven hundred and eighty-eight, whereby the Constitution of the United States of America was ratified, and also, all Acts and parts of Acts of the General Assembly of this State, ratifying amendments of the said Constitution, are hereby repealed; and that the union now subsisting between South Carolina and other States, under the name of "The United States of America," is hereby dissolved.

THE

UNION

IS

DISSOLVED!

A handbill announcing South Carolina's secession from the Union.

half free," and "that the public mind must rest in the belief that Slavery is in the course of ultimate extinction."

By February 1, 1861, six more states had declared themselves out of the Union. Texas was the last to act because its governor, staunch old Jacksonian Sam Houston, had refused to assemble the legislature for a convention call, but secessionist leaders called an irregular convention which authorized secession. Only there was the decision submitted to a referendum, which the secessionists carried handily. In some places the vote for delegates revealed a close division, especially in Georgia and Louisiana, but secession carried. On February 4 a convention of the seven states met in Montgomery; on February 7 they adopted a provisional constitution for the Confederate States of America, and two days later they elected Jefferson Davis its president. He was inaugurated February 18, with Alexander Stephens of Georgia as vice-president.

In all seven states of the southernmost tier a solid majority had voted for secessionist delegates, but their combined vote would not have been a majority of the presidential vote in November. What happened, it seemed, was what often happens in revolutionary situations: a determined and decisive group acted quickly in an emotionally charged climate and carried its program against a confused and indecisive opposition. Trying to decide whether or not a majority of the whites actually favored secession probably is beside the point—a majority were vulnerable to the decisive action of the secessionists.

BUCHANAN'S WAITING GAME History is full of might-have-beens. A bold stroke, even a bold statement, by the president at this point might have changed things. "Oh, for one moment of Jackson!" many a Unionist lamented, but there was no Jacksonian will in Buchanan. Besides, a bold stroke might simply have hastened the conflict. No bold stroke came from Lincoln either, nor would he consult with the administration during the long months before his inauguration on March 4. He inclined all too strongly to the belief that secession was just another bluff and kept his public silence. Buchanan followed his natural bent, the policy on which he had built a career: make concessions, seek a compromise to mollify the South. In his annual message on December 3 Buchanan made a forthright argument that secession was illegal, but that he lacked authority to coerce a state. "Seldom have we known so strong an argument come to so lame and impotent a conclusion," the Cincinnati *Enquirer* editorialized. There was, however, a hidden weapon in the president's reaffirmation of a duty to "take care that the laws be faithfully executed" insofar as he was able. If the president could enforce the law upon all citizens, he would have no need to "coerce" a state. Indeed his position became the policy of the Lincoln administration, which fought a war on the theory that individuals but not states as such were in rebellion.

Buchanan held firmly to his resolve, with some slight stiffening by the end of December 1860, when secession became a fact and the departure of two southerners removed the region's influence in his cabinet. He would retain positions already held, but would make no effort to assert federal authority provocatively. As the secessionists seized federal property, arsenals, and forts, this policy soon meant holding to isolated positions at Fort Pickens in Pensacola Harbor, some remote islands off southern Florida, and Fort Sumter in Charleston Harbor.

On the day after Christmas the small garrison at Fort Moultrie had been moved into the nearly completed Fort Sumter by Maj. Robert Anderson, a Kentucky Unionist. Anderson's move, designed to achieve both disengagement and greater security, struck South Carolina authorities as provocative, a violation of an earlier "gentleman's agreement" that the administration would make no changes in its arrangements, and commissioners of the newly "independent" state peremptorily demanded withdrawal of all federal forces.

They had overplayed their hand. Buchanan's cabinet, with only one southerner left, insisted it would be a gross violation of duty, perhaps grounds for impeachment, for the president to yield. His backbone thus stiffened, he sharply rejected the South Carolina ultimatum to withdraw: "This I cannot do: this I will not do." His nearest approach to coercion was to dispatch a steamer, *Star of the West*, to Fort Sumter with reinforcements and provisions. As the ship approached Charleston Harbor, Carolina batteries at Fort Moultrie and Morris Island opened fire and drove it away on January 9. It was in fact an act of war, but Buchanan chose to ignore the challenge. He decided instead to hunker down and ride out the remaining weeks of his term, hoping against hope that one of several compromise efforts would yet prove fruitful.

LAST EFFORTS AT COMPROMISE   Forlorn efforts at compromise continued in Congress until dawn of inauguration day. On December 18 Sen. John J. Crittenden of Kentucky had proposed a series of amendments and resolutions the central features of which were the recognition of slavery in the territories south of 36° 30'; and guarantees to maintain slavery where it already existed. A Senate Committee of Thirteen named to consider the proposal proved unable to agree. A House Committee of Thirty-three under Thomas Corwin of Ohio adopted two concessions to the South: an amendment guaranteeing slavery where it existed and granting statehood to New Mexico, presumably as a slave state. But the committee finished by submitting a set of proposals without endorsing any of them. The fight for a compromise was carried to the floor of each house by Crittenden and Corwin, and subjected to intensive debate during January and February.

Meanwhile a Peace Conference met in Willard's Hotel in February 1861, at the call of the Virginia legislature. Twenty-one states sent delegates and former president John Tyler presided, but the convention's proposal, substantially the same as the Crittenden Compromise, failed to win the support of either house of Congress. The only compromise proposal that met with any success was Corwin's amendment to guarantee slavery where it existed. Many Republicans, including Lincoln, were prepared to go that far to save the Union, but they were unwilling to repudiate their stand against slavery in the territories. As it happened, after passing the House the amendment passed the Senate without a vote to spare, by 24 to 12, on the dawn of inauguration day. It would have become the Thirteenth Amendment, with the first use of the word "slavery" in the Constitution, but the states never ratified it. When a Thirteenth Amendment was ratified in 1865, it did not guarantee slavery—it abolished slavery.

FURTHER READING

Two works which survey the coming of the Civil War are Allan Nevins's *Ordeal of the Union* (2 vols., 1947) and David M. Potter's *The Impending Crisis, 1848–1861* (1976).° Interpretive essays can be studied in Eric Foner's *Politics and Ideology in the Age of the Civil War* (1980)° and Joel H. Silbey's *The Partisan Imperative* (1985).

Numerous works cover various aspects of the political crises of the 1850s. Chaplain W. Morrison's *Democratic Politics and Sectionalism: The Wilmot Proviso Controversy* (1967) focuses on the initial dispute. William R. Brock's *Parties and Political Conscience: American Dilemmas, 1840–1850* (1979), examines the disruption of the two-party balance. Holman Hamilton's *Prologue to Conflict: The Crisis and Compromise of 1850* (1964) probes that crucial dispute. Michael F. Holt's *The Political Crisis of the 1850s* (1978)° traces the demise of the Whigs. Eric Foner provides a good introduction to how events and ideas combined in the formation of a new political party in *Free Soil, Free Labor, Free Men: The Ideology of the Republican Party before the Civil War* (1970).° Also good on the Republicans is Hans L. Trefousse's *The Radical Republicans: Lincoln's Vanguard for Racial Justice* (1969) and David H. Donald's *Charles Sumner and the Coming of the Civil War* (1960).

Robert W. Johannsen's *Stephen A. Douglas* (1973) analyzes the issue of popular sovereignty. A more national perspective is provided in James A. Rawley's *Race and Politics: "Bleeding Kansas" and the Coming of the Civil War* (1969). On the role of John Brown in the sectional crisis, see Stephen B. Oates's *To Purge This Land with Blood: A Biography of John Brown* (2nd ed., 1984).° Two other issues that divided the nation can be studied in Stanley W. Campbell's *The Slave Catchers* (1970),° on attempts to enforce the Fugitive Slave Act, and Don E. Fehrenbacher's *Slavery, Law, and Politics* (1981),° on the Dred Scott case.

The growing alienation of southerners from national trends is explored in David M. Potter's *The South and the Sectional Conflict* (1968). Studies of southern states include J. Mills Thornton III's *Politics and Power in a Slave Society: Alabama, 1800–1860* (1978),° Michael P. Johnson's *Toward a Patriarchial Republic: The Secession of Georgia* (1977), and Steven A. Channing's *Crisis of Fear: Secession in South Carolina* (1970).°

To gauge the role played by Lincoln in the coming crisis of war, see the biographies listed in Chapter 17; particularly good for Lincoln during the 1850s is Don E. Fehrenbacher's *Prelude to Greatness* (1962). Harry V. Jaffa's *Crisis of the House Divided* (1959) details the Lincoln-Douglas debates, and Richard N. Current's *Lincoln and the First Shot* (1963) treats the Fort Sumter controversy.

°These books are available in paperback editions.

17

THE WAR OF THE UNION

END OF THE WAITING GAME

During the four long months between his election and in-auguration Lincoln would say little about future policies and less about past positions. "If I thought a *repetition* would do any good I would make it," he wrote to an editor in St. Louis. "But my judgment is it would do positive harm. The secessionists *per se,* believing they had alarmed me, would clamor all the louder." So he stayed in Springfield until February 11, 1861, biding his time. He then boarded a train for a long, roundabout trip, and began to drop some hints to audiences along the way. To the New Jersey legislature, which responded with prolonged cheering, he said: "The man does not live who is more devoted to peace than I am. . . . But it may be necessary to put the foot down." At the end of the journey he reluctantly yielded to rumors of plots against his life, passed unnoticed on a night train through Baltimore, and slipped into Washington before daybreak on February 23.

The ignominious end to his journey reinforced the fears of eastern sophisticates that the man lacked style. Lincoln, to be sure, lacked a formal education and training in the rules of eti-quette. His clothing was hardly modish, even for the times. His tall frame shambled awkwardly, and he had an unseemly pen-chant for funny stories. But the qualities that first called him to public attention would soon manifest themselves. His prose, at least, had style—and substance. So did his politics. What Hawthorne called his "Yankee shrewdness and not-to-be caughtness" guided him through the traps laid for the unwary in Washington. Whatever else people might think of him, they soon learned that he was not easily dominated.

LINCOLN'S INAUGURATION   Buchanan called for Lincoln at Willard's Hotel on a bright and blustery March 4. Together they rode in an open carriage to the Capitol, where Chief Justice Taney administered the oath on a platform outside the East Portico. At the start, Stephen A. Douglas reached out to hold Lincoln's hat as a gesture of unity. In his inaugural address Lincoln repeated views already on record by quoting from an earlier speech: "I have no purpose, directly or indirectly, to interfere with the institution of slavery in the States where it exists. I believe I have no lawful right to do so, and I have no inclination to do so."

But the immediate question had shifted from slavery to secession, and most of the speech emphasized Lincoln's view that "the Union of these States is perpetual." The Union, he asserted, was older than the Constitution itself, dating from the Articles of Association in 1774, "matured and continued" by the Declaration of Independence and the Articles of Confederation. But even if the United States were only a contractual association, "no State upon its own mere motion can lawfully get out of the

The scene at the East Front of the Capitol during Abraham Lincoln's inauguration as president, March 4, 1861. The Capitol dome was then under construction.

Union." Lincoln promised to hold areas belonging to the government, collect duties and imposts, and deliver the mails unless repelled, but beyond that "there will be no invasion, no using of force against or among the people anywhere." The final paragraph, based on a draft by Seward, was an eloquent appeal for harmony:

> I am loath to close. We are not enemies, but friends. We must not be enemies. Though passion may have strained, it must not break, our bonds of affection. The mystic chords of memory, stretching from every battlefield and patriot grave to every living heart and hearthstone all over this broad land, will yet swell the chorus of the Union, when again touched, as surely they will be, by the better angels of our nature.

Lincoln not only entered office amid the gravest crisis yet faced by a president, but he also faced unusual problems of transition. Republicans, in power for the first time, crowded Washington, hungry for office. Four of the seven new cabinet members had been rivals for the presidency: William H. Seward at State, Salmon P. Chase at the Treasury, Simon Cameron at the War Department, and Edward Bates as attorney-general. Four were former Democrats and three were former Whigs. They formed a group of better-than-average ability, though most were so strong-minded they thought themselves better qualified to lead than Lincoln. It was only later that they were ready to acknowledge with Seward that "he is the best man among us."

THE FALL OF FORT SUMTER   For the time being Lincoln's combination of firmness and moderation differed little in effect from his predecessor's stance. Harsh judgments of Buchanan's waiting game overlook the fact that Lincoln kept it going. Indeed his only other choices were to accept secession as an accomplished fact or to use force right away. On the day after he took office, however, word arrived from Charleston that time was running out. Major Anderson had supplies for a month to six weeks, and Fort Sumter was being surrounded by a Confederate "ring of fire." Most cabinet members favored evacuation of Fort Sumter and defense of Fort Pickens at Pensacola, where relief ships were already offshore.

Events moved quickly to a climax in the next two weeks. On April 4 Lincoln decided to reinforce Fort Pickens and resupply Fort Sumter. On April 6 he notified the governor of South Carolina that "an attempt will be made to supply Fort Sumter with provisions only. . . . " On April 9 President Jefferson Davis and his cabinet in Montgomery decided against permitting Lincoln to maintain the status quo. On April 11 Confederate Gen. Pierre G. T. Beauregard demanded a speedy surrender of Sumter. Major Anderson refused, but said his supplies would be used up in three more days. With the relief ships approaching, Anderson received an ultimatum to yield. He again refused, and at 4:30 A.M. on April 12 the first gun sounded at Fort Johnson on James Island, and Fort Sumter quickly came under a crossfire from Sullivan's and Morris Islands as well. After more than thirty hours, his ammunition exhausted, Anderson agreed to give up, and on April 14 he lowered his flag. The only fatalities were two men killed in an explosion during a final salute to the colors, the first in a melancholy train of war dead.

The guns of Charleston signaled the end of the waiting game. On the day after Anderson's surrender, Lincoln called upon the loyal states to supply 75,000 militiamen to subdue a combination "too powerful to be suppressed by the ordinary course of judicial proceedings." Volunteers rallied around the flag at the recruiting stations. On April 19 Lincoln proclaimed a blockade of southern ports which, as the Supreme Court later ruled, confirmed the existence of war.

TAKING SIDES In the free states and the Confederate states the proclamation reinforced the patriotic fervor of the day. In the upper South it brought dismay, and another wave of secession which swept four more states into the Confederacy. Many in those states abhorred both abolitionists and secessionists, but faced with a call for troops to suppress their sister states, decided to abandon the Union. Virginia acted first. Its convention had met intermittently since February; now it convened again and passed an ordinance of secession on April 17. The Confederate Congress then chose Richmond as its new capital, and the government moved there in June.

Three other states followed Virginia in little over a month: Arkansas on May 6, Tennessee on May 7, and North Carolina on May 20. The Tar Heel state, next to last to ratify the Constitution, was last in secession. All four of the holdout states, especially Tennessee and Virginia, had areas (mainly in the mountains) where both slaves and secessionists were scarce and where Union support ran strong. In Tennessee the mountain counties would supply more volunteers to the Union than to the Confederate cause. Unionists in western Virginia, bolstered by a Union army from Ohio under Gen. George B. McClellan, contrived a loyal government of Virginia which gave its consent to the formation of a new state. In 1863 Congress admitted West Virginia to the Union with a constitution that provided for gradual emancipation of the few slaves there.

Of the other slave states, Delaware, with but a token number of slaves, remained firmly in the Union, but Maryland, Kentucky, and Missouri went through bitter struggles for control. The secession of Maryland would have made Washington but a Union enclave within the Confederacy, and in fact Baltimore's mayor for a time did cut all connections to the capital. On April 19 a mob attacked the Sixth Massachusetts Regiment on its way through Baltimore and inflicted a toll of four dead and thirty-six wounded. To hold the state Lincoln took drastic measures of dubious legality: he suspended the writ of habeas corpus (under which judges could require arresting officers to produce their prisoners and justify their arrest) and rounded up pro-Confederate leaders and threw them in jail. The fall elections ended the threat of Maryland's secession by returning a solidly Unionist majority in the state.

Kentucky, native state of both Lincoln and Davis, home of Crittenden and Breckinridge, was torn by divided loyalties. But May and June elections for a state convention returned a thump-

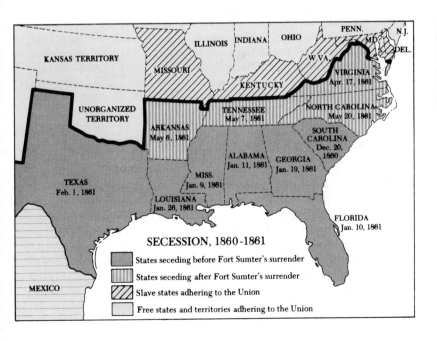

SECESSION, 1860-1861

States seceding before Fort Sumter's surrender

States seceding after Fort Sumter's surrender

Slave states adhering to the Union

Free states and territories adhering to the Union

ing Unionist majority, and the state legislature proclaimed Kentucky's "neutrality" in the conflict. Lincoln recognized the strategic value of his native state, situated on the south bank of the Ohio. "I think to lose Kentucky is nearly the same as to lose the whole game," he said. He promised to leave the state alone so long as the Confederates did likewise, and reassured its citizens that a war against secession was not a war against slavery. Kentucky's fragile neutrality lasted until September 3, when a Confederate force occupied Hickman and Columbus. Gen. Ulysses S. Grant then moved Union soldiers into Paducah, at the mouth of the Tennessee River. Kentucky, though divided in allegiance, for the most part remained with the Union. It joined the Confederacy, some have said, only after the war.

Lincoln's effort to hold a middle course in Missouri was upset by the maneuvers of less patient men in the state. Unionists there had a numerical advantage, but Confederate sympathies were strong and St. Louis had large numbers of both. For a time the state, like Kentucky, kept an uneasy peace. But elections for a convention brought an overwhelming Union victory, while a pro-Confederate militia under the state governor began to gather near St. Louis. In the city Unionist forces rallied and on May 10 they surprised and disarmed the militia at its camp. They pursued the pro-Confederate forces into the southwestern part of the state, and after a temporary setback on August 10, the Unionists pushed the Confederates back again, finally breaking their resistance at the battle of Pea Ridge (March 6–8, 1862), just over the state line in Arkansas. Thereafter border warfare continued in Missouri, pitting rival bands of gunslingers who kept up their feuding and banditry for years after the war was over.

A "BROTHERS' WAR"   Robert E. Lee epitomized the agonizing choice facing many men of the border states. Son of "Lighthorse Harry" Lee, a Revolutionary War hero, and married to a descendant of Martha Washington, Lee had served in the United States Army for thirty years. Master of Arlington, an estate which faced Washington across the Potomac, he was summoned by Gen. Winfield Scott, another Virginian, and offered command of the Federal forces in the field. After a sleepless night pacing the floor, Lee told Scott that he could not go against his "country," meaning Virginia. He resigned his commission, retired to his estate, and soon answered a call to the Virginia—later the Confederate—service. The course of the war might have been different had Lee made another choice.

Soldier group. *Neither side in the Civil War was prepared for the magnitude of this first of "modern" wars.*

The conflict sometimes became literally a "brothers' war." At Hilton Head, South Carolina, Percival Drayton commanded a Federal gunboat while his brother, Brig. Gen. Thomas F. Drayton, led Confederate land forces. Franklin Buchanan, who commanded the *Virginia* (formerly the *Merrimac*), sank the Union ship *Congress* with his brother on board. John J. Crittenden of Kentucky had a son in each army. J. E. B. Stuart of the Confederate cavalry was chased around the peninsula below Richmond by his Federal father-in-law. Lincoln's attorney-general had a son in the Confederate army, and Mrs. Lincoln herself had a brother, three half-brothers, and three brothers-in-law in the Confederate forces.

Neither side was ready for war, not even for the kind that had been fought before. And certainly neither could foresee the consuming force of this one, with its total mobilization of men and materials. This first of "modern" wars brought into use devices and techniques never before employed on such a scale: railroad transport, artillery, repeating rifles, ironclad ships, the telegraph, balloons, the Gatling gun (a rudimentary machine-gun), trenches, and wire entanglements.

ECONOMIC ADVANTAGES   If the South seceded in part out of a growing awareness of its minority status in the nation, a balance sheet of the sections in 1860 shows the accuracy of that perception. To begin, the Union held twenty-three states, including four border slave states, while the Confederacy had eleven, claiming also Missouri and Kentucky. Ignoring conflicts of allegiance within various states, which might roughly cancel each other out, the population count was about 22 million in the Union to 9 million in the Confederacy, and about 3½ million of the latter were slaves. The Union therefore had an edge of about four to one in potential manpower.

An even greater advantage for the North was its industry. In gross value of manufactures, the Union states had a margin of better than ten to one in 1860. The states that joined the Confederacy produced just under 7.4 percent of the nation's manufactures on the eve of conflict. What made the disparity even greater was that little of this was in heavy industry. The only iron industry of any size in the Confederacy was the Tredegar Iron Works in Richmond, which had long supplied the United States Army. Tredegar's existence strengthened the Confederacy's will to defend its capital. The Union states, in addition to making most of the country's shoes, textiles, and iron products, turned out 97 percent of the firearms and 96 percent of the railroad equipment produced in the nation. They had most of the trained mechanics, most of the shipping and mercantile firms, and the bulk of the banking and financial resources.

Even in farm production the northern states overshadowed the bucolic South, for most of the North's population was still rooted in the soil. As the progress of the war upset southern output, northern farms managed to increase theirs, despite the loss of workers to the army. The Confederacy produced enough to meet minimal needs, but the disruption of transport caused shortages in many places. One consequence was that the North produced a surplus of wheat for export at a time when drought and crop failures in Europe created a critical demand. King Wheat supplanted King Cotton as the nation's main export, the chief means of acquiring foreign money and bills of exchange to pay for imports from abroad.

The North's advantage in transport weighed heavily as the war went on. The Union had more wagons, horses, and ships than the Confederacy, and an impressive edge in railroads: about 20,000 miles to the South's 10,000. The actual discrepancy was even greater, for southern railroads were mainly short lines built to different gauges, and had few replacements for rolling stock which broke down or wore out. The Confederacy had only one east-west connection, between Memphis and Chattanooga. The latter was an important rail hub with connections via Knoxville into Virginia and down through Atlanta to Charleston and Savannah. The North, on the other hand, already had an intricate railroad network. Three major lines gave western farmers an outlet to the eastern seaboard and greatly lessened their former dependence on the Mississippi River.

MILITARY ADVANTAGES Against the weight of such odds the wonder was that the Confederacy managed to survive four years. Yet at the start certain things evened the odds. At first the South had more experienced military leaders. A number of circumstances had given rise to a military tradition in the South: the long-standing Indian danger, the fear of slave insurrection, an archaic punctilio about points of honor, and a history of expansionism. Military careers had prestige, and military schools multiplied in the antebellum years, the most notable West Points of the South being the Citadel and Virginia Military Institute. West Point itself drew many southerners, producing an army corps dominated by men from the region, chief among them Winfield Scott. Many northern West Pointers, like George B. McClellan and Ulysses S. Grant, dropped out of the service for civilian careers. A large proportion of the army's southern officers resigned their commissions to follow their states into the Confederacy. The head of the Louisiana Seminary of Learning and Military Academy (precursor of Louisiana State University), William Tecumseh Sherman, went the other way, rejoining the United States Army.

The general loyalty of the navy, which retained most of its southern officers, provided an important balance to the North's losses of army men. At the start Union seapower relied on about 90 ships, though only 42 were on active service and most were at distant stations. But under the able guidance of Secretary Gideon Welles the Union navy eventually grew to 650 vessels of all types. It never completely sealed off the South, but it raised to desperate levels the hazards of blockade running. On the inland waters navy gunboats and transports played an even more direct role in ultimately securing the Union's control of the Mississippi and its larger tributaries, which provided easy routes into the center of the Confederacy.

THE WAR'S EARLY COURSE Amid the furies of passion after the fall of Fort Sumter, hearts lifted on both sides with the hope that the war might end with one sudden bold stroke, the capture of Washington or the fall of Richmond. Strategic thought at the time remained under the spell of Napoleon, holding that everything would turn on one climactic battle in which a huge force, massed against an enemy's point of weakness, would demoralize its armies and break its will to resist. Such ideas had been instilled in a generation of West Point cadets, but these lessons neglected the massive losses Napoleon had suffered, losses that finally turned his victories into defeat.

General Scott, the seventy-five-year-old commander of the Union army, saw a long road ahead. Being older—his career dated from the War of 1812—he fell under the Napoleonic spell less than others. He proposed to use the navy to blockade the long Atlantic and Gulf coastlines, and then to divide and subdivide the Confederacy by pushing southward along the main water routes: the Mississippi, Tennessee, and Cumberland Rivers. As word leaked out, the newspapers impatiently derided his "Anaconda" strategy, which they judged far too slow, indicative of the commander's old age and caution. To the end, however, the Anaconda strategy of attrition remained Union policy: there was no Napoleonic climax.

Like Lincoln, President Davis was under pressure to strike for a quick decision. Davis let the battle-hungry Gen. P. G. T. Beauregard hurry his main forces in Virginia to Manassas Junction, about twenty-five miles from Washington. Lincoln seems meanwhile to have been persuaded that Gen. Irwin McDowell's newly recruited army of some 30,000 might overrun the outnumbered Confederates and quickly march on to Richmond. But Gen. Joseph E. Johnston had another Confederate force of some 12,000 in the Shenandoah Valley around Winchester. These men slipped over the Blue Ridge and down the Manassas Gap Railroad. Most arrived on the scene the day before the battle.

On July 21, 1861, McDowell's forces encountered Beauregard's army dug in behind a little stream called Bull Run. The generals adopted markedly similar plans—each would turn the other's left. Beauregard's orders went astray, while the Federals nearly achieved their purpose early in the afternoon. Beauregard then rushed his reserves to meet the offensive, which reached its climax around the Henry House Hill. Amid the fury, Gen. Barnard Bee rallied his South Carolina volunteers by pointing to Thomas J. Jackson's brigade: "There stands Jackson like a stone wall." After McDowell's last assault had faltered, he decided that discretion was the better part of valor. An orderly retreat in battle is one of the most difficult of maneuvers, and as it

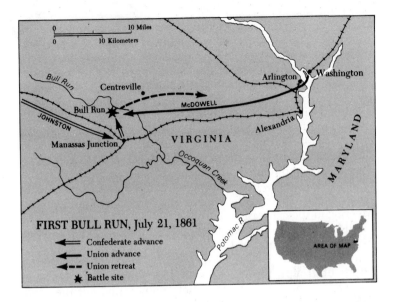

FIRST BULL RUN, July 21, 1861

◄═══ Confederate advance
◄─── Union advance
◄--- Union retreat
★ Battle site

AREA OF MAP

happened, was too much for the raw Federal recruits. On the road back to Washington a bridge at Cub Run collapsed, and in the traffic jam that ensued, retreat turned into panic.

Fortunately for the Federals, the Confederates were about as demoralized by victory as the Federals by defeat. In any case a summer downpour the next day turned roads into sloughs. The quick decision for which both sides had reached proved beyond their grasp. Beauregard, however, was promoted to full general, one of five in the Confederate service, while the Union set about building Washington's defenses. To replace the hapless McDowell, Lincoln named Gen. George B. McClellan, fresh from his victories in western Virginia where he had secured the route of the Baltimore and Ohio Railroad.

MILITARY DEADLOCK

MOBILIZING VOLUNTEERS   After the Battle of Bull Run (or Manassas)° both sides realized that the war would be more than a triumphant march. But even then mobilization was so haphazard that a Prussian general later remarked that the war was fought by little more than armed mobs on both sides. When secession

°The Federals most often named battles for natural features, the Confederates for nearby towns, thus Bull Run (Manassas), Antietam (Sharpsburg), Stone's River (Murfreesboro), and the like.

came, the United States Army numbered only 16,400 men and officers, most of whom were out west. The army remained a separate and very small part of the Union forces. Both sides, in the time-honored American way of war, looked to militia and volunteers to beef up their armies, and in the beginning were swamped with lighthearted recruits.

Lincoln's first emergency call for 75,000 militiamen produced about 80,000, but most of these three-month men were nearly due to go home by the time of Bull Run. On May 3 Lincoln called for 45,000 volunteers in 40 regiments to serve for three years. So overwhelming was the response that 208 regiments quickly materialized. This was the beginning of a great volunteer army. Meeting in special session on July 4, 1861, Congress authorized a call for 500,000 more men, and after Bull Run added another 500,000. By the end of the year the first half million had enlisted, as a result mainly of state initiative and in many cases the efforts of groups, towns, and even individuals who raised and equipped regiments. This pell-mell mobilization left the army with a large number of "political" officers, commissioned by state governors or elected by the recruits.

The Confederate record was much the same. The first mass enlistment put an even greater strain on limited means. By act of February 28, 1861, the Provisional Congress authorized President Jefferson Davis to accept for terms of one year state troops or volunteer units offered by governors. On March 6 Davis was empowered to call 100,000 twelve-month volunteers and to employ state militia up to six months. In May, once the fighting had started, he was authorized to raise up to 400,000 three-year volunteers "without the delay of a formal call upon the respective states." Thus by early 1862, despite the leavening of three-year men, most of the veteran Confederate soldiers were nearing the end of their terms without having encountered much significant action. They were also resisting the incentives of bonuses and furloughs for reenlistment.

THE DRAFT   The Confederates were driven to adopt conscription first. By act of April 16, 1862, all male white citizens, eighteen to thirty-five, were declared members of the army for three years and those already in service were required to serve out three years. In September 1862 the upper age was raised to forty-five, and in February 1864 the age limits were further extended to cover all from seventeen to fifty, with those under eighteen and over forty-five reserved for state defense.

Comprehensive as the law appeared on its face, it was weakened in practice by two loopholes. First, a draftee might escape service either by providing an able-bodied substitute not of draft age or by paying $500 in commutation. Second, exemptions, designed to protect key civilian work, were all too subject to abuse by men seeking "bombproof" jobs. Exemption of state officials, for example, was flagrantly abused by the governors of Georgia and North Carolina, who were in charge of defining the vital jobs. The exclusion of teachers with twenty pupils inspired a sudden educational renaissance, and the exemption of one white man for each plantation with twenty or more slaves led to bitter complaints about "a rich man's war and a poor man's fight."

The Union took nearly another year to decide that volunteers would be too few after the first excitement. Congress flirted with conscription in the Militia Act of July 1862, which invited states to draft 300,000 militiamen, but this move produced only about 65,000 soldiers. Then Congress offered bounties of $100 ($300 by 1864) for enlistments, but the system was grossly abused by "bounty-jumpers" who would collect in one place and then move on to enlist somewhere else.

Congress finally acted in March 1863 to draft men aged twenty to forty-five. Exemptions were granted to specified federal and state officeholders and to others on medical or compassionate grounds, but one could still buy a substitute or, for $300, have one's service commuted. An elaborate machinery of enforcement passed down quotas to states and districts; conscription was used only where the number of volunteers fell short of the quota, an incentive for communities to supplement the federal bounties. In both the North and the South conscription spurred men to volunteer, either to collect bounties or to avoid the disgrace of being drafted. Eventually the draft in the North produced only 46,000 conscripts and 118,000 substitutes, or about 6 percent of the Union armies.

The draft flouted an American tradition of voluntary service and was widely held to be arbitrary and unconstitutional. In the South the draft also sullied the cause of states' rights by requiring the exercise of a central power. It might have worked better had it operated through the states, some of which had set up their own drafts to meet the calls of President Davis. The governor of Georgia, who had one of the best records for raising troops at first, turned into a bitter critic of the draft, pronouncing it unconstitutional and trying to obstruct its enforcement. Few of the other governors gave it unqualified support, and Vice-President Stephens remained unreconciled to it throughout the war.

Widespread opposition limited enforcement of the draft acts

both North and South. In New York City, which had long enjoyed commercial ties with the South, the announcement of a draft lottery on July 11, 1863, led to a week of rioting in which mobs turned on black scapegoats, lynched Negroes caught on the streets, and burned down a Negro orphanage. The violence and pillaging ran completely out of control; seventy-four persons died, and an estimated $2 million in property was destroyed before soldiers brought from Gettysburg restored order.

As important as the problem of manpower were those of supply and logistics. If wars bring forth loyalty, they also bring forth greed, and this war's pell-mell mobilization offered much room for profiteering. Simon E. Cameron, the machine politician whom Lincoln appointed secretary of war to round out his political coalition, tolerated wholesale fraud. Lincoln eased him out in January 1862, and his successor, Edwin M. Stanton, brought order and efficiency into the department. But he was never able entirely to eliminate the plague of overcharging for shoddy goods.

NAVAL ACTIONS   After Bull Run, both sides mobilized for a longer war, and for the rest of 1861 into early 1862 the most important actions involved naval war and blockade. The one great threat to the Union navy proved to be short-lived. The Confederates in

The Merrimack (center, top) *and the* Monitor (center, bottom) *exchange fire at Hampton Roads on March 9, 1862. This print is based on a sketch done at the scene.*

Norfolk fashioned an ironclad ship from an abandoned Union steam frigate, the *Merrimack*. Rechristened the *Virginia*, it ventured out on March 8, 1862, and wrought havoc among Union ships at the Chesapeake entrance. But as luck would have it, a new Union ironclad, the *Monitor*, arrived from New York in time to engage the *Virginia* on the next day. They fought to a draw and the *Virginia* returned to port, where the Confederates destroyed it when they had to give up Norfolk soon afterward.

Gradually the "anaconda" tightened its grip on the South. At Fortress Monroe, Virginia, Union forces under Benjamin F. Butler held the tip of the peninsula between the James and the York, the scene of much colonial and revolutionary history. The navy extended its bases farther down the coast in the late summer and fall of 1862. Ben Butler's troops then captured Hatteras Inlet on the Outer Banks of North Carolina in August, a foothold soon extended to Roanoke Island and New Bern on the mainland. In November 1861 a Federal flotilla appeared at Port Royal, South Carolina, pounded the fortifications into submission, and seized the port and nearby sea islands.

From there the navy's progress extended southward along the Georgia-Florida coast. To the north the Federals laid siege to Charleston; by 1863 Fort Sumter and the city itself had come under bombardment from Morris Island. In the spring of 1862 Flag Officer David Glasgow Farragut forced open the lower Mississippi and surprised New Orleans, which had expected any attack to come downstream. Farragut won a surrender on May 1, then moved quickly to take Baton Rouge in the same way. An occupation force moved in under General Butler.

ACTIONS IN THE WEST Except for the amphibious thrusts along the southern coast, little happened in the Eastern Theater (east of the Appalachians) before May 1862. The Western Theater (from the mountains to the Mississippi), on the other hand, flared up with several encounters and an important penetration of the Confederate states. In January, Gen. George H. Thomas cleared eastern Kentucky by a decisive defeat of the Confederates at Mill Springs. The main routes southward, however, lay farther west. There Confederate Gen. Albert Sidney Johnston had perhaps 40,000 men stretched over some 150 miles, with concentrations at Columbus and Bowling Green, Kentucky, each astride a major north-south railroad. At the center, however, only about 5,500 men held Fort Henry on the Tennessee and Fort Donelson on the Cumberland.

Early in 1862 Ulysses S. Grant made the first thrust against

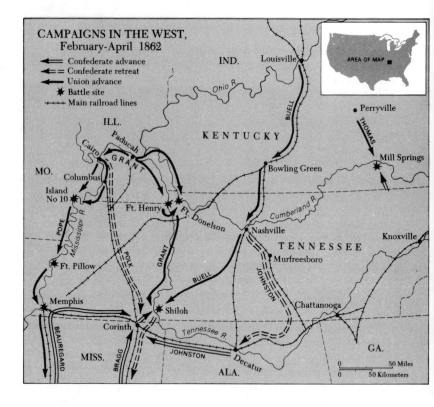

Johnston's center. Moving out of Cairo and Paducah with a gunboat flotilla under Commodore Andrew H. Foote, he swung
southward up the Tennessee River toward Fort Henry. After a
pounding from the Union gunboats, Fort Henry fell on February
6. Grant then moved quickly overland to attack Fort Donelson,
while Foote ran his gunboats back to the Ohio and up the Cumberland. Donelson proved a harder nut to crack, but on February
16 it gave up with some 12,000 men. Grant's terms, "unconditional surrender," and his quick success sent a thrill through the
Union. U. S. "Unconditional Surrender" Grant had not only
opened a water route to Nashville, but had thrust his forces between the two strongholds of the western Confederates. A. S.
Johnston therefore had to give up his foothold in Kentucky and
abandon Nashville to Don Carlos Buell's Army of the Ohio (February 25) in order to reunite his forces at Corinth, Mississippi,
along the Memphis and Chattanooga Railroad.

SHILOH Thus, quickly, the Union regained most of Kentucky
and western Tennessee, and stood poised in 1862 to strike at the

Deep South. On the Mississippi itself, Confederate strong points at Island No. 10 and at Fort Pillow fell on April 7 and 13 respectively, and Memphis on June 6, to a combined force under Commodore Foote and Gen. John Pope. Meanwhile Grant moved farther southward along the Tennessee River, hoping to link up with Buell's army near the southern border of Tennessee. At Pittsburg Landing, their rendezvous, Grant made a deadly mistake. While planning his attack on Corinth, he failed to set up defensive lines. The morning of April 6 the Confederates struck suddenly at Shiloh, a country church, and after a day of bloody confusion, pinned Grant's men against the river. But under the cover of gunboats and artillery at Pittsburg Landing, reinforcements from Buell's army arrived overnight. The next day the tide turned and the Rebels withdrew to Corinth, with Grant's army too battered to pursue.

Shiloh was the costliest battle in which Americans had ever engaged, although worse was yet to come. Combined casualties of nearly 25,000 exceeded the total dead and wounded of the Revolution, the War of 1812, and the Mexican War combined. Among the dead was Albert Sidney Johnston, an artery in his leg severed by a gunshot. The Union, too, lost for a while the full services of its finest general. Grant had been caught napping and was too shattered by his heavy losses to press the advantage. The Confederates had missed their chance to prevent Grant's linkage with Buell, but as at Bull Run, the victors were as demoralized by victory as the losers by defeat.

Gen. Henry W. Halleck, who first replaced Frémont in Missouri and then took overall command in the West, now arrived to take personal command of the Union forces in the field. He shelved Grant in an insignificant position as second in command, giving the troops Grant had been leading to George H. Thomas. Halleck, "Old Brains," the textbook strategist of offensive war, proved in the field to be unaccountably timid. Determined not to repeat Grant's mistake, he moved with profound caution on Corinth, taking at face value every inflated report of Rebel strength. But outnumbered better than two to one, P. G. T. Beauregard (Johnston's successor) abandoned Corinth to the Federals on May 30, falling back on Tupelo.

Halleck let slip the chance to overwhelm Beauregard. Instead, before being summoned back to Washington in June, he dispatched units in several directions. Grant remained on the scene, guarding Corinth and other points. Buell withdrew to Nashville to prepare an offensive against Chattanooga. The Confederate force, commanded by Braxton Bragg after the loss of Corinth,

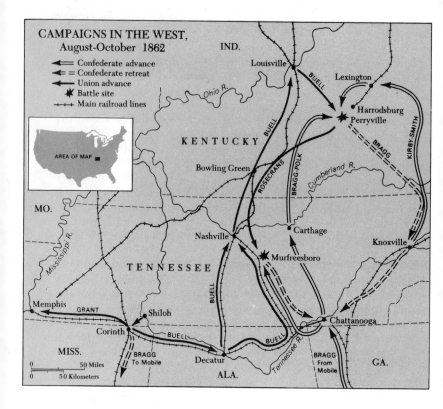

CAMPAIGNS IN THE WEST,
August-October 1862

moved via Mobile to Chattanooga. For the remainder of 1862
the chief action in the Western Theater was a series of inconclusive maneuvers and two sharp engagements. Bragg took his army
to Kentucky, threatened Louisville, and was stopped by Buell's
Army of the Ohio at Perryville on October 8. Kentuckians failed
to rally to the Confederate flag and Bragg pulled back into Tennessee. Buell, meanwhile, under pressure to sever the rail line at
Chattanooga, proved to be one of the many Union generals who
Lincoln said had "the slows." The administration replaced him
with William S. Rosecrans, who moved out of Nashville and met
Bragg in the costly engagement at Murfreesboro (or Stone's
River), December 31 to January 3, after which Bragg cleared out
of central Tennessee and fell back on Chattanooga. But Lincoln
still coveted eastern Tennessee both for its many Unionists and
for its railroads, which he wanted to cut to get between the
Rebels and their "hog and hominy."

MCCLELLAN'S PENINSULAR CAMPAIGN   The Eastern Theater, aside
from the coastal operations, remained fairly quiet for nine

months after Bull Run. When George B. McClellan took command in Washington after Bull Run, he vigorously set about getting men back to their units, getting them organized, and keeping them busy—in short, he built an army out of the fragments left from the first battle. In November 1861, upon General Scott's retirement, which McClellan impatiently awaited, he became general-in-chief. The newspapers dubbed him Little Napoleon, and a photographer posed him with his right hand inside his jacket. But these impressions were misleading. On the surface McClellan exuded confidence and poise, and a certain flair for parade-ground showmanship. Yet his knack for organization never went much beyond that.

Time passed, the army grew, and McClellan kept building his forces to meet the superior numbers that always seemed to be facing him. His intelligence service, headed by the private detective Allen Pinkerton, tended to overestimate enemy forces. Before moving, there was always the need to do this or that, to get 10,000 or 20,000 more men, always something. McClellan's Army of the Potomac was nine months in gestation after Bull Run, and then moved mainly because Lincoln insisted. In General Order No. 1, the president directed McClellan to begin forward movement by Washington's Birthday, February 22, 1862. The president's idea was that the army should move directly toward Richmond, keeping itself between the Confederate army and Washington. But McClellan had another idea, and despite his reluctance to move, very nearly pulled it off. The idea was to enter Richmond by the side door, so to speak, up the neck of land between the York and James Rivers, site of Jamestown, Williamsburg, and Yorktown, at the tip of which Federal forces already held Fortress Monroe, about seventy-five miles from Richmond.

Lincoln consented but specified, to McClellan's chagrin, that a force be left under McDowell to guard Washington. In mid-March 1862 McClellan's army finally embarked. Advancing slowly up the thinly defended peninsula, taking no chances, McClellan brought Yorktown under siege from April 5 until May 4, when the Confederates slipped away, having accomplished their purpose of allowing Gen. Joseph E. Johnston to get his army in front of Richmond. Before the end of May McClellan's advance units sighted the church spires of Richmond. But his army was divided by the Chickahominy River, which splits the peninsula north and east of Richmond, and though Richmond lay south of the Chickahominy, part of the Confederate army was on the north bank to counter any southward move from Washington by McDowell.

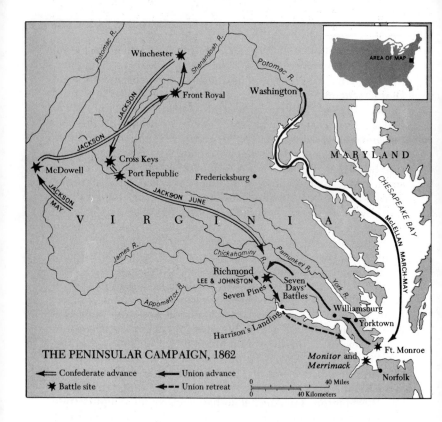

McDowell, however, was delayed by more urgent matters, or
what seemed so. President Davis, at the urging of military ad-
viser Robert E. Lee, sent Stonewall Jackson into the Shenandoah
Valley on what proved to be a brilliant diversionary action. From
March 23 to June 9, Jackson and some 18,000 men pinned down
two separate armies with more than twice his numbers by striking first at Frémont's forces in the western Virginia mountains,
then at Nathanial P. Banks at the northern end of the valley.
While McDowell braced to defend Washington, Jackson hastened back to defend Richmond.

On May 31 Johnston struck at Union forces isolated on the
south bank by the flooded river. In the battle of Seven Pines (Fair
Oaks), only the arrival of reinforcements, who somehow crossed
the swollen river, prevented a disastrous Union defeat. Both
sides took heavy casualties, and General Johnston was severely
wounded. At this point Robert E. Lee assumed command of the
Army of Northern Virginia. Lee quickly sized up the situation.
Reunited with the elusive Jackson, Lee would hit the Union

forces north of the Chickahominy with everything he had, leaving a token force in front of Richmond.

On June 26, Lee and Jackson struck the Union's extreme right at Mechanicsville, and kept up the assault on successive days at Gaines' Mill, Savage's Station, and White Oak Swamp. As the Federals withdrew they inflicted heavy losses on the Rebels, frustrating Lee's purpose of crushing the right flank. McClellan managed to get his main forces on the south side of the river, and established a new base at Harrison's Landing on the James. Lee's final desperate attack came at Malvern Hill (July 1), where the Confederates suffered heavy losses from Union artillery and gunboats in the James. The Seven Days' Battles (June 25 to July 1) had failed to dislodge the Union forces. McClellan was still near Richmond, with good supply lines on the James River.

On July 9, when Lincoln visited McClellan's headquarters on the James, the general complained that the administration had failed to support him adequately and handed the president a strange document, the "Harrison's Landing Letter," in which, despite his critical plight, he instructed the president at length on war policies. It was ample reason to remove the general. Instead Lincoln returned to Washington and on July 11 called Henry Halleck from the west to take charge as general-in-chief, a post that McClellan had temporarily vacated.

SECOND BATTLE OF MANASSAS   The new high command decided to evacuate the peninsula, which had become the graveyard of the last hope for a short war. McClellan was ordered to leave the peninsula and join the Washington defense force, now under John Pope, for a new overland move on Richmond. As McClellan's Army of the Potomac began to pull out, Lee moved northward to strike at Pope before McClellan arrived. Once again he adopted an audacious stratagem. Dividing his forces, he sent Jackson on a sweep around Pope's right flank to attack his supply lines. At Cedar Mountain on August 9 Jackson pushed back an advance party under General Banks, and on August 26 struck suddenly through Thoroughfare Gap to seize and destroy the Federal supply base at Manassas Junction. At Second Bull Run (or Second Manassas), fought on almost the same site as the earlier battle, Pope assumed that he faced only Jackson, but Lee's main army by that time had joined in. On August 30 a crushing attack on Pope's flank by James Longstreet's corps of 30,000 drove the Federals from the field. In the next few days the Union forces pulled back into the fortifications around Washington, where McClellan once again took command and reorganized.

Union soldiers encamped at Manassas, Virginia, in July 1862.

ANTIETAM But Lee gave him little time. Still on the offensive, early in September 1862 he invaded western Maryland. His purpose was in part to get the fighting out of Virginia during harvest season, in part to score a victory on Union soil for the sake of prestige and possible foreign recognition. By a stroke of fortune a Union soldier picked up a bundle of cigars with an order from Lee wrapped around them. The paper revealed that Lee had again divided his army, sending Jackson off to take Harpers Ferry. But McClellan delayed, still worried about enemy strength, and Lee got most of his army back together behind Antietam Creek. On September 17, at the Battle of Antietam (Sharpsburg), just as the Confederate lines seemed ready to break, the last of Jackson's men arrived to bolster them. At this point McClellan backed away, letting Lee get away across the Potomac. Lincoln, discouraged by McClellan's failure to follow up, removed him once and for all and assigned him to recruiting duty in New Jersey. McClellan would never again have a command.

FREDERICKSBURG   In his search for a fighting general Lincoln now made the worst choice of all. He turned to Ambrose E. Burnside, whose main achievements to that time had been to capture Roanoke Island and grow his famous side-whiskers. Burnside had twice before turned down the job on the grounds that he felt unfit for so large a command. But if the White House wanted him to fight, he would fight even in the face of oncoming winter. On December 13 he sent his men across the Rappahannock River to face Lee's forces, entrenched west of Fredericksburg on Marye's

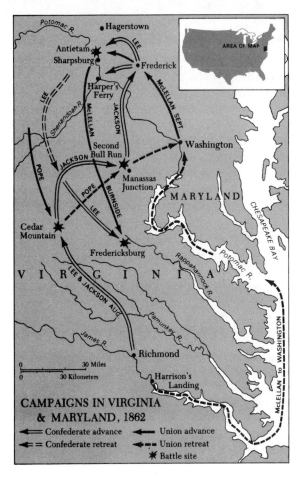

CAMPAIGNS IN VIRGINIA
& MARYLAND, 1862
◀━━ Confederate advance   ◀━━ Union advance
◀═ = Confederate retreat   ◀━∙━ Union retreat
✳ Battle site

Lincoln and his staff at Antietam, 1862.

Heights. Confederate artillery and small-arms fire chewed up the blue columns as they crossed a mile of bottomland outside the town. Six times the Union's suicidal assaults melted under the murderous fire issuing from protected positions above and below them. After taking more than 12,000 casualties compared to fewer than 6,000 for the Confederates, Burnside retired across the river.

The year 1862 ended with forces in the East deadlocked and the Union advance in the West stalled since mid-year. Union morale reached a low ebb. Northern Democrats were calling for a negotiated peace. At the same time Lincoln was under pressure from the Radicals of his own party who were pushing for more stringent war measures, questioning the competence of the president, and demanding the removal of Secretary of State Seward. Burnside was under fire from his own officers, some of whom were ready to testify publicly to his shortcomings.

But the deeper currents of the war were turning in favor of the Union: in a lengthening war its superior resources began to tell. In both the Eastern and Western Theaters the Confederate counterattack had been turned back. The year ended with forces under Rosecrans and Bragg locked in combat at Stone's River (Murfreesboro) in Tennessee. There again, after three more days of bloody stalemate, the Confederates fell back. And even while the armies clashed on that darkling plain in Tennessee, Lincoln by the stroke of a pen had changed the conflict from a war for the Union into a revolutionary struggle for abolition. On January 1, 1863, he signed the Emancipation Proclamation.

EMANCIPATION

It was the product of long and painful deliberation. In Lincoln's annual message of December 3, 1861, he had warned Congress to be "anxious and careful" that the war did not "degenerate into a violent and remorseless revolutionary struggle." At the outset he had upheld the promise of his party's platform to restore the Union but accept slavery where it existed. Congress too endorsed that position in the Crittendon-Johnson Resolutions, which passed both houses soon after the Battle of Bull Run with few dissenting votes. Once fighting began, the need to hold the border states dictated caution on the issue of emancipation. Beyond that, some other things deterred action. For one, Lincoln had to cope with a deep-seated racial prejudice in the North. Even the antislavery impulse derived often from the will to keep both slavery and blacks in the South. Lincoln himself harbored doubts about his authority to act so long as he clung to the view that the states remained legally in the Union. The only way around the problem would be to justify emancipation on the bases of military necessity and the president's war powers, as in fact John Quincy Adams had foreseen many years before.

A MEASURE OF WAR The war forced the issue. Fugitive slaves began to turn up in Union camps. In May 1861 at Fortress Monroe, Virginia, Benjamin F. Butler declared them "contraband of war" and put them to work on his fortifications. "Con-

Former slaves, or "contrabands," on a farm in Cumberland Landing, Virginia, 1862.

trabands" soon became a common name for runaways in Union lines. But John C. Frémont pressed the issue one step too far. As commander of the Department of the West, in August 1861 he simply liberated the slaves of all who actively helped the Rebel cause, an action which risked unsettling the yet-doubtful border states. Lincoln demanded that Frémont conform to the Confiscation Act of 1861, which freed only those slaves used by Rebel military services, as Butler's first "contrabands" had been. Then in May 1862 Gen. David Hunter declared free all slaves in South Carolina, Georgia, and Florida. He had no runaway slaves in his lines, he said, although some runaway masters had fled the scene. Lincoln quickly revoked the order, and took the brunt of the rising outrage among congressional Radicals.

Lincoln himself meanwhile edged toward emancipation. In March 1862 he proposed that federal compensation be offered any state which began gradual emancipation. The cost in the border states, he estimated, would about equal the cost of eighty-seven days of the war. The plan failed in Congress because of border-state opposition, but on April 16, 1862, Lincoln signed an act which abolished slavery in the District of Columbia, with compensation to owners; on June 19 another act excluded slavery from the territories, without offering owners compensation. A Second Confiscation Act, passed on July 17, liberated the slaves of all persons aiding the rebellion. Still another act forbade the army to help return runaways.

To save the Union, Lincoln finally decided, complete emancipation would be required for several reasons: slave labor bolstered the Rebel cause, sagging morale in the North needed the lift of a moral cause, and public opinion was swinging that way as the war dragged on. Proclaiming a war on slavery, moreover, would end forever any chance that France or Britain would suport the Confederacy. In July 1862 Lincoln first confided to his cabinet that he had in mind a proclamation that under his war powers would free the slaves of the enemy. At the time Seward advised him to wait for a Union victory in order to avoid any semblance of desperation.

The delay lasted through the long weeks during which Lee invaded Maryland and Bragg moved into Kentucky. As late as August 22, 1862, Lincoln responded to Horace Greeley's plea for emancipation: "My paramount object in this struggle is to save the Union and is not either to save or destroy slavery." The time to act finally came a month later, after Antietam. It was a dubious victory, but it did result in Lee's withdrawal. On September 22 Lincoln issued a preliminary Emancipation Proclamation, in

Two views of the Emancipation Proclamation. *The Union view* (top) *shows a thoughtful Lincoln composing the Proclamation with the Constitution and the Holy Bible in his lap. The Confederate view* (bottom) *shows a demented Lincoln with his foot on the Constitution using an inkwell held by the devil.*

which he repeated all his earlier stands: that his object was mainly to restore the Union and that he favored proposals for compensated emancipation and colonization. But the main burden of the document was his warning that on January 1, 1863, "all persons held as slaves within any state, or designated part of a state, the people whereof shall be in rebellion against the United States, shall be then, thenceforward and forever free."

In his annual message of December 1862 Lincoln once again raised the question of border-state compensation and ended with one of his most eloquent passages:

> We, even we here, hold the power and bear the responsibility. In giving freedom to the slave we assure freedom to the free—honorable alike in what we give and what we preserve. We shall nobly save or meanly lose the last, best hope of earth. Other means may succeed; this could not fail. The way is plain, peaceful, generous, just—a way which if followed the world will forever applaud and God must forever bless.

But this peroration was delivered with one eye to justifying the emancipation he had already promised. On January 1, 1863, Lincoln signed the second Emancipation Proclamation, giving effect to his promise of September, again emphasizing that this was a war measure based on his war powers. He also urged blacks to abstain from violence except in self-defense, and added that free blacks would now be received into the armed service of the United States. For all its eloquence, the document set forth its points in commonplace terms. A newspaper in faraway Austria got the point better than many closer home: "Lincoln is a figure *sui generis* in history. No pathos, no idealistic flights of eloquence, no posing, no wrapping himself in the toga of history. The most formidable decrees which he hurls against the enemy and which will never lose their historic significance, resemble— as the author intends them to—ordinary summonses sent by one lawyer to another on the opposing side. . . . " But as Henry Adams wrote from the London embassy, the Proclamation had created "an almost convulsive reaction in our favour."

REACTIONS TO EMANCIPATION Among the Confederate states, Tennessee and the occupied parts of Virginia and Louisiana were exempted from its effect. The document, with few exceptions, freed no slaves who were within Union lines at the time, as cynics noted. Moreover, it went little further than the Second Confiscation Act. But these objections missed a point which black slaves readily grasped. "In a document proclaiming liberty," wrote the historian Benjamin Quarles, "the unfree never bother to read the fine print." Word spread quickly in the quarters, and in some cases masters learned of it first from their slaves. Though most slaves deemed it safer just to wait for the "day of jubilee" when Union forces arrived, some actively claimed their freedom. One spectacular instance was that of the black pilot Robert Smalls, who one night took over a small Confederate gunboat, the *Planter*, and sailed his family through Charleston Harbor out to the blockading Union fleet. Later he served the Union navy as a pilot and still later became a congressman.

BLACKS IN THE MILITARY   From very early in the war Union commanders found "contrabands" like Smalls useful as guides to unfamiliar terrain and waterways, informants on the enemy, and at the very least common laborers. While menial labor by blacks was familiar enough, military service was something else again. Though not unprecedented, it aroused in whites instinctive fears. For more than a year the administration warily evaded the issue, although the navy began to enlist blacks before the end of 1861.

Even after Congress authorized the enlistment of Negroes in the Second Confiscation Act of July 1862, the administration ordered no general mobilization of black troops. It did, however, permit Gen. Rufus Saxton to raise five regiments in the Sea Islands, forming the First South Carolina Volunteer Regiment under Col. Thomas Wentworth Higginson, which sallied forth in late 1862 on raids along the Georgia-Florida coast. On January 1, 1863, Lincoln's Emancipation Proclamation reaffirmed the policy that blacks could enroll in the armed services and sparked new efforts to organize all-black units. The first northern all-Negro unit was the Massachusetts Fifty-fourth Regiment under Col. Robert Gould Shaw. Rhode Island and other states soon followed suit. In May the War Department authorized general recruitment of blacks all over the country.

By mid-1863 black units were involved in significant action in both the Eastern and Western Theaters. On July 18 the Massachusetts Fifty-fourth led a gallant if hopeless assault on Battery Wagner, at the entrance to Charleston Harbor. This action, and the use of Negro units in the Vicksburg campaign, did much to win acceptance for both black soldiers and for emancipation, at least as a proper strategem of war. Commenting on Union victories at Port Hudson and Milliken's Bend, Mississippi, Lincoln reported that "some of our commanders . . . believe that . . . the use of colored troops constitutes the heaviest blow yet dealt to

Company E of the Fourth U.S. Colored Infantry. *These determined soldiers helped defend Washington, D.C.*

the rebels, and that at least one of these important successes could not have been achieved . . . but for the aid of black soldiers."

Altogether, between 180,000 and 200,000 black Americans served in the Union army, providing around 10 percent of its total. Some 38,000 gave their lives. In the Union navy the 29,500 blacks accounted for about a fourth of all enlistments; of these more than 2,800 died. Not only black men but black women as well served in the war; Harriet Tubman and Susie King Taylor, for instance, were nurses with Clara Barton in the Sea Islands.

As the war entered its final months freedom emerged more fully as a legal reality. Three major steps occurred in January 1865 when both Missouri and Tennessee abolished slavery by state action and the House of Representatives passed an abolition amendment introduced by Sen. Lyman Trumbull of Illinois the year before. Upon ratification by three-fourths of the states, the Thirteenth Amendment became part of the Constitution on December 18, 1865, and removed any lingering doubts about the legality of emancipation. By then, in fact, slavery remained only in the border states of Kentucky and Delaware.

GOVERNMENT DURING THE WAR

Striking the shackles from 3.5 million slaves was a momentous social and economic revolution. But an even broader revolution got under way as power shifted from South to North with secession. Before the war southern congressmen had been able at least to frustrate the designs of both Free Soil and Whiggery. But once the secessionists abandoned Congress to the Republicans, a dramatic change occurred. The protective tariff, a transcontinental railroad, a homestead act—all of which had been stalled by sectional controversy—were adopted before the end of 1862. The National Banking Act followed in 1863. These were supplemented by the Morrill Land Grant Act (1862), which provided federal aid to state colleges of "agriculture and mechanic arts," and the Contract Labor Act (1864), which aided the importation of immigrant labor. All of these had great long-term significance.

UNION FINANCES   The more immediate problem for Congress was how to finance the war, because expenditures generally ran ahead of expectations while revenues lagged behind. Three expedients were open: higher taxes, issues of paper money, and borrowing. The higher taxes came chiefly in the form of the Morrill Tariff and excise duties which one historian said "might be described with a near approach to accuracy as a tax on everything." Excises taxed manufactures and the practice of nearly every profession. A butcher, for example, had to pay thirty cents for every head of beef he slaughtered, ten cents for every hog, five for every sheep. On top of the excises came an income tax which started in 1861 at 3 percent of incomes over $800 and increased in 1864 to a graduated rate rising from 5 percent of incomes over $600 to 10 percent of incomes over $10,000. To collect these the Revenue Act of 1862 created a Bureau of Internal Revenue.

But tax revenues trickled in so slowly—in the end they would meet 21 percent of wartime expenditures—that Congress in 1862 forced upon a reluctant Treasury Secretary Chase the expedient of printing paper money, backed up only by the proviso that it was legal tender for all debts. Beginning with the Legal Tender Act of February 1862, Congress ultimately authorized $450 million of the notes, which soon became known as "greenbacks" because of their color. The amount of greenbacks issued was limited enough to tide the Union over its financial crisis without causing the ruinous inflation which the unlimited issue of paper money caused in the Confederacy.

The net wartime issue of $431 million in greenbacks was only about a sixth of the total wartime indebtedness. From the beginning Chase had intended to rely for funds chiefly on the sale of bonds. Sales went slowly at first, although the issue of greenbacks, which depreciated in value against gold, encouraged the purchase of 6 percent bonds with the cheaper currency. But after October 1862 a Philadelphia banker named Jay Cooke (sometimes tagged "The Financier of the Civil War") mobilized a nationwide machinery of agents and propaganda for the sale of bonds. Eventually bonds amounting to more than $2 billion were sold, but not all by the patriotic ballyhoo of Jay Cooke and Company. New banks formed under the National Banking Act were required to invest part of their capital in the bonds, and encouraged to invest even more as security for the national banknotes they could issue.

For many businessmen wartime ventures brought quick riches which were made visible all too often in vulgar display and extravagance. "The world has seen its iron age, its silver age, its golden age and its brazen age," the New York *Herald* commented. "This is the age of shoddy . . . shoddy brokers in Wall Street, or shoddy manufacturers of shoddy goods, or shoddy contractors for shoddy articles for shoddy government. Six days a week they are shoddy businessmen. On the seventh day they are shoddy Christians." Not all the wartime fortunes, however, were made dishonestly. And their long-run importance was in promoting the capital accumulation with which American businessmen fueled later expansion. Wartime business laid the groundwork for the fortunes of such nabobs as Morgan, Rockefeller, Mellon, Carnegie, Stanford, Huntington, Armour, and Swift.

CONFEDERATE FINANCES Confederate finances were a disaster from the start. The Confederacy's treasury secretary was appointed more to give South Carolina a place in the cabinet than for his financial skill or tact. But even the most tactful genius might never have overcome popular reluctance, congressional stalling, and limited governmental structure, all of which hindered efforts to finance the Confederacy. In the first year of its existence the Confederacy levied export and import duties, but exports and imports were low. It enacted a tax of one-half of 1 percent on most forms of property, which should have yielded a hefty income, but the Confederacy farmed out its collection to the states, promising a 10 percent rebate on the take. The result was chaos. All but three states raised their quota by floating loans, which only worsened inflation.

In April 1863 the Confederate Congress passed a measure which, like Union excises, taxed nearly everything. A 10 percent tax in kind on all agricultural products did more to outrage farmers and planters than to supply the army, however. Enforcement was so poor and evasion so easy that the taxes produced only negligible amounts of depreciated currency.

Altogether, taxes covered no more than 5 percent of Confederate costs, perhaps less; bond issues accounted for less than 33 percent; and treasury notes for more than 66 percent. The last resort, the printing press, was in fact one of the early resorts. The first issue of $1 million in treasury notes in February 1861 was only the beginning: $20 million was authorized in May and $100 million in August, launching the Confederacy on an extended binge for which the only cure was more of the same. Altogether the Confederacy turned out more than $1 billion in paper money. By March 1864 a wild turkey was offered in the Richmond market for $100, flour at $425 a barrel, home calls by doctors at $30, meal at $72 a bushel, and bacon at $10 a pound. Country folk were likely to have enough for subsistence, perhaps a little surplus to barter, but townspeople on fixed incomes were caught in a merciless squeeze.

CONFEDERATE DIPLOMACY   Civil wars often become international conflicts. The foundation of Confederate diplomacy in fact was the hope of help from the outside in the form of supplies, diplomatic recognition, or perhaps even intervention. The Confederates indulged the pathetic hope that diplomatic recognition would prove decisive, when in fact it more likely would have followed decisive victory in the field, which never came. An equally fragile illusion was the conviction that King Cotton, as an Atlanta newspaper affirmed, would "bring more wooing princes to the feet of the Confederate states than Penelope had."

Indeed, to help foreign leaders make up their minds, the Confederates imposed a voluntary embargo on shipments of cotton until the Union blockade began to strangle their foreign trade. European textile manufacturers meanwhile subsisted on the carryover from their purchase of the record crops of 1859 and 1860. By the time they needed cotton, it was available from new sources in Egypt, India, and elsewhere. Cotton textiles aside, the British economy was undergoing a boom from wartime trade with the Union and blockade-running into the Confederacy.

The first Confederate emissaries to England and France took hope when the British foreign minister received them informally after their arrival in London in May 1861; they even got a promise from Napoleon III to recognize the Confederacy if Britain would lead the way. The key was therefore in London, but the foreign minister refused to receive the Confederates again, partly because of Union pressures and partly out of British self-interest.

One incident early in the war threatened to upset British equanimity. In November 1861 the Union warship *San Jacinto* stopped a British mail packet, the *Trent*, and took into custody two Confederate commissioners, James M. Mason and John Slidell, en route from Havana to Europe. Celebrated as a heroic deed by a northern public still starved for victories, the *Trent* affair roused a storm of protest in Britain. An ultimatum for the captives' release was delivered to Washington, confronting Lincoln and Seward with an explosive crisis. But to interfere with a neutral ship on the high seas violated long-settled American principle, and Seward finally decided to face down popular clamor and release Mason and Slidell, much to their own chagrin. As martyrs in Boston's Fort Warren they were more useful to their own cause than they could ever be in London and Paris.

In contrast to the futility of King Cotton diplomacy, Confederate commissioners scored some successes in getting supplies. The most spectacular feat was the procurement of Confederate raiding ships. Although British law forbade the sale of warships to belligerents, a Confederate commissioner contrived to have the ships built and then, on trial runs, to escape to the Azores or elsewhere for outfitting with guns. In all, eighteen such ships were activated and saw action in the Atlantic, Pacific, and Indian Oceans, where they sank hundreds of Yankee ships and threw terror into the rest. The most spectacular of the Confederate raiders were the first two, the *Florida* and the *Alabama*, which took thirty-eight and sixty-four prizes respectively.

A much greater threat to Union seapower came when the Confederate Commissoner contracted with England's Laird Shipyard for fast ironclad ships with pointed prows. Named the "Laird rams," they were meant to smash the Union's wooden vessels, break its blockade, and maybe even attack northern ports. Perhaps in response to news of Union victories at Gettysburg and Vicksburg, however, the British government decided to hold the Laird rams in port. Thereafter the British showed little disposition to ignore Confederate transgressions of British law, although one Rebel raider, the *Shenandoah*, did escape British port in October 1864, and was still burning Yankee whalers in the Bering Sea as late as July 1865, when a passing British ship brought word that the war was over.

UNION POLITICS AND CIVIL LIBERTIES   On the home fronts there was no moratorium on politics, North or South. Within his own party

Lincoln faced a Radical wing composed mainly of prewar abolitionists. By the end of 1861 they were getting restless with the policy of fighting solely to protect the Union. The congressional Joint Committee on the Conduct of the War, created December 20,1861, became an instrument of their cause. Led by men like Thaddeus Stevens and George W. Julian in the House, and Charles Sumner, Benjamin F. Wade (the chairman), and Zachariah Chandler in the Senate, they pushed for confiscation and emancipation, and a more vigorous prosecution of the war. Still, the greater body of Republicans backed Lincoln's more cautious approach. And the party was generally united on economic policy.

The Democratic party was set back by the loss of its southern wing and the death of its leader, Stephen A. Douglas, in June 1861. By and large, northern Democrats supported a war for the "Union as it was" before 1860, giving reluctant support to war policies but opposing wartime restraints on civil liberties and the new economic legislation. "War Democrats" like Sen. Andrew Johnson and Secretary of War Edwin M. Stanton fully supported Lincoln's policies, however, while a Peace Wing of the party preferred an end to the fighting, even at risk to the Union. An extreme fringe of the Peace Wing even flirted with outright disloyalty. The "Copperheads," as they were called, organized secret orders with such names as Sons of Liberty for purposes that were none too clear and often suspect. They were strongest in states such as Ohio, Indiana, and Illinois, all leavened with native southerners, some of whom were pro-Confederate.

Coercive measures against disloyalty were perhaps as much a boost as a hindrance to Democrats, who took up the cause of civil liberty. Early in the war Lincoln assumed the power to suspend the writ of habeas corpus and subjected "disloyal" persons to martial law—often on vague suspicion. The Constitution said only that it should be suspended in cases of rebellion or invasion, but congressional leaders argued that Congress alone had authority to act, since the provision fell in Article 1, which deals with the powers of Congress. When Congress, by the Habeas Corpus Act of March 1863, finally authorized the president to suspend the writ, it required officers to report the names of all arrested persons to the nearest district court, and provided that if the grand jury found no indictment, those arrested could be released upon taking an oath of allegiance.

There were probably more than 14,000 arrests made without a writ of habeas corpus. One celebrated case arose in 1863 when Federal soldiers hustled Clement L. Vallandigham out of his home in Dayton, Ohio. Brought before a military commission, Ohio's most prominent Copperhead was condemned to confinement for the duration of the war because he had questioned arbitrary arrests. The muzzling of a political opponent proved such an embarrassment to Lincoln that he commuted the sentence, but only by another irregular device, banishment behind the Confederate lines. Vallandigham eventually found his way to Canada. In 1863 he ran as the Democratic candidate for Ohio governor *in absentia*, and in 1864 slipped back into the country. He was left alone at Lincoln's order, took part in the Democratic national convention, and ultimately proved more of an embarrassment to the Democrats than to the president.

In the midterm elections of 1862 the Democrats exploited war weariness and resentment of Lincoln's war measures to gain a startling recovery, though not control of Congress. At their 1864 national convention in Chicago the Democrats called for an armistice to be followed by a national convention which would restore the Union. They named Gen. George B. McClellan as their candidate, but McClellan distanced himself from the peace platform by declaring that agreement on Union would have to precede peace.

Radical Republicans, who still regarded Lincoln as soft on treason, trotted out two candidates, first Salmon P. Chase, who failed to get the support of his own state, then John C. Frémont, but too late. Lincoln outmaneuvered them at every turn, and without public announcement of a choice, brought about the vice-presidential nomination of Andrew Johnson, a War Democrat from Tennessee, on the "National Union" ticket, so named to minimize partisanship. As the war dragged on through 1864, with Grant taking heavy losses in Virginia, Lincoln fully expected to lose. Then Admiral Farragut's capture of Mobile in August and Sherman's capture of Atlanta on September 2 turned the tide. McClellan carried only New Jersey, Delaware, and Kentucky, with 21 electoral votes to Lincoln's 212, and 1.8 million popular votes (45 percent) to Lincoln's 2.2 million (55 percent).

CONFEDERATE POLITICS   Unlike Lincoln, Jefferson Davis never had to contest a presidential election. Both Davis and Vice-President Stephens, named first by the Provisional Congress, were elected without opposition in 1861 and began single terms of six years on Washington's Birthday, February 22, 1862. But discontent flourished as things went from bad to worse, and came very close to home in the Richmond bread riot of April 2, 1863, which

Jefferson Davis, president of the Confederacy.

ended only when Davis himself persuaded the mob to disperse. After the congressional elections of 1863, the second and last in the confederacy, about a third of the legislators were antiadministration. Although parties as such did not figure in the elections, it was noteworthy that many ex-Whigs and other opponents of secession were chosen.

Davis, like Lincoln, had to contend with dissenters. Large pockets of Union loyalists appeared in the German counties of Texas, the hill country of Arkansas, the North Carolina Piedmont, and most of all along the Appalachian spine that reached as far as Alabama and Georgia. Many Unionists followed their states into the Confederacy reluctantly, and were receptive to talk of peace. They were less troublesome to Davis, however, than the states'-rights men who had embraced secession and then guarded states' rights against the Confederacy as zealously as they had against the Union. Georgia, and to a lesser degree North Carolina, were strongholds of such sentiment, which prevailed widely elsewhere as well. They challenged, among other things, the legality of conscription, taxes on farm produce, and above all the suspension of habeas corpus. Never mind that Davis, the legal-minded leader of a revolution, never suspended habeas corpus until granted congressional authority on February 27, 1862, and then did so sparingly. Vice-President Alexander Stephens carried on a running battle against Davis's effort to establish "military despotism," left Richmond to sulk at his Georgia home for eighteen months, and warned the Georgia legislature in 1864, on the eve of Sherman's march, against the "siren song, 'Independence first and liberty afterwards.' " The ultimate failure of the Confederacy has been attributed to many things. One of many ironies was that the fight for slavery suffered from a doctrinaire defense of liberty. Among other things, the Confederacy died of dogma.

THE FALTERING CONFEDERACY

In 1863 the hinge of fate began to close the door on the brief career of the Confederacy. After the Union disaster at Fredericksburg, Lincoln's search for a general turned to one of Burnsides's disgruntled lieutenants, Joseph E. Hooker, whose pugnacity had given him the name of "Fighting Joe." Hooker took over the Army of the Potomac near the end of January. After the appointment, Lincoln wrote his new commander, "there are some things in regard to which, I am not quite satisfied with you." Hooker had been saying the country needed a dictator, and word reached Lincoln. "Only those generals who gain successes can set up dictators," the president wrote. "What I now ask of you is military success, and I will risk the dictatorship." But the risk was not great. Hooker was no more able than Burnside to deliver the goods. He failed the test at Chancellorsville, May 1–5.

CHANCELLORSVILLE With a force of perhaps 130,000, the largest Union army yet gathered, and a brilliant plan, he suffered a loss of control, perhaps a failure of nerve, at the critical juncture. Lee, with perhaps half that number, staged what became a textbook classic of daring and maneuver. Hooker's plan was to leave his base, opposite Fredericksburg, on a sweeping movement upstream across the Rappahannock and Rapidan to flank Lee's position. John N. Sedgwick was to cross below the town for a major diversion with 40,000 men. Lee, however, leaving about 10,000 men at Marye's Heights, pulled his main forces back to meet Hooker. At Chancellorsville, after a preliminary skirmish, Lee divided his army again, sending Jackson with more than half the men on a long march to hit the enemy's exposed right flank.

On May 2, toward evening, Jackson surprised the right flank at the edge of a wooded area called the Wilderness, throwing things into chaos, but the fighting died out in confusion as darkness fell. The next day, while Jeb Stuart held Hooker at bay, Lee

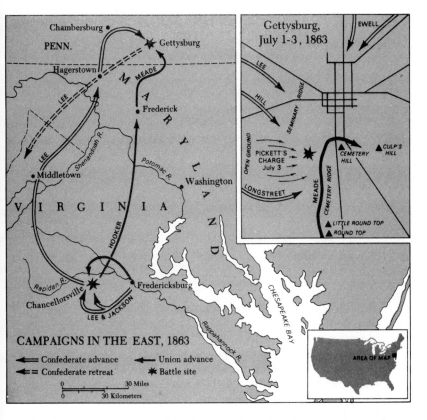

CAMPAIGNS IN THE EAST, 1863

⬅= Confederate advance ⬅— Union advance
⬅= Confederate retreat ✳ Battle site

0 ————— 30 Miles
0 ————— 30 Kilometers

Gettysburg,
July 1-3, 1863

had to turn around and fend off Sedgwick, who had stormed
Marye's Heights and advanced on Lee's rear. Lee struck him and
counterattacked on May 3–4, after which Sedgwick recrossed
the Rappahannock. The following day Hooker did the same, although he was still left in a strong position. It was the peak of
Lee's career, but Chancellorsville was his last significant victory.
And his costliest: the South suffered some 12,000 casualties and
more than 1,600 killed, among them Stonewall Jackson, mistakenly felled by his own men upon his return from a reconnaisance.

VICKSBURG While Lee held the Federals at bay in the East, they
had resumed a torturous advance in the West. Since the previous
fall Ulysses Grant had been groping his way toward Vicksburg,
which along with Port Hudson, Louisiana, was one of the last two
Rebel strongholds on the Mississippi. Located on a bluff 200 feet
above the river, Vicksburg had withstood naval attacks and a
downriver expedition led by William T. Sherman, which had
stormed Chickasaw Bluffs north of the city in December. Be-

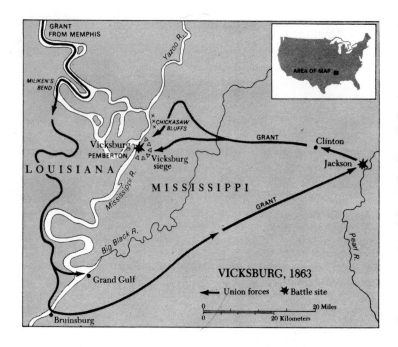

GRANT
FROM MEMPHIS

MILIKEN'S
BEND

Yazoo R.

AREA OF MAP

×CHICKASAW
× BLUFFS

Vicksburg
PEMBERTON

GRANT

Clinton

Jackson

Vicksburg
siege

LOUISIANA

MISSISSIPPI

Mississippi R.

GRANT

Pearl R.

Big Black R.

VICKSBURG, 1863

Grand Gulf

Union forces ✳ Battle site

0   20 Miles
0   20 Kilometers

Bruinsburg

cause the rail lines were vulnerable to hit-and-run attacks, Grant
resolved to use naval supply lines downriver. He positioned his
army about fifteen miles north of the city, but the Delta region
there was laced with bayous which baffled efforts to reach the
goal. At first Grant thought to use these waterways to advantage,
and during the winter he made bold efforts along two routes.
Well to the north, opposite Helena, Arkansas, he blasted a hole
in the levee and floated gunboats and transports through to the
Tallahatchie River. There ensued a strange progress along winding waterways choked with vegetation and covered by overhanging branches, where the Union navy stood in danger of
capture by the Confederate army. That effort, and a similar try
up Steele's Bayou farther south, was soon abandoned.

Grant finally gave up the idea of a northern approach. He
crossed over to Louisiana at Milliken's Bend, and while the navy
ran gunboats and transports past the Confederate batteries at
Vicksburg, he moved south to meet them, crossed back, and
fetched up on dry ground south of Vicksburg at the end of April.
From there Grant adopted a new expedient. He would forget
supply lines and live off the country. John C. Pemberton, the
Confederate commander at Vicksburg, was thoroughly baffled.
Grant then swept eastward on a campaign which Lincoln later
called "one of the most brilliant in the world," took Jackson,

where he seized or destroyed supplies, then turned westward and on May 18 emerged from the "tunnel" he had entered two weeks before to pin Pemberton's army of 30,000 inside Vicksburg.

GETTYSBURG   The plight of Vicksburg put the Confederate high command in a quandary. Joseph E. Johnston, now in charge of the western forces but with few men under his personal command, would have preferred to focus on the Tennessee front and thereby perhaps force Grant to relax his grip. Robert E. Lee had another idea for a diversion. If he could win a victory on northern soil he might do more than just relieve the pressure at Vicksburg. In June he moved into the Shenandoah Valley and northward across Maryland.

Hooker followed, keeping himself between Lee and Washington, but demoralized by defeat at Chancellorsville and quarrels with Halleck, he turned in his resignation. On June 28 Maj.-Gen. George C. Meade took command. Neither side chose Gettysburg, Pennsylvania, as the site for the climactic battle, but a Confederate party entered the town in search of shoes and encountered units of Union cavalry on June 30. The main forces quickly converged on that point. On July 1 the Confederates pushed the Federals out of the town, but into stronger positions on high ground to the south. Meade hastened reinforcements to his new lines along the heights: on the map these resembled an inverted fishhook with Culp's Hill and Cemetery Hill curved

Harvest of Death. *T. H. O'Sullivan's grim photograph of the dead at Gettysburg.*

around the top; Cemetery Ridge extended three miles down the shank to Round Top and Little Round Top. On July 2 Lee mounted assaults at both the extreme left and right flanks of Meade's army, but in vain.

On July 3 Lee staked everything on one final assault on the Union center on Cemetery Ridge. Confederate artillery raked the ridge, but with less effect than intended. About 2 P.M. 15,000 men of Gen. George E. Pickett's command emerged from the woods west of Cemetery Ridge and began their advance across open ground commanded by Union artillery. It was as hopeless as Burnside's assault at Fredericksburg. Only 5,000 of Pickett's men reached the ridge, and the few who got within range of hand-to-hand combat were quickly overwhelmed.

With nothing left to do but retreat, on July 4 Lee's dejected army, with about a third of its number gone, began to slog back through a driving rain. They had failed in all their purposes, not the least being to relieve the pressure on Vicksburg. On that same July 4 Pemberton reached the end of his tether and surrendered his entire garrison of 30,000 men, whom Grant paroled and permitted to go home. Four days later the last remaining Confederate stronghold on the Mississippi, Port Hudson, under siege since May by Union forces, gave up. "The father of waters," Lincoln said, "flows unvexed to the sea." The Confederacy was irrevocably split, and had Meade pursued Lee he might have delivered the *coup de grace* before the Rebels could get back across the flooded Potomac.

CHATTANOOGA The third great Union victory of 1863 occurred in fighting around Chattanooga, the railhead of eastern Tennessee and gateway to northern Georgia. In the late summer Rosecrans's Union army moved southeastward from Murfreesboro, and Bragg pulled out of Chattanooga to gain room for maneuver. Rosecrans took the city on September 9 and then rashly pursued Bragg into Georgia, where his forces met the Confederates at Chickamauga. The battle (September 19–20) had the makings of a Union disaster, since it was one of the few times when the Confederates had a numerical advantage (about 70,000 to 56,000). On the second day Bragg smashed the Federal right, and only the stubborn stand of the left under George H. Thomas (thenceforth "the Rock of Chickamauga") prevented a general rout. The battered Union forces fell back into Chattanooga, while Bragg cut the railroad from the west and held the city virtually under siege from the heights to the south and east.

Rosecrans seemed stunned and apathetic, but Lincoln urged

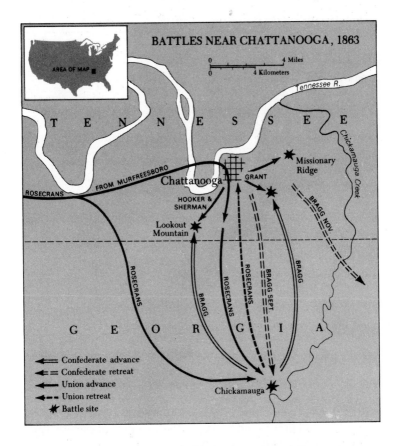

BATTLES NEAR CHATTANOOGA, 1863

0   4 Miles
0   4 Kilometers

AREA OF MAP ■

Tennessee R.

T E N N E S S E E

Chickamauga Creek

FROM MURFREESBORO

Chattanooga   GRANT   Missionary
                                    Ridge

ROSECRANS

HOOKER &
SHERMAN

BRAGG NOV.

Lookout
Mountain

ROSECRANS   BRAGG ROSECRANS ROSECRANS BRAGG SEPT. BRAGG

G   E   O   R   G   I   A

← ⇐ Confederate advance
← = Confederate retreat
← Union advance
←- - Union retreat
✷ Battle site

Chickamauga ✷

him to hang on: "If we can hold Chattanooga, and East Tennessee, I think rebellion must dwindle and die." Following the Confederate example the Union command sent Joe Hooker with
reinforcements from Virginia, Grant and Sherman with more
from the west. Grant, given overall command of the West on October 16, pushed his way into Chattanooga a few days later, forcing open a supply route as he came. He replaced Rosecrans,
putting Thomas in command. On November 24 the Federals
began to move, with Hooker and Sherman hitting the Confederate flanks at Lookout Mountain and Signal Hill while Thomas
created a diversion at the center. Hooker took Lookout Mountain in what was mainly a feat of mountaineering, but Sherman
was stalled. On the second day of the battle Grant ordered
Thomas forward to positions at the foot of Misssionary Ridge.
Successful there, but still exposed, the men spontaneously began
to move on up toward the crest 400 to 500 feet above. They
might well have been cut up badly, but the Rebels were unable

Gen. Ulysses S. Grant.

to lower their big guns enough and in the face of thousands swarming up the hill they panicked and fled.

Bragg was unable to get his forces together until they were many miles to the south, and the Battle of Chattanooga was the end of his active career. Jefferson Davis, who had backed him against all censure, reluctantly replaced him with Johnston and called Bragg back to Richmond as an advisor. Soon after the battle the Federals linked up with Burnside, who had taken Knoxville, and proceeded to secure their control of eastern Tennessee, where the hills were full of Unionists.

Chattanooga had another consequence. If the battle was won by the rush on Missionary Ridge, against orders, the victory nonetheless confirmed the impression of Grant's genius. Lincoln had at last found his general. In March 1864 Grant arrived in Washington to assume the rank of lieutenant-general and a new position as general-in-chief. Halleck became chief-of-staff and continued in his role as channel of communication between the president and commanders in the field. Within the Union armies at least, a modern command system was emerging; the Confederacy never had a unified command.

THE CONFEDERACY'S DEFEAT

The main targets now were Lee's army in Virginia and Johnston's in Georgia. Grant personally would accompany

Meade, who retained direct command over the Army of the Potomac; operations in the West were entrusted to Grant's longtime lieutenant, William T. Sherman. As Sherman put it later, "he was to go for Lee, and I was to go for Joe Johnston. That was his plan."

GRANT'S PURSUIT OF LEE   They began to go for both of them in May 1864, while lesser offensives kept the Confederates occupied all across the map. The Army of the Potomac, numbering about 115,000 to Lee's 65,000, moved south across the Rappahannock and the Rapidan into the Wilderness, where Hooker had come to grief in the Battle of Chancellorsville. In the Battle of the Wilderness (May 5–6) the armies fought blindly through the woods, the horror and suffering of the scene heightened by crackling brush fires. Grant's men took heavier casualties than the Confederates, but the Rebels were running out of replacements. Always before, Lee's adversaries had pulled back to nurse their wounds, but Grant slid off to his left and continued his relentless advance southward, now toward Spotsylvania Court House.

There Lee's advance guard barely arrived in time to stall the movement and the armies settled down for five days of bloody

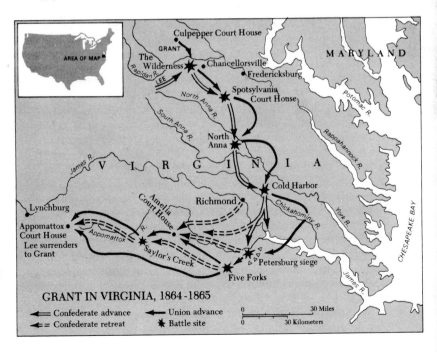

GRANT IN VIRGINIA, 1864-1865

warfare, May 8–12, in which the Federals failed to break the Confederate center, the "Bloody Angle." Before it was over Grant sent word back to Halleck: "I propose to fight it out along this line if it takes all summer." But again Grant slid off to his left, tested Lee's defenses along the North Anna River (May 16–23), and veered off again over the Pamunkey and back to the scenes of McClellan's Peninsula Campaign. There, along the Chickahominy, occurred the pitched battle of Cold Harbor (June 1–3). Battered and again repulsed, Grant cut away yet again. For several days Lee lost sight of the Federals while they crossed the James on a pontoon bridge and headed for Petersburg, the junction of railroads into Richmond from the south.

Petersburg was thinly held by Confederates under Beauregard, but before Grant could bring up his main force Lee's men moved into the defenses. Grant dug in for a siege along lines that extended for twenty-five miles above and below Petersburg. On July 30 a huge mine exploded in a tunnel under the Confederate line. In the ensuing Battle of the Crater, the soldiers who were supposed to exploit the opening milled around aimlessly in the pit while Rebels shot them like fish in a pond. For nine months the two armies faced each other down while Grant kept pushing toward his left flank to break the railroad arteries that were Lee's lifeline. He would fight it out along *this* line all summer, all autumn, and all winter, generously supplied by Union vessels moving up the James while Lee's forces, beset by hunger, cold, and desertion, wasted away. Petersburg had become Lee's prison while disasters piled up for the Confederacy elsewhere.

SHERMAN'S MARCH   When Grant headed south, so did Sherman—toward the railroad hub of Atlanta, with 90,000 men against Joe Johnston's 60,000. Sherman's campaign, like Grant's, developed into a war of maneuver, but without the pitched battles. As Grant kept slipping off to his left, Sherman kept moving to his right, but Johnston was always one step ahead of him—turning up in secure positions along the North Georgia ridges, drawing him farther from his Chattanooga base, harassing his supply lines with Joe Wheeler's cavalry, and keeping his own main force intact. But Johnston's skillful tactics caused an impatient President Davis finally to replace him with the combative but reckless John B. Hood. Three times in eight days Hood lashed out, each time meeting a bloody rebuff. Sherman at first resorted to a siege of Atlanta, then slid off to the right again, cutting the rail lines below Atlanta. Hood evacuated on September 1, but kept his army intact.

William Tecumseh Sherman.

Sherman now laid plans for a march through central Georgia where no organized armies remained. Hood meanwhile had hatched an equally audacious plan. He would cut away to northern Alabama and push on into Tennessee, forcing Sherman into pursuit. Sherman refused to take the bait, although he did send Thomas back to Tennessee to keep watch with 30,000 men. So the curious spectacle unfolded of the main armies moving off in opposite directions. But it was a measure of the Confederates' plight that Sherman could cut a swath across Georgia with impunity while Hood was soon outnumbered again. In the Battle of Franklin (November 30), Hood sent his army across two miles of open ground. Six waves broke against the Union lines, leaving the ground strewn with Confederates. Total Rebel casualties numbered 6,000. With what he had left, Hood dared not attack Nashville, nor did he dare withdraw for fear of final disintegration. Finally, in the Battle of Nashville (December 15–16), Thomas broke and scattered what was left of the Confederate Army of Tennessee. The Confederate front west of the Appalachians had collapsed, leaving only Nathan Bedford Forrest's cavalry and a few other scattered units in the field, mainly around Mobile.

During all this, Sherman was marching through Georgia, pioneering the modern practice of total war against a people's resources and against their will to resist. On November 15, 1864, he destroyed Atlanta's warehouses and railroad facilities while spreading fires consumed about a third of the city. The Union army moved out in four columns over a front twenty to sixty

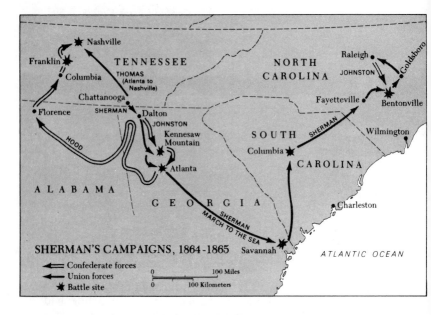

SHERMAN'S CAMPAIGNS, 1864-1865

⇐ Confederate forces
← Union forces
★ Battle site

0   100 Miles
0   100 Kilometers

miles wide, living off the land and destroying any stores or provisions that might serve Confederate forces. Bands of stragglers and deserters from both armies joined in looting along the flanks, while Joe Wheeler's cavalry destroyed Rebel stores to keep them out of enemy hands. When, after a month, Sherman fetched up near Savannah he had cut a swath of desolation 250 miles long. On December 21 Sherman marched into Savannah, and three days later Lincoln got a dispatch tendering the city as a Christmas gift.

Pushing across the river into that "hell-hole of secession," South Carolina, his men wrought even greater destruction. More than a dozen towns were consigned to the flames in whole or part, including the state capital of Columbia, captured February 17, 1865. On the day Sherman entered Columbia, Charleston's defenders abandoned the city and pulled north to join an army which Joseph E. Johnston was desperately pulling together. Johnston was able to mount one final attack on Sherman's left wing at Bentonville (March 19–20), but that was his last major battle.

APPOMATTOX   During this final season of the Confederacy, Grant kept pushing, probing, and battering the Petersburg defenses. Raids by Philip H. Sheridan had desolated Lee's breadbasket in the Shenandoah Valley, and winter left his men on short rations. News of Sherman's progress added to the gloom and the impulse to desert. By March the Confederate lines had thinned out to about 1,000 men per mile. Lee began to lay plans to escape and join Johnston in North Carolina. At Five Forks (April 1, 1865) Grant finally cut the last rail line to Petersburg, and the next day Lee abandoned Richmond and Petersburg in a desperate flight toward Lynchburg and rails south. President Davis gathered what archives and treasure he could and made it out by train ahead of the advancing Federals, only to be captured by Union cavalry on May 10 at Irwinton, Georgia.

By then the Confederacy was already dead. Lee moved out with Grant in hot pursuit, and soon found his escape route cut by forces under Sheridan. On April 9 (Palm Sunday) he met Grant in the parlor of the McLean home at Appomattox to tender his surrender, four years to the day after Davis and his cabinet decided to attack Fort Sumter. Grant, at Lee's request, let the Rebel officers keep their side arms and permitted soldiers to keep private horses and mules. On April 18, Johnston surrendered to Sherman at the Bennett house near what would soon be the thriving tobacco town of Durham. On May 4 at Citronelle, Alabama, General Taylor surrendered the remaining forces east of the Mississippi to General Canby, leaving only the forces under Edmund Kirby Smith west of the river. On May 26 Kirby Smith capitulated to Canby at New Orleans.

In Charleston, the Confederate "holy of holies," the first occupation troops to arrive in February were black units, including

Ruins of Georgia R.R. Roundhouse at Atlanta, 1864. *In the wake of Sherman's march, abandoned locomotives and twisted rails marked the destruction in Atlanta.*

Robert E. Lee. *Mathew Brady took this photograph in Richmond eleven days after Lee's surrender at Appomattox.*

the Third and Fourth South Carolina Regiments, some of whom had been among the city's slaves in 1860. It was little more than four years since the secession convention had met at Institution Hall, not quite five years since the disruption of the Democratic party in the same building. Soon after the occupation the War Department began plans for a massive celebration at Fort Sumter on the fourth anniversary of its fall. On April 14, 1865, the fort filled with dignitaries, including William Lloyd Garrison and Henry Ward Beecher, the orator of the day, and a few hundred black soldiers brought out by the *Planter*, the boat on which Capt. Robert Smalls had fled slavery three years before. At noon Major Anderson ran up the flag he had lowered just four years previously, while gaily decorated ships and all the forts in the harbor sounded a salute.

The same day President Lincoln spent the afternoon discussing postwar policy with his cabinet. That night Mr. and Mrs. Lincoln went to the theater.

FURTHER READING

The most comprehensive treatment of the Civil War period is Allan Nevins's *The War for the Union* (4 vols., 1959–1971). Also good for an overview are William C. Davis's *The Imperiled Union* (3 vols.,

1982–   ), James M. McPherson's *Ordeal by Fire: The Civil War and Reconstruction* (1982),° and James G. Randall and David H. Donald's *The Civil War and Reconstruction* (2nd ed., rev., 1969).° The many military histories by Bruce Catton are extremely readable; begin with *This Hallowed Ground* (1956).° *The Image of War, 1861–1865* (6 vols., 1981–   ), edited by William C. Davis, is a useful collection of photographs.

The Civil War period features a number of firsthand accounts. Among the better are *Mary Chesnut's Civil War* (1981),° edited by C. Vann Woodward, and *The Children of Pride* (1972; abridged ed., 1984),° edited by Robert M. Myers. The life of the common soldier is well treated by Bell I. Wiley in *The Life of Johnny Reb* (1943) and *The Life of Billy Yank* (1943).

For emphasis on the South, turn first to Emory M. Thomas's *The Confederate Nation, 1861–1865* (1979). Older, but still reliable, is Clement Eaton's *A History of the Southern Confederacy* (1954).

Shelby Foote's *The Civil War* (3 vols., 1958–1974) gives the most thorough treatment of the military conflict from the southern perspective. The war in the Eastern Theater is handled in the several biographies of Robert E. Lee, among them Douglas S. Freeman's *R. E. Lee: A Biography* (4 vols., 1934–1936) and Thomas L. Connelly's *Marble Man* (1977).° A cultural interpretation of Confederate military behavior is Grady McWhiney and Perry D. Jamieson's *Attack and Die* (1982). MacKinlay Kantor's *Andersonville* (1955)° covers that tragedy.

Treatments of northern politics during the war include David H. Donald's *Charles Sumner and the Rights of Man* (1970), Harold M. Hyman's *A More Perfect Union* (1973), and Allan G. Bogue's *The Earnest Men: Republicans of the Civil War Senate* (1981). Diplomatic relations with Europe are covered in Glyndon Van Deusen's *William Henry Seward* (1967).

The central political figure, Abraham Lincoln, is the subject of many books. Good single-volume biographies are Stephen B. Oates's *With Malice toward None* (1977)° and Benjamin P. Thomas's *Abraham Lincoln* (1952). Carl Sandburg's *Lincoln: The War Years* (4 vols., 1939) gives the fullest treatment of his presidential career. Varying interpretations of Lincoln can be found in David H. Donald's *Lincoln Reconsidered* (1956) and Richard N. Current's *The Lincoln Nobody Knows* (1958). On Lincoln's assassination, see William Hanchett's *The Lincoln Murder Conspiracies* (1983).

The emphasis is also on Lincoln in a number of works dealing with northern military strategy. A fine interpretive work is T. Harry Williams's *Lincoln and His Generals* (1952).° Biographical studies of the northern military leaders include T. Harry Williams's *McClellan, Sherman and Grant* (1962) and William S. McFeely's *Grant: A Biography* (1981).° The views of northern intellectuals on the war is the subject of George M. Fredrickson's fine work, *The Inner Civil War* (1965).

°These books are available in paperback editions.

How the emancipated slave fared during the war has drawn recent scholarly attention. The standard overview is Benjamin Quarles's *The Negro in the Civil War* (1953).° The career of the black soldier is found in Dudley T. Cornish's *The Sable Arm* (1956). Willie Lee Rose's *Rehearsal for Reconstruction: The Port Royal Experiment* (1964) and Louis S. Gerteis's *From Contraband to Freedman: Federal Policy toward Southern Blacks, 1861–1865* (1973) both trace the federal government's policies. For Lincoln's viewpoint, see LaWanda Cox's *Lincoln and Black Freedom: A Study in Presidential Leadership* (1981).° The Confederate viewpoint is handled in Robert F. Durden's *The Gray and the Black* (1972).

18

RECONSTRUCTION: NORTH AND SOUTH

The War's Aftermath

In the spring of 1865 the wearying war was over, a war whose cost in casualties was greater than all foreign wars down to World War II, and in proportion to population, greater than all other American wars down to the present day. At this frightful cost some old and tenacious issues were finally resolved. As the historian David Potter so graphically put it, "slavery was dead, secession was dead, and six hundred thousand men were dead." American nationalism emerged triumphant, its victory ratified in 1869 when the Supreme Court stamped its approval on the decision of arms. In the case of *Texas v. White*, the Court firmly denied any legality to Rebel state governments while it affirmed the existence of "an indestructible Union, composed of indestructible states." Pursued at first to preserve that Union, the war had turned into a crusade for the total abolition of chattel slavery. Before the end of 1865 all but two border states had voted emancipation. Ratification of the Thirteenth Amendment in December 1865 ended the remnants of slavery in Delaware and Kentucky and overrode any lingering doubts about the legitimacy of Lincoln's Emancipation Proclamation.

DEVELOPMENT IN THE NORTH   To some the war had been a Second American Revolution. It was more truly a social revolution than the War of Independence, for it reduced the once-dominant

697

In celebration of victory, Union forces parade down Pennsylvania Avenue, Washington, D.C., in the Grand Review, May 1865.

power of planter agrarians in the national councils and elevated that of the "captains of industry." It is easy to exaggerate the profundity of this change, but government did become subtly more friendly to businessmen and unfriendly to those who would probe into their activities. The wartime Republican Congress had delivered on the major platform promises of 1860, which had cemented the allegiance of northeastern businessmen and western farmers to the party of free labor.

In the absence of southern members, Congress during the war had passed the Morrill Tariff, which brought the average level of duties up to about double what it had been on the eve of conflict. The National Banking Act created a uniform system of banking and banknote currency, and helped to finance the war. Congress also passed legislation guaranteeing that the first transcontinental railroad would run along a north-central route from Omaha to Sacramento, and donated public lands and public bonds to ensure its financing. In the Homestead Act of 1862, moreover, Congress voted free homesteads of 160 acres to actual settlers who occupied the land for five years, and in the Morrill Land Grant Act of the same year conveyed to each state 30,000 acres of public land per member of Congress from the state, the proceeds from the sale of which went to colleges of "agriculture and mechanic arts."

DEVASTATION IN THE SOUTH   The South, where most of the fighting had occurred, offered a sharp contrast to the victorious North. Along the path of the army led by General Sherman, one observer reported in 1866, the countryside still "looked for many miles like a broad black streak of ruin and desolation." Columbia, South Carolina, said another observer, was "a wilderness of ruins," Charleston a place of "vacant houses, of widowed women, of rotting wharves, of deserted warehouses, of weed-wild gardens, of miles of grass-grown streets, of acres of pitiful and voiceless barrenness." In the valley of the Tennessee, a British visitor reported: "The trail of war is visible . . . in burnt-up gin houses, ruined bridges, mills, and factories." The border states of Missouri and Kentucky had gone through a guerrilla war which lapsed into postwar anarchy perpetrated by marauding bands of bushwhackers turned bank robbers, such as the notorious James boys, Frank and Jesse.

Property values had collapsed. Confederate bonds and money became worthless; railroads and rolling stock were damaged or destroyed. Stores of cotton that had escaped destruction were seized as Confederate property or in forfeit of federal taxes. Emancipation at one stroke wiped out perhaps $4 billion invested in human flesh and left the labor system in disarray. The great age of expansion in the cotton market was over. Not until 1879 would the cotton crop again equal the record crop of 1860; tobacco production did not regain its prewar level until 1880; the sugar crop of Louisiana not until 1893; and the old rice industry of the Tidewater and the hemp industry of the Kentucky Blue Grass never regained their prewar status.

Virginia's Capitol, designed by Thomas Jefferson, looms over the ruins of Richmond, April 1865.

According to a former Confederate general, recently freed blacks had "nothing but freedom."

LEGALLY FREE, SOCIALLY BOUND The newly freed slaves suffered most of all. According to Frederick Douglass, the black abolitionist, the former bondsman "was free from the individual master but a slave of society. He had neither money, property, nor friends. He was free from the old plantation, but he had nothing but the dusty road under his feet. He was free from the old quarter that once gave him shelter, but a slave to the rains of summer and the frosts of winter. He was turned loose, naked, hungry, and destitute to the open sky."

Even dedicated abolitionists in large part shrank from the measures of land reform that might have given the freedmen more self-support and independence. Citizenship and legal rights were one thing, wholesale confiscation and land distribution quite another. Instead of land or material help the freedmen more often got advice and moral platitudes.

In 1865 Rep. George Julian of Indiana and Sen. Charles Sumner of Massachusetts proposed to give freedmen forty-acre homesteads carved out of Rebel lands taken under the Confiscation Act of 1862. But their plan for outright grants was replaced by a program of rentals since, under the law, confiscation was effective only for the lifetime of the offender. Discussions of land distribution, however, fueled rumors that freedmen would get "forty acres and a mule," a slogan that swept the South at the end of the war. Its source remains unknown, but the aspirations which gave rise to it are clear enough. As one black man in Mississippi put it: "Gib us our own land and we take care ourselves;

but widout land, de ole massas can hire us or starve us, as dey please." More lands were seized as "abandoned lands" under an act of 1864, and for default on the direct taxes that Congress had levied early in the war, than under the Confiscation Act. The most conspicuous example of confiscation was the estate of Robert E. Lee and the Custis family, which became Arlington National Cemetery, but larger amounts were taken in the South Carolina Sea Islands and elsewhere. Some of these lands were sold to freedmen, some to Yankee speculators.

THE FREEDMEN'S BUREAU   On March 3, 1865, Congress set up within the War Department the Bureau of Refugees, Freedmen, and Abandoned Lands, to provide "such issues of provisions, clothing, and fuel" as might be needed to relieve "destitute and suffering refugees and freedmen and their wives and children." The Freedmen's Bureau would also take over abandoned and confiscated land for rental in forty-acre tracts to "loyal refugees and freedmen," who might buy the land at a fair price within three years. But the amount of such lands was limited. Under Gen. Oliver O. Howard as commissioner, and assistant commissioners in each state of the former Confederacy, agents were entrusted with negotiating labor contracts (something new for both freedmen and planters), providing medical care, and setting up schools, often in cooperation with northern agencies like the American Missionary Association and the Freedmen's Aid Society. The bureau had its own courts to deal with labor disputes

The Freedmen's Bureau set up schools such as this throughout the former Confederate states.

and land titles, and its agents were further authorized to supervise trials involving Negroes in other courts.

This was as far as Congress would go. Beyond such temporary measures of relief, no program of reconstruction ever incorporated much more than constitutional and legal rights for freedmen. These were important in themselves, of course, but the extent to which even these should go was very uncertain, to be settled more by the course of events than by any clear-cut commitment to equality.

THE BATTLE OVER RECONSTRUCTION

The problem of reconstruction arose first at the very beginning of the Civil War, when the western counties of Virginia refused to go along with secession. In 1861 a loyal state government of Virginia was proclaimed at Wheeling and this government in turn consented to the formation of a new state called West Virginia, duly if irregularly admitted to the Union in 1863. The loyal government of Virginia then carried on from Alexandria, its reach limited to that part of the state which the Union controlled. As Union forces advanced into the South, Lincoln in 1862 named military governors for Tennessee, Arkansas, and Louisiana. By the end of the following year he had formulated a plan for regular governments in those states and any others that might qualify.

LINCOLN'S PLAN AND CONGRESS'S RESPONSE Acting under his pardon power, President Lincoln issued on December 8, 1863, a Proclamation of Amnesty and Reconstruction under which any Rebel state could form a Union government whenever a number equal to 10 percent of those who had voted in 1860 took an oath of allegiance to the Constitution and the Union, and had received a presidential pardon. Participants also had to swear support for laws and proclamations dealing with emancipation. Excluded from the pardon, however, were certain groups: civil and diplomatic officers of the Confederacy; high officers of the Confederate army and navy; judges, congressmen, and military officers of the United States who had left their posts to aid the rebellion; and those accused of failure to treat captured Negro soldiers and their officers as prisoners of war. Under this plan loyal governments appeared in Tennessee, Arkansas, and Louisiana, but Congress recognized them neither by representation nor in counting the electoral votes of 1864.

In the absence of any specific provisions for reconstruction in the Constitution, there was disagreement as to where authority properly rested. Lincoln claimed the right to direct reconstruction under the clause that set forth the presidential pardon power, and also under the constitutional obligation of the United States to guarantee each state a republican form of government. Republican congressmen, however, argued that this obligation implied a power of Congress to act.

The first congressional plan for reconstruction appeared in a bill sponsored by Sen. Benjamin Wade of Ohio and Rep. Henry Winter Davis of Maryland, which proposed much more stringent requirements than Lincoln had. In contrast to Lincoln's 10 percent plan, the Wade-Davis Bill required that a majority of white male citizens declare their allegiance and that only those who could take an "ironclad" oath (required of federal officials since 1862) attesting to their *past* loyalty could vote or serve in the state constitutional conventions. The conventions, moreover, would have to abolish slavery, exclude from political rights high-ranking civil and military officers of the Confederacy, and repudiate debts incurred "under the sanction of the usurping power."

Passed during the closing day of the session, the bill was subjected to a pocket veto by Lincoln, who refused to sign it but issued an artful statement that he would accept any state which preferred to present itself under the congressional plan. The sponsors responded with the Wade-Davis Manifesto, which accused the president, among other sins, of usurping power and attempting to use readmitted states to ensure his reelection.

Lincoln's last public words on reconstruction came in his final public address, on April 11, 1865. Speaking from the White House balcony, he pronounced the theoretical question of whether the Confederate states were in the Union "bad as the basis of a controversy, and good for nothing at all—a mere pernicious abstraction." These states were simply "out of their proper practical relation with the Union," and the object was to get them "into their proper practical relation." It would be easier to do this by merely ignoring the abstract issue: "Finding themselves safely at home, it would be utterly immaterial whether they had been abroad." At a cabinet meeting on April 14, Lincoln proposed to get state governments in operation before Congress met in December. He was reported to have said: "There were men in Congress who, if their motives were good, were nevertheless impracticable, and who possessed feelings of hate and vindictiveness in which he did not sympathize and could not participate." He wanted "no persecution, no bloody work."

THE ASSASSINATION OF LINCOLN   That evening Lincoln went to Ford's Theater and his rendezvous with death. Shot by John Wilkes Booth, a crazed actor who thought he was doing something for the South, the president died the next morning in a room across the street. Accomplices had also targeted Vice-President Johnson and Secretary of State Seward. Seward and four others, including his son, were victims of severe but not fatal stab wounds. Johnson escaped injury, however, because his chosen assassin got cold feet and wound up in the barroom of Johnson's hotel. Had he been murdered, the presidency would have gone to a man whose name is virtually unknown today: Lafayette Sabine Foster, president pro tem of the Senate, a moderate Republican from Connecticut.

Martyred in the hour of victory, Lincoln entered into the national mythology even while the funeral train took its mournful burden north to New York and westward home to Springfield. The nation extracted a full measure of vengeance from the conspirators. Pursued into Virginia, Booth was trapped and shot in a burning barn. Three collaborators were brought to trial by a military commission and hanged, along with the woman at whose boarding house they had plotted. Against her the court had no credible evidence of complicity. Three others got life sentences, including a Maryland doctor who set the leg Booth had broken when he jumped to the stage. All were eventually pardoned by President Johnson, except one who died in prison. The doctor achieved lasting fame by making common a once obscure expression. His name was Mudd. Apart from those cases, however, there was only one other execution in the aftermath of war: Henry Wirz, who commanded the infamous prison at Andersonville, Georgia, where Union prisoners were probably more the victims of war conditions than of deliberate cruelty.

JOHNSON'S PLAN   Lincoln's death suddenly elevated to the White House Andrew Johnson of Tennessee, a man whose state was still in legal limbo and whose party affiliation was unclear. He was a War Democrat who had been put on the Union ticket in 1864 as a gesture of unity. Of humble origins like Lincoln, Johnson had moved as a youth from his birthplace in Raleigh, North Carolina, to Greeneville, Tennessee, where he became proprietor of a moderately prosperous tailor shop. Self-educated with the help of his wife, he had made himself into an effective orator of the rough-and-tumble school, and had become an advocate of the yeomanry against the privileges of the aristocrats. He was one of the few southern men who championed a homestead act. He had

Andrew Johnson.

served as mayor, congressman, governor, and senator, then as military governor of Tennessee before he became vice-president.

Some of the most advanced Radicals at first thought Johnson, unlike Lincoln, to be one of them—an illusion created by Johnson's gift for strong language. "Treason is a crime and must be punished," he had said. "Treason must be made infamous and traitors must be impoverished." Ben Wade was carried away with admiration. "Johnson, we have faith in you," he said. "By the gods, there will be no trouble now in running this government." But Wade would soon find him as untrustworthy as Lincoln, if for different reasons. Johnson's very loyalty to the Union sprang from a strict adherence to the Constitution. Given to dogmatic abstractions which were alien to Lincoln's temperament, he nevertheless arrived by a different route at similar objectives. The states should be brought back into their proper relation to the Union not by ignoring as a pernicious abstraction the theoretical question of their status, but because the states and the Union were indestructible. And like many other whites, he found it hard to accept the growing Radical movement toward suffrage for blacks. By May 1865 he was saying "there is no such thing as reconstruction. Those States have not gone out of the Union. Therefore reconstruction is unnecessary."

Johnson's plan of Reconstruction thus closely resembled Lincoln's. A new Proclamation of Amnesty (May 1865) added to those Lincoln excluded from pardon everybody with taxable property worth more than $20,000. These were the people Johnson believed had led the South into secession. But special applications for pardon might be made by those in the excluded groups, and before the year was out Johnson had issued some 13,000 such pardons. In every case Johnson ruled that pardon, whether by general amnesty or special clemency, restored one's property rights in land. He defined as "confiscated" only lands already sold under court decree. This applied to lands set aside by order of General Sherman, who had allocated for the exclusive use of freed Negroes a coastal strip thirty miles wide from Charleston south to the St. John's River in Florida.

Johnson's rulings nipped in the bud an experiment in land distribution that had barely begun. More than seventy years later one freedman, born a slave in Orange County, North Carolina, spoke bluntly of his dashed hopes: "Lincoln got the praise for freeing us, but did he do it? He give us freedom without giving us any chance to live to ourselves and we still had to depend on the southern white man for work, food and clothing, and he held us through our necessity and want in a state of servitude but little better than slavery." Later, a South Carolina Land Commission, established by the Radical state government in 1869, distributed lands to more than 5,000 black families. One black community in the up-country, Promised Land, still retained its identity more than a century later, an obscure reminder of what might have been.

On the same day that Johnson announced his amnesty, he issued another proclamation which applied to his native state of North Carolina, and within six more weeks came further edicts for the other Rebel states not already organized by Lincoln. In each a native Unionist became provisional governor with authority to call a convention elected by loyal voters. Lincoln's 10 percent requirement was omitted. Johnson called upon the conventions to invalidate the secession ordinances, abolish slavery, and repudiate all debts incurred to aid the Confederacy. Each state, moreover, was to ratify the Thirteenth Amendment. Lincoln had privately advised the governor of Louisiana to consider a grant of suffrage to some blacks, "the very intelligent and those who have fought gallantly in our ranks." In his final public address he publicly endorsed a limited black suffrage. Johnson repeated Lincoln's advice. He reminded the provisional governor of Mississippi, for example, that the state conventions might "with perfect safety" extend suffrage to blacks with education or with military service so as to "disarm the adversary"—the adversary being "radicals who are wild upon Negro franchise."

The state conventions for the most part met Johnson's requirements, although South Carolina and Mississippi did not repudiate their debt and the new Mississippi legislature refused to ratify the Thirteenth Amendment. Presidential agents sent south to observe and report back for the most part echoed General Grant's finding after a two-month tour: "I am satisfied that the mass of thinking men of the south accept the present situation of affairs in good faith." But Carl Schurz of Missouri found "an *utter absence of national feeling* . . . and a desire to preserve slavery . . . as much and as long as possible." The discrepancy between the two reports is perhaps only apparent: southern whites accepted the situation because they thought so little had changed after all. Emboldened by Johnson's indulgence they ignored his counsels of expediency. Suggestions of Negro suffrage were scarcely raised in the conventions, and promptly squelched when they were.

SOUTHERN INTRANSIGENCE When Congress met in December 1865, for the first time since the end of the war, it had only to accept the accomplished fact that state governments were functioning in the South. But there was the rub. Southern voters had acted with extreme disregard of northern feelings. Among the new members presenting themselves were Georgia's Alexander H. Stephens, late vice-president of the Confederacy, now claiming a seat in the Senate, four Confederate generals, eight colonels, six cabinet members, and a host of lesser Rebels. That many of them had counseled delay in secession, like Stephens, or actu-

Slavery Is Dead (?) *Thomas Nast's cartoon suggests that, in 1866, slavery was only legally dead.*

ally opposed it until it happened, made little difference given the temper of the times. The Congress forthwith excluded from the roll call and denied seats to all members from the eleven former Confederate states. It was too much to expect, after four bloody years, that Unionists would welcome Rebels like prodigal sons.

Furthermore, the action of southern legislatures in passing repressive Black Codes seemed to confirm Schurz's view that they intended to preserve slavery as nearly as possible. The codes extended to blacks certain rights they had not hitherto enjoyed, but universally set them aside as a separate caste subject to special restraints. Details varied from state to state, but some provisions were common. Existing marriages, including common-law marriages, were recognized, and testimony of Negroes was accepted in legal cases involving Negroes—and in six states, in all cases. Blacks could hold property. They could sue and be sued in the courts. On the other hand Negroes could not own farm lands in Mississippi or city lots in South Carolina. In some states they could not carry firearms without a license to do so.

The codes' labor provisions seemed to confirm the worst suspicions. Blacks were required to enter into annual labor contracts, with provision for punishment in case of violation. Dependent children were subject to compulsory apprenticeship and corporal punishment by masters. Vagrants were punished with severe fines and could be sold into private service if unable to pay. To many people it indeed seemed that slavery was on the way back in another guise. The new Mississippi penal code virtually said so: "All penal and criminal laws now in force describing the mode of punishment of crimes and misdemeanors committed by slaves, free negroes, or mulattoes are hereby reenacted, and decreed to be in full force against all freedmen, free negroes and mulattoes."

Faced with such evidence of southern intransigence, moderate Republicans drifted more and more toward Radical views. Having excluded southern members, the new Congress set up a Joint Committee on Reconstruction, with nine members from the House and six from the Senate, to gather evidence and submit proposals. Headed by the moderate Sen. William Pitt Fessenden, the committee fell under greater Radical influence as a parade of witnesses testified to the Rebels' impenitence. Initiative on the committee fell to determined Radicals who knew what they wanted: Ben Wade of Ohio, George W. Julian of Indiana—and most conspicuously of all, Thaddeus Stevens of Pennsylvania and Charles Sumner of Massachusetts.

THE RADICALS   Their motivations were mixed, and perhaps little purpose is served in attempting to sort them out. Purity of motive is rare in an imperfect world. Most Radicals had been connected with the antislavery cause. While one could be hostile to both slavery and blacks, many whites approached the question of Negro rights with a humanitarian impulse. Few could escape the bitterness bred by the long and bloody war, however, or remain unaware of the partisan advantage that would come to the Republican party from Negro suffrage. But the party of Union and freedom, after all, could best guarantee the fruits of victory, they reasoned, and Negro suffrage could best guarantee Negro rights.

The growing conflict of opinion brought about an inversion in constitutional reasoning. Secessionists—and Johnson—were now arguing that their states had remained in the Union, and some Radicals were contriving arguments that they had left the Union after all. Rep. Thaddeus Stevens spun out a theory that the Confederate states were now conquered provinces, subject to the absolute will of the victors. Sen. Charles Sumner advanced a thesis that the southern states, by their pretended acts of secession, had in effect committed suicide and reverted to the status of unorganized territories subject to the will of Congress. But few ever took such ideas seriously. Republicans converged instead on the "forfeited rights theory," later embodied in the report of the Joint Committee on Reconstruction. This theory held that the states as entities continued to exist, but by the acts of seces-

Two leading Radicals: Charles Sumner (left) and Rep. Thaddeus Stevens.

sion and war had forfeited "all civil and political rights under the constitution." And Congress was the proper authority to determine conditions under which such rights might be restored.

JOHNSON'S BATTLE WITH CONGRESS   A long year of political battling remained, however, before this idea triumphed. Radical views had gained a majority in Congress, if one not yet large enough to override presidential vetoes. But the critical year 1866 saw the gradual waning of Johnson's power and influence; much of this was self-induced, for he betrayed as much addiction to "pernicious abstraction" as any Radical. Johnson first challenged Congress in February, when he vetoed a bill to extend the life of the Freedmen's Bureau. The measure, he said, assumed that wartime conditions still existed, whereas the country had returned "to a state of peace and industry." No longer valid as a war measure, the bill violated the Constitution in several ways. It made the federal government responsible for the care of indigents. It was passed by a Congress in which eleven states were denied seats. And it used vague language in defining the "civil rights and immunities" of Negroes. The Congress soon moved to correct that particular defect, but for the time being Johnson's prestige remained sufficiently intact that the Senate upheld his veto.

Three days after the veto, however, Johnson undermined his already weakening prestige with a gross assault on Radical leaders during an impromptu speech on Washington's Birthday. The Joint Committee on Reconstruction, he said, was "an irresponsible central directory" which had repudiated the principle of an indestructible Union and accepted the legality of secession by entertaining conquered-province and state-suicide theories. From that point forward moderate Republicans backed away from a president who had opened himself to counterattack. He was "an alien enemy of a foreign state," Stevens declared. He was "an insolent drunken brute," Sumner asserted—and Johnson was open to the charge because of an incident at his vice-presidential inauguration. Weakened by illness at the time, he had taken a belt of brandy to get him through the ceremony and, under the influence of fever and alcohol, had become incoherent.

In mid-March 1866 Congress passed the Civil Rights Act, which Sen. Lyman Trumbull of Illinois had introduced along with the Freedmen's Bureau Bill. A response to the Black Codes, this bill declared that "all persons born in the United States and not subject to any foreign power, excluding Indians not taxed," were citizens entitled to "full and equal benefit of all laws." The grant of citizenship to native-born blacks, Johnson fulminated, went beyond anything formerly held to be within the scope of federal power. It would, moreover, "foment discord among the races." This time, on April 9, 1866, Congress overrode the presidential veto. On July 16 it enacted a revised Bureau Bill, again overriding a veto. From that point on Johnson steadily lost ground.

THE FOURTEENTH AMENDMENT   To remove all doubt about the constitutionality of the new Civil Rights Act, which was justified as implementing freedom under the Thirteenth Amendment, the Joint Committee recommended a new amendment which passed Congress on June 16, 1866, and was ratified by July 28, 1868. The Fourteenth Amendment, however, went far beyond the Civil Rights Act. It merits close scrutiny because of its broad impact on subsequent laws and litigation.

In the first section it did four things: it reaffirmed state and federal citizenship for persons born or naturalized in the United States, and it forbade any *state* (the word "state" was important in later litigation) to abridge the "privileges and immunities" of citizens; to deprive any *person* (again an important term) of life, liberty, or property without "due process of law"; or to deny any person "the equal protection of the laws." The last three of these

Extract Const. Amend. *Referring to the recently ratified Fourteenth Amendment, Uncle Sam advises the president in this cartoon, "Now, ANDY, take it right down. More you Look at it, worse you'll Like it."*

clauses have been the subject of long and involved lawsuits resulting in applications not widely, if at all, foreseen at the time. The "due process clause" has come in the twentieth century to mean that state as well as federal power is subject to the Bill of Rights, and the "due process clause" has been used to protect corporations, as legal "persons," from "unreasonable" regulation by the states. Other provisions of the amendment had less far-reaching effect. One section specified that the debt of the United States "shall not be questioned," but declared "illegal and void" all debts contracted in aid of the rebellion. Another section specified the power of Congress to pass laws enforcing the amendment.

Johnson's home state was among the first to ratify. In Tennessee, which had harbored probably more Unionists than any other Confederate state, the government had fallen under Radical control. The state's governor, in reporting the results to the secretary of the Senate, added: "Give my respects to the dead dog of the White House." His words afford a fair sample of the growing acrimony on both sides of the reconstruction debates. In May and July bloody race riots in Memphis and New Orleans added fuel to the flames. Both incidents amounted to indiscriminate massacres of blacks by local police and white mobs. The carnage, Radicals argued, was the natural fruit of Johnson's policy. "Witness Memphis, witness New Orleans," Sumner cried. "Who can doubt that the President is the author of these tragedies?"

RECONSTRUCTING THE SOUTH

THE TRIUMPH OF CONGRESSIONAL RECONSTRUCTION As 1866 drew to an end, the congressional elections promised to resolve differences in the direction of policy. In August Johnson's friends staged a National Union Convention in Philadelphia. Men from Massachusetts and South Carolina marched down the aisle arm in arm to symbolize national reconciliation. The Radicals countered with a convention of their own and organized a congressional campaign committee to coordinate their propaganda.

Johnson responded with a stumping tour of the Midwest, a "swing around the circle," which turned into an undignified contest of vituperation. Subjected to heckling and attacks on his integrity, Johnson responded in kind. "I have been called Judas Iscariot and all that," he said in St. Louis. "If I have played the Judas, who has been my Christ that I have played the Judas with? Was it Thad Stevens? Was it Wendell Phillips? Was it Charles Sumner?" Johnson may have been, as Secretary Seward claimed,

This cartoon appeared at the time of the 1866 congressional elections. It shows "King Andy I" approving the execution of Radical leaders in Congress.

the best stump speaker in the country. The trouble was, as another cabinet officer responded, the president ought not to be a stump speaker. It tended to confirm his image as a "ludicrous boor" and "drunken imbecile," which Radical papers projected. When the returns of the congressional elections came in, the Republicans had well over a two-thirds majority in each house, a comfortable margin with which to override any presidential vetoes.

The Congress in fact enacted a new program even before new members took office. Two acts passed in January 1867 extended the suffrage to Negroes in the District of Columbia and the territories. Another law provided that the new Congress would convene on March 4 instead of the following December, depriving Johnson of a breathing spell. On March 2, 1867, two days before the old Congress expired, it passed three basic laws of congressional reconstruction over Johnson's vetoes: the Military Reconstruction Act, the Command of the Army Act (an amendment to an army appropriation), and the Tenure of Office Act.

The first of the three acts prescribed new conditions under

which the formation of southern state governments should begin all over again. The other two sought to block obstruction by the president. The Command of the Army Act required that all orders from the commander-in-chief go through the head-quarters of the general of the army, then Ulysses S. Grant, who could not be reassigned outside Washington without the consent of the Senate. The Radicals had faith in Grant, who was already leaning their way. The Tenure of Office Act required the consent of the Senate for the president to remove any officeholder whose appointment the Senate had to confirm in the first place. The purpose of at least some congressmen was to retain Secretary of War Edwin M. Stanton, the one Radical sympathizer in Johnson's cabinet, but an ambiguity crept into the wording of the act. Cabinet officers, it said, should serve during the term of the president who appointed them—and Lincoln had appointed Stanton, although, to be sure, Johnson was serving out Lincoln's term.

The Military Reconstruction Act, often hailed or denounced as the triumphant victory of "Radical" Reconstruction, actually represented a compromise that fell short of a thoroughgoing radicalism. As first reported from the Reconstruction committee by Thaddeus Stevens, it would have given military commanders in the South ultimate control over law enforcement and would have left open indefinitely the terms of future restoration. More moderate elements, however, pushed through the "Blaine amendment," which scrapped the prolonged national control under which Radicals hoped to put through the far more revolutionary program of reducing the Rebel states to territories, plus programs of land confiscation and education. With the Blaine amendment in place the Reconstruction program boiled down to little more than a requirement that southern states accept black suffrage and ratify the Fourteenth Amendment. Years later Albion W. Tourgée, after a career as a carpetbagger in North Carolina, wrote: "Republicans gave the ballot to men without homes, money, education, or security, and then told them to use it to protect themselves. . . . It was cheap patriotism, cheap philanthropy, cheap success!"

The act began with a pronouncement that "no legal state governments or adequate protection for life and property now exists in the rebel States. . . . " One state, Tennessee, which had ratified the Fourteenth Amendment, was exempted from the application of the act. The other ten were divided into five military districts, and the commanding officer of each was authorized to keep order and protect the "rights of persons and property." To that end he might use military tribunals in place of civil courts when he judged it necessary. The Johnson governments remained intact for the time being, but new constitutions were to be framed "in conformity with the Constitution of the United States," in conventions elected by male citizens twenty-one and older "of whatever race, color, or previous condition." Each state constitution had to provide the same universal male suffrage. Then, once the constitution was ratified by a majority of voters and accepted by Congress, and once the state legislature had ratified the Fourteenth Amendment, and once the amendment became part of the Constitution, any given state would be entitled to representation in Congress once again. Persons excluded from officeholding by the proposed amendment were also excluded from participation in the process.

Johnson reluctantly appointed military commanders under the act, but the situation remained uncertain for a time. Some people expected the Supreme Court to strike down the act, and for the time being no machinery existed for the new elections. Congress quickly remedied that on March 23, 1867, with the Second Reconstruction Act, which directed the commanders to register for voting all adult males who swore they were qualified. A Third Reconstruction Act, passed on July 19, directed registrars to go beyond the loyalty oath and determine each person's eligibility to take it, and also authorized district commanders to remove and replace officeholders of any existing "so-called state" or division thereof. Before the end of 1867 new elections had been held in all the states but Texas.

Having clipped the president's wings, the Republican Congress moved a year later to safeguard its program from possible interference by the Supreme Court, which had shown a readiness to question certain actions related to Reconstruction. In *Ex parte Milligan* (1866) the Court had struck down the wartime conviction of an Indiana Copperhead tried by court-martial for conspiracy to release and arm Rebel prisoners. In *Cummings v. Missouri* (1866) the Court had ruled void, as *ex post facto*, a Missouri statute which excluded ex-Confederates from certain professions. *Ex parte Garland* (1867) led to a similar ruling against a test oath which barred ex-Confederates from practice before the Court. In a case arising from Mississippi, *Ex parte McCardle*, a Vicksburg editor arrested for criticizing the administration of the Fourth Military District sought release under the Habeas Corpus Act of 1867. Congress responded on March 27, 1868, by simply removing the power of the Supreme Court to review cases arising under the law, which Congress clearly had the right to do under its power to define the Court's appellate jurisdiction. The Court accepted this curtailment on the same day it affirmed the principle of an "indestructible union" in *Texas v. White* (1869). In that case it also asserted the right of Congress to reframe state governments.

THE IMPEACHMENT AND TRIAL OF JOHNSON   Congress's move to restrain the Supreme Court preceded by just two days the trial of the president in the Senate on an impeachment brought in by the House. Johnson, though hostile to the congressional program, had gone through the motions required of him. He continued, however, to pardon former Confederates in wholesale lots and replaced several district commanders whose Radical sympathies offended him. He and his cabinet members, moreover, largely ignored the Test Oath Act of 1862 by naming former Confederates to post offices and other federal positions. Nevertheless a lengthy investigation by the House Judiciary Committee, extending through most of the year 1867, had failed to convince the House that grounds for impeachment existed.

The occasion for impeachment came when Johnson deliberately violated the Tenure of Office Act in order, he said, to test its constitutionality in the courts. Secretary of War Edwin M. Stanton had become a thorn in the president's side, refusing to resign despite his disagreements with the president's policy. On August 12, 1867, during a recess of Congress, Johnson suspended Stanton and named General Grant in his place. Grant's political stance was ambiguous at the time, but his acceptance implied cooperation with Johnson. When the Senate refused to confirm Johnson's action, however, Grant returned the office to Stanton. The president thereupon named Gen. Lorenzo Thomas as secretary of war after a futile effort to interest Gen. William T. Sherman. Three days later, on February 24, 1868, the House voted impeachment, to be followed by specific charges. In due course a special committee of seven brought in its report.

Of the eleven articles of impeachment, eight focused on the charge that he had unlawfully removed Stanton and had failed to give the Senate the name of a successor. Article 9, the "Emory article," accused the president of issuing orders directly to Gen. William H. Emory in violation of the Command of the Army Act. The last two in effect charged him with criticizing Congress by "inflammatory and scandalous harangues" and by claiming that the Congress was not legally valid without southern representatives. But Article 11 accused Johnson of "unlawfully devising and contriving" to violate the Reconstruction Acts, contrary to his obligation to execute the laws. At the least, Johnson had tried to obstruct Congress's will while observing the letter of the law.

House of Representatives managers of the impeachment proceedings and trial of Andrew Johnson. Among them were Benjamin Butler (R.-Mass., seated left) and Thaddeus Stevens (R.-Pa., seated with cane).

The Senate trial opened on March 5 and continued until May 26, with Chief Justice Salmon P. Chase presiding. Seven managers from the House, including Thaddeus Stevens and Benjamin F. Butler, directed the prosecution. The president was spared the humiliation of a personal appearance. His defense counsel shrewdly insisted on narrowing the trial to questions that would be indictable offenses under the law, and steered the questions away from Johnson's manifest wish to frustrate the will of Congress. Such questions, they contended, were purely political in nature. In the end enough Republican senators joined their pro-Johnson colleagues to prevent conviction. On May 16 the crucial vote came on Article 9: 35 votes guilty and 19 not guilty, one vote short of the two-thirds needed to convict. On Articles 2 and 3 the vote was exactly the same, and the trial adjourned.

In a parliamentary system Johnson probably would have been removed as leader of the government long before then. But by deciding the case on the narrowest grounds, the Senate made it unlikely that any future president could ever be removed except for the gravest personal offenses, and almost surely not for flouting the will of Congress in his execution of the laws. Impeachment of Johnson was in the end a great political mistake, for the failure to remove the president was damaging to Radical morale and support. Nevertheless the Radical cause did gain something. To blunt the opposition, Johnson agreed not to obstruct the process of Reconstruction, named a secretary of war who was committed to enforcing the new laws, and sent to Congress the new Radical constitutions of Arkansas and South Carolina. Thereafter his obstruction ceased and Radical Reconstruction got under way.

REPUBLICAN RULE IN THE SOUTH   In June 1868 Congress agreed that seven states had met the conditions for readmission, all but Virginia, Mississippi, and Texas. Congress rescinded Georgia's admission, however, when the state legislature expelled twenty-eight black members on the pretext that the state constitution had failed to specify their eligibility, and seated some former Confederate leaders. The military commander of Georgia then forced the legislature to reseat the Negro members and remove the Confederates, and the state was compelled to ratify the Fifteenth Amendment before being admitted in July 1870. Mississippi, Texas, and Virginia had returned earlier in 1870, under the added requirement that they too ratify the Fifteenth Amendment. This amendment, submitted to the states in 1869, ratified in 1870, forbade the states to deny any person the vote on grounds of race, color, or previous condition of servitude.

Long before the new governments were established, Republican groups began to spring up in the South, chiefly under the aegis of the Union League, founded at Philadelphia in 1862 to promote support for the Union. Emissaries of the league enrolled Negroes and loyal whites, initiated them into the secrets and rituals of the order, and instructed them "in their rights and duties." The league emphasized the display of such symbols as the Bible, the flag, the Constitution, and the Declaration of Independence. The sign of recognition was the recital of the "four Ls": Lincoln, Liberty, Loyal, League. Agents of the Freedmen's Bureau, northern missionaries, teachers, and soldiers aided the cause and spread its influence. When the time came for political action, they were ready. In October 1867, for instance, on the eve of South Carolina's choice of convention delegates, the league reported eighty-eight chapters, which claimed to have enrolled almost every adult black male in the state.

BLACKS IN SOUTHERN POLITICS   It was the new role of Negroes in politics on which attention focused then and afterward. If largely illiterate and inexperienced in the rudiments of politics, they were little different from millions of whites enfranchised in the age of Jackson or immigrants herded to the polls by political bosses in New York and other cities after the war. Some freedmen frankly confessed their disadvantages. Beverly Nash, a black delegate in the South Carolina convention of 1868, told his colleagues: "I believe, my friends and fellow-citizens, we are not prepared for this suffrage. But we can learn. Give a man tools and let him commence to use them, and in time he will learn a trade. So it is with voting."

Brought suddenly into politics in times that tried the most skilled of statesmen, a surprising number of blacks rose to the occasion. Yet it would be absurd to claim, in the phrase of the times, that the "bottom rail" ever got on top. To call what happened "black Reconstruction" is to exaggerate black influence, which was limited mainly to voting, and to overlook the large numbers of white Republicans, especially in the mountain areas of the upper South. Only one of the new conventions, South Carolina's, had a black majority, 76 to 41. Louisiana's was evenly divided between blacks and whites, and in only two other conventions were more than 20 percent of the members black: Florida's, with 40 percent, and Virginia's, with 24 percent. The Texas convention was only 10 percent black, and North Carolina's, 11 percent—but that did not stop a white newspaper from calling it "Ethiopian minstrelsy, Ham radicalism in all its glory," a body consisting of "baboons, monkeys, mules, Tourgée, and other jackasses."

In the new state governments, any Negro participation was a novelty. No black man ever served as governor and few as judges, but there were two Negro senators in Congress, Hiram

Hiram R. Revels. Senator from Mississippi, Revels was also a Methodist minister and, later, president of Alcorn College.

Revels and Blanche K. Bruce, both from Mississippi, and fourteen black members of the House during Reconstruction. Among these were some of the ablest congressmen of the time. Blacks served in every state legislature, and in South Carolina they made up a majority in both houses for two years.

CARPETBAGGERS AND SCALAWAGS   The top positions in southern state governments went for the most part to white Republicans, whom the opposition whites soon labeled "carpetbaggers" and "scalawags," depending on their place of birth. The men who allegedly came south with all their belongings in carpetbags to pick up the political pelf were more often than not men who had arrived as early as 1865 or 1866, drawn south by the hope of economic opportunity and by other attractions that many of them had seen in Union service. Many were teachers or preachers who came on missionary endeavors. Albion W. Tourgée, for instance, a badly wounded Union veteran, moved to North Carolina in 1865, seeking a milder climate for reasons of health. He invested $5,000 in a nursery, and promptly lost it. He would have needed a fine crystal ball indeed to see two years in advance the chance for political office under the Radical program. As it turned out, he served in the state constitutional convention of 1868 and later as a state judge.

The "scalawags," or native white Republicans, were even more reviled and misrepresented. Most had opposed secession, forming a Unionist majority in many mountain counties as far south as Georgia and Alabama, and especially in the Tennessee hills. Not a few in both hills and flatlands attested to the power of what has been labeled "persistent Whiggery." Old Whigs often found Republican economic policies to be in keeping with Henry Clay's American System. Unionists, whether Whig or Democratic before the war, and even some secessionists, agreed with Georgia's Confederate governor and later Democratic senator: "The statesman like the businessman should take a practical view of questions as they arise." For the time a practical view dictated joining the Republicans. Mississippi's James L. Alcorn, wealthy planter and former Whig, was among the prominent whites who joined the Republicans in the hope of moderating Radical policies. Such men were ready to concede Negro suffrage in the hope of influencing Negro voters. Alcorn became the first Republican governor of Mississippi.

THE REPUBLICAN RECORD   The new state constitutions were objectionable to adherents of the old order more because of their origins than because of their contents, excepting their provisions for Negro suffrage and civil rights. Otherwise the documents were in keeping with other state constitutions of the day, their provisions often drawn from the basic laws of northern states. Most remained in effect for some years after the end of Radical control, and later constitutions incorporated many of their features. Conspicuous among Radical innovations were such steps toward greater democracy as requiring universal manhood suffrage, reapportioning legislatures more nearly according to population, and making more state offices elective.

Given the circumstances in which the Radical governments arose and the intense hostility which met them, they made a surprising record of achievement. For the first time in most of the South they established state school systems, however inadequate and ill-supported at first. The testimony is almost universal that Negroes eagerly sought education for themselves and their children. Some 600,000 black pupils were in southern schools by 1877. State governments under the Radicals gave more attention than ever before to poor relief and to public institutions for the disadvantaged and handicapped: orphanages, asylums, institutions for the deaf, dumb, and blind of both races. Public roads, bridges, and buildings were repaired or rebuilt. Blacks achieved new rights and opportunities that would never again be taken away, at least in principle: equality before the law, and the right to own property, carry on business, enter professions, attend schools, and learn to read and write.

In the annals of Reconstruction, partisan historians long denounced the Republican regimes for unparalleled corruption and abuse. That abuses proliferated in those years there is no question. Public money and public credit were often voted to privately owned corporations, especially railroads, under conditions which invited influence-peddling. But governmental subsidies—especially for transportation—were common before and after Reconstruction (and still are), and the extension of public aid had general support among all elements, including the Radicals and their enemies. Contracts were let at absurd prices and public officials took their cut. Taxes and public debt rose in every state. Yet the figures of taxation and debt hardly constitute an unqualified indictment of Radical governments, since they then faced unusual and inflated costs for the physical reconstruction of public works in the South. Most states, moreover, had to float loans at outrageous discounts, sometimes at 50–75 percent of face value, because of uncertain conditions.

Nor, for that matter, were the breaches of public morality lim-

ited to the South or to Republicans. The Democratic Tweed Ring
at the time was robbing New York City of more than $75 million,
while the Republican "Gas Ring" in Philadelphia was lining its
pockets. In national politics a number of scandals plagued the
Grant administration. Corruption was neither invented by the
Radical regimes, nor did it die with them. Louisiana's carpetbag
governor found a certain Latin zest in the game: "Why," he said,
"down here everybody is demoralized. Corruption is the fashion." In three years Louisiana's printing bill ran to $1.5 million,
about half of which went to a newspaper belonging to the young
governor, who left office with a tidy nest egg and settled down to
a long life as a planter. But a later Democratic state treasurer de-
camped for Tegucigalpa in 1890 with the accounts over $1 mil-
lion short, far outstripping the governor's record or anybody
else's. About the same time Mississippi's Democratic state treasurer was found to have embezzled over $315,000. During Re-
publican rule in Mississippi, on the other hand, there was no
evidence of major corruption.

WHITE TERROR   The case of Mississippi strongly suggests that
whites were hostile to Republican regimes less because of their
corruption than their inclusion of blacks. Most white southerners
remained unreconstructed, so conditioned by slavery that they
were unable to conceive of blacks as citizens or even free agents.
In some places hostility to the new regimes took on the form of
white terror.

The prototype of terrorist groups was the Ku Klux Klan, first
organized in 1866 by some young men of Pulaski, Tennessee, as
a social club with the costumes, secret ritual, and mumbo-jumbo
common to fraternal groups. At first a group of Merry Andrews
devoted to practical jokes, the founders eventually realized, as
two of them wrote in a later account, that they "had evoked a
spirit from 'the vasty deep' [which] would not down at their bid-
ding." Pranks turned into intimidation of blacks and white Republicans, and the KKK and imitators like Louisiana's Knights of
the White Camellia spread rapidly across the South in answer to
the Union League. Klansmen rode about the countryside hiding
under masks and robes, spreading horrendous rumors, issuing
threats, harassing assertive Negroes, and occasionally running
amok in violence and destruction. "Typically the Klan was a re-
actionary and racist crusade against equal rights which sought to
overthrow the most democratic society or government the South
had yet known," wrote one historian. During its brief career it
"whipped, shot, hanged, robbed, raped, and otherwise outraged

This Thomas Nast cartoon chides the Ku Klux Klan and the White League for promoting conditions "worse than slavery" for southern blacks after the Civil War.

Negroes and Republicans across the South in the name of preserving white civilization."

Militia groups formed by the Radical regimes were hardly able to cope with the underground tactics of the Klan, although their presence may have prevented worse violence. Congress struck back with three Enforcement Acts (1870–1871) to protect Negro voters. The first of these measures levied penalties on persons who interfered with any citizen's right to vote. A second placed the election of congressmen under surveillance by federal election supervisors and marshals. The third (the Ku Klux Klan Act) outlawed the characteristic activities of the Klan—forming conspiracies, wearing disguises, resisting officers, and intimidating officials—and authorized the president to suspend habeas corpus where necessary to suppress "armed combinations." President Grant, in October 1871, singled out nine counties in up-country South Carolina as an example, suspended habeas corpus, and pursued mass prosecutions which brought an abrupt halt to the Klan outrages. Elsewhere the Justice Department carried out a campaign of prosecution on a smaller scale, while a congressional committee gathered testimony on Klan activity which ran to twelve volumes. The program of federal enforcement broke the back of the Klan, whose outrages declined steadily as conservative southerners resorted to more subtle methods.

CONSERVATIVE RESURGENCE   The Klan in fact could not take credit for the overthrow of Republican control in any state. Perhaps its most important effect, one historian has suggested, was to weaken Negro and Republican morale in the South and strengthen in the North a growing weariness with the whole "southern question." Yankees had other fish to fry anyway. Onrushing expansion into the West, Indian wars, economic growth, and political controversy over the tariff and the currency distracted attention from southern outrages. Republican control in the South gradually loosened as "Conservative" parties—Democrats used that name to mollify former Whigs—mobilized the white vote. Scalawags, and many carpetbaggers, drifted away from the Radical ranks under pressure from their white neighbors. Few of them had joined the Republicans out of concern for Negro rights in the first place.

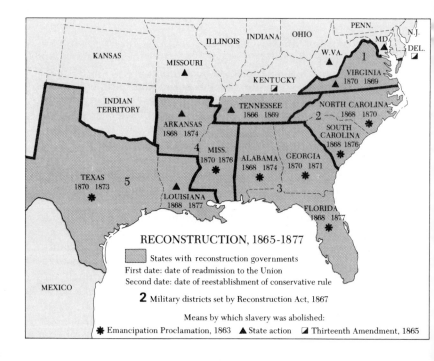

RECONSTRUCTION, 1865-1877

☐ States with reconstruction governments
First date: date of readmission to the Union
Second date: date of reestablishment of conservative rule

2 Military districts set by Reconstruction Act, 1867

Means by which slavery was abolished:
✳ Emancipation Proclamation, 1863   ▲ State action   ◩ Thirteenth Amendment, 1865

Republican control collapsed in Virginia and Tennessee as early as 1869, in Georgia and North Carolina in 1870, although North Carolina had a Republican governor until 1876. Reconstruction lasted longest in the Deep South states with the heaviest Negro population, where whites abandoned Klan masks for barefaced intimidation in paramilitary groups like the Mississippi Rifle Club and the South Carolina Red Shirts. By 1876 Radical regimes survived only in Louisiana, South Carolina, and Florida, and these all collapsed after the elections of that year. Later the last carpetbag governor of South Carolina told William Lloyd Garrison that "the uneducated negro was too weak, no matter what his numbers, to cope with the whites."

THE GRANT YEARS

GRANT'S ELECTION   Ulysses S. Grant, who presided over this fiasco, brought to the presidency less political experience than any man who ever occupied the office, except perhaps Zachary Taylor, and perhaps less political judgment than any other. But in 1868 the rank-and-file voter could be expected to support "the Lion of Vicksburg" because of his record as a war leader. Both parties wooed him, but his falling-out with President Johnson pushed him toward the Republicans and built trust in him among the Radicals. They were, as Thad Stevens said, ready to "let him into the church." Impeachment proceedings were still in progress when the Republicans gathered in Chicago to name their candidate. Grant was the unanimous choice and House Speaker Schuyler Colfax of Indiana became his running mate. The platform endorsed the Reconstruction policy of Congress, congratulating the country on the "assured success" of the program. One plank cautiously defended Negro suffrage as a necessity in the South, but a matter each northern state should settle for itself. Another urged payment of the national debt "in the utmost good faith to all creditors," which meant in gold. More important than the platform were the great expectations of a soldier-president and his slogan: "Let us have peace."

The Democrats took the opposite position on both Reconstruction and the debt. The Republican Congress, the platform charged, instead of restoring the Union had "so far as in its power, dissolved it, and subjected ten states, in the time of profound peace, to military despotism and Negro supremacy." As to the public debt, the party endorsed the "Ohio idea" that since most bonds had been bought with depreciated greenbacks, they should be paid off in greenbacks unless they specified payment in gold. With no conspicuously available candidate in sight, the convention turned to Horatio Seymour, war governor of New York and chairman of the convention. His friends had to hustle him out of the hall to prevent his withdrawal. The Democrats made a closer race of it than showed up in the electoral vote. Eight states, including New York and New Jersey, went for Seymour. While Grant swept the electoral college by 214 to 80, his popular majority was only 307,000 out of a total of over 5.7 million votes. More than 500,000 black voters accounted for Grant's margin of victory.

EARLY APPOINTMENTS   Grant had proven himself a great leader in the war, but in the White House he seemed blind to the political forces and influence peddlers around him. He was awe-struck by men of wealth and unaccountably loyal to some who betrayed his trust. The historian Henry Adams, who lived in Washington at the time, noted that to his friends "Grant appeared as intermittent energy, immensely powerful when awake, but passive and plastic in repose. . . . They could never measure his character or be sure when he would act. They could never follow a mental process in his thought. They were not sure that he did think." His conception of the presidency was "Whiggish." The chief executive carried out the laws; in the formulation of policy he passively followed the lead of Congress. This approach endeared him at first to party leaders, but it left him at last ineffective and others disillusioned with his leadership.

President Ulysses S. Grant.

At the outset Grant consulted nobody on his cabinet appointments. Some of his choices indulged personal whims; others simply betrayed bad judgment. In some cases appointees learned of their nomination from the newspapers. As time went by Grant betrayed a fatal gift for losing men of talent and integrity from his cabinet. Secretary of State Hamilton Fish of New York turned out to be a happy exception; he guided foreign policy throughout the Grant presidency.

At first it looked as if Grant's free-wheeling style of choosing a cabinet signaled a sharp departure from the spoils system. But once Grant had taken care of his friends and relatives, he began to take care of party leaders. Cabinet members who balked at the procedure were soon eased out. This strengthened a nascent movement for a merit system in the civil service, modeled on systems recently adopted in Great Britain, Germany, and France. Grant finally approved a measure to set up a commission to look into the matter in 1872, a good gesture in a political year. The group duly brought in recommendations which in turn were duly shelved and forgotten once the election was over.

THE GOVERNMENT DEBT The "sound money" men had more success than the reformers. They claimed that Grant's election had been a mandate to save the country from the Democrats' "Ohio idea." The underlying purpose of the movement to pay off the government debt in greenbacks was to bring about an inflation of the currency. Many debtors and aggressive businessmen rallied to the cause of "easy money," joined by a large number of Radicals who thought a combination of high tariffs and easy money would bring about more rapid economic growth. But creditors stood to gain from payment in gold, and they had the greater influence in Republican circles. They also had the benefit of a strong Calvinistic tendency in the public mind to look upon the cause of hard money as a moral one; depreciated currency was somehow a fraud. In his inaugural address Grant endorsed payment of the debt in gold not as a point of policy but as a point of national honor. On March 18, 1869, the Public Credit Act endorsing that principle became the first act of Congress he signed. Under the Refunding Act of 1870 the Treasury was able to replace 6 percent Civil War bonds with a new issue promising 4–5 percent in gold.

But whatever Grant's convictions respecting a "sound currency," he was not ready to risk a sharp contraction of the greenbacks in circulation. After the war the Treasury had assumed that the $400 million in greenbacks would be retired from circulation. To that end in 1866 Congress gave the Treasury discretionary power to begin the process at a rate of $10 million in the first six months and $4 million a month thereafter. In 1868, however, "soft money" elements in Congress stopped the process, leaving $356 million outstanding. There matters stood when Grant took office.

REFORM AND SCANDAL   Long before Grant's first term was out, a reaction against the Reconstruction measures, and against incompetence and corruption in the administration, had incited mutiny within the Republican ranks. Open revolt broke out first in Missouri where Carl Schurz, a German immigrant and war hero, led a group which elected a governor with Democratic help in 1870 and sent Schurz to the Senate. In 1872 the Liberal Republicans (as they called themselves) held a national convention at Cincinnati which produced a compromise platform condemning the party's southern policy and favoring civil service reform, but remained silent on the protective tariff. The meeting, moreover, was stampeded toward an anomalous presidential candidate: Horace Greeley, editor of the New York *Tribune*, a strong protectionist, and longtime champion of just about every reform of his times. His image as a visionary eccentric was complemented by his record of hostility to Democrats, whose support the Liberals needed. The Democrats nevertheless swallowed the pill and gave their nomination to Greeley as the only hope of beating Grant.

The result was a foregone conclusion. Republican regulars duly endorsed Radical Reconstruction and the protective tariff. Grant still had seven carpetbag states in his pocket, generous support from business and banking interests, and the stalwart support of the Radicals. Above all he still evoked the imperishable glory of Missionary Ridge and Appomattox. Greeley, despite an exhausting tour of the country—still unusual for a presidential candidate—carried only six southern and border states and none in the North. Greeley's wife had died during the campaign, and worn out with grief and fatigue, he too was gone three weeks after the election.

Within less than a year of his reelection Grant was adrift in a cesspool of scandal. The first hint of scandal had touched Grant in the summer of 1869, when the crafty Jay Gould and the flamboyant Jim Fisk connived with the president's brother-in-law to corner the gold market. Gould concocted an argument that the government should refrain from selling gold on the market because the resulting rise in gold prices would raise temporarily

The People's Handwriting on the Wall. *An 1872 engraving comments on the corruption engulfing Grant.*

depressed farm prices. Grant apparently smelled a rat from the start, but was seen in public with the speculators. As the rumor spread on Wall Street that the president had bought the argument, gold rose from $132 to $163 an ounce. When Grant finally persuaded his brother-in-law to pull out of the deal, Gould began quietly selling out. Finally, on "Black Friday," September 24, 1869, Grant ordered the Treasury to sell a large quantity of gold and the bubble burst. Fisk got out by repudiating his agreements and hiring thugs to intimidate his creditors. "Nothing is lost save honor," he said.

During the campaign of 1872 the public first learned about the financial buccaneering of the Crédit Mobilier, a construction company which had milked the Union Pacific Railroad for exorbitant fees to line the pockets of insiders who controlled both firms. Rank-and-file Union Pacific shareholders were left holding the bag. One congressman had distributed Crédit Mobilier shares at bargain rates where, he said, "it will produce much good to us." The beneficiaries had included Speaker Schuyler Colfax, later vice-president, and Rep. James A. Garfield, later president. This chicanery had transpired before Grant's election in 1868, but it touched a number of prominent Republicans. Of thirteen members of Congress involved, only two were censured by a Congress which, before it adjourned in March 1873, voted itself a pay raise from $5,000 to $7,500—retroactive, it decided, for two years. A public uproar forced repeal, leaving the raises voted the president ($25,000 to $50,000) and Supreme Court justices.

Even more odious disclosures soon followed, and some involved the president's cabinet. The secretary of war, it turned out, had accepted bribes from Indian traders at army posts in the West. He was impeached, but resigned in time to elude trial by the Senate. Post-office contracts, it was revealed, went to carriers who offered the highest kickbacks. The secretary of the treasury had awarded a political friend a commission of 50 percent for the collection of overdue taxes. In St. Louis a "Whiskey Ring" bribed tax collectors to bilk the government of millions in revenue. Grant's private secretary was enmeshed in that scheme, taking large sums of money and other valuables in return for inside information. Before Grant's second term ended, the corruption crossed the Atlantic when the minister to London unloaded worthless stock in "Emma Mines" on gullible Britons. Only a plea of diplomatic immunity and a sudden exit spared him from British justice. There is no evidence that Grant himself was ever involved in, or that he personally profited from, any of the fraud, but his poor choice of associates earned him the public censure that was heaped upon his head.

PANIC AND REDEMPTION Economic distress followed close upon public scandal. Contraction of the money supply and expansion of the railroads into sparsely settled areas had made investors cautious. During 1873 the market for railroad bonds turned sour as some twenty-five roads defaulted on their interest payments before the end of August. The investment-banking firm of Jay Cooke and Company, unable to sell the bonds of the Northern Pacific Railroad, financed them with short-term deposits in hope that a European market would develop. But in 1873 the opposite happened when a financial panic in Vienna forced many financiers to unload American stocks and bonds. Caught short, Cooke and Company went bankrupt on September 18, 1873. The ensuing stampede forced the stock market to close for ten days. The Panic of 1873 set off a depression that lasted for six years, the longest and most severe that Americans had yet suffered, marked by widespread bankruptcies, unemployment, and a drastic slowdown in railroad building.

Hard times and scandals hurt Republicans in the midterm elections of 1874. The Democrats won control of the House of

Representatives and gained in the Senate. The new Democratic House immediately launched inquiries into the scandals and unearthed further evidence of corruption in high places. The panic meanwhile focused attention once more on greenback currency.

Since greenbacks were valued less than gold, they had become the chief circulating medium. Most people spent greenbacks first and held their gold or used it to settle foreign accounts, which drained much gold out of the country. The postwar retirement of greenbacks had made for tight money. To relieve deflation and stimulate business, therefore, the Treasury reissued $26 million in greenbacks previously withdrawn, raising the total in circulation to about $382 million.

For a time the advocates of easy money were riding high. Early in 1874 they pushed through a bill to issue greenbacks up to the wartime level of $400 million. Here the administration drew the line, however. Grant vetoed the bill in April and in his annual message of December 1874 called for the gradual resumption of specie payments—that is, the redemption of greenbacks in gold. This would make greenbacks "good as gold" and raise their value to a par with the gold dollar. In January, before the Republicans gave up control of the House, Congress obliged by passing the Resumption Act of 1875. The redemption in specie began on January 1, 1879, after the Treasury had built a gold reserve for the purpose and reduced the value of greenbacks in circulation.

THE COMPROMISE OF 1877   Grant, despite everything, was eager to run again in 1876, but the recent scandals discouraged any challenge to the two-term tradition. James G. Blaine of Maine, late Speaker of the House, emerged as the Republican front-runner, but he too bore the taint of scandal. Letters in the possession of James Mulligan of Boston linked Blaine to some dubious railroad dealings. Blaine cajoled Mulligan into turning over a packet of letters, from which he read to Congress selected passages exonerating him. But the performance was a shade too clever. It left doubts which were strengthened by the disclosure of still other "Mulligan letters" that found their way into print.

The Republican convention in Cincinnati therefore eliminated Blaine and several other hopefuls in favor of Ohio's favorite son, Rutherford B. Hayes. Three times elected governor of Ohio, most recently as an advocate of sound money, Hayes had also made a name as a civil service reformer. But his chief virtue was that he offended neither Radicals nor reformers. As Henry Adams put it, he was "a third rate nonentity, whose only recommendation is that he is obnoxious to no one."

A Republican campaign piece from the 1876 election: "Yankee Doodle, that's the talk—/ We've found an honest dealer;/ And o'er the course we ride or walk,/ We'll go for Hayes *and* Wheeler.*"*

The Democratic convention in St. Louis was abnormally harmonious from the start. The nomination went on the second ballot to Samuel J. Tilden, millionaire corporation lawyer and reform governor of New York who had directed a campaign to overthrow first the Tweed Ring in New York City and then another ring in Albany which had bilked the state of millions.

The campaign generated no burning issues. Both candidates favored the trend toward conservative rule in the South. During one of the most corrupt elections ever, both candidates favored civil service reform. In the absence of strong differences, Democrats waved the Republicans' dirty linen. In response, Republicans waved the bloody shirt, which is to say that they engaged in verbal assaults on former Confederates and the spirit of Rebellion. The phrase "waving the bloody shirt" originated at the impeachment trial of President Johnson when Benjamin F. Butler, speaking for the prosecution, displayed the bloody shirt a Mississippi carpetbagger had been wearing when hauled out of bed and beaten by Ku Kluxers. Reporting such atrocities came to be known to Democrats as "grinding the outrage mills." "Our strong ground," Hayes wrote to Blaine, "is the dread of a solid South, *rebel rule*, etc., etc. . . . It leads people away from 'hard times,' which is our deadliest foe."

On the night of the election early returns pointed to a victory for Tilden, but the Republican national chairman refused to concede. As it fell out, Tilden had 184 electoral votes, just one short of a majority, but Republicans claimed nineteen doubtful votes from Florida, Louisiana, and South Carolina, while Democrats laid a counterclaim to Oregon. But the Republicans had clearly carried Oregon. In the South the outcome was less certain, and given the fraud and intimidation perpetrated on both sides, nobody will ever know what might have happened if, to use a slogan of the day, "a free ballot and a fair count" had prevailed. As good a guess as any may be, as one writer suggested, that the Democrats stole the election first and the Republicans stole it back.

In all three of the disputed southern states rival canvassing boards sent in different returns. In Florida, Republicans conceded the state election, but in Louisiana and South Carolina rival state governments also appeared. The Constitution offered no guidance in this unprecedented situation. Even if Congress was empowered to sort things out, the Democratic House and the Republican Senate proved unable to reach an agreement.

Finally, on January 29, 1877, the two houses decided to set up a special Electoral Commission which would investigate and report back its findings. It had fifteen members, five each from the House, the Senate, and the Supreme Court. Members were so chosen as to have seven from each major party with Justice David Davis of Illinois as the swing man. Davis, though appointed to the Court by Lincoln, was no party regular and was in fact thought to be leaning toward the Democrats. Republicans who voted for the commission, James A. Garfield said, were "fair-minded asses" who thought that "truth is always half way between God and the Devil." The panel appeared to be stacked in favor of Tilden.

But as it turned out, the panel got restacked the other way. Short-sighted Democrats in the Illinois legislature teamed up with minority Greenbackers to name Davis their senator. Davis accepted, no doubt with a sense of relief. From the remaining justices, all Republicans, the panel chose Joseph P. Bradley to fill the vacancy. The decision on each state went by a vote of 8 to 7, along party lines, in favor of Hayes. After much bluster and threat

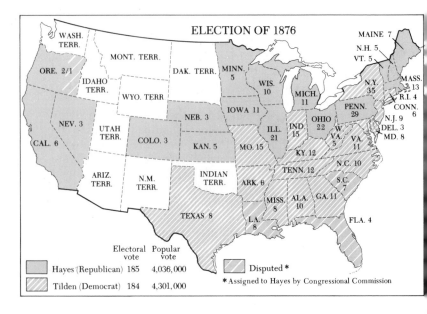

ELECTION OF 1876

	Electoral vote	Popular vote
Hayes (Republican)	185	4,036,000
Tilden (Democrat)	184	4,301,000

Disputed *
* Assigned to Hayes by Congressional Commission

of filibuster by Democrats, the House voted on March 2 to accept the report and declare Hayes elected by an electoral vote of 185 to 184.

Critical to this outcome was the defection of southern Democrats who had made several informal agreements with the Republicans. On February 26, 1877, a bargain was struck at the Wormley House, a Washington hotel, between prominent Ohio Republicans and powerful southern Democrats. The Republicans promised that, if elected, Hayes would withdraw federal troops from Louisiana and South Carolina, letting the Republican governments there collapse. In return the Democrats promised to withdraw their opposition to Hayes, to accept in good faith the Reconstruction amendments, and to refrain from partisan reprisals against Republicans in the South.

With this agreement in hand, southern Democrats could justify deserting Tilden because this so-called Compromise of 1877 brought a final "redemption" from the "Radicals" and a return to "home rule," which actually meant rule by white Democrats. Other, more informal promises, less noticed by the public, bolstered the Wormley House agreement. Hayes's friends pledged more support for Mississippi levees and other internal improvements, including federal subsidy for a transcontinental railroad along a southern route. Southerners extracted a further promise that Hayes would name a white southerner as postmaster-general, the cabinet position with the most patronage jobs at hand.

In return, southerners would let Republicans make James A. Garfield Speaker of the new House.

THE END OF RECONSTRUCTION   After Hayes took office, most of these promises were either renounced or forgotten. They had served their purpose of breaking the crisis. In April, Hayes withdrew federal troops from the state houses in Louisiana and South Carolina, and the Republican governments there collapsed— along with much of Hayes's claim to legitimacy. Hayes chose a Tennessean and former Confederate as postmaster-general. But after southern Democrats failed to permit the choice of Garfield as Speaker, Hayes expressed doubt about any further subsidy for railroad building, and none was voted.

As to southern promises regarding the civil rights of blacks, only a few Democratic leaders, such as the new governors of South Carolina and Louisiana, remembered them for long. Over the next three decades those rights crumbled under the pressure of white rule in the South and the force of Supreme Court decisions narrowing the application of the Reconstruction amendments. The Compromise of 1877, viewed in the light of its consequences, might justly bear the label that one historian gave it: "The betrayal of the Negro." But "betrayal" implies that a promise was made in the first place, and Reconstruction never offered more than an uncertain commitment to equality before the law. Yet it left an enduring legacy, the Thirteenth, Fourteenth, and Fifteenth Amendments—not dead but dormant, waiting to be warmed back into life.

FURTHER READING

Reconstruction has long been "a dark and bloody ground" of conflicting interpretations. Among the recent surveys of the period are John Hope Franklin's *Reconstruction after the Civil War* (1961) and Kenneth M. Stampp's *The Era of Reconstruction, 1865–1877* (1965).° James M. McPherson's *Ordeal by Fire: The Civil War and Reconstruction* (1982)° and James G. Randall and David H. Donald's *Civil War and Reconstruction* (2nd ed., rev., 1969)° are also valuable.

More specialized works give closer scrutiny to the aims of the principal political figures. Peyton McCrary's *Abraham Lincoln and Reconstruction* (1978) deals with the Lincoln policies as they were carried out in Louisiana. Eric L. McKitrick's *Andrew Johnson and Reconstruction* (1960), LaWanda Cox and John H. Cox's *Politics, Principle, and Preju-*

°These books are available in paperback editions.

dice, 1865–1866 (1963), and William R. Brock's *An American Crisis* (1963) criticize Johnson's policies. Why Johnson was impeached is detailed in Michael Les Benedict's *The Impeachment and Trial of Andrew Johnson* (1973)° and Hans L. Trefousse's *Impeachment of a President* (1975).

Recent scholars have been fairly sympathetic to the aims and motives of the Radical Republicans. See, for instance, Herman Belz's *Reconstructing the Union* (1969). The ideology of these Radicals is explored in Michael Les Benedict's *A Compromise of Principle: Congressional Republicans and Reconstruction* (1974).

The intransigence of southern white attitudes is examined in Michael Perman's *Reunion without Compromise* (1973).° Allen W. Trelease's *White Terror* (1971)° covers the various organizations that practiced vigilante tactics, chiefly the Ku Klux Klan. The difficulties former planters had in adjusting to the new labor system are documented in James L. Roark's *Masters without Slaves* (1977).° Recent books on southern politics during Reconstruction include Michael Perman's *The Road to Redemption* (1984), Terry L. Seip's *The South Returns to Congress* (1983), Mark W. Summers's *Railroads, Reconstruction, and the Gospel of Prosperity* (1984), Dan T. Carter's *When the War Was Over* (1985), and George C. Rable's *But There Was No Peace* (1984).

Numerous works have appeared on the freedmen's experience in the South. Start with Leon F. Litwack's *Been in the Storm So Long* (1979),° which wonderfully covers the transition from slavery to freedom. Willie Lee Rose's *Rehearsal for Reconstruction* (1964) examines Union efforts to define the social role of former slaves during wartime emancipation. Joel Williamson's *After Slavery* (1965)° argues that South Carolina freedmen took an active role in pursuing their political and economic rights. Peter Kolchin's *First Freedom* (1972), a study of Alabama freedmen, is also useful. The role of the Freedman's Bureau is explored in William S. McFeely's *Yankee Stepfather: General O. O. Howard and the Freedmen* (1968).°

The land confiscation issue is discussed in Eric Foner's *Politics and Ideology in the Age of the Civil War* (1980);° Beth Bethel's *Promiseland* (1981), on a South Carolina black community; and Janet S. Hermann's *The Pursuit of a Dream* (1981),° on the Davis Bend experiment.

The politics of corruption outside the South is depicted in Allan Nevin's *Hamilton Fish: The Inner History of the Grant Administration* (1936) and William S. McFeely's *Grant: A Biography* (1981).° The political maneuvers of the election of 1876 and the resultant crisis and compromise are explained in C. Vann Woodward's *Reunion and Reaction* (1951)° and William Gillette's *Retreat from Reconstruction, 1869–1879* (1979).°

APPENDIX

THE DECLARATION OF
INDEPENDENCE

WHEN IN THE COURSE OF HUMAN EVENTS, it becomes necessary for one people to dissolve the political bands which have connected them with another, and to assume the Powers of the earth, the separate and equal station to which the Laws of Nature and of Nature's God entitle them, a decent respect to the opinions of mankind requires that they should declare the causes which impel them to the separation.

We hold these truths to be self-evident, that all men are created equal, that they are endowed by their Creator with certain unalienable rights, that among these are Life, Liberty, and the pursuit of Happiness. That to secure these rights, Governments are instituted among Men, deriving their just powers from the consent of the governed. That whenever any Form of Government becomes destructive of these ends, it is the Right of the People to alter or to abolish it, and to institute new Government, laying its foundation on such principles and organizing its powers in such form, as to them shall seem most likely to effect their Safety and Happiness. Prudence, indeed, will dictate that Governments long established should not be changed for light and transient causes; and accordingly all experience hath shown, that mankind are more disposed to suffer, while evils are sufferable, than to right themselves by abolishing the forms to which they are accustomed. But when a long train of abuses and usurpations, pursuing invariably the same Object evinces a design to reduce them under absolute Despotism, it is their right, it is their duty, to throw off such Government, and to provide new Guards for their future security.—Such has been the patient sufferance of these Colonies; and such is now the necessity which constrains them to alter their former Systems of Government. The history of the present King of Great Britain is a history of repeated injuries and usurpations, all having in direct object the establishment of an absolute Tyranny over these States. To prove this, let Facts be submitted to a candid world.

He has refused his Assent to Laws, the most wholesome and necessary for the public good.

He has forbidden his Governors to pass Laws of immediate and press-

A1

ing importance, unless suspended in their operation till his Assent should be obtained; and when so suspended, he has utterly neglected to attend to them.

He has refused to pass other Laws for the accommodation of large districts of people, unless those people would relinquish the right of Representation in the Legislature, a right inestimable to them and formidable to tyrants only.

He has called together legislative bodies at places unusual, uncomfortable, and distant from the depository of their public Records, for the sole purpose of fatiguing them into compliance with his measures.

He has dissolved Representative Houses repeatedly, for opposing with manly firmness his invasions on the rights of the people.

He has refused for a long time, after such dissolutions, to cause others to be elected; whereby the Legislative powers, incapable of Annihilation, have returned to the People at large for their exercise; the State remaining in the mean time exposed to all dangers of invasion from without, and convulsions within.

He has endeavoured to prevent the population of these States; for that purpose obstructing the Laws of Naturalization of Foreigners; refusing to pass others to encourage their migrations hither, and raising the conditions of new Appropriations of Lands.

He has obstructed the Administration of Justice, by refusing his Assent to Laws for establishing Judiciary powers.

He has made Judges dependent on his Will alone, for the tenure of their offices, and the amount and payment of their salaries.

He has erected a multitude of New Offices, and sent hither swarms of Officers to harass our People, and eat out their substance.

He has kept among us, in times of peace, Standing Armies without the Consent of our legislature.

He has affected to render the Military independent of and superior to the Civil Power.

He has combined with others to subject us to a jurisdiction foreign to our constitution, and unacknowledged by our laws; giving his Assent to their Acts of pretended Legislation:

For quartering large bodies of armed troops among us:

For protecting them, by a mock Trial, from Punishment for any Murders which they should commit on the Inhabitants of these States:

For cutting off our Trade with all parts of the world:

For imposing taxes on us without our Consent:

For depriving us of many cases, of the benefits of Trial by jury:

For transporting us beyond Seas to be tried for pretended offences:

For abolishing the free System of English Laws in a neighbouring Province, establishing therein an Arbitrary government, and enlarging its Boundaries so as to render it at once an example and fit instrument for introducing the same absolute rule into these Colonies:

For taking away our Charters, abolishing our most valuable Laws, and altering fundamentally the Forms of our Governments:

For suspending our own Legislatures, and declaring themselves invested with Power to legislate for us in all cases whatsoever.

He has abdicated Government here, by declaring us out of his Protection and waging War against us.

He has plundered our seas, ravaged our Coasts, burnt our towns, and destroyed the lives of our people.

He is at this time transporting large armies of foreign mercenaries to compleat the works of death, desolation, and tyranny, already begun with circumstances of Cruelty & perfidy scarcely paralleled in the most barbarous ages, and totally unworthy the Head of a civilized nation.

He has constrained our fellow Citizens taken Captive on the high Seas to bear Arms against their Country, to become the executioners of their friends and Brethren, or to fall themselves by their Hands.

He has excited domestic insurrections amongst us, and has endeavoured to bring on the inhabitants of our frontiers, the merciless Indian Savages, whose known rule of warfare, is an undistinguished destruction of all ages, sexes, and conditions.

In every stage of these Oppressions We have Petitioned for Redress in the most humble terms: Our repeated Petitions have been answered only by repeated injury. A Prince, whose character is thus marked by every act which may define a Tyrant, is unfit to be the ruler of a free people.

Nor have We been wanting in attention to our British brethren. We have warned them from time to time of attempts by their legislature to extend an unwarrantable jurisdiction over us. We have reminded them of the circumstances of our emigration and settlement here. We have appealed to their native justice and magnanimity, and we have conjured them by the ties of our common kindred to disavow these usurpations, which, would inevitably interrupt our connections and correspondence. They too must have been deaf to the voice of justice and of consanguinity. We must, therefore, acquiesce in the necessity, which denounces our Separation, and hold them, as we hold the rest of mankind, Enemies in War, in Peace Friends.

WE, THEREFORE, the Representatives of the UNITED STATES OF AMERICA, in General Congress, Assembled, appealing to the Supreme Judge of the world for the rectitude of our intentions, do, in the Name, and by Authority of the good People of these Colonies, solemnly publish and declare, That these United Colonies are, and of Right ought to be FREE AND INDEPENDENT STATES; that they are Absolved from all Allegiance to the British Crown, and that all political connection between them and the State of Great Britain, is and ought to be totally dissolved; and that as Free and Independent States, they have full Power to levy War, conclude Peace, contract Alliances, establish Commerce, and to do all other Acts and Things which Independent States may of right do. And for the support of this Declaration, with a firm reliance on the Protection of Divine Providence, we mutually pledge to each other our Lives, our Fortunes, and our sacred Honor.

The foregoing Declaration was, by order of Congress, engrossed, and signed by the following members:

John Hancock

NEW HAMPSHIRE
Josiah Bartlett
William Whipple
Matthew Thornton

MASSACHUSETTS BAY
Samuel Adams
John Adams
Robert Treat Paine
Elbridge Gerry

RHODE ISLAND
Stephen Hopkins
William Ellery

CONNECTICUT
Roger Sherman
Samuel Huntington
William Williams
Oliver Wolcott

NEW YORK
William Floyd
Philip Livingston
Francis Lewis
Lewis Morris

NEW JERSEY
Richard Stockton
John Witherspoon
Francis Hopkinson
John Hart
Abraham Clark

PENNSYLVANIA
Robert Morris
Benjamin Rush
Benjamin Franklin
John Morton
George Clymer
James Smith
George Taylor
James Wilson
George Ross

DELAWARE
Caesar Rodney
George Read
Thomas M'Kean

MARYLAND
Samuel Chase
William Paca
Thomas Stone
Charles Carroll,
  of Carrollton

VIRGINIA
George Wythe
Richard Henry Lee
Thomas Jefferson
Benjamin Harrison
Thomas Nelson, Jr.
Francis Lightfoot Lee
Carter Braxton

NORTH CAROLINA
William Hooper
Joseph Hewes
John Penn

SOUTH CAROLINA
Edward Rutledge
Thomas Heyward, Jr.
Thomas Lynch, Jr.
Arthur Middleton

GEORGIA
Button Gwinnett
Lyman Hall
George Walton

Resolved, That copies of the Declaration be sent to the several assemblies, conventions, and committees, or councils of safety, and to the several commanding officers of the continental troops; that it be proclaimed in each of the United States, at the head of the army.

ARTICLES OF CONFEDERATION

To ALL TO WHOM these Presents shall come, we the undersigned Delegates of the States affixed to our Names send greeting.

Whereas the Delegates of the United States of America in Congress assembled did on the fifteenth day of November in the Year of our Lord One Thousand Seven Hundred and Seventy-seven, and in the Second Year of the Independence of America agree to certain articles of Confederation and perpetual Union between the States of Newhampshire, Massachusetts-bay, Rhodeisland and Providence Plantations, Connecticut, New York, New Jersey, Pennsylvania, Delaware, Maryland, Virginia, North-Carolina, South-Carolina and Georgia in the Words following, viz.

"Articles of Confederation and perpetual Union between the States of Newhampshire, Massachusetts-bay, Rhodeisland and Providence Plantations, Connecticut, New-York, New-Jersey, Pennsylvania, Delaware, Maryland, Virginia, North-Carolina, South-Carolina and Georgia.

ARTICLE I. The stile of this confederacy shall be "The United States of America."

ARTICLE II. Each State retains its sovereignty, freedom and independence, and every power, jurisdiction and right, which is not by this confederation expressly delegated to the United States, in Congress assembled.

ARTICLE III. The said States hereby severally enter into a firm league of friendship with each other, for their common defense, the security of their liberties, and their mutual and general welfare, binding themselves to assist each other, against all force offered to, or attacks made upon them, or any of them, on account of religion, sovereignty, trade or any other pretence whatever.

ARTICLE IV. The better to secure and perpetuate mutual friendship and intercourse among the people of the different States in this Union, the free inhabitants of each of these States, paupers, vagabonds and fugitives from justice excepted, shall be entitled to all privileges and immunities of free citizens in the several States; and the people of each State shall have free ingress and regress to and from any other State, and shall enjoy therein all the privileges of trade and commerce, subject to the same duties, impositions and restrictions as the inhabitants thereof respectively, provided that such restrictions shall not extend so far as to prevent the removal of property imported into any State, to any other State of which the owner is an inhabitant; provided also that no imposition, duties or restriction shall be laid by any State, on the property of the United States, or either of them.

If any person guilty of, or charged with treason, felony, or other high misdemeanor in any State, shall flee from justice, and be found in any of the United States, he shall upon demand of the Governor or Executive power, of the State from which he fled, be delivered up and removed to the State having jurisdiction of his offence.

Full faith and credit shall be given in each of these States to the records, acts and judicial proceedings of the courts and magistrates of every other State.

ARTICLE V. For the more convenient management of the general interests of the United States, delegates shall be annually appointed in such manner as the legislature of each State shall direct, to meet in Congress on the first Monday in November, in every year, with a power reserved to each State, to recall its delegates, or any of them, at any time within the year, and to send others in their stead, for the remainder of the year.

No State shall be represented in Congress by less than two, nor by more than seven members; and no person shall be capable of being a delegate for more than three years in any term of six years; nor shall any person, being a delegate, be capable of holding any office under the United States, for which he, or another for his benefit receives any salary, fees or emolument of any kind.

Each State shall maintain its own delegates in a meeting of the States, and while they act as members of the committee of the States.

In determining questions in the United States, in Congress assembled, each State shall have one vote.

Freedom of speech and debate in Congress shall not be impeached or questioned in any court, or place out of Congress, and the members of Congress shall be protected in their persons from arrests and imprisonments, during the time of their going to and from, and attendance on Congress, except for treason, felony, or breach of the peace.

ARTICLE VI. No State without the consent of the United States in Congress assembled, shall send any embassy to, or receive any embassy from, or enter into any conference, agreement, alliance or treaty with any king, prince or state; nor shall any person holding any office of profit or trust under the United States, or any of them, accept of any present, emolument, office or title of any kind whatever from any king, prince or foreign state; nor shall the United States in Congress assembled, or any of them, grant any title of nobility.

No two or more States shall enter into any treaty, confederation or alliance whatever between them, without the consent of the United States in Congress assembled, specifying accurately the purposes for which the same is to be entered into, and how long it shall continue.

No State shall lay any imposts or duties, which may interfere with any stipulations in treaties, entered into by the United States in Congress assembled, with any king, prince or state, in pursuance of any treaties already proposed by Congress, to the courts of France and Spain.

No vessels of war shall be kept up in time of peace by any State, except such number only, as shall be deemed necessary by the United States in Congress assembled, for the defence of such State, or its trade; nor shall any body of forces be kept up by any State, in time of peace, except such number only, as in the judgment of the United States, in Congress assembled, shall be deemed requisite to garrison the forts necessary for the defense of such State; but every State shall always keep up a well regulated and disciplined militia, sufficiently armed and accoutred, and shall provide and constantly have ready for use, in public stores, a due number of field pieces and tents, and a proper quantity of arms, ammunition and camp equipage.

No State shall engage in any war without the consent of the United States in Congress assembled, unless such State be actually invaded by enemies, or shall have received certain advice of a resolution being formed by some nation of Indians to invade such State, and the danger is so imminent as not to admit of a delay, till the United States in Congress assembled can be consulted: nor shall any State grant commissions to any ships or vessels of war, nor letters of marque or reprisal, except it be after a declaration of war by the United States in Congress assembled, and then only against the kingdom or state and the subjects thereof, against which war has been so declared, and under such regulations as shall be established by the United States in Congress assembled, unless such State be infested by pirates, in which case vessels of war may be fitted out for that occasion, and kept so long as the danger shall continue, or until the United States in Congress assembled shall determine otherwise.

Article VII. When land-forces are raised by any State of the common defence, all officers of or under the rank of colonel, shall be appointed by the Legislature of each State respectively by whom such forces shall be raised, or in such manner as such State shall direct, and all vacancies shall be filled up by the State which first made the appointment.

Article VIII. All charges of war, and all other expenses that shall be incurred for the common defense or general welfare, and allowed by the United States in Congress assembled, shall be defrayed out of a common treasury, which shall be supplied by the several States, in proportion to the value of all land within each State, granted to or surveyed for any person, as such land and the buildings and improvements thereon shall be estimated according to such mode as the United States in Congress assembled, shall from time to time direct and appoint.

The taxes for paying that proportion shall be laid and levied by the authority and direction of the Legislatures of the several States within the time agreed upon by the United States in Congress assembled.

ARTICLE IX. The United States in Congress assembled, shall have the sole and exclusive right and power of determining on peace and war, except in the cases mentioned in the sixth article—of sending and receiving ambassadors—entering into treaties and alliances, provided that no treaty of commerce shall be made whereby the legislative power of the respective States shall be restrained from imposing such imposts and duties on foreigners, as their own people are subjected to, or from prohibiting the exportation or importation of and species of goods or commodities whatsoever—of establishing rules for deciding in all cases, what captures on land or water shall be legal, and in what manner prizes taken by land or naval forces in the service of the United States shall be divided or appropriated—of granting letters of marque and reprisal in times of peace—appointing courts for the trial of piracies and felonies committed on the high seas and establishing courts for receiving and determining finally appeals in all cases of captures, provided that no member of Congress shall be appointed a judge of any of the said courts.

The United States in Congress assembled shall also be the last resort on appeal in all disputes and differences now subsisting or that hereafter may arise between two or more States concerning boundary, jurisdiction or any other cause whatever; which authority shall always be exercised in the manner following. Whenever the legislative or executive authority or lawful agent of any State in controversy with another shall present a petition to Congress, stating the matter in question and praying for a hearing, notice thereof shall be given by order of Congress to the legislative or executive authority of the other State in controversy, and a day assigned for the appearance of the parties by their lawful agents, who shall then be directed to appoint by joint consent, commissioners or judges to constitute a court for hearing and determining the matter in question: but if they cannot agree, Congress shall name three persons out of each of the United States, and from the list of such persons each party shall alternately strike out one, the petitioners beginning, until the number shall be reduced to thirteen; and from that number not less than seven, nor more than nine names as Congress shall direct, shall in the presence of Congress be drawn out by lot, and the persons whose names shall be so drawn or any five of them, shall be commissioners or judges, to hear and finally determine the controversy, so always as a major part of the judges who shall hear the cause shall agree in the determination: and if either party shall neglect to attend at the day appointed, without reasons, which Congress shall judge sufficient, or being present shall refuse to strike, the Congress shall proceed to nominate three persons out of each State, and the Secretary of Congress shall strike in behalf of such party absent or refusing; and the judgment and sentence of the court to be appointed, in the manner before prescribed, shall be final and conclusive; and if any of the parties shall refuse to submit to the authority of such court, or to appear or defend their claim or cause, the court shall nevertheless proceed to pronounce sentence, or judgment, which shall in like manner be final and decisive, the judgment or sentence and other procedings being in either case transmitted to Congress, and lodged among the acts of Congress for the security of the parties concerned: provided that every commissioner, before he sits in judgment, shall take an oath to be administered by one of the judges of the supreme or superior court of the State where the cause shall be tried, "well and truly to hear and determine the matter in question, according to the best of his judgment, without favour, affection or hope of reward:" provided also that no State shall be deprived of territory for the benefit of the United States.

All controversies concerning the private right of soil claimed under different grants of two or more States, whose jurisdiction as they may respect such lands, and the states which passed such grants are adjusted, the said grants or either of them being at the same time claimed to have originated antecedent to such settlement of jurisdiction, shall on the petition of either party to the Congress of the United States, be finally determined as near as may be in the same manner as is before prescribed for deciding disputes respecting territorial jurisdiction between different States.

The United States in Congress assembled shall also have the sole and exclusive right and power of regulating the alloy and value of coin struck by their own authority, or by that of the respective States—fixing the standard of weights and measures throughout the United States—regulating the trade and managing all affairs with the Indians, not members of any of the States, provided that the legislative right of any State within its own limits be not infringed or violated—establishing and regulating post-offices from one State to another, throughout all of the United States, and exacting such postage on the papers passing thro' the same as may be requisite to defray the expenses of the said office—appointing all officers of the land forces, in the service of the United States, excepting regimental officers—appointing all the officers of the naval forces, and commissioning all officers whatever in the service of the United States —making rules for the government and regulation of the said land and naval forces, and directing their operations.

The United States in Congress assembled shall have authority to appoint a committee, to sit in the recess of Congress, to be denominated "a Committee of the States," and to consist of one delegate from each State; and to appoint such other committees and civil officers as may be necessary for managing the general affairs of the United States under their direction—to appoint one of their number to preside, provided that no person be allowed to serve in the office of president more than one year in any term of three years; to ascertain the necessary sums of money to be raised for the service of the United States, and to appropriate and apply the same for defraying the public expenses—to borrow money, or emit bills on the credit of the United States, transmitting every half year to the respective States an account of the sums of money so borrowed or emitted,—to build and equip a navy—to agree upon the number of land forces, and to make requisitions from each State for its quota, in proportion to the number of white inhabitants in such State; which requisition shall be binding, and thereupon the Legislature of each State shall appoint the regimental officers, raise the men and cloath, arm and equip them in a soldier like manner, at the expense of the United States; and the officers and men so cloathed, armed and equipped shall march to the place appointed, and within the time agreed on by the United States in Congress assembled: but if the United States in Congress assembled shall, on consideration of circumstances judge proper that any State should not raise men, or should raise a smaller number of men than the quota thereof, such extra number shall be raised, officered, cloathed, armed and equipped in the same manner as the quota of such State, unless the legislature of such State shall judge that such extra number cannot be safely spared out of the same, in which case they shall raise officer, cloath, arm and equip as many of such extra number as they judge can be safely spared. And the officers and men so cloathed, armed and equipped, shall march to the place appointed, and within the time agreed on by the United States in Congress assembled.

The United States in Congress assembled shall never engage in a war, nor grant letters of marque and reprisal in time of peace, nor enter into any treaties or alliances, nor coin money, nor regulate the value thereof, nor ascertain the sums and expenses necessary for the defence and welfare of the United States, or any of them, nor emit bills, nor borrow money on the credit of the United States, nor appropriate money, nor agree upon the number of vessels to be built or purchased, or the number of land or sea forces to be raised, nor appoint a commander in chief of the army or navy, unless nine States assent to the same: nor shall a question on any other point, except for adjourning from day to day be determined, unless by the votes of a majority of the United States in Congress assembled.

The Congress of the United States shall have power to adjourn to any time within the year, and to any place within the United States, so that no period of adjournment be for a longer duration than the space of six months, and shall publish the journal of their proceedings monthly, except such parts thereof relating to treaties, alliances or military operations, as in their judgment require secresy; and the yeas and nays of the delegates of each State on any question shall be entered on the Journal, when it is desired by any delegate; and the delegates of a State, or any of them, at his or their request shall be furnished with a transcript of the said journal, except such parts as are above excepted, to lay before the Legislatures of the several States.

ARTICLE X. The committee of the States, or any nine of them, shall be authorized to execute, in the recess of Congress, such of the powers of Congress as the United States in Congress assembled, by the consent of nine States, shall from time to time think expedient to vest them with; provided that no power be delegated to the said committee, for the exercise of which, by the articles of confederation, the voice of nine States in the Congress of the United States assembled is requisite.

ARTICLE XI. Canada acceding to this confederation, and joining in the measures of the United States, shall be admitted into, and entitled to all the advantages of this Union: but no other colony shall be admitted into the same, unless such admission be agreed to by nine States.

ARTICLE XII. All bills of credit emitted, monies borrowed and debts contracted by, or under the authority of Congress, before the assembling of the United States, in pursuance of the present confederation, shall be deemed and considered as a charge against the United States, for payment and satisfaction whereof the said United States, and the public faith are hereby solemnly pledged.

ARTICLE XIII. Every State shall abide by the determinations of the United States in Congress assembled, on all questions which by this confederation are submitted to them. And the articles of this confederation shall be inviolably observed by every State, and the Union shall be perpetual; nor shall any alteration at any time hereafter be made in any of them; unless such alteration be agreed to in a Congress of the United States, and be afterwards confirmed by the Legislatures of every State.

And whereas it has pleased the Great Governor of the world to incline the hearts of the Legislatures we respectively represent in Congress, to approve of, and to authorize us to ratify the said articles of confederation and perpetual union. Know ye that we the undersigned delegates, by virtue of the power and authority to us given for that purpose, do by these presents, in the name and in behalf of our respective constituents, fully and entirely ratify and confirm each and every of the said articles of confederation and perpetual union, and all and singular the matters and things therein contained: and we do further solemnly plight and engage the faith of our respective constituents, that they shall abide by the determinations of the United States in Congress assembled, on all questions, which by the said confederation are submitted to them. And that the articles thereof shall be inviolably observed by the States we respectively represent, and that the Union shall be perpetual.

In witness thereof we have hereunto set our hands in Congress. Done at Philadelphia in the State of Pennsylvania the ninth day of July in the year of our Lord one thousand seven hundred and seventy-eight, and in the third year of the independence of America.

THE CONSTITUTION OF
THE UNITED STATES

WE THE PEOPLE OF THE UNITED STATES, in order to form a more perfect Union, establish Justice, insure domestic Tranquility, provide for the common defence, promote the general Welfare, and secure the Blessings of Liberty to ourselves and our Posterity, do ordain and establish this Constitution for the United States of America.

ARTICLE. I.

Section. 1. All legislative Powers herein granted shall be vested in a Congress of the United States, which shall consist of a Senate and House of Representatives.

Section. 2. The House of Representatives shall be composed of Members chosen every second Year by the People of the several States, and the Electors in each State shall have the Qualifications requisite for Electors of the most numerous Branch of the State Legislature.

No Person shall be a Representative who shall not have attained to the Age of twenty five Years, and been seven Years a Citizen of the United States, and who shall not, when elected, be an Inhabitant of that State in which he shall be chosen.

Representatives and direct Taxes shall be apportioned among the several States which may be included within this Union, according to their respective Numbers, which shall be determined by adding to the whole Number of free Persons, including those bound to Service for a Term of Years, and excluding Indians not taxed, three fifths of all other Persons. The actual Enumeration shall be made within three Years after the first Meeting of the Congress of the United States, and within every subsequent Term of ten Years, in such Manner as they shall by Law direct. The Number of Representatives shall not exceed one for every thirty Thousand, but each State shall have at Least one Representative; and until such enumeration shall be made, the State of New Hampshire shall be entitled to chuse three, Massachusetts eight, Rhode-Island and Providence Plantations one, Connecticut five, New-York six, New Jersey four, Pennsylvania eight, Delaware one, Maryland six, Virginia ten, North Carolina five, South Carolina five, and Georgia three.

When vacancies happen in the Representation from any state, the Executive Authority thereof shall issue Writs of Election to fill such Vacancies.

The House of Representatives shall chuse their Speaker and other Officers; and shall have the sole Power of Impeachment.

Section. 3. The Senate of the United States shall be composed of two Senators from each State, chosen by the legislature thereof, for six Years; and each Senator shall have one Vote.

Immediately after they shall be assembled in Consequence of the first Election, they shall be divided as equally as may be into three Classes. The Seats of the Senators of the first Class shall be vacated at the Expiration of the second Year, of the second Class at the Expiration of the fourth Year, and of the third Class at the Expiration of the sixth Year, so that one third maybe chosen every second Year; and if Vacancies happen by Resignation, or otherwise, during the Recess of the Legislature of any State, the Executive thereof may make temporary Appointments until the next Meeting of the Legislature, which shall then fill such Vacancies.

No Person shall be a Senator who shall not have attained to the Age of thirty Years, and been nine Years a Citizen of the United States, and who shall not, when elected, be an Inhabitant of that State for which he shall be chosen.

The Vice President of the United States shall be President of the Senate, but shall have no Vote, unless they be equally divided.

The Senate shall chuse their other Officers, and also a President pro tempore, in the Absence of the Vice President, or when he shall exercise the Office of President of the United States.

The Senate shall have the sole Power to try all Impeachments. When sitting for that Purpose, they shall be on Oath or Affirmation. When the President of the United States is tried, the Chief Justice shall preside: And no Person shall be convicted without the Concurrence of two thirds of the Members present.

Judgment in Cases of Impeachment shall not extend further than to removal from Office, and disqualification to hold and enjoy any Office of honor, Trust or Profit under the United States: but the Party convicted shall nevertheless be liable and subject to Indictment, Trial, Judgment and Punishment, according to Law.

Section. 4. The Times, Places and Manner of holding Elections for Senators and Representatives, shall be prescribed in each State by the Legislature thereof, but the Congress may at any time by Law make or alter such Regulations, except as to the Places of chusing Senators.

The Congress shall assemble at least once in every Year, and such Meeting shall be on the first Monday in December, unless they shall by Law appoint a different Day.

Section. 5. Each House shall be the Judge of the Elections, Returns and Qualifications of its own Members, and a Majority of each shall constitute a Quorum to do Business; but a smaller Number may adjourn from day to day, and may be authorized to compel the Attendance of absent Members, in such Manner, and under such Penalties as each House may provide.

Each House may determine the Rules of its Proceedings, punish its Members for disorderly Behaviour, and, with the Concurrence of two thirds, expel a Member.

Each House shall keep a Journal of its Proceedings, and from time to time publish the same, excepting such Parts as may in their Judgment require Secrecy; and the Yeas and Nays of the Members of either House on any question shall, at the Desire of one fifth of those Present, be entered on the Journal.

Neither House, during the Session of Congress, shall, without the Consent of the other, adjourn for more than three days, nor to any other Place than that in which the two Houses shall be sitting.

Section. 6. The Senators and Representatives shall receive a Compensation for their Services, to be ascertained by Law, and paid out of the Treasury of the United States. They shall in all Cases, except Treason, Felony and Breach of the Peace, be privileged from Arrest during their Attendance at the Session of their respective Houses, and in going to and returning from the same; and for any Speech or Debate in either House, they shall not be questioned in any other Place.

No Senator or Representative shall, during the Time for which he was elected, be appointed to any civil Office under the Authority of the United States, which shall have been created, or the Emoluments whereof shall have been encreased during such time; and no Person holding any Office under the United States, shall be a Member of either House during his Continuance in Office.

Section. 7. All Bills for raising Revenue shall originate in the House of Representatives; but the Senate may propose or concur with Amendments as on other Bills.

Every Bill which shall have passed the House of Representatives and the Senate shall, before it become a Law, be presented to the President of the United States; If he approve he shall sign it, but if not he shall return it, with his Objections to that House in which it shall have originated, who shall enter the Objections at large on their Journal, and proceed to reconsider it. If after such Reconsideration two thirds of that House shall agree to pass the Bill, it shall be sent, together with the Objections, to the other House, by which it shall likewise be reconsidered, and if approved by two thirds of that House, it shall become a Law. But in all such Cases the Votes of both Houses shall be determined by yeas and Nays, and the Names of the Persons voting for and against the Bill shall be entered on the Journal of each House respectively. If any Bill shall not be returned by the President within ten Days (Sundays excepted) after it shall have been presented to him, the Same shall be a Law, in like Manner as if he had signed it, unless the Congress by their Adjournment prevent its Return, in which Case it shall not be a Law.

Every Order, Resolution, or Vote to which the Concurrence of the

Senate and House of Representatives may be necessary (except on a question of Adjournment) shall be presented to the President of the United States; and before the Same shall take Effect, shall be approved by him, or being disapproved by him, shall be repassed by two thirds of the Senate and House of Representatives, according to the Rules and Limitations prescribed in the Case of a Bill.

Section. 8. The congress shall have Power To lay and collect Taxes, Duties, Imposts and Excises, to pay the Debts and provide for the common Defence and general Welfare of the United States; but all Duties, Imposts and Excises shall be uniform throughout the United States.

To borrow Money on the credit of the United States;

To regulate Commerce with foreign Nations, and among the several States, and with the Indian Tribes;

To establish an uniform Rule of Naturalization, and uniform Laws on the subject of Bankruptcies throughout the United States;

To coin Money, regulate the Value thereof, and of foreign Coin, and fix the Standard of Weights and Measures;

To provide for the Punishment of counterfeiting the Securities and current Coin of the United States;

To establish Post Offices and Post Roads;

To promote the Progress of Science and useful Arts, by securing for limited Times to Authors and Inventors the exclusive Right to their respective Writings and Discoveries;

To constitute Tribunals inferior to the supreme Court;

To define and punish Piracies and Felonies committed on the high Seas, and Offences against the Law of Nations;

To declare War, grant Letters of Marque and Reprisal, and make Rules concerning Captures on land and Water;

To raise and support Armies, but no Appropriation of Money to that Use shall be for a longer Term than two Years;

To provide and maintain a Navy;

To make Rules for the Government and Regulation of the land and naval Forces;

To provide for calling forth the Militia to execute the Laws of the Union, suppress Insurrections and repel Invasions;

To provide for organizing, arming, and disciplining, the Militia, and for governing such Part of them as may be employed in the Service of the United States, reserving to the States respectively, the Appointment of the Officers, and the Authority of training the Militia according to the discipline prescribed by Congress;

To exercise exclusive Legislation in all Cases whatsoever, over such District (not exceeding ten Miles square) as may, by Cession of particular States, and the Acceptance of Congress, become the Seat of the Government of the United States, and to exercise like Authority over all Places purchased by the Consent of the Legislature of the State in which the Same shall be, for the Erection of Forts, Magazines, Arsenals, dock-Yards, and other needful Buildings;—And

To make all Laws which shall be necessary and proper for carrying into Execution the foregoing Powers, and all other Powers vested by this Constitution in the Government of the United States, or in any Department or Officer thereof.

Section. 9. The Migration or Importation of such Persons as any of the States now existing shall think proper to admit, shall not be prohibited by the Congress prior to the Year one thousand eight hundred and eight, but a Tax or duty may be imposed on such Importation, not exceeding ten dollars for each Person.

The Privilege of the Writ of Habeas Corpus shall not be suspended, unless when in Cases of Rebellion or Invasion the public Safety may require it.

No Bill of Attainder or ex post facto Law shall be passed.

No Capitation, or other direct, Tax shall be laid, unless in Proportion to the Census or Enumeration herein before directed to be taken.

No Tax or Duty shall be laid on Articles exported from any State.

No Preference shall be given by any Regulation of Commerce or Revenue to the Ports of one State over those of another: nor shall Vessels bound to, or from, one State, be obliged to enter, clear, or pay Duties in another.

No Money shall be drawn from the Treasury, but in Consequence of Appropriations made by Law, and a regular Statement and Account of the Receipts and Expenditures of all public Money shall be published from time to time.

No Title of Nobility shall be granted by the United States: And no Person holding any Office of Profit or trust under them, shall, without the Consent of the Congress, accept of any present, Emolument, Office, or Title, of any kind whatever, from any King, prince, or foreign State.

Section. 10. No State shall enter into any Treaty, Alliance, or Confederation; grant Letters of Marque and Reprisal; coin Money; emit Bills of Credit; make any Thing but gold and silver Coin a Tender in Payment of Debts; pass any Bill of Attainder, ex post facto Law, or Law impairing the Obligation of Contracts, or grant any Title of Nobility.

No State shall, without the Consent of the Congress, lay any Imposts or Duties on Imports or Exports, except what may be absolutely necessary for executing it's inspection Laws: and the net Produce of all Duties and Imposts, laid by any State on Imports or Exports, shall be for the Use of the Treasury of the United States; and all such Laws shall be subject to the Revision and Controul of the Congress.

No State shall, without the Consent of Congress, lay any Duty of Tonnage, keep Troops, or Ships of War in time of Peace, enter into any Agreement or Compact with another State, or with a foreign Power, or engage in War, unless actually invaded, or in such immiment Danger as will not admit of delay.

ARTICLE. II.

Section. 1. The executive Power shall be vested in a President of the United States of America. He shall hold his Office during the term of four

Years, and, together with the Vice President, chosen for the same Term, be elected, as follows.

Each State shall appoint, in such Manner as the Legislature thereof may direct, a Number of Electors, equal to the whole Number of Senators and Representatives to which the State may be entitled in the Congress: but no Senator or Representative, or Person holding an Office of Trust or Profit under the United States, shall be appointed an Elector.

The Electors shall meet in their respective States, and vote by Ballot for two Persons, of whom one at least shall not be an Inhabitant of the same State with themselves. And they shall make a List of all the Persons voted for, and of the Number of Votes for each; which List they shall sign and certify, and transmit sealed to the Seat of the Government of the United States, directed to the President of the Senate. The President of the Senate shall, in the Presence of the Senate and House of Representatives, open all the Certificates, and the Votes shall then be counted. The Person having the greatest Number of Votes shall be the President, if such Number be a Majority of the whole Number of Electors appointed; and if there be more than one who have such Majority, and have an equal Number of Votes, then the House of Representatives shall immediately chuse by Ballot one of them for President; and if no Person have a Majority, then from the five highest on the List the said House shall in like Manner chuse the President. But in chusing the President, the Votes shall be taken by States, the Representation from each State having one Vote; A quorum for this Purpose shall consist of a Member or Members from two thirds of the States, and a Majority of all the States shall be necessary to a Choice. In every Case, after the Choice of the President, the Person having the greatest Number of Votes of the Electors shall be the Vice President. But if there should remain two or more who have equal Votes, the Senate shall chuse from them by Ballot the Vice President.

The Congress may determine the Time of chusing the Electors, and the Day on which they shall give their Votes; which Day shall be the same throughout the United States.

No Person except a natural born Citizen, or a Citizen of the United States, at the time of the Adoption of this Constitution, shall be eligible to the Office of President, neither shall any Person be eligible to that Office who shall not have attained to the Age of thirty five Years, and been fourteen Years a Resident within the United States.

In Case of the Removal of the President from office, or of his Death, Resignation, or Inability to discharge the Powers and Duties of the said Office, the Same shall devolve on the Vice President, and the Congress may by Law provide for the Case of Removal, Death, Resignation or Inability, both of the President and Vice President, declaring what Officer shall then act as President, and such Officer shall act accordingly, until the Disability be removed, or a President shall be elected.

The President shall, at stated Times, receive for his Services, a Compensation, which shall neither be encreased or diminished during the Period for which he shall have been elected, and he shall not receive within that Period any other Emolument from the United States, or any of them.

Before he enters on the Execution of his Office, he shall take the following Oath or Affirmation:—"I do solemnly swear (or affirm) that I will faithfully execute the Office of President of the United States, and will to the best of my Ability, preserve, protect and defend the Constitution of the United States."

Section. 2. The President shall be Commander in Chief of the Army and Navy of the United States, and of the Militia of the several States, when called into the actual Service of the United States; he may require the Opinion, in writing, of the principal Officer in each of the executive Departments, upon any Subject relating to the Duties of their respective Offices, and he shall have Power to grant Reprieves and Pardons for Offences against the United States, except in Cases of Impeachment.

He shall have Power, by and with the Advice and Consent of the Senate, to make Treaties, provided two thirds of the Senators present concur; and he shall nominate, and by and with the Advice and Consent of the Senate, shall appoint Ambassadors, other public Ministers and Consuls, Judges of the supreme Court, and all other Officers of the United States, whose Appointments are not herein otherwise provided for, and which shall be established by Law; but the Congress may by Law vest the Appointment of such inferior Officers, as they think proper, in the President alone, in the Courts of Law, or in the Heads of Departments.

The President shall have Power to fill up all Vacancies that may happen during the Recess of the Senate, by granting Commissions which shall expire at the End of their next Session.

Section. 3. He shall from time to time give to the Congress Information of the State of the Union, and recommend to their Consideration such Measures as he shall judge necessary and expedient; he may, on extraordinary Occasions, convene both Houses, or either of them, and in Case of Disagreement between them, with Respect to the Time of Adjournment, he may adjourn them to such Time as he shall think proper; he shall receive Ambassadors and other public Ministers; he shall take Care that the Laws be faithfully executed, and shall Commission all the Officers of the United States.

Section. 4. The President, Vice President and all civil Officers of the United States, shall be removed from Office on Impeachment for, and Conviction of, Treason, Bribery, or other high Crimes and Misdemeanors.

ARTICLE. III.

Section. 1. The judicial Power of the United States, shall be vested in one supreme Court, and in such inferior Courts as the Congress may from time to time ordain and establish. The Judges, both of the supreme and inferior Courts, shall hold their Offices during good Behavior, and shall, at stated Times, receive for their Services, a Compensation, which shall not be diminished during their Continuance in Office.

Section. 2. The judicial Power shall extend to all Cases, in Law and Equity, arising under this Constitution, the Laws of the United States, and Treaties made, or which shall be made, under their Authority;—to all Cases affecting Ambassadors, other public Ministers and Consuls;—to all Cases of admiralty and maritime Jurisdiction;—to Controversies to which the United States shall be a Party;—to Controversies between two or more States;—between a State and Citizens of another State;—between Citizens of different States;—between Citizens of the same State claiming Lands under Grants of different States, and between a State, or the Citizens thereof, and foreign States, Citizens or Subjects.

In all cases affecting Ambassadors, other public Ministers and Consuls, and those in which a State shall be Party, the supreme Court shall have original Jurisdiction. In all the other Cases before mentioned, the supreme Court shall have appellate Jurisdiction, both as to Law and Fact, with such Exceptions, and under such Regulations as the Congress shall make.

The Trial of all Crimes, except in Cases of Impeachment, shall be by Jury; and such Trial shall be held in the State where the said Crimes shall have been committed; but when not committed within any State, the Trial shall be at such Place or Places as the Congress may by Law have directed.

Section. 3. Treason against the United States, shall consist only in levying War against them, or in adhering to their Enemies, giving them Aid and Comfort. No Person shall be convicted of Treason unless on the Testimony of two Witnesses to the same overt Act, or on Confession in open Court.

The Congress shall have Power to declare the Punishment of Treason, but no Attainder of Treason shall work Corruption of Blood, or Forfeiture except during the Life of the Person attainted.

ARTICLE. IV.

Section. 1. Full Faith and Credit shall be given in each State to the public Acts, Records, and judicial Proceedings of every other State. And the Congress may by general Laws prescribe the Manner in which such Acts, Records and Proceedings shall be proved, and the Effect thereof.

Section. 2. The Citizens of each State shall be entitled to all Privileges and Immunities of Citizens in the several States.

A Person charged in any State with Treason, Felony, or other Crime, who shall flee from Justice, and be found in another State, shall on Demand of the executive Authority of the State from which he fled, be delivered up, to be removed to the State having Jurisdiction of the Crime.

No Person held to Service or Labour in one State, under the Laws thereof, escaping into another, shall, in Consequence of any Law or Regulation therein, be discharged from such Service or Labour, but shall be delivered up on Claim of the Party to whom such Service or Labour may be due.

Section. 3. New States may be admitted by the Congress into this Union; but no new State shall be formed or erected within the Jurisdiction of any other State; nor any State be formed by the Junction of two or more States, or Parts of States, without the consent of the Legislatures of the States concerned as well as of the Congress.

The Congress shall have Power to dispose of and make all needful Rules and Regulations respecting the Territory or other Property belonging to the United States; and nothing in this Constitution shall be so construed as to Prejudice any Claims of the United States, or of any particular States.

Section. 4. The United States shall guarantee to every State in this Union a Republican Form of Government, and shall protect each of them against Invasion; and on Application of the Legislature, or of the Executive (when the Legislature cannot be convened) against domestic Violence.

Article. V.

The Congress, whenever two thirds of both Houses shall deem it necessary, shall propose Amendments to this Constitution, or, on the Application of the Legislatures of two thirds of the several States shall call a Convention for proposing Amendments, which, in either Case, shall be valid to all Intents and Purposes, as Part of this Constitution, when ratified by the Legislatures of three fourths of the several States, or by Conventions in three fourths thereof, as the one or the other Mode of Ratification may be proposed by the Congress; Provided that no Amendment which may be made prior to the Year One thousand eight hundred and eight shall in any Manner affect the first and fourth Clauses in the Ninth Section of the first Article; and that no State, without its Consent, shall be deprived of its equal Suffrage in the Senate.

Article. VI.

All Debts contracted and Engagements entered into, before the Adoption of this Constitution, shall be as valid against the United States under this Constitution, as under the Confederation.

This Constitution, and the Laws of the United States which shall be made in Pursuance thereof; and all Treaties made, or which shall be made, under the Authority of the United States, shall be the supreme Law of the Land; and the Judges in every State shall be bound thereby, any Thing in the Constitution or Laws of any State to the Contrary notwithstanding.

The Senators and Representatives before mentioned, and the Members of the several State Legislatures, and all executive and judicial Officers, both of the United States and of the several States, shall be bound by Oath or Affirmation, to support this Constitution; but no religious Test shall ever be required as a Qualification to any Office or public Trust under the United States.

ARTICLE. VII.

The Ratification of the Conventions of nine States, shall be sufficient for the Establishment of this Constitution between the States so ratifying the Same.

Done in Convention by the Unanimous Consent of the States present the Seventeenth Day of September in the Year of our Lord one thousand seven hundred and Eighty seven and of the Independence of the United States of America the Twelfth. In witness thereof We have hereunto subscribed our Names,

G°: WASHINGTON—Presid¹
and deputy from Virginia

New Hampshire	{ John Langdon Nicholas Gilman	Delaware	{ Geo: Read Gunning Bedford jun John Dickinson Richard Bassett Jaco: Broom
Massachusetts	{ Nathaniel Gorham Rufus King		
Connecticut	{ Wᵐ Samˡ Johnson Roger Sherman	Maryland	{ James McHenry Dan of Sᵗ Thoˢ Jenifer Danˡ Carroll
New York	Alexander Hamilton		
New Jersey	{ Wil: Livingston David A. Brearley. Wᵐ Paterson. Jona: Dayton	Virginia	{ John Blair— James Madison Jr.
Pennsylvania	{ B. Franklin Thomas Mifflin Robᵗ Morris Geo. Clymer Thoˢ. FitzSimons Jared Ingersoll James Wilson Gouv Morris	North Carolina	{ Wᵐ. Blount Richᵈ Dobbs Spaight. Hu Williamson
		South Carolina	{ J. Rutledge Charles Cotesworth Pinckney Charles Pinckney Pierce Butler.
		Georgia	{ William Few Abr Baldwin

AMENDMENTS TO THE CONSTITUTION

ARTICLES IN ADDITION TO, and Amendment of the Constitution of the United States of America, proposed by Congress, and ratified by the Legislatures of the several States, pursuant to the fifth Article of the original Constitution.

Amendment I.

Congress shall make no law respecting an establishment of religion, or prohibiting the free exercise thereof; or abridging the freedom of speech, or of the press; or the right of the people peaceably to assemble, and to petitition the Government for a redress of grievances.

Amendment II.

A well regulated Militia, being necessary to the security of a free State, the right of the people to keep and bear Arms, shall not be infringed.

Amendment III.

No Soldier shall, in time of peace be quartered in any house, without the consent of the Owner, nor in time of war, but in a manner to be prescribed by law.

Amendment IV.

The right of the people to be secure in their persons, houses, papers, and effects, against unreasonable searches and seizures, shall not be violated, and no Warrants shall issue, but upon probable cause, supported by Oath or affirmation, and particularly describing the place to be searched, and the persons or things to be seized.

Amendment V.

No person shall be held to answer for a capital, or otherwise infamous crime, unless on a presentment or indictment of a Grand Jury, except in cases arising in the land or naval forces, or in the Militia, when in actual service in time of War or public danger; nor shall any person be subject for the same offence to be twice put in jeopardy of life or limb; nor shall be compelled in any criminal case to be a witness against himself, nor be deprived of life, liberty, or property, without due process of law; nor shall private property be taken for public use, without just compensation.

Amendment VI.

In all criminal prosecutions, the accused shall enjoy the right to a speedy and public trial, by an impartial jury of the State and district wherein the crime shall have been committed, which district shall have been previously ascertained by law, and to be informed of the nature and cause of the accusation; to be confronted with the witnesses against him; to have compulsory process for obtaining witnesses in his favor, and to have the Assistance of Counsel for his defence.

Amendment VII.

In Suits at common law, where the value in controversy shall exceed twenty dollars, the right of trial by jury shall be preserved, and no fact tried by a jury, shall be otherwise re-examined in any Court of the United States, than according to the rules of the common law.

Amendment VIII.

Excessive bail shall not be required, nor excessive fines imposed, nor cruel and unusual punishments inflicted.

Amendment IX.

The enumeration in the Constitution, of certain rights, shall not be construed to deny or disparage others retained by the people.

Amendment X.

The powers not delegated to the United States by the Constitution, nor prohibited by it to the States, are reserved to the States respectively, or to the people. [The first ten amendments went into effect December 15, 1791.]

Amendment XI.

The Judicial power of the United States shall not be construed to extend to any suit in law or equity, commenced or prosecuted against one of the United States by Citizens of another State, or by Citizens or Subjects of any Foreign State. [January 8, 1798.]

Amendment XII.

The Electors shall meet in their respective states, and vote by ballot for President and Vice-President, one of whom, at least, shall not be an inhabitant of the same state with themselves; they shall name in their ballots the person voted for as President, and in distinct ballots the person voted for as Vice-President, and they shall make distinct lists of all persons voted for as President, and of all persons voted for as Vice-President, and of the number of votes for each, which lists they shall sign and certify, and transmit sealed to the seat of the government of the United States, directed to the President of the Senate;—The President of the Senate shall, in the presence of the Senate and House of Representatives, open all the certificates and the votes shall then be counted;—The person having the greatest number of votes for President, shall be the President, if such number be a majority of the whole number of Electors appointed; and if no person have such majority, then from the persons having the highest numbers not exceeding three on the list of those voted for as President, the House of Representatives shall choose immediately, by ballot, the President. But in choosing the President, the votes shall be taken by states, the representation from each state having one vote; a quorum for this purpose shall consist of a member or members from two-thirds of the states, and a majority of all the states shall be necessary to a choice. And if the House of Representatives shall not choose a President whenever the right of choice shall devolve upon them, before the fourth day of March next following, then the Vice-President shall act as President, as in the case of the death or other constitutional disability of the President.—The person having the greatest number of votes as Vice-President, shall be the Vice-President, if such number be a majority of the whole number of Electors appointed, and if no person have a majority, then from the two highest numbers on the list, the Senate shall choose the Vice-President; a quorum for the purpose shall consist of two-thirds of the whole number of Senators, and a majority of the whole number shall be necessary to a choice. But no person constitutionally ineligible to the office of President shall be eligible to that of Vice-President of the United States. [September 25, 1804.]

Amendment XIII.

Section 1. Neither slavery nor involuntary servitude, except as a punishment for crime whereof the party shall have been duly convicted, shall exist within the United States, or any place subject to their jurisdiction.

Section 2. Congress shall have power to enforce this article by appropriate legislation. [December 18, 1865.]

Amendment XIV.

Section 1. All persons born or naturalized in the United States, and subject to the jurisdiction thereof, are citizens of the United States and of the State wherein they reside. No State shall make or enforce any law which shall abridge the privileges or immunities of citizens of the United States; nor shall any State deprive any person of life, liberty, or property, without due process of law; nor deny to any person within its jurisdiction the equal protection of the laws.

Section 2. Representatives shall be apportioned among the several States according to their respective numbers, counting the whole number of persons in each State, excluding Indians not taxed. But when the right to vote at any election for the choice of electors for President and Vice President of the United States, Representatives in Congress, the Executive and Judicial officers of a State, or the members of the Legislature thereof, is denied to any of the male inhabitants of such State, being twenty-one years of age, and citizens of the United States, or in any way abridged, except for participation in rebellion, or other crime, the basis of representation therein shall be reduced in the proportion which the number of such male citizens shall bear to the whole number of male citizens twenty-one years of age in such State.

Section 3. No person shall be a Senator or Representative in Congress, or elector of President and Vice President, or hold any office, civil or military, under the United States, or under any State, who, having previously taken an oath, as a member of Congress, or as an officer of the United States, or as a member of any State legislature, or as an executive or judicial officer of any State, to support the Constitution of the United States, shall have engaged in insurrection or rebellion against the same, or given aid or comfort to the enemies thereof. But Congress may by a vote of two-thirds of each House, remove such disability.

Section 4. The validity of the public debt of the United States, authorized by law, including debts incurred for payment of pensions and bounties for services in suppressing insurrection or rebellion, shall not be questioned. But neither the United States nor any State shall assume or pay any debt or obligation incurred in aid of insurrection or rebellion against the United States, or any claim for the loss or emancipation of any slave; but all such debts, obligations and claims shall be held illegal and void.

Section 5. The Congress shall have power to enforce, by appropriate legislation, the provisions of this article. [July 28, 1868.]

Amendment XV.

Section 1. The right of citizens of the United States to vote shall not be denied or abridged by the United States or by any State on account of race, color, or previous condition of servitude—

Section 2. The Congress shall have power to enforce this article by appropriate legislation.—[March 30, 1870.]

Amendment XVI.

The Congress shall have power to lay and collect taxes on incomes, from whatever source derived, without apportionment among the several States, and without regard to any census or enumeration. [February 25, 1913.]

AMENDMENT XVII.

The Senate of the United States shall be composed of two senators from each State, elected by the people thereof, for six years; and each Senator shall have one vote. The electors in each State shall have the qualifications requisite for electors of the most numerous branch of the State legislature.

When vacancies happen in the representation of any State in the Senate, the executive authority of such State shall issue writs of election to fill such vacancies: *Provided,* That the legislature of any State may empower the executive thereof to make temporary appointments until the people fill the vacancies by election as the legislature may direct.

This amendment shall not be so construed as to affect the election or term of any senator chosen before it becomes valid as part of the Constitution. [May 31, 1913.]

AMENDMENT XVIII.

After one year from the ratification of this article, the manufacture, sale, or transportation of intoxicating liquors within, the importation thereof into, or the exportation thereof from the United States and all territory subject to the jurisdiction thereof for beverage purposes is hereby prohibited.

The Congress and the several States shall have concurrent power to enforce this article by appropriate legislation.

This article shall be inoperative unless it shall have been ratified as an amendment to the Constitution by the legislatures of the several States, as provided in the Constitution, within seven years from the date of the submission thereof to the States by Congress. [January 29, 1919.]

AMENDMENT XIX.

The right of citizens of the United States to vote shall not be denied or abridged by the United States or by any State on account of sex.

The Congress shall have power by appropriate legislation to enforce the provisions of this article. [August 26, 1920.]

AMENDMENT XX.

Section 1. The terms of the President and Vice-President shall end at noon on the twentieth day of January, and the terms of Senators and Representatives at noon on the third day of January, of the years in which such terms would have ended if this article had not been ratified; and the terms of their successors shall then begin.

Section 2. The Congress shall assemble at least once in every year, and such meeting shall begin at noon on the third day of January, unless they shall by law appoint a different day.

Section 3. If, at the time fixed for the beginning of the term of the President, the President-elect shall have died, the Vice-President-elect shall become President. If a President shall not have been chosen before the time fixed for the beginning of his term, or if the President-elect shall have failed to qualify, then the Vice-President-elect shall act as President until a President shall have qualified; and the Congress may by law provide for the case wherein neither a President-elect nor a Vice-President-elect shall have qualified, declaring who shall then act as President, or the manner in which one who is to act shall be selected, and such person shall act accordingly until a President or Vice-President shall have qualified.

Section 4. The Congress may by law provide for the case of the death of any of the persons from whom the House of Representatives may choose a President whenever the right of choice shall have devolved upon them, and for the case of the death of any of the persons from whom the Senate may choose a Vice-President whenever the right of choice shall have devolved upon them.

Section 5. Sections 1 and 2 shall take effect on the 15th day of October following the ratification of this article.

Section 6. This article shall be inoperative unless it shall have been ratified as an amendment to the Constitution by the legislatures of three-fourths of the several States within seven years from the date of its submission. [February 6, 1933.]

AMENDMENT XXI.

Section 1. The eighteenth article of amendment to the Constitution of the United States is hereby repealed.

Section 2. The transportation or importation into any State, Territory or possession of the United States for delivery or use therein of intoxicating liquors, in violation of the laws thereof, is hereby prohibited.

Section 3. This article shall be inoperative unless it shall have been ratified as an amendment to the Constitution by convention in the several States, as provided in the Constitution, within seven years from the date of the submission thereof to the States by the Congress. [December 5, 1933.]

AMENDMENT XXII.

Section 1. No person shall be elected to the office of the President more than twice, and no person who has held the office of President, or acted as President, for more than two years of a term to which some other person was elected President shall be elected to the office of the President more than once. But this Article shall not apply to any person holding the office of President when this Article was proposed by the Congress, and shall not prevent any person who may be holding the office of President, or acting as President, during the term within which this Article becomes operative from holding the office of President or acting as President during the remainder of such term.

Section 2. This article shall be inoperative unless it shall have been ratified as an amendment to the Constitution by the legislatures of three-fourths of the several states within seven years from the date of its submission to the States by the Congress. [February 27, 1951.]

Amendment XXIII.

Section 1. The District constituting the seat of government of the United States shall appoint in such manner as the Congress may direct:

A number of electors of President and Vice-President equal to the whole number of Senators and Representatives in Congress to which the District would be entitled if it were a State, but in no event more than the least populous State; they shall be in addition to those appointed by the States, but they shall be considered, for the purposes of the election of President and Vice-President, to be electors appointed by a State; and they shall meet in the District and perform such duties as provided by the twelfth article of amendment.

Section 2. The Congress shall have the power to enforce this article by appropriate legislation. [March 29, 1961.]

Amendment XXIV.

Section 1. The right of citizens of the United States to vote in any primary or other election for President or Vice President, for electors for President or Vice President, or for Senator or Representative in Congress, shall not be denied or abridged by the United States or any State by reason of failure to pay any poll tax or other tax.

Section 2. The Congress shall have power to enforce this article by appropriate legislation. [January 23, 1964.]

Amendment XXV.

Section 1. In case of the removal of the President from office or of his death or resignation, the Vice President shall become President.

Section 2. Whenever there is a vacancy in the office of Vice President, the President shall nominate a Vice President who shall take office upon confirmation by a majority vote of both Houses of Congress.

Section 3. Whenever the President transmits to the President pro tempore of the Senate and the Speaker of the House of Representatives his written declaration that he is unable to discharge the powers and duties of his office, and until he transmits to them a written declaration to the contrary, such powers and duties shall be discharged by the Vice President as Acting President.

Section 4. Whenever the Vice President and a majority of either the principal officers of the executive departments or of such other body as Congress may by law provide, transmit to the President pro tempore of the Senate and the Speaker of the House of Representatives their written declaration that the President is unable to discharge the powers and duties of his office, the Vice President shall immediately assume the powers and duties of the office as Acting President.

Thereafter, when the President transmits to the President pro tempore of the Senate and the Speaker of the House of Representatives his written declaration that no inability exists, he shall resume the powers and duties of his office unless the Vice President and a majority of either the principal officers of the executive departments or of such other body as Congress may by law provide, transmit within four days to the President pro tempore of the Senate and the Speaker of the House of Representatives their written declaration that the President is unable to discharge the powers and duties of his office. Thereupon Congress shall decide the issue, assembling within forty-eight hours for that purpose if not in session. If the Congress, within twenty-one days after receipt of the latter written declaration, or, if Congress is not in session, within twenty-one days after Congress is required to assemble, determines by two-thirds vote of both Houses that the President is unable to discharge the powers and duties of his office, the Vice President shall continue to discharge the same as Acting President; otherwise, the President shall resume the powers and duties of his office. [February 10, 1967.]

Amendment XXVI.

Section 1. The right of citizens of the United States, who are eighteen years of age or older, to vote shall not be denied or abridged by the United States or by any State on account of age.

Section 2. The Congress shall have power to enforce this article by appropriate legislation [June 30, 1971.]

PRESIDENTIAL ELECTIONS

Year	Number of States	Candidates	Parties	Popular Vote	% of Popular Vote	Electoral Vote	% Voter Participation
1789	11	**GEORGE WASHINGTON**	No party			69	
		John Adams	designations			34	
		Other candidates				35	
1792	15	**GEORGE WASHINGTON**	No party			132	
		John Adams	designations			77	
		George Clinton				50	
		Other candidates				5	
1796	16	**JOHN ADAMS**	Federalist			71	
		Thomas Jefferson	Democratic-Republican			68	
		Thomas Pinckney	Federalist			59	
		Aaron Burr	Democratic-Republican			30	
		Other candidates				48	
1800	16	**THOMAS JEFFERSON**	Democratic-Republican			73	
		Aaron Burr	Democratic-Republican			73	
		John Adams	Federalist			65	
		Charles C. Pinckney	Federalist			64	
		John Jay	Federalist			1	

Year	Number of States	Candidates	Parties	Popular Vote	% of Popular Vote	Electoral Vote	% Voter Participation
1804	17	**THOMAS JEFFERSON**	Democratic-Republican			162	
		Charles C. Pinckney	Federalist			14	
1808	17	**JAMES MADISON**	Democratic-Republican			122	
		Charles C. Pinckney	Federalist			47	
		George Clinton	Democratic-Republican			6	
1812	18	**JAMES MADISON**	Democratic-Republican			128	
		DeWitt Clinton	Federalist			89	
1816	19	**JAMES MONROE**	Democratic-Republican			183	
		Rufus King	Federalist			34	
1820	24	**JAMES MONROE**	Democratic-Republican			231	
		John Quincy Adams	Independent			1	
1824	24	**JOHN QUINCY ADAMS**	Democratic-Republican	108,740	30.5	84	26.9
		Andrew Jackson	Democratic-Republican	153,544	43.1	99	
		Henry Clay	Democratic-Republican	47,136	13.2	37	
		William H. Crawford	Democratic-Republican	46,618	13.1	41	

Year	Number of States	Candidates	Parties	Popular Vote	% of Popular Vote	Electoral Vote	% Voter Participation
1828	24	**ANDREW JACKSON**	Democratic	647,286	56.0	178	57.6
		John Quincy Adams	National Republican	508,064	44.0	83	
1832	24	**ANDREW JACKSON**	Democratic	688,242	54.5	219	55.4
		Henry Clay	National Republican	473,462	37.5	49	
		William Wirt	Anti-Masonic	101,051	8.0	7	
		John Floyd	Democratic			11	
1836	26	**MARTIN VAN BUREN**	Democratic	765,483	50.9	170	57.8
		William H. Harrison	Whig			73	
		Hugh L. White	Whig	739,795	49.1	26	
		Daniel Webster	Whig			14	
		W. P. Mangum	Whig			11	
1840	26	**WILLIAM H. HARRISON**	Whig	1,274,624	53.1	234	80.2
		Martin Van Buren	Democratic	1,127,781	46.9	60	
1844	26	**JAMES K. POLK**	Democratic	1,338,464	49.6	170	78.9
		Henry Clay	Whig	1,300,097	48.1	105	
		James G. Birney	Liberty	62,300	2.3		
1848	30	**ZACHARY TAYLOR**	Whig	1,360,967	47.4	163	72.7
		Lewis Cass	Democratic	1,222,342	42.5	127	
		Martin Van Buren	Free Soil	291,263	10.1		

Year	Number of States	Candidates	Parties	Popular Vote	% Popular Vote	Electoral Vote	% Voter Participation
1852	31	**FRANKLIN PIERCE**	Democratic	1,601,117	50.9	254	69.6
		Winfield Scott	Whig	1,385,453	44.1	42	
		John P. Hale	Free Soil	155,825	5.0		
1856	31	**JAMES BUCHANAN**	Democratic	1,832,955	45.3	174	78.9
		John C. Frémont	Republican	1,339,932	33.1	114	
		Millard Fillmore	American	871,731	21.6	8	
1860	33	**ABRAHAM LINCOLN**	Republican	1,865,593	39.8	180	81.2
		Stephen A. Douglas	Democratic	1,382,713	29.5	12	
		John C. Breckinridge	Democratic	848,356	18.1	72	
		John Bell	Constitutional Union	592,906	12.6	39	
1864	36	**ABRAHAM LINCOLN**	Republican	2,206,938	55.0	212	73.8
		George B. McClellan	Democratic	1,803,787	45.0	21	
1868	37	**ULYSSES S. GRANT**	Republican	3,013,421	52.7	214	78.1
		Horatio Seymour	Democratic	2,706,829	47.3	80	

ADMISSION OF STATES

Order of Admission	State	Date of Admission	Order of Admission	State	Date of Admission
1	Delaware	December 7, 1787	26	Michigan	January 26, 1837
2	Pennsylvania	December 12, 1787	27	Florida	March 3, 1845
3	New Jersey	December 18, 1787	28	Texas	December 29, 1845
4	Georgia	January 2, 1788	29	Iowa	December 28, 1846
5	Connecticut	January 9, 1788	30	Wisconsin	May 29, 1848
6	Massachusetts	February 7, 1788	31	California	September 9, 1850
7	Maryland	April 28, 1788	32	Minnesota	May 11, 1858
8	South Carolina	May 23, 1788	33	Oregon	February 14, 1859
9	New Hampshire	June 21, 1788	34	Kansas	January 29, 1861
10	Virginia	June 25, 1788	35	West Virginia	June 30, 1863
11	New York	July 26, 1788	36	Nevada	October 31, 1864
12	North Carolina	November 21, 1789	37	Nebraska	March 1, 1867
13	Rhode Island	May 29, 1790	38	Colorado	August 1, 1876
14	Vermont	March 4, 1791	39	North Dakota	November 2, 1889
15	Kentucky	June 1, 1792	40	South Dakota	November 2, 1889
16	Tennessee	June 1, 1796	41	Montana	November 8, 1889
17	Ohio	March 1, 1803	42	Washington	November 11, 1889
18	Louisiana	April 30, 1812	43	Idaho	July 3, 1890
19	Indiana	December 11, 1816	44	Wyoming	July 10, 1890
20	Mississippi	December 10, 1817	45	Utah	January 4, 1896
21	Illinois	December 3, 1818	46	Oklahoma	November 16, 1907
22	Alabama	December 14, 1819	47	New Mexico	January 6, 1912
23	Maine	March 15, 1820	48	Arizona	February 14, 1912
24	Missouri	August 10, 1821	49	Alaska	January 3, 1959
25	Arkansas	June 15, 1836	50	Hawaii	August 21, 1959

POPULATION OF THE UNITED STATES

Year	Number of States	Population	Percent Increase	Population per Square Mile
1790	13	3,929,214		4.5
1800	16	5,308,483	35.1	6.1
1810	17	7,239,881	36.4	4.3
1820	23	9,638,453	33.1	5.5
1830	24	12,866,020	33.5	7.4
1840	26	17,069,453	32.7	9.8
1850	31	23,191,876	35.9	7.9
1860	33	31,443,321	35.6	10.6
1870	37	39,818,449	26.6	13.4
1880	38	50,155,783	26.0	16.9
1890	44	62,947,714	25.5	21.2
1900	45	75,994,575	20.7	25.6
1910	46	91,972,266	21.0	31.0
1920	48	105,710,620	14.9	35.6
1930	48	122,775,046	16.1	41.2
1940	48	131,669,275	7.2	44.2
1950	48	150,697,361	14.5	50.7
1960	50	179,323,175	19.0	50.6
1970	50	203,235,298	13.3	57.5
1980	50	226,504,825	11.4	64.0
1985	50	237,839,000	5.0	67.2

PRESIDENTS, VICE-PRESIDENTS, AND SECRETARIES OF STATE

President	Vice-President	Secretary of State
1. George Washington, Federalist 1789	John Adams, Federalist 1789	T. Jefferson 1789 E. Randolph 1794 T. Pickering 1795
2. John Adams, Federalist 1797	Thomas Jefferson, Dem.-Rep. 1797	T. Pickering 1797 John Marshall 1800
3. Thomas Jefferson, Dem.-Rep. 1801	Aaron Burr, Dem.-Rep. 1801 George Clinton, Dem.-Rep. 1805	James Madison 1801
4. James Madison, Dem.-Rep. 1809	George Clinton, Dem.-Rep. 1809 Elbridge Gerry, Dem.-Rep. 1813	Robert Smith 1809 James Monroe 1811
5. James Monroe, Dem.-Rep.-1817	D. D. Tompkins, Dem.-Rep. 1817	J. Q. Adams 1817
6. John Quincy Adams, Dem.-Rep. 1825	John C. Calhoun, Dem.-Rep. 1825	Henry Clay 1825
7. Andrew Jackson, Democratic 1829	John C. Calhoun, Democratic 1829 Martin Van Buren, Democratic 1833	M. Van Buren 1829 E. Livingston 1831 Louis McLane 1833 John Forsyth 1834
8. Martin Van Buren, Democratic 1837	Richard M. Johnson, Democratic 1837	John Forsyth 1837
9. William H. Harrison, Whig 1841	John Tyler, Whig 1841	Daniel Webster 1841

President	Vice-President	Secretary of State
10. John Tyler, Whig and Democratic 1841		Daniel Webster 1841 Hugh S. Legare 1843 Abel P. Upshur 1843 John C. Calhoun 1844
11. James K. Polk, Democratic 1845	George M. Dallas, Democratic 1845	James Buchanan 1845
12. Zachary Taylor, Whig 1849	Millard Fillmore, Whig 1848	John M. Clayton 1849
13. Millard Fillmore, Whig 1850		Daniel Webster 1850 Edward Everett 1852
14. Franklin Pierce, Democratic 1853	William R. D. King, Democratic 1853	W. L. Marcy 1853
15. James Buchanan, Democratic 1857	John C. Breckinridge, Democratic 1857	Lewis Cass 1857 J. S. Black 1860
16. Abraham Lincoln, Republican 1861	Hannibal Hamlin, Republican 1861 Andrew Johnson, Unionist 1865	W. H. Seward 1861
17. Andrew Johnson, Unionist 1865		W. H. Seward 1865
18. Ulysses S. Grant, Republican 1869	Schuyler Colfax, Republican 1869 Henry Wilson, Republican 1873	E. B. Washburne 1869 H. Fish 1869

CHRONOLOGY OF
SIGNIFICANT EVENTS

16,000–14,000 B.C.	Likely period for first crossing of land bridge from Old World to New World
5000 B.C.	Hunting and gathering established as a way of life in New World
2000–1500 B.C.	Permanent towns appear in Mexico
800 B.C.–A.D. 600	Adena-Hopewell culture (northeast United States)
400 B.C.–present	Pueblo-Hohokam culture (southwest United States)
A.D. 300–900	Mayan culture
600–1500	Mississippian culture (southeast United States)
1000	Leif Ericsson sights Newfoundland
1215	Magna Carta adopted in England
1300–1519	Aztec culture
1300–1598	Inca culture
1440	Gutenberg invents movable type
1477	Marco Polo's *Travels* published
1492–1504	Columbus's four voyages to New World
1493	Pope declares demarcation line
1517	Martin Luther launches Protestant Reformation
1519	Cortés conquers Aztec empire
1536	John Calvin publishes *The Institutes*
1558–1603	Reign of Queen Elizabeth I
1565	Town of St. Augustine founded by the Spanish

1692	Salem witch trials
1700	Population of English colonies in America at 250,000
1702–1713	Queen Anne's War (War of the Spanish Succession)
1704	First enduring newspaper published in America
1732	Georgia founded
1732–1757	Benjamin Franklin publishes *Poor Richard's Almanack*
1734	Great Awakening begins in colonies
1735	Trial of John Peter Zenger
1740–1748	King George's War (War of the Austrian Succession)
1754–1763	French and Indian War (Seven Years' War)
1763	Proclamation of 1763
1764	The Sugar Act
1764	The Currency Act
1765	The Stamp Act
1766	Declaratory Act
1767	Townshend Act
1768	John Dickinson publishes *Letters of a Pennsylvania Farmer*
1768	Samuel Adams's Massachusetts Circular Letter
1769	Virginia Resolves
1770	Boston Massacre
1773	Boston Tea Party
1774	Coercive Acts
1774	First Continental Congress
1775	Battles of Lexington and Concord
1775	Second Continental Congress
1775	Battle of Bunker Hill
1776	Thomas Paine's *Common Sense*
1776	Declaration of Independence
1777	American victory at Saratoga
1777	Congress adopts the Articles of Confederation
1778	Franco-American alliance set
1781	Battle of Yorktown
1782	Crevecoeur's *Letters from an American Farmer*
1783	Peace of Paris
1784	*Empress of China* sails for Canton

1822	Cotton mills opened in Lowell, Massachusetts
1823	Monroe Doctrine
1826	James Fenimore Cooper's *The Last of the Mohicans*
1828	Andrew Jackson elected president
1828	Calhoun's *South Carolina Exposition and Protest*
1829–1837	Battle over recharter of the Bank of the United States
1830	Webster-Hayne debate
1830	Indian Removal Act
1830–1847	The Mormon trek west
1830–1860	Hudson River school of painting
1831	*Cherokee Nation v. Georgia*
1831	William Lloyd Garrison begins publication of *The Liberator*
1831	Nat Turner's rebellion
1832	South Carolina Ordinance of Nullification
1833	Chicago founded
1836	Siege of the Alamo
1836	Texas declares its independence
1836–1850	Transcendentalism spreads in New England
1836	Ralph Waldo Emerson's *Nature*
1837	Panic of 1837
1837	*Charles River Bridge v. Warren Bridge*
1840	Edgar Allan Poe's *Tales of the Grotesque and Arabesque*
1842	Webster-Ashburton treaty
1844	Samuel F. B. Morse invents the telegraph
1844–1846	Dispute with Great Britain over Oregon territory
1845	United States annexes Texas
1846	Americans declare California an independent republic
1846	United States declares war on Mexico
1846	Wilmot Proviso
1846	Potato famine in Ireland
1848	Gold discovered in California
1848	Treaty of Guadalupe Hidalgo
1848	Seneca Falls convention on women's rights
1850	Compromise of 1850
1850	Nathaniel Hawthorne's *The Scarlet Letter*
1850	Clayton-Bulwer Treaty

ILLUSTRATION CREDITS

Note: The number preceding each credit is the page number on which the illustration is located.

CHAPTER 1   2 / Museum of the American Indian, Heye Foundation. 5 / Lee Boltin. 7 / Milwaukee Public Museum. 9 / Denver Convention & Visitors Bureau. 15 / New York Public Library. 16 / New York Public Library. 20 / British Museum. 21 / Library of Congress. 25 / The British Library. 31 / Editorial Photocolor Archives. 32 / Musée Historique de la Reformation. 33 / The Warder Collection. 37 / National Maritime Museum, London. 39 / Library of Congress.

CHAPTER 2   44 / National Portrait Gallery, London. 46 / National Portrait Gallery, London. 47 / Bulloz. 53 / Library of Congress. 54 / Society of Antiquaries, London. 56 / New York Public Library. 61 / Pilgrim Society, Boston. 62 / American Antiquarian Society. 64 / American Antiquarian Society. 66 / The Warder Collection. 70 / National Portrait Gallery, London. 73 / University of North Carolina. 74 / New York Public Library. 76 / New York Public Library. 80 / Historical Society of Pennsylvania. 81 / Museum of Fine Arts, Boston. 83 / The Mariners Museum, Newport News, Virginia.

CHAPTER 3   90 / From John J. McCusker and Russell R. Menard, *The Economy of British America, 1607–1789* (Chapel Hill: University of North Carolina Press, 1985), Fig. 10.1, p. 218. 92 / The Worcester Art Museum. 93 / National Gallery of Art, Washington, D.C. 94 / National Gallery of Art, Washington, D.C. 97 / Connecticut Historical Society. 98 / New York Public Library. 101 / Metropolitan Museum of Art. 103 / American Antiquarian Society. 105 / The Abby Aldridge Rockefeller Folk Art Center, Williamsburg, Virginia. 107 / (top) Library of Congress; (bottom) Museum of Modern Art. 109 / Historic Christ's Church, Virginia. 111 / The Warder Collection. 114 / American Antiquarian Society. 115 / Metropolitan Museum of Art. 118 / From Ralph Gardiner, *England's Grievance Discovered*, 1655. 120 / York County Historical Society, York, Pennsylvania. 125 / Essex Institute. 126 / New York

Public Library. 131 / Harvard University. 132 / American Antiquarian Society. 135 / Yale University Art Gallery.

CHAPTER 4 142 / Winterthur Museum. 144 / The Warder Collection. 146 / National Maritime Museum, London. 148 / National Portrait Gallery, London. 152 / The Colonial Williamsburg Foundation. 155 / The Library Company of Philadelphia. 157 / University of Virginia Library. 169 / Historical Society of Pennsylvania. 172 / National Army Museum, London. 173 / The National Gallery of Canada, Ottawa.

CHAPTER 5 179 / Courtauld Institute of Art. 180 / Independence National Historical Park Collection. 185 / Collection, Washington University, St. Louis. 186 / Christ Church, Oxford. 187 / British Museum. 191 / Historical Society of Pennsylvania. 193 / Brown University Library. 195 / Historical Society of Pennsylvania. 196 / Museum of Fine Arts, Boston. 199 / (top) Library of Congress; (bottom) Boston Public Library. 202 / Massachusetts Historical Society. 204 / Library of Congress. 205 / New York Public Library. 208 / British Museum. 211 / (top and bottom) New York Public Library. 212 / National Gallery of Art. 215 / Independence National Historical Park Collection. 216 / American Antiquarian Society. 217 / Library of Congress.

CHAPTER 6 221 / Brown University Library. 223 / Pennsylvania Academy of the Fine Arts. 225 / New York Public Library. 227 / Historical Society of Pennsylvania. 230 / The Frick Collection. 232 / Library of Congress. 241 / The British Library. 249 / Maryland Historical Society. 251 / Massachusetts Historical Society. 253 / National Gallery of Art. 254 / Museum of Art, Rhode Island School of Design. 258 / Yale University Art Gallery.

CHAPTER 7 264 / Independence National Historical Park Collection. 271 / Wethersfield Historical Society. 272 / The Library Company of Philadelphia. 274 / Boston Athenaeum. 276 / Historical Society of Pennsylvania. 277 / The Smithsonian Institution. 280 / Library of Congress. 283 / Library of Congress. 285 / Independence National Historical Park Collection. 293 / New-York Historical Society.

CHAPTER 8 296 / Museum of the City of New York. 297 / The Brooklyn Museum. 300 / The Smithsonian Institution. 304 / Library of Congress. 308 / Library Company of Philadelphia. 312 / White House Collection. 316 / Frick Art Reference Library. 317 / Detroit Public Library. 320 / The Warder Collection. 323 / New York Public Library. 325 / National Gallery of Art. 326 / American Antiquarian Society. 328 / The Warder Collection. 329 / Henry E. Huntington Library and Art Gallery. 332 / New York Public Library.

CHAPTER 9 339 / New York Public Library. 340 / Maryland Historical Society. 341 / Library of Congress. 343 / New York Public Library. 345 / The Cincinnati Historical Society. 348 / The Bettmann Archive, Inc. 351 / Missouri Historical Society. 353 / New-York Historical Society. 354 / New York Public Library. 359 / Historical Society of Pennsylvania. 361 / New-York Histori-

Congress. 585 / Library of Congress. 587 / Oberlin College Archives. 588 / Metropolitan Museum of Art. 592 / (left) Library of Congress; (right) New-York Historical Society.

CHAPTER 16   603 / Library of Congress. 605 / The Bancroft Library, Berkeley. 607 / Metropolitan Museum of Art. 609 / Library of Congress. 612 / The Smithsonian Institution. 613 / New-York Historical Society. 616 / Library of Congress. 618 / Library of Congress. 623 / New York Public Library. 626 / (left) Missouri Historical Society; (right) National Archives. 629 / Library of Congress. 632 / Library of Congress. 635 / The Warder Collection. 637 / Library of Congress. 638 / Library of Congress. 641 / New York Public Library.

CHAPTER 17   646 / Library of Congress. 651 / Library of Congress. 658 / New York Public Library. 666 / Library of Congress. 668 / National Archives. 669 / Library of Congress. 671 / (top and bottom) Library of Congress. 674 / Library of Congress. 681 / National Archives. 685 / Library of Congress. 688 / Library of Congress. 691 / National Archives. 693 / National Archives. 694 / Library of Congress.

CHAPTER 18   698 / Library of Congress. 699 / Library of Congress. 700 / Library of Congress. 701 / Library of Congress. 705 / Library of Congress. 707 / Harper's Weekly. 709 / (left) Library of Congress; (right) National Archives. 711 / The Warder Collection. 713 / Library of Congress. 717 / National Archives. 719 / Library of Congress. 723 / Library of Congress. 726 / Library of Congress. 729 / Library of Congress. 732 / Library of Congress.

INDEX